LORI WICK

The Yellow Rose Trilogy

EVERY LITTLE THING ABOUT YOU
A TEXAS SKY
CITY GIRL

HARVEST HOUSE PUBLISHERS

EUGENE, OREGON

Contents

LORI WICK

Every Little Thing About You

HARVEST HOUSE PUBLISHERS

EUGENE, OREGON

Scripture references are taken from the King James Version of the Bible.

Cover design by Dugan Design Group, Bloomington, Minnesota

This is a work of fiction. Characters, places, and incidents are products of the author's imagination or are used fictitiously. Any resemblance to actual persons, living or dead, or to events or locales, is entirely coincidental.

EVERY LITTLE THING ABOUT YOU
Copyright © 1999 Lori Wick
Published by Harvest House Publishers
Eugene, Oregon 97402

ISBN-13: 978-0-7394-9555-1

Printed in the United States of America.

Acknowledgments

$\mathcal{Z} \cdot \mathcal{Z} \cdot \mathcal{Z}$

What a time it's been. This book has been with me for literally years. I was ready to begin writing in 1992, but the Kensington Chronicles came along. They in turn led to other works, so Texas was shelved for a time. But because of that, the Yellow Rose Trilogy has taken on better form and dimension, and I think the books might be better than the first drafts in my mind.

All this to say, I'm so excited to finally put this first book down on paper. The people I need to acknowledge have patiently helped me come to this point. A huge thank-you goes to:

Phil Caminiti. Your wisdom as we walk through the book of Mark has been invaluable to me. Thank you for your insight, love of the Word, and humble desire to be more like Jesus Christ. Thank you for teaching the student, not the lesson. My world is a bigger place because of you.

Denise Caminiti. The time in your Bible study has been a joy and a delight. I love your honest approach and easy agenda. Thank you for your patience with me and for never failing to show me love and acceptance. I consider you a friend so dear.

The women from Bible study. If I try to name all of you, I will be sure to miss someone. Please allow me to thank all of you for your love and kindness. I learn so much from you and Thursday mornings are a highlight of the week for me.

The elders' wives at BECC. Thank you for what you've shared and taught me. I am privileged beyond measure to know and fellowship with you. Thank you for your hunger and humility and the way you bring glory to God.

My own precious Bob. You hung in there, Wickie! This book was put on the back burner so many times, and still you waited in silence. Thank you for being patient and for cheering the loudest along the way.

Did I laugh before you were born?
Not quite so often, I'm sure.
Did I know about a mother's love before you?
Not by half.
Keep growing, keep trusting,
and never forget that I love you.
For my Tin Man.

Prologue

September 1881
Austin, Texas

THE MIDAFTERNOON SUN beat down unmercifully as the cowboy, a Texas Ranger, rode into town. Heat waves shimmered on the horizon, and the blowing dust caused the horse's eyes to squint as Slater Rawlings tethered the dark roan animal to the hitching post. Other than seeing that the horse could reach the water trough, Slater gave little heed to Arrow's comfort. For weeks the rider had been working on the courage to tell his boss about his decision, and now it was time to do the job. It was a relief to arrive at the Austin office and walk in the door.

🌿 🌿 🌿

"Why can't you do both, Slate?" Marty Bracewell asked one of his best rangers just 15 minutes later. "Why does this faith thing mean you have to leave?"

"It's not my faith—just as it is, Brace," the younger man tried to explain. "And it's not the job itself. It's the travel. I'm tired of tracking and being out on the trail. I want to settle in someplace for the winter, possibly longer." What Slater Rawlings didn't try to explain was the need to get to church on Sundays—the ache inside of him for fellowship. Brace, whose life was the Rangers, would never have understood.

"You'll be back," Brace said with confidence, the desk chair creaking as he leaned back with ease. "It's in your blood, just like it's in Dakota's. You'll be back."

Slater didn't even reply. He stood, lifting his hat to his head.

"Take care, Brace."

"I'll do that. You do the same. I want you coming back fit."

Not only did Slater not reply to this, he didn't even look back as he placed his badge on the desk. With a hand to the doorknob, he quietly let himself out. Just moments later he was back astride Arrow and headed out of town. With a thought of how cool the hills would be, he headed west.

One

October 1881
Shotgun, Texas

FRIDAY AFTERNOONS WERE normally quiet. Saturday nights were a little more rambunctious, but most days and evenings in Shotgun were peaceful. It was for this reason that Liberty Drake was surprised to be needed. Being called out of the sheriff's office to one of the saloons was the last thing she expected, but Shotgun had laws about carrying firearms into the saloons or after sunset, so she had a job to do. She strapped on her holster and followed Jep, the saloon owner's 11-year-old son, down the street. The boy ran, but Liberty walked, not apathetic, but not certain she needed to be out of breath when she arrived.

And indeed, things were quiet when she pushed through the swinging doors of the Brass Spittoon. Jep's father, Gordie, nodded his head to a table in the corner. Liberty took in three men. Two were daytime regulars, but the blond was a stranger. There wasn't even a drink in front of him, but Liberty had no choice.

"Excuse me," Liberty began politely, waiting for the man to look at her. "I need you to surrender your firearm to me. Shotgun has outlawed firearms in the saloons and after dark."

Slater looked up at the woman beside him. She was dressed in baggy men's clothes, which did nothing to hide her gender, and he could only stare. *Was that really a sheriff's badge on her vest?* His hesitation cost him. With a move so fast and smooth that Slater blinked, the woman's gun cleared leather as swiftly as she lifted his own gun from the holster at his hip.

"You'll need to come with me, sir," Liberty said calmly.

"What?" Slater returned, finally uttering his first word.

Liberty gestured with the gun and moved so he could stand. "This way, please," she ordered congenially but watching every move as he slowly rose. One of the other men handed saddlebags to Liberty, and after she'd thanked him and draped them over her arm, she moved Slater again with the motion of her gun.

As though he'd been frozen from the cold, Slater moved very slowly as he walked through the saloon. At the table he had stopped just short of reaching for his pocket to show his Ranger's badge when he remembered it wasn't there. He also remembered what such a move would look like. He didn't want to run the risk of having this woman shoot him. She had cleared leather very smoothly, but that didn't mean she could shoot straight. Barely managing to keep his amazement concealed, he walked ahead of her and out onto the street. He made the mistake of turning to her as soon as he was outside and felt cold steel press into his ribs.

"Just turn back around," she said evenly, "and lead the way straight up the walk."

Now seething inside, Slater turned and obeyed. He didn't know when he'd been so angry. At six foot, he was not a huge man, but this small woman with the badge, clearly too full of herself, had him at her mercy. With a prayer for calm that was slow in coming, Slater did as he was told. They hadn't walked for a minute when she spoke.

"In here," she directed, and Slater, already aware of the location, went through the door of the sheriff's office. He heard the door shut behind him and turned.

"Empty your pockets onto the desk, please," Liberty ordered, all business, as she put the saddlebags out of reach on the floor. "Nice and slow will do fine."

Slater did so without ever taking his eyes from her, which meant he couldn't miss the way she watched him in return. She was calm; he had to give her that. As he looked into her eyes, he knew with a bone-chilling certainty that she would shoot if she felt she had to.

"Now your boots," she instructed.

Slater hesitated and heard the gun cock.

"All right," he said smoothly. "I'll just tell you, though, I do have a knife in my boot. I won't use it—I just wanted you to know."

"Put the knife on the desk," Liberty said, taking a second to eye the Bowie knife that appeared. Not a heartbeat later her eyes were back on her prisoner, who was removing his boots with slow, measured movements.

"Your belt now," Liberty said as soon as he stood back to full height.

He was a taller man than she liked to deal with, but she didn't think he was going to threaten her. She couldn't, however, take any chances.

"Turn around," was the next order, once all of Slater's belongings were on the desk. "Head into the cell."

Slater did so, the feeling of unreality washing over him again. He turned as soon as he was inside and watched as the door was shut and locked. He also watched as Liberty holstered her gun, set his on the desk, and began to speak.

"Dinner comes at 6:00 this evening, and breakfast tomorrow at 7:00. You're expected to be neat and quiet. Unless you're wanted for something, the charge to get out is ten dollars."

"*Ten dollars!*" Slater growled in outrage. "You can't be serious."

Liberty shrugged. "We need a new jail, and this seems like the most obvious way to come up with the money."

Slater's mouth fell open. He couldn't believe what he had just heard. How in the world had he thought this was a nice little town?

"I don't suppose you have it," Liberty said now, her voice resigned as she studied him.

"Why would you say that?" Slater was just irritated enough to ask.

Liberty's brows rose. "You can't even afford a haircut and a shave." There was no censure in her voice, only calm reason. Slater swallowed his rage as she turned away. He turned his back on the bars. The cell was standard fare, but he saw what she meant—repairs were needed.

With a sigh that he made no attempt to hide, Slater walked to the bed and collapsed on the straw mattress, which sent up a musty odor. He leaned against the wall and tried to stay calm. Nothing worked. Wrong as it was, he was furious, and for right now he was going to stay that way.

Ten dollars, he thought once again. *That'll be the day.*

❧ ❧ ❧

"How'd it go?" Griffin Drake asked the moment he stepped into the sheriff's office—his office.

"Just a newcomer in town. He wouldn't give up his gun."

Griffin's eyes went to the cell, where he could see long legs stretched out from the bunk but no body or face.

"Did he give you any trouble?"

"No, but he's bigger than I like to deal with."

Griffin smiled. Liberty was always honest.

Brother and sister both heard movement in the cell just then and turned to see the prisoner coming to stand at the bars.

"I'm Griffin Drake," Liberty's brother volunteered, "sheriff here in Shotgun. What's your name?"

"Slater Rawlings," the prisoner said, his eyes going between them. "You're the sheriff?"

"Yes."

"And you want ten dollars from me?"

"Unless you're wanted, and then no amount will gain your release."

"How was I supposed to know about guns in the saloon?"

"It's posted above the bar," Griffin told him calmly.

"I didn't go to the bar. I don't even drink."

"Then what were you doing in the saloon?"

I can't spend all my money on the luxury of a hotel room, and there's no place else to go in this town after you've slept out in the woods, Slated thought to himself, but he wasn't about to admit that to them.

Griffin waited calmly for an answer, but the man turned away. Griffin and Liberty exchanged a glance.

"He doesn't like you, big brother," Liberty said, her voice low but her eyes lit with a smile. "He was much nicer for me."

Griffin smiled back. "Let me guess, Lib. You were holding your gun."

Liberty laughed a little and stood. "I'd better get home so I can help Mam with dinner."

"All right," Griffin said as he walked Liberty outside. "Thanks for your help." There was no missing the contentment in his voice as he looked up and down the street and even back at the sheriff's office, not new by any stretch of the imagination.

Liberty said her own goodbyes, thinking not for the first time that her brother was the perfect man to act as sheriff in Shotgun. He loved this town, believed in it, and trusted the people who helped run it.

❧ ❧ ❧

When Griffin moved back inside to his desk, he saw that his prisoner had returned to stand at the bars.

"Don't tell me you let your sister walk the streets alone." Slater's voice was mildly sarcastic. "It's getting dark. She might be harmed."

Griffin did not rise to the bait. On the way to the desk, he said, "Not my sister. She's the fastest gun in town."

Slater shook his head in disgust. Was the man a fool? He certainly didn't look tough enough to be the sheriff. He wasn't small, but he had the face of a boy—merry eyes, smooth cheeks, and all.

"I don't suppose you want to tell me if you're wanted anywhere,"

Griffin commented as he lifted a stack of wanted posters and flyers onto the desktop from a drawer. "It might save me some time."

"I'm not wanted," Slater said coldly, knowing the lawman would have to check anyway. Slater watched him start on the stack. Twice Griffin rose to hold a picture up to the fading light at the window and then look toward the bars. But he only went back to the desk.

"So tell me," Griffin began after a good ten minutes. "Why didn't you just give up your gun?"

Slater sighed. "You wouldn't believe me."

"Try me."

"I was stunned. I honestly didn't think she could be serious."

"I believe you," Griffin said conversationally. "It's happened before." This said, Griffin reached for the wallet Slater had been commanded to put on the desk. He could see a few bills without even opening it. "If I don't find you in this stack, it looks like you could pay your way out of here."

"Don't count on it." Slater's voice was decidedly cool. "Ten dollars is robbery, and we both know it."

Griffin shrugged. "The food's not bad, and it doesn't get noisy until Saturday night."

Slater didn't reply. Neither did Griffin. It would be easier for the sheriff not to have a man locked up, but he would leave it up to him.

The stack was still rather high when Griffin needed to move around a bit. He scooped up Slater's belongings and took them to the safe in the corner. There wasn't much inside, but the wallet, knife, timepiece, papers, belt, and saddlebags just about filled it. He then checked the boots for weapons and set them by the bars.

"What time is it?" Slater asked.

"Coming onto 6:00. Supper will be here soon."

"I can't say as I'm very hungry."

"Suit yourself," Griffin replied in his calm way, and Slater knew a moment of respect. One of the hallmarks of a good Ranger was calmness. Another was politeness, and he knew he'd failed there. But this was so irritating, and at the moment he couldn't think why God would put him in this place. He had fought the Lord for weeks about leaving the Rangers, and now that he'd talked with Brace, he found himself in jail.

Slater shook his head as he went back to the bunk. He could well imagine Brace's face if that man could see where he was, not to mention his brother Dakota's. Slater made himself sit back against the wall before he tried praying again.

🥀 🥀 🥀

"All right, Libby," Kate Peterson, Liberty's mother, said as she adjusted the candles on the table and moved the basket full of biscuits. "I think that just about does it. Duffy is carving the meat."

"I'll put the gravy in the blue boat just before we sit down."

"Good. Where are Zach and Laura?"

"You sent them out to wash."

"Oh, that's right. Some days I think my head has rolled off my shoulders and I haven't noticed."

"It's still there, Mam," Liberty smilingly told her.

Kate smiled back and said, "I think I'll have you run a plate of food over to your brother."

"He's at the jail with a prisoner."

"Oh, who did he bring in?"

"I brought him in, and his name is Slater Rawlings."

Kate was instantly alert. Since Griffin's deputy had moved across state a month back, Liberty had been filling in. It was not the first time, nor was it an ideal situation, but at times a matter of life and death.

"Everything all right?" Kate asked her daughter.

"Yes. He's new to town and didn't know the rules. He hesitated, and I felt I had no choice but to lift his weapon."

Kate nodded. She didn't fear Liberty's being shot—the younger woman was very competent with a firearm—it was more the things men said to her that Kate objected to. No mother wanted vulgar things said to her children, but when the child was a young, unmarried woman, it was all the harder. At times Kate wanted a different life for her daughter, a life without Griffin's refitted pants or a gun. Kate honestly believed that would be best, but for the moment, this was where God had them.

"I washed," five-year-old Laura announced as she came to the dining room doorway.

"Thank you, dear. Please tell your father we're all ready in here."

"Papa!" Laura dashed from the room on that note, and both women turned as Zach entered. He was a serious six-year-old with a heart of gold.

"Are you washed, Zach?" Liberty asked her young half-brother.

"Yes, but I got my shirt a little wet."

"It will dry," Liberty said kindly as she touched his fair head.

"Laura says we're ready!" Duffy Peterson, one of Shotgun's doctors and Kate's second husband, said as he came on the scene just then, a platter of roast pork in his hands. He added it to the table, and in his warm, wonderful way invited everyone to sit down. He then asked them to bow in prayer.

"Family is so special, Lord," he said reverently, "and we thank You for the ones You've gathered here. Thank You for the sweet fellowship we have in You. Thank You for this food, and for the strong bodies You've given to us. Help us to be filled without being greedy, and to remember that every bite is from Your hand. In Jesus Christ's name I pray. Amen."

The meal began on that good note and only got better. Duffy had been called upon that day to deliver twins—always fun news. He was peppered with questions for a good ten minutes; questions he patiently answered.

"Boys or girls?"

"One of each."

"Who was born first?"

"The boy. I think they're calling him John after his father."

"Did they cry hard?"

"Yes, but we kept them warm, and they settled right down for their mother."

"Is their mother all right?"

"She's doing very well."

"Will you see her again this week?"

"If they call me, yes."

"We'll have to get over with a basket of baked goods," Kate suggested in an effort to stem the tide.

"The pantry's full right now, so that shouldn't be a problem," Liberty said as she remembered she had not brought in the gravy. She rose to do this, giving husband and wife a moment to speak.

"She brought a man in today," Kate said for her husband's ears alone.

"Did it go all right?"

"She said it did. Griffin is still at the jail with him."

"I can bake," Laura put in suddenly.

"What's that, honey?" her mother asked, needing to let the other conversation drop. Her husband watched her for a moment.

"I can bake for the babies too."

"Yes, you can, and we'll just do that. All right?"

Laura nodded, looking pleased.

"Tell me, Zach," his father said conversationally, "what was the funnest thing that happened in school today?"

"We got to read outside."

"Oh, that is fun. Did you all have books, or did Mrs. Murch read to you?"

"She read to us first, but then the older kids took turns."

"Very good. You'll be having your turn before you know it."

Zach smiled up at his father, his favorite person in the world. While other boys wanted to chase after frogs and go fishing, Zach Peterson wanted to sit with a book and read. Some of the children at school had said that such things were sissy, but not Zach's father. Duffy had told him that reading was wonderful and that he should never feel ashamed of his love for it. Right after that, Zach had found himself very interested in fishing, and he tried it with his father, who made it the greatest outing of the entire summer.

"I'm sorry about this gravy," Liberty apologized as she returned with the dark blue gravy boat and set it on the table. "I'm going to start parroting you, Mam, about my head falling off."

"Did you help Griff today?" Zach suddenly asked.

"Yes, I did. I was there for a few hours."

"Did you put someone in jail?" This came from Laura, and Liberty nodded.

"Did you need your gun?"

"Yes. The man waited a little too long to do as I asked, and I couldn't take any chances."

"Is Griff with him now?"

Again Liberty nodded. "That was the plan."

Kate was thankful that the subject was dropped after that. They finished the meal on another topic, and she wasn't forced to keep her feelings hidden. Thoughts of Liberty helping Griffin played in her mind the entire evening, but she prayed and worked to give her two oldest children to the Lord. It was a huge relief, however, when it was time for her younger children to go to bed. She kissed Liberty goodnight and finally gained the privacy of her bedroom. Duffy wasn't far behind her. He found his wife sitting on the edge of the bed, facing away from the door. Duffy slipped his shoes off and climbed onto the mattress. With gentle fingers he unbuttoned the back of her dress and then softly kissed her neck.

"Are you all right?"

"I think so," Kate answered honestly as she slipped from her cotton dress and sat back down in her petticoat and chemise, turning a little so she could look at her husband. "She's so calm, Duffy."

"She has to be, Kate. You don't want her carrying her emotions on her sleeve when she has to pull that gun."

Kate's breath caught in her throat, and Duffy pulled her into his arms and held her close. Kate clung to him. She didn't want to cry, but she felt a desperate need to be held. Duffy was only too happy to oblige.

He hadn't seen her coming. He hadn't known she was going to walk into his life when she did. They had known each other for years, lived in the same town, and gone to the same church, but he hadn't noticed her until almost a year after Thomas Drake died. Kate had been teaching school in those days—the town's sheriff had not been able to leave a huge legacy behind—and still trying to do her job as a mother to Griffin and Liberty, the only two of her five children to make it past infancy. Then she had taken ill. Duffy would never forget Liberty's pale face as she came to his office.

"Mam is sick," the slim 12-year-old had said.

"Who is sick?" Duffy questioned her.

"Mam. She's hot and quiet."

Duffy had finally figured out that Liberty was referring to her mother. He had hung a sign on his door and followed her home. And Kate had been sick—very sick. Duffy still remembered asking God if He would take the children's mother as well as their father.

Some days passed before he felt she was out of the woods, and even then she wasn't back in the schoolhouse for more than two weeks. And that first day when school dismissed, Duffy was there. He used her health as an excuse for a long time but eventually gained the courage to ask if he could court her. He thought his heart would burst when she said yes.

"I was married to Thomas and had two babies by the time I was Libby's age," Kate said suddenly; Liberty was not long past her twenty-first birthday. "I don't want Libby to marry for anything but love, Duffy, but I find myself wishing she would show more interest in some of the young men who like her."

"Kate," Duffy said seriously, waiting for her to look at him, "you're trying to change circumstances that are out of your control rather than serving God in the midst of them. And you're worrying."

Kate looked up into his wonderful face. Older than she was by ten years, he'd never planned to marry. But he had suddenly found himself in love with her, and in time, Kate had loved him back. The day she married him was one of the happiest of her life. And his faith was so alive. He had been busy as a doctor, but not having a wife or children for so many years had left him with great amounts of time for Bible study and prayer. She learned something from him every week.

"You're right. I need to give her back to the Lord."

"And you need to keep asking God, in His will, to bring someone into her life. You've been happily married, you've seen Libby with people, and you naturally think she would flourish in marriage and parenthood. I do too. So we both need to keep going to God about this."

"She is special, isn't she, Duff?"

"Very. And although some of the men here are fine young men, I think it's going to take someone just as special as she is, someone who understands how multifaceted she is, to claim her heart."

Kate nodded, thinking not for the first time that it was wonderful to know he loved Griffin and Liberty as he did Zach and Laura. She kissed him and thanked him before rising to ready for bed. The week had been long, and she was weary. Thirty minutes later, her husband beside her, she drifted off to sleep, but not before asking God to help her take Duffy's advice: Serve God where you are; don't ask Him to take you elsewhere before you obey. She had made it flowery—that was more her way—but the meaning was still clear.

Two

LIBERTY'S NEAT HAND MOVED across the paper, her head bent as she filled out a report on Slater Rawlings' arrest. There wasn't much to tell, but Griffin was particular about details. He had been ready to do the report himself until he remembered that Liberty was coming in because he had a meeting with the mayor and two members of the town council. He had nearly dragged his sister outside before he left.

"Lunch will be coming while I'm gone, so you be careful."

"I will, Griff, but he doesn't seem that dangerous to me."

"I don't know," Griffin replied with a small shake of his head. "He's probably not, but there's something about this guy, some kind of inner turmoil. I can see it in his eyes. He's angry about being in there, but I know he could pay his way out. He wasn't all too happy this morning when I gave him breakfast, so just be on guard."

Liberty had nodded. "I'll watch myself—him too."

"All right. Thanks, and be sure to thank Mam for those sweet-rolls."

"I'll do it. Hey," Liberty called to him before he could get far. "What about tomorrow?"

"If he hasn't paid his way out, I'll bring him along."

Liberty smiled. "Let's hope you have a quiet night tonight."

Griffin only waved and continued down the street. Liberty went back inside to start the paperwork and give the office a complete dusting. She knew that the prisoner stood at the bars for a while and watched her, but she didn't speak to him or even look in his direction.

"I need something out of my saddlebags," Slater suddenly said.

"You'll have to wait for the sheriff to get back for that," Liberty told him, not bothering to raise her head.

"When will that be?"

"I'm not sure."

"What do I call you, by the way?"

"Deputy."

"What's the matter with this town that a woman has to act as deputy?" Slater muttered, but the woman at the desk just kept writing. Feeling even more irate, he watched her, but in the corner of his mind knew that he was being unjust. He was a prisoner, which meant he had few rights. If she didn't want to talk with him, it was her privilege. Slater let his head rest against the bars and was still in that position when the door opened.

"Oh, Liberty, it's you!" a female voice exclaimed.

Slater watched the woman at the desk laugh.

"It's nice to see you too, Tess."

"I'm sorry." Tess Locken was contrite as she came to stand before the desk. "I was so hoping to find Griff."

"I can't imagine why," Liberty teased. "I'm more fun than he is."

"You are fun, Lib," Tess said sincerely, "but," and here she sighed a little, "I'm not in love with you."

"Oh, well," Liberty shrugged as if the loss were hers. "Can I do anything for you?"

"Only if you know whether Griff is free for dinner Monday night."

Again Liberty shrugged. "I wish I could help."

"Well, I'll just—oh!"

Liberty followed Tess' gaze, knowing she'd just spotted their guest. Slater was still standing, his hands protruding through the bars so his forearms could rest comfortably, his look expressionless as he stared out at them.

"Is he dangerous?" the other woman asked, her voice dropping to a stage whisper.

"He hasn't been so far."

"Did you bring him in?" Tess' voice had risen, but she moved closer to Liberty.

"Yesterday."

Liberty's friend lowered her brow. "He needs a haircut."

The deputy's eyes sparkled as her hand came to her mouth, a movement Slater couldn't miss. He stood very still, doing everything he could not to glare at them. To be talked about as if he wasn't there was maddening.

"Well, I'd better scoot," Tess said quietly. "Tell Griff hello."

"Do you want me to mention Monday night?"

Tess' head cocked to the side in a way that made her look like a scatterbrained female, something she was not. It didn't help that her blue eyes were as innocent as a child's.

"I guess you can go ahead and tell him, but also say that I'll check back with him. Mother said to be sure and tell him to come even if he can only make it for dessert."

Liberty smiled at her. Tess' expression had turned so hopeful.

"I'll relay all of it, Tess."

"Thanks, Libby."

The other woman left on that note, but not before taking one more look at the man behind the bars. The fear in her eyes was not comfortable to Slater, but as he'd been doing for almost 24 hours, he hardened his heart.

"When's lunch?" he asked rudely.

"As soon as it arrives."

Liberty had gone back to the paperwork, and Slater saw that he would get nothing more. Ignoring the voice that reminded him he knew better than to act this way, he stretched out on the bunk and lay still until the noon meal arrived.

🌹 🌹 🌹

"I'm headed to church this morning," Griffin said to Slater as he gave him breakfast on Sunday morning. "I'll have to cuff you, but you can join me if you've a mind to."

Slater thought fast; two nights on that bunk was having an effect. Nevertheless, he still said, "I'm not very fresh for church."

"I'll get some extra water to you."

"I'd need my saddlebags."

"I can get out what you need."

Slater saw it for the olive branch it was. There was no denying that this man had been more than fair. Slater knew he was being stubborn about paying.

"I'd appreciate that" was all Slater said before turning to the bunk to eat the food and drink the coffee that arrived on the tray.

"I'll be back in about an hour," Griffin said as he went out the door. Not anticipating trouble, he certainly hoped to learn a little more about the man who at present was quite the mystery. Griffin guessed Slater to be in his midtwenties, but there was a worldliness about him that made the sheriff think he knew his way around. That wasn't all. From time to time Griffin also saw regret in Slater's light blue eyes and wondered what plagued him. He hadn't honestly thought Slater would accept the offer to attend church—not many did when they learned they had to be cuffed—but Griffin was pleased nonetheless.

Riding home, Griffin let himself in the back door of his own house and began to ready himself for the day. He never relished wearing his guns with a suit, so he opted for clean denim pants, a nice shirt, and a narrow tie. He shaved carefully, looking forward to the service but also to possibly catching sight of Tess. He was sorry he'd missed her the day before. He didn't know if going to her house for dinner was wise, but saying no to the invitation would have been easier if he could have spent a few minutes with her. Now he found himself wanting to accept the invitation just to see her.

His heart sighed with the quandary of it all even as he moved through the house to leave. Having someone love him had never been part of his plan; loving her back was even less so. With a prayer for continued wisdom and kindness, he mounted his horse, Tess on his mind until he arrived back at the jailhouse to help Slater with his saddlebags.

🌹 🌹 🌹

Griffin watched Slater take his Bible in cuffed hands. The sheriff nearly shook his head in wonder as he directed Slater out the jailhouse door. A little more of the mystery was solved. Whether or not this man had accepted the words of Scripture and claimed them for his own, he was clearly under some type of conviction. *No wonder he was so angry*, Griffin thought as he waited until the service started and then escorted his prisoner to the corner of a rear pew. The congregation was on their feet joined in prayer, which allowed Griffin to bring Slater in unobtrusively.

The men sat down with the rest of the worshipers when the pastor closed the prayer, and Griffin saw Liberty rise from the other side of the church to head to the piano. He glanced at the man beside him and saw that he'd noticed as well. A mischievous thought passed through Griffin's mind, a hunch he had to try out. He spoke when Slater glanced at him.

"She looks different in a dress, doesn't she?"

For several heartbeats Slater frowned at the sheriff in confusion before his eyes flew back to the woman at the piano. He stared in disbelief. *Could that actually be the deputy?* Slater had all he could do to keep his mouth closed.

Looking utterly feminine in a bright yellow dress, Liberty readied herself at the keys, completely unaware of Slater's scrutiny. That man took in the way she'd swept her hair off her neck, thinking he'd never seen her without a hat. The dress had long, fitted sleeves, and Slater was surprised by how small her arms and shoulders were; there was never a hint of form in the baggy clothes she wore. The neckline of the dress was rounded with white lace, and it looked as though she had a locket at her throat. Slater had to tear his eyes away when Griffin handed him the hymnal. He didn't know the song at all but did his best. Anything to keep his mind on why he was there.

Slater suddenly gave up and began to pray the way he should have prayed two days before. He stopped trying to sing and poured his heart out to God, confessing his pride and anger. He knew when the song ended but was not quite ready to open his eyes. Not until Griffin leaned over and asked if he was all right did he open his eyes, his heart feeling pounds lighter with the load lifted.

Why do I fight everything You want me to do? Slater asked the Lord when three other people stood and moved to the front, not toward the piano, but toward the pastor. Slater thought they were going to sing until he saw that Liberty had left the piano bench.

"We have a little skit for you this morning," Pastor Ross Caron told the congregation as his wife, Felicia, their daughter, Mayann, and their son, Tanner, came forward. Pastor Caron had a way with drama, and his parishioners were accustomed to his putting a Bible passage or an illustration into skit form.

Tanner and Mayann went off to the right side of the church, but Felicia stood right in front of the pulpit, a mixing bowl and spoon in her hands. Ross came onto the scene from the side.

"Felicia, have you seen Mayann? I asked her to bring me those notes I have upstairs. She's been gone for 20 minutes."

Felicia shook her head, her arm cradling the bowl as she stirred. "I asked her to bring the clothes in off the line, but when I looked out a minute ago, nothing had been done."

Ross walked away shaking his head. Felicia kept up her stirring for a moment and then set the bowl aside. "I guess I'll have to do it myself," she said as she walked to the side of the room.

Ross came back to the center now, and on his way, he stumbled and righted himself.

"What in the world? Mayann, where are you? I just tripped over your skates. You left them right in the hall. Mayann!" he tried again, but when he received no answer, he shook his head and went back the other way.

As soon as he was gone, Mayann and Tanner walked slowly across the front.

"You mean it?" Mayann asked. "You want me to be in charge of the money?"

"Yes," Tanner told her. "You're good with numbers, and we want to be sure that all the proceeds go to the new hymnals."

"I'd love to do it. I can't wait to tell my folks."

Ross and Felicia came back to the middle then, and Mayann wasn't long in joining them.

"You'll never believe what happened!" Mayann nearly shouted. "I've been asked to be in charge of the hymnal money. Isn't that great?"

"The hymnal money?" Ross said with surprise. "That fund is growing fast, Mayann. That's a large responsibility. I'm not sure you can do it."

"Yes, I can," she told her parents. "I've always been good with numbers."

"But there's more to it than that, Mayann," her mother put in. "You've got to be responsible with the account book and all the receipts."

"I will be," the girl assured her parents, who looked at her for a moment.

"Where are the sermon notes I asked you to get me?" Ross finally questioned her.

Mayann's hand came to her mouth.

"Did you fold the laundry when you got it off the line, Mayann, or just throw it in the basket?"

"Oh, no!" she said. "I forgot all about that."

"You also forgot where your skates belong. I tripped on them."

Mayann hung her head. Ross ended the skit by saying, "We've got some work to do."

Slater took in the words of each actor, impressed with the idea and point that was made. He was staring straight at the pastor when that man stepped behind the pulpit and asked, "How good is your reputation? Mayann's wasn't very good with her parents, was it? That wasn't a complicated skit. Anyone could figure it out. But the message needs to hold a lot of weight with all of us. How good is your reputation? How good is *my* reputation? Can the people of this congregation come to me if they feel I'm wrong, or do they fear I'll be angry and send them away? Can I come to you and know that you'll listen to me? Is your reputation that good?

"As we look again in our Bibles at the life of Nehemiah, we see that his reputation was excellent. Let me give you just a few examples. Nehemiah is saddened by sin as we see in chapter 1, verse 4, and his first response is to pray and recognize God's greatness, verse 5. He's humble, verse 6; repentant, verse 7; and he claims God's redemption, verse 10. Go to chapter 2 and see that he's bold, a trusted worker, organized, discreet, tactful, and gives credit where credit is due."

Pastor Caron looked up from his Bible and notes. "I don't know about you, but I can learn from this man."

So can I, Slater thought. He realized he'd never even read the book of Nehemiah. The Texas Ranger who had led him to the Lord had urged him to study in the New Testament. Beyond that, Slater had spent so little time in church that his training had been very limited. This was one of the reasons he'd walked away from his job.

Slater had let his mind wander further than he intended. Surprised when everyone stood for the closing prayer, he didn't have a chance to bow his head. Since the sheriff was already leading him outside, he had all he could do not to drop his Bible with cuffed hands. He looked forward to getting back to the jail and paying his way out. He was surprised again when Sheriff Drake did not return him to the jail.

🌿 🌿 🌿

"Then what did you do?" Liberty asked Laura, their faces close as the little girl sat in her sister's lap.

"I just looked away," Laura told her, working not to let her voice quiver.

"You did well," Kate inserted from her seat nearby. "I'm glad you didn't pinch back."

Laura nodded and looked down at the dark bruise on her arm. One of the other children at church had pinched her.

"I didn't cry," Laura told them, "but I think Zach wanted to."

"Zach loves you," Liberty put in. "He hurts when you hurt."

"I love Zach too."

Liberty kissed her sister's soft temple and hugged her close. Laura had always treated Liberty like another mother—both children did—and their mother had never done anything to alter that.

"All right, Laura," Kate instructed after she kissed her youngest daughter too. "Will you please help me get things ready for dinner?"

Laura nodded.

"Please take your dolls off that chair. Your brother brought a guest today."

"Who is it?"

"You'll meet him when he gets here. Where is Zach?"

"I think he's outside."

"Please go tell him we're almost ready to eat."

Griffin and Slater, both sitting in the parlor, listened to this last sentence in silence. Slater had not uttered a word since Griffin had led him from the church, and Griffin had done little more than lead him up the street, into the front door of a two-story home, and to a satin-covered chair in a very comfortable room, where he now sat.

Not thinking that the sheriff was inclined to visit, Slater let his eyes roam the walls. Clearly a woman lived here. Family pictures were displayed on tables and walls; lace curtains graced windows and doilies sat on the arms of upholstered furniture. And everything was freshly dusted.

"We're ready," a female voice called from the other room.

Griffin stood and approached Slater. "This is my family," he told the prisoner. "I think you'd be more comfortable without the cuffs, and I think I can trust you, but if I'm wrong, I won't hesitate to take you out."

Slater nodded, knowing the man had no choice. Slater only wished he had his wallet so he could lose the cuffs for good. It was a relief to rub his wrists once they were gone, and his enjoyment of that caused him to forget that he might see the sheriff's sister. When he walked into the dining room and saw her, he had all he could do not to gawk. If he'd thought her lovely across the church, he didn't know what to think now. Why hadn't he noticed before the deep hazel of her eyes or the red highlights in her hair?

"Duffy—" Griffin's voice brought Slater back. "This is Slater Rawlings. He's a guest of the jailhouse right now."

"Hello, Slater." Duffy shook his hand and took over. "This is my wife, Kate, my daughter Liberty, my son Zach, and my younger daughter, Laura."

"Thank you for letting me join you," Slater said quietly, taking the chair Griffin indicated. Heads bowed and Duffy prayed. Slater looked up after the close, an ache in his throat for his own family. He was glad that the bowls of food were immediately passed.

"Will she go to hell?" Laura suddenly asked.

"What?" Her father turned to her, a spoonful of mashed potatoes frozen in his hand as he looked at her in astonishment.

"We didn't explain to you, Duffy," Kate put in, not looking at Liberty, who had her hand over her mouth, her eyes brimming with merriment. "Someone pinched Laura at church."

"I see," Duffy said quietly, now in the same state as his stepdaughter. He made himself finish with the potatoes and pass them on, then turned to Laura, all the while working to keep a straight face.

"Did you say it was another girl?" Duffy clarified.

Laura nodded. "I can't tell names unless you tell me to, or it's gossip."

"All right," Duffy nodded over being reminded of his own rule. "This little girl might be lost, Laura, but not because she pinched you.

It was wrong of her to pinch you, but she would only go to hell if she never accepted Christ's forgiveness in her life. Do you understand?"

Laura nodded again, and Duffy went back to his food.

Slater glanced around the table and noticed the way all the other adults were busy with their plates as well. He watched Liberty and Griffin share a glance, but other than Liberty's eyes sparkling, she gave nothing away. He wished he could keep watching her. From where he sat, she and Zach were very clear.

Griffin spoke up with a tidbit of news that Zach thoroughly enjoyed, and that seemed to get the conversation ball rolling. Slater remained very quiet and forced himself not to stare or wolf down the delicious food, both of which were strong temptations.

"Who's for pie?" Kate asked after a time.

No one declined. An apple pie came to the table that was so mounded with fruit that it had a hump in the middle. Slater had decided not to speak, but after tasting this pie, he could not contain himself; it was the best he'd ever had.

"This is excellent," he said quietly.

"Libby made it," Kate said, smiling down the table at her.

Slater welcomed a reason to look at her, but she was not looking his way. He stared for several bites of pie, and she eventually looked up, but he couldn't read her expression. Regret knifed through him. She wouldn't see him as anything more than a two-bit drifter, and he had no one to thank but himself. It was almost a relief to have the meal end and Griffin tell him they had to be on their way.

🌢 🌢 🌢

"If you'll give me my wallet, I'll get the ten dollars for you."

Griffin looked at the man he'd just uncuffed and nodded. He went to the safe, opened it, and removed the rest of Slater's things. The moment Slater had his wallet, he settled things with Shotgun's sheriff. He then began to fill his pockets with his possessions.

"Where will you head from here?" Griffin asked after he'd sat on the desk, his legs dangling down the side.

Slater looked to the window. "I don't know. I like Shotgun, especially the church. Maybe I'll stick around."

Griffin nodded. "What took you so long to decide?"

Slater shook his head. "Stubborn-mule pride, and I just quit my job. Ten bucks is a lot of money."

"What do you do?"

Slater looked him in the eye. "I was a Texas Ranger until last month."

Griffin's brows rose as a dozen more questions rolled through his mind. When did a man question and when did a man leave a person his privacy? Griffin thought of one safe inquiry.

"Did the church service this morning have anything to do with your decision?"

"It had a lot to do with it. There's nothing like hearing about Nehemiah's qualities to make me see how short I am."

"I felt that same way."

Slater threw his saddlebags over one shoulder and started to say thank you. Griffin cut him off.

"Have you got a place to sleep tonight?"

Slater's mouth quirked. "You mean other than the woods?"

Griffin smiled. "I live next door to my mother and Duffy. You're welcome to one of the bedrooms."

Slater nodded. "Thank you."

"If I'm not there when you get in, use the back door and take any bedroom upstairs."

"I'll plan on that."

"One more thing," Griffin said. "The hotel gives a full plate of food for 15 cents. It's not fancy, but it's always hot and filling."

Slater's hand came out. "Thank you, sheriff."

"You can call me Griffin."

Slater nodded, shook the man's hand, and went to the door. It was a quiet Sunday afternoon, the sun shining, but the breeze was cool as he walked down the street. Slater held his expectations at bay, but on the way to church that morning he thought he'd spotted a bathhouse. It might not be open, but he had to give it a try. If that didn't work, he'd get Arrow from the livery and ride out until he found a deep spot in the creek.

Three

"THAT YOU, SLATER?" GRIFFIN CALLED when he heard the back door open after 8:00 that night.

"Yeah. I couldn't tell if you were here or not."

Griffin appeared at the doorway, a lantern in his hand. He set it on the kitchen table, noticed Slater's slicked-back hair, and grinned.

"If I'd known you were looking for a bath, I'd have told you to use my tub."

Slater shook his head. "The bathhouse was closed, and I couldn't find any privacy on the creek. I had to wait until after dark. That water is cold."

"Come on through here," Griffin invited. He led the way to the living room where he'd been cleaning a gun. This room had gas lighting that cast a warm glow to every corner but didn't penetrate the dark curtains over the windows. The house had looked dark and deserted when Slater rode up. He had taken the liberty of stabling his horse in the back and letting himself in.

"How far did you ride up the creek?"

"About a mile. It's pretty country."

"I think so. Did you get some supper?"

"The hotel. I'm not crazy about lamb, but I've had worse. By the way, do you live alone? Should I be watching not to scare the life out of someone?"

"No, I'm on my own. This was Duffy's mother's house. I moved over when she died."

"Duffy's not your father?"

"No. My father died when I was a kid. Mam married Duff about two years later."

"And had Zach and Laura."

"Yeah," Griffin smiled. There was little that got to his heart faster than his little brother and sister. He suddenly remembered Laura's question at the table and chuckled.

Slater had thought of it too. "Unless I miss my guess, she's something of a character."

"Laura? Yes. She makes me laugh every time I talk to her."

"I thought your sister would choke."

"Libby's like another mother to Laura but with very little discipline; Mam and Duffy see to that. It's the same with Zach."

"He seems like a bright young man."

"He's better read than some adults my age. He has a sensitive heart too."

Slater wanted to ask if Griffin would marry and have his own brood, but he knew it wasn't his affair. The pretty blonde who had come into the jailhouse was clearly willing. Slater wondered if Shotgun's sheriff was holding back for some reason.

"I was in bed late and up early," Griffin suddenly said, finishing his work and putting it aside. "I hope you won't mind if I turn in."

"Not at all. I was hoping to turn in soon."

The men said their goodnights, but Griffin ended up showing Slater to the most comfortable room. He told him to come downstairs if he needed anything and left him alone with the lantern. Slater climbed into bed, intent on reading the whole book of Nehemiah. But he only got halfway through. He was asleep just five seconds after turning down the lantern.

🌿 🌿 🌿

Pulling the belt on her dressing gown tightly around her, Liberty slipped out of the house on Monday morning and dashed across to Griffin's house. She had left her revolver in his kitchen—he had volunteered to clean it for her—but she didn't know if he'd gotten to it or not. She was headed to the office this morning and didn't want to forget.

Liberty slipped in the back door and groped around until she had the lantern lit. Griffin was a fairly light sleeper, and Liberty hoped she could get out without disturbing him. She was still looking for the gun when she heard him at the door.

"Sorry, Griff," Liberty spoke while facing the counter. "I just thought I'd better get my gun before I head downtown."

"Why would you leave your gun here?" Slater asked before he thought.

Liberty had only just laid her hands on the weapon. She spun so fast that Slater blinked. The gun was up and aimed at his chest.

"When did you get out?"

"Yesterday, right after lunch."

"What are you doing here?" Her voice was deadly calm, the gun completely steady.

"I just got up." Slater was a little sleepy but waking fast.

"Where's my brother?"

"Probably asleep."

"If you've hurt him—" Liberty began, but Slater cut her off, having just remembered the night before.

"You'll what?" he asked mildly. "Shoot me with a gun that has no bullets?"

"How do you know whether or not it has bullets?" Liberty asked, still not dropping her guard or the weapon.

"Because that's the gun I watched your brother clean last night, and somehow I don't think he loaded it."

Liberty didn't answer. He was probably right, but until she saw Griffin . . .

"What's up, Libby?" the man of her worries asked as he came in behind Slater. He summed up the scene in a moment, leaning against the opposite wall to address her. "I asked him to spend the night."

Liberty slowly lowered the gun, feeling foolish.

"Fix your robe, Lib," Griffin said softly, and Liberty fell completely apart. She nearly dropped the gun as she set it aside, only to scoop it up the moment she'd drawn the front of her dressing gown back together. She was on the verge of leaving when she realized what she'd done. Liberty made herself turn back and meet Slater's eyes.

"I'm sorry."

He was not given a chance to reply. Liberty quietly thanked Griffin for cleaning the gun and hurried back out the door.

The kitchen was very quiet on her exit. Slater had his eyes on the door but looked over to see Griffin staring at him, his expression one of complete puzzlement.

"I've never seen her so rattled," he said, almost to himself.

"She must have been embarrassed." Slater's hand went to his bare chest. "It never occurred to me that you might have company this early in the morning, or I'd have stayed in my room."

"Well," Griffin shrugged, "she lives next door, and we all kind of come and go as we please." Griffin paused and looked at his guest. This man was nothing like he had first figured. The line about being a Texas Ranger could all be a farce, but Griffin didn't think so. Something inside of him wanted to reach out. "If you find work, Slater, and want to live here, you're welcome. If that ends up being the case, I'll warn the family."

Slater, who had been praying about that very thing, nodded his head and thanked Griffin.

"How did you sleep?" the law officer wished to know.

"Very well. The bed and room are comfortable. Can we set up some type of rent system if I find work here in town?"

"That would be fine, but I'm not worried about it right now."

Slater nodded, taking him at his word on that subject but quite certain there was something else on the man's mind. Slater felt it was best to leave him with his thoughts.

"I'll clean up now," the visitor said.

"Sure. There's water in the bucket there."

Slater used the pitcher that sat close by, filled it, and exited the room. He wasn't gone a second before his head came back around the door frame.

"*You* clean Liberty's gun?"

Griffin laughed before he said, "It's my own fault. I did it for her once, and she liked it so well, I've been roped into it ever since. She's the fast hand and I'm the gunsmith."

"Where did she learn to draw?" Slater couldn't help asking.

"Our father. He worked with both of us from the time we were small, but Liberty was different. She took to handling weapons like a kitten takes to its mother. For as long as I can remember, it's been as natural as breathing for her."

Slater suddenly felt out of words. After a look at his host to see if he expected a reply, Slater turned and made his way upstairs. This was a most unusual situation, and he didn't know how he felt about it. The family he'd met yesterday had been warm and caring. But if they cared, how could they put one of their women in such a dangerous position? Slater did not understand. It made him uncomfortable, but at the same time he wanted to know them better. He wished to be invited into their home as a guest, not a prisoner. For this reason alone, he held his tongue about the things that confused him. Maybe in time it would be clear.

Slater stepped in front of the mirror, the one that sat over the washbowl in his room. He scowled at his reflection. His desire to grow a beard was waning. His hair was just light enough that the attempt only made him look unkempt. Knowing he needed a trip to the barber anyway, he opted to leave the beard until he got downtown.

A shave and a haircut, and then off to find work.

Liberty stood in her bedroom, her brow drawn into serious contemplation. At the moment she wondered if she would ever comfortably walk into her brother's house again. She shook her head, thinking she had never been so surprised. The sheriff's office, the saloons, and even the streets of Shotgun were places she had to be on guard—never here at home and never at Griffin's. Now all that felt as though it had changed. Liberty worked at not being angry at her brother or the blond cowboy who had wandered into town.

"Libby," her mother called from down the stairs, "should I put some pancakes on for you?"

"Yes, please," Liberty called back. She hurried to button the baggy shirt she'd put on before placing the vest over the top. She didn't bother to look in the mirror; it was easier that way.

Oh, stop it! she chided herself. *What do you care what you look like right now? You have a job to do! People are counting on you.* But it wasn't quite that simple. For some reason the blond cowboy's eyes kept coming to mind. He had looked at her when she arrested him, and even in the jail, but the eyes he'd turned on her at the dinner table the day before had been entirely different.

"It's just that it's never happened before," she said softly, her feet leaving the last step and turning toward the dining room. "Everyone else in town is used to seeing you both ways."

"Were you talking to us, dear?" her mother asked.

"No, just to myself."

Kate took in Liberty's face and felt concern. Duffy must have seen something too because he asked from his place at the table, "Are you all right, Lib?"

Liberty thought of the way she'd held a gun on her brother's houseguest that morning. It would have been easy to say no, she wasn't all right, but she wasn't up to explaining right then.

"I'm just thinking," Liberty told them.

Kate and Duffy let it go, but both were watchful.

"Can I go to work with you today, Libby?" Laura asked.

"Don't talk with food in your mouth," her mother corrected.

Laura swallowed with great show and asked again.

"Not today, Laura. If Griffin is with me you might come sometime, but if I'm on my own and needed, you'd be left by yourself."

"I could sit at the desk."

"That's true, but I would want someone with you."

"Zach has a desk at school, and Mam has one in the kitchen."

Liberty only smiled at her before looking at her parents, who had been taking in the whole exchange. Zach's going off to school had been very hard for Laura, and the year had just begun. Duffy and Kate had been talking about getting her a small desk for Christmas, and it seemed that might still be a good idea.

Liberty tucked into her food, all the while listening to Zach tell about the book he was reading. Liberty remembered reading that very book when she was about his age and almost shook her head at the difference. Zach was most impressed with the way the boy had worked to earn money to buy his teacher a present; Liberty remembered little but the girl in the story and the way she took care of her baby sister. She chalked it up to the difference between the genders and then remembered the incident from the morning.

"We're still quite far apart," she mumbled to herself as she headed out the door for work.

🌹 🌹 🌹

"Shave and a haircut?" the barber asked solicitously, now that Slater was in the chair.

"Yes, please."

"You're a polite one," the man with the razor commented as he laid Slater back and began to lather his face.

"Why wouldn't I be?"

"No reason, but I don't often see young cowboys stopping to help ladies with their bags or children when their dog runs off."

Slater's eyes went to the large windows that overlooked Main Street.

"You don't miss much, do you?"

The barber grinned unrepentantly. "Nope."

Little more was said as the barber got down to business. Slater had slept well but felt himself relaxing under the man's capable hands. He still had gainful employment on his mind and suddenly realized whom he could talk to.

"Any work to be had in town?" Slater asked as the barber started on his hair.

"What do you do?"

"A little of everything, I guess."

The barber looked at him in the mirror for a moment.

"Hank Hathaway's boy just left for the bright lights of Austin. Hank builds houses. He might be looking for a hand."

Slater's brows rose. It had been a while since he'd worked with a hammer, but he didn't think he'd forgotten any of the basics.

"Do you know where I might find him?"

"A few blocks over. He's puttin' a covered porch on the back of Mrs. Tobler's house. Should have done it years ago; nothing but west sun for hours every day."

Slater smiled a little. If he'd wanted information, he'd come to the right place.

🌸 🌸 🌸

"You ever even held a hammer?" the scruffy-looking old man asked Slater about 15 minutes after he left the barbershop.

"Yes, sir. I've done some building."

"You won't get rich," Hank said.

"I didn't plan on it. Some food and covering the rent would be nice, maybe a new shirt now and again."

Still Hank weighed him. He wasn't as big as his son, but then not many men were. He was polite enough; Hank had to give him that.

"I'll give you a try and pay you when you work, but if I say you're gone, you're gone."

"Yes, sir."

"You can start by lifting the other end of that board and holding it in place. Hold it steady now."

Slater immediately bent to the task, glad he'd seen fit to return his horse to the stable at Griffin's. He'd asked God to help him find work. He now asked His help in not shrinking from any task.

🌸 🌸 🌸

Griffin came in reading the mail. He stood a few feet from the desk, his mind otherwise occupied, so it took several minutes for him to realize his sister was staring at him from the desk chair.

"What's up?" he asked.

"Whatever compelled you to ask him to spend the night at your house?"

Remembering how embarrassed she'd been, Griffin put the mail aside.

"He's not a bad guy, Lib. I was really impressed with the way he wanted to go to church and the way he followed along in his Bible. He found the book of Nehemiah without a bit of help from me."

"He agreed to go to church with you yesterday?"

"Yes, we sat in the back."

This gave Liberty pause; she had not expected this. Griffin often asked prisoners to join him in church, but few accepted.

"I feel worse now," Liberty admitted.

"Why?"

"While he was still behind bars, he wanted something from his saddlebags. I told him he'd have to wait for you, and then I never told you. He probably wanted his Bible."

"Don't be too hard on yourself, Lib. He admitted to me that he was being stubborn about paying the fine. If he'd wanted out enough to get his Bible, he could have paid the ten dollars at any time."

Liberty was thankful for her brother's understanding but still felt uncomfortable about that whole ordeal. *Ah, well, he'll be miles from here in no time. I'll just have to put it from my mind.*

"Were things quiet this morning?" Griffin asked, the other subject slipping from his mind.

"No trouble, but Maddie Flowers stopped to say that her neighbors were on a drunken binge all weekend. She said they've been making their own brew and that we'd do well to burn down that barn of theirs, since that's where the trouble always starts."

Griffin shook his head. "And of course Maddie's brew is only for medicinal purposes, so we should leave her still alone."

Liberty grinned.

"Let's go out in the morning," Griffin suggested. "You'll be in?"

"Midmorning. Right after Bible study."

"All right. I'll see you then."

Liberty left the jailhouse and sheriff's office, thinking it was a nice day for a walk. She untied her horse's reins but didn't climb into the saddle. She even went the long way home. She worked on Monday and Tuesday mornings, and at odd times when Griffin needed her. So far Griffin had not met anyone he felt qualified for the job. The town was getting big enough to consider more law enforcement, but that didn't mean men were available.

"Libby! Is that you?"

Liberty looked over to see old Mrs. Tobler waving a dishtowel in her direction.

"Hi, Mrs. Tobler."

"Come in here!" the old gal demanded. "I can't find my needle. Come in and look for it."

Liberty changed directions without hesitation. Mrs. Tobler was a dear old thing, if a little bossy. It never occurred to her to ask for anything—it was always demanded—but beyond that, she was kindness itself.

"It's slipped down the cushion, I'm sure!" Mrs. Tobler informed Liberty as she neared. "I don't know how I'm supposed to get anything done without my needle."

"What are you working on right now?"

"Pillow slips! And Christmas right around the corner."

Liberty hid a smile as she went in the old woman's front door. Not for anything would she have mentioned that Christmas was well over two months away or that Mrs. Tobler's closet was so full of things she'd made that she probably could give up sewing for the rest of her life.

"All right," Liberty said, standing in the overcrowded living room. "Where were you sitting?"

"Right here. I like to keep an eye on the work out back, so I moved my chair."

"What's going on out back?" Liberty asked as she dropped to her knees and began to search.

"A covered porch," Mrs. Tobler said absently, having moved to the window to peer out. "No, no!" the older woman suddenly exclaimed and dashed out of the room. Liberty could hear the side door bang and Mrs. Tobler's voice raised in irritation. Shotgun's deputy only shook her head and kept searching. She pulled the cushion from the chair, but that only produced some popcorn kernels and a button. The floor was next.

Liberty was searching, her nose nearly on the rug, when she spotted them. Liberty stared at the cowboy boots in confusion, until she realized someone was wearing them. She tipped her head back and literally gawked into the face of Slater Rawlings. With his haircut and beard gone, he was a different man.

"Aren't you going to pull your gun?" he asked quietly.

Liberty blinked before saying, "Why should I do that?"

"That's what you've done every time you've seen me, so I thought you might have gotten into the habit."

Liberty bit her lip but it didn't work; a smile peeked through, and then a laugh. She moved to get up, and Slater's hand was suddenly right there to help her.

"I really am sorry about this morning."

"It's all right," Slater said. Having seen the way she looked without the men's clothes, he could now see the real Liberty Drake, even in this outfit. She had the most amazing hazel eyes, more gold than anything else. And that hair! Slater wanted to stare and stare.

"You're very understanding."

"And you're looking for something. What is it?"

"A needle."

Comprehension dawned on Slater's face. "That's what she sent me in to do—look for a needle with you."

Liberty frowned. "How do you know Mrs. Tobler?"

"I'm working on her porch with Hank Hathaway."

Liberty's eyes went to the window and back to Slater.

"You're working here in town?"

"Yep." Slater's thumbs went to his belt loops, and he rocked back on his heels. "Hired just four hours ago. I'm the town's newest carpenter."

Liberty found him so cute that she couldn't stop her second smile.

"And why" she asked now, a smile still in her voice, "did Mrs. Tobler think I needed help with the needle?"

"Well, I didn't understand it at the time, but I realize now that she said, 'You might as well help Lib find the needle. I've got to set this old man straight.'"

Hand to her mouth, Liberty dissolved into laughter, and without thinking, she collapsed into the chair, a position that lasted for only a second before she was on her feet again.

"I found it!" she gasped, just stopping short of clutching her stinging backside.

Slater's eyes flew to the seat and there it was, protruding point-side up. It wasn't hard to imagine why Liberty had not stayed in the chair. Slater bent to retrieve it just as Mrs. Tobler came in the door.

"You've found it," she said matter-of-factly. "I knew Liberty could do it with some help." With that the old woman plucked the needle from Slater's fingers. "Now get back out there and keep an eye on him. He knows what he's supposed to do, but you'd better watch him.

"Libby! You come with me. I want you to see that new quilt I put on my bed."

Liberty nodded and even smiled. She followed Mrs. Tobler with a wave at Slater. Slater waved back before moving to exit the room. Before he left, however, he looked back to see Liberty following their hostess, her hand now reaching back to rub the pin hole. Slater stopped for a moment, his heart wrung with tenderness. Even as he proceeded back out to work, the scene remained on his mind along with another emotion, one he couldn't quite define.

Four

"THANK YOU, MRS. LOCKEN," Griffin said kindly on Monday evening. "Everything was great."

"You're welcome, Griffin. Would you like some coffee on the porch?"

Griffin looked at Tess, and she nodded.

"I'll help you, Mama," Tess offered.

"I'm fine, dear. If I need help, I'll ask your father. You go ahead."

Tess led the way but wished she didn't have to. She never wanted it to look as if she'd conspired to get Griffin alone. For this reason she took a chair that sat off on its own when she reached the front porch.

Griffin noticed and even understood why. Tess had never pushed herself at him. This, along with dozens of other facts about this woman, made his feelings even harder to accept. He hadn't planned to love anyone. And he certainly hadn't planned on a sweet, godly woman loving him.

"Was it busy today?" Tess asked, always interested in his work.

"Pretty quiet. Lib was in this morning, but she said it was quiet too."

Tess smiled. "I like Libby so much. She's so fun and smart."

"You're smart too, Tess," Griffin said. He knew she struggled with her self-image. She was a very beautiful woman, with pale blonde hair, skin like cream, and huge blue eyes. And since most people thought that was all there was to her, she had begun to believe it. It didn't help that her father and older brothers were men who had little time for family. Making money was their main concern.

"That's what Libby always says, but when you're with someone as capable as Libby, it's hard to believe."

Griffin didn't answer. Tess hadn't been looking directly at him, so when it got quiet she looked up to find his eyes on her. His face looked boyish, as it often did. It made Tess smile.

"You don't look tough enough to be the sheriff."

"And you're too wonderful to be in love with an old hound dog like me."

"Oh, Griff," Tess said softly.

Griffin watched her look away, her eyes filling. He had talked with Duffy and Pastor Caron, and they had asked him if he was trusting God. He thought that he was, but did trust mean being blind to the facts? When a man had his type of job—the type of job that had killed his father—did he go into marriage without a backward glance? And what if they had children? He would not only leave Tess alone, but his kids too.

Griffin looked out over the quiet street the Lockens lived on. He had been happy to be single, but then Tess moved into town a year ago and came to church with her mother. At first he thought there wasn't much under those pale blonde curls or behind that ready smile, but then she'd visited Mam and Duffy's house at Liberty's invitation, and Griffin learned otherwise. She was a woman whose faith in God was genuine and whose courage was deep.

"Here's coffee," Mrs. Locken said as she used her hip to push open the screen door, the tray in her hands. Griffin rose to take it from her.

"If you don't mind, I think I'll go in and have mine with Albert. Call if you need something."

"Thank you, Mrs. Locken."

Tess rose to pour the coffee and offered him a cup. She fixed it just the way he liked. The light was fading, but when she sat with her own cup, Griffin could see that Tess' eyes were still moist.

"Maybe I shouldn't stay, Tess," Griffin forced himself to say.

"You don't have to if you don't want to," she said to him, and Griffin had to close his eyes. She was so special.

"What do you want me to do?" he finally asked.

Tess took a big breath. "I want you to play me in checkers. You beat me the last two times, and I want a rematch."

For a long moment the sheriff could only look at her. Not able to help himself and not willing to try, Griffin reached over and let one finger slide down her soft cheek.

"I'll get the board."

Tess' eyes closed the moment he stood, her heart wondering how she would make it. Every moment with him was sweet torture. She wanted to sob her eyes out but heard him coming back through the house.

If he isn't for me, Lord, please work a miracle in my heart so it doesn't break in two.

❧ ❧ ❧

"A shave *and* a haircut," Griffin said when he got home that night and found Slater in the living room. "Did you go for a job or courtin'?"

Slater laughed. "I didn't think it would hurt to look my best."

"Where'd you go—the bank?"

Slater's look was smug. "You happen to be looking at Shotgun's newest contractor."

Griffin was not long in catching on. "I'd heard that Price Hathaway headed to Austin. You must have taken his job. How do you like working for Hank?"

Slater's eyes grew comically. "He knows what he's doing, and he knows what he wants me to do; it's just a matter of getting him to remember that he thought about the order but didn't tell me. I think I know why Price left town."

"Hank's a case, but you're right, he does know how to build. Are you by any chance at Mrs. Tobler's right now?"

"That's the place. She wants a covered porch on the back side of her house. It's only going to shade two windows, but she wants it."

"She's got a big heart but also a mind of her own. Libby went there as a little girl for sewing lessons."

"She was there today."

"For sewing lessons?"

"No. Mrs. Tobler lost her needle and expected your sister to find it."

"Did she?"

"Not until after she sat on it."

Griffin's brow lowered. "Is she all right?"

"That's not a question I could really ask her. I think it smarted, but she might have been more surprised than anything."

"How did you learn about the needle?"

Slater gave Griffin a rundown and that man's face became very thoughtful.

"Did I say something wrong?" Slater had been watching him closely.

"No, not at all," Griffin told him honestly but knew that the rest of his thoughts would have to stay inside. Slater wouldn't thank him and neither would Liberty. *Not to mention the fact that you can't figure out what you're doing in your own relationship, Griffin, let alone getting involved in someone else's.*

"How do you think you'll like a hammer and nails after law enforcement?" Griffin asked in an effort to shift his thoughts.

Slater thought for a moment, his head leaning back against the softly padded chair; it was a question he'd been asking himself all day.

"It's going to take some getting used to," Slater finally admitted.

Griffin nodded but still didn't ask the question that had come to his mind the moment he'd learned this man was a Texas Ranger. That question might take some time or turn out to be one he could never ask.

"There's a church picnic this Sunday afternoon," Griffin told him instead. His mother had let him know that day. "We must have come in after it was announced."

"Right after church?"

"Yes, at the Millers', on the creek."

"Do we bring something?"

"My mother and Libby usually take pity on me and bring enough for a threshing crew. Unless you're in the mood to cook, don't worry about it."

"My skills in the kitchen can't compare to your mother's. I wouldn't starve, but a home-cooked meal always tastes like a feast."

Griffin laughed, but such words made him think of Tess. She was a great cook. With sudden clarity he realized something that had never been evident to him. In the last two months, when Tess' feelings and his own had become clear, he'd talked to Pastor Caron and Duffy. They had been very helpful, but he'd never spoken to his mother—the woman who had been widowed because she'd been married to the town's sheriff.

Sitting across the room, Slater watched the emotions chase across Griffin's face but kept silent. Clearly the man had much on his mind. If memory served him correctly, this was the night the blonde woman had wanted him to come for dinner. Had Liberty called her Tess? Is that where he'd been when Slater found the house empty? Much as Slater wondered, he knew he would never ask.

"I'm for bed," Slater said instead, wanting to give this man who had offered him a home even more privacy.

"I'll bet you are. Waking up to have a gun pointed at you takes it out of a man."

Slater laughed. "When I saw your sister today, I asked her why she didn't draw."

"Did she blush or laugh?"

"A little of both, I guess." Slater stood. "Good night, Griffin."

"Good night, Slater."

Griffin watched him walk from the room, reminding himself that it was way too early to take a full measure of this man, but the temptation to let his mind wander was strong. Liberty needed someone special. The thought no more formed than Griffin's mouth quirked. What brother didn't feel that way? That Tess' brothers might not care suddenly came to mind. As Griffin was coming to expect, it didn't take much to make him think of that woman.

※ ※ ※

"Do you have to work?" Laura asked Liberty the next day. Bible study had just ended.

"Yes. Griffin and I have to check on something."

"Can you give Griff a hug for me?"

"I certainly can. Is there some special reason?"

Laura only shook her head no, seeming in no hurry to leave her sister's lap. Their mother was sitting beside Liberty, and the younger woman decided to question her if she had a chance. The opportunity came a few minutes later. Their hostess, Mrs. Caron, offered cookies to the children, and Laura, looking only mildly interested, left her sister's lap.

"Did you hear what she said?" Liberty asked quietly.

"About the hug? Yes. She's been so clingy, Lib. I think she's coming down with something. She cried this morning when she got juice on her hand."

Liberty's eyes widened in surprise. Her little sister was a very plucky gal. Spilled juice would not normally get her down.

"You look tired, Mam." Liberty had just seen it. "Maybe the two of you have a little bug going."

"Maybe."

"I think you should see the doctor," Liberty said, her eyes sparkling a little. "I hear he gives very personal service."

Kate laughed and put a hand on her daughter's arm. *If* she was coming down with something, just talking to Liberty would make her feel better.

"I'll think about your advice."

"All right. I'd better go. Griff and I have a case to check on. I won't stay any longer than I have to in case Laura gets worse."

"Thank you, dear. Don't forget to eat lunch."

Liberty thanked their hostess and went out front to where she had tethered Morton. Already dressed for work, she swung easily into the saddle. Mrs. Tobler's house was close enough that Liberty could hear the hammers pounding, but she made herself ride for downtown.

Why would you stop, Libby? She couldn't have lost another needle, and there's no other reason to go there right now.

This was all the further Liberty would allow these thoughts to roam. Knowing that she had to go with Griffin to confront the Potters, a consistently risky event, Liberty forced her mind to concentrate on her job. A good thing too. As soon as Griffin spotted her, he exited the office and climbed into the saddle of his own mount, Benny.

"Has there been more word?" Liberty asked, after telling Griffin that Laura had sent him a hug.

"Yes. Mrs. Flowers was back in this morning. The party was still going on last night."

"Ned Potter was nothing short of belligerent the last time I saw him."

"When was this?"

"About two weeks back. He was giving Miss Amy a hard time over the price of eggs and looked mad enough to kill when I stepped in."

"Why didn't you tell me?"

Liberty shrugged. "I forgot about it until just now."

"Well, I hope he remembers."

"Why?"

"Because this is just the first. Ned and his boys have thought themselves above the law just one time too many. I won't take action today, and maybe not even this year, but this is the beginning of the end. I'm going to put enough pressure on to make them uncomfortable."

Liberty agreed with the action but couldn't help wondering what they'd be letting themselves in for.

"Will we see Maddie Flowers too?"

"Yep. She's a little too self-righteous for my comfort. I want her to know that I'm aware of what she's up to, and that just because she doesn't have drunken binges does not make her judge and jury."

They fell silent for the rest of the ride. The Potters lived a ways outside of town. Their place was large and run down, a marked contrast to Mrs. Flowers' spotless paint and yard. They had to pass Mrs. Flowers' house on the way, and both officers caught the way she smugly watched them from the window, but neither sibling waved or acknowledged her call.

Things were quiet at the Potter house. A dog as old and broken-down as most of the rusty farm equipment in the yard barked a hoarse yap at them, but he didn't have enough ambition to move from his place under the porch, not even when Griffin went up the steps and pounded on the door. It was answered by Critter, the youngest of three sons.

"Pa's not here," the teen scowled at him, his eyes squinting against the sun.

"Mind if I come in and look?"

"Yeah, I do!" Critter growled, but Griffin's hand had already pushed the door wide. Liberty was right behind him.

"Get out," Critter said. The officers ignored him. He started a string of curses but stopped when he realized no one was listening. The house was in awful shape, and Liberty couldn't help but wonder how they all stood the smell and the filth. She had never needed to come in here before, but Griffin seemed to know his way around.

"What'd ya want?" Critter tried again as Griffin slipped upstairs, but again no one paid him any heed.

Still taking in the broken furniture, stained walls, and liquor bottles, Liberty thought she and Critter couldn't be too many years apart in age, but their lives had been lived in separate worlds.

"I think I'll have a look at the barn," Griffin said casually as he came slowly back down the stairs.

It wasn't lost on either sibling the way Critter came to attention.

"Pa don't like anybody nosin' out there."

"Well, come with us," Griffin offered mildly. "Give us the grand tour."

Critter seemed at a momentary loss before turning to the door, his body saying very clearly that the law in Shotgun was unjust.

As always, Liberty kept to the rear. More than once she had protected her brother's back, and as Griffin swung the barn door open, hinges howling, she took her standard position. Critter was mutinously silent. He walked in behind the sheriff, not seeming to notice the way Liberty hung back.

"What's in here?" Griffin asked as he approached a wagon covered by a tarpaulin. Without permission, Griffin untied the edge and threw it back.

"Nice load of corn, Critter. It's a little late in the year for planting."

The eyes that followed him were dark with rage. Watching him, Liberty thought he might still be a little done-in from the night before, which would slow his reaction time. His reputation, however, did not lead to trust. She watched while Griffin came from the stall, his head tipped back inspecting the rafters. With a move that gave nothing away, he approached Critter.

"The shinin's going to stop, Critter. I just want you to know that." Griffin walked as he talked, and the youngest Potter, against his will, was backed up to the wall. "You give your Pa and brothers a message from me: I'm going to shut you down. I can't have you out here gettin' drunk, lightin' fires, and shootin' off shotguns all night. It's gotta stop."

Griffin had Critter flat against the wall now, his eyes hard and serious. Critter's own gaze was no more friendly, and when he suddenly felt a sickle on the wall, he started to reach for it. He had barely moved when the wood near his fingers splintered from a bullet. Critter froze. He'd completely forgotten the deputy. He could have lost part of his hand!

"Have I made myself clear?" Griffin asked.

"You wouldn't be so tough if Pa was here!" Critter spat. The fear had swiftly left, and he was angry again. "He won't be too pleased to know you were here nosin' around."

"He's welcome to come by the jailhouse and lodge a complaint." This said, Griffin held the younger man's eyes for several seconds and then pushed away from the wall. He walked from the barn, Liberty having already moved ahead of him this time, her eyes watching Critter. She was satisfied when he took his eyes from them. Critter's hand went to the back of his neck, and he leaned against the wall with a shake of his head. Liberty had already holstered her gun but now felt free to turn and mount her horse.

Griffin had been watching as well and climbed into his own saddle after Liberty was settled. They turned and rode from the Potters' yard, the dog letting out a few more obligatory woofs.

"Why now, Griff?" Liberty asked as they rode back up the road toward Maddie Flowers'. "You've been sheriff for three years. Why are you putting the pressure on the Potters now?"

"Because Shotgun is growing. I've not wanted to disturb the waters since they've always lived so far out, but the town is moving out here fast. I can't have townspeople in danger because of the Potters' moonshine."

Liberty nodded but still worried. What would old man Potter do when he discovered Griffin had been out? She found herself praying for their safety and also that God would bring a peaceful end to this. Never once did she pray for patience, something she desperately needed once they entered Maddie Flowers' house and were forced for the next hour to listen to her excuses about making moonshine.

🌿 🌿 🌿

"I thought you said you weren't any good in the kitchen?" Griffin accused Slater on Thursday evening.

Slater laughed. "Spoken like a hungry man."

"No, Slater, I mean it. It was very good."

Slater inclined his head modestly and rose to clear the table. Griffin started peeling a bar of soap into a basin of hot water, thinking that Slater was as easy to live with as any man could be. He was quiet, polite, clean, generous with the rent money and food he bought, and pulled his weight in the kitchen. But one question still lingered in Griffin's mind: Why had he left the Rangers? For some odd reason Griffin was hesitant to ask, fearing the answer would be very personal. But he genuinely liked the man. For this reason he extended the invitation.

"I'm headed next door tonight. Mam and Laura are under the weather, and Laura needs a little cheering up. Would you like to come?"

"If you're sure I won't be in the way."

"Not at all. We'll go right after cleanup."

Which is precisely what they did. Slater had offered to cook that evening. He'd been overrun with homesickness that day and wanted to make a beef dish that his family often had on the ranch. The weather was cooler now—he could head home anytime—but something compelled him to stay on in Shotgun; more specifically, to stay on with Griffin. He'd sent word to his oldest brother and folks about where he was, but right now he couldn't leave. Walking next door and going through the back, just like family, made him very glad he'd stayed.

Griffin led the way through the kitchen, through the dining area they'd eaten in last Sunday, and into the parlor. Zach was reading a book, Liberty had sewing in her lap, and Laura was swathed in quilts on the chair, bright-eyed with fever and remarkably wide awake.

"Hi, Griff." Zach was the first to spot him.

"Hey, Zach," Griffin said as he leaned down to hug the boy. "How was your day?"

"It was good. I lasted three rounds in the spelling bee."

"Good job. Do you remember Mr. Rawlings? He lives with me now."

"Hello," Zach said with a smile.

"Hi, Zach. You can call me Slater if you want to."

"All right. My sister's sick."

"I heard about that."

Griffin took a seat, so Slater did the same thing. From his place next to Zach, Griffin looked over at his younger sister.

"Are you going to come and see me, Laura?"

"Papa says I'm not supposed to run around."

Liberty's hand came to her mouth, and Griffin smiled.

"It won't be running around just to come over here to my lap."

Laura looked to Liberty, but that woman only smiled at her. Dragging along one small blanket and a stuffed bunny that had seen better days, Laura left the chair and went to Griffin's lap on the davenport.

"Where's Mam?" Griffin asked Liberty as soon as he hugged and kissed his very warm sister.

"She feels miserable, so Duff is putting her to bed."

Griffin looked down at the hot bundle in his lap. "Did you share your cold with Mam?"

"I think so, but her throat doesn't hurt."

"And yours does?"

"I'm not supposed to talk."

"Well, we both know how long that's going to last."

Laura only smiled and laid her head against him.

"How's the work on the porch going, Mr. Rawlings?" Liberty asked.

"I would say we're about half done. Mrs. Tobler doesn't want us there before 8:00, so by midafternoon the sun gets a little intense."

"It's anyone's guess why she doesn't want you there earlier," Griffin speculated.

"I think she said something about disturbing her breakfast."

"I'm amazed that Hank puts up with it. He's pretty much his own man," Liberty commented.

"He's not as eager to work as he once was," Griffin said. "Has he talked to you, Slater, about missing Price?"

"Not in so many words, but one day he expected me to lift the wagon for him and muttered something about Price never having any trouble. It made me wonder about the man I've replaced."

"Price is big," Laura suddenly put in, and Zach came alive.

"He lifted Miss Amy's horse right out of the creek. I saw it! He didn't even groan."

"I think they should have been married," Laura stated, and the occupants of the room stared at her.

"Who?" Griffin finally asked.

"Price and Miss Amy. He won't find a nice girl like her in Austin."

Zach looked at her as if she'd grown two heads, but the adults in the room were all working not to laugh. Griffin hugged her close so he could hide his face, and Slater dropped his head down to check for stains on the front of his shirt. Liberty became very involved with her sewing.

"That's just dumb, Laura," Zach told her mildly. "Why would Price want to get married?"

"Because it's fun," Laura told him. "Mam and Papa have fun, and when I marry Bobby Fossett, I'll have fun too."

"Bobby Fossett is a whole year older than me," Zach felt a need to remind her, his voice very logical.

"Well, Papa is older than Mam," Laura argued.

"I thought we decided that you weren't supposed to talk," Duffy said as he came into the room and stood looking down at his daughter.

"I had to set Zach straight."

Duffy looked at her sternly. "It's not your job to set anyone straight, and you need to be quiet when your throat is sore. Do you understand?"

Laura nodded, and Duffy turned away. Griffin was behind him, but Slater and Liberty could not miss the way his eyes lit with laughter and tenderness the moment Laura could not see him.

Five

"Do you have family, Slater?" Duffy asked after he'd taken a seat and they'd all talked a little more about the day.

"I do. I'm the youngest of three boys."

"Are you from Texas?"

"Not originally, and in fact, my parents moved back to St. Louis about five years ago. But my grandmother is still in Texas, and so are both my brothers."

"What do they do?" Liberty asked.

"One is a Texas Ranger, and the other runs the family ranch in Kinkade."

"So would you consider Kinkade home for you?"

"Yes. I was thinking about heading in that direction when I found myself detained in Shotgun."

Liberty and Griffin both smiled at his dry tone.

"Why have you stayed?" Duffy asked. This young man seemed very straightforward, but he was living with Kate's son, and it wasn't unusual to see his eyes stray in Liberty's direction. Duffy wanted to take him at face value, but he wasn't going to be heedless.

"Mostly the church. If I hadn't found work so easily, I probably wouldn't have had much choice but to move on. Griffin's hospitality was a draw too."

"Has he complained of your snoring yet, Griff?" Liberty asked.

"If I could get up, you'd be in trouble," Griffin told her. Laura had fallen asleep on him.

"I can hear it," Slater admitted, "but it doesn't keep me awake."

Liberty enjoyed sending a teasing look at her brother.

"What did you enjoy about the church?" Duffy asked.

"The way your pastor preached from the Word, and the way he didn't skip around the issues or make excuses. He's obviously studied, and I learned quite a bit. I've been reading in Nehemiah all week, and I'm looking forward to going back."

"There's a picnic," Zach told him, and Duffy looked surprised.

"You were so quiet, Zach, that I forgot you were there. I think you'd best head up to bed."

"All right. Are you coming?"

"Indeed, I am. Get changed and wash your face. I'll be right along."

"Mam told me about the picnic," Griffin explained to Duffy after Zach had kissed Liberty and Griffin and told Slater goodnight. "Do you think she'll feel up to going?"

"I don't know," Duffy admitted. "She tells me she's been tired lately. I think maybe she should stay home just so she can rest."

"It's not the picnic itself, Duff," Liberty put in. "It's all the work beforehand. I can take care of it, but she can't stand to lie around."

"I'll talk with her, Liberty," he said, sounding very much like a doctor. "But it wouldn't hurt for either of you to realize you don't need to bring enough food to feed the entire congregation. Everyone brings food to pass, and we always have an abundance."

Liberty nodded, knowing he was right. They always brought food home. Liberty was still thinking about it, even going so far as to figure out what she would make this time—two or three dishes to share instead of the usual four or five would be reasonable—when she realized she was alone with Slater. Duffy had gone up to tuck Zach into bed, and Griffin had carried Laura to her room. Slater was staring at her, his expression unreadable.

"That was rude of me," Liberty said. "I was thinking and didn't realize we were alone."

"I don't need to be entertained," Slater said politely.

The moment he said this, Liberty became thoughtful again. She looked at Slater and made no pretense that she was doing otherwise.

"It's terribly rude for a man to ask a lady what she's thinking, but I must tell you I'm very tempted."

"I'll tell you," Liberty said. "I'm trying to figure out which man is the real Slater Rawlings: the man who spent 48 hours in the jailhouse, or the man I see now."

Slater nodded, regret knifing through him once again. "I can't begin to tell you how sorry I am for the way I handled myself, Miss Drake. I was completely wrong. It's not surprising that you don't know what to think of me."

Liberty was impressed with his humility and said, "I'm glad you understand, but please don't think I'm looking for something. I'm not watching to see you slip up or make a wrong move, but it does take a little getting used to. Everyone calls me Libby, by the way."

"I hope you'll call me Slater."

"That's an unusual name."

"A family name from my mother's side. My oldest brother is named after my father but goes by a nickname. And my middle brother was named after the territory my father always wanted to visit. My mother finally got her way with me."

Liberty smiled at him and the story. Slater Rawlings was so straightforward and courteous. People had come and gone over the years, and Liberty's family had helped out whenever they could. Some made more of an impression than others. After she met Slater, he had glared at her; just days later he teased her. For some reason the contrast stayed in her mind. As Duffy and Griffin came back to the room and suggested a board game, Liberty knew that even if this man left town the next day, she would never completely forget him.

🌹 🌹 🌹

"It looks good, Hank," Griffin complimented the old man, who grunted but still managed to look pleased. He slapped the horse and set the wagon into motion.

Slater watched his boss for a moment, still amazed at how few words the man said. Some days he worked them both like there was no tomorrow, but not on Saturday. After a few hours of work, Hank wanted to start the weekend early. Griffin rode up just as they finished for the day.

"Don't tell me you'll actually be a man of leisure today," Griffin teased Slater as he stacked some large boards against the house, his final chore.

"Well, someone has to do it."

"What in the world?" Slater suddenly heard Griffin exclaim. He looked to find the lawman watching a man who was backing toward them. He had come around the corner of the house, clearly watchful, and it took him some moments to realize Griffin was approaching from the rear.

"What are you doing, Critter?"

"Nothing!" The younger man was instantly belligerent. "And you can stop tryin' ta pin things on me I didn't do. Just leave me be. I won fair and square!"

Griffin's gaze narrowed as he watched him stalk away. He hadn't gone 15 steps before he was back to looking over his shoulder and moving behind trees and houses.

"I think I'll check on Lib," Griffin said quietly.

"Mind if I come along?" Slater asked, his voice belying the way his heart slammed in his chest upon the mention of Griffin's sister.

"Not at all," was all Griffin said in return. A minute later they both rode for downtown.

🌿 🌿 🌿

"Can you come?" old Davis Marks panted as he hobbled into the jailhouse on Saturday afternoon. Liberty immediately stood.

"What's up?"

"Guy with a whip. He says young Potter cheated in cards, and he's mad. Potter made off, but this guy's still cracking that thing and . . ."

Liberty didn't wait to hear more. Checking her gun for bullets, she jumped into Morton's saddle and rode for the Crescent Moon Saloon at the far end of town. Slowing as she neared and eventually dropping off Morton's back, Liberty moved close to the window for a look. She was glad to see he was at the rear wall. No one else was in sight, but the man was talking wildly, which meant the others were probably all against the walls, a wise place to be if the whip was as long as it looked.

Seeming for all the world to be on an afternoon stroll, Liberty walked down the boardwalk and through the swinging doors of the saloon. She stopped inside, her eyes scanning the room and summing up the situation. The afternoon was growing long, and the saloon was already getting crowded. A good 25 customers were backed away from the angry man, who for a moment was in profile to her.

"I want him found," he said, his voice low as he lashed at a chair.

"Is he looking for Critter?" Liberty asked Smiley, who tended the bar.

"Yeah, but Stumpy was at the table, and he said nobody cheated."

The man turned suddenly, his eyes scanning the room.

"Don't nobody move until I find him."

"We'll find him for you, but you have to put the whip down," Liberty told him, taking a few more steps inside. The man seemed to notice her for the first time. He wasn't a big man, but the bullwhip looked to be a dozen feet long, and even with his staggering gait, he looked like he could use it. Crescent Moon's bouncer was against one wall, a red slash on his face and one on his arm. The only disadvantage to Shotgun's laws concerning firearms in the saloons was the owner's inability to protect himself or his clientele.

"What did you say to me?"

"I said, put the whip down. No one wants to fight with you. Just put it away." Liberty's voice held authority, but it didn't carry like Griffin's. She wasn't sure she would get any response at all.

The whip suddenly cracked with terrific force, giving Liberty her answer. Nevertheless, she held her ground.

"Do you know what I can do to you?" he started to say, but Liberty drew and put a bullet past his ear.

"I want the whip put down," she said, her voice deadly calm. She also heard riders but couldn't be certain that help was on the way. She tried again. "Set it gently on the floor and take a seat at the table there."

The man watched her suspiciously. He noticed that she was holding a gun, but he still wasn't certain she had fired the shot. He shook his head a little and went to sit down, the whip still in his hand.

"What's his name?" Liberty asked of Smiley.

"I think Leonard something."

"Listen to me, Leonard," Liberty said as she approached. "You need to drop the whip and kick it toward me."

"You can't have my whip!" he stood with a roar as he shouted, the whip going into action again. Liberty had stayed well back, and from the corner of her eye she caught Griffin and Slater as they entered. Keeping her target in view, she shot the hat from Leonard's head. That man stopped in surprise, reeling a little in his boots. He turned in a deliberate fashion when he heard the cock of a shotgun from his other side.

"Put the whip down, or I'll take your arm off," Griffin said, his tone telling everyone in the room that he meant it. Slater had moved around and was coming at him from behind. When he drew close enough, he stepped on the whip and waited. He certainly hoped the man would do as he was told. It wasn't fun to shoot any man. It was extremely hard to shoot a drunk, when your heart told you he would act differently when sober.

"I want my whip," the man said pathetically, and Slater was close enough to see it go loose in his grasp. He removed the whip gently, the man having never seen him, and stepped back against the wall, where he began to wind it into a circle. Griffin moved toward him, and Liberty repositioned herself in case Leonard had more tricks up his sleeve. Griffin was cuffing him when Slater reached her side.

"Are you all right?" He dropped his head slightly to see her face beneath the brim of her hat.

Liberty blinked in surprise. "I'm fine."

Slater nodded, but his heart smarted a little in his chest. Did no one ever check with her? Was she ever frightened or rattled? He had all he could do not to shake his head. He would be treating this woman like a precious flower, not like a gunman. He stopped the judgment going on in his mind. It wasn't his place. He didn't have all the facts. He was also out of time. Griffin was taking the cuffed man away. After taking the whip from his hand and thanking him, Liberty followed in her brother's wake.

☙ ☙ ☙

"And I hope ya'll can join us at the picnic," Pastor Caron said after the closing prayer. "If you've never joined us at one of our fellowships, just ask and someone will give you directions to the Millers'. We picnic on the creek at the back of their place. We'll gather for a blessing under the big oak tree in about 30 minutes. I hope you can all come."

Slater stood, his Bible going under his arm and his hat in his hand. He smiled at the two young ladies who kept looking back at him and then moved out the door, wishing Griffin could have been there. Griffin said his mother usually made plenty, but not expecting to be on his own, Slater felt very awkward in just assuming he was welcome to their food.

"Slater," Zach piped up, suddenly speaking from his side.

"Hi, Zach."

"Papa asked me to tell you that you can come with us."

"Oh, thank you, Zach. I'll do that."

The little boy smiled up at him, and Slater saw Griffin's dark eyes.

"You can come with me, and I'll show you the wagon."

"All right."

Slater passed a group of young ladies—others had joined the two who had smiled at him after the service—and he would have been blind not to see their interest. Even if he had been blind, he would have still heard someone say his name as he walked away. They all looked sweet—nice girls—but his mind was elsewhere at the moment.

"Thank you, Zach," Duffy said as soon as he and Slater neared. "We weren't sure if you knew the way."

"Thank you, sir. I was hoping Griffin would get here, but I don't see him."

"Maybe he'll join us later."

"We need to go by the house, Duff," Liberty reminded him.

"All right. Laura, are you sitting down?"

The little girl's seat landed fast. "Yes."

"Is your mother still not well, Libby?" Slater asked from the seat beside her. The wagon had one wide seat. The younger two children were in the back.

"She is feeling better but still tired. She was ready to come, but Duffy put his foot down."

"You make me sound like an ogre," Duffy said, his hands controlling the reins.

"I think the word Mam used was beast, Duffy; never think of yourself as an ogre."

Duffy shook his head. For all Liberty's rather quiet ways, she could be quite a card.

She was also a good cook, and the food they brought from the kitchen not many minutes later smelled wonderful.

"Gingerbread?" Zach asked after peeking into the basket.

"Yes, just like you asked me."

"Thanks, Lib."

"You're welcome, Zach."

Brother and sister shared a smile, and watching them, Slater thought he might have missed something by not having a sister.

"The Millers have water in their backyard," Laura told Slater. "They can get wet anytime they want."

"That sounds fun," Slater responded as he turned to talk with her. "Will you get wet today?"

"If I'm lucky," Laura said in all seriousness and turned back around.

Slater faced forward again, his shoulders shaking a little. "Has she always been so profound?"

"No," Liberty told him. "She couldn't talk until she was two."

Smiling to himself, Slater suddenly knew just where she'd picked up her charming wit.

🌹 🌹 🌹

"What a privilege this is, Father God," Bill Miller prayed from his place under the big oak tree after the group had quieted, "to gather in Your name for fellowship and food. We thank You for each person here, and pray that our time in You would be sweet. Bless this food as we partake. In Christ's name we pray. Amen."

Tables had been set up. Baskets, pots, bowls, and platters had been laid out. Towels were lifted and the contents displayed. Plates in hand, the congregation lined up to make their choices. A few mothers had to coax children from the water's edge, but most of the younger set were ready.

"It's time to eat," Liberty told Laura and Zach.

"Do you think they catch fish in here?" Zach asked, his eyes on the creek bed and the minnows that swam near the bank.

"I'll bet they do. You should ask Mr. Miller if you can fish here sometime."

"I could too," Laura put in. "I won't poke anyone with the hook."

"Papa won't let you fish yet, Laura," Zach said, his voice regretful. "You might get hurt."

Laura looked stubborn over this until she caught her brother's look. It was impossible to get mad at him when he *wanted* her to fish.

"We could ask," she said in a quiet voice, all stubbornness gone. "You could ask, Zach . . . you could."

Zach contemplated this. His father wouldn't get angry, but if he said no, Laura would be disappointed. Zach's soft heart could hardly handle the thought. He wished she hadn't even asked.

"Are you ready to eat?" Duffy called as he came toward them. Liberty had come off the quilt she had laid out and was holding the plates, but she didn't answer for the children. She was too busy trying not to watch Slater. He was surrounded by a group of women.

Zach stood staring up at his father until Duffy lowered his brow in puzzlement. Laura was pulling on her brother's sleeve.

"Papa," Zach began, "could Laura come fishing with us sometime?"

"Sure, Zach. I think that's a great idea. You were very kind to think of her."

There was no missing the little boy's sigh. He grinned at his sister, who grinned right back, and then smiled up at his father in a way that always melted the hearts of those who loved him.

"Let's eat," Duffy said softly, and the four proceeded across the grass. Liberty had a plate for Slater, but she suddenly felt awkward. She approached the food tables, fully expecting him to already have a plate in hand. She hadn't counted on Laura.

"Here," Laura said, as they neared the group that Slater was a part of and she took a dinner plate from her sister. Her family watched as she stepped right into the midst and handed it to Slater.

"Here's your plate, Slater. Are you going to come to our quilt?"

"I am. Thank you, Laura. I'll just come and stand in line with you right now. Excuse me, ladies."

Liberty could have sunk into the grass. She hadn't put Laura up to anything, but the looks on the female faces that watched Slater leave the circle were certainly speculative, or were they just fascinated with this new man?

"I hope I didn't hold you up," Slater said as they gathered at the rear of the line.

"Not at all," Duff put in before Liberty could speak. "We hope we didn't interrupt your conversation."

Slater didn't answer, but Liberty could have hugged her stepfather. He must have seen her strained, surprised look when Laura took things into her own hands. Indeed, her stepfather was bending over to speak to Laura right then. It wasn't hard to guess that she was being reprimanded over interrupting.

"Did Griffin happen to tell you how long he would be?" Slater asked Liberty.

"I didn't talk to him at all. Did he have to stay at the jail?"

"Yes. It was a busy night last night. He didn't get in until quite late." Liberty nodded.

"Do you never work on Saturday nights?" Slater asked, no longer able to squelch his curiosity over the arrangement.

"Not usually, but that's why I go in on Monday and Tuesday mornings, so he can do a little catching up on his rest."

It was on the tip of Slater's tongue to ask how long she had been at this, along with a dozen other questions, but he felt he'd asked enough. Pastor Caron had taken most of the service that morning to tell them what a prayer warrior Nehemiah had been. Slater determined to emulate that Bible character and to start immediately.

Covertly watching Slater, Liberty tried to figure out what he might be thinking. Had he been very disappointed to be taken from the group? Had Laura rescued him, or was he being polite to a little girl? Liberty had no idea how she could find out and made herself rest in the matter. Easier said than done. She found herself glancing at him often to see where he was looking. She was quite fascinated to note that she never once saw him glancing back to the group of young women who had finally fallen into line.

"I don't like beets," Liberty heard Laura say. She watched as Duffy gave her something else. Zach's plate wobbled a little, but before Liberty could reach for it, Slater's hand was there. For the briefest of moments, Liberty had the unwanted feeling of not being needed but managed to push it away and concentrate on getting her food. While she did this, she had a stern talk with herself.

You enjoy Slater's company, and he's chosen to eat with your family. After all, Griffin invited him. Now, you can relax and take pleasure in this, or you can examine every move the man makes and be miserable. You're too old to be so distracted by a pair of warm blue eyes, a tall build, wavy blond hair, broad shoulders, a great smile . . . Stop it, Libby! Liberty shouted to herself just in time.

"Why don't I take our plates, Libby." Slater turned and offered, "and you can get our drinks?"

"Oh—all right," Liberty said but moved away from the crowd only a little and stood looking at him.

"I'm getting that look again," he said, his eyes smiling.

Liberty's eyes narrowed in an effort to hide her feelings. "I'm still figuring you out."

Slater smiled slowly. "Well, I hope you keep at it."

Liberty had no idea what he meant by this, so she simply said, "I think there's coffee, lemonade, and water. Which would you like?"

"Lemonade, please," Slater said, watching her closely and thinking he found her a little more fascinating every time they talked.

Liberty ended up with a tray holding five lemonades and then walked beside Slater back to the quilt. The Millers had a quilt next to theirs, and Laura joined their family to be with little Kathy Miller. Slater waited until Liberty had doled out the drinks and taken a seat on the quilt and then gave her her plate. Watching his solicitous manner, Duffy couldn't stop his smile.

"You're looking pleased with yourself, Duffy Peterson," Liberty said, knowing her stepfather well and reading his sparkling eyes.

"Am I?" he evaded.

Liberty only looked at him and smiled when he winked. She might have given him a hard time, but Zach suddenly said, "It's Griff and Tess! Over here, Griffin."

The couple made their way over to the quilt, Tess' mother coming with them. It was on Liberty's mind to find out what Duffy had been thinking, but the afternoon suddenly rushed on, and she never got back to it.

Six

"DID YOU POP THE QUESTION?" Liberty came right out and asked her brother.

"No," he told her honestly, his voice mild.

"Why not?"

They were still at the picnic, but Laura had wandered too close to the bank and fallen completely into the water. Slater had plucked her out, and Mrs. Miller had told Duffy to bring her to the house. Slater had gone with them. Zach had wandered off with a schoolmate, and Tess and Mrs. Locken had gone to see the Carons, who were sitting closer to the house.

"I have my reasons," Griffin said, effectively shutting the door in his sister's face. Griffin didn't realize this until he looked over at her. Liberty's eyes, large and somber as she looked at the children playing near the water, were hurt.

"I didn't mean it that way, Lib. I have some more thinking to do and someone I must talk to. I just know it's not time right now. It may never be time."

Liberty stared at him. "Then why do you spend so much time with her, Griff?"

Griffin sighed before admitting, "Because I'm selfish and unfeeling. I want to be with her—I want to see her—even if it hurts later."

Liberty nodded, glad that he had been so honest. Knowing she needed to be careful about what she said, she reminded herself that her brother was not answerable to her; she was not in charge.

"Griffin," Liberty said suddenly, "Slater is headed this way, and I want to ask him something. You may not like it, so I won't if you don't want me to."

"About what?"

"Marriage and law enforcement."

Griffin shrugged. "I don't care."

"Is this a bad time?" Slater asked as he neared—little wonder with the serious looks on Liberty's and Griffin's faces.

"No," Griffin told him. "Please join us."

"Does Duffy need me to do anything with Laura?" Liberty asked Slater.

"I don't think so. She had Mrs. Miller laughing when I left."

"What did she say this time?"

"She assumed the Millers had special get-wet clothes. When Kathy didn't know what she was talking about, Laura asked, 'So you just get wet in whatever you're wearing?' "

Griffin laughed, and Liberty shook her head.

"Her logic is always a challenge," Griffin said.

"I was looking at her as her head came out of the water. She was very shocked to have fallen in," Slater told them.

"Well," Liberty said, "Duff told her she couldn't wade in because it meant removing her stockings, but I know she still wanted to. I don't think getting completely wet was in her mind at all."

"Probably not. I think I heard a few tears when she thanked me."

"I'm glad she remembered to do that," Griffin said quietly.

"Slater," Liberty began, choosing that moment to plunge in, "may I ask you a question about your family?"

"Shoot."

"Did you say your brother is a Texas Ranger?"

"Yes."

"Is he married?"

"No."

Liberty nodded but didn't go on.

Slater watched her.

"Why did you ask, Libby?" Surprisingly enough, this came from Griffin, who felt she'd left Slater at sea.

"I just wondered if he had any views on the subject because of his job, or if he wasn't married because the right girl hadn't come along."

"His job requires him to move around a lot, and Dakota, that's my brother," Slater explained, "enjoys his work, even though it doesn't make marriage very practical."

"Do you think he worries about leaving a widow if he were to marry?"

"I would say he does. He's not at all easy on people who break the law, but he's usually very polite and caring of women. I think he would consider marriage a serious move for someone in his position."

Liberty nodded. She'd gotten her answer, but it wasn't one that would comfort Tess if she'd heard it. Liberty glanced at Griffin but only found him staring at Slater. He appeared to be waiting for something, and Liberty wondered if Griffin had wished she'd kept her mouth shut.

Slater, on the other hand, thought that Liberty's questions stemmed entirely from her own situation. Did she fear marrying someone because her job was so dangerous? Again, Slater was pained at the thought that she had to live like this. His own gaze swung to Griffin, whom Slater felt was very responsible for his sister. But that man was watching Tess and her mother return to the quilt. Asking God to help him be patient over matters that might never become clear, Slater shifted his mind away from the torturous thoughts.

❦ ❦ ❦

"How are you feeling?" Liberty asked Kate first thing Monday morning. Kate was still in bed; Duffy had gone downstairs to start breakfast.

"As well as can be expected," Kate said, her voice light.

Liberty stared at her mother, and Kate smiled at her.

"Duffy and I were talking last night and again this morning. Sometimes surprises are very nice things."

Liberty caught on swiftly, her eyes growing in size. "Oh, Mam, are you really?"

"Well, Duffy thinks so, but he's only a doctor."

Liberty rushed over and hugged her mother for a long time. Kate eventually pushed up against the headboard and the two sat talking.

"You didn't have Laura's cold at all."

"I don't think I did. I'm just tired."

"Not queasy?"

"Only around certain food."

"When do you think the baby is due?"

"Well, by my calculations, sometime in June—mid to late."

Liberty smiled. "Remember Zach's first day of school? You cried, not only because he was leaving, but because you knew that next year Laura would be gone too."

"I do remember that." Kate's voice was fond. "I asked the Lord to give me strength on that day and all the ones to come, but not to worry about tomorrow. It never occurred to me that we would have more children, but I can't tell you how pleased I am."

"When will you tell Zach and Laura?"

"Not until I'm ready for the whole world to know."

Liberty laughed. "But, Mam, Laura would tell the world in such a warmhearted manner. It might not be something we'd want to miss."

"This sounds like fun," Duffy offered as he came in the door with a steaming mug of coffee for his wife. Zach was close on his heels.

"Thank you, dear," Kate said as she took a sip and then set the drink aside so Zach could come close and cuddle with her. "Are you all ready for school?"

"Yes. We had oatmeal."

"Was it good?"

"Yes, but I think it's the only breakfast Papa can make." Zach looked over at his father. "What did you eat before you married Mam?"

"Oatmeal," Duffy told him, and Zach laughed at the way his eyes crossed.

Their voices woke Laura, who did not always rise with the rest of the family. Tousled and sleep-warm in a small flannel gown, she came in to snuggle next to her mother as well. Liberty had to be at the jail-house soon, but she made time before she left to thank God for this new little person and to pray for his safe arrival. As she watched her family—Duffy was on the bed too—she didn't think that God could give another child to a more godly, loving couple. In her opinion, next June couldn't come soon enough.

🌸 🌸 🌸

Did you pop the question? Why not? The questions Liberty had asked Griffin more than two weeks earlier were almost constantly on his mind. He had even double-checked with his sister to make sure she wasn't upset by his cold reply.

And why had he been so formal with her? He had thought it might help to speak with his mother, but Griffin used the excuse that she wasn't feeling well long after it was valid. No longer. Slater had left for work, Liberty was at the jailhouse, Zach was at school, and Duffy would also have gone to work. It was time to pay a visit to his mother. Griffin spent some time in prayer about their meeting and then went next door, hoping very much that she didn't have plans or company for the morning.

"Well, Griff," Kate greeted him warmly as they exchanged a hug, "I was just about to have some coffee and read my Bible. Would you like a cup?"

"I would if it wouldn't be interrupting."

"Not at all. You've been busy lately, and I don't want to miss a chance to talk with you."

Griffin realized that she always did that: made him feel special and wanted.

"Unless I miss my guess, you have something on your mind," Kate said as she put a steaming mug in front of him, not even giving him a chance to ask how she was feeling, especially with the baby coming.

"How did you know?"

"Because Libby told me she said something to you at the picnic and felt bad about it. She got the impression that you were upset by her probing. Did she not get back to you as she planned?"

"Well, I had to talk to her about the way I acted, and she tried to make sure I was all right with her, but now that you mention it, I think I was a little too busy making sure she wasn't upset with me to listen."

Kate nodded. "You're in terrible pain, Griff. I can see it."

Griffin dropped his head, his hand going to the back of his neck.

"All this time I should have been talking to you, but it never occurred to me. I think you could give me some answers—you have insight into being a lawman's wife—and it only just recently occurred to me to ask."

Kate smiled. "Sometimes we're like that, a little slow to start."

"Hi, Griff!" a cheery voice called just before Laura launched herself at her oldest brother. "I didn't know you were here."

Griffin gave her a hug and kissed her cheek. "How are you today?" he asked.

"I'm drawing a picture of our house. I did Mam and Papa's room and the kitchen."

"Well, you still have a lot of rooms to cover."

Laura agreed with a nod of her head but still plopped down in a kitchen chair as if she had all day.

"Laura," her mother said gently, "I need you to play on your own for a little longer."

Laura looked between the two adults.

"Are you talking to Griffin?"

"Yes."

"Is it because he loves Tess?" Laura asked, a little frown on her brow.

"That is none of your concern," her mother told her, and Laura tucked her lower lip under her teeth and gave Griffin an apologetic look. She left, looking back at them only once, and when she was gone, Griffin smiled.

"Just so long as she doesn't see you laughing," Kate told her son. "She's precocious enough as it is, and at times, nosey. Now! Let's get back to you. Ask me anything, Griff, and I'll try to answer."

Griffin sighed. "You married Thomas Drake before he was a sheriff, but did you know he wanted to be the sheriff?"

"Yes, I did. I can't say that I didn't worry, Griff, but I will admit that I didn't worry much. My father hadn't died from a bullet wound, so I didn't have that on my mind like you do. I knew the risks, but not until your father pushed to have the laws changed did I really start to see how dangerous his job would become."

"Tell me about the firearms law," Griffin requested. "I can't remember how long he waited to implement that."

"Less than a year after he took the job. And then he died not long after it went into effect. Because of that, there were some who said the law didn't do any good. All this clamping down on guns, only to have your father shot while enforcing the new statute. But he was the only one killed for a long time, and even though the job came with risks, we both believed in it. I still do. And thankfully, so did the town fathers. Innocent people still die, Griffin—they always will—but there's no comparison to what it used to be like."

"And you would have no trouble with my marrying a woman who could end up alone like you did?"

"It's crazy to say I don't have any trouble with it. I would be crushed if I lost you, but I remind myself of one thing: God is still in control. If it is God's will that you die, then you could go swimming with Tess on your honeymoon and drown. If it isn't God's will that you die, then a thousand bullets fired at you wouldn't make it happen."

In so many words, both Duffy and Pastor Caron had voiced the same thoughts to him. It was good to be reminded. Too often he wanted God to reveal His will before it was time. Griffin knew he was suffering from a lack of trust and that he needed to grow in this area.

"Thanks, Mam," Griffin said. "I'm still not certain what would be the wise course, but I needed that reminder."

"I'll keep praying for you, Griff, and if you need to talk again, come straight back. You know Duffy feels the same way."

"Can I come back in now?"

"*May* I come back in," Kate corrected, "and, yes, you may."

Laura flew through the doorway, kissed her mother, and scrambled into Griffin's lap. Watching her, Kate's prayers intensified for her son. It was so easy to skip through life without thought of the future. Griffin was wise to take it seriously. Looking at Laura, Kate was reminded that she might someday be forced to look at Griffin's children, just as she had her own, and wish that their father was still there to hold them.

🌹 🌹 🌹

I don't know her well—at least not yet, Slater prayed a few weeks later. He was on his horse and headed to dinner at the Carons'. *But I like her . . . I like her so much. I've been here only six weeks, and already I feel at home and cared for. Can that be possible? I loved my job, Lord. I fought You tooth and nail about leaving it. But I don't miss the long rides, unpredictable hours, and meager pay. I've never known such a sense of completeness. I want to stay in Shotgun. I miss taking care of folks, and it's not always easy to work with Hank, but the thought of leaving Griffin and his family, especially Libby, really bothers me.*

I need to know Your will in this. The letters from the ranch have been encouraging. I'm glad they want me to stay here since I've found a good church, but I should probably visit them sometime soon. I'm still surprised that Dakota hasn't shown up. Please be with him, Father; touch his heart wherever he is.

Slater could have prayed on for the next hour, but the Carons' house was in sight. He had honestly appreciated being asked over, but he had been more thankful before Duffy extended an invitation for the same night. He'd had no choice but to go to the Carons'—he'd been asked there first—but it was hard to see Griffin head next door and know that he had to go elsewhere. With a prayer for a thankful heart, Slater tethered his horse and went to the door.

🌹 🌹 🌹

"Do you think he's cute?" Mayann asked her mother while they were preparing the coffee tray.

"Mr. Rawlings? Yes, he's very nice-looking," Felicia said kindly, but she was not going to do too much encouraging. Mayann was growing up fast, but she was not ready to be in a relationship, especially one with a man Slater's age. Felicia wasn't certain, but she figured him somewhere in his midtwenties; not to mention the fact that they were still getting to know him. However, Betsy, their oldest daughter, suddenly sprang to mind. Felicia was not about to start pushing her daughter at anyone—she did not want to play God in the matter—but if Slater should show some interest in Betsy, Felicia didn't think she'd have any trouble with that at all. Felicia determined to discuss it with Ross later that evening.

"I think Betsy is in love," Mayann said, her voice a little too loud. Felicia came and put a hand on her daughter's shoulder.

"I don't want you to talk like that, Mayann. If Betsy has feelings for Mr. Rawlings, then we'll deal with that in its time, but don't you start planting ideas."

"All right. But do you think he likes her?"

Mayann had Felicia there. In truth, she had never seen Slater Rawlings give any of the young women preferential treatment. He was extremely polite, a real gentleman, but not at any time did she feel he was playing games with the young women of the church.

"Papa sent me out to help," Tanner, suddenly appearing in the doorway, said. "Do you want me to carry the tray?"

"Thank you, Tanner," Felicia responded, but his question brought her up short. How many minutes had she stood here daydreaming?

Lord, she prayed as she followed her children out of the kitchen and into the living room. *Mr. Rawlings needs my love and hospitality, not my matchmaking skills. Please help me to want his spiritual growth more than a husband for my daughter.*

"So where will we go after Nehemiah?" Felicia heard Slater ask her husband as she entered.

"I think the book of Mark. I try to alternate Old and New Testament books, but before we do that, I have some topics I feel we need to cover. Tell me, Slater, does sharing your faith come easily to you?"

"Not as a rule. I don't know how to open the subject with strangers."

"That's my point exactly. So often I think we try to press Jesus Christ onto someone who has given no sign of interest. What if we got to know our neighbors? What if we loved the people we worked with, without ever mentioning our faith, and then when they noticed the difference in us—*making sure they've seen one*—we lovingly explained why we're different and how they can be different too?"

Slater sat back and stared at him. "I almost want to laugh with the irony of your suggestion. I work with Hank Hathaway, and it's been on my mind to share with him, but he never wants to talk. He never lets me into his world, even a little, and for that reason I just haven't felt free to mention my decision for Christ. You've put it so well. He needs to see a difference in my life first."

Ross Caron nodded, thinking this young man was a balm for his heart. Unless he missed his guess, both his daughters thought he was nice to look at, but that wasn't Pastor Caron's main concern. He believed the church needed strong male leadership. If Slater Rawlings stayed around and continued to grow, he could be a help in leading this church to strength and maturity.

"When did you come to Christ, Mr. Rawlings?" Felicia now asked.

"Less than two years ago. A man I'd been working with talked to me. I had a tendency to search in all the wrong places. Some of my family had come to Christ, but I didn't think it was for me." Slater smiled. "I'll never forget that day. I told the Lord that I didn't think I would be any good as His child, that I could never love and serve Him like my brother was trying to do, but if He wanted a rotten sinner like me, I would do my best." Again Slater smiled. "I was in for quite a surprise. The Bible, a book I had always found dry as dust, became so exciting to me that I couldn't get enough of it."

Slater was on the verge of saying that that was just the beginning when he looked over to see the oldest Caron girl, he thought she had been introduced as Betty, staring at him with a dreamy look on her face. Slater smiled at her but stopped just short of pulling at his collar, which suddenly felt tight. Had he been invited over here as a prospective son-in-law? The thought chilled Slater to the bone, until a glance at his hosts put him at ease. They were looking at their daughter, neither one happy, and when the younger Caron girl saw it, she dropped her eyes and turned red. Slater busied himself with his coffee cup and was glad when Tanner changed the subject.

They fellowshipped for the next hour, and everyone, even Betsy after she realized what she'd been doing, joined in the conversation and had fun. Slater left, his heart at peace and very thankful as he rode through town toward Griffin's house. The church family was wonderful. All he'd wanted to do was escape to the cool of the mountains. Never in his wildest dreams did he think God would—

Slater's mind ceased its wandering. From the corner of his eye he'd caught movement on a downtown roof not far from the bank. He thought he heard a raised voice, but one of the saloons was nearby and he couldn't be sure of the direction. A second later he brought Arrow to a full halt. Another man was on the roof, and this one looked like Griffin. Slater was out of the saddle in a flash, tying Arrow's reins to a post and moving silently toward the alley between the buildings. Slater had gone only ten feet into the alley when someone moved ahead of him. Thinking that the bank was being robbed or cased, Slater touched the Bowie knife in his boot for reassurance and crept forward, not making a sound. A moment later he grabbed the guy in front of him with an arm around the neck, and Slater knew in an instant that this was not a man. With a swift hand to what was sure to be Liberty's mouth, he pulled her into the shadows.

"It's Slater," he whispered in her ear to stop her struggling and to also keep from being shot. The moment she calmed, he turned her to face him but did not let her out of his arms. He bent again to catch her ear. "What are you doing in this alley?"

"Leonard is drunk again," she spoke against his chest. "He's on the roof with his whip."

"Where's Griffin?"

"Up there with him. He wanted me here."

Slater sighed. Her voice was so pragmatic. Didn't anyone know this wasn't normal?

"What does he expect you to do?"

"Just to keep watch if something should happen, or if he calls."

Slater sighed again, this time over his emotions. Even in what was sure to be her deputy outfit, she smelled so nice, and holding her, even loosely in his arms, was nothing short of delightful.

"How do I let Griffin know that I'm here to help?" Slater, making himself concentrate, asked.

"I don't know. He wants me to stay quiet."

"Put it down!" The shout came from overhead, and Liberty scrambled loose and ran, Slater right behind her. They both heard Leonard's drunken wailing and the crack of the whip as they raced up the alley. Liberty, knowing the town well, ran for a ladder at the side of the bank building. She started to climb but found herself lifted by the waist and set back on her feet.

"Give me your gun!" Slater said in a voice that was not to be argued with. Liberty obeyed automatically. "Stay put!" was the next order before Slater started up the ladder. Liberty stood in shock. It took her a moment to realize she was not up there to take care of Griffin. Would Slater really know what to do? All cowboys carried guns, and she had originally found Slater with one, but did that mean he knew how to use it? In the next moment more shouting came to Liberty's ears, and without thought she climbed the ladder. She had just reached the top when she heard Griffin's voice.

"I've got him, Slater. Do you have the whip?"

"Yes. How do we get him down that ladder?"

"We don't. There's a stairway at the back here."

Liberty stepped across the roof then, and both men spotted her.

"We've got him, Lib," was all Griffin had to say.

"Good."

Slater, on the other hand, was speechless. He could not believe she'd come up that ladder. He opened his mouth to say something but closed it again. Now was not the time. They had a drunk to put in jail, but in his mind, the incident was not over.

🌹 🌹 🌹

"I take it Leonard's moved into town, since he's still here?" Liberty asked Griffin.

"Smiley tells me that he lives out a ways, but when he gets lonely, he brings his whip to town for a drink."

"Smiley needs to get smart and have his bouncer take the whip away from Leonard while he's still in his right mind."

"I'll have to tell him," Griffin said. "In fact, I need to head over there right now and confirm what happened. Can you stay here for about 30 minutes?"

"Sure."

"All right. Thanks for your help, Slater. I'll be back long enough to check on him and then I'll come home."

"All right."

Both Liberty and Slater watched Griffin leave. Liberty walked to the cell and looked in to where Leonard was sleeping off his bottle before turning back to Slater. His look gave her pause. Indeed, after seeing the intensity of his gaze, she stopped a few paces short of the desk and stood very still.

Slater wasn't still at all. With the reach of one long arm, he hooked a finger in the bandana Liberty had knotted around her neck and pulled her toward him.

Seven

THE BANDANA AND HIS FINGER still holding Liberty captive, Slater spoke when their faces were scant inches apart.

"I thought I told you to stay put at the bottom of that ladder."

Liberty looked hesitant before her chin rose just a little. "Just because you have a gun doesn't mean you can handle it."

Slater's eyes narrowed, his finger still in place.

"All right," he began, his voice saying he would let it go this time. "But just for the record, Liberty Drake, I can handle a gun."

Liberty nodded, her eyes on the ones that watched her so sternly. She stood still while he removed his finger and even when he brushed that finger gently across her chin, but her heart was trying to beat a hole in her rib cage.

"How long did Griffin say he would be?" Slater asked.

"Thirty minutes."

"I'll stick around and walk you back."

"All right. Slater?"

"Yeah?"

"How did you happen to be in the alley?"

Slater explained where he'd been, and Liberty worked hard to quell an emotion she'd never before experienced: jealousy. For a moment, all she could see was Betsy Caron's face. Betsy was a good friend—a remarkably sweet woman—but Liberty had a hard time seeing her with Slater. Liberty almost shook her head. She had no right to picture Slater with *anyone*. His life was not her business.

"Did I hurt your neck just now?" Slater asked.

"No," Liberty said with some surprise. "Why did you ask that?"

"You got so quiet all of a sudden."

"I'm not hurt. I was just thinking, and before I forget to say it, thank you, Slater, for going up and helping Griff."

"You're welcome. I was glad to do it." *I would do it all the time if I could just figure out a way.*

"Where'smywhip?" was suddenly slurred from the cell, and both Liberty and Slater heard a thump. Investigating the noise confirmed to them that Leonard had rolled onto the floor. Liberty began to get the key, but Slater's voice stopped her.

"I would leave him there. He'll be stiff in the morning, but this way he won't fall off again and possibly hurt himself."

"All right," Liberty said, but she couldn't help but notice the way he spoke. He was so confident, more so than she would have thought he would be. Her mind recalled the way he had climbed that ladder going to Griffin's defense, seemingly without a qualm. Was there something they were all missing?

"Okay, Libby," Griffin called as he came back through the door. "Oh, Slater, you're still here."

"I told Libby I would walk her home."

"Well, be my guest. I'm going to make sure Leonard is settled and then head home myself."

"He fell off the bunk," Slater put in. "He's probably safer there."

Liberty nodded. She knew that if Leonard woke and caused a fuss, someone would just head to Griffin's house and shout him out of bed.

"Thanks again, Slater," Griffin said.

"You're welcome."

Slater and Liberty headed out the door then, both a little quiet. Slater was still thinking about the way Liberty seemed to withdraw from him just before Griffin returned, and Liberty was still speculating on the way Slater handled himself. Griffin, staying back at the jail for a few minutes longer, reminded himself not to start matchmaking when clearly he was no expert.

🌹 🌹 🌹

Slater woke early. It was still dark out, but his body told him he was done sleeping. Thankful for an untroubled night, he rolled to his side, lit the lantern, and reached for his Bible. He was still studying Nehemiah's life, wanting to keep up with Pastor Caron, but he was also spending time in 1 Corinthians. The early church was teaching him a great deal. Slater was now in the seventh chapter and began to read there. Reading verse one, he was ready to move on but got no further. Slater read it a second time.

Now concerning the things whereof ye wrote unto me: It is good for a man not to touch a woman.

Slater felt his breath leave him in a rush. The verses right before this had spoken of the sacredness of the body. Because a believer was bought with a great price—God's blood—his body was God's temple.

So what were you thinking in the alley last night, Rawlings? You knew immediately that it wasn't a man, and as soon as you figured out it was Liberty, you hugged her and held her as if you had the right. Slater rolled to his back and looked at the ceiling.

She was so soft and smelled so good, but she's not mine, Lord. I've got to apologize to her. I've got to put things right. I can't have intimate thoughts about her. It's wrong. You have better for me. As You do Liberty. She was so quiet as I walked her home. I can only imagine how offended she must have been.

Slater was sincere in his confession and planned to make amends, but his heart was still heavy. He had a feeling that it would be until he could go next door and ask to speak to the woman who occupied his thoughts so much of the time.

❧ ❧ ❧

"Here, let me try," Liberty said, as she worked on the button on Zach's pants. He had to leave for school soon. "The problem is, Zach," she continued, panting a little, "if it's this hard for me, how will you ever get them off to use the privy at school?"

"I don't know," the little boy worried. "Should I change? Do I have time?"

"Let me work the hole for a few more seconds," Liberty suggested. "Maybe that will loosen it."

"I even soaked those," Kate said as she put a platter of eggs and toasted bread on the table. "New denim pants should be outlawed."

"Now you try," Liberty encouraged Zach.

She was still watching him as he tried to unbutton and button his pants when his mother said he had to eat. Zach had just taken his place at the table when Liberty heard a knock at the door. Laura, fork in hand, began to rise.

"I'll get it," her older sister said. Liberty went through the house, opened the front door, and found Slater on the porch.

"May I see you a moment, Libby?" Slater said as soon as he saw her, relieved that she had answered the door.

"Certainly. Come in."

Slater cleared his throat. "I think out here might be better."

At a complete loss as to what could be going on, Liberty joined him on the porch and shut the door behind her. She watched Slater turn his hat in his hands and waited.

"I acted inappropriately last night, Libby, and I want to tell you I'm sorry."

Liberty's mind raced but she came up blank.

"I grabbed you in the alley and should have let go as soon as I knew it was you. I didn't, and that was wrong of me."

Liberty had forgotten all about it, but she was suddenly standing in his arms again. He was taller than she was, and his arms had been very gentle. The recollection was not unpleasant.

"I hope you can forgive me."

"Of course, Slater. Don't give it another thought."

Slater studied her eyes to see if she truly was all right and then nodded. It was so tempting to tell her how sweet she was and how lovely she'd been to hold, but that would have canceled everything he'd just said.

"I hope in the future you won't be afraid to be around me or untrusting of me because of the way I acted."

Liberty's mouth nearly fell open, but she saw the pain in his eyes and knew she had to make him understand.

"You don't feel threatening to me, Slater, not in the least. And as for the hug in the alley, I had forgotten about it, but I can honestly tell you that I wasn't offended." *Quite the opposite* were the words in her head, but she wisely held them, along with Slater's eyes, as she looked up at him.

Slater thought he could get lost in her gaze. She was so sweet, and unless he missed his guess, she had not objected to the hug. Slater was on the verge of asking when the verse came to mind. She was not his.

"I was reading in 1 Corinthians this morning about the fact that a man shouldn't touch a woman, and I realized what I'd done."

Liberty nodded. "I know the verses, the ones that go on to say that each man should have his own wife and such."

Slater nodded but realized he hadn't kept reading; he would have to do that.

"Thank you, Libby," Slater said.

"Thank you, Slater."

Slater put his hat on but still stood for a moment. He had to get to work—it wasn't wise to be late—but it was certainly hard not to stay and talk with this woman.

"Are you and Griffin still coming to dinner tonight?" Liberty asked, working not to read anything into the look he gave her.

"I wouldn't miss it," Slater told her before forcing his eyes away and admitting that he had to get to work.

"Take care," Liberty wished him and then watched as he left the porch, hoping he would turn so she could wave. He did that just before he disappeared around the corner. Liberty went back inside, a smile on her face as she thought about the evening to come.

🌿 🌿 🌿

"I have something I need to thank you for," Liberty told Duffy over lunch that very day.

"What's that?"

"Do you remember when I told you I'd fallen into a slump in my Bible study and prayer time?"

"Yes, I do remember."

"Well, you told me that I had lost my wonder over the cross, and you know what? You were right."

Duffy smiled. They had been planning to go to lunch all week and were now at the hotel, just the two of them at a quiet corner table.

"So what did you do?"

"I began looking at those passages that cover Christ's death, and I realized I wasn't thankful, not deeply thankful, for the sacrifice God made on my behalf. I was saved when I was so young, Duffy, that it's too easy to take it for granted. I've been thankful and, I think, more obedient lately because my focus has changed."

"That's great news. I've been reading in the book of Revelation. There's so much to come, Lib, and we can't waste a moment in sin; it's just not worth it."

The waitress came with their lunch. They ate in silence for several minutes, but Liberty had something more on her mind and could wait no longer.

"Slater was over first thing this morning," Liberty told him. "Right after you left."

"Oh?" Duffy's coffee cup went to his mouth. "Something wrong?"

"He thought so," Liberty said, watching Duffy's brows shoot upward.

"But you didn't?"

Liberty gave a quick rundown on what had happened in the alley. She ended by saying, "I honestly didn't think anything of it, Duff. I didn't even remember it until he brought it up, but that's not my biggest problem."

Duffy waited, but she didn't tell him. Finally he asked. "What is, Libby?"

"I enjoyed it," she said so softly that he almost missed it.

Duffy's eyes lit with tenderness. "I'm going to say something that may surprise you, Libby girl. I'm glad."

"Why, Duffy?"

"Because it could have scared you, and I wouldn't want you to have that kind of memory. I don't know who the Lord has for you, and Slater was right, he had no business hugging you, but your response was normal. If it causes your thoughts to wander where they shouldn't, that will be very hard for you. But God made us to enjoy one another. I would not have chosen for it to happen, but now that it has, it's good to know that you'll enjoy your husband's embrace someday."

"I think about him a lot," Liberty admitted. "You're right, we don't know who the Lord has, but Slater is the first man I've even been able to imagine. Is that bad, Duffy?"

"Not if you handle it well. You can't be in a hurry, no matter what your emotions or body says. If God has a plan for the two of you, He will reveal it in His time. Neither you nor Slater should rush or push the point."

Liberty smiled at her stepfather. He was a gift to all of them. The subject shifted soon afterward to various topics—dinner that night, the barn raising on Saturday, and eventually the baby and how Liberty could help Kate take it easy from time to time. The tender light in Duffy's eyes caused Liberty to pray and ask God to let this child be healthy and live to fill their hearts for many years to come.

❧ ❧ ❧

Nevertheless, to avoid fornication, let every man have his own wife, and let every woman have her own husband. Slater knew there was much more to chapter 7 than the verse he'd read that morning and the one now, but for the moment he stopped.

It was late at night, and he had just gotten home from next door and an evening full of good food, fellowship, and fun. Liberty Drake was one of the most special women he'd ever met. She was bright and talented. Slater smiled when he remembered her at the piano. She was compassionate and caring—he smiled again over the way she helped Duffy with the kids so Kate could put her feet up. And the whole family had made him feel welcome, even when Griffin had to leave right after dinner to go on duty.

At the moment, Slater was never more glad that he had saved himself for marriage. His parents, although not believers, were very moral people and had strong convictions on the subject. Respect for women and future mates was instilled from a young age. Slater had been unbelievably tempted over the years to throw it all away, but he had not. Even though his faith was new, he did not regret his actions in that area of his life.

Sometime after midnight, Slater woke to find the lantern still burning. He blew it out, realizing he must have fallen asleep while praying. It took a moment to remember what had been on his mind. Liberty floated back into his consciousness just before sleep, and right after he told the Lord he would talk to Him in the morning.

❧ ❧ ❧

Liberty knew that being called to the saloon on a Saturday before noon was nothing to worry about. Saturdays didn't heat up until evening, and mornings were especially quiet, stemming from Friday late-nighters. For these reasons, Liberty walked into the Brass Spittoon with confidence, a confidence that died as soon as she spotted him. Like the last time, the room was sprinkled with regulars. The gun-toting stranger stood out like a sore thumb. And he was big—big and dark—making him look all the more menacing. Liberty approached, praying for calm and for her own safety, and stood next to the table until he looked up.

"Excuse me, sir," she began politely, "I'll need you to surrender your firearm to me. Shotgun has outlawed firearms in the saloons and after dark."

Liberty steeled herself when his hand instantly went down to his side. All he did, however, was set his side arm on the table and keep his hand on top of it. It seemed to be going fine until he didn't move his hand. Black eyes weighed Liberty, and with more calm than she felt, Liberty stared right back. This was the reason she knew the exact minute his gaze shifted behind her.

"You're going to get yourself shot," she said in a voice that was measured and in control, "as well as whoever you're looking at behind me, if you don't gently push the gun across the table."

The dark man did just that, his touch light, his eyes back on Liberty.

"Thank you," she said simply. "Do you have any more?"

"No, ma'am," he replied softly.

"You're welcome to pick this up at the jailhouse later today. It's a block and a half down, on this side."

The black-haired, black-eyed man nodded, and Liberty glanced at the man at the table with him, his crooked-tooth smile in place.

"Well, at least ya didn't haul this one away."

Liberty shook her head. "As always, you're a big help, Lance."

The man only cackled, and Liberty turned to go. She glanced around but didn't see anyone who appeared to know the stranger. Realizing there was still a chance that he could be ornery enough to pull a hidden gun or a knife and get her from the back, she made herself walk away. He had certainly looked big, without even standing up. She spoke with Gordie before going back to the jailhouse, all the time hoping Griffin would be back before the man at the table came looking for his gun.

🌹 🌹 🌹

"Did that really just happen," Dakota Rawlings asked his brother the moment he exited the saloon, "or did I imagine the whole thing?"

Slater smiled. "At least you didn't get thrown in jail."

Dakota's look was shrewd. "Meaning you did?"

Slater nodded, and Dakota's gaze narrowed a bit more.

"Why didn't you come inside?"

Slater shrugged. "You didn't seem to need me."

Again, this response was carefully weighed as Dakota's eyes narrowed. "Where can we talk?" he asked bluntly.

"You mean, where can we go so you can give me the third degree and then lecture me?"

"That about sums it up," the older Rawlings said without apology.

Slater had all he could do not to laugh, but he didn't think Dakota, his senior by just one year, was in the mood for levity. Slater turned and started down the boardwalk. Dakota moved to untie a huge black horse at the hitching post and then followed slowly behind his brother.

Dakota missed little. His experience with the Texas Rangers had made his senses as honed as the knife in his boot. He noticed the way Slater walked with ease and even greeted by name some of the folks he passed, and how they passed the sheriff's office on the way out of the downtown and into a residential neighborhood. The last thing he noticed was the way Slater walked right in the back door of the house he approached.

Dakota saw the barn out back but opted to tie Eli's reins to a tree before following his brother inside. Slater was waiting in what Dakota found to be the kitchen, but the younger man turned and led the way the moment Dakota shut the door. When he walked into a nicely furnished living room and sat down like he owned the building, Dakota was more intrigued than ever.

"Start talking," Dakota, recovering swiftly, ordered, his seat having just hit the chair opposite Slater's.

"About what?"

"Don't play games with me, Slate. I've seen Brace, and I've been tracking you for days. Now I want to know why you left the Rangers."

"You won't like the answer."

Slater's voice and expression calmed Dakota immediately. He loved his brother; he was devoted to him. The last thing he wanted to do was make him feel attacked over his beliefs. He was, however, desperate to understand.

"Can you tell me this?" Dakota began again. "Why don't you think God wants us to keep law and order in Texas?"

"I do think that God wants that, Dak. I know He does. But I can't keep roaming around the country. I can't keep on the move like I have been. I want to be settled in one place and regularly attending church. I need consistent teaching and fellowship, not grabbing what I can, when I can."

"And Shotgun gives you that? How did you even hear of this place?"

"I didn't. I was just traveling at an easy pace and found myself in jail. When the sheriff asked me to church, I went. I haven't wanted to leave. It's not any more complicated than that."

Dakota didn't agree, but for the moment he kept silent. In his opinion, this whole thing was miserably complicated. He was still getting used to the first change in Slater; now he'd gone and made another one.

"Just so I have it straight," Dakota began. "You now believe the way Grandma and Cash do—that the only way to heaven and happiness on this earth is through the Christ?"

"Yes."

Dakota nodded before asking, "What was wrong with your life, Slate, that you needed that?"

Slater had to think about that one. The question didn't stump him, but wording the answer for his brother did.

"If you've never experienced a gnawing ache, Dak, then this won't make any sense," Slater began, his voice soft and serious as he remembered the pain. "But gnawing ache is the best way I can describe how I felt. Texas is a big land. It's easy to look at the sky and landscape and feel completely insignificant. I felt that way often. I found myself asking more and more what the point was. I believed in my work, and I was glad when I did a good job, but the fulfillment I once had was gone. I knew I had to find something that gave my life more meaning.

"That's why I talked with Desmond Curtis. I know there are men who can both walk the path God has laid out for His children and travel. Des is a good example of that. But I couldn't, Dakota. That's all the more I can tell you."

Dakota worked to calm the frustration rising inside of him. Slater was a good Ranger. He needed to be on the job. Dakota had just figured out what to say to him concerning that very subject when Slater stood.

"I've got to get cleaned up."

"We're not done talking." In the blink of an eye, Dakota became authoritative again.

"I'm afraid we are," Slater said calmly. "I'm going to a barn-raising party. Now, you're welcome to join me—in fact, I hope you do—but for right now the discussion is over."

"Slater," Dakota began, but the blond man was already headed toward the stairs. Dakota rose, went to the bottom step, and called his name again.

"We have to leave here in about 30 minutes, Dak," was all Slater would say. He didn't even turn around. "You won't want to smell like a horse."

For the first time in days, a smile threatened at Dakota's mouth. His brother knew just where to hit. With a shake of his head, he went for his saddlebags, seeing no help for it but to get cleaned up so he could accompany his little brother and keep an eye on the whole situation.

Eight

No one knew exactly how the fire started, but the Copper-smiths' barn had burned down three weeks back. The stock was rescued, but the building was lost. The townsfolk, many of them from the church, now gathered on the third Saturday of November to build a new structure. A level wooden floor had been laid on a stone foundation, and the plan for the day was to raise the walls and the roof before dark—all of this after the square dance.

Wagons arrived bearing families, baskets of food, and tools for the workers. Stacks of lumber, boxes of nails, and work supplies were set in place for the main event. Quilts were laid out, but many tables were set up too. The children chased each other, the adults visited, and in one corner of the barn, a small trio was tuning up—two fiddles and a strum bucket. In no time at all, the floor was being used.

By the time Slater and Dakota arrived, the square dance was in full swing. From her place under a tree, Liberty happened to look up and see Slater joining a group of men as they were talking. She noticed the dark-haired man with him but didn't make the connection. She was telling herself not to stare when Tess joined her.

"Hi, Tess."

"Hi, Libby." Tess smiled in her direction, but Liberty could see that she was not her bubbly self.

"How are you?"

"I'm okay. How are you?"

"Fine," Liberty said honestly but kept an eye on Tess. "Are you sure you're all right?"

"How's your mom, Libby?" Tess asked, ignoring the question.

"She's feeling pretty good. Duffy had to work until 2:00, so she'll come with him then."

The women were silent for a moment. The floor was quite full now, and the music was wonderful. Both women enjoyed a good square dance, but each wanted to be asked only by certain men. Liberty suddenly caught sight of Slater again. This time many women had joined the group, and as Liberty watched, one put her hand on his arm. Liberty glanced at Tess in an effort to shift her gaze and knew she had to forget herself and ask the question again.

"Tess?" Liberty's voice was soft. "Are you sure you're all right?"

Tess sighed and admitted, "I will be, but Papa said he would come today, and then he backed out. Mama didn't want to come either, so I rode with the Millers. I was okay until I got here and saw all the families grouped off. It makes me feel a little lonely."

Liberty's heart ached for her, and wishing to be a comfort, she said, "Maybe you'll have a family of your own one day, Tess."

"I suppose it could happen," Tess said. "I guess I have to keep trusting."

"Is that your way of saying that you haven't been?"

Tess' blue eyes met Liberty's gaze. "I will admit to you, Lib, that it's been pretty hard lately." Tess gave a little shake of her head. "It's so awful, Libby—all this hurt. I really am glad for your family that Griffin is still alive, but it occurred to me just as I was turning in last night, that for me, he might as well be dead."

Liberty's breath caught in her throat. The pain on Tess' face was unlike any she'd ever seen. Her words only confirmed the fact that this was miserable for her.

"I'm wicked, aren't I?" Tess whispered, tears coming to her eyes.

"No, Tess," Liberty whispered right back, a hand going to the other woman's arm. "I would never think that. And do you know what? You're right. I wish it wasn't so, but you're completely right about Griff. There's nothing anyone can do. There's certainly nothing I can say. I wish there were."

Tess nodded, her eyes going to her hands, which were fiddling with the pleats in her dress. Liberty dropped her own hand, thinking she would have both of them sobbing if she didn't let the subject go. For a time the women sat in silence. Liberty was slowly growing more stunned over what Tess had revealed, and Tess felt guilty for having the thought and admitting it.

"Hello, ladies." Slater was suddenly in front of them, his eyes smiling and kind. Liberty thought him adorable in a crisp plaid shirt and dark denim pants. His light-colored hat was in place, and Liberty thought as she had before that the hat always worked to accentuate his eyes.

"How are you, Mr. Rawlings?" Tess asked.

"I'm fine. Are you enjoying yourself?"

Tess smiled, not wanting to lie, and said, "It's certainly a nice day for a barn raising."

"Indeed. Is your family around?" Slater asked now, this time of Liberty.

"They're coming in a little while," she explained. For a moment she had been rather lost in the sight of him, but her gaze had drifted as she wondered whether Griffin knew of Tess' thoughts.

"Would you care to join me in the next set?"

Probably not. Tess said that it had just occurred to her last night.

"Would you like to dance, Libby?"

Then again, they may have seen each other earlier today. I'd like to think that this news would affect Griffin like it has me, so maybe he doesn't know after . . .

"Libby!" Tess' voice came through to the daydreaming deputy at the same time she shook her arm. "Mr. Rawlings is trying to ask you something."

"Oh, I'm sorry." Liberty looked to Slater to find him smiling in great amusement.

"Would you care to dance?"

Liberty blinked. "You want me to dance?"

Slater's smile grew. "Well, we could start to work with the hammer and nails, but I thought dancing might be a bit more fun."

Liberty laughed and stood. Slater offered her his arm, and just a minute later they had joined a group. There was no time for talking, something that suited Liberty fine. She smiled and laughed as they spun around, changed partners, stood opposite each other, and promenaded from one end of the floor to another. They were breathless when the set was through and only too glad to turn the floor over to the next group.

"Thank you," Slater said as they stepped off the floor. "How about some water?"

"That sounds good, thank you."

They stood in line with the other couples for a chance at the dipper, and it was there that Slater caught Liberty looking back at Tess. He looked as well and saw that Griffin had joined her. Liberty's eyes took on a look he hadn't seen before.

"Here you go, Libby," Slater said as he offered her the ladle. Liberty drank and handed it back. She watched Slater drink, realizing only then that she'd been distracted. Even so, she took one more peek at Tess and her brother.

"Why don't we come over here out of the way," Slater was saying, her hand captured in his as he urged her along. "You might even feel like telling me what's bothering you."

It was said so smoothly that for a moment Liberty missed it. When they stopped and she looked up at him, his raised brows told her she had heard him right.

"I'm sorry I was so distracted, Slater. Did it ruin the dance for you?"

"Not at all, but you could have told me no; I would have understood that Tess needed you."

Liberty was horrified to feel tears fill her eyes.

"Did you see the size of this gopher mound?" Slater quickly asked, his hand to Liberty's arm now as he moved her a few feet away. "They sure make a mess of things."

Liberty worked to catch her breath as he turned her away from the gathering and chattered inanely.

"Thank you, Slater," Liberty said when she had herself under control.

"My pleasure."

Liberty smiled a little. "Do you have a sister, Slater?"

"No, why?"

Liberty shrugged, almost sorry she'd said anything. "You just seem to know what to say. It makes me think some older sister influenced you."

Slater laughed. "My mother would be pleased to know that all of her work paid off."

"Did she keep on you?"

"On all three of us, yes. She had very definite ideas, and woe to the son who forgot to hold the door or let a lady go first."

"What would she do if you forgot?"

Slater shuddered a little. "She'd give us the eye."

Liberty found this highly amusing.

"You wouldn't laugh if you could see it," her told her, his eyes filled with dramatic fear. "She was tough."

"You poor baby." Liberty was teasing him when she saw that Tess and Griffin were approaching. She was relieved to see that Tess was looking more like herself, but her heart still speculated on what the other woman had said to her. The four of them talked for a few minutes, but the two walls that were built were ready to go into place, and the walls remaining to be built needed crews of men. Hank Hathaway was giving orders as though the barn were his, and Slater and Griffin went over to put their hands to the task. Some of the women started to lay out the tablecloths and set out the food, plates, and flatware. Tess and Liberty joined them.

"Is it my imagination, or is Mr. Rawlings rather interested in you, Libby?"

"I don't know," Liberty told her honestly, although she wished it was true. "Have you seen something that makes you think that?"

Tess smiled. "You mean, other than the way he stares at you and then asks you to dance?"

"Oh," Liberty said quietly, suddenly at a loss.

Tess put a hand on her arm. "Oh, Lib, sometimes I think you don't have a clue."

Liberty laughed a little. "Why is that?"

"You're so busy looking for lawbreakers, you never notice how cute any of them are or how much they watch you."

"Tess Locken!" Liberty had a good laugh over this. "Where do you come up with this stuff?"

Tess' jaw dropped. "Libby, it's true. I swear to you."

"Swearing, Tess? I'm ashamed of you."

Both women turned to see a smiling Dr. Duffy Peterson behind them.

"She's been coming up with all sorts of wild notions, Duff," Liberty told him. "You might hear anything out of her."

"Yes, Dr. Peterson," Tess chimed right in, hands on her hips, a smile in her voice and eyes. "I was telling Libby how men notice her, and she thinks I don't know what I'm talking about."

Duffy turned such a surprised face to Liberty that that woman shook her head.

"No, Duff," she began. "Don't join Tess and tease me about this."

Duffy looked a little more stunned, his brows rising slightly, as he saw that his stepdaughter was quite serious.

"Duffy?" Liberty began, her face now showing that she was very confused. Duffy put a hand on her arm.

"We'll have to get back to this, Lib. All right? Don't give it any more thought right now."

Liberty's eyes went back and forth between the two of them, their faces reminding her how much they cared. This was a subject she would need to know more about, but Duffy was right. This was not the time or place.

"Hi, Tess. Hi, Libby," Laura greeted them as she arrived. "Did you dance yet?"

"I did," Liberty said, glad to have the subject changed. Her mother was coming, Zach in tow, and all hands fell to food preparation as Duffy went to help the men. In no time at all dozens of people would be gathering to eat. Time for small talk had ended.

🦋 🦋 🦋

"My brother is in town," Slater told Griffin when he had the chance.

"He is? That's great."

Slater nodded, his face thoughtful.

"Is it great, Slater?" the lawman asked sensitively.

"It is," Slater agreed, "but he came looking for some answers, and I know he won't like everything he hears."

"Well, let me know if I can help."

"Thanks, Griffin."

"Oh, and don't hesitate to have him stay at the house for as long as he needs."

"Okay."

"Where is he, by the way?"

Slater nodded his head toward a large, dark man some 30 feet away who was driving nails into the wood with one blow. Griffin, surprised that he was even there, stared at Dakota for a moment and then turned his attention back to Slater.

"Was your brother in the saloon earlier today?"

Slater smiled. "Yep. Libby was ready to put him away, but he gave up the gun."

"She said it was some big guy with dark hair. Does she know he's your brother?"

"No. I'm not sure how long he'll stick around or how much he'll want to become known. He moved away from me the moment we arrived. Actually, I was surprised that he even came here today. I'm going to invite him to everything but let him make the choice," Slater chuckled, "not that I could do much else."

"Is he older than you?" Griffin thought Slater might have said but couldn't remember.

"Yes, but not by as much as it looks. Do you want to meet him now or later?"

"Later is fine. Be sure and tell him that Mam and Duffy are expecting us after church tomorrow."

"I'll do that. I'll be very satisfied if he joins me for either one." This said, Slater went back to work, his heart asking God to let Dakota stay long enough to have contact with folks who could make such a difference in his life.

※ ※ ※

"When did you meet her?" Dakota asked the minute they were in the door that evening.

"Who?"

"The woman you're going to marry."

Slater blinked. "You spent too much time bending over a hammer today, Dak. Get some rest."

"Not until you tell me."

"How can I tell you when I don't know what you're talking about?"

"I'll tell you what I'm talking about. You arrive and every female under 25 comes crowding around. They look at you as if you've just dropped from heaven, but do you ask one of them to dance? No. You leave them all for the small, dark-haired beauty who wanted to put me in jail this morning."

Slater was speechless. Dakota had perfectly described the scene. So why had the younger Rawlings thought that no one would notice his special interest in Liberty Drake?

"I haven't asked Libby to marry me, not even close," was all Slater could think to say.

"What's her name?" Dakota pressed him.

Slater closed his mouth. If Dakota wasn't going to stay in town long, he wasn't sure how much he wanted to share with him.

"You can meet her tomorrow," Slater finally said, "if you're sticking around that long."

Dakota's eyes narrowed. Slater had always held Dakota in high regard, and Dakota respected Slater in return, but if Dakota ever wanted the upper hand, he knew just how to get it. Having his younger brother refuse him anything or not answer a question took some getting used to.

"I take it she goes to your church."

"Yes, she does, but that's not where you would meet her. Griffin and I go to lunch at her parents' home on Sundays."

"And Griffin is the one who owns this house?" Dakota asked as he gestured to the room in general.

"Yes."

"How is he tied into this Libby woman?"

Slater opened his mouth but shut it again. Finally he said, "Why don't you come tomorrow and find out?"

Those dark eyes narrowed in his direction again but nothing more was said. Griffin came in a short time later, met Dakota Rawlings, and then took himself downtown to check on the Saturday night activity. Both Slater and Dakota turned in without another word on the subject.

❧ ❧ ❧

Slater didn't know when he'd been so distracted. Never in his wildest dreams did he think that Dakota would be sitting next to him in church. His presence caused Slater to listen with new ears. Things that made complete sense to him caused him to wonder if Dakota had a clue. His brother had not seemed overly intrigued or even resigned, but fairly early that morning he had come to Slater's room and asked when he needed to be ready for church. Slater was glad that he had some time alone after telling him. He spent that time praying, thanking God for His work, and asking Him to soften Dakota's heart.

"I want you to pay close attention to Nehemiah's prayer life," Pastor Caron instructed now. "Almost a dozen times the verses tell us that Nehemiah engaged in prayer. I'm just going to point out a few. He goes to God in prayer starting in chapter 1:4, and then while he's talking to the king in 2:4. Chapter 4 has several verses on the subject; 6:9 is a prayer, and the book ends with a plea to God from Nehemiah." Pastor Caron went back and read those verses before pausing and meeting the eyes of his congregation.

"As I've been saying for weeks now, this man teaches me so much. Is he teaching you? Are you trying to serve God without talking to Him? Are you forgetting that after we believe, He is with us always? How many of you can spend hours in someone's presence and not utter a word to him?"

Slater had to stop himself from smiling. Thinking that if Hank Hathaway were present he could raise his hand, he forced himself to concentrate on the sermon.

"If your goal is to grow and to serve the Lord, you've got to be praying. I don't know that any of us will be called to do something as huge as Nehemiah did, but no matter what your task, God is standing by to help you. He doesn't want to just observe; He delights in the prayers of His children and wants to give you the power and strength to succeed."

Slater felt Dakota shift beside him, and for a moment he thought he might rise and leave. In an effort to accept God's will in his brother's life, no matter what it was, Slater prayed and steeled himself for the worst, but nothing came of it. The service ended and Dakota headed right for the door, but not a mention was made of the service. Slater found him by the horses, asked him if he wanted to go to the Petersons', and took his quiet nod as a yes. Tempted as he was to question the older man's look, Slater held his tongue, praying all the way down the street.

🌿 🌿 🌿

"Zach can read," Laura told Dakota, leaning from her chair to make sure he could hear. "He goes to school."

"Does he?" Dakota's words were soft, his tone warm. The change had come over him as soon as he met Laura Peterson. "Do you go to school?"

"Next year. I'll be big then."

Dakota smiled, learning swiftly what many already knew: Laura was a heartwarmer.

"Is your horse the big black one?"

"Yes, it is."

"He looks like you," she announced.

"Laura!" Zach's shocked voice could be heard as he entered the room.

"Oh," Laura's eyes widened. "I'm sorry," she apologized. She had learned what Zach's looks meant. She wasn't sure what she had said, but her brother was looking horrified.

"That's all right," Dakota reassured her. "I guess Eli and I do look alike."

"His name is Eli?" Her face showed her disillusionment. "I was hoping it was a girl."

Dakota smiled before exchanging looks with Slater, who was glad to sit back and take this all in.

"I'm glad you don't have handcuffs on," Laura proclaimed.

Dakota blinked at her. "What?"

"Slater did when he first came."

This got another shocked tone out of Zach, even as Dakota turned compelling eyes onto his brother. Laura simply sat back and shut her mouth. The last time she had said too much she experienced a visit to the pantry with the wooden spoon. Laura had only just made her wise decision when Liberty came through the door.

"I think we're ready to eat," she announced.

The children scooted from the parlor on this note, but both men stood on her entrance, Slater ready to do the honors.

"Libby, this is my brother, Dakota. Dakota, this is Liberty Drake."

Liberty's eyes told the men that she was thinking fast, even while she heard Dakota say, "I've been wondering what you would look like for a long time."

"Dakota," his brother warned, but Liberty only looked confused. A moment later, still not having heard what Dakota said, she made the connection she'd been working through her mind.

"Oh, my," she said softly. "I didn't know." Indeed, Liberty was shocked. With his hat off, a freshly shaved face, and warm eyes, Dakota took some moments to place.

"It's all right." Dakota came to her rescue. "You were just doing your job."

Liberty suddenly bit her lip. "I did the same thing to Slater," she admitted on a laugh, relieved when the men joined her.

"Did Slater say the name was Liberty?" Dakota asked after she invited them to follow her to the dining room.

"Yes."

"Born on the Fourth of July?" Dakota asked, his eyes not missing a thing.

Liberty laughed again. "As a matter of fact, I was," she told him, all the time causing Slater to wonder why he had never asked.

"Here you are," Duffy said as they entered. "I'm sorry we didn't get to do more than meet you, Dakota. Did Laura do a good job as hostess?"

"Yes." Dakota told the truth, but Laura's eyes darted to their guest and swiftly away.

"Do we need to talk, Laura?" her father asked quietly.

"I shocked Zach two times," she admitted.

Duffy's hand came to his mouth, but he managed, "Well, did you say you were sorry?"

"I think so." She looked on the verge of tears, and Slater, feeling free to do so, stepped in.

"She handled it very well, as did Zach."

"Thank you, Slater," Duffy said with a nod. "Good job, children." He smiled at both of them before bowing his head. "What a privilege it is, Father, to gather around this table to eat, and also to have Slater's brother join us this day. We thank You for all Your blessings, from the food to the warm shelter You have lovingly placed over us. In Your will and timing, we ask that Griffin's business downtown will go smoothly, so that he may join us for dinner. In Your Son's holy name I pray. Amen."

The bowls were passed, and in an instant, Dakota was experiencing what Slater had experienced the first time he sat at this table. He hadn't heard anything too disagreeable from the preacher that morning, but he didn't think he wanted to go to church all the time. He was, however, gaining a glimpse of why Slater wanted to stay in this town. Dakota thought he might stick around himself.

"Hello," Griffin suddenly called as he came through from the kitchen. "Any food left?"

"Oh, Griff." Kate shook her head at him. "As if I would let you starve on the one day you let me feed you."

Griffin smiled before kissing his mother's cheek, taking a seat, and serving himself. He was in the midst of telling them what had happened downtown when someone else came in the back door.

"Doc! Doc!" the man cried frantically.

"In here," Duffy said calmly but started to rise.

Pat Brewster came panting to the doorway, his face a mask of fear. "Meg's pains have started. Doc, can you come?"

"I'm on my way," Duffy told him.

"I'd better get back," Pat panted, suddenly whipping the hat off his head. "I'm sorry, Mrs. Peterson," he said to Kate.

"It's all right, Pat. Tell Meg I'm thinking of her."

"Thank you, ma'am."

In the next few seconds Pat left and Duffy grabbed his bag, kissed Kate, took a hug from Laura, and made his way from the room. The diners had all fallen silent.

"My Papa's going to make a baby be born," Laura said after a moment. The pride in her voice made the rest of the room smile.

Nine

"Was Laura serious about your handcuffs?" Dakota asked much later that day as both men rode on horseback along the creek line. The men had spent most of the afternoon with the Petersons. They were still there when Duffy returned to announce that he had delivered a healthy baby girl.

"I'm afraid so," Slater replied, shaking his head with regret. "I told you I went to jail."

"True, but why would the sheriff take you to his mother's house?"

Slater gave him a rundown and watched Dakota's brows lift. He didn't have to say it. It was written all over his face: Were these people real? Since Slater believed their actions were all spiritually based, he was glad when Dakota didn't press him over answers he wouldn't believe.

"Do you think Libby will like being a Ranger's wife?" Dakota asked.

"You'll have to ask her when you propose," Slater replied calmly, not rising to the bait.

"That's not what I meant, and you know it."

"Well, then she knows some other Ranger, because I turned in my badge."

The look Dakota sent him was dark, and not just from the color of his eyes. He looked ready to begin a lecture but turned away, his eyes on the water.

"How long do you plan to keep this up?" Dakota asked, his voice soft.

Slater sighed. "I'm not on vacation, Dak."

"Then what would you call it?"

Slater weighed his words and spoke, a slight edge to his voice. "I don't know where all of this is going to lead, but rare are the times in my life when I've felt such a peace. I felt a peace when I told Brace, and I felt a peace the first Sunday I sat in that church and was taught from the Word. I don't think I can tell you how much I needed that. If you have peace right now, I'm glad for you, and I will welcome your questions, but badgering me will stop, Dakota. I'm staying here right now, and that's the end of it. If you stay around, you'd better know one thing: I'm not going to have you constantly on my back."

Dakota nodded but kept silent. Lately Slater had become very even-natured. He hadn't been as a child, so there was no missing the change. It wasn't often in the last two years that he grew angry or overly passionate on an issue, so when he did, his family had learned to listen. It was on Dakota's mind to tell Slater that he would go along but that his eyes would be open. He changed his mind. Why would he want to threaten his brother? Much as he disagreed with his decision, the idea was ludicrous. They eventually turned and rode silently back toward town. No tension lingered between them—they cared for each other too much for that—but each brother wondered what the future would bring.

🌹 🌹 🌹

"Hey, Griff," Liberty said softly as she followed Griffin out the door.

"Yeah?" He turned while still on the porch. The sun was falling fast, but they could still see each other well. The already visible moon was full.

"Did you see Tess today?"

"Not to talk to. Why?"

Liberty opened her mouth but hesitated.

"What's the matter?" Griffin asked, his voice telling her he wanted an answer.

"She was having a pretty hard time at the barn raising yesterday. I just wondered how she was today."

"Was it something to do with me or her family?"

"Some of both. She didn't talk to you?"

"Not a word."

Liberty nodded, saddened by the fact. She wanted to help her friend—she wanted to help Griffin—but the situation seemed impossible.

"What did her family do?"

Liberty explained the way they had backed out of coming and how lonely she felt.

"How did my name come up?" Griffin asked, no censure in his voice.

"Oh, Griff." Liberty sounded annoyed. "Sometimes I'm such a dolt. I told Tess that maybe someday she'd have a family of her own. She was already upset. I don't know what I was thinking." Liberty stopped and then admitted, "Then she told me some of her most recent thoughts. I wanted to sob for her."

Griffin could see that she didn't want to go on, but he had to know. "Tell me, Libby," Griffin said, his voice indicating he was at a loss in the whole situation.

"You won't thank me, Griff—not if it hits you as hard as it did me."

Griffin gave a mirthless laugh. "Sometimes I think a hit is just what I need. Please tell me."

Liberty looked up at him. "She said she was glad for your family's sake that you were alive, but where she's concerned, you might as well be dead."

Griffin could barely find air to fill his lungs. He put his hands on his sister's upper arms, harder than he intended, and brought her up close.

"Did she really, Libby—did she actually say that?"

A small cry broke Liberty's voice. "I'm sorry, Griff. I'm so sorry."

Griffin slowly let go of his sister, his arms dropping to his side. What a fool he'd been. All this fear of leaving her when he'd already abandoned her. He looked over to see Liberty staring at him, tears caught on her lower lids.

"Did I hurt you?"

"No," she replied, shaking her head. "Not at all. I just feel so bad."

"I've got to go see her," Griffin said, his voice still stunned. "I'll talk to you later."

"Okay."

Griffin was ten steps off the porch when he turned and ran back. He hauled Liberty into his arms and hugged her tightly.

"Thanks, Lib," he whispered.

Liberty stood still long after her brother moved out of sight. Her heart in her throat, she prayed that God would give Griffin wisdom and that Tess would just keep trusting.

❧ ❧ ❧

"Well, Griffin," Mrs. Locken said with a smile, "come in."

"Thank you, Mrs. Locken," Griffin said as he removed his hat, "but could I possibly see Tess here on the porch?"

Mrs. Locken smiled. This man had never done anything to make her worry, but it was a cold evening.

"Tess is in the kitchen, Griffin; you won't be disturbed in there."

"Thank you," he said softly as he crossed the threshold. The house was warm, and with his heart trying to jump into his mouth, he began to perspire.

"Just go on through, Griffin," the lady of the house invited. "Tess is working on a pie."

Griffin greeted Mr. Locken as he passed through the living room, but he only waved his hand and kept the newspaper to his face. His legs feeling weighted, Griffin made his way to the kitchen at the back of the house. Whoever had built this home had not spared in space. It was roomy and comfortable. The dining room was dim, but more light peeked from under the closed door to the kitchen. Griffin pushed open the door without knocking, standing just inside until Tess looked up from her work.

"Well, Griffin," she said in surprised delight.

In just a few strides, Shotgun's sheriff covered the distance between them and took Tess' flour-covered hand in his.

"Marry me, Tess," he barely managed through suddenly dry lips.

Tess closed her eyes for a moment and sighed. She then smiled into his worried gaze and said, "Just name the date, Griffin, and I'll be there."

"Oh, my wonderful Tess," the sheriff breathed as he drew her gently into his arms. "I love you so."

"Oh, Griffin." Tears were coming now, and Tess could not stop them. "I never thought . . ." she began.

"I know," he said as he moved back and smoothed the hair from her brow. "I just didn't understand until Lib told me what you said."

Tess wasn't long in catching on. "It was horrible of me."

"It wasn't," Griffin said emphatically. "It was horrible of me, but to be honest, I really thought I was doing the right thing. Now I see that you're right: I might as well be dead for you if I'm going to keep us apart."

Tess couldn't take it. She sobbed into his shirt front and couldn't stop, even when she heard the door open again.

"I'm sorry," Griffin said, turning to see Mrs. Locken. "I didn't know she would cry."

"What is it, Griffin? Has something happened?"

"I asked her to marry me."

As though he was watching the scene all over again, Mrs. Locken began to cry too. She and Tess came together in a hug and then laughed at each other's teary faces.

"I'm sorry," Mrs. Locken told Griffin. "You can't have bargained on both of us sobbing all over the place."

"Well, I left my sister in tears when I came over here, and something tells me my mother will do the same."

"So Libby knew?" Tess asked. "What did she think?"

"No, she didn't know, but she told me what you'd said and that was upsetting."

Tess briefly explained the conversation from the day before, and Mrs. Locken hugged her again.

Ready for a lighter subject, the older woman said, "Tell me, Tess, a big wedding or a small affair?"

Tess looked at Griffin. "I don't care, just as long as I become Mrs. Drake."

"Oh my, Tess," her mother complained. "You'll have me going again. Come. Let's go tell your father."

The next few minutes went much better than Griffin could have anticipated. Mr. Locken actually put his reading material down long enough to smile at his daughter, congratulate the both of them, and ask about the date, something that would have to be considered. One of Tess' brothers even came home from downtown and heard the news as well before going off to his room. When Griffin was finally ready to leave, Tess walked him onto the porch.

"I won't sleep tonight," Tess said, "and that means I'll have bags under my eyes. If I see you tomorrow, you'll change your mind."

Griffin laughed. "That's not going to happen."

Tess could only stare at him. "I love you, Griffin."

"I love you, Tess, so very much. Thank you for helping me see what I'm missing."

Tess nodded. "We have to trust. For all we know, something could happen to me."

"I hope not," Griffin said softly. "I hope we're still gazing into each other's eyes 30 years down the road."

All Tess could do was smile. It was the last thing Griffin saw before he turned and headed for home—not home exactly but more like the house next door, where just as he suspected, his mother, joined by his sister, cried when they heard the news.

🌹 🌹 🌹

The man working with Hank Hathaway when Slater landed on the job the next morning was one of the biggest men Slater had ever seen. A vague remembrance of someone lifting a horse from the creek passed through his mind even as he went forward to see if he still had a job.

"I'm Slater Rawlings," he said as he put out his hand to the stranger.

"Price Hathaway," the huge man said in return, just before he engulfed Slater's hand in a gentle grip. "I hear you've been fillin' in."

"Yes," Slater said congenially, even as his heart sank. It sounded as though he was no longer needed.

"I've been in Austin," Price informed him.

"I'd heard that. How was it?"

An odd light flickered in the larger man's eyes. "Not like I thought."

"Did you make friends there?"

"I thought I would, but I didn't."

Slater ached a little for this gigantic young man. He had the face and eyes of a boy, and maybe the heart of one too.

"What do you want Slater to do, Pa?" Price turned and asked.

"Same as always," the older Hathaway grunted, not bothering to look up.

Price turned back to Slater with a huge grin. "Pa's as informative as ever."

Slater smiled before he went for a hammer. He came back and began to stack and organize the lumber. Right now they were building a house. It wasn't long before Price was working beside him.

"You ever been to Austin?" the young Hathaway asked.

"I have, yes."

"It's big," he said with awe. "I had heard that, but I wanted to see for myself."

"Did you get work there?"

"I tried, but nothing panned out."

"What did you want to do?"

"I wanted to build houses—big, fancy ones—but everyone I met told me I should be in the saloons. I finally ran out of money and had no choice. I was hired right away."

Slater took in the pained look on his face. Yes, he was the perfect size for a bouncer but clearly not a rough individual. The combination would not have worked.

"How'd you get home?" Slater asked as he began to place a board against the studs and nail it into place. Price worked on a plank of his own.

"I finally saved enough to go. They actually owed me a little more pay, but I wanted out."

Slater wanted to ask if it was nice to be home, but the pain on Price's face was too raw.

"Where is that saw I asked for?" Hank called.

Unlike Price's last communication with his father, this time he didn't smile. His look was clearly longsuffering as he turned to help his parent. Slater watched the two of them for just a moment, wondering what the week would bring.

☙ ☙ ☙

"I'm here for my gun," Dakota told Liberty as soon as he opened the office door.

Liberty laughed as she stood and took the weapon from the wall cabinet.

"I really am sorry," she said as she handed it over, eyes brimming with pleasure.

"You look sorry," he teased back and then shook his head. "It wasn't a very nice welcome to your fine town."

"That's true," Liberty had to admit.

"Think of my feelings. You've got some patching to do."

Liberty laughed again. "All right, I'm *very, very* sorry."

Dakota shook his head. "That won't do. Nothing short of lunch with me will help."

Liberty's mouth opened in surprise, and she gave an incredulous laugh. He was certainly smooth, but she was not going to agree. When her features were composed once again, she told him plainly, "I'm going home to have lunch with my mother and sister. You're free to join us, but that's my final offer."

Dakota smiled. He liked a lady who would not let anyone push her around. Not getting her alone would make it harder to find out her feelings for Slater, but maybe he'd learn something after all.

"Your mother won't mind?" Bold as he'd been, he felt a need to check.

"No." Liberty shook her head. "I've brought stray pups home before; Mam will understand."

Dakota fought hard not to smile, but it wasn't working. He had seen how fun she was on Sunday but not had it directed at him. He'd just found a comeback when a woman's stringent voice cut through the air.

"I tell you I want something done!"

Both Liberty and Dakota turned as Griffin came through the door, closely followed by Maddie Flowers.

"I swear those Potters were up all night! Now, are you the law in this town or not?"

"Have a seat, Mrs. Flowers," Griffin returned calmly as he took the desk chair and pulled out his report folder. He began to write, his head bent, while the lady in front of the desk went puce with outrage.

"My dog's hair is falling out! If they shot those guns once, they shot them a hundred times, and I want to know what you're going to do!"

Griffin took a few notes and then looked up.

"I'll come out and check on things, probably later today or this week for sure."

"Why not now?"

"Because if they roughhoused until that late, they'll all be dead asleep for most of the day."

"Well, you wake 'em up! That's your job."

Griffin let her rail for a time but eventually turned a deaf ear.

"How'd it go?" he asked Liberty.

"Fine. I never left the office. Duffy stopped by with the mail. I left it there for you."

"All right. Thanks, Lib. What are you up to, Dakota?"

"I just talked my way into lunch at your mother's," he answered, but went on to say what he was thinking. "Has Slate ever mentioned what I do?"

"Yes, he has," Griffin remembered even as he said it.

Dakota nodded. "If I can be of help while I'm in town, please say the word."

"Thank you."

Maddie's voice had quieted, but she was still sitting there seething and muttering to herself. Knowing that Griffin would best know how to deal with her, Liberty moved to the door, Dakota on her heels.

"Tell me, Libby," Dakota asked almost as soon as they were outside, "how did you become the deputy?"

"My father taught me to shoot, and I've filled in as Griffin's deputy ever since he's had the office. I think most of Griff's deputies have come into the job with stars in their eyes. They think it's going to be exciting and action-packed, but Shotgun's a very peaceful town. Deputies hear of something bigger or better and move on."

"But not you."

"No, not me. I grew up here, and I love it. My father was the sheriff for years. He died in the line of duty."

"And what compelled him to teach you to fast-draw?"

Liberty shrugged. "He worked with Griff, and I was interested. He let me try." Liberty shrugged again, and Dakota, even though he'd never seen her draw, sensed that there was more to it than that. He might have tried to find out, but the house was in sight. Much as he wanted to know more about Liberty's work with a gun, Dakota actually hoped that her heart would be revealed at lunch.

※ ※ ※

"My brother is getting married," Laura told Dakota, her eyes shining with the news. They had just sat down to eat.

"He is?" Dakota asked; the Ranger had not heard this.

Laura nodded. "He loves Tess."

Dakota smiled. He had certainly seen Shotgun's sheriff with a lovely blonde on Saturday but not made any suppositions.

"I get to watch," Laura went on. "Mam and Papa said. I just have to stay quiet."

Dakota smiled again and looked up to see Kate watching her daughter, her eyes alight with love.

"Well," Dakota put in, "let me offer my congratulations on your getting a new sister-in-law."

Laura's eyes widened, and she told her mother. "Another sister! And she's going to help Libby when she helps Griffin with the law."

"No, dear," Kate said gently and explained Tess' title to Laura. The little girl did a lot of nodding but waited only until Kate turned away before whispering to Dakota, "Did Tess break the law?"

Dakota could not stop laughing. He had never encountered a child quite like her. She was so full of wonder and news. He was still trying to compose himself when Liberty tried to explain. More nodding followed, but no one was very certain if Laura understood.

"Dakota," Kate began kindly, thinking they all needed a change, "did Slater say you are older than he is?"

"Yes, ma'am, by just a year."

"And I can't remember if you have other siblings."

"I'm the middle of three brothers. Cash runs the family ranch in Kinkade."

"Well, if you don't think you can make it home for Thanksgiving, the church always has a dinner. We attend, and we'd be happy to have you join us."

"Thank you, Mrs. Peterson, I think Slater talked about doing that, so I'll probably tag along."

"What will your family do?" Liberty asked.

"My parents, who moved back to St. Louis about five years ago, will dine with friends, but my brother will do as you're doing, meet with families from the church he attends. My grandmother, who lives in Hilldale but visits the ranch each winter, will probably do the same thing."

Dakota said all this very politely and had no qualms about sharing, but he did have a motive. He wanted to know more about *this* family—more specifically, Liberty. He spent the next hour hoping some tidbit would be revealed, but it was not to happen. Much as he enjoyed the meal and company, he left the house feeling as though he hadn't accomplished a thing.

🌿 🌿 🌿

Liberty suddenly made the connection from the comment in the sheriff's office. Dakota was the brother who was a Texas Ranger. Liberty had already changed into her dress, but she felt a need to check on Griffin. Heading from the house with a brief word to her mother, she moved swiftly back downtown.

"What's up?" Griffin asked when she came in panting just a little.

"I just realized I heard you say you might go to the Potters'. I wondered if you needed me."

"Thanks, Lib, but Dakota's going with me. He was just in to check about it and went back to get his horse. I figure now is as good a time to go as any. They might be a little more docile if they're still feeling the effects."

Liberty nodded, working successfully to hide the confusion and hurt inside of her. Never before in her life could she remember Griffin not needing her. It was one of the most awful sensations she'd ever experienced.

"Well," she said to hide the hurt, "let me know how you fare, and be careful."

"I'll do that," Griffin said sincerely, but he wasn't looking directly at her. He might have seen her confusion if he had been.

Liberty took that moment to make her exit, hoping against all hope that Dakota would not be coming down the street. She slipped away, going a strange, indirect route in an effort not to see him. She slowed her pace when she thought it was safe and tried to pray and think clearly. She knew she could talk to her mother, but what would she say exactly? *Griff didn't need me, and I've never been so crushed and rejected.* Even to her own ears, she sounded like a five-year-old. It was, however, exactly how she felt.

"Hey, Lib," a male voice suddenly said.

Liberty looked up to see Price Hathaway next to a half-built home, a hammer in one hand, a board in the other.

"Well, Price, when did you get back into town?"

Price gave his boyish smile. "When in actual time, or how I feel?"

Liberty laughed as she moved toward him. It had been a long time since they'd talked; the two of them had been in school together, and she had always cared for this gentle giant. And right now she welcomed the chance to get Griffin and Dakota off her mind.

Ten

"You still totin' a gun?" Price teased Liberty as soon as she was near.

"Yes, I am, so you'd better not have brought any bad habits back from Austin. They could land you in trouble."

"If you'd stay at the jailhouse and talk to me, I wouldn't mind," he returned, flirting with her a little.

"What would Miss Amy say?"

A sad light filled Price's eyes. "She wasn't too happy when I left."

"Does she know you're back?"

"I haven't talked to her, so I don't know."

Liberty nodded but didn't press him. She glanced around and heard pounding but couldn't see who it was.

"Did you meet Slater Rawlings?"

"Sure," Price said easily enough.

"Did your father keep him on or is he out looking for work?"

"He's around the corner, trying to please Pa."

As if Slater had heard the calling of his name, he suddenly appeared from around the other side of the building. He paused when he saw Liberty, but only because he was a sweaty mess. He thought as he always did that she looked wonderful.

"Hi, Slater," Liberty greeted him, giving no thought to the signs of hard work on his shirt or face.

"Hi, Libby. What are you up to?"

"I'm headed home," she said, trying not to think of her conversation with Griffin.

"*Price!*" Hank suddenly bellowed from around the corner, and that man withdrew from Slater and Liberty.

"I'll talk to you later, Price," Liberty called to him.

"All right, Lib. Take care."

Liberty watched him move away and then noticed Slater's eyes on her. She smiled in genuine pleasure.

"I'm glad you didn't lose your job, Slater."

Slater's brows rose a little. "It's been an interesting day."

Liberty nodded, not needing much more of an explanation. Hank Hathaway's reputation preceded him. Price's desire to leave had been no mystery.

"Price and I were in school together," Liberty put in. "I've always liked him."

"There isn't much not to like."

"That's true. I've always hoped he would marry a certain woman here in town, but I don't know."

"Miss Amy?"

Liberty looked hopeful. "Did he talk of her?"

Slater shook his head no. "Some of the neighbors around here are a might busy. One came by and asked him questions for far longer than I would have allowed."

"He's so kindhearted. I don't suppose he wanted to wound Mrs. Hurst."

Slater smiled at the way she knew exactly who it was.

They talked for a few minutes more, but Slater knew he had to get back to work. Liberty went on her way, and Slater returned to help Hank and Price. The temptation to simply follow Liberty and talk to her for the remainder of the day was powerful indeed, but he resisted. Instead, he prayed for her almost the entire afternoon.

🌹 🌹 🌹

"And how long have they been giving the town trouble?" Dakota asked as they rode away from the Potters' house.

"For as long as anyone can remember. Maddie Flowers didn't mind for a long time, and they're far enough out that not much was said by anyone else, but Maddie's getting older and more intolerant of the noise."

"And you say she has her own still."

"Yes. If rumor can be trusted, Rush and Possum Potter built it for her. Maybe that's why she stayed quiet for so long."

"What will you do next?" Dakota asked as they arrived in Shotgun's downtown area.

"I'll lie low. Critter is as mean as a rattlesnake, and Ned can be. If I rush things, someone will die. I want to avoid that, but my eventual goal is to shut them down. If I succeed at that, they'll probably move on. I wouldn't wish that on any other town, but I've got to think of how fast our city is growing."

Dakota was impressed. He'd been impressed for a long time, but his respect was steadily growing. His first meeting of the town sheriff had not given him much to hope for, but behind that smooth, young face was an intelligent, clear-thinking sheriff—one who cared about the people as much as he did his job.

They parted company after they reached the jailhouse, Dakota heading to Griffin's house and Griffin into his office. Dakota had not thought of Slater and Liberty since earlier that day, but now they came to mind; more specifically, Liberty did. He wished that she had gone to the Potters' with them so he could see her in action.

🌿 🌿 🌿

"Thanks for putting the kids down, Lib," her mother said that evening. "I swear, some days I don't think I'll even get up the stairs to put myself to bed."

Liberty came over and kissed her mother's cheek.

"What was that for?"

"That was from Laura. She said you needed another one."

Kate chuckled and began to loosen the pins in her hair. If they had unexpected company, she'd have to put it back up in a hurry, but right now it felt too good to massage her scalp.

"Why don't you head up?" Duffy asked as he watched her.

"Because I'm not sleepy, just weary. And when I go to bed too early, I wake so early that I have to just lie quiet or wake Zach." Zach was the light sleeper in the family. He was very good about staying in bed, but his mother knew how much he needed his rest in this first year of school.

"Duffy?" Liberty had sat down, but she was not relaxed. Duffy looked over to see her perched on the edge of the davenport.

"Yes?"

"I need to ask you about something. Are you too tired?"

"Not at all," the doctor said sincerely. "What's up?"

Liberty took a moment to start, and Kate looked to Duffy for answers. His raised brows told her he was in the dark, so they both waited.

"Do you remember talking to Tess and me as soon as you got to the barn raising on Saturday?"

Now knowing exactly what was on her mind, Duffy nodded.

"Duffy, do you really agree with Tess that I don't see when men are interested in me?"

Duffy did not immediately answer. He weighed his words and then started. "I don't want you to misunderstand me, Lib, and you might because the single women in our church so dreadfully outnumber the single men. I do agree with Tess that you don't seem aware of the looks that come your way, but most of the time I'm glad you don't see the attention of those men, since they're probably not the ones for you. Does that make sense?"

"Yes, but I still don't see it," she told him, frustration punctuating every word. "I think you and Tess are doing more hopeful thinking than witnessing any great male interest in Liberty Drake."

"That's easy to understand," Kate suddenly inserted. Both Duffy and Liberty stared at her.

"How do you figure?" Duffy asked.

"Well, she's a deputy. She has to keep her eyes open. She hasn't had time to relax like a lot of her friends have." Kate suddenly looked sad. "I wish she had."

Liberty sat back. For the first time in her life she asked herself if she might be too involved in her work. She suddenly found her eyes on her mother and had to ask her a question.

"Do you wish I wasn't helping Griff, Mam?"

Kate smiled. "Now that's a hard one, Lib. Do I want both my children in danger or do I want one of them in extreme danger because he has no one to back him up?"

Liberty nodded. That made very clear sense, but there was more. As seemingly slow as she was about men, Liberty now asked herself what godly mother didn't want her daughter to meet and marry a wonderful man?

"I keep praying that God will send the right man to help Griff, but so far that hasn't happened," Kate continued.

"I pray for the same thing," Duffy added. "Every day."

Liberty felt as if she'd been hit. She had never once asked God to send someone to replace her. Why was that? The question gave Liberty pause. She suddenly wasn't sure that she wanted to know.

A moment later Duffy asked Liberty if she was all right. Admitting that she didn't know, she was ready to change the subject. She double-checked with her mother about Thursday's preparations. They talked of Thanksgiving for the next hour. When she finally went to bed, her mind immediately moved to Slater, Griffin, and her job. She pushed them all away and repositioned her mind to the baking she wanted to get done for Thanksgiving, telling herself she didn't want to rush this holiday time away with all sorts of other thoughts. It was not a solid reason and Liberty knew that, but she just kept justifying it by reminding herself that all too soon it would be December, with Christmas rushing up on the calendar.

❧ ❧ ❧

"Do you know what happened to me on Sunday?" Tess whispered to Griffin in the general store. She had been shopping and turned to find him next to her, something that never failed to delight her.

"What?"

"A very wonderful man asked me to marry him."

"No kidding?" Griffin's eyes were impressively large.

"No kidding," Tess answered, her own eyes alight with pleasure as she looked up at him. "I said yes."

"Did you?" Griffin smiled down at her. "When is the big event?"

"Well," her brow dropped in the way he loved, "I'm free tomorrow."

"Tomorrow is Thanksgiving," he reminded her, feeling intoxicated by her nearness.

"Friday then?" Tess asked hopefully, and Griffin had to laugh.

Tess smiled complacently and then noticed the eyes that watched them, mostly older women who should have known better.

"I can tell this is going to be interesting," Tess said as she turned to examine a row of shoes and belts.

"Why is that?" Griffin asked, studying her profile with pleasure.

"You might be the most well-known person in town. It's like courting in a house made of glass."

Griffin had noticed the attention as well, but there was little he could do or say. He opted for a lighter note.

"You sound as though you're changing your mind."

No longer caring who might be watching, Tess' eyes met his.

"Not even close," she said softly.

Griffin reached for her hand, their fingers entwining for several seconds.

Not long afterward, Griffin went back to work, comforted by the fact that in two days he could see her almost all day. Nevertheless, he asked God to help him concentrate on the job. Remembering Tess' sweet smile and love for him, he thought he might endanger someone if he even touched his gun.

❧ ❧ ❧

The second week in December was cold. Slater had not paid much attention to the weather so far, working with Price and Hank no matter what. But today his head felt full, and every time he bent over the hammer, his forehead and cheeks pounded. He told himself he could make it all day, but by midafternoon, he knew he had to get inside.

"I don't feel well," Slater wasted no words in telling his boss. "I'm going to head home. I'll try to work tomorrow."

Hank looked up, a frown on his face, but Slater's glassy eyes and red face softened him a little.

"Just take off till it's gone, or you'll have us all sick."

Slater did little more than wave as he turned away.

"Hey, Slater," Price stepped in, "Miss Amy carries some medicine for colds. Stop by for some on your way home. Doc Bergram's or something like that."

"Thanks, Price."

Slater hadn't really decided to stop, but since he hadn't ridden Arrow to the job that day, he felt nearly frozen by the time he reached downtown. He stepped into the general store just to get his lungs out of the cold. Miss Amy happened to be standing right inside.

"May I help you?"

"Oh." Slater tried to smile and be polite, his mind fuzzy with the headache. "I'm looking for something for colds. I think Price said it was Doc Berg's or some name like that."

"Doc Bergrin's?"

"Yeah, that must be it."

"Right this way."

Slater followed her in something of a daze. She had a large selection of tonics and such. He watched as she plucked one off the shelf and handed it to him.

"That one will take all pain away—it's pretty potent. This one," she said, handing him another bottle, "doesn't have any alcohol in it at all, but it's still good stuff. Typically, husbands buy the first one and wives buy the second one."

No contest in Slater's mind. He took the second bottle and turned toward the counter, wanting nothing more than to get home and climb into bed.

"Price sent you, didn't he?" Miss Amy asked quietly as Slater was fishing for coins.

"Yes. He said you might have something."

"He hasn't been in since he got back," she murmured. A note in her voice got through to Slater. Working to ignore his own discomfort, he looked at the tall, well-built woman behind the cash register. She didn't appear to be quite as young as Price, but there was no mistaking the interest in her eyes.

"Maybe he doesn't know you'd like him to come in," Slater offered.

"Well," Miss Amy's gaze dropped, "I hope someone tells him." With that, she slid Slater's change across the counter, shut the drawer, and turned away. Slater watched her take a feather duster to shelves that looked immaculate, his heart turning over in compassion. He felt simply awful, but that did not stop him from praying for Price and Miss Amy and asking God to open the door if he should tell his coworker what this woman had said.

※ ※ ※

"Oh! Dakota!" Liberty said when the door was opened, "I didn't know you were back."

Dakota had been called to work just after Thanksgiving and hadn't been in town since.

"I'm just in," he explained. "Come on in."

"Well, I don't want to be in the way, but Mam thought she saw Slater come in and wanted to send this soup for him. Is he here?"

"I don't think so, but maybe he is. Come on through and I'll check."

Dakota held the door wide, and Liberty took the pot of warm soup straight through to the kitchen. Since her brother had gained a housemate, she did not come and go as she pleased through his back door.

"Let me see if he's here now," Dakota said.

Liberty put the pot on the stove top and went ahead and added a little wood to the fire in the oven. The house felt chilly to her.

"He's sound asleep," Dakota announced when he returned from upstairs.

Liberty nodded. "He mentioned on the weekend that he thought he'd caught something. Well, tell him to rest, and hopefully the soup will help."

"All right. Thanks."

Liberty started back toward the front door, Dakota on her heels.

"Should I take this as a good sign?" Dakota suddenly asked, causing Liberty to turn before she reached the doorknob.

"For what?"

"Well," Dakota smiled charmingly. "When a lady brings a gentleman hot soup, I would say that means she cares."

Liberty's eyes lit with amusement. "My mother sent the soup, and to answer your question, yes, she cares very much."

"Come on, Libby," he coaxed now, "give a guy a break."

"Dakota," Liberty replied, trying not to laugh at his pleading look, "I don't know what you want."

His black eyes narrowed as they always did when he was in thought.

"All right," he finally said, "I'll play my hand. How do you feel about Slater?"

Liberty's look was remarkably calm. "That, Mr. Rawlings, is a question the gentleman himself will have to ask me."

"But you could give me a hint."

"No, I couldn't," Liberty said on a laugh. She thought he was so funny. "And while we're on the subject, what is it to you?"

"I'll tell you what. He's going to let you get away if he isn't careful."

Liberty shook her head. "I don't think I've ever seen the like."

"What's that?"

"A Texas Ranger with nothing better to do than play matchmaker."

Dakota was opening his mouth in outrage when Liberty slipped out the door. She didn't look back or even wave, but she smiled to herself all the way back to her own front door.

🌹 🌹 🌹

"Did I hear Liberty's voice?" Slater asked when Dakota checked on him about 20 minutes later.

"Yes. Are you going to marry that lady or not?"

"This afternoon," Slater said as he rolled over to go back to sleep. "Didn't I tell you?"

Dakota took compassion when he heard Slater's rough voice. Thinking his throat had to be sore, he took himself from the room. It didn't look as though anything he could say or do would induce Slater back to the Rangers, but where Liberty Drake was concerned, he wasn't going to leave things so up in the air. He decided that before he left town he was going to wring a few promises out of his little brother.

🌹 🌹 🌹

A high-noon bank robbery the day after Christmas was not what Griffin and Liberty had been expecting, but that was exactly what they got.

It was a Monday, and Liberty was due to go off duty when a terrified Miss Amy came running to tell her what she'd witnessed across the street. Liberty knew better than to go alone. Thankfully, Griffin was in the mayor's office, and within minutes the two of them were making their way to the bank building. The only way in was through the front door, so they started to inch their way down the boardwalk. They had just gained positions at the window when a shot was fired and at least two women screamed. Wasting no more time, the Drakes rushed in.

"Don't do it!" a wild-eyed man screamed, his gun pointed right at them. "Get your hands up. I swear I'll shoot again."

Liberty and Griffin did exactly as they were told, coming in and leaving the door wide open. The man kept turning, moving around so fast that he gave them no time to reach for their weapons. At the same time, he didn't seem to notice their gun belts. Standing with her hands in the air, helpless for the moment, Liberty took in the scene and felt very sick.

Seven people stood against the tellers' windows. One of them was three-year-old Josie Frank, who stood frozen as she stared at her mother's body. What had compelled this man to shoot Desna Frank was unclear, but the pool of blood underneath her and her motionless form did not look good.

Liberty forced her mind back onto the robber just in time to see him spot Griffin. It seemed as though he had forgotten him.

"You there!" he screamed. "Get that gun off and shove it away from you."

The robber was so wild-eyed that it was terrifying to watch him, but Griffin slowly removed his weapon and quietly placed it on the floor. He pushed it away with the flick of his boot, his calm face seeming to irritate the man even more.

"Now come here! Help him," he ordered, gesturing wildly with the gun. "Help him put money in the bag."

Griffin went slowly forward. Liberty didn't dare move. She was small enough not to be seen behind Griffin's back if she wanted to pull her gun, but if the robber caught any movement, Griffin would be right in the line of fire.

"What bag do you want me to use?" Griffin asked calmly. The man looked panicky until he remembered and pulled a sack from his waistband.

Griffin had deliberately moved between the gunman and the innocent folks against the counter, but now the head teller had no choice but to move out of their ranks and join Griffin. The gunman started to follow but pulled back. Suddenly grabbing Bill Miller, who had come in to withdraw some funds, he pulled him close and held the gun to his head.

"Make it fast!" he yelled.

Griffin and the teller did just that, taking money from the drawers and shoving the bills into the bag. They were finished in less than two minutes, but the man was so agitated it looked as though he would shoot anyway. He had to let go of Bill to grab the money, and when he did, Griffin stepped in such a way as to put himself between them. The gunman was instantly irate.

"What are you doing?"

"Just waiting on you," Griffin said. He was close enough to see that the man was out of his head.

"I'll shoot him if I want to," he said suddenly and gestured with his gun. "Move!"

"I can't let you shoot him," Griffin said calmly, and the man lost control. He brought the gun directly in front of him and aimed at Griffin, giving Liberty no choice. The look of surprise on the man's face as the bullet entered his body was pathetic. He froze, dropped everything from both hands, and crumpled to the floor.

In the next instant, Liberty was across the room taking Josie in her arms. She scooped the child up—she was stiff with shock—and cradled her close. Looking to Griffin, who motioned her out with his head, she turned for the door. She didn't expect to see Slater and Dakota, who had just slipped in the door, both with guns pulled. The look on Slater's face shocked Liberty. She had never seen such a look of revulsion, and it was directed at her. In an instant she was angry.

"This baby's mother is gone, and Griffin was next," she said quietly. "I suppose you wanted me to slap his hand for that."

This said, Liberty pushed past both men and the crowd that had started to gather outside. Questions about what happened flew at her, but she ignored them. She had to get to the Franks'. She had to find this little girl's father. She only hoped that in time the memory would fade. There was no chance that Liberty would ever forget, but she prayed that Josie would never remember a thing about this day.

Eleven

"How are you?" Duffy asked Liberty as he joined her in the living room several hours later. Kate had called Duffy home as soon as she'd heard. She had given Zach and Laura a snack at the table, but Liberty had wanted to be alone. She'd opted to grab her Bible and sit in the living room where she could hear their voices, but she had yet to open the book.

"I feel bruised all over," she said as she looked at him. "I never get used to it, Duffy. Today's not the first time, but it might as well be. The shock and hurt are just the same."

"If you did get used to it, I'd be worried about you."

Liberty nodded.

"Thank you, Libby," he said now.

"What for?"

"For saving our Griffin."

Liberty cried then. "I had to, Duff, I had to do it. He was going to kill Griff!"

Duffy moved to put an arm around her. She hadn't cried yet, and this was what she needed. Not even her mother's arms had provided the needed cathartic, but having Duffy, who loved them as though they were his own, thank her for her brother's life had been enough.

Duffy had yet to go to the Franks', but he was headed there next. He left as soon as Liberty fell asleep on the sofa and he'd covered her with a quilt. He held Kate for the longest time and then his children. The Frank family went to church with them, but it was more than that: As a doctor, Duffy had to check on that little girl.

❧ ❧ ❧

"Why have you never asked me to be your deputy?" Slater asked later that afternoon. It had been an emotional day for all of them, but Slater could not keep his thoughts to himself any longer. He had even asked Dakota to take off for a while to give him and Griffin privacy.

Griffin, who was headed to Tess' for dinner, looked at him from across the room and was suddenly all ears. He took in Slater's intense eyes and had sudden hope.

"Tell me something, Slate," Griffin requested right back. "Why have you never told me why you left the Rangers?"

Slater looked confused. "I thought I did."

This was not what Griffin expected at all. "Tell me again" was all the sheriff said.

"I couldn't keep on the trail for the Rangers, constantly moving around and never having a home church. It was wreaking havoc with my walk with Christ. I knew I had to settle somewhere; most Rangers can't do that. I don't understand why knowing that is so important."

"I wasn't sure it would be, but for all I knew, you'd accidentally killed an innocent man or a child and never wanted to be in law enforcement again. You had opportunity at one point to tell Liberty you were a Ranger, but you didn't do it. Other than me, I've never heard you tell anyone what you were. I didn't know what to think about that. Much as I need a new deputy, I have to be pretty selective about who I have at my back. I think you can probably understand."

Slater nodded. He had no idea Griffin's thoughts had run along that line. No wonder he'd not said a word. But there was more, and Slater thought it was time to come out with it.

"I would like to serve as your deputy, Griffin; I think I would do well. But there's more to it than that. I don't want Libby working as your deputy. I've had a hard time with that from day one. I don't think she should be in such a dangerous position."

"Liberty takes care of herself very well." Griffin defended his sister with calm self-assurance. "And she has a natural ability. Not to mention I use her only when I have to."

Slater still shook his head. "I can't tell you what to do, Griffin, and I won't leave in a huff, but I don't like it. No, that's not true, I hate it. I want to marry your sister, Griffin. It's not fair of me to tell you before I've spoken to her, but that's the fact. I don't want her packing a gun and putting her life in danger, no matter how good she is. I'm glad she saved your life today and possibly the lives of others, but I don't like Libby being an option when you don't have help."

Griffin nodded very slowly. Liberty had never let him down—he would be the first to say that—but had he done the right thing by her? Sheriff Drake questioned this for the first time. He knew this was going to take some thinking.

"Can you use me?" Slater asked, naturally wanting an answer.

Griffin looked him in the eye. "Yes, and with you on as deputy, Liberty can go back to her own life."

Slater nodded but didn't let his satisfaction go too far. That Griffin would use Liberty at all told him his bias was altogether different. But he would have to be content with that for now. Thanking him, Slater stood.

"Are you headed out too?" Griffin asked. "I could give you a rundown on a few things before I have to go."

"Is there any way it can wait for morning, or even later this evening?"

"That's fine."

Slater put his hat on his head. "I've got to find Hank Hathaway and tell him I've got another job. I'll ask him if he needs me to put some time in until he finds someone else. Then I need to see your sister."

Griffin looked at the grim line around the other man's mouth and said, "Something tells me you're not going to propose."

"You're right. I'm not even sure she'll speak to me, but I've got some explaining to do."

"I'll give you one word of advice," Griffin offered.

"What's that?"

"They don't think like we do." Griffin's voice was dry. "Don't expect Liberty to be the exception."

Serious as Slater's business was, he found himself laughing on the way to the door.

❧ ❧ ❧

"Mrs. Peterson," Slater began as he stood at her door some time later, hat in hand. "May I see Libby?"

Kate hesitated. Liberty had said something about seeing Slater and Dakota at the bank, and even though she had not explained, her mother could see that it had upset her even more.

"Please," Slater tried again.

"She's sleeping, Slater," Kate said honestly. "I'm not sure what Libby would want, but I can't ask you to wait because she's asleep in the living room."

Slater was nodding and trying to fight his discouragement when a disheveled Liberty appeared behind her mother.

"Did I hear the door, Mam?" she asked in a small, croaky voice. A moment later, she spotted Slater, stiffened, and turned away.

"You misunderstood my look," Slater promptly said, looking past Kate to see her. "I'd like to explain."

When Liberty stopped and looked back at him, Kate slipped away. Slater took this as consent, stepped inside, and shut the door. Dim as the light was, Slater could see Liberty's eyes as he walked forward and stopped in front of her. His hand came up, and with just the tips of his fingers, he touched the hair at her temple.

"How are you doing?"

"I just woke up."

"You might feel drained for a few days," he offered.

Liberty nodded. "I always have in the past."

Slater had all he could do not to close his eyes and sigh with pain. How could she do this? How could this be so normal for all of them? He had to force his mind back to why he was here.

"I'm sorry you misunderstood my look," he repeated, his eyes looking directly into hers. "I was sick inside that you had to go through that. I was sick inside over that poor woman lying in her own blood. And all I was thinking was that I wish I'd been there to spare you. I would have done exactly as you did," he told her softly, "but I'm sorry *you* had to do it."

Liberty bit her lip and admitted, "I thought you despised me."

"Not even close. I just wish I had been on the scene faster."

Liberty shook her head. "I think I should tell you, Slater, that that's not really anything I've ever expected."

"I can understand how you would feel that way, and it's time I told you that I was a Texas Ranger, Libby. I gave up that job right before I came here."

Liberty blinked, taking a moment to let it sink in. Finally, "Why, Slater? Why did you give it up?"

"I want to tell you—it's not even that complicated—but right now I need to let you know that I asked Griffin whether he could use me as deputy, and he hired me. I hope you're pleased. If not, I hope you'll talk to me. It may not have been my place to tell you, but I wanted you to know."

"Oh, Slater, that's wonderful. I'm very pleased," Liberty said sincerely even as she took in the full impact of his news. She didn't have to back up her brother or stay on edge any longer. She didn't have to worry about someone being there to protect her brother's back. A former Texas Ranger would be on the job to do it. Liberty was slightly amazed, so much so that it took a moment for her to hear her mother calling.

"Yes?" she answered after the second call.

"Can you come here a moment, Lib?"

"Excuse me," Liberty said to Slater and slipped around into the dining room where she followed her mother into the kitchen.

"Are you all right? Did you need me to rescue you?"

"No, thank you, Mam. He was just explaining what his expression meant earlier. I had completely misunderstood."

Kate smiled at the daughter she adored. "Would you like to invite Slater for dinner? We have plenty."

"I'll ask him."

Intent on doing that, Liberty went back to the hallway but found Slater leaning against the wall, his eyes closed. She hesitated, and almost instantly he opened his eyes.

"Are you all right?" she asked.

"Yes," he answered right away. "I was just praying. I—"

Liberty waited, but it took a moment for him to continue. Slater had just told Griffin that he wanted to marry Liberty, but he suddenly realized that he wasn't ready to ask her on the spot. He suspected that she might need some time as well.

"There's so much in my heart, Libby. Sometimes I think I could burst with all the things I'm keeping inside. Does that make sense?"

Liberty nodded.

"I guess I just wanted you to know that. I want to have a chance to figure out what I'm feeling toward you. I don't want us to rush, but I want you to know I'm feeling things and to ask if you might be feeling some things too."

"I am, Slater. I have been for a time now," Liberty said, not able to keep the breathlessness and fear from her voice. "It's all so new."

Slater nodded. The light caught her face for a moment, and he thought she looked so pale. He chastised himself for his timing.

"I should have waited to talk to you, Libby. It's been a rough day. I am glad to learn, however, that I'm not in this alone."

Liberty felt a wonderful warm feeling spiral through her. He was so honest and open. Her mother had told her that women seemed to deal better with their thoughts and feelings than men did, but she wondered if Slater might be an exception.

"My mother said you could stay for dinner," Liberty suddenly said, wishing she'd come up with something a little more profound.

"I'd like that," Slater replied, not wishing for any other words from her. For right now it was enough just to stand with her, knowing she was not upset with him anymore and that the subject of the future—their future—was an open one.

🌹 🌹 🌹

"How are you?" Tess asked Griffin the moment she saw him. For more than two weeks they had been planning to celebrate their Christmas the day after, but neither one had expected the evening to follow a bank robbery and shooting.

"I'm all right."

"How about Libby?"

"I stopped for a moment before I came over here. She's pale, but they were just sitting down to dinner, and she seemed to be doing fairly well."

"Who was the man, Griff? Was he from around here?"

"Not that I'm aware of. I did find a poster that looked like him, but I'll have to write some letters and check it out." Griffin shook his head. "He didn't seem to be in his right mind."

They fell silent for a moment. They were the only ones in the living room—Tess' mother had said she would finish preparing dinner, and her father and brothers were not yet home. They never waited dinner for the men—they would starve if they tried—so Tess wondered what the evening would be like.

"I'm sorry I couldn't get over here sooner," Griffin said. "Slater needed to talk with me."

"Was he upset?"

"Yes, but mostly because of Libby," Griffin told her before explaining Slater's past work experience, their conversation, and Slater's new position as deputy.

"I hope Lib will be pleased."

Griffin gave her a shrewd look. "Do you have some doubt about that?"

Tess looked surprised. "Don't you, Griff?"

"I didn't, no."

Tess bit her lip.

"Talk to me, Tess," he said in that tone she could never argue with.

Tess hesitated but still said, "I don't want to be too harsh on Libby, but I wouldn't have said she could give it up that easily. But then you know her better than I do, Griff. If you say she'll be fine, I'm sure you're right."

Griffin felt the air leave his lungs. What was Tess saying that made him feel so breathless? He wasn't exactly sure, but doubts about

Liberty handling this change began to assail him. She had honestly looked very calm that night at the dinner table, but would that be the end of it?

"Have I upset you?" Tess asked after studying his thoughtful face.

"Yes, but that's good. I'm going to have to keep my eyes open."

Not really knowing what he was referring to, Tess innocently said, "Maybe Slater isn't the man for Libby after all."

"Why do you say that?"

"Well, you've told me when you were explaining about the change that Slater didn't want Libby in that job and was glad to become your deputy." She suddenly smiled. "Maybe I've misunderstood all these years, but I've always thought that when a woman loved a man enough to marry him, she would be willing to do anything he wants."

Griffin smiled a little but couldn't speak. Was Tess right? Would Liberty still want to work for him even if it meant losing Slater?

Tess missed all of this turmoil. She heard a bang in the kitchen and told Griffin she was headed to check on her mother. By the time she returned, Griffin calmed his thoughts. He knew that time and prayer were needed here, but right now it was more important that he celebrate Christmas with the family he would be joining.

"Dinner's not ready yet," Tess said as she returned to her place across from Griffin. "Did I tell you that my father came home and told me you were all right?"

"No, you didn't. How did he know?" Griffin asked, working hard to get back into Tess' life.

"He saw you downtown and came home and told me." Tess gave a small, incredulous laugh. "You could have pushed me over with a small breeze. My father left the office and came all the way home to tell me you were all right. He went back as soon as he'd let me know. My mother and I could only stare at each other after he left."

"Maybe with your getting married and leaving, he has realized how much he's missed."

Tess smiled hugely. "I love it when you talk about our getting married."

Griffin smiled back at her. "Then you should get downtown more—that's all I hear from people. And they all want a date set right now."

"Well, maybe we'd better do that," Tess said softly.

"We don't have to . . ." Griffin's tone was just as hushed.

It was not logical to people who knew of their plans, but Tess Locken did not want to set a wedding date too soon. She hadn't thought she would ever be engaged to the man of her dreams, and she wasn't about to rush things. It wasn't that she didn't look forward to being married—she looked forward to it all the time—but this was special. This was a once-in-a-lifetime experience for her, and she wanted to savor it.

"Maybe we could at least pick a season," Tess capitulated. "Would people be pleased about that?"

Griffin shook his head. "We don't have to do anything. I was just teasing."

"I suppose everyone would be crushed if we just up and married one of these days."

Griffin could only stare at her. A moment later Tess caught his expression.

"What is it, Griff?"

"You're so easy to love, Tess."

"Why is that?"

"You're never the same, but everything I discover is wonderful."

"Oh, Griffin," was all Tess could say; she was so much in love with this man. She couldn't be having intimate thoughts about him, not yet anyway, but the desire to crawl into his lap was so very strong.

"Dinner," Mrs. Locken called from the other room.

Griffin stood immediately, took Tess' hand, and pulled her from the chair. With his hand under her chin, he bent and kissed her mouth.

"Merry Christmas, Tess."

"Merry Christmas, Griffin."

They walked hand-in-hand to the dining room where Mrs. Locken was waiting. It seemed that some weeks her husband and sons never ceased to cause her pain with the way they overlooked her and took her efforts for granted, but this couple who loved the Lord and each other was like a gift from God and the best Christmas gift she could possibly imagine.

❧ ❧ ❧

Dakota could not dispel Liberty's image from his mind. He had tried closing his eyes, which only made it worse. He had tried concentrating on the creek line, dark as it was, but he could still see her in the bank building. He shook his head a little at how fast she had been. He'd seen many a quick draw in his business, and he thought she might rank among the smoothest. And her aim! If it hadn't been so sad, he would have called it beautiful. That thought today, however, only made him ache.

"I wanted to see her in action," he said quietly, causing Eli's ears to twitch, "but not like this."

Slater had asked him to head out for a time. Dakota had been only too glad to oblige him. He needed to be alone. He needed to think. For a moment his mind lingered on some of the things he'd seen and heard from the pastor and the church family, but it didn't take long for him to feel uncomfortable with his thoughts. He pushed them away to concentrate on his brother. As though he'd never had a problem with Slater giving up his job, Dakota was now resolute.

Slate should stay here, he decided. *Slate needs to step in as deputy. I don't know why I didn't see it before. I'm still not certain what to do with the change in him, but he's made a life here. A man with his skill and level head shouldn't be building houses. He should be helping Griffin with the law, not Libby. And I'm going to tell him as soon as I get back.*

🌸 🌸 🌸

"This is my room," Laura told Slater after dinner, her drawing of the house in her lap. The whole family was gathered in the living room. "It used to be Griffin's room, but he moved next door, and Mam gave it to me. It's my very own."

"What's this?" Slater pointed to a circle on the floor.

"My rug. It's all red and blue and green colors."

"It sounds nice."

"Libby's is almost the same, only hers has some yellow."

Slater nodded and smiled down at her.

"If you marry Libby, then you can come upstairs and see all the rugs."

"Laura May Peterson!" Duffy wasted no time in exclaiming.

The little girl looked across at him, clearly upset and uncertain, but her silence didn't last for more than a few seconds. Tears already filling her eyes and her chin tilted upward, she said, "Well, he should marry Libby and make her smile all the time!"

The room was silent with shock—not just over her talking back—but at the words as well.

"Libby's sad because she had to shoot that man, and when Slater comes she always smiles." With that Laura put her face in her hands and sobbed. Kate was sitting closer than Duffy, so she was the one to move and put her arms around the little girl. It took some time for her to calm, the others quietly waiting.

Laura would not look at anyone, but they all had eyes on her. Duffy waited but could see that she was going to keep her face buried against her mother's side. He went to her, hunkered down in front of both his wife and daughter, and spoke quietly.

"Laura, you need to look at me."

Laura obeyed at once, her little face blotchy and tearstained.

"I know you meant well, but Slater and Libby's relationship is not your business. If you have questions, you may ask Mam or me, but you can't just sit and give your opinion whenever you feel like it. Understood?"

Laura nodded, and her father gave her knee a little squeeze.

"You need to apologize." This said, Duffy returned to his seat, fully expecting to be obeyed.

"I'm sorry, Libby," Laura said to the big sister who sat across the room.

"I forgive you, Laura."

"I'm sorry, Slater."

"Thank you, Laura, and I want you to know that I do appreciate the nice words you said."

"I can be nice sometimes," Laura told him, "but not always."

Slater had to smile over this. He looked over at Liberty to find her smiling at Laura too. He was still watching her when she noticed him. Duffy asked Zach a question just then, and the little boy began to answer, but it took several minutes for Slater and Liberty to hear.

Twelve

"I WANT TO TALK TO YOU," Dakota greeted Slater the moment he walked in the door.

"All right. Let me get my coat off."

Dakota waited with ill-concealed impatience, and Slater wanted to laugh. It was always clear to him when Dakota had a mission.

"When are you headed back to work, Dak?" Slater asked as he sauntered his way toward the living room and took a seat on the davenport.

"Not until I'm through with you, at the very least. Now, I've been doing some thinking."

"About my life or yours?"

"My life is fine," Dakota clarified for him. "Yours could use a little work."

Slater laughed, which only got him glared at.

"Are you going to listen?"

"Yes." Slater schooled his features and worked not to smile.

"Now, I think the most logical thing for you to do is apply as deputy of Shotgun. You're good enough to be the sheriff, but Griffin already has the job, and he's doing fine. However, a man with your talents has no business pounding nails for a living, and I don't want to hear any arguments.

"My first choice would be to have you come back to the Rangers, but since you're being mule stubborn about that, this is the next best thing. I'll also concede," Dakota went on even as both men heard the back door open and close, "that there's a very sweet lady in town who makes staying a very palatable option. *But,* if I find out that you've let her get away, you'll have some fast explaining to do."

"Hello," Griffin greeted the men as he walked in and took a chair. He saw that Slater was on the sofa, relaxed as a cat, but Dakota was standing as though giving a lecture. Griffin, not worrying about offending anyone, spoke to Slater.

"Did you tell Dakota about the job as deputy?"

"Not yet," Slater replied and let his gaze swing back to his older sibling.

Not surprisingly, Dakota was looking right back at Slater.

"You could have stopped me," the older man said.

"That wouldn't have been half as much fun."

Dakota dropped into a chair and shook his head.

"Someone should fill me in," Griffin suggested.

Slater did the honors, and both men had a laugh on Dakota.

"How's Tess?" Slater asked when the laughter died down.

"She's fine."

"Price asked me this morning if the two of you had a date."

"That seems to be the common question. Tonight Tess suggested that we just up and marry."

"That would be fun," Dakota agreed.

"Spoken like a man," Griffin stated. "I know I would like it, but somehow I think the women in my life, namely Kate Peterson, Liberty Drake, and Rebecca Locken, would not find it so amusing."

"You never know," Slater put in. "Our mother wanted to elope, but our father wouldn't hear of it."

"Did she really?"

"That's what they've always told us," Slater confirmed. "Our father hailed from modest means, and our mother had been reared in the lap of luxury. *Her* mother desperately wanted a large wedding, the kind befitting a young socialite, but our mother had had that her whole life. I guess Grandma Slater, who had a terrible time accepting our father, was won over in an instant when he took his future mother-in-law's side and opted for a grand wedding."

"What did your mother say?"

"She was ready to call the whole thing off," Dakota continued. "She can be rather stubborn, but our father talked her around."

Griffin looked between the two of them, so mismatched in appearance.

"By the way, where do you two get your coloring?"

Both Rawlings laughed.

"He should see Cash," Dakota said to Slater.

"What does Cash look like?" Griffin took the bait.

"Dark red hair, brown eyes."

Griffin's brows rose. The two men before him were so different. One was blond with blue eyes, and the other had black hair with eyes so black you couldn't even see the pupils.

"And you all have the same mother and father?" Griffin clarified.

Both brothers nodded, smiles on their faces.

"No sisters?"

"Nope," Dakota supplied, "but if you're giving up Laura, I'll take her."

"She's a card, all right," Griffin agreed with a small sigh. "She's another reason not to just up and marry."

"She gets to watch it happen," Slater supplied the words, "if she's quiet."

"I'm not sure that's possible." Griffin's tone was dry. "Actually, I shouldn't be surprised at how different you two look, considering Zach and Laura are like day and night in personality."

"Zach's a nice little guy," Dakota said, and with that the men fell quiet. It had been a long day, emotionally and physically. And speaking of the children reminded them of a little girl who no longer had a mother. It wasn't long before all three men opted to turn in, knowing that the next few days promised to be just as draining. On Wednesday they would all be attending the funeral of Desna Frank.

🌿 🌿 🌿

"Are you up to this?" Duffy asked Kate Wednesday morning. She had been crying since she rose and hadn't wanted anything for breakfast. She now washed the dishes with slow, distracted movements.

Kate shrugged. "Even if I'm not, I can't stay away. Desna was my friend, and I need to see Lloyd and Josie."

Duffy eyed her face. Her color wasn't good, and he naturally thought of her condition.

"Stop looking at me, Duffy," she told him as she handed him a plate to dry.

"That's like telling me not to be a doctor, Kathleen," he replied firmly. "Now, you're not going if there's more than grief going on here. Do you hear me?"

"Yes, but it is grief, Duffy; I know it is. That can bring about problems of its own, but I'm not feeling *that* feeling or anything like that."

To just about anyone else, those words would have been cryptic, but to Kate, who had been expecting so many times, and for the doctor she was married to, it made perfect sense that she was in tune with her pregnancy. Duffy continued to watch her for a moment, and finally Kate came to him. Duffy slipped his arms around her and held her close.

"I don't want to lose you, Duff," she admitted. "I want you here with me. When I think of Lloyd I can hardly stand it."

Duffy pressed a kiss to her temple; he'd had the same thoughts about her. He held her a little closer, already feeling the baby between them. He never tired of touching or holding her. He wasn't a lot taller than she was, but the difference in their heights gave him wonderful access to her soft hair and brow, where he kissed her again.

"We should always have the attitude that we're not staying here permanently, but there's nothing like a death to remind us of how frail we are."

"I'm glad school was canceled. I want the children with me."

"I'd have kept them home anyway," Duffy told her. "Laura told me she wants to talk to Josie, but I told her I'd have to think about it."

"She means so well, but I'm a little afraid of what she'll come up with."

They heard noises behind them then and weren't surprised when Zach came forward and hugged his father from the side. Duffy slipped an arm down to hold him.

"Where are Libby and Laura?"

"Both crying in Libby's room."

"Maybe I should go up," Kate said and moved a little, but steps could be heard on the stairs. Sure enough, the teary-eyed sisters joined the family in the kitchen, and 15 minutes later, they headed for the cemetery.

🌹 🌹 🌹

"Second Corinthians 5 says, 'Therefore, we are always confident, knowing that, while we are at home in the body, we are absent from the Lord. For we walk by faith, not by sight. We are confident, I say, and willing rather to be absent from the body, and to be present with the Lord,'" Pastor Caron read these words to the crowd as they huddled close against the cold wind. Rain was threatening.

"Can there ever be good news at a funeral?" the pastor asked. "I just read verses to you that would give a resounding yes!" Pastor Caron went on to say, "Desna Frank was 24 years old. She was born in Dallas on May 1, 1857, to the late Henry and Lottie Jeffers. She lived most of her life in Dallas and moved to Shotgun after she married Lloyd Frank in 1876. Her daughter Josie was born to her in 1878. Desna is also survived by two sisters and a brother, all of whom live in the Dallas area.

"Desna wanted to be a schoolteacher but met Lloyd before she completed her training. She was actively involved in the church where she attended and was a regular at the women's Bible study. Desna also enjoyed attending the quilting bees that the Ladies' Legion holds each month. She was quoted just a few weeks back as saying, 'I love Shotgun. I hope we can raise all of our children here.'"

Pastor Caron took a moment to compose himself. He had just recently learned that Desna had been expecting. For an instant he wanted to sob with the loss of both lives. Almost a minute later he took a breath and continued.

"I had a long talk with Lloyd yesterday. He talked to me about Desna, a woman he'd known and loved for more than six years. Lloyd is confident, as am I, that Desna is indeed present with the Lord. Lloyd was with Desna the day they both realized they needed a Savior. He told me all about the camp meeting where they both sat, hungry for the truth about eternity, and how they needed to fill the ache inside, an ache that was spiritually based. Both Lloyd and Desna were saved that day.

"I didn't know Desna before she and Frank moved to Shotgun and began attending the church where I pastor, but we spoke many times, and on several occasions she told me about her life. Frank wanted me to talk about Desna today, but also to let you know that you can have the same hope in Christ that she had.

"I don't say that Desna is in heaven because she was a good person. Those of you who know me know that I would make no such claim. She's in heaven today because she repented of her sin and accepted God's Son as her Savior."

Taking in the words as best she could, Liberty stood very still at the graveside. She felt like her insides were crumbling, but she didn't want to break down. She was thankful beyond what she could express that her friend was in heaven, but Lloyd's pale face and Josie's confused eyes were almost too much to bear. When the service ended, many people went forward to have a word with Lloyd, but Liberty hung back until they were almost all gone. Griffin was close by, Dakota and Slater behind him.

"I'm sorry I didn't get there in time, Lloyd," Liberty said, tears coming without invitation. "I can't tell you how sorry."

"It's not your fault, Libby. I'm just glad no one else was hurt."

Tears fell as she nodded and shifted her gaze to Josie, who was standing next to some of Lloyd and Desna's family. As she watched, Laura came up to the other little girl.

"Hi, Josie. Mam said you can come and play with me. Do you want to come and play sometime?"

Josie nodded and Laura gave her a hug, one that the younger girl returned.

"We'll plan on that," the woman next to Lloyd now said. She was Desna's sister.

"Call on us," Griffin told him, his hand extended in friendship. "We'll do whatever we can, Lloyd."

"Thanks, Griff."

It was time to move on, but Liberty didn't want to. She stood in momentary indecision. Since she was ready to leave, Laura made it a little easier. She took Liberty's hand and even turned away. They hadn't gone ten feet when the five-year-old stumbled over the uneven ground and nearly fell. Slater was suddenly there, scooping her up to sit on his arm and taking Liberty's hand in his own.

"If I had just been a little faster," Liberty said quietly.

"Don't do this to yourself." Slater's voice came softly to her. "It won't help to go over it again and again."

Liberty turned her head to look up at him. It was too easy to forget that he would know that. The news about his past job was still so foreign. Dakota seemed like a Texas Ranger, but for some reason Slater did not. A moment of disquiet filled her. Was he capable of being Griffin's deputy? Had Griffin known what he was doing, or was the decision made in the heat of emotion? On top of these upsetting thoughts, Liberty abruptly realized how warm and solid his hand was and how confidently he'd taken over with Laura. Even amid her doubts about his serving as deputy, Liberty still thought him the most wonderful man she'd ever met.

"Here you go," he said gently, helping her into Duffy and Kate's wagon.

"Come and have some lunch," Kate invited Slater, her eyes taking in Griffin and Dakota as well.

"You're welcome to come by the house for lunch," Duffy cut in, his voice mild, "but your hostess will be lying down."

Kate's hand went to her mouth, and she looked away. She was just holding on, and her husband knew it.

"Do you want company, Lib?" her brother asked.

She nodded yes. It wasn't hard to guess that she found that easier than being on her own. The wagon pulled away then, and the men moved to their horses. Once at the house, her husband seeing to the task of settling Kate upstairs, all hands joined in to help with the meal. It was light fare, and because her mother was not with them, Liberty was committed to acting as normally for Zach and Laura as she could. Neither one of them had eaten a good breakfast, and she determined to see food into them now. Slater was feeling the same way about Liberty, and Dakota watched it all in silence. Not until the meal was over and he was in the living room with Zach and Griffin did he start to relax. It didn't last long, however, as the little boy began to talk with his brother.

"I don't like cemeteries, Griff."

"Why not, Zach?"

The little boy shrugged. "They scare me a little."

Griffin nodded.

"I'm not scared now, but I'm afraid I'll think of it tonight when I go to bed."

"Come here, Zach," Griffin invited, putting an arm around him when he joined him in the large chair. "Do you know one of the things I love about God, Zach? It's the way He's everywhere all the time. Do you know what that's called?"

Zach shook his head no.

"Omnipresent. That's a long, funny word, but it simply means that God is everywhere 100 percent of the time. I love that. When I have to ride into a dangerous situation, I know that He's with me, but that He's also where I'm headed. When I lie down at night He's with me, but He's also with Tess. I take great comfort in that.

"And now tonight, I'll be thinking of you especially. I'll be so glad that when God is with me, He's also with you in your bed, and with Josie Frank where she's sleeping, and even at the cemetery. There's no reason to fear if God is with us, Zach, and He always is."

"Papa has told me that, but I think I forgot."

"Well, I'll pray that you'll remember it the next time you're scared. You can pray that Josie will understand and remember too."

Without warning or word to anyone, Dakota suddenly stood and left the room. Zach looked to his brother, his eyes questioning. Griffin's eyes met the younger ones.

"I think maybe Dakota could use the same prayers too, Zach."

The six-year-old was still nodding when Griffin tightened his arm around him and bent to give him a kiss.

🌷 🌷 🌷

"How are you?" Slater asked Liberty as he took the wet bowl from her hand.

"I'm all right. I'm always surprised at how much it affects me physically. I still feel bruised all over."

"You might be in a way," Slater surmised.

Liberty looked up at him in question.

"You move very fast when you draw, Libby. That's bound to affect your muscles."

"I've never thought of that," Liberty said slowly. She had just handed another bowl to Slater when Dakota burst through the door.

"Oh," he seemed momentarily stopped. "I, um, I mean, thanks for lunch, Libby."

"Are you all right?" Slater asked before Liberty could reply.

"Yeah," Dakota answered, but he was clearly agitated. "I've got to go."

Both Slater and Liberty watched in surprise as he moved for the back door and left in a hurry.

"I need to see what's wrong," Slater said, even as he was setting the towel down and moving out the door.

Liberty didn't try to comment; she didn't want to distract him, but she stepped away from the washtub to see Slater catch up with Dakota halfway between the houses.

"Are you all right?" Slater asked again, this time taking his brother's arm.

"No, I'm not all right," he gritted. "But it's nothing you could possibly understand."

"Try me."

Dakota speared him with angry eyes. "I suppose you thought the service was great. I suppose you agreed with every word."

"I did, yes."

Dakota shook his head in disgust. "What's the matter with all of you, Slater? A woman is dead. Her husband and baby stood there in terrible grief, and who do we hear about? Jesus Christ! Unbelievable."

It was cold out, but neither man seemed to notice. Slater's mind scrambled fast for a reply, his mind praying for wisdom.

"What did you want Pastor Caron to say, Dak? What would you have deemed appropriate?"

"A little more about the woman herself, for starters. He turned it into a sermon!"

"What if the woman was who she was because of Jesus Christ, Dak?"

"What do you mean?"

"Well, you heard what he said. She was a changed person because of her faith."

Dakota's eyes narrowed. Slater knew he was not happy with that answer, but he went on anyway.

"If I'm a different person because of my beliefs, Dakota, and I were to die, I would want other people to know they could have the same hope. Lloyd Frank clearly feels the same way." Slater took a breath and said, "Maybe you should be listening instead of criticizing."

"My life is *fine*," Dakota did not hesitate to clarify.

"If that's true, then why does this have you so upset? If everything is fine, you should be able to shrug this off and go on with your life."

Dakota's eyes became dangerously black, but Slater held his ground.

"I'm leaving," he finally gritted out.

Slater stood still as Dakota stormed away and slammed into the house. Not until he reappeared with his saddlebags and gear did Slater see how serious he was and follow him to the barn to try again.

"Please don't leave like this, Dak. Don't leave in a rage."

"I'm not angry at you, Slate," Dakota said tightly, throwing tack onto Eli in a hurry. "You're just a little confused right now, and I know how that can be. I just need to get away for a time. Maybe when I return you'll have come down off this cloud that says your way is the only way."

Slater had no idea how to reply. He believed with all of his heart that God's Son *was* the only way, but clearly that was the last thing he could say right now. Dakota mounted Eli and said goodbye, leaving Slater standing by the small barn. As he watched him ride away, Slater thought it most fitting that it had finally begun to rain.

🌸 🌸 🌸

"I brought you some soup," Liberty said as she entered her mother's room.

"Thank you, dear." Kate sat up and reached for her robe; the room was chilly.

"Did Zach and Laura eat lunch?"

"Yes. I think I got quite a bit into them."

"And what about you?"

Liberty chuckled. "Slater kept pushing food my way. He must have had the same plan I had for the kids."

Kate took a sip from the mug of soup and watched her daughter. A blush had stolen over her cheeks, and her eyes, which had a dreamy light in them, had gone toward the window.

"You're falling for this man, Libby," her mother said.

"I think you're right." Liberty bit her lip and met her mother's eyes. "I didn't know I could feel this way about anyone, Mam. I think he's wonderful."

"Are you going to be able to move slowly?"

Liberty nodded. "I do have feelings, though, ones I've never experienced before. I also have a lot of questions. We haven't talked about when he came to Christ, and he said he'd get back to me about why he left the Rangers."

"Cover all of it, Lib. I can't give you better advice than that."

"When did you and Duffy find time to talk?"

Kate smiled. "It wasn't easy. I had two children and he had a busy practice, but we made it work. I also listened to the people who were close to me. If someone I loved and trusted had felt any doubts, I would have slowed down or stopped."

"Do you and Duffy have doubts about Slater?"

"Not doubts, but we do want you to go slowly. We think Slater is wonderful. We're delighted that he's taking the deputy's position, but that doesn't mean he's the man God has for you."

Liberty nodded. "I think about what Tess said too—you know, about my never noticing male attention before. Maybe all I'm feeling is a first-time infatuation."

"That's what time will determine, dear. Give yourself lots of it."

Liberty stood and kissed her mother's cheek.

"Send the kids up, will you, Lib? I want to see how they're doing."

"Will do. Are you up to coming to the table for dinner?"

"I feel up to it, yes, but Duffy may come home and order me back to bed. I'll be down in about an hour."

"All right."

Zach and Laura were already in the hallway when she left the room, their little faces anxious.

"Can we see Mam, Libby?" Zach asked.

"Yes, Zach. She was just asking for you."

Liberty smiled as they raced down the hall and heard her mother's cry of delight. Again she prayed that God would allow this fifth child to come safely into their world.

Thirteen

"So HE JUST STORMED OFF?" Griffin asked.

"Yep. He's fighting what he's hearing, I'm sure. That's not like Dakota, but then I guess I did a good deal of fighting myself."

"What do you suppose brought it on?" Tess asked; the three of them were at the sheriff's office the next day.

"The funeral," Slater said, filled her in, and went on. "He's not a man who cares how other people live as long as they obey the law, so this is a surprise. I haven't had hope until now."

"Zach and I were talking in Mam's living room yesterday when he left so suddenly."

"What were you discussing?"

"God's omnipresence."

Slater nodded.

"I find it so interesting that he wanted Pastor Caron to talk more about Desna," Tess said. "Do you remember what you pointed out to me, Griff, about the way the disciples wanted to talk about themselves when Jesus mentioned His death?"

Griffin nodded. "It's the same today. You talk about Christ's work on the cross, and most people start telling you how good they've been. They want to talk about themselves, not about Christ's death for their sins."

Slater's brows rose. That was exactly what he did for a time, but he eventually got so miserable that all the fight went out of him.

"Do you think he'll come back?" Griffin now asked.

"Yes, but probably not for a time. I know he thinks I need to get my head on straight. I'm not real anxious to have him return, knowing there will probably be another confrontation."

"Maybe not," Tess put in. "Maybe he'll run into the man who led you to Christ, and he'll have an impact."

"I only hope and pray that it happens," Slater said sincerely.

"Oh, there's Libby," Tess exclaimed, spotting her across the street. "Maybe she'll come over."

Slater's head whipped around at the sound of that name, and he was out the door so fast the other two almost didn't see him move. Griffin and Tess' eyes met, both people smiling in delight.

🌹 🌹 🌹

"I think the pink calico," Liberty said to Miss Amy. "The one with the small flowers."

"Six cents a yard," Miss Amy quoted as she laid it on the counter. "I just got this in."

"And the navy flannel?"

"Eleven cents a yard" was the price as this bolt came down from the shelf.

"Thank you. I need to see a little of the blue-striped ticking too."

"That goes for twelve cents a yard."

"Okay. Thanks, Miss Amy. I'll look these over and do some figuring."

"Okay. I've got a special on buttons. There're some red ones that would be nice if you want that navy flannel for a shirt."

"Okay."

Liberty was fingering fabric and working sums on her paper when Slater approached. He said nothing but stood at her shoulder and watched her work. Without warning Liberty's head came up, and she swung around to look at the buttons. What she encountered was Slater's chest.

"Hello," he said quietly, a smile in his eyes.

"I'm sorry. I didn't see you."

"I saw you," he told her warmly, and watched as she smiled, bit her lip, and dropped her eyes.

"How did you know I was in here?"

"Tess is across the street talking to Griffin. She spotted you."

Liberty nodded.

"What are you shopping for?"

"Mam gave me a list of things. Zach needs a shirt, and two of Laura's dresses are rather short."

"Nothing for yourself?" Slater asked, wishing he could purchase something for her, something as lovely and feminine as she looked right now.

"Not today."

"How are you doing, Libby?" he suddenly asked so seriously that Liberty wanted to lay her head against his shoulder and cry.

"Why did you ask me that?"

"Because with a list like that, it sounds as though your mother knew you needed to get out."

Liberty nodded. "She probably did."

"Is your mother feeling better?"

"Yes. She's up and around, and Duffy has stopped watching her like a hawk."

It was in that instant that Slater realized there was more to Duffy's actions the day before than his concern about his wife's grief. He felt a jolt of concern shoot through him. Griffin had once mentioned all the babies his mother had been forced to bid goodbye, and he found himself hoping and praying that this one would not be added to the list.

"Tell her I'm praying for her, will you, Libby?"

"I'll do that."

Liberty felt it again—that warm feeling spiraling through her over this man. He was so gentle and kind. Griffin and Duffy were that way as well, but this was different. Slater looked at her as if he couldn't pull his eyes away. Knowing that did strange things to Liberty's heart.

"Are you shopping for something?" Liberty asked, also happening to notice several pairs of eyes on them. She dropped her own and added, "I'm afraid we're drawing a crowd."

Slater glanced around, causing eyes to look away, but he still didn't move.

"I have a little time off after lunch," he said quietly. "Would you be free to go for a walk?"

Liberty nodded.

"I'll see you then," he assured her, his eyes warm and direct until he was forced to turn away.

Liberty watched him leave and then made herself go back to her list. She was still looking at the buttons when she felt a large presence beside her. Certain that Slater had returned, she looked up with a smile. Price Hathaway stood beside her, his brow showing determination.

"There are some goods in the back you need to see, Libby," he said. "Come this way."

Liberty was given no chance to argue. Her upper arm was taken in his huge fist, and she was urged along toward the rear of the store, and not just out of sight: Price walked her until they were at the far corner of the storeroom—cans of lima beans to Liberty's back and sacks of flour at her heels.

"Are you going to marry Slater?" Price wasted no time in asking.

"Of all things!" Liberty exclaimed. "Price Hathaway, what's come over you?"

Price bent until his face was close. "Slater Rawlings is the reason Amy and I are together again. He told me she still cared. Now if he's in love with you and wants to marry you, I want that for him."

Liberty blinked. There were so many things she could say to that, but all she could manage was "You want that for him? What about me?"

"He's a good man, Lib. I've never known a man like him. He works hard, and he's fair. You can't believe what he put up with with Pa and never said a word. He even invited me to church. Not since I've been grown has anyone ever done that."

"Are you going to go?"

"I don't know yet. Amy and I are still talking about it. Marry him, Libby. If he asks you, marry him."

Liberty saw the earnestness in his eyes.

"For the record, and just between the two of us, he hasn't asked me, but we are going for a walk today. And I do care, Price; I care very much."

Price stood to full height and smiled. "I knew he was the one for you. I just knew it. He believes like you do, and he's a lawman. He probably can't outshoot you, but you can still make it work."

Liberty had a good laugh over that, and Price continued to smile as though he'd won a ticket to the fair.

"I think I'd better get back to my list."

"Did you talk?" Miss Amy's anxious voice came toward them as she nearly ran into the storeroom.

"Yes," Price told her.

Miss Amy came right up to Liberty. "He told Price I still wanted to see him, Libby. I was never so glad in all my life."

Liberty smiled up at her. She was the perfect size for a huge man like Price, but Liberty had always found her so reserved. Not now, however. Her eyes were lit up with pleasure and love for Price, and all because Slater had gone between them.

"So when is *your* date?" Liberty felt free to demand of the two before her.

They both smiled, and Liberty's eyes grew.

"You didn't!"

"We did. Just before Christmas."

"When are you going to announce it?"

"Mama's planning a big party on January 14. You'll be invited."

Liberty hugged Price, who squeezed her in return. Miss Amy surprised Liberty by hugging her next, but Liberty returned the embrace just the same.

"Congratulations!" Liberty told them warmly, but then her eyes grew serious. "I hope you do come to church. I play the piano, so I sit down on the left-hand side. Just look for me and sit with me. You don't know how welcome you would be." This said, Liberty smiled and turned away. She gave a wave but didn't turn back when Miss Amy thanked her.

Not since I've been grown has anyone ever done that.

Liberty could not get the words from her mind. *How many people do I see every day? I've been keeping my eye on the behavior in this town and missing the lost souls.* Liberty finished her list—fabric, buttons, and all—but the subject stayed at the front of her mind for the next several hours. Indeed, she and Kate were still speaking of it when Slater arrived for their walk.

🌵 🌵 🌵

"His name is Desmond Curtis. He's been a Ranger forever. I was working with him, and he noticed how unsettled I was. I'm not an angry person, but I tend to get antsy and have to move around all the time. I just thought that was the way I was, but he asked me what I was running from. I didn't like that, just like Dakota didn't like it when I challenged him, but it got me to thinking."

"So you did know about Christ?" Liberty asked. They had planned to take a walk, but rain had threatened so they sat alone in the Petersons' living room.

"Yes. Both my grandmother and my oldest brother had come to Christ and had talked with me on several occasions, but I was convinced there was nothing wrong with my life." Slater shook his head. "I was blind for a long time."

"What was the turning point?"

"I think God used the solitude of my job to make me see. I was alone so much of the time and becoming lonely in the bargain. I would be on the trail and thinking about how insignificant I was. I found myself wanting to cry all the time. I would look at the magnificent world around me and think, 'If all this just happened, then what's the point? Why go on? Why try at all?' One day when I was in the midst of feeling that way, I realized someone was riding toward me. It was Des. Here I'm sitting in the saddle, tears pouring down my face, and Desmond Curtis rides slowly up.

"I'll never forget it. He stopped his horse right next to mine, looked me in the eye, and said, 'Would you like to talk about it, Slate?' All I could do was nod. We never moved or even got off our horses. He told me that Christ's love was so huge that it had sent Him to the cross for my sins. I was so hungry for that love. Des listened to me while I prayed."

"Oh, Slater," Liberty said, breathless with emotion.

Slater smiled. "I wasn't saved a year when I knew God wanted me to settle down someplace. I fought that one like a madman, but in the end, I gave up the Rangers and ended up here. I didn't know Shotgun existed, and I don't believe that a man should just wander around looking for signs from God, but I ended up here and felt I should stay."

Liberty couldn't take her eyes from him. "I'm so glad you did."

"Are you, Libby? It means a lot to hear you say that."

Liberty's head tipped and she admitted, "You came so suddenly. Sometimes I'm sure I'm going to wake up and find you've gone."

"I wouldn't do that, not to you or Griffin."

Liberty nodded, her heart very full. She wanted to tell this man she was falling for him but opted for a change in subject.

"How will you like the job?"

"I like it already. Griffin is great to work for."

Liberty nodded; she knew that very well. She was genuinely glad that Slater had the job, but on occasion she felt a twinge of regret. This worried her since it had been only a few days.

Someone knocked on the front door right then, and Laura, having been told to play in the kitchen, came running, glad for an excuse to escape.

"Hi, Tess!" they heard her say. "Come on in."

"Thank you, Laura. Are your mother and Libby home?"

"Yes. Mam is in the kitchen, and Libby is visiting with Slater. I'm not allowed in there."

Tess laughed.

"Hi, Tess." Kate had come around the corner. The two women hugged.

"I have news," Tess told her future mother-in-law. "I'd like to tell you all at the same time."

"Of course. Slater and Lib are right in here."

"We have a date!" Tess announced to the occupants of the living room just moments later.

"When?"

"January 21. Three weeks from this Saturday. We know it's short notice, but we didn't want anything too fancy."

"Will you be able to find a dress?" Liberty asked.

"I'm going to wear Mama's. She's so excited."

"When did you decide?"

"Just today."

"And I get to watch?"

"Yes, Laura, you do."

"Oh, I can't wait to tell Zach."

Kate happened to look over just then toward Slater. That man was just starting to get glassy-eyed.

"Did you want to ask what the dress looks like, Slater?" Kate teased.

He gave a small laugh. "That was on my mind," he told her and then shook his head and stood. "I hope I won't offend anyone, but I think this might be a good time for me to get back to work."

The women all laughed at his expense, but Liberty took pity on him and walked him to the door.

"Thanks for the walk," she said.

Slater smiled. "We'll do it again very soon, Miss Drake, and you can tell me your story."

Liberty nodded. Slater slipped out the door, and she peeked out to watch him walk away. Her brother was getting married in three weeks. For the first time in Liberty's life, she wished the wedding was hers.

�"""🌾🌾🌾

Price and Amy Hathaway's party did not turn out to be overly crowded, but a good time was had by all, including the smiling newlyweds, whose eyes were constantly turned to each other in love. That they had managed to keep their marriage a secret so long was nothing short of amazing. It was also amazing when Hank Hathaway approached Slater and offered him a room.

"In your house?" Slater had to clarify.

"Well, Price won't be needin' it! And the sheriff is gettin' himself hitched too."

Slater nodded slowly. "How about I come back on Monday?"

"Suit yourself," the crotchety old man said as he turned away. Slater looked to Liberty with raised brows.

"He's always a surprise, isn't he?"

"Yes, but Mrs. Hathaway is one of the best cooks in town, so you might want to consider it."

"Did he talk to you?" Korina Hathaway came up as if she'd heard her name.

"He did, Mrs. Hathaway. Did you know he was going to ask me?"

"It was my idea," she beamed at them. "Hank has talked about what a good worker you are, and I thought it sounded just right. Hank always tries to please me."

Both Slater and Liberty managed to smile, but they were stunned. It wouldn't seem that Hank tried to please anyone. Clearly he was not the same man at home that he was in public.

"Everyone seems to be settled in with their cake and coffee. Why don't I show the room to you right now?"

"All right," Slater agreed. He would not have suggested it, but he saw no harm in agreeing.

"Would you like to come too, Libby?" their hostess asked.

"Thank you," Liberty smiled and followed Korina up the stairs, Slater bringing up the rear.

"Price is so big that we've always given him the large room. We talked about switching, but we like where we are."

This didn't really make sense until they were upstairs, but in truth, both rooms were spacious and separated by a large closet that Mrs. Hathaway proudly showed them. Nevertheless, Slater questioned Mrs. Hathaway about disturbing them.

Brushing it off, she responded, "We both sleep like the dead. Price has always come and gone, and we never hear a thing. Lucky for us he's such a good boy because we would never have stayed awake to catch him in his mischief."

The room was lovely—spacious and beautifully furnished. The curtains even matched the bedspread. Slater found himself agreeing to the rent they wanted—a buy because it included meals—and asking when he could move in. Griffin and Tess were to be married in one week's time, and he thought the sooner he vacated, the better.

"Anytime," he was told, and looking at the immaculate room, Slater could see that it was in fact ready for occupation.

"That was a nice surprise," Liberty said when they finally joined the party back downstairs, and their hostess hurried away to see to the refreshments.

"Wasn't it? I would never have guessed."

"Do you have some reservations?"

"A few, but I'd already checked into the boarding house. If this doesn't work out, I can still try there."

Liberty made a face.

"You're spoiled," Slater told her, watching that adorable nose wrinkle.

"I'm sure you're right."

As had become normal for her in the last few weeks, Liberty

looked around the Hathaways' home and tried to picture herself as wife and homemaker in a home of her own. It wasn't hard to do with a certain tall blond standing next to her.

Slater suddenly turned and looked at her, his eyes searching her face. The act made her wonder if her thoughts had shown, and she blushed at the very idea.

"I don't suppose you want to tell me why you're blushing," Slater asked, his voice low as he bent toward her.

Liberty refused to look at him.

"I'll find out," he teased, but Liberty only smiled.

The temptation to ask him how he would learn her thoughts was strong, but that might be stepping onto intimate ground, something Liberty was struggling with anyway. She made herself shift her thoughts and gladly took the cake and fresh coffee she was offered. Slater did the same, causing Liberty to wonder if he wasn't struggling with the same thing. With a heart asking for an extra measure of patience, Liberty asked the Lord to strengthen them both.

❧ ❧ ❧

Griffin and Slater had not been back from the Hathaways' party an hour when Maddie Flowers came in. She was obnoxious and shrill, but since Griffin's plan was to keep a close eye on the Potters' dealings, the men mounted up and rode out.

Griffin filled Slater in as they rode, and by the time they arrived, the new man felt prepared. He wasn't prepared, however, to have shots fly at them when they were still a ways off. Griffin wasn't either.

"That's enough, Ned!" Griffin bellowed at him from behind an outcropping of rocks.

"I didn't know it was you," the man called back. "I thought it was that Flowers woman."

"You and the boys come on out to the porch, Ned. Just leave your guns inside."

The front door opened soon after, and all four men trooped out.

"We weren't going to shoot the old bat, only shut her up a bit."

Griffin shook his head. "I oughta run you all in."

Ned was a mean one, but even the threat of jail time made his face pale. He'd been locked up twice in his life. Jail was a dry place.

"We won't shoot anymore," he told them in a petulant voice; he sounded like a spoiled child.

"Who's that?"

"Shut your mouth, Critter," his father turned on him, but Griffin answered.

"That's my deputy, Critter." The sheriff's voice was cold. "You take a good look at him. You too, Rush and Possum. We are not going to put up with this any longer. You'd best keep that in mind."

While Griffin held his shotgun on all of them, he ordered Slater to collect the guns.

"You can come for them in two weeks. Not a day before. Now keep it clean, boys, or I'll run the lot of you in and raid the house and barn."

The lawmen did not stick around much longer, but both were aware of the dark, angry eyes that followed them.

"It's going to come to a head one of these days, and someone is going to get hurt," Griffin predicted.

"I'm sure you're right. Some things you can avoid, and some you have to deal with when they come. Unless they up and move, it's probably going to get worse before it gets better."

Griffin couldn't have agreed with him more, but right now he had no solution. Ideas and plans shifted through his mind all the way back into town. They did battle with thoughts of his wedding in a week's time. Not for the first time, he asked God to let him be there for Tess.

Fourteen

"WHAT DO YOU MEAN, NO?"

"Just that, Libby. The answer is no."

Liberty stared at the man she thought she might be in love with and wondered if she knew him at all. The wedding had been wonderful. Tess had been stunningly beautiful, and Griffin's eyes had been full of love as they joined hands and vowed their lives to one another. Now it was Monday morning, and all that had faded. Liberty had gotten up, climbed into her work clothes, and headed to the jail, only to have Slater tell her to go home.

"Slater," she tried a new tact. "Griff and Tess don't come back until Wednesday."

"Be that as it may, you can't fill in."

"What if something dangerous comes up?"

"I'll call Price."

Liberty was instantly angry. "Price is no lawman!"

"But he does know how to use a gun, and he told me to call him if I needed him." Slater spoke with more calm than he felt. Liberty's coming to work was the last thing he'd expected. They had never talked about this, and now he wished they had. It was past time for her to know how he felt on this issue.

"You're going to get your fool head shot off," Liberty retorted, her anger still evident.

"At least it won't be yours" was all the deputy said, sending Liberty storming from the office.

Liberty was some ways up the street before she realized she'd left without Morton. She stormed back up the walk, swung into the saddle, and heeled him too hard for the short ride home. The poor horse had never been treated so roughly. By the time she stabled the beast and hit the kitchen door, she was in the finest rage she'd ever known.

"Liberty!" her mother exclaimed, naturally surprised. "What in the world?"

Liberty was ready to explode, but reason took over. Laura had come off the floor where she was playing, and a sudden view of her mother's expanding waistline caused Liberty to remember that she was not the only person in the world. Willing herself to calm down, she took a seat at the table and accepted the mug of coffee her mother set before her.

"Laura . . ." Kate began.

"You want me to play somewhere else, don't you?"

"Well," Kate hesitated, hoping she didn't do this too often, "only if you want to."

"I don't. I want to know why Libby's face is all red."

The room was silent for several seconds. Kate had no idea what to do, and Liberty was still working on calming down. She finally looked at her small sister's concerned face.

"It's nice of you to care so much, Laura," Liberty said. "I would like to talk with Mam. Do you think you could give us a few minutes alone?"

"Are you mad at me?"

"Not at all, and I'm very sorry that I acted that way when I came in."

Laura nodded. Liberty's voice had returned to normal. All was right in the world. Both older women watched the little girl skip from the room, and when she left, Kate sat opposite the small table in the kitchen.

"What's up?" She didn't hesitate; Laura would not want to stay gone all morning.

"I just had an argument with Slater."

"About?"

"My working. He told me that I couldn't fill in and to go home."

"I would think you would be glad of that, Lib. I thought you'd been rather relieved."

Liberty knew it was time for the truth. "I haven't been near so relieved as I've let on."

"Meaning?"

"I just don't feel needed by Griffin any longer," she said, finally telling the truth. "Slater has fit in so well. I thought Griff would need me from time to time. I know it hasn't been that long, but I feel so left out."

"So Griffin didn't ask you to go down there this morning and help?"

"He shouldn't have to ask me. He knows I'll just naturally fill in."

"But he didn't ask you, did he, Libby?" her mother asked again.

"No."

"So Slater's telling you to leave did not sit well."

Liberty shook her head in confusion. "I know he needs me, Mam. Why can't he see that?"

For the first time ever Kate saw how unhealthy her daughter's situation might be. It never occurred to her that Liberty wouldn't be able to give up the job. She'd always been too busy being thankful that her daughter could be there for her son. Clearly, Slater had other ideas. Kate was in a sudden quandary. Her natural bent was toward her child, but she certainly admired Slater's desire to keep Liberty safe.

"What was his reason?" Kate asked.

"I don't think he wants me hurt," Liberty said, some disgust coming back into her voice. "I can take care of myself, Mam. I think I've more than proved that."

Kate's brow lowered. "What's really going on here, Liberty? It doesn't sound to me as though you want to help so much as you want to prove that you can."

Liberty looked so crushed that Kate almost retracted the words, but she took long enough to decide that Liberty's face changed again.

"I don't know," Liberty admitted. "I want to say that's not true, but you might be right. Clearly my pride is involved, or I wouldn't have gotten so angry."

Kate only nodded.

"I think I'll head up to my room now. Tell Laura I'll play with her in a little while."

"All right. What are you going to do?"

"Spend some time reading my Bible and praying. I've got a lot of thinking to do."

Kate stayed where she was as Liberty left the room. She had work to do—lots of it—but right now her daughter needed prayer. She was still praying for her when Laura returned. Kate carried on, seeming as normal as ever to Laura, but her heart was full of doubts and questions, all of which she had to leave with the Lord. No easy task. It was close to lunchtime before she surrendered and knew God's peace.

❧ ❧ ❧

He divided the sea, and caused them to pass through; and he made the waters to stand up as a heap. In the daytime also he led them with a cloud, and all the night with a light of fire. He cleaved the rocks in the wilderness, and gave them drink as out of the great depths. He brought streams also out of the rock, and caused waters to run down like rivers. And they sinned yet more against him by provoking the most High in the wilderness. And they tempted God in their heart by asking for meat for their lust.

Liberty read these verses in Psalm 78 several times. The children of Israel had been brought from slavery and bondage, but all they did was complain about what they'd been forced to leave behind. God had given them an abundance. Every need was met. He showed His love for them over and over, but they still complained and wanted more.

I'm just like they are, Liberty now told the Lord, tears clogging her throat. *You've given me so much to thank You for, but I want something different. You allowed me to help Griffin, but when Slater doesn't want me, I grow angry. I'm sorry, Lord. I'm so willful and full of pride. I think Mam is right. I want to prove that I can do this. I've never seen it that way before.*

Liberty suddenly rolled onto her back. "I'm terrified," she whispered, her eyes on the wood molding at the edge of the ceiling. Liberty said the words, but not even that made it clear to her. She knew she was frightened, but she wasn't sure of what. Not being wanted? Not being good enough? The answer wasn't obvious to her, but one thing was: She had to go back to the jailhouse and apologize to Slater. She had behaved terribly. Griffin had put him in charge, and she'd treated him with contempt because she didn't get her way.

Liberty did take time to put a puzzle together with Laura, but when she left the house an hour later, she was in one of her best dresses, her hair brushed away from her face and falling long down her back. There hadn't been much color in her face when she left, but just the thought of facing Slater made her blush, and she knew there would be more than enough color when she saw him.

It was something of a letdown to find the office empty, but she was not put off. She paced around the small confines and hoped he wouldn't be hours. She was determined to see him before she left. She turned when she heard boot steps on the boardwalk, and sure enough, he opened the door a moment later. Liberty watched him freeze and then come in slowly. She spoke the moment the door was shut.

"I'm sorry."

Slater covered the distance between them in an instant, coming to stand close in front of her.

"Thank you," he said softly, his eyes taking in every detail of the face he loved.

"It was presumptuous of me and disrespectful. I am very sorry, Slater."

Slater's hand came up, and with the backs of his fingers he stroked her baby-soft cheek, wishing with all his might that it could be his lips instead.

"I was going to talk with you," he finally said. "I'm so glad you came to me. The time was dragging because I wanted to see you so much."

"Oh, Slater. Have you always been so understanding?"

He smiled. "Did you think I would order you into the street?"

Liberty chuckled. "No, but I wouldn't have been too surprised if you didn't want to speak to me for a while."

"That's never going to happen. Do you hear me?"

Liberty nodded. She desperately wanted to tell him what was in her heart—the fears, the love—all of it, but it had to come from him first. She thought he might be ready for that, but until it happened, she couldn't be sure. The silence was making her tense, so she invited him to dinner.

"I'd like to come, but I'm not sure I can spare the time."

Liberty understood. She had watched her brother as sheriff for a long time.

"Can you tell me something, Slater?" Liberty asked, wondering why she hadn't asked him before.

"Sure."

"Why didn't you want my help? Have I done something that makes you think you can't trust me?"

"Not at all. I know how good you are, but my answer may not be the one you want to hear."

Liberty frowned. He could very well be right, but she still wanted to know.

"Will you tell me anyway?"

"If you want me to, yes." Wondering if she could handle his feelings on the matter, Slater looked at her for a moment and then plunged in. "I haven't liked this arrangement from the beginning. I don't think Griffin should be using you as a backup. I think it's too dangerous."

Libby blinked in surprise but still said, "Slater, what does Griffin do when there's no one else?"

Slater tenderly put his hands on Liberty's shoulders, his touch light. "Don't misunderstand me right now, Libby. I'm glad that Griff is still here because you have a clear head and good aim, but I don't think Griff should even use you as an option. I can't help but wonder if he might not have looked a little harder for a deputy if you hadn't been so available."

Liberty's head was spinning. This was so new to her. They had always done it this way. Her father had taught her, and she had carried on to do what was needed, always feeling that even though he was gone, she had his blessing. She shook her head a little. She wanted to be available for Griffin, and right now she wasn't convinced that she couldn't do that.

"Are you all right?" Slater asked.

"I am, Slater, but I can't tell you that I agree. I don't know what I'm feeling right now. I've got to think."

Slater could only nod. He expected no less, but that didn't change his disappointment. This was a major issue in his mind. The pain in his heart forced him to go to the Lord, the only good thing he could see in this situation. Liberty didn't stick around much longer, but that wasn't all bad. He found he needed time to think as badly as she did.

❧ ❧ ❧

"A baby?" Laura's little face showed her shock and delight.

"That's right," Duffy told her. "This summer he or she will be here."

"Can he sleep with me?" Zach wished to know.

"Well," Kate told him gently, "the baby will have his own bed, but maybe when he's a little older."

"Does Libby know?" Laura asked.

"Yes."

"And Griffin and Tess?"

"Yes."

"Does Slater?" she tried again, and her parents laughed; she simply had to share this news.

"I don't think he does," Duffy said. "Did you need to tell someone?"

Laura nodded and looked down at her mother's stomach.

"You're going to get fat, aren't you, Mam?"

Kate smiled. "I suppose I am."

"Laura!" Zach looked shocked. "Mam will never be fat. It's not the same when you have a baby."

Laura nodded—she was always amazingly contrite when Zach rebuked her—but her eyes still strayed to her mother's waistline. Kate was increasing rapidly now, being over the halfway point. It was one of those things a child wouldn't notice unless told, and Laura was now noticing plenty.

"Does the baby make you tired, Mam?" Zach asked sweetly, and Kate leaned to kiss him.

"At times, yes. Have I been crabby with you?"

"No, but you fell asleep in the kitchen that one day, and I wondered."

"That was very observant of you, Zach," his father praised. "A woman does tire easily when she's expecting."

"Will there be more?" the six-year-old asked.

"We don't know. We didn't know that God would send us this baby, but we know that God knows what's best for us."

Zach sighed. "A baby. I've always wanted a baby."

Duffy and Kate shared a warm smile. God had surely given them the most precious children in the world. They were still thinking on this when Laura scrambled from her mother's lap.

"Where are you going?" Duffy wished to know.

"To the front porch in case someone walks by," she answered as she went.

"Why?" Zach asked first.

"So I can tell him Mam is having a baby."

"Laura." Duffy called her back even as Kate and Zach dissolved into laughter. Kate didn't know what God had planned for them, but if it was another Laura, it was sure to be fun.

🌹 🌹 🌹

"How is it?" Tess look anxiously across the table at her mate.

"Very good," Griffin told her after he swallowed. "Were you worried?"

Tess nodded a hesitant yes.

"Why?"

"Oh, well, I'm still getting used to a different stove, and this is a new recipe. I wanted everything to be just right."

Griffin sat back a little. "I was crazy not to marry you the first time I laid eyes on you."

Tess smiled. "Well, *I* think so, but sometimes it takes you a little longer."

Griffin reached over and took her hand. "I love you, Tess."

The bride sighed. "It's funny, but I can't hear that too much."

"I'll have to remember that," Griffin responded.

They continued to eat, but as Tess watched her husband, she could tell something was on his mind.

"Did anything happen today, Griff?"

Griffin looked at her. "Slater told me that he and Libby had it out while we were away."

Tess put her fork aside. "Why did he wait almost a week to tell you?"

"I don't know. Maybe he was still trying to gauge whether he should."

"Can you tell me what happened?"

"He didn't go into great detail, but he wanted to know if I had asked her to come and fill in while I was gone. She evidently arrived all ready for work, and he told her she couldn't stay."

"And she was unhappy about that," Tess stated.

"I think you were right, Tess. She is more attached to the job than I thought. I don't know how I feel about that."

"Do you think it would help to talk with her?"

"I would say yes, but I don't want her to feel that Slater snuck around her and reported. He said it ended well; she even came and apologized. I guess I'm hoping she'll mention it to me."

"And if she doesn't?"

"I don't know," he said honestly.

"Will you continue to ask her to work?"

Griffin stared at his wife. That really was the sticking point in all of this. When he needed help, his sister came to mind so easily. But Slater was so against it, and Griffin had such a high regard for his new deputy . . .

"I don't know," he said one more time and went back to his food. Both husband and wife were thoughtful for the next several minutes.

☙ ☙ ☙

"This fabric is nice," Mrs. Tobler told Liberty the second week of February. "I think this color would be good on you too."

"I've never had a purple dress." Liberty forced herself to be honest, even amid the generosity. "I guess I had blue or green in mind."

"Well, I've got those too. Just give me a minute!"

Mrs. Tobler was in the mood to sew. Liberty had never known her to be in any other mood, but this was the plan in her mind when she stopped by the day before and vowed to start with Liberty, move to Laura, and then make a dress for Kate, and even one for the baby if it was a girl. The ladies were all naturally pleased, and because Liberty felt at loose ends lately, she was glad that Mrs. Tobler wanted to start the next day.

"How's this blue?"

"Oh, this is beautiful."

"I like it too, but let's not be too hasty!"

Liberty smiled. Mrs. Tobler was always the same.

"What is that noise?" she exclaimed in irritation. "I just keep hearing it!"

Liberty thought she heard something too, but her host had gone back to excavating in the closet and grumbling again, so she wasn't sure.

Bolts of fabric and an hour later, they agreed on one. It was a deep green piece with a tiny yellow flower all over it. The yellow flower seemed to make Liberty's eyes come alive. Once Mrs. Tobler saw it draped over her, she would not look at anything else. In just a matter of minutes, Liberty was being fitted with a pattern.

❧ ❧ ❧

"I think there's been a murder," Keaton Saint said almost as soon as he walked in the door.

"Why do you think that, Mr. Saint?" Griffin asked. He and Slater had come to full attention.

"Because my neighbor, Mrs. Mills, is missing, and I've been hearing strange noises."

"What kind of noises?"

"Digging."

Griffin took a moment to compute this.

"Her nephew was visiting, wasn't he?"

"He's still there."

"We'll check it out for you, all right?"

The tall man solemnly thanked him, turned, and went on his way.

"How reliable is he?" Slater asked as soon as the door closed.

"Very. He's lived here for years. He's retired now, but he used to run the library and teach part-time."

"Where does he live?"

"Two doors down from Mrs. Tobler. The house he's talking about would be next to hers as well."

"A small, two-story white house?"

"That's the one."

The men had exchanged all of this as they moved to their horses. They rode without haste toward the Mills place, both hoping Mr. Saint was wrong but knowing that such an announcement could not be ignored. Griffin led the way up to the front door, and it took several knocks for someone to answer.

"Yes?" an impeccably dressed man answered as he stood looking out at them. He had an eastern air about him, and his voice was clipped and precise.

"I'm Sheriff Drake," Griffin said congenially. "Could I please talk to Mrs. Mills?"

"My aunt is out of town right now," the man said.

"I see. And you would be?"

"Her nephew, Davis Mills."

"Well, Mr. Mills, when do you expect her back?"

"She didn't say," he said very swiftly and then seemed to reconsider. "Actually, I just remembered a letter she sent. Maybe she mentions her return date. I'll check."

Griffin and Slater exchanged a glance, both men wishing Griffin hadn't given him such an easy way out and also wishing that Davis had left the door open.

"Not a word, I'm afraid," the nephew told them the moment he reopened the portal.

"Where has she gone?" Slater asked.

"Dallas," he said very smoothly.

"And you have no idea when she plans to return?"

"I'm afraid not." His smile was almost angelic.

"Well, please do us a favor, Mr. Mills, and ask her to come by the office when she returns," Griffin said. "I'd like to speak with her."

"I'll do that."

The door was shut again, and the men had no choice but to move away, but neither one was buying the story. Plans bounced around in both men's minds, and they waited only until they were back at the office to discuss them.

Fifteen

"Since Mr. Saint came to us," Slater began, "I wonder if he would be open to our using his home for surveillance."

"I was thinking the same thing. I would guess that he wouldn't care to be disturbed, but the very fact that he came to the office might indicate some willingness."

"How long do we want to wait?"

Griffin's look was grim. "If Mrs. Mills is dead, then there's no hurry to help her, but if Davis is planning to escape or do something with the body, then we need to keep tabs on him."

The door opened suddenly, and both men were surprised to see Mr. Saint enter.

"Did you speak to Mrs. Mills?" he wasted no time in asking; he wasn't nearly so composed as earlier. "Did you see her?"

"I'm afraid not, Mr. Saint. Her nephew says she's out of town."

The man dropped into a chair.

"She does like to travel, but she always tells me when she goes. This nephew has visited before, and she did go away the last time he was here, but not for this long. She seems very tense when he comes, and his manner is so stiff and formal. I suppose it's terrible to accuse him of anything, but something is not right in that house. I just know it."

"When was the last day you saw her?"

"Thursday. She was in her front yard and waved to me as I came down the street."

"This is Tuesday," Griffin murmured out loud, taking a minute to gather his thoughts. "I think I need to know more, Mr. Saint. Tell me everything you've heard and seen in the last five days."

Mr. Saint recounted things as best he could. There were times when he heard short bouts of the digging noise during the day, but it was especially loud and continuous at night. He talked to the men for the better part of an hour, and when he was done, Griffin knew what he wanted to do. Mr. Saint was very cooperative, and Griffin sent Slater home before lunch to get some rest. They would start their work right after sundown.

🌹 🌹 🌹

"All right, Libby. I'm going to sew for a while. You come back in the morning for a fitting."

"Okay. Thank you, Mrs. Tobler."

The woman didn't even answer. She was already bent over her machine. Liberty let herself out the back door. She had walked instead of ridden and was all set to head for home when she heard the sound. It was coming from Mrs. Mills' and sounded like digging. Liberty had been wandering in and out of these homes since she was a child. For this reason she approached the back porch, opened the door, and called inside.

"Mrs. Mills? Are you here?"

Liberty heard nothing, which only caused her to move more fully inside.

"Mrs. Mills, it's Libby. I was just next door at Mrs. Tobler's and thought I would stop to say hi." Liberty didn't add that she wanted to know if she was all right. Some of the older ladies in town took offense to that idea.

"Mrs. Mills?" she tried again, this time moving through the kitchen toward the living room. What she saw caused her to blink. The rug was rolled back and there was a huge hole in the living room floor. The boards had been brought up, and even from several feet away, she could see a mound of dirt so high that it was above the line of the floor.

"What in the world are you up to?" Liberty said softly as she approached. She stared down at the bags still in the hole, her eyes huge. They looked like money sacks.

"Mrs.—" she looked up to try again but stopped. A man calmly stood to one side of the room. He held a derringer. It was pointed right at her.

"You shouldn't have come in here," he said congenially. "I wish you hadn't."

"Well, I can leave again," Liberty said, trying to be calm.

"I'm afraid that won't do at all. I've seen you around. You know too many people in town."

Liberty swallowed. "I just wanted to check on Mrs. Mills."

"Why is everyone so interested in Mrs. Mills today?" The man sounded testy. With that he motioned with the gun, and Liberty backed herself into the kitchen. She thought she might be able to bolt for the door but took too long to decide. The man came forward, shut it, and ordered her to sit at the table.

"Where is Mrs. Mills?" Liberty asked quietly, her eyes straying back to the hole in the floor. To her surprise the man smiled.

"You think I've murdered my aunt? How barbaric."

"Where is she?"

"Out of town. Just like I told the sheriff. I don't know why people can't leave well enough alone."

Liberty waited for him to take his eyes from her so she could make some kind of move, but he never did.

"I guess it will have to be the closet. The one by the front door locks."

"When will Mrs. Mills be back?" Liberty asked in an attempt to stay calm.

"I'm not entirely sure," he replied absently as he tried to think.

"Are you really her nephew?"

"On her late husband's side, yes."

"Does she know what you're up to?"

"Come along," he commanded, ignoring the question this time. "Back through the living room, and watch the hole."

Liberty moved as slowly as she could get away with. It wasn't much floor space to cross, but she moved at a snail's pace. The front door was almost in reach, but Davis took that moment to put the gun right against her back.

"All right now," he said as he opened the closet. It was full of coats, but there was plenty of room to stand. "In you go."

Liberty stepped inside and turned to look at him. She tried for her sternest deputy look.

"What's your name?"

"Davis. And yours?"

"Liberty."

His brows rose and he chuckled. "Rather ironic, isn't it? I'm locking freedom in the closet."

The door shut in her face, and she heard the key turn before she listened to the hollow sound of his shoes as he walked away. For several seconds she felt as though she were dreaming. Not in all of her years of law enforcement had she been held captive. Now here she was—no gun—and locked in a closet.

"Are you going to put up with this?" Liberty said to the darkness around her. With that she began to pound and yell. She kicked on the door, throwing herself against it with such force that she fell out when it opened. She would have continued to yell, but there was a derringer in her face.

"You can't do this," Davis said softly. His voice was still congenial, but his eyes were hard. "I have to leave town soon, and I can't have you disturbing me. Now you need to stay in here and be quiet. Have I made myself clear?"

Liberty nodded, very real fear covering her features. Davis turned her with a hand to her arm and closed the door while her back was still to him.

"That was stupid, Libby," she breathed. "He could have shot you."

She groped for the wall and slid down to a sitting position, her legs drawn up and her arms around her knees.

Show me what to do, Lord. Show me a way out of this. I don't know if Mrs. Mills is all right or not, but I could get myself shot. He's obviously stolen that money. He needs to go to jail for that.

Liberty stopped when she realized he had said he was leaving town soon. She let her head fall back against the wall and prayed again, wishing there was some way to go for help.

🌹 🌹 🌹

"This is for Libby when she comes home," Laura told Kate as they sat down to lunch.

"What is it?"

"A picture of our family with the new baby."

"Let me see."

"This is Papa and this is Zach. Libby is by me, and I'm holding the baby."

"Where am I?"

"You're still in bed."

Kate laughed. "I don't know whether to thank you or to be insulted."

Laura frowned at her, since the word "insulted" was new, but Kate only blew a kiss in her direction. Weary from a morning of work, Kate sat back a little in the chair, a sigh escaping her as she took a bite of sandwich.

At times like this, Lord, I feel as though I'm going to be tired for the rest of my life. My attitude has been anxious, and I feel achy and grumpy all the time. That's not fair to You or any of my family. Please help me to . . .

Laura was going to ask her mother for more milk but saw that her eyes were closed. Her mother's limp hand and sandwich lay in her lap, and for a moment Laura just stared at her. When she didn't open her eyes, Laura, carrying her own sandwich, moved to the chair right next to her mother and simply sat still until she awakened.

🌹 🌹 🌹

Liberty had moved as quietly as she knew how, but in the still confines of the closet it sounded so loud. She only hoped that all the digging and movement from the living room was muffling the sound.

Liberty had pushed the hem of her dress under the door as far as she could get it. She then proceeded to use first a hairpin, then the slim heel of a shoe she encountered, and finally what she thought might be a knitting needle, to try to push the key from the lock. She knew the sound of the key dropping might give her away, but she was determined to get out of this closet. She had sat quietly for the longest time before realizing that Mr. Mills was working. Feeling that she had little to lose, she decided to try. She thought she might have just gotten it when the door opened.

Without a word from her captor the sewing implement was plucked from her hand, and she looked up into enraged features.

"The thought of trussing you up is abhorrent to me, but if that's what it takes to keep you quiet, I'll do it. You must understand that I won't let anything stop me from leaving here. Now this is my last warning."

The door closing once again, Liberty let her shoulders slump. This was such a mess. How long would it be before she was missed at home? Quite possibly hours. Her mother knew what Mrs. Tobler was like and would assume that she'd wanted her to stay all day. Liberty worked to keep her head clear, but it was getting hard. For the first time since she could remember, she wanted to panic.

Stretching out on her side, she prayed and tried to calm her heart. She thought of every verse that would come to mind, going slowly over the words and even singing hymns in her heart. While mentally going through the song she was supposed to play in church on Sunday morning, her fingers moving over imaginary keys, she must have fallen asleep. She hadn't planned to do that, but the door was suddenly opening again and she'd heard no footsteps.

"I have to take care of this now," her jailer began by saying. "I won't have your death on my mind."

Liberty stared at him as he set a basket, presumably of food, and a jug beside her.

"You'll have to eat sparingly, but you won't starve."

"You can't be serious!" Liberty said in outrage, coming awake in a hurry. "You can't leave me in here."

"I don't think it will be long. Aunt likes her home too much. She should be back any day now."

Liberty had come to her feet, causing Davis to back away a little.

"If I die," she said fiercely, "it'll be on your head. Don't try to tell yourself anything else!"

"You'll be fine," he said with an irritating confidence, the door starting to close. "And don't forget," he immediately opened it again to say, "I will tie you up if you make a single noise."

Liberty had never known such frustration. To be this helpless was maddening. She made herself sit back down and take slow, even breaths. Bumping the jug, she realized she was thirsty. She'd missed lunch, but as soon as she'd had a drink, her mind went back to obtaining her freedom. It might take some time, but she *would* come up with a plan.

🌹 🌹 🌹

"And then Mam fell asleep during her sandwich," Laura told Griffin. Knowing he would have to work late, he had stopped by the house and found her home with Tess. "She was tired."

"What did you do?"

"I just sat there beside her."

"That was nice of you. Did Libby get you the milk you wanted?"

"Libby wasn't home. She's been at Mrs. Tobler's all day getting a new dress. She didn't even come home for lunch or to help Mam start dinner."

Griffin's entire frame stiffened. Mr. Saint, Mrs. Mills, and Mrs. Tobler had been on his mind since he'd started making plans for that night. But this news about Liberty could not wait that long.

"I need to head out for a little bit," Griffin rose and said. "I'll check back with you, Tess." He gave her a swift kiss.

"All right," Tess said calmly, thinking of the little girl next to her. But she knew something was wrong and began to pray.

"'Bye, Laura," he said as he kissed the top of her head.

"'Bye."

Griffin tried not to run. He debated going all the way to the Hathaways' to get Slater but decided to swing by the office instead. His heart slowed with relief to see Arrow out front.

"I need you" was all he said, his head going swiftly inside and back out again. Slater was fast to respond, and on the way to the Mills', Griffin gave him the news.

"I hope it's just an uncomfortable hunch that doesn't pan out."

"You and me both," Slater agreed. Hunch or not, it needed to be checked. If Liberty was there and they didn't follow this lead, they would never forgive themselves.

In the next few seconds Griffin told Slater what he wanted to do. They had given Davis Mills the benefit of the doubt earlier that day and knocked on the front door. Griffin was not going to make that mistake again.

🌣 🌣 🌣

Liberty listened to the noise of doors opening or furniture moving, she couldn't decide which. She did know one thing, however—if he was moving furniture, that meant that the hole was covered and he was getting ready to leave. Even if he had the gun with him again, Liberty was not going to take this lying down. The pointed-heel shoes in her hands, she launched her assault against the door with a vengeance.

"Let me out! Do you hear me? I said, GET ME OUT OF HERE!"

Liberty continued to shout, kick, and beat against the door until her hair flew in her face and her throat felt raw. She screamed for all she was worth, and when the door was opened, she attacked the man with the shoes, her arms swinging in a desperate attempt to gain the upper hand.

She found herself subdued, arms locked at her sides in a tight grasp. It happened so swiftly that for a moment she couldn't breathe. When she did find her breath, she looked up into Slater Rawlings' face.

"Oh, Slater," Liberty whispered. "Did I hurt you?"

Slater smiled, but the answer was clear: His cheek was bleeding and one eyelid was already beginning to swell.

"Are you all right?" was all he wanted to know.

"Yes. Oh, Slater," she cried again.

"What happened here, Libby?"

It was Griffin. Liberty hadn't even seen him. For the first time in her life, Liberty began to babble. Both Griffin and Slater listened to words like "dirt mounds, money sacks, water jug, derringer, front door, key, shoes," and so on. They both tried to take in the sequence, but she kept changing directions on them, all the time gesturing to the room and pointing out the dust that lay in thick layers on the furniture.

"Take her home," Griffin said. "I'll make a final check here and with Mr. Saint, then see if the neighbors spotted anyone."

Liberty told herself to offer her services, but Griffin had looked at her strangely. It was then that she realized this had been more upsetting than she first thought.

"I'm sorry," she heard herself say.

Griffin hugged her. "We're just glad you're all right."

"I should be helping you."

Griffin shook his head. "I'll be by later and we'll talk about it, okay?"

Liberty nodded, and Slater took her by the arm. She was shocked to see it was almost dark out. Why had she thought that just a few hours had passed? And when had she left Mrs. Tobler's to head home?

"Here we go," Slater said, and Liberty looked up to see that he'd brought his horse close to the step and was reaching for her. Liberty automatically lifted her arms, and a moment later she was sitting across the front of Arrow's saddle. Slater's arms came around her to hold the reins, and Liberty let herself relax against him. Actually, she gave no thought to what she was doing. She just didn't have the strength right now to sit up straight.

"Slater?"

"Yeah?"

"He took the floor apart and had bags of money buried in the dirt."

"In the living room?"

"Yes. He wouldn't let me out of the closet." She sighed a little. "I thought about you."

"Good thoughts?"

She nodded against him, and Slater had everything he could do not to tip her head back and kiss her. It was so nice to have her close.

Liberty's full weight was leaning against Slater by the time they arrived at the house, and for an instant he wondered if she might have fallen asleep. She wasn't asleep, but he had to steady her on her feet once they dismounted.

"Well, Libby," her mother said as soon as they both walked in the kitchen door, "Mrs. Tobler must have been sewing with a vengeance."

Liberty shrugged a little as her mother got a better look at her.

"Is Duffy here, Kate?" Slater asked.

"In the living room reading with Zach," she answered while taking in the marks on his face. "What's happened?"

The next hour was spent explaining and checking wounds. Liberty changed clothes and ate with the family, but her disappointment over Slater not staying was keen. He'd gone back to check on Griffin.

When Griffin learned that no one had seen a thing, he'd gone back to the office, searched through the wanted circulars, and filled out a report, readying it completely to be mailed the next day. He'd also gone back to the house and checked out what Liberty had told Slater about the living room floor, but there was nothing else he could do. Davis Mills had to be miles out of town by now, and Shotgun's sheriff had to leave it at that. He only hoped that Mrs. Mills would return soon and not be buried under her own living room floor.

🌹 🌹 🌹

"All this time, Duff—" Kate said after they were in bed that night. "All this time I thought if Libby wasn't in law enforcement, she'd be safe, and here she gets grabbed just trying to check on Mrs. Mills. I can't help but wonder what things are coming to."

"It's like we've talked about before, Kate. Don't expect things to get better. It won't happen."

Kate nodded. Sometimes Duffy's logical mind infuriated her, but not now. She needed to think clearly, or she would never let Liberty out of the house again.

"I'm so glad Griffin and Slater were there, Duffy, so very glad. I don't know if I could lose my Libby. I don't think I can."

Kate's first tears flowed. She had wanted to cry when she heard what happened but held herself in check, trying to be strong for her daughter, who still looked a little shocked and confused during dinner.

"She's always been the calm one, Duffy," Kate sobbed. "She looked just like a lost child, and then I saw Slater's face. I know he loves her. I know it killed him to have to leave before she came back downstairs."

Duffy held her and thought about God's promises. Never did He tell His children that this life would be safe and pain free. Indeed, every book in the Bible indicated otherwise. Nevertheless, God did promise never to desert His loved ones or give them more than they could handle. Picturing Liberty in that closet was a sickening thing. The man could have done anything, but they all had to choose to take God at His Word, which meant Liberty wasn't alone. The all-powerful God of the universe had been right there beside her at every moment.

"I have to sleep now," Kate said, her voice slurred with fatigue.

"Okay. I'm going to check on the kids one more time. I'll see you in the morning."

"I love you, Duffy."

"I love you too, Kate," he said before kissing her cheek.

The doctor slipped quietly from the room, heading down the hall to see Laura and Zach, and finally to knock gently before opening Liberty's door a crack. There was no light on, but the moonlight coming from the window told him Liberty was standing at the glass looking out.

"Are you all right?" her stepfather asked.

"Just a little restless," Liberty told him as she turned and let the curtain fall back into place. "I can't stop thinking about everything he said and trying to decipher if he gave any clues as to where he was headed."

"Will you take some advice?"

"Certainly."

"Stop being an officer of the law and try to sleep. All of this will still be here in the morning."

"All right," Liberty agreed and even thanked Duffy as he shut the door, but his words took her off in another direction. *Stop being an officer of the law.* Why did that one simple sentence hurt so much? Right now Liberty didn't have a clue, and the prospect of finding out made her feel pretty helpless.

Seeing no other option, she climbed into bed, willing herself to sleep. It took some time and some confessing, since she'd started to worry, but by the time she drifted off to sleep, she was ready to leave the whole affair in God's capable hands.

❧ ❧ ❧

Three mornings after the uproar at Mrs. Mills' house, a newcomer walked from the hotel, his eyes taking in the neat, even streets of Shotgun's small community. He'd arrived rather late the night before and opted to bunk at the hotel for that night. The room had been comfortable and warm, and he felt rested as he started up the street.

He hadn't gone far when he spotted Shotgun's deputy. Slater stood in front of the general store with a mountain of a man and a tiny, enraged woman.

"I tell you it's robbery!" Mrs. Swenson insisted, her whole frame vibrating in irritation. "And I want this man arrested."

"Mrs. Swenson." Slater's voice was remarkably patient. "Price and Amy may charge whatever they want. It's their store."

"Nonsense! Why, only last year I paid half that much for a tin of peaches. I tell you it's against the law."

Price tried to reason with her, but she would have none of it. She ended up storming down the boardwalk, muttering all the way.

"She'll cool down," Amy said as she came on the scene. "My guess is she'll be back in the morning and pay without a whimper."

Slater nodded as the couple thanked him and went back inside. Slater turned up the street, only then seeing the tall, slim man with the dark red hair who had come from the hotel. He'd leaned against the side of the building, watching the whole scene with great interest. Slater thought he had the warmest brown eyes in Texas. It wasn't hard to figure that Dakota must have headed straight home. Slater began to smile. Cash Rawlings had come to town.

Sixteen

As soon as the brothers were back at the sheriff's office, they embraced for a long time.

"I've missed you, Cash," Slater said, feeling strangely choked up as they drew back.

"You could have come home," the oldest Rawlings said, not unkindly.

"I planned on it but found it wasn't so easy."

Cash smiled. "Dak says her name is Libby."

Slater laughed. "She's not the only reason, but she's a good one."

"What's she like?"

"Oh, Cash," Slater sighed. "How much time have you got?"

Cash smiled again; somehow he'd always known that softhearted Slater would be the first to fall.

"Does she know?" he asked next.

"Not directly, but we're getting there."

"So she loves you in return?"

"I hope so."

For a moment they were silent.

"Grandma sends her love."

"How is she?"

"Doing well. Surprisingly enough, she's getting a little more independent. She cut her visit short this last time and headed home. Said she had things to do."

Slater laughed, wishing he could see their father's mother, who, although her son and daughter-in-law had returned to St. Louis, had stayed in Texas.

"I take it Dak came home?" Slater asked.

"On the verge of apoplexy. Said you needed straightening out."

Slater's look was telling.

"I knew it was probably the other way around," Cash confessed, knowing which of his brothers needed more guidance at the moment. "What happened?"

Slater gave his brother a detailed account of the bank shooting, the death of Desna Frank, and Desna's funeral service. Cash had no trouble catching on.

"I wonder how long he's going to fight this."

"I don't know, but this is the most riled up I've ever seen him. He's still angry with me over leaving the Rangers, and it's not like him to carry things around. He left here in a huff. I hated to have him go like that. With our jobs, it could be the last time we ever lay eyes on each other, but he didn't give me much choice."

"No, he didn't, but you did the right thing by letting him go. Dak is a big boy—too old to be leaving in a rage—but to beg him to stay wouldn't have been wise. He needs to see that you're man enough to make this choice and not just his kid brother anymore."

"He's certainly protective. If I hadn't met Libby's family, he probably would have trussed me up, thrown me over his saddle, and carried me off."

"So he has at least seen that you've made a life here?"

"Yes. In fact, I think he was on his way to accepting that, but the service set him off. He'd even been coming to church with me, and he's threatened me if I let Libby get away."

Cash suddenly frowned. "He also mumbled something about her arresting you."

Slater took some time to explain the way he'd met Liberty, and then said, "You can pray for us, Cash, because her acting as deputy is something I can't live with."

"I will pray, and although I'm not an expert, I will tell you: You're doing well to remember that you can't marry her and expect to change her."

They suddenly smiled at each other, remembering that their mother had learned this the hard way. Charles Rawlings Sr. was as independent a man as any they'd ever known. He raised his boys to be the same way. As much as he loved Virginia Rawlings, Charles was not going to be slowed down. If he wanted to travel, he traveled. Virginia was welcome to go along, but if she didn't want to go, he went without her. He was as faithful as any husband could be, but having a wife and children was not going to alter his lifestyle. Following in the wake of her vagabond husband, Virginia had seen much of the countryside.

"So when can I meet her?" Cash wanted to know.

"It just happens that I'm invited to dinner tonight. I can't stay long since I'll be on duty, but I'm sure they would welcome you with open arms."

"All right. Should I leave my gear at the hotel?"

"Not if you don't mind sharing a bed. It's fairly wide, and as I recall, you don't snore too loudly."

Cash only snorted in disbelief and asked, "By the way, what happened to your eye and cheek?"

"I was attacked by a pair of shoes."

Cash's right brow winged upward. "I think I need to hear about this."

"You will," Slater decided swiftly, "but only *after* you meet Libby."

Cash smiled again. It was so good to see his brother, but seeing him also reminded him of how little time they'd spent together in the last few years. For his part, Cash didn't care if Slater snored all night. The day, however, had the possibilities of dragging. He was most anxious to meet this woman named Libby.

$\clubsuit$ $\clubsuit$ $\clubsuit$

"When Mam has her baby, I'll help her because I'm the big sister. Even if the baby is a boy, I'll still be the big sister."

"I'm sure you'll do a fine job," Cash said seriously. He was being welcomed as his brothers had, by witnessing Laura firsthand and falling just as swiftly in love with her.

"Do you have a baby?" Laura wished to know.

"No. I'm not married."

Laura nodded seriously. "You can share ours when you come to town."

"Thank you very much."

Liberty took that moment to slip into the room. She sat next to Zach and whispered, "What is Laura sharing?"

"The baby."

Liberty's eyes became hysterically round, and Zach had to cover his mouth to muffle laughter. Cash chose that moment to look up at them.

"Cash Rawlings," Slater began, having been waiting for this moment, "please meet Liberty Drake."

"The pleasure is all mine," Cash said as he rose, moving to shake Liberty's hand and bending slightly over her, his eyes alight with pleasure.

"You're tall," Liberty told him.

"Yes. Dakota got the strength; Slater got the manners; and I'm just tall."

Looking at those broad shoulders and the way he bent to catch her eye, Liberty wasn't fooled. She was still smiling at him when Duffy called them to the table.

"Your brother's nice," Liberty had a chance to say softly to Slater as he seated her at the table.

"I was hoping you would think so."

"I can't remember—are any more of you going to show up?"

Slater smiled. "No. Just the three of us. Had enough?"

"Since I haven't figured *you* out—yes."

"What's to figure out?"

Liberty's look was pointed, but Slater had no time to question her.

"So tell us, Cash," Kate began, "how large is your ranch?"

That started the conversation ball rolling, and in seemingly no time at all, Slater said he had to get to work, thanked his host and hostess, and stood.

"I'll walk you out," Liberty offered after Cash told him he would see him that night at the Hathaways'.

Slater stopped on the porch, turning to Liberty as she came out and shut the door.

"So what's to figure out?"

"What?" Liberty questioned right back.

"That's right. What?"

Liberty laughed. "I think next time I'll keep my mouth shut."

"Don't do that. I'll never find out."

Liberty could hear the smile in his voice. There was so much she wanted to say but found her mouth empty.

"Griff will be looking for me," Slater spoke when she didn't. "I'd better scoot."

"Okay. Thanks for coming."

"Thank *you*. Take care of Cash for me."

"We'll do that."

Slater hesitated. There had been one advantage about working construction: Come darkness, you had to quit. Seeing no hope for it, he bid Liberty goodnight and went on his way, asking himself when he was going to have time to get to know this woman better.

❧ ❧ ❧

"It was nice of you to show me the way, Libby," Cash said as they walked toward the Hathaways'. "It's too bad Slater couldn't be with us."

When Liberty didn't answer, Cash pressed her a little more.

"You do wish Slater could join us, don't you, Libby?"

"I wouldn't have believed it!" she exclaimed suddenly.

"What?" Cash asked from some distance over her head, his voice indicating true confusion.

"Your Texas Ranger brother was something of a matchmaker too. I wouldn't have thought it could run in the family."

Cash hooted with laughter, but just as soon as he found his breath, he tried again.

"What did Dak learn?"

"No more than you're going to."

"Come on, Libby," he coaxed, having swiftly fallen into easy familiarity with her. "Just a hint."

Liberty stopped in the street and looked up at him, dark as it was. "What is it you want to know?"

"Just how you feel about Shotgun's deputy. Nothing more."

"Is that all? Well, if I had known that . . ."

Liberty began walking again, and Cash fell into step beside her.

"In case you haven't noticed, Dak and I think a lot of Slater," he said after half a block. "Watching him with you makes us care about you as well."

Liberty stopped suddenly, her heart coming to her throat. "What do you see when he's with me?"

"Ah, Libby," Cash replied, his voice gentle. "He'll have to tell you that."

Cash heard her sigh in the dark.

"Going to finish walking me to the house now?"

"I already did. That's the Hathaways' right there."

Cash looked toward the trim two-story and back to his companion. "Well, thank you, Libby. I appreciate your showing me."

"You're welcome, Cash. I'm glad you can stay a few days. It should be fun."

"Indeed."

"Goodnight," Liberty said and started away, coming to a stop only when Cash fell into step beside her. "Where are you going?"

"I'm going to walk you back," Cash said simply. "I can't let a lady walk all the way home after dark. And besides," he added outrageously, "I just might get some information out of you yet."

They started back toward the Peterson house to the sound of Liberty's laughter.

❧ ❧ ❧

"Oh, you're cold. Have you been outside?" Tess asked as Griffin climbed into bed late Friday night.

"Yes. We had to check out a disturbance at the Potters'—one that turned out to be nothing at all—and Maddie Flowers kept us standing on her porch until she was completely dressed."

"And all for nothing."

"Yes. The Potters must have started early in the day, because everyone but Rush was passed-out drunk."

"What had Mrs. Flowers wanted?"

"She said she heard noises, and this time we thought we'd catch them in the act. It was dead quiet by the time we arrived, and she was ready for bed."

Tess laughed at his disgruntled tone. Griffin kissed her.

"Your man is freezing in the cold, and all you can do is laugh."

Tess chuckled again.

"If I wasn't so tired, I'd kiss you again," he threatened.

Tess only snuggled close. "There's always the morning."

Griffin sighed and talked to himself. "It's like you've known for some time now, Griff, you should have married the woman the moment you laid eyes on her."

Tess chuckled softly this time, thanking God as she often did that He had brought her husband home safely one more time.

❧ ❧ ❧

"Okay," Liberty said to her small charges the next morning, "we're going into the general store next. Josie, you stick close to Laura, and both of you remember to look with your eyes, not your hands."

Little heads bobbed in agreement, and Liberty watched as her sister, an old pro at shopping, led Josie down the aisle that displayed the toys. When she saw that they were safely ensconced, she began on her list. So much had been on her mind lately. She could still feel herself in that closet; Desna Frank's funeral often came to mind; the Lord was showing her new things in the book of Romans; she was still trying to sort out Slater's feelings on her wearing a badge—and then there was Slater himself. It was a relief for her mother to ask her to shop.

"We've got to stop meeting like this," a soft voice whispered in her ear.

Liberty couldn't stop her smile as she turned to see Slater at her shoulder.

"How are you?" he asked warmly.

"I'm fine. How about yourself?"

"Better all the time."

Liberty smiled into his eyes, her thoughts very loving, and then caught herself.

"We had fun with Cash last night," she said, pretending to be interested in the set of bowls on the shelf.

"He said he enjoyed it too," Slater answered as he studied her profile. He thought her nose turned up in the most adorable way. "He said a very pretty lady escorted him home."

Liberty laughed. "Did he tell you he escorted her right back?"

"He didn't have to. I would have been surprised if he'd done anything else."

Liberty shook her head. "I think the mold was broken after the Rawlings boys were born. I've never known such manners."

"I'll tell Mother next time I write."

"How often do you hear from her?" Liberty wondered aloud.

"Every few months."

"Are they pleased with what you're doing here? I mean, do they wish you'd settled closer to them or the ranch?"

"They know that we're Texans through and through, but my mother would like to see us more often."

"Not your father?"

Slater smiled. "He loves us, but that man is an adventurer. As long as we write and tell him what we're doing and what we've seen, he's happy."

The thought crossed Liberty's mind that his father's feelings might change if there were grandchildren involved. She thought about saying so and then realized how embarrassing that would be.

"Are you blushing?" Slater asked without thinking, causing Liberty to turn even redder.

Slater's manners kicked in at that point and he turned away, only to see Laura and Josie coming toward him.

"Hello, girls," he said quietly. Much as he wanted to question her, he turned away to give Liberty a chance to compose herself. "How are you today?"

"This is my friend Josie. She likes toys too."

"I think toys are pretty fun. Did you have a favorite, Josie?"

"Is the deputy in here?" a man's voice called from the door, and Slater turned away to answer. The three females didn't hear why he was needed. Liberty was tempted to follow and see if she could help, but she would not leave the girls in anyone else's care, not with Josie along. They went on with their shopping before heading to Duffy's office for a visit. Liberty, never knowing where her sister's mind would head, was glad that Laura waited to talk to her until they were gone from the general store, their purchases wrapped in neat brown paper.

"I want to tell you something but not have you be shocked," Laura said as they neared Duffy's office door, Josie going in ahead of them.

"I'll do my best not to be shocked," Liberty told her, already wanting to laugh.

"I hope you marry Slater."

"Why do you hope that?"

"So you can protect each other with your guns."

Liberty only smiled, leaned close, and kissed her soft cheek.

"Now, can I tell you something?"

Laura nodded yes.

"Thank you for not saying anything in front of Slater or anyone else. As long as you always talk quietly to me about Slater, without everyone listening, I won't be shocked. Deal?"

"Deal."

The two joined Josie in Duffy's office, and he was delighted to have them. Liberty, on the other hand, spent some time looking out the window that gave a view of Main Street. She could hear the girls' chatter and Duffy's soothing replies, but her mind was elsewhere; namely, on why Slater had been called away. It was all Liberty could do not to head home, change, and go to his aid. That he wouldn't thank her for this did not enter her mind. She only knew she wanted to protect and be with that man.

🌿 🌿 🌿

Slater and Cash made their way up to the Petersons' front door. Ready as they were for Sunday dinner, they moved slowly. They had the rest of the day together, but Cash was leaving in the morning, and they didn't know when they would see each other again.

"I knew from your letter, Slate, that you were growing in your church, but it was good to be here and see it firsthand. Pastor Caron does a fine job."

"He's taught me a lot. Griffin has too and probably doesn't even know it."

"It will be great to give such a good report to Grandma, but I know that Dakota is not going to be happy with me. He'll want to have heard that I came here and straightened you out."

"Tess Drake said something to me one day that was a big help with that. She said that Dakota might run into the same man that led me to Christ. I haven't forgotten that. I had had some contact with Des, but never did I dream he would have such an impact on me. I need to be reminded that I'm not the only person who could talk to Dakota or who prays that he'll see the truth. By the time you see him again, Cash, it could be that he'll have done some real soul-searching."

Cash looked at his youngest sibling.

"When did you grow up, Slater?"

Slater smiled a little, but his eyes were thoughtful. "Funny, but some days I find I have so much to learn that I think I'm still a child."

Cash reached to put an arm around his shoulders.

"When I forget how good God has been to me, Slate, I have only to remind myself of the way He reached down and saved Grandma, me, and then you. Considering how self-centered we all were, I call that a miracle."

"I'll miss you, Cash," Slater said, his eyes having to look up a little.

"I'll miss you too. Don't be a stranger."

The men went inside then, Cash so glad that he'd come and Slater having a sudden daydream. He'd like to go home, he'd like it very much, but he wanted to go with a certain woman on his arm; God willing, his wife.

Seventeen

THE GUNSHOTS STARTED AT DAWN, just 24 hours after Cash left town. The house sat off a piece, but the nearest structure was the schoolhouse. Had it been a weekend, Griffin might have let her get it out of her system, but not on a school day. And because it was Bernie, he had to have Liberty. Not even noticing the tightening of Slater's mouth when he told him, he mounted his horse and rode for his mother's, Slater right behind him. And all the time the shots could be heard.

"I need Libby, Mam," he said as he met her in the kitchen.

"I heard the shots, so I think Libby must have too. I'll go up and check."

Kate slipped away, and some time later Liberty arrived on the scene, dressed in work clothes. She looked as calm and confident as ever.

"Bernie?" she asked, strapping on her gun belt.

"Yes. She's a little early this year."

"Too bad she couldn't wait for the weekend."

Slater didn't question any of this but understood that Bernie must be a regular.

The three rode out as soon as Morton had been saddled, Slater stepping forward to do this against his better judgment. The sky was lighting fast, always a help. They rode toward Bernice Shambles' house, coming in on the barn side. She never shot that way. Every year they confiscated her gun, but she always managed to come up with another one. Daryl Shambles had left Bernie more than ten years before, but she had never gotten over it. Every winter she took shots at the tree he'd planted, the main problem being that the tree sat between Bernice's and the schoolhouse.

"We'll have to get around, Lib, or she'll never hear us. The side we tried last year didn't work. Let's go to the other side this time."

"That will give me a better view of the windows," Liberty said. "Let's hope she stops firing long enough to listen."

The horses had been tied, and the three now made their way along the far side of the barn, their steps punctuated by gunshots.

"What is she shooting at?" Slater finally asked.

"The huge tree on the west side of the house."

"Right toward the school," Slater muttered.

"She would be crushed if she hit anyone," Liberty filled in, "but she never thinks of that ahead of time."

"How often does she do this?"

"Once a year too often," Liberty said.

They were in position now, and Griffin tried to holler up at her. He waited for the shots to stop and then began.

"Bernie, put the weapon down!"

More shots were his answer, so the next time they slowed, Liberty gave it a try.

"I want to come in and talk to you, Bernie, but you have to put the gun . . ."

There was no point in going on.

They were patient. They tried calling to her for close to 20 minutes, but it was no use. Liberty finally got disgusted enough to take the upper hand. Stepping out just enough, she systematically took out four of Bernie's windows.

Dead silence followed and then a small voice.

"Libby? Is that you?"

"I'm out here," she called back.

"Why didn't you say so?"

"I've been trying, but you just kept shooting. Are you hurt?"

"No, but I'm sad."

Liberty started forward but suddenly found herself hauled backward.

"Don't even think about it," Slater said in a voice not to be argued with. He had taken Liberty by the waist and pulled her back until she was against his chest in a no-nonsense hold.

"She'll be calm now," Griffin explained. "We can all go. The only person she'll ever put her gun down for is Libby."

"Then I'll go first," Slater said, moving Liberty behind him and leading the way, knowing he could die in the next instant. Every town had its regulars, but no one could predict everything. As it was, not another shot was fired. The three moved to the door, and Bernie was even there to let them in.

"This is the day," Bernie said, but Liberty didn't comment. Bernie always said the same thing, but over the years the date had fluctuated. Liberty believed that when a person hung onto grief, he or she changed.

"We'll come in and talk to you for a while," Liberty said as she took the gun from her hand.

"You're welcome to talk to Bernie, Lib, but it will have to be at the jailhouse."

This said, Griffin took the cuffs from his belt and handcuffed Bernie's hands behind her back. "This has to stop, Bernie," he went on. "I don't know how else to get through to you. I've been dealing with you since I became sheriff, and how many years had it gone on before that?"

Both Bernie and Liberty stared at him in shock. Griffin ignored his sister and continued to address his prisoner.

"Too long, I'll be bound. Maybe a little time in jail and a hefty fine will make you think about someone other than yourself next year."

"But I miss him," Bernie whined pitifully, but Griffin was not moved.

"You think you miss him? How do you think the parents of the child you shoot will feel? Daryl left here of his own free will. The child or schoolmarm you hit will be a victim."

Liberty was still in shock when Griffin began to lead Bernie away, Slater falling in behind him. Since none of them climbed back onto their horses, they had a bit of a walk as they headed toward town. Bernie was very subdued, and Liberty was angry. She had never seen Griffin act like this toward a woman. What had changed? Slater was an incredible gentleman, but could he have had a hand in this action?

"In you go," Griffin said to Bernie as he opened the cell door. He removed her cuffs but shut and locked the door without looking back. Slater had put Bernie's gun on the desk, and Griffin now tagged it and locked it up.

"Could I see you a moment, Griffin?" Liberty asked, her voice tight.

Griffin had been expecting as much, but not quite so soon.

"Can it wait a few hours, Lib?"

Liberty nodded, but she was not happy. Knowing that her job was done, she told Griffin she'd see him later and bid Slater goodbye, but she didn't go right home. She was so overcome with fury that she didn't think she could be civil even to her own family. She completely disagreed with the way Griffin had handled Bernie, and she never remembered a time when her brother wouldn't allow her to speak to him.

"I don't even know him anymore," Liberty muttered to herself in rage. She wasn't even watching where she was headed and suddenly realized she was on the way back to Bernie's. Another angry spark lit inside of her.

Take a woman off without even letting her gather some things! Well, I'll just do it myself. I'll take things to Bernie and make her the most comfortable prisoner we've ever had. Leave it to a man not to understand.

Liberty all but stomped into the house and began searching for things Bernie might want. Her emotions spiraling completely out of control, she carried on in a fury. The few times she let her mind tell her she was wrong, she pushed the thought away. At the moment she thought she might never speak to her brother, or any man, ever again.

🌹 🌹 🌹

"The sheriff asked me to come by and tell you to ring the school bell right on time, Miss Winters. The shooting's over."

"Oh, thank you, Deputy Rawlings. I appreciate your stopping."

The couple was standing on the school steps. Slater had knocked and been ready to go in, but Miss Winters had suddenly come out and nearly run into him.

"I've got coffee on," she said. "It's a cold morning; may I bring you a cup?"

"Yes, please," Slater said sincerely. He was cold—very cold. They had been out early and then stood in the cold. Then, just after he'd gotten back inside the jailhouse, Griffin had sent him out to the school.

"Here you go," Miss Winters came with two mugs; she had also slipped into her coat.

"Thank you. This is good," Slater told her as he took a sip. "I just remembered that you were coming out to do something. I should drink this and let you get back to work."

"Oh, I just have to hang a sign. I shouldn't have come out without my coat in the first place."

"Do you want some help?"

"I'd love some," she admitted, looking very young and in need of a rescue. "The last time I tried to pound a nail, I hit my hand."

"We can't have that." Slater put his mug aside. "Just show me where you want it."

The next few minutes were filled with hilarity as Slater's cold hands fumbled with the nails, dropping two of them and moving too slowly to catch them before they disappeared into the spaces between the boards. He and Miss Winters were laughing so hard at one point that they couldn't even work. Slater ended up leaning against the building to catch his breath, laughing once again when the schoolteacher commented that it didn't feel that cold anymore.

Across the field, just coming out of Bernie's house, Liberty took in this scene and froze in her steps. She had gathered two bags of items for Bernie, but in the process her anger had cooled. Now, watching the man she loved as he laughed and enjoyed the company of another woman, all anger left her.

There's probably a perfectly good explanation for what I'm seeing, Liberty thought, reason having once again returned. *And if I hadn't been so het up about coming here, I wouldn't have seen them together at all.*

Turning slowly back inside, Liberty replaced the items. By the time she came out the front door again, the steps of the schoolhouse were empty and all was quiet. Liberty climbed into Morton's saddle and turned toward home, wishing she'd repented sooner and was already back in the warmth of that house. She also hoped that Griffin would forget that she wanted to talk to him. She had changed her mind.

🌸 🌸 🌸

"Hi," Griffin said kindly as he came to the house just before lunch. "Did you still want to see me, Lib?"

"No," his sister said honestly.

Griffin stared at her as she sat at the kitchen table and calmly frosted a batch of molasses cookies. She had never been secretive with her feelings, but something wasn't right.

"Are you sure?" he tried again, but Laura came into the room.

"Hi, Griff!" she greeted him with a huge smile. Griffin swung her up into his arms for a hug. He could see that she wanted to talk, and most of the time he let her, but not today.

"I need to see Libby. You go find Mam."

"All right," she agreed with such a wistful little face that Griffin had to harden his heart, but he felt compelled to get back to Liberty. He was ready to launch into a discussion the moment he sat at the table with her, but Liberty started first.

"Tell me, Griff. Have you ever known women who control the people around them, even their husbands, by pouting or getting angry?"

"Lots of them."

"Me too," Liberty nodded. "I was upset with you when you put

Bernie in jail. I even went to her house to get some of her things so she would be more comfortable, but then I realized where I was. I was at Bernie's house: the woman who shoots at a tree every year because a man left her. I've never known Bernie to say she was wrong or do anything more than whine about how miserable she is. It suddenly became very clear to me why Daryl left."

Griffin studied her. Unless he missed his guess, she'd had a hard morning but was doing better now.

"You're not like Bernie, Lib. I hope you know that."

"But I could be," Liberty said quietly, her eyes on the cookie in her hand. "I didn't see it until today. I've always had things my way, Griff, so there's never been a need to fight you, but today I wanted to argue and interfere. That's not the same as covering for you."

Griffin's heart swelled with love for her. "You're one in a million, Libby."

Liberty smiled over the compliment, her own heart swelling a bit. She was very content right now that she had not made a scene. It had taken several hours for her to calm down completely, but she didn't have to apologize to Griffin or Slater over anything she said.

In the next few minutes, Griffin explained to Liberty why he'd locked Bernie up, and Liberty thought his views were very sound. She returned the kiss he placed on her cheek when he went to find Laura and Mam, thanked him, and went on with the frosting.

She was very glad she didn't have to repent to Slater, but her heart was not quite as settled where that man was concerned. Liberty was finding that not knowing exactly where she stood was terribly unsettling. Each day was filled with thinking of him, praying for him, and wondering where he was, what he was doing, and if he thought of her in return. Today's thoughts, however, were also full of Shotgun's pretty young schoolteacher.

❧ ❧ ❧

"I'm so sorry, Libby," Mrs. Mills said for the fifth time, tears coming to her eyes. "How awful for you. I'm surprised you even want to set foot in here again."

Liberty smiled at her and said honestly, "Nothing has changed, Mrs. Mills."

The living room looked remarkably different than it had a week ago. Everything was spotlessly clean, but it wasn't hard for Liberty to picture the way it had been.

"He was really quite devious, wasn't he, Mrs. Mills?" Liberty said thoughtfully.

"Yes. I haven't been comfortable with him for the last few visits, so I began to travel when he came. It was just a month back when I returned to find things covered with dust. Davis had a reason, but I was so put off with the mess that I didn't listen very well." The woman looked at the floor. "I wouldn't have guessed what he was up to in a hundred years."

"Griffin told me he's had a meeting with all the neighbors and that you've had secure locks put on all the doors."

"Indeed, I have. I don't care if he is family, I'll not have him use my home to store stolen money—or come again for that matter."

Liberty nodded, thinking about the few facts they had. Mrs. Mills had told them where Davis lived, and Griffin had been in touch with the law there, but they hadn't heard of any significant bank robberies. The bags of money Liberty had seen had been part of a large job.

"Griffin told me that dozens of cases go unsolved every year," Mrs. Mills said. "I fear this might be one we'll have to live with."

"Will it make things awkward for you when you see your husband's family?" Liberty asked.

"No. We're so spread out these days, and in truth, my brother-in-law and I are not on good terms. He doesn't like the way I've never settled down. As if every woman must be dominated and ruled by a husband. Well, some of us just won't be!" These last words were said with an indignant sniff, and Liberty had all she could do not to ask Mrs. Mills how she'd become a Mrs. when she felt that way. Or maybe that was it: She had been ruled and dominated in her marriage and was glad to have the man gone. Liberty wondered if the older woman might explain, but someone knocked on the door just then. Liberty was sitting with a perfect view of that portal and couldn't stop the thundering of her heart when she saw that it was Slater.

"Why, Mr. Rawlings," Mrs. Mills nearly gushed. "Come in."

"Thank you, Mrs. Mills. I hope I'm not disturbing you."

"Not at all. Libby is here visiting me. Come right in."

Slater's hat had come off, and he gave Liberty a smile as he took the chair his hostess indicated.

"What can we do for you, Mr. Rawlings?" Mrs. Mills asked.

"Actually, I just came by to ask Libby if I could see her home."

For all her seemingly negative ideas about marriage and men, Mrs. Mills beamed at them.

"Of course, what a wonderful idea. Libby and I were just visiting—something we can do anytime."

Liberty didn't remember too much more as she found herself embarrassed, not only by Mrs. Mills' obvious efforts to put them together, but by her own thoughts about Slater and Miss Winters. But she did suddenly find herself outside with Slater, that man taking the reins of both horses in one hand and leading the way.

"I hope that was all right, Libby. I hope I didn't interrupt."

"Not at all. How did you know I was there?"

"I have the rest of the day off, so I went to your house and your mother told me where to find you."

"Were you looking for me for a reason?"

"Do I need a reason?" he asked softly, and Liberty gave him a sideways glance but didn't answer.

"How was your day?" he now tried. They had seen each other so briefly that morning, and he had known she was upset over Griffin's treatment of Bernice. Slater wondered if Griffin had told Liberty how Bernice had taken it. That woman had curled up on the bunk and gone sound asleep for the next four hours.

"Enlightening," she said cryptically.

"Oh!" was all Slater could think to say.

They walked in silence for a time.

"Are you going to enlighten *me*?" Slater finally ventured.

Liberty laughed. "Not exactly. Let's just say I learned some things about myself that were very helpful."

Slater studied her profile and waited for her to look at him. When she did, she couldn't look away from his eyes. She even stumbled in the road a little, but that only caused Slater to take her hand. He held it all the way to the small barn at the back of the Petersons' house.

Without a word of conversation, Slater tied Arrow to the hitching post outside the barn and went inside to stable Morton. Liberty followed, pulling hay from the rack so the horse could reach it, applying the water bucket, and then standing back against the wall, out of the way, until Slater was done. Slater eventually turned to see where she'd disappeared to and found her in the shadows. Like a powerful magnet, he went to her, his hands going to the wall around her, as he leaned close.

"I thought about you all day," he admitted.

"Oh, Slater."

"Tell me that means you thought of me too."

"It does."

Slater sighed and didn't even try to fight the temptation. Not rushing or hesitating, his head lowered. His lips caught Liberty's in a kiss that sent both their senses staggering. Not content to keep his arms free of her, with hands to her waist, he pulled her close. Liberty needed no other prompting. Her own arms went around his neck, and she kissed him back.

They were both gasping when Slater broke away, only to study Liberty's face and kiss her again. She was a wonderful fit in his arms, and for long moments she was his only thought.

"I have to go inside!" Zach's young voice suddenly shouted. He was up by the house but must have been calling to the boys who'd walked with him from school. The sound was just enough to bring Slater back to earth. He began to move away, but Liberty caught his arm; she was still in a fog of sensation.

"Slater?"

"Yes?"

"Will you come to dinner tonight? Are you free?"

He nodded, his eyes still on her face and then her mouth. "The usual time?"

"Yes," Liberty said softly. She had never been kissed before, and now she'd been kissed by the man she loved. The thought of being separated from him made her anxious.

"I'll see you then."

"Okay."

Liberty wasn't sure why she didn't invite him inside right then, but with a final look into his eyes, she made her way across the back-yard and to the house. Slater watched her go, his arms still aching to hold her, but his heart telling him how wrong he'd been.

"What a mess," he said softly, causing Morton's ears to twitch. It was a good thing that he had some time before dinner; he had a good deal of thinking to do and a fair measure of confessing. He wasn't playing games where Liberty Drake was concerned, but she was not his to hold and kiss as he'd just done.

"And it's time you remember that," he said, pulling himself into Arrow's saddle and going for a long ride.

🌹 🌹 🌹

"Maybe I shouldn't have invited Slater," Liberty said to her mother as she checked on her in her room.

"Not at all, Libby," Kate said genuinely, but she was too tired to rise. "I'm glad you did, but I'm not feeling the best, so I think I'll stay right here."

"All right. I'll bring something up for you. Do you want it before we eat or later?"

Liberty felt alarmed when her mother didn't answer but then

realized she'd fallen asleep that fast. She was glad, however, that as she was leaving the room, Duffy was coming down the hall.

"Zach told me she's not feeling well."

"That's what she told me. She fell asleep almost in midsentence."

"I'll check on her and be down soon."

"We'll wait for you."

Duffy thanked her, and Liberty continued on downstairs, only to find Slater in the kitchen with her brother and sister.

"May I see you a moment, Libby?" he asked without preamble.

"Certainly."

Liberty was on the verge of asking where, when Slater turned toward the door. Liberty followed him.

"I had no right to kiss you," Slater began as soon as the door was shut. They stood facing each other on the step. "I've confessed to the Lord, and now I'm repenting to you. I'm sorry I did that."

"I started feeling pretty awful about 30 minutes after you left. I'm sorry too, Slater."

"Liberty," Slater said, moving so close and bending over her that had Liberty not known better, she might have thought she would be kissed again. "I'm not playing games here. I want you to understand that. With whom do I talk? Do I go to Griffin or Duffy and tell him I want to court you? Just tell me, and I'll take care of it as soon as I can."

"Duffy," Liberty barely managed, wanting to kiss him all over again.

Slater nodded and worked to study her face in the dusky light.

"You do things to my heart, Liberty Kathleen. I want you to know that."

Liberty thought that if he could feel her own heart, he'd know he wasn't alone, but no words would come.

"Libby?" Laura called through the door. "Are you out there?"

Slater reached to squeeze Liberty's hand and then opened the back door for her to go in. He didn't know how he would manage the waiting. He wanted to be married right now. He wanted to move fast, but the only way they would be sure not to make a mistake was to go slowly.

Slater joined the family for dinner that night, his heart light with the knowledge that Liberty was open to his suit. It would be some days before he remembered the issue that was not settled between them, and hoping it would go away was not going to make it happen.

Eighteen

"WELL, HELLO, SLATER," Duffy said the following day. He'd only just arrived at his office and was not expecting anyone for almost an hour.

"Is this bad timing, Duffy?"

"Not at all."

This was normally the time Duffy read his Bible, but he could see that Slater had something on his mind.

"How is Kate?" the younger man asked. His eyes showed that he cared, but his stance carried a good deal of tension.

"Much better. We think she was just tired. She was up early this morning and ready to go."

"Good," Slater said and then fell quiet. This was so much easier when it was just he and Liberty. With Duffy looking at him, kind as he was, Slater felt oddly tongue-tied. When he didn't say anything, Duffy caught on and also saw a way to have a little fun at Slater's expense.

"Are you not feeling well, Slater?"

"No, I'm fine," Slater assured him.

"There are colds going around. You're sure you haven't caught something?"

"I'm sure not."

"Old Mrs. Featherpenny—" Duffy went on expansively, making up a name, "she was in recently with a horrible rash. Itched and itched. Thought she would go mad. I gave her some ointment, but sometimes these things take a while. You don't have a rash, do you?"

Slater shook his head, now looking at Duffy as though the man had lost his senses.

"This is only mid-February, but you know we do have our fair share of fevers in the spring, people fancying themselves in love and mooning about with their heads in the clouds."

Catching the glint in the doctor's eyes, Slater finally smiled.

"And can a doctor help with that?"

"Well, it depends on the doctor. I might be a bit of help in Libby or Laura's case, but I wasn't much help to Tess."

"Now that you've mentioned Libby . . ." Slater, seeing his opportunity, eased in. "She said I should talk to you."

"About a rash?" Duffy teased one more time.

Slater laughed.

"Sometimes I think that would be easier."

"What's hard about Libby?"

"Going slow."

Duffy nodded wisely. He well-remembered that he was ready to marry Kate long before the date arrived.

"Are you here today to tell me you love my girl, Slater?"

"That just about sums it up. You can see how little I have. I don't even have my own place. But I'd like to visit with Libby with the intent of finding out what we have here."

"My blessing doesn't hinge on the answer to this question, but do you plan to stay in Shotgun?"

"I do, yes. I love the church here, and I can easily see myself settled down in this town."

"Liberty would be glad to know that. She loves Shotgun."

"It's a fine town. People care."

"Indeed, they do. Well, Slater, I think I can speak for both Kate and myself. You're free in our eyes to see Libby and to court her. You did say that she told you to talk to me?"

"Yes."

"Then I assume you have her consent."

"It certainly looks that way."

"How long have you been living here?" Duffy could not remember.

"A little over four months. It seems longer, maybe because Libby and I have seen each other a lot during that time."

"That'll do it."

Both men were thankful that Dr. Peterson's first patient waited until that moment to come through the door. Entering any sooner might have made it awkward all around. Slater was able to leave knowing he'd done what he set out to do. The only problem that remained the rest of the day was keeping his mind on the job. Liberty seemed to be crowding in more than she ever had before.

❧ ❧ ❧

"He asked whom he should talk to, Griffin or Duffy," Liberty told Tess that same morning. "He told me he's not playing games."

Tess gave Liberty a squeeze, wanting to holler with delight.

"What did you say?" Tess asked as she dragged Liberty into the living room.

"That he should go to Duffy. I don't know when he will, but he said he'd take care of it soon."

Tess sighed. "He's wonderful, Libby. Griff thinks so much of him."

"He is wonderful. Even the way his family has come into town and liked us all so much seems like more evidence that we're to be together."

"And how do you feel, Lib? Would you say you're in love, or are you still thinking on it?"

"I think I'm in love. I feel something for Slater that I've never felt for anyone. I know we have to be careful not to just follow our hearts, but feelings do play a part, don't they, Tess?"

"Yes, they do, but you're right, we can only go on emotions when every thought and action is biblical."

Liberty blinked. "I think I want you to explain that to me."

"Well, when I met Griff, I was instantly attracted. Had my family not liked him, or had he proven to be a nonbeliever or someone who said he believed but didn't live it, then I would have to have taken a step back, no matter what my heart said.

"If at any point I had started to feel that I couldn't live without him, then I would have had to examine my own heart and see that as sin. The only Person I can't live without is Christ."

"That's why you felt such a peace about marrying Griff, even in his line of work?"

"Yes. Don't misunderstand me, Libby. I want Griffin with me forever, but if God has a better plan, I have to be open to that."

Liberty nodded, and for a moment Tess hesitated in indecision. It was on her heart to ask Liberty if she and Slater had ever worked out the issue of Liberty's acting as deputy. Tess didn't know why, but she was afraid to open the subject.

"I told Mam I would help her with the laundry," Liberty said, rising slowly. She wanted to sit and dream with Tess all day.

"I'd better get to work too," Tess said, feeling guilty. "My mother asked us to dinner, and I said I would make dessert."

"Thanks for letting me come over and share."

"Anytime," Tess said lightly, her heart telling her that she was letting an opportunity slip away.

Liberty waved and went on her way, completely unsuspecting. Her heart still in a quandary, Tess stood for a time after she left, planning to ask Griffin about it as soon as he got home.

🌿 🌿 🌿

Slater wondered how many times Liberty had done this. Moving slowly on his way to the Brass Spittoon, he thought this had to be much like her first encounter with him. Having seen Griffin's way of handling these situations, Slater went right to the bar and spoke with Gordie. That man nodded in the direction of a corner table. Slater turned. Even with his back to the main room, there was no missing Dakota Rawlings.

Slater went toward him, his sense of danger draining away. He walked until he stood beside him, but Dakota didn't look up.

"Hand it over," Slater ordered, wasting no time.

Dakota, on the other hand, tipped his hat back and looked slowly up at Slater as though he had all the time in the world.

"Something wrong, deputy?"

Slater put his hand out.

Looking rather amused, Dakota put the pistol in Slater's hand.

"I would think you'd have other things to do," Slater muttered and turned away. Dakota rose and stayed right with him. Slater was well aware of Dakota behind him, but remembering the way the older Rawlings had left things, he was suddenly angry. They were half a block down the street before Slater gave vent to it.

"And if you think," Slater suddenly turned and said with quiet fierceness, "that everything is fine between us after you left here like a spoiled child, you can think again!"

Dakota was not given time to answer, so he slowly followed Slater down the street. The deputy headed to the office and took a seat behind the desk. Dakota came through the door in time to see him unload the gun, tag it, and put it on one corner of the desk. Slater then looked at him, and as stern as Slater appeared, Dakota took a seat and spoke.

"I'm sorry, Slate. I did leave here like a child, and I wasn't ten miles down the trail before I was regretting it."

"Why didn't you return?" Slater asked, his voice having calmed completely.

"Because I still don't agree. I'd have paid dearly if anything had happened to you before I returned, but I still don't agree."

"Tell me, Dak. Exactly what is it that you find so impossible to accept?"

Dakota looked at him. "Maybe it's the change. I didn't think you needed saving from anything, but you are different. I think I'm all right, and I'm happy with that belief. I don't feel I need more."

Slater nodded but still said, "Do you remember the fights Mother used to have with Father? They never ended without Father saying, 'Your mother and I can agree, just as long as I don't confuse her with the facts.' We used to laugh about that, but sometimes I think it's very true. The facts are staring you in the face, Dak, but you're happy with what you have." Slater shook his head in wonder. "No man knows how long he's going to live. I hope you won't take too long deciding if what you have will take you through eternity."

"Maybe there is no eternity," Dakota stated. "Preachers have been spooking people with that line for years."

"I guess you used the operative word, Dak—*maybe*. I believe with all my heart that we are eternal beings. You're not sure. It sounds to me as though you need to be as prepared as I am when death knocks on your door."

Dakota would not have said so at the moment, but Slater had given him something to think about. He was quiet while he digested all of this, unaware of the way Slater watched him.

"How long are you in town for?" Slater asked.

"That depends on you."

"Meaning?"

"If you want me to leave, I'll go."

"Don't be ridiculous, Dak. I didn't want you to leave the first time."

Dakota took the olive branch that Slater offered him. He would have to head back out on the trail soon—he hated the thought of doing that, something he'd never experienced before. He knew it was because of the way he'd left.

"Griffin ever get married?"

"Indeed," Slater told him and went on to say where he was living and that Dakota would be welcomed at the Hathaways'. They talked for a time before Slater headed out to walk the streets and keep an eye on things. Dakota accompanied him, the conversation turning to Cash's visit. For right now the younger brother knew he had to let the other subject go. It didn't stop his praying though—something he did fervently—asking God for another chance to share his faith.

🌸 🌸 🌸

"Anybody here?"

The afternoon was slipping away fast, and the temperature was dropping as Tess stepped into Kate's kitchen and called to her.

"In the living room, Tess," her mother-in-law answered.

Tess went through the house and found Kate and Liberty rehanging curtains.

"Hi, Tess," Kate greeted her. "Be prepared to get dusty."

Tess laughed. "That's fine. As long as I don't have to sit by myself, I can stand a little dust."

Both women were instantly alert.

"Bad news?" Liberty asked.

"It's hard to say. Griffin stopped for an extra gun. Mrs. Flowers was in again. He and Slater are headed to confront the Potters. It doesn't sound as though he'll give them any quarter this time."

"Oh, Tess," Kate began, but Liberty cut her off.

"I've got to go," she said softly and moved toward the door.

Tess watched Kate as she went utterly still. She waited for the older woman to say something to stop Liberty, but it didn't happen. Tess felt torn inside. Another gun would be so helpful, but she also knew that Slater would not find it worth the risk. Neither woman spoke, and in almost record time, Liberty was back downstairs, clothes changed, gun belt in place.

"Please be careful," her mother finally managed.

"Yes, Libby, do," Tess was able to add.

Liberty called her assurance back to them, and moments later they heard Morton's hooves. The swiftness of her actions caused Tess' heart to sink with dread. She didn't like rushed things. Too often one was left to repent for a long time to follow.

"Let's pray," Kate suggested.

Tess had no argument with that. She didn't know if she would see her husband again, but Kate had more on the line: Half of her children were riding into battle. No, Tess didn't need to be asked twice. She sat with her mother-in-law, content to pray for as long as she wanted.

🌹 🌹 🌹

The men were on their horses, their faces grim. Both had known it would come to this, but neither man looked forward to it. Maddie Flowers had just come and said that the Potters had caroused all night. Griffin felt he'd given them enough time. Slater wished that Dakota hadn't left to run an errand, but he hoped he wouldn't be gone long and would find the note he left.

"What in the world?" Griffin exclaimed. Slater looked up to follow his gaze. Coming toward them, her face full of determination, was Liberty. Slater didn't waste any time. His mouth tight with equal resolve, he turned back to the sheriff.

"I'll handle this," he told Griffin as soon as their eyes met, and from the look in his deputy's eyes, Griffin wouldn't have argued for the world.

Slater was already off his horse when Liberty arrived, and just as soon as she slid off Morton's back, ready to ask about the plan, Slater took her hand. He led her into the office and spoke with his face just inches from her own.

"I don't want you to do this."

"Slater," Liberty returned, ready to explain, "you don't know the Potters like I do. You and Griffin need me."

"I don't want you to do this, Libby, and I mean it."

Liberty began to shake her head, so Slater placed his hands gently on either side of her face and held it still.

"No, Liberty."

Her look was nothing short of longsuffering.

"I'll ask Griff," she said, and would have moved toward the door if Slater hadn't caught her hand.

Giving her no time to anticipate his next move, he led her into one of the cells. Bending once again to catch her eye, he said, "I can't put you at risk." Slater then exited, locked the door, and hung the key out of reach.

"Slater," Liberty said on a laugh, sure he could not be serious. "Stop fooling around."

Slater only shook his head. How could he have let this go unsettled? Now was not the time to speculate, but that didn't change his actions. She was not coming to the Potters'.

"I don't want you hurt," he said gently. "I think it would kill me."

"The Potters will probably do that for you."

She'd said it with such conviction that Slater sadly shook his head. "You really are arrogant, Libby. You don't think anyone else can do this."

She was getting ready to argue with him again, but he turned away. He glanced back just as he went out the door. She wasn't happy with him, but neither was she ready to panic. Something wasn't right, but right now he couldn't put his finger on it. Slater felt he had no choice but to shut the door and walk away.

※ ※ ※

Never before had Liberty Drake been tempted to pinch herself. She thought she must be in a dream. Had Slater just locked her in jail? Had he really taken it that far? Liberty thought the man was amazing.

You'd think I was a criminal, and here I am trying to help.

With a shake of her head, she turned away from the bars. Griffin Drake was no fool. Every lawman had heard stories of getting locked in his own jail. Griffin had never been one to take chances. Liberty was in front of the bunk now, getting ready to count the bricks, climb up, and fetch the hidden key. Whether Slater Rawlings thought so or not, Liberty knew she was needed.

The opening of the door stopped all movement. With as casual a shift as she could muster, Liberty turned to see who had come in.

"Dakota!"

"Hi, Libby." His voice held just the right amount of amusement and surprise. "I can't say as I expected to find you in there."

"Would you let me out?" she asked sweetly.

Dakota paused. "Why are you in there?"

Liberty thought fast. "You know Slater. He can be such a joker."

Dakota watched her.

"In fact," she lied again, "you just missed him. If you'll let me out, I'll take you to him."

Dakota was amused again but not swayed. She looked awfully cute behind bars, those hazel eyes making their appeal, but his brother had given him strict orders.

"How have you been?" Dakota asked, causing Liberty to blink. Her mind raced as she studied his expression and knew she'd been set up.

"Dakota," she began, all trace of congeniality gone. "I want out of here."

"Can't do that, Lib."

"Why not?"

"Slater's orders were very clear."

"But they need me."

"Slater doesn't seem to think so."

"Did you ask Griffin?"

"I didn't have to. My brother knows what he wants, and he wants you safe."

Liberty knew very real frustration for the first time. She knew she would have to keep calm to get out, but that was taking an effort.

"Why don't you go," she now tried. "They went to the Potters', and they're going to need all the help they can get."

"I can't do that either."

"Why not?" Liberty asked, although she believed she knew the answer.

"Because Slater thinks you know a way out of here."

Liberty was stunned. How had Slater figured that out? Surely Griffin wouldn't have told. Liberty's frustration rose yet again. She was suddenly so angry that tears filled her eyes.

Dakota had been headed to the desk chair to sit down but saw Libby's brimming eyes and approached.

"Libby?"

Thinking fast, Liberty played the tears for all they were worth.

"I really think they need me, Dak," she managed in a quivery voice.

"Libby." Dakota's voice was most tender. "If you could just trust that—"

Liberty waited only until he drew close. In a move he wouldn't have believed if he hadn't seen it, Liberty lifted his gun from the holster. For a second he was stunned. Then he smiled.

"What are you going to do with that?"

"Let me out of here, Dakota," she said, her voice level.

"No."

"I'm not going to say it again."

Dakota was in the act of turning away, seeing no point in arguing, when a shot was fired and his hat flew off. He whirled back to face Liberty with blazing eyes.

"I don't like to be shot at, Miss Drake!"

Liberty didn't appear to have heard. With the gun still aimed at him, she spoke in that same measured tone.

"Now the next one is going to hurt. You won't die, but you'll be in pain and probably bleed all over your clothes."

Dakota was so angry he could have spit. When he'd come upon Slater and Griffin leaving, having just been joined by Price who drove a huge wagon, he thought his brother's idea for keeping an eye on Liberty sounded fun. He hadn't bargained on how badly she wanted out of that cell. He didn't honestly think she would shoot him, but knowing how much she wanted her freedom, he could not deny her.

He went for the key, just barely keeping his temper. He didn't know what was worse, having to face his brother when he found that Liberty had gotten around him, or having to face a woman who was upset enough to take shots at him to gain her release. None too happy with himself or anyone else, Dakota fetched the key, wishing he'd stayed out of town one more day.

Nineteen

THE POTTERS WERE NOT PREPARED for a visit from the sheriff. Indeed, the drinking in the barn had started a little early this day. It put Rush and Possum in a good mood, but both Ned and Critter were none too happy to see Shotgun's law enforcement arriving.

"Let me do the talkin'!" the father of the clan snapped at his boys.

"I think this should do the talkin'," Critter proclaimed, a shotgun in his hand.

"Gimme that!" Ned ordered, but Critter was having none of it. They scuffled around a bit, all four hands on the weapon, and froze when the gun went off.

Four sets of eyes rounded in fear, just as the first shots came from without. The Potters hit the dirt. From behind a small outcropping of rocks, Griffin and Slater let off a steady stream of bullets as the four inside scrambled for cover. The barn being ancient, daylight could be seen from every crack and crevice, with new holes appearing all the time and wood splintering around them. Ned thought he would kill Critter himself if he could get close enough.

"Ned!" The firing finally stopped, and that man heard his name being called. "Do you hear me?"

It was Griffin.

"Yeah, I—" Ned began, but Critter jumped in.

"We hear ya, Sheriff, and all you're gonna hear is this!"

Critter fired one shot, and the bullets started up again. For what seemed like many minutes, the Potters hid in the barn and waited yet again for silence, each one wondering how many guns the law had brought.

At last it was quiet, but Griffin did not shout toward the barn. From next to him, Slater held his peace as well.

"Going to let them sweat a little," Griffin said, almost to himself.

"Something tells me Ned would talk to you."

"I think you're right. He'll do anything to stay out of jail, but he hasn't learned to control Critter in all these years, and now he's going to pay."

"My guess is Critter won't be able to last much longer."

As though on cue, Critter let off two shots, and both Slater and Griffin went at it again. This went on for much longer than either man would have cared for, the youngest Potter shooting one or two bullets, and the lawmen answering with a round. Things happened to be quiet when they heard the voices.

"Knock it off!" one of the Potters thundered.

"Shut up! Get away from me."

Not surprisingly, a few shots came outside, and for the last time Griffin and Slater went into action, staying well back since Critter was firing on them as well. It took a little more time at this point, but at last the guns fell quiet. The barn was quiet too.

"If you've had enough," Griffin tried again, "throw the guns out ahead of you and come out of there with your hands up!"

Slater and Griffin were both peeking out when the barn door slowly swung open, creaking like the stays in a tight corset. A moment later a shotgun was tossed far from the door, and out walked Ned. Behind him came Rush and Possum, Critter between them. That they had landed a few blows in his direction was obvious. He was staggering a bit and the men on either side of him were clearly keeping him on his feet. When Griffin, Slater, and now Price, who had come into position, stepped out with guns drawn, they dropped Critter on his face to put their hands in the air.

"Very nice, boys," Griffin congratulated them. "Just step apart a little, not too close to the gun, and keep those hands right where we can see them. Easy now, Critter," Griffin said to him as he came to his hands and knees.

There wasn't a single argument at this point, mostly due to the fact that Critter's mouth was too swollen for talking. The three men moved in on them, and in fairly short order, the four Potters were cuffed and loaded into the wagon. That was when Slater spotted him.

To the side of a small outcropping of rocks stood Dakota. Slater told himself to stay calm, but even as he thought it, he felt his temper rising. It didn't help to suddenly spot Liberty's horse.

Seeing that he'd been spotted, Dakota started toward him. The men met halfway.

"Where is she?"

"Sitting behind the rocks."

Slater's mouth tightened. "What happened?"

"She got my gun away from me. I don't think she would have hurt me, but knowing how much she wanted out, Slate, I let her go. I'm sorry."

"It's not you who needs to apologize," Slater gritted, coming around Dakota to head to the rock. He didn't know when he'd been so disappointed and angry. They should have had this out a long time ago, but even at that, Liberty should have known he just wanted her to be safe. Slater walked until he stood just a few feet from her. She was sitting quite still, her back against the rock, and finally looked up at him.

"I can't believe you've done this," he said quietly. "I thought I knew you, Libby. I thought you were the one."

"Slater," she began softly, but he cut her off with a downward slash of his hand.

"Don't talk to me." Slater uttered the very words he believed he would never say. "I don't want to hear any excuses right now. I wanted to marry you, Libby, but you don't trust anyone but yourself. You're a law unto yourself. I'm just now seeing that."

Liberty sat very still as he turned and walked away. She didn't know when she'd been in such pain. In a haze of misery, she heard the wagon start into motion and couldn't be sure if her brother and Slater's horses had left as well. She didn't even hear Dakota come up, but he was suddenly there.

"I'll ride back with you, Libby," he said.

"You don't have to, Dakota."

"I want to."

Liberty nodded. In reality she wanted to be alone, but she saw that Dakota was offering his friendship. Liberty came slowly to her feet and moved toward Morton. She had little interest in doing anything right now but made herself climb into the saddle and turn the horse toward home.

Riding quietly beside her, Dakota took in her white features and searched for something to say. He hadn't actually heard Slater's words, but it wasn't hard to guess that they hadn't been too welcoming. It was on Dakota's mind to ask Liberty why coming had been so important, but she looked like a fragile piece of crystal to him right now. One move and she might break into a million tiny bits.

"Dakota?" Liberty suddenly spoke, surprising him just as they hit the edge of town.

"Yeah?"

"I think I'll stop by and see Duffy."

"Okay."

"Thank you for riding back with me."

"Anytime."

Liberty pulled off a little then and moved Morton to the right side of the street. Dakota watched her stop in front of the office and even as she sat for a moment and then slid out of the saddle. He wanted to leave her some privacy, so he forced himself to turn away. Not knowing quite what to do with himself, he went ahead to the jailhouse, thinking he might be a help. He also thought his brother might need someone to talk to.

❧ ❧ ❧

Duffy heard the door open, but no one answered his greeting. He had his hands full of bottles at the moment, and then he needed to wash, so it took a minute for him to move into the other room. The last person he expected to see was his daughter.

"Well, Libby. What's up?"

Liberty didn't look directly at him, and Duffy, ever the kind and sensitive parent, came and sat down on one of the chairs across from her. Only then did Liberty's eyes meet his.

"I've done it this time, Duffy," she began.

"Okay," Duffy said simply, wanting her to know he was listening.

"I went someplace I shouldn't have, and I've ruined everything."

Duffy didn't believe that but told himself not to be too hasty. "Can you tell me about it?" he asked gently.

"I suppose I should explain everything, but for right now I just need you to know that I've been shot."

"Where, Libby?" Duffy forced himself to remain calm, even as he took in her bloodless lips and glazed eyes with new understanding.

"In the side. I think the bullet must have ricocheted off a rock, but even at that, it burns something fierce. I never knew it would hurt like this." Duffy watched in amazement as she stood. "I'm going to head home now—I just wanted you to know."

"This way, Libby," Duffy said softly, also having come to his feet. Letting the doctor in him completely take over, he continued, "I need you to come back here and lie down on the table."

"I should help Mam with dinner," Liberty said in a strange voice, and Duffy knew that shock was setting in. She did as she was told, however, and a minute later Duffy was pushing aside her jacket and cutting away the bloodstained shirt at her left side. He worked to tamp down every emotion as he labored over her injury. That this had happened to one of his own—his precious Liberty—was turning out to be very hard.

"Oh, Duffy," Liberty gasped as he cleansed the wound. The bullet had passed through, but it had made a mess.

Duffy didn't answer her. He was a surgeon at work now, having to turn his emotions off almost to the point of indifference. He cleansed and stitched, not letting himself think about the possible infections that could set in and what they could do, and especially not letting himself think about who had let this happen, not letting his mind stray to the woman he loved above all others or the child within her and the way this was going to affect them both.

Almost an hour passed before the bleeding stopped. It was not an effusive wound, but loss of blood from someone as petite as Liberty scared him a little. She was silent now, her eyes staring blankly at the ceiling. In all this time she hadn't fainted or even closed her eyes. He had known she was strong but had not expected her to be able to speak so coherently.

"Are you wrapping it?"

"Yes."

"So you're almost done?"

"Yes."

"I want to go home and lie in my own bed, Duffy."

"You shouldn't move. I've got the bleeding stopped, but you need to lie still."

Liberty shook her head. "I want you to help me home. I ache with things I haven't told you yet, Duffy. I can't tell you how much I need to go home."

It was the first time he'd heard emotion in her voice, and for some reason it scared him more than the wound. She was crushed about something that brought her more pain than a bullet wound. Duffy found himself unable to argue with her.

"Give me a few minutes," he said. "I'll help you, but stay put for right now."

Waiting for her to nod, Duffy went out back to hitch Cotton to the buggy. This all set, he slipped around to the front, grabbed Morton's reins, and took him to the back. By the time he came in the back door, Liberty was rising from the table. She stood, her hands leaning on the surface, her mouth open as she gasped for air.

"All right," Duffy said, thinking to save the lecture for later. It was probably too late anyway; she most surely had started bleeding again.

With an arm supporting her, he led her to the back door. Not until he maneuvered her into the buggy did he go back for his bag and to get the lamps.

🦋 🦋 🦋

The ride home was a complete loss for Liberty. For the next several minutes she didn't know where she was or what was going on around her. The pain had intensified, and when Slater's face moved through her mind, she wanted to be sick. She didn't remember the buggy jostling her much or even the walk up the steps, but she was suddenly in the kitchen, her mother's concerned face coming into view.

"I just want to go to bed, Mam," Liberty said.

Biting her lip to keep from speaking, Kate moved into Zach's view when she saw the blood on her daughter's coat.

"Up you go," Duffy now said, not giving anything more than a swift glance at his wife. He would explain it all to her, but not until Liberty was in bed and his youngest children were out of earshot.

Not surprisingly—with a word to Zach and Laura—Kate followed her husband and daughter. She told the children to stay in the kitchen and went to help Liberty settle in.

"I want you to know," Kate said, not looking at anyone as she eased Liberty's jacket from her shoulders and started on the buttons on her shirt, "that I've spent the entire afternoon and evening giving my children to the Lord. I won't say that I'm not upset, but I feel that God prepared me for this." Kate turned and stared into her husband's eyes. "All of this to say, I'm all right, and I don't want to be told to go lie down."

In the process of pulling the covers down on the bed, Duffy calmly met her gaze but did not comment. He found Liberty's nightgown hanging on the back of the door and brought it to the end of the bed.

"Sit down," he commanded his daughter, removing her boots after she'd lowered herself onto the mattress. He did not slip out of the room as the rest of Liberty's things were removed but stayed to recheck her wound, which had started to bleed again, and keep track of Kate's reaction when she saw that her daughter had actually been shot. None of this took an extreme amount of time, and after padding the wound some more and laying an extra sheet on the bed, Liberty was finally lying with the covers close around her.

"I should spank you," Kate whispered as she sat on the edge and held Liberty's hand, her eyes just now filling with tears. "Getting yourself shot. Of all things."

Liberty only looked at her, and for a moment Kate was alarmed.

"Liberty? I didn't mean that."

"It's all right, Mam," Liberty said as she shut her eyes. "It's all right."

Kate looked to Duffy, her expression fearful.

"Sleep now, Lib," Duffy said, having just checked her side one more time. "And try to lie still."

Liberty nodded against the pillow, and Duffy, with an arm around Kate, took her from the room. The lantern was still burning, but Duffy left it, knowing he would be back to check on her again soon, and probably all through the night.

"We need to go back down, Kate, and tell Zach and Laura what's happened. We can't leave them sitting frightened in the kitchen."

Kate could only nod. She had said she was all right but found herself shaking and very glad that her husband was in charge. They arrived in the kitchen to see Zach getting a glass of water for Laura. Kate went to help him. After she'd kissed his cheek and thanked him, they sat at the table where Laura was watching them with serious eyes.

"Is Libby sick?" she asked.

"Yes," Duffy told her.

"She went to help Griffin today and got hurt," Kate filled in. Duffy had not heard the specifics but was not surprised.

Zach's little face paled. "Is she shot?"

"Yes, Zach," Duffy said. "And she hurts quite a bit, but I think she's going to be fine."

"Does she need water?" Laura wanted to know. "I could give her mine."

"That's very kind of you, honey, but right now she just needs to rest."

"Where was she shot?" Zach now asked.

"In the side. The bullet is out, and I think she'll heal quickly, but she's going to need lots of rest."

Their little faces were so sober. Kate could see that they were not going to eat another bite.

"Why don't we go into the living room and read," she suggested.

The children were still nodding solemnly when Duffy suggested, "I think we should go up and take a peek at Libby. She might be awake, and you can tell her you're praying for her and love her."

Not for the first time, Kate thanked God for her husband's wisdom. The children's faces brightened instantly, and they were swift to accompany Duffy upstairs. Kate brought up the rear and found herself fighting tears as Laura talked with her sister.

"We're here, Libby. You don't need to be worried anymore. Zach and I are here to pray for you."

Liberty's eyes, which had opened at the sound of their coming, now closed, but she smiled and moved her fingers in a little wave.

"I love you, Libby," tenderhearted Zach said, his little hand coming up to touch hers.

"I love you too, Zach. You too, Laura."

"Okay," Duffy said now. "Why don't you go back down with Mam, and I'll join you in just a bit."

The children left with a final glance at their sister. It was so hard to see her in bed. She was always the strong one.

"Here we go," Kate said, keeping her voice as normal as possible.

As their footsteps receded in the hall and Duffy touched her forehead, Libby opened her eyes.

"Duffy?"

"I'm right here."

"I've been so selfish. Please don't let Mam be upset. Tell her to take it easy. If the baby doesn't make it because of me, I'll never forgive myself."

Duffy was checking Liberty's side for bleeding, which seemed to have stopped, and didn't immediately speak.

"We'll have to get a garment that opens on the side, Lib. This long nightgown ends up all bunched under you."

"Duffy, didn't you hear what I said?"

"I heard," he said quietly, as he settled the bedcovers back in place and placed a hand on either side of her to look directly into her eyes. "But just as I want your mother to look after herself right now, I want you to concentrate on getting better. You've lost a good deal of blood, and you're not going to be jumping out of that bed in the morning."

Liberty looked up at him but didn't comment.

"I'm going to go down now and spend some time with the kids and then put them to bed. Sleep if you can and lie still. I could give you something."

Liberty shook her head no.

"All right."

Duffy kissed Liberty's brow and slipped from the room, this time turning the lantern down a bit on his way out. He wanted to sit with her. He wanted to keep an eye on how much she moved in her sleep. But he knew that would have to wait until Zach and Laura were in bed. He found them flanking Kate on the davenport and listening as she read. He did not interrupt but sat on Zach's other side and listened as well.

"Libby will be all right," Laura leaned around her mother to tell the doctor.

"You're interrupting Mam, Laura," he told her.

Laura looked up at her mother. "She wants Libby to be all right too."

Duffy didn't try to correct her, and Kate stopped reading. Maybe it was best to talk about what had happened and not try to distract the children with a story. Maybe the time would be better spent in prayer.

"I think that Libby will be all right too, Laura, but tell me why you think so."

"Well, she's always been all right before, and we're going to pray for her," she offered, her little heart speaking with great confidence.

Duffy thought about how confident believers could be in God, even if things didn't turn out exactly as they hoped for, and for this reason he only smiled at his daughter, thanked her, and suggested they turn in a little early. Kate finished reading the story she was on, and Duffy said it was time to head up.

"Kiss Mam," he ordered, not wanting her to move from her seat.

The children embraced her warmly, and Kate held them tight, but she was nothing short of relieved that Duffy was putting them to bed. Her first thought was to run to Liberty's side and be with her, but she tried to act as normally as possible.

Rising and putting the book away, she went to the kitchen. She had not eaten but still wasn't hungry. She filled a plate for her husband and put it on the stove to stay warm. Then she started the cleanup, something so routine that it gave her a chance to pray continuously. She was just finishing the dirty dishes when the back door opened and Griffin walked in.

"Hi, Mam," he said, kissing her cheek when he saw how drained she looked.

"Hello, dear."

"How's Libby?" Griffin asked innocently. She was the reason he'd come, but not for the reason his mother thought.

"The bleeding has stopped, and she's resting quietly. Duffy thinks she'll be fine, but she's awfully—" Kate stumbled to a halt as she watched her son's face. "Griffin, what is it?"

"Why is Libby bleeding?"

Kate was stunned. No wonder he hadn't come earlier, or for that matter, taken her to Duffy's office.

"She was shot today, Griffin. I had no idea you didn't know."

"Where is she?" he asked, already moving toward the door.

"In her room, but Griff—" his mother stopped him, "Duffy just put the kids down; please don't go rushing up there and frighten them if they're still awake."

Griffin put his hand up in understanding. He nodded and took some deep breaths, this time moving slowly to the stairs. Kate didn't go with him but could tell that he was walking at a more controlled pace. And indeed she was right. Griffin's pace was slow, giving complete lie to the way his heart nearly pounded through his chest.

Oh, Father in heaven, Libby's been hit. I didn't know, Lord, I didn't know. My sister, who I love so much. I can't believe it. I've wrestled with this whole issue, not really wanting to face it, and now this has happened. Please help her. Please touch her and heal her.

Griffin was at the doorway of Liberty's room now and found Duffy in the rocking chair by the bed, his Bible open in his hand and his head turned to catch the soft light of the lantern. Griffin spoke when the older man looked up.

"I didn't know."

Duffy nodded. He had wondered why Griffin and Slater had not been around, but his main thought was Liberty.

Griffin came in, his eyes glued to Liberty's colorless cheeks. He came to the side of the bed and just stood looking down at her.

"How bad?" he whispered to Duffy without shifting his gaze.

"It passed clear through. She thought it might have ricocheted."

"Where was she hit?"

"Her left side."

Griffin licked his lips, wishing she would wake up so he could talk to her. He could count on one hand the amount of times he had been this upset. His father's death came to mind, as did the night Liberty told him that Tess thought he might as well be dead. Now his sister lay hurt and vulnerable, and something deep inside Griffin told him he could have prevented it. His father's death was beyond his control. When he learned of Tess' feelings, he had instantly acted. Not so with Liberty. He had been thinking about her involvement for a long time, and now he'd waited too long.

Griffin broke from his reverie when he heard movement at the door. He turned to see his mother enter. The fullness under her apron was another reminder of the many people who were affected. He watched his mother as she stepped up and joined him. If Liberty's even breathing was any indication, she was deeply asleep; nevertheless, they whispered.

"Tell me, Griffin," Kate commented, having recovered enough to question him, "if you didn't know Libby was hurt, why did you come?"

He shook his head. "Slater was not at all happy that Libby came out to the Potters'. He was pretty hard on her."

The words were no more out of his mouth than a thunderstruck look crossed his face.

"Slater!" he whispered in soft dismay.

"He doesn't know?"

"No."

Kate was relieved. She had worried that Slater was deliberately staying away.

Griffin, still watching Liberty's face, put his hat back on. He knew how he would feel if he'd been hard on Tess and she was harmed before he'd made it right. Maybe Liberty had needed to hear what Slater said, but that wouldn't change the way he felt when he learned she was hurt and he'd just ridden away. Much as he knew his deputy would be upset, Griffin had to tell him. Telling his family he would be back as soon as he could and to tell Liberty he'd been there, he left the room, intent on finding Slater and explaining as gently as he could.

Twenty

LIBERTY THOUGHT SHE MIGHT BE FLOATING. She was warm, almost hot, and for some time she couldn't tell where she was. She saw flowers along the creek bank, little yellow ones. They were so pretty and so early for this time of year. Reaching out with her arm, she bent to pick one but found herself gasping in pain. Her eyes flew open, and after a moment, she found herself staring at the ceiling in her own bedroom. Her sigh was very soft as memory returned.

I never believed it would come to this, Lord. I never thought I would not be able to let go. Giving up the job has been hurting and bothering me for a long time, but I didn't think I was capable of doing what I did today.

Liberty shuddered with shame as she remembered. It was as if she had taken leave of her senses, but that hadn't happened. Completely in her right mind, she'd been desperate to be involved, sure that no one else could handle it. Arrogant. Just as Slater had said.

Liberty's whole frame shook for a moment. She couldn't think of Slater—not now—not ever. He was sure to be gone soon. *I thought you were the one. I wanted to marry you.* Both statements in the past tense. He might stay until Griffin could find a replacement, but he'd only come through town on a whim in the first place. It would just be a matter of time before he went on his way. Liberty knew she mustn't do anything to stop him. She would make sure she apologized and thanked him for taking her measure so correctly, but she must never make him feel that he must stay.

But first, she had to see Dakota. Liberty prayed even now that he was still in town. There was no excuse for the way she'd treated him, but she would still ask for his forgiveness and hope that he didn't despise her.

A noise at the door just then carried Liberty's eyes that way. Duffy came in quietly even when he saw that she was awake. He laid a hand on her cheek. She was getting warm, but that might be the covers.

"Are you too warm?" he asked.

"No. My feet are cold."

Duffy took the quilt from the brass footboard and laid it across her feet and lower legs. He then came back to the rocking chair and pulled it even closer so he could talk with her.

"Griff was here."

"Was I asleep?"

"Yeah. He was pretty shaken."

Liberty looked away.

"What happened out there, Libby, that no one knew of this?"

Liberty did not answer. She was ashamed of her actions, but it was more than that. She didn't feel she could explain yet how blameless the men had been. She thought that whatever she said, Duffy would think they should have come to her aid.

"Oh, Libby," Duffy whispered softly. "What's happened to hurt you so much?"

Liberty's heart broke over the caring in his voice.

"My own sin, mostly, a complete lack of trust. And I think that's the reason it's so hard for me to talk about it."

"Have you confessed it?"

"Yes."

"Then there's no reason for you to be ashamed in front of me."

Liberty felt as though she had been released. Going slowly, working to gather her thoughts and remember the details, she filled Duffy in, not surprised that his eyes were full of compassion even when she admitted to what she considered reprehensible actions toward the Rawlings brothers, especially Dakota.

"Slater will want to see you, honey," Duffy said when she had finished.

Liberty smiled sadly. "I guess he probably will. I'll have to find a way to tell him he did the right thing."

Duffy knew this was not the time to argue, but Slater should have let Liberty speak. The doctor somehow knew that he would regret that more than anything else.

"I'm going to pray for Slater," Duffy said. "I think he'll need it."

Liberty nodded. It was just like Duffy to be willing to walk in the other man's shoes. Had Liberty seen Griffin just then, she'd have also known how timely her stepfather's prayers would be.

❧ ❧ ❧

"Could I see you both a moment?" Griffin asked Slater and Dakota the moment he stepped into the Hathaways' living room. The men were buried in the newspaper, Mr. Hathaway as well. Mrs. Hathaway had opened the front door, looking delighted that "her boys" had company.

"If you need privacy," Mrs. Hathaway said as she joined them, "feel free to talk in the kitchen."

"Thank you," Griffin replied as she handed him a lantern. He went in the direction she pointed and waited until Slater and Dakota were both inside the door.

"Dakota," Griffin wasted no time in asking, "did you ride back with Libby today?"

"Yes. She went to Duffy's as soon as she got to town."

Griffin nodded. "She was shot out there today."

Not surprisingly, both men looked thunderstruck.

"Where?" Slater asked, his voice hoarse.

"In the side. It's clean, but she's lost some blood. Duffy says she'll be all right."

Slater began to move away and turned back. "Is she home?"

"Yes."

There was no need for other words. Dakota went through to tell their hosts that they would be out for a while, and by the time he got back, Slater had already jumped onto Arrow's bare back and started down the street.

Slater had never felt like this. He had not lost anyone he loved, unusual for a man in his position, and although he'd been saddened by death many times, his heart had never been deeply involved. Knowing that Liberty was hurt and realizing that he hadn't been there for her were the most painful things he could ever recall.

Arriving on the Petersons' street, Slater rode between the two houses. Not bothering to tie Arrow's reins, he entered the kitchen without knocking. Kate and Tess were talking at the table. Slater looked between them and then toward the door.

"Duffy's up there, Slater," Kate said kindly. "I'm sure it will be fine if you go up."

"Thank you." The words came automatically as he moved through the kitchen.

Realizing he wasn't going to know the way, Kate followed him. She directed him toward the light spilling into the dark hall and stood back as he filled the doorway.

"I was just thinking of you, Slater," Duffy said. His gaze swung to Liberty for a moment. "She just fell back to sleep."

Slater tried to speak, but there was no moisture in his mouth. He moved toward the bed, his heart frozen with fear. She might not get up again. She might die before he could tell her how sorry he was and how much he loved her. They might never have a life together, and he wanted that so much.

"Duffy?" Liberty said with her eyes closed.

"I'm right here."

"I have to see Dakota. I have to make it right."

"Okay. If he comes, I'll tell him. Would you like to see Slater?"

Liberty sighed. "He'll just feel bad," she said, her voice fading. "He shouldn't feel bad."

"Libby," Slater tried her name, having drawn close, but Liberty only mumbled and fell back to sleep.

Slater stared at her face, her dark hair in a riot around her head and on the pillow. She was the prettiest little thing he'd ever seen. Her dark lashes, always so thick and long, made little fans on her pale cheeks. Slater felt his breath catch in his throat. Never had anyone been so precious to him. It was as if she were already his. It felt as though she'd been his for all time.

"Sit down," Duffy directed softly, having given up his chair.

Slater obeyed without thought. He stared at Liberty a time longer and then turned to her stepfather.

"Did she tell you what happened?"

"Just that one of Critter's bullets must have ricocheted."

Slater nodded. "Did she tell you she tried to speak to me and I wouldn't let her?"

"Yes."

"Was she going to tell me she was hurt or something else?"

Duffy's silence was answer enough. It was almost more than the tall blond cowboy could take. His eyes went upward as they filled with tears.

You left her! You wouldn't even let her speak!

Noise at the door brought both men's heads around. Griffin was there, Dakota just behind him. They were on their way into the room when Liberty spoke, her eyes still closed.

"Mam?"

"I'm here," Kate said as she came in behind the men, followed by Tess.

For a moment she didn't say anything, so Duffy spoke.

"You have quite a bit of company here, Libby."

"Do any of them have any candy? I wish I had a peppermint."

Griffin didn't even try to hold his laughter. Liberty smiled when she heard it and opened her eyes.

"Here we are," Griffin began, "scared to death, and you want candy."

Liberty smiled a little, but her eyes found Dakota, and her face grew sad.

"I'm sorry," she said to him, her eyes filling. "I was such a fool. Everyone misses, and if I had missed when I shot at you, I might have hurt or killed you. Please forgive me, Dakota."

"It's all right, Libby," he said, barely able to speak. She might not believe him, but he really did understand.

Movement out of the corner of her eye caused her to look that way. Not until that moment had she seen Slater, who was by her side near her pillow.

"I'm sorry, Libby," were the first words out of his mouth. "I should have let you talk."

Liberty's hand went up and he took it.

"I shouldn't have been there. I've never been so foolish, Slate. I just hope you can forgive me."

He kissed the back of her hand and tenderly held onto it.

Griffin had gone to the far side of the bed, as had Tess, and when they'd all caught her eye long enough to smile or speak to her, Duffy ushered them from the room. Kate stayed a moment longer to kiss her cheek, but the last one to be seen out by the doctor was Slater.

"I'll see you tomorrow," he said quietly to Libby. "Sleep well."

Liberty nodded and watched him leave. She didn't speak until his steps told her he was down the hall.

"Tell him he doesn't have to come," Liberty told Duffy.

"I can't do that."

"Why not?"

"Because he does have to come."

Liberty blinked. "Says who?"

"Says me." Duffy bent and kissed her brow. "Go to sleep. I'll check on you later."

Liberty didn't have much choice; she was already sleepy. But not at any time before she dropped off did she understand what he meant.

❧ ❧ ❧

"And then the little horse said he didn't like his hay," Laura said from the foot of Liberty's bed almost a week after the shooting. The patient was sitting up against the headboard, swathed with quilts and bolstered with pillows. There had been a slight fever, but the wound was healing fast. Weakness from the loss of blood, however, was still apparent.

"What did his mother do?"

"I don't know," she said, her little brow perplexed. "I'm still figuring that part of the story out."

Liberty would have laughed, but she'd learned her lesson about laughing too much when Laura had come in to talk to her every day.

"Maybe she should take the hay away from him because he isn't thankful."

Laura looked amazed. "That's good, Libby," she said intently. "We should write that down."

Liberty had to laugh then, even though it caused her to gasp. And as her little nurse had started to do, she came close, careful not to bump Liberty's side, and took her sister's hand in both of hers, praying that the pain would go away soon. Liberty thought that if her feelings for Laura were any more tender, she would melt into a puddle.

"Hey, Libby," Zach announced as he joined them, "I have to go to school."

"Okay. Thanks for coming in to say goodbye."

"I'll have a new book to read you when I get home today."

"Great. I'll look forward to it."

The little boy came over to kiss her, Liberty leaning toward him as best she could. The kiss usually landed in midair, but they always caught each other's smiles, and Liberty thought about him all day once he was gone.

Zach hadn't been gone from the room five minutes when Kate came in. She shooed Laura downstairs to eat, pulled Liberty's curtains open, cracked the window, and made sure Libby could reach the cup of coffee she'd just brought in. She then took Laura's place at the foot of the bed.

"How'd you sleep?"

"Not so well. I kept waking up and wanting to turn on my bad side. Did I keep you awake?"

"A little."

"I do wonder when I'm going to feel like getting out of this bed."

"It'll come. It would seem that everyone will still be here, so take your time."

Liberty found that comment odd, even as she realized her mother had said it the day before.

"What do you mean 'everyone will still be here'?"

"Your brother, Tess, and the Rawlings have just about moved in. I thought you knew that."

Liberty's mouth opened. "Mam, you can't do that! You can't be entertaining all these people and still be taking it slow."

"Liberty, they haven't let me do a thing. If the church family isn't bringing something, Tess is cooking. Dakota walks Zach to and from school every day, and unless Slater is working or sleeping, he's here cleaning something, trying to cook, or seeing to the kids."

Liberty was flabbergasted. She had done a lot of sleeping, that was certainly true, but that life was being lived below stairs in such a surprising way was a little hard to take in.

"Why?" was the only word she could find.

Kate looked very sympathetic. "How else are they going to be near you, Lib? Slater especially. He can't exactly sit around your bedroom."

Sadness overwhelmed Liberty. She didn't want Slater hanging around because he felt guilty. She was glad that everyone had come and taken the burden from her mother, but Liberty had reconciled herself to not having the life she'd envisioned. For a moment she thought she might be selling both God and Slater short, but that didn't seem likely.

"How about some breakfast?" Kate asked.

"That sounds good."

Kate was gone for a long time, and when she returned with a breakfast tray, it was also to explain that Dakota had just been there.

"He said to tell you goodbye and that he'd come back through as soon as he could."

"I take it he has to go back to work?"

"Yes. He wished he could see you, but I told him you'd understand."

"Yes, I do. I appreciate how gracious he's been."

"Yes. As special as he is right now, it's wonderful to think of who he would be if he came to Christ."

"Slater and I have talked about that very thing."

Kate took in the wistful expression that came into her daughter's eyes and knew that it was about more than Dakota's need for salvation. With a word about checking on her soon, Kate made sure Libby had the Bible, pencil, and paper she'd asked for and slipped from the room. Liberty had not asked to be alone, but it wasn't hard to see that this was just what she needed.

❧ ❧ ❧

"We have to talk to you," Griffin said the next day, coming into her room one week to the day after Liberty had been hurt.

Liberty looked into Tess and Griffin's faces. They would certainly be more happy if a baby was on the way, but she hoped that their news was good.

"We owe you an apology, Lib," Tess began. "I feel very much at fault for waiting so long. Griffin said he's to blame, but I've been very cowardly."

Liberty still looked between them, her face open.

"Libby," Griffin sad down in the rocker and leaned close. "It's been on my mind for some time now, especially knowing how Slater feels, that I shouldn't be using you to back me up. I felt the Lord speaking to my heart, but it was easier to depend on you. I called on you for help with Bernie and then thought afterward that maybe she lets herself go just to get you to come.

"And I can't help but wonder if I had put in my vote of disapproval about your coming last week and not left the whole thing in Slater's hands you might have listened. I'm sorry, Libby. I'm sorry I didn't obey the Lord and prevent this from happening in the first place."

"And I didn't speak to you as a friend, Libby," Tess now put in. "I knew the way Slater felt but never asked you about it. I'm sorry."

Liberty nodded and said quietly, "I must admit that I've always taken the family's support as a positive sign, but Slater's strong feelings have certainly made me think."

They fell silent for a moment before Tess said, "Are you all right, Libby?"

Liberty's thoughts had turned to Slater, causing the region around her heart to ache, but she forced herself to nod and smile. Griffin rescued her by turning the conversation to business.

"The circuit judge will be through in about two weeks. The Potters are back on the farm, but they've stayed very quiet, especially because I told them one of their bullets hit and could have killed someone."

"Slater and Griffin went out to Maddie Flowers' too," Tess added. "Her still is gone as well."

"I can guess how she took that," Liberty said dryly.

Griffin chuckled. "I thought she would faint, but she was quiet even when we smashed her *medicinal* bottles."

Liberty now laughed a little too. "And what of Davis Mills? Any word yet?"

Griffin shook his head. "Only that the law in Austin thinks he must have pulled a lot of little jobs and been storing the money under his aunt's floor, since there's been no report of a large bank holdup. He's left almost no trail, but I plan to keep my eyes and ears open."

Liberty smiled at him, thinking he was the man to do it. Hard as her own situation was, Liberty believed with all her heart that her brother was a fine lawman. Shotgun was blessed to have him.

Griffin and Tess didn't stay much longer, something for which Liberty was grateful. She had some more thinking to do and that, along with their visit, seemed to wear her out. She settled against her pillow, knowing that if she had it to do over again, out of her love for Slater, she would do whatever he asked.

It wouldn't come easily to me, Father. Not only am I comfortable with a gun, I'm also too quick to want to do Your job, but I would try. I would try with all my heart. I can see now that Slater only wanted to protect and take care of me. I wish he still did.

Liberty fell asleep while telling God that she didn't think she'd ever get over him.

❧ ❧ ❧

"You're certainly in a good mood," Griffin commented to his deputy on the first day of March.

"I am," Slater agreed.

"Going to tell me why?"

"Well," he drew the word out, clearly having a fine time. "As a matter of fact, a little bird told me that a certain lady was out of bed yesterday for the first time. I'm hoping I'll find her downstairs when I go by at lunch."

Griffin tried not to smile when he said, "I don't suppose I'll get another moment of work out of you until you see her."

"Probably not," Slater said unrepentantly, looking out the window, hands behind his back as he rocked on his heels.

"Someone could probably be holding up Price and Amy, and you would just smile."

"Now, that I wouldn't do," Slater turned and said with mischievous eyes. "It might keep me from seeing your sister."

Griffin could only laugh. "Get out of here, Slate. I don't want to see your face until Libby smiles at you and you're ready to work."

Slater was not going to argue. With hat in place and a certain Drake on his mind, he made a beeline for the door. It was a little early for lunch, but Liberty still might be downstairs.

The separation had been torture. Slater found himself able to be downstairs with Tess, the children, or Kate, people he cared for very much but didn't feel desperate to see. When he asked after Liberty's health, he knew they told him the truth, but he had a natural need to see her for himself; and not just see her, but be close, talk to her, and watch her face for signs of the old Liberty.

"Well, Slater," Kate said when he knocked and slipped in the kitchen door, "this is a surprise."

Slater smiled. Not until he'd gotten very close to Liberty's mother had he discovered that she had a very subtle sense of humor. You had to spend a great amount of time with her to see it, but it was there.

"I just thought you might need me to sweep the floor or burn some trash."

Kate could barely keep from smiling. "Actually," she began, turning back to the pudding she was stirring in order to hide her gleaming eyes, "I was hoping you could dust the living room."

"I'll do it," he said, hoping she was only kidding but ready to do as she asked.

"Just go on through. I think you'll know what to do when you get there."

Slater did not waste any time. He left his hat by the door, smoothing his hair and trying to keep his pace normal as he went. Still, he must have been heard because Liberty's and Laura's faces were turned to him as soon as he stepped across the threshold.

"Slater!" Laura cried, launching herself in his direction.

Slater swung her up into his arms for a hug and kissed her small cheek.

"How are you today?"

"I'm very good. Libby and I are very good."

Slater finally let his eyes swing to where Liberty sat quietly on the sofa. She wore a black and white checked dress with tiny pink flowers running over the fabric. Her feet were on the footstool, and she had a thick quilt over her legs and lap. Slater moved toward her now, sitting in the chair closest to the sofa and fighting the urge to sit right beside her. He settled Laura in his lap and spoke.

"Do you agree with Laura's diagnosis? Are you very good?"

Liberty smiled. "Yes, I would say I am. I don't care to pull myself into a buggy or throw a ball, but I'm doing fine."

"You look wonderful," Slater said softly, his eyes not missing a thing, not even when her cheeks turned a little pink and she shifted her gaze to the window.

"Are you working today?" Liberty asked, her eyes and hands busy with the quilt now.

"Yes, I'm just taking a long lunch."

Liberty nodded. "How's Griff?"

"Doing fine. He had a meeting with the town council this morning. They've voted to hire more men. Griff is thinking about putting ads in the Austin papers to get a little more exposure."

Liberty smiled. "My mother still has the newspaper clipping from San Antonio that my father answered to get the job here."

"I'd like to see that."

"I can ask her," Laura volunteered, startling both adults. They had been so preoccupied with one another that Laura had been momentarily forgotten.

"That would be nice of you, Laura," Liberty said with a smile, not realizing the little girl meant to go right then. Not until she moved from the room did Liberty realize her mistake. She didn't feel emotionally ready to be alone with this man she still loved, but it was too late. She looked over to find his eyes on her and knew he was ready to speak.

Twenty-One

"I WANT TO THANK YOU," Liberty blurted before Slater could utter a word.

"Thank me?"

"Yes," Liberty nodded, still embarrassed and having a hard time meeting his eyes. "I never saw my actions for what they were. I was arrogant and untrusting. You helped me to see that. If I had it to do over again, I would do it differently. That's why I'm thanking you."

"When you were still laid up, my mind wandered and I had some moments when I feared you might hate me," Slater admitted. "All I ever wanted to do was protect you, but I think I came across as overbearing and stubborn."

"You were overbearing and stubborn at times, Slater, but it was over something you believed in. That makes complete sense to me now."

Slater had so much he wanted to say, but fell rather silent for a moment. The silence allowed Slater to hear Kate and Laura in the kitchen. It reminded him of how hard it was to find time alone with Liberty. For this reason, Slater moved forward a little bit in his chair, his forearms resting on the top of his thighs as he leaned closer.

"Every little thing about you fascinates me, "Slater surprised Liberty by saying. "I've never known a woman with such a wide range of talents, Libby, and I mean that. I can't tell you how my thoughts whirled to find the woman who'd pulled a gun on me in a saloon walking up the aisle to play the piano at church. And playing beautifully, I might add. Then at lunch, I see you helping with the meal.

"Added to that, you're a marvelous care giver. You love and take care of others so naturally. You take food to folks in need, you check on the older women in town like a loving daughter, you're like another pair of hands for your mother, and you cherish Laura and Zach as if they were your own.

"And each time I think of them losing you, I die a little inside. That's what I wrestle with every time you put on that gun. I want to take care of you, but with that gun you don't need me." Saying this, Slater saw Liberty go pale and wished he'd waited to speak of this.

"Libby," Slater said urgently, taking in her stricken face. "I'm sorry to have said this to you now. You've been hurt, and I shouldn't have tried—"

Liberty put her hand out to stop him, and Slater took it. She shook her head, and he held her hand in both of his and waited. He also prayed, hoping she would tell him her thoughts so he could make it right.

"I've always protected the people and the town I love, but you've given me much to think about, Slater. Don't ever apologize for that."

Did that mean . . . ? Slater found himself thinking, but was afraid to hope or ask the question aloud. It didn't, however, change the strong urge to gently take this woman in his arms and tell her he loved her. The thought was so powerful within him that his face flushed. He could only stare at her, which caused Liberty's own cheeks to redden before she looked away, gently reclaiming her hand just as Laura shot into the room.

"Libby, Mam wants to know if you want lunch in here or in the kitchen. We're having pudding," she added, as if this might be the deciding factor.

"I'll come to the table," Liberty told her, already moving the quilt from her lap.

Slater stood, ready to help, but other than moving very slowly, Liberty seemed totally normal. Slater wrestled with the things he'd said. Had it been too soon? Her words and actions would not indicate so, but he was still tempted to worry. What Slater didn't know was how good it had been for Liberty to be able to thank him. She didn't honestly believe that they would end up married, but she wanted him to know that he'd been a help in showing her how untrusting she'd been.

"Slater," Kate asked once they were seated, "will you pray for us?"

"Certainly. Father in heaven, we thank You for Your love and grace to us, for Your protecting hand and mercy. Thank You that Libby is able to be in the kitchen, moving on her own. Thank You for Kate, Laura, and the baby, and the special family You've put in this place.

Thank You for this wonderful food. I pray all this in Christ's holy name. Amen."

"You didn't thank God for yourself, Slater," Laura noted as soon as her eyes were open.

"Didn't I?" Slater asked as he took a roll and passed the basket to Liberty.

"No. Don't you thank God for you?"

"Well," Slater replied as he thought about this, "I thank God for everything He's done for me. Does that help?"

"I think so," she said, her brow lowered in that intense way he loved.

"You could thank God for Slater," Kate suggested.

Laura nodded, her mouth moving as she chewed but again looking very thoughtful. She swallowed, opened her mouth to say something about being thankful if Liberty and Slater got married, but suddenly caught her big sister's eye.

"Oh," she said softly, shutting her mouth.

"Oh, what?" Kate asked innocently.

Laura looked so uncertain that her mother dropped it. Not having to think long before understanding dawned, Kate went back to her plate without looking at Slater or Liberty.

Liberty cast a sidelong look at her sister and one at Slater. If he suspected anything, he was hiding it very well.

Suddenly Libby was tired. It was enough for her body to work on healing without adding emotions to the mix. But what else could she feel when Slater was in the room? Her sigh was more internal than anything else, but heartfelt nonetheless. She continued to eat, listening to what Kate had to say about plans for the day but also asking God to help her survive the emotions running through her. Right now she didn't think she would.

🌹 🌹 🌹

"You're grinning again today like you did yesterday," Griffin commented the next morning. "Are you planning another long lunch?"

"No, I won't need much time," Slater said, still looking like the cat with the cream.

"Going back to talk to her?"

"*Talk to her?*" Slater replied, looking surprised. "I'm not going to talk, I'm going to tell her she has to marry me and that's the end of it."

Griffin laughed. "I take it Dakota was on your trail before he left."

"As if I needed him," Slater said with a shake of his head. "But he did threaten to ask for me if I didn't do the job soon. I wanted to ask her yesterday if she'll marry me and let me take care of her."

"She's sure healing fast. Duff is very pleased."

"She looks wonderful," Slater said quietly, his eyes on nothing in particular. Griffin couldn't stop his smile as he studied the other man. He felt as though he'd waited a long time for a Slater Rawlings to walk in the door. Slater was a man who would love his sister and appreciate the woman she was. Griffin understood now why Slater had never wanted Liberty to pack a gun. His own relationship with Tess had been a big help to him on that too, and they were both thankful that Slater had never stopped loving Liberty.

Both men were needed before Slater could get away for lunch, but that didn't change Slater's thoughts, or Griffin's for that matter. Just as soon as there was a break and Griffin told Slater he could spare him, Slater went to the Petersons', his mind on what he intended to say. Griffin watched him go, somehow feeling a burden to pray for his sister. She'd been through quite a bit since Slater Rawlings rode into town. Griffin only hoped she was still thinking clearly enough to know a good man when he was standing in front of her.

⚘ ⚘ ⚘

Slater found Liberty in the living room again, this time alone. She appeared to be hemming a dress. She did look up to greet him but immediately bent back over her work. This time he sat right next to her.

"What's this?" Slater asked, lifting the fabric a little.

"A dress of Laura's. Mam was smart enough to make it big, but now the hem has to come down."

"She's growing fast. I can just see her in school this fall."

"It'll be awfully quiet around here."

Slater didn't comment. His eyes were on her profile, and he stared until she looked at him.

Liberty was so surprised by the warm look in his eyes that she didn't look away.

"Marry me," he ordered softly.

Surprised as she was, Liberty shook her head. "You don't have to do this, Slater."

It took Slater a moment to figure out what she meant, and when he did, he said, "Let me get this straight. I feel guilty about the way I handled things at the Potters', so now I'm proposing to make up for it?"

"Something like that," Liberty admitted.

"So you don't love me?" he asked, putting everything on the line.

"I didn't say that," Liberty said swiftly before going back to her needle.

Silence hung heavily between them, and Liberty had all she could do not to howl when she shoved the needle into her thumb. Finally, she chanced a look in his direction and found him still watching her, a tender smile on his face.

"So your answer is no?" he clarified.

"That's right."

A large smile crossed his features.

"What does that mean?" Liberty had to ask.

"If you're talking about the smile, I was just thinking of how fun it's going to be to convince you." He leaned close before adding in a whisper, "And don't forget, Liberty Kathleen, I'm a very patient man."

Liberty's mouth swung open as he pushed to his feet, bent to kiss her cheek, put his hat on, told her he would see her later, and walked from the room. No one looking at Slater Rawlings as he made his way back to the sheriff's office would have believed that his proposal had been turned down—least of all Griffin—who stood in anticipation when he was back so soon.

"She must have said yes," Griffin began.

"On the contrary—she turned me down flat."

Griffin hesitated. The smile on the blond man's face belied those words, but something told Griffin they were true.

"Why did she say no?"

"Because she thinks I only asked out of guilt."

"Guilt about what?"

"The way I treated her at the Potter place."

Griffin was so stunned that he sat back down. He thought for a moment and then offered, "Do you want me to talk to her?"

"There's no need," Slater said calmly. "I'll talk her around."

Griffin could see that he meant it and decided to leave well enough alone. Not long after, he went home for his own lunch, prayers for Slater and his sister filling his heart.

Slater, not at all sorry to be on his own, also thought of Liberty and prayed for her. He could tell that her mind was made up, but that didn't daunt him in the least. Indeed, he smiled again now and rocked back on his heels, just thinking about how swiftly she went back to her sewing when he asked if she loved him.

"Oh, yes, Libby," Slater said to the empty office as he sat down at the desk to get back to work. "I'll get around you. Just see if I don't."

🌹 🌹 🌹

"You're awfully quiet tonight, Lib," Duffy said that evening. The children were in bed, and the three adults sat in the living room. "How are you feeling?"

"All right. I moved a little suddenly today and regretted that, but other than the itching, it's not bad."

"I noticed that when Slater was here today," Kate put in, her head bent over some needlework, "he looked like a man with a mission."

"He wants to marry me," Liberty informed them.

Both Duffy, who had been reading the paper, and Kate froze and then looked at her.

"You don't seem too excited," Duffy mentioned carefully.

"I turned him down."

Kate could not control herself. Tears filled her eyes, and she looked across at Liberty.

"I'm sorry, Mam," Liberty whispered. "I didn't know it would hurt you."

"It's not me, Libby." Kate's voice was just as hushed. "I thought you loved Slater."

"I do. I love him like I've never loved anyone, but I think he just feels bad about what happened. I can't have him thinking he's in love when all he feels is guilt."

Liberty's face held an expression her parents had never seen before. She seemed so vulnerable that it shook them terribly. Not for anything would they scold her or try to convince her that Slater did in fact love her. They both believed he did, but this had to come from her heart, not theirs.

"Follow your heart," Duffy said, needing to voice the words. "We think Slater is a fine man, but if you're doubting, Libby girl, don't let anyone rush you anywhere."

"Thank you, Duffy."

Kate smiled at her. Her eyes were still suspiciously moist, but she was able to agree with her spouse. "It's a big step, Libby. A woman would be a fool to start out with doubts."

Liberty nodded, but even as her mother said the word *doubts*, she began to struggle with her own. Maybe she was being too hard on Slater. After all, he'd showed her that he cared long before the Potter incident.

"I think I'll head up," Liberty said, not needing to feign exhaustion in an effort to be alone. She was remarkably weary. As she readied for bed, Slater came to mind again. Liberty thought how nice it would be to have him there, talking to her or maybe helping with the buttons on her dress or the pins in her hair. Tears poured down her face as she changed clothes and climbed beneath the covers. She was too tired to do anything more than cry and ask the Lord if she would ever survive this.

❧ ❧ ❧

"Did you say painting the fence out by the barn?" Slater asked Kate just two days later.

"Yes."

Slater stared at the woman, waiting for her to laugh in jest. That didn't happen.

"Why is she doing that?" Slater asked.

Kate looked hesitant but eventually admitted, "I think she needs to keep busy right now."

Again Slater thought. "Is that your way of saying she's having second thoughts about saying no to me?"

Kate bit her lip. "I don't know that for certain, Slater, but I think she prefers to be shot again rather than hurt you or be hurt by you. She's going to have to keep busy to pull that off."

Slater's eyes narrowed. He looked so much like Dakota just then that Kate missed the older Rawlings terribly and prayed for him wherever he was.

"I think I'll go out to see her."

"All right. Send Laura in if you need to."

The deputy nodded, thanked her, and moved out the door. While he was still a way off, he spotted them, both with their backs to the house, Liberty in an old dress, her right arm moving slowly with the brush, Laura talking sixteen to the dozen beside her. Slater could see how easy it would be to keep her back to him, so he circled the barn and came up opposite Liberty, looking at her over the top of the fence.

"Hi," he said, startling her a little.

"Hello," she said and smiled some, but the greeting appeared strained.

"What made you decide to paint?"

"The fence has needed it for a while," Laura put in, and Liberty smiled down at her.

"Does this hurt your side, Libby?" Slater asked.

"No. I couldn't do it if I was left-handed, but it's not bad."

He wanted to ask what Duffy thought of the idea but chose not to baby her.

"Laura," Kate called from the house, "Josie Frank is here to see you."

"Oh, Libby! Oh, Libby," the little girl flapped, "I have to go."

"That's all right. I'll just keep painting."

Laura took off then, and Slater smiled as he watched her dress and hair fly.

"She takes good care of you."

"Yes, she does."

They fell quiet then, Slater leaning against the fence as though he had all day, his whole head showing over the top as he watched Liberty work. She was starting to grow nervous under his gaze and finally frowned, wishing she could think of some snappy thing to say. Slater went first.

"I never thought about how cute you would look with paint on your eyelashes and cheek."

Liberty shot a look at him and said, "Did you come by for some special reason, Slater?"

"Only to tell you that I love you."

Liberty nearly dropped the brush.

"It's the silliest thing," Slater went on conversationally. "You know I want to marry you and take care of you, but not how much I love you. I get things switched around sometimes."

Liberty began to paint as though she were under the gun. She told herself not to look up but to get the job done and get inside. She worked along steadily for some time and finally chanced a glance at Slater. He was gone.

Liberty's head whipped around, but he was not in sight. It was time to paint the lower half of the section she was in, so Liberty dropped to her knees. However, the brush didn't move for quite some time, and Liberty got more paint on her face attempting to wipe away the tears that she couldn't seem to stop.

¾ ¾ ¾

Liberty told herself to breathe. She had survived not being able to play the piano in church the day before and hadn't broken down, even when Slater came to sit by her. She told herself that if she could just keep busy, she would make it. Then Monday came, and she went to get the mail. Why she opened Dakota's letter just outside the building, she didn't know, but she had, and now she must find Slater.

The jailhouse was empty. She thought about heading to Hathaways' house but was fairly certain he wouldn't still be there. She had just decided to go ask Tess if she knew where Griffin was so, she could ask him about Slater, when the door opened and the man she loved stepped in.

"Hi," he said warmly, a smile coming to his face the moment he saw her. He came close but didn't try to speak. Liberty's face looked strained, and he thought she might cry if he touched her.

"You see, it's like this," Liberty began with no warning. "I just like you so much, Slater." Tears came to her eyes, but she kept on. "I have from the start. I don't know when that turned to love, but it did, and it just won't go away. But all my love, Slater, doesn't change the fear, this horrible terror inside of me, that you only feel obligated."

"I don't Libby," Slater clarified. "I promise you."

"That's what Dakota said," she told him as she handed him the letter.

Slater read, *Dear Libby, nothing would induce Slater to marry a woman out of guilt. He's always loved you. Never forget that. Dakota.*

Slater looked down at her, his heart in his eyes. "I can't tell you how true this is, Libby. I love you so much. I ache with what I feel. I wish I could have done things differently at the Potters', if only to convince you that for weeks now, I've known you were the one."

"Oh, Slater." Liberty wanted to stop crying but couldn't. "Please ask me again."

Slater's arms were around her before she saw him coming.

"Marry me?"

"Yes."

He held her gently, so very careful of her side. Liberty would have raised both arms to hold him close but could only manage one. Slater kissed her sweetly, first her soft cheek and then her mouth.

"I love you, Libby. Don't you ever forget it."

"I won't, Slater, but you can remind me anytime you want."

Slater had to laugh. The only thing fuller than his arms right now was his heart, and that was fair to bursting.

You did it, Lord, his heart cried in joy as he held Liberty with the utmost care. *I didn't know how and I didn't know when. I only knew You would. I'll spend the rest of my days thanking You for this miracle You performed on my behalf.*

$$\mathcal{Epilogue}$$

June 1882

THE TELEGRAM READ: *Dakota hurt. Come swiftly. D. Curtis.* Slater had left for Desmond's house within the hour. Now, a week later, he moved swiftly toward Duffy and Kate's, one thought on his mind: seeing his wife.

It was getting late. Darkness was falling fast, but Slater took little notice. He heeled Arrow to just short of a run as he moved toward the home his in-laws were sharing with them until he and his wife could find a place, his heart hoping he would find Liberty on her own.

Slater took Arrow back to the barn, stabled him as swiftly as he could, and walked in ground-eating strides toward the kitchen door. All he could do was smile and lean against the door when he found Liberty at the kitchen table, a recipe book open in front of her. She was bent over reading something and took a moment to look up to see who had entered. An instant later she flew into his arms.

"I missed you," she said as soon as she could breathe.

Slater wanted only to kiss her again.

"How's Dakota?" she finally got out.

"Hurt bad," Slater said as he led her to a chair, sat in it, and invited her to sit in his lap. "He's lost a lot of blood, and he'll be at Desmond's place for a while, but he's strong. And the best news of all, Libby," Slater added, "he came to Christ."

"Oh, Slater!"

"It's true. Cash was there too. Dakota told us he's never been so scared. The bullets just kept coming, and he knew he couldn't do a thing. He said that he's never before seen how lost he was, and at that moment was completely terrified of dying. He talked to Desmond as soon as he woke up, but not until Cash and I got there did he tell anyone he was ready to talk to the Lord."

"Oh, Slater." Liberty hugged him tightly. "I've been praying and praying. I must admit that I thought the Lord might use this injury in Dakota's life, but I didn't know how completely."

Slater's sigh was heartfelt. "You should have seen his face, Lib. He looked so at peace. He's a shot-up mess, but all the fear and defensiveness are gone." Slater couldn't go on. He was suddenly too choked up to speak. He and Liberty sat quietly together until Slater heard a noise. It sounded like a tiny baby's cry.

"What was that?" Slater asked, wondering if Zach and Laura had gotten a kitten.

Liberty grinned hugely. "That's my baby sister."

Slater's mouth fell open. "Your mother had her baby?"

Liberty still grinned. "Last night, just before midnight. Come see her."

Slater was in a state of shock as Liberty led him to the living room. It was empty, save for the small person in the cradle, who was just starting to make noise.

"Well, now," she said tenderly as she scooped up the light bundle, "did you think we'd all forgotten you? You have to wake up and meet your big brother-in-law." Liberty bounced her a little and coaxed, "Come on, Jeanette, wake up and talk to us."

Liberty and Slater laughed when the baby would have none of it. She turned her face toward Liberty and went back to sleep. The three of them sat on the sofa then, and Slater took Jeanette in his arms.

"I've never seen anything so perfect," he said as he lifted her tiny hand and examined each finger. Jeanette's tiny head was beautifully shaped and covered with soft, dark fuzz. She was feather-light to hold, and for a time Slater was transfixed with this precious infant.

"How's your mother?" he suddenly remembered to ask.

"Doing great. Up and around already and feeling strong. Duffy's plan is for her to take it easy on the stairs—only two trips down a day—so I'll be bringing Jeanette down here with me so Mam can sleep and not think she's hearing the baby cry all the time."

Their eyes went back to the baby then, and for a time they just watched her. Jeanette's next cry was a real one. In no time at all, she was awake and howling, obviously ready to be fed. Liberty took her upstairs to Kate and then rejoined her husband on the sofa. They had not been apart since they'd been married in April. They spent some time catching up, both glad for a little time alone.

"We could have one of our own," Slater offered, his arms holding Liberty tightly.

"Indeed. I'm all for it," Liberty said with a smile.

Slater moved to kiss her, accidently bumping her nose.

"I'm sorry," he apologized.

Liberty shrugged it off, saying, "My aim has always been better."

Slater couldn't hold his laughter. Indeed, he was still laughing when Liberty kissed him, and as he expected, her aim was perfect.

LORI WICK

A Texas Sky

HARVEST HOUSE PUBLISHERS

EUGENE, OREGON

Scripture references are taken from the King James Version of the Bible.

Cover design by Dugan Design Group, Bloomington, Minnesota

A TEXAS SKY
Copyright © 2000 by Lori Wick
Published by Harvest House Publishers
Eugene, Oregon 97402

ISBN-13: 978-0-7394-9555-1

Printed in the United States of America.

Acknowledgments

I had such fun with this book, during which many lives touched my own. This page is to thank...

Merry Hahn. Thank you for letting me borrow the spelling of your name. You, Norm, and the kids are so precious to our family. We thank God for you. May we long serve Christ together, honing and sharpening each other as the Word commands.

Mary Vesperman. This is the one that fell apart, Mary. Thank you, dear friend, for giving me permission to start over. When all is said and done, I think this was the best work. God bless you.

Diane Barsness. It's so fun to have a friend who loves a good romance and laughs in all the right places. Thanks for being there on days when I wonder if I'm going to survive parenthood. Our friendship is such a good reminder that through God's help, our mothers did.

The Caminiti kids. Thank you for being great friends to our gang. Your examples do not go unnoticed. No matter where your paths lead, I pray that all of you will walk strong in obedience and trust in our saving God.

My Bob. The vocabulary lessons never end. From *constabulary* to *coffers*, from *tertiary* to *tributary*, thank you for always bringing in new words, explaining them with clarity and patience, and expanding my world in this small way. Of all the things you say, however, my favorite is about your love for me. We don't live under a Texas sky, but my Wisconsin sky would be very small without you.

Prologue

June 1882
Wellsville, Texas

"HOW IS HE?" MARTY BRACEWELL ASKED anxiously as he entered the bedroom, not remembering to remove his hat or offer any of the standard greetings.

"Doing a little better," Desmond Curtis said. "Slate and Cash were just here, and although Dakota's as weak as a girl, he's in a good frame of mind." Desmond, knowing how Brace would feel if he knew the whole truth, did not elaborate, but he knew that Dakota was doing as well as he was because of how significant his brothers' visit had been.

"Hey, Dak," Brace said softly, watching the Ranger's eyes come open a little. As a point in fact, all three men were Texas Rangers, but only one of them had nearly bled to death from numerous gunshot wounds, and he was still very injured.

"Hi, Brace," Dakota tried to say, but his mouth was too dry. Desmond helped him with a drink, but they had to go slowly—they would probably have to go slowly for a long time.

"Sorry I took so long. I was up north and just got back."

"It's all right," Dakota managed.

"What happened out there?" Brace asked, not really expecting an answer. Dakota tried anyway.

"I thought I had the jump on them, but there were more men than I figured. I went down fast. Had no choice."

Brace felt his throat close. This man was one of his best. To see him shot-up and helpless was hard. He cleared his throat, telling himself this was no time for tears.

"You'll be back soon, ornery as ever."

"No doubt," the man in the bed agreed, a small smile coming to his lips. "I'll see you in a few weeks."

Brace was suddenly angry. That this would happen to one of his best infuriated him!

"If you so much as show your face near my office inside of six months, I'll shoot you myself," Brace warned. "And I mean it!"

Dakota could only nod. Right now six months sounded too soon. Sleep was coming in again, but that was all right. For the first time in his life, Dakota James Rawlings had Someone he could talk to.

ৡৡৡ

Dakota heard gunshots a few days later, as real as the ones that had taken him down. His eyes flew open and he gasped, remembering with painful clarity where he was.

"Easy…" Desmond's voice came softly to his ears, and Dakota turned to find him sitting next to the bed.

Dakota tried to tell Desmond he was thirsty but couldn't manage it. Thankfully the older Ranger knew the signs. He lifted a cup for the injured man. Dakota thanked him with a slight raise of his hand, amazed at how spent he was.

"Better?"

"Yeah. Is it hot in here, or is it me?"

"Both I would guess. It is June."

Dakota nodded a little, and Desmond thought he would fall right back to sleep. Drained as he seemed, Dakota's eyes stayed on a far-away spot on the wall, and he began to speak.

"Do you know what I thought of when everything started to go black?"

"No. What?"

"Something Slate said to me," Dakota said as he licked his lips. "Of all the things to remember, I recall something he said when I was angry." Dakota's mind went back to a cloudy day in Shotgun. As the result of a senseless shooting, a woman had just been buried. At the funeral Dakota thought they should have talked about the woman and not about God.

"What did you want Pastor Caron to say, Dak?" his brother asked him. "What would you have deemed appropriate?"

"A little more about the woman herself, for starters. He turned it into a sermon!"

"She was a changed person because of her faith."

Dakota's eyes narrowed, telling Slater he was not happy with that answer, but his brother went on anyway.

"If I'm a different person because of my beliefs, Dakota, and if I were to die, I would want other people to know they could have the same hope. Maybe you should be listening instead of criticizing."

"My life is fine!" Dakota did not hesitate to clarify.

"If that's true, then why does this have you so upset? If everything is fine, you should be able to shrug this off and go on with your life."

Dakota's eyes now met Desmond's.

"In so many words, Slater said it shouldn't bother me if I didn't believe as he did—but it didn't work that way. It bothered me so much, I left angry."

"So the turning point came when Slate and Cash were here?"

Much as it hurt, Dakota's chest lifted with his sigh. "My very last thought before I lost consciousness was that I had waited too long. When I woke up and they were sitting here, I knew I'd been given a second chance." Another sigh escaped the injured man. "As you well know, I've been a fool many times, but not this time. I grabbed that second chance."

Desmond had a comment on his mind, but he could see that it was going to have to wait.

"Do you think he can eat something?" Geneva Curtis asked from the doorway.

"No," her husband answered with a shake of his head. "He just slipped back out."

Geneva came and stood close, her hand on Desmond's shoulder.

"He will make it, won't he, Des?"

"I think so," that man replied with his eyes on Dakota's face. "As Dak just put it, he's been given a second chance. I've been wrong before, but something tells me he'll get out of this bed and want to know everything God has ever said—and in the first hour, if I can tell him."

Geneva chuckled softly and exited the room ahead of her husband. Her only thought was *Look out, Texas, Dakota Rawlings is nearly on the loose.*

One

July 1882

IF YOU SO MUCH AS SHOW YOUR FACE NEAR my office inside of six months, I'll shoot you myself.

Sitting alone by the window, Dakota Rawlings remembered the words of his supervisor from just a month earlier and sat back, a thoughtful frown between his brows. He didn't know if he could stand five more months of inactivity. When Brace had first uttered these words, it had been an emotional time. Dakota had been certain he hadn't meant a literal six months, but his first letter—telling Brace when he thought he could come back—was hotly returned in a no-nonsense way.

Dakota's hosts, Desmond and Geneva Curtis, were out at the moment, so the house in Wellsville was quiet. Their home sat right in the middle of town, but the street was not a busy one, and for a moment, Dakota thought he was very much alone. He'd just eaten a large lunch and still had half a cup of coffee to drink, but he was not particularly eager to continue sitting at the window.

As a new believer in Jesus Christ, he'd spent almost two hours studying the Bible that morning and had understood some new truths. Desmond had been a great help in this area, and Dakota was still amazed at how pertinent the Bible was to his life right now. Not many months back, he would have said that old Book was outdated and unrealistic. He was learning every day just how wrong he'd been.

Knowing he did not want the rest of the coffee, Dakota went to the sink, rinsed out his mug, and wandered onto the front porch. It was blistering hot, much as it was every day at this time. That was Texas in July—something they all had to live with.

He wrote a quick note and took himself out for a walk. It was too hot to be out for long, but he had to stretch his legs. He hadn't planned to feel this good. Only five weeks ago he'd been shot so badly they thought he would die, but God had had other ideas.

"I shot you first," a child's voice yelled from nearby. Dakota turned to see two little boys scoot up the alley, firing sticks at each other. Though he hoped they would never actually experience that pain, he nevertheless found himself smiling at their antics. He continued slowly up the street and turned right onto the main street of town.

Interesting as the storefronts were, Dakota was beginning to sweat. He thought he might have overdone and should turn back, but his sister-in-law had celebrated a birthday a few weeks ago, and he hadn't sent her anything. Not that he'd been in any shape to do that.

"What are you doing out here?" Desmond suddenly spoke as he came up behind Dakota.

Dakota turned with innocent eyes. "Just strolling."

Feeling like a father, Desmond pointed back up the street. "Get home!"

Worried as she was to see Dakota's pale face, Geneva laughed from her place beside her husband.

"You sounded as if you were scolding the dog."

Dakota laughed as well, but he did want to shop for Liberty, who was married to his younger brother, Slater. He said as much to the Curtises.

"As if Libby will be expecting anything with the way you were hurt," Geneva said with a mild shake of her head.

"Even a firecracker would do the trick, Gen. She was born on the Fourth."

"And she'll enjoy a late gift," Desmond said, his hand to the younger man's arm as he turned and directed him back up the boardwalk.

Dakota wanted to argue, but he was suddenly feeling very warm and weak. By the time he reached the house, he was sweating profusely, and two of the bullet wounds were starting to burn. Geneva brought him a cool drink of water and waited for him to lie down on the sofa.

"It looks as though you need to give it more time, Dak. I'm sorry."

Dakota sighed. "I guess I could write to Libby."

"She would probably enjoy that, but even as little as I know her, I can't think she would expect anything from you at this point."

Dakota nodded and thanked his hostess, who returned to the kitchen, and then let his mind drift backward to when Geneva had met Liberty Drake, now Liberty Rawlings.

The wedding had been on Saturday, April 22. The whole family had gathered, including his parents, who had come all the way from St. Louis. Special friends like Desmond and Geneva Curtis and Marty Bracewell had also been invited. Closing his eyes, Dakota could still see how pretty Liberty looked in her dress, her eyes shining with love for Slater as her stepfather, Duffy Peterson, walked her down the aisle.

He and Cash, Dakota's older brother, had both known that Slater would be the first to fall. They were only thankful that he'd found a girl like Liberty. Dakota thought that if another Liberty could be found, he too might be tempted to marry. Almost as soon as the thought materialized, he pushed it away. His was not a job that was suited to family life. Hours on the trail, uncertain pay, and the dangers of being a Texas Ranger played hard in his mind. Desmond had made it work, but a career in the Rangers had its drawbacks. The fact that the Curtises had never been able to have children had been a factor.

Suddenly Dakota wanted to get up. He felt lazy, as though his not trying hard enough was slowing the healing process. But wanting to get up and actually doing it were proving to be two different matters.

Just help me, Lord, Dakota prayed. *Just help me to rest and give it some more time—even a few weeks.* Dakota fell asleep while still wondering what he would do with himself in the months to come.

ॐ ॐ ॐ

August

Dakota could not believe the difference just four weeks had made. He was feeling very strong. His last little escapade had set him back, but as he left the church with Desmond and Geneva for the second week in a row, that incident was already receding from his thoughts. His mind was on the sermon for some of the ride back to the house, but Dakota waited only until they sat down to eat Sunday dinner to tell his hosts what was really in his thoughts.

"I need to thank both of you for your care and hospitality, but I have some good news for you."

Desmond looked up from cutting his meat.

"A statement like that could mean only one of two things," the older Ranger began. "Either you're pulling out soon, or one of the women who were falling over themselves to catch your eye this morning did in fact catch your eye, and you're getting married."

Dakota had a good laugh before saying, "The first one is correct."

"Where are you headed?" Geneva wished to know.

"Back to work," Dakota replied calmly while buttering a piece of bread with complete ease.

"I thought you said Brace didn't want you for the full six months."

"That's right.

"But you're going anyway?"

"Yep."

"And what of Brace?" Desmond asked.

Dakota smiled his slow, warm way. "He'll get over it."

Knowing how much Marty Bracewell liked to have his own way, Geneva enjoyed a good laugh over this.

The next morning, however, her laughter was not to be found. Tears welled in her eyes as she hugged their guest. Dakota had come to Christ under their roof and grown so much in the few months they'd had with him. She could have easily had him stay on.

"Thanks, Gen. Thanks, Des."

"You know the door is always open" were Desmond's parting words to the young Ranger.

Husband and wife stood together as he rode away, Geneva with a hankie to her face and Desmond watching for signs of hurt or discomfort. Not that he actually expected to see any—Dakota was as tough as they came—but he was concerned too, and missing him already.

"Will he be all right?" Geneva asked, her eyes still on the dark figure as he rounded a corner and moved from sight.

Desmond slipped an arm around her.

"Don't forget who indwells him now, Gen. He'll be more all right than he's ever been before."

❧ ❧ ❧

Austin, Texas

Marty Bracewell entered his office as he did most mornings, sat at his desk, and began to open the mail; it was always a large stack. As a Ranger, Marty had traveled extensively for many years, but now he kept the home office fires burning. He kept track of new men, deaths, countless details, and payroll for the area. It wasn't that he never went out on patrol, but most weeks he was needed at the office.

"What in the world?" Brace was muttering over some confusing correspondence when the door opened and someone stepped inside. He looked up to see a familiar face and smiled in delight.

"You must be feeling better," he said as he stood and came around the desk.

Darvi Leigh Wingate warmly accepted her uncle's embrace and smiled into his eyes when he stepped back.

Darvi was a smallish strawberry blonde who appeared more frail than she actually was. However, this time she had been very ill. She had come by train and stagecoach all the way from St. Louis, and had picked up an illness en route. For the first few days of her visit she had been laid up in bed, miserably achy and sick to her stomach.

"I do feel better," she admitted with conviction, taking a chair when the Ranger returned to his desk. "For a few days there I was dreadfully sorry I had come, but now I'm raring to go."

"Where are you headed first?"

"To the bank and then to see Merry. Did you need anything? I'd be glad to pick it up." Darvi had asked the question, but Brace didn't answer. He sat staring at his niece for several seconds, his face uncertain.

"What is it, Uncle Marty?"

"She's married now, Darv. Didn't you know that?"

"Merry? Of course I knew. She was engaged when I last saw her."

"She's also moved away. She and the doc moved about six months after the wedding."

Now it was Darvi's turn to stare.

"She doesn't live in Austin?"

He slowly shook his head. "Up in the hills. A small town outside of Blake called Stillwater."

Darvi continued to stare, her mouth slightly agape. This couldn't be true. She'd been dying to see her friend for close to three months and only now was able to make time to come to Austin. How could this have happened?

"I can't believe it," she muttered softly.

"It's been four years since you've visited, Darv. A lot can change in that time."

Her shoulders drooped a little.

"Yes, they can, and we never tried to stay in touch outside of my visits. There was never a need. We were always able to pick up right where we left off."

"I'm sorry, Darv. I wish you had known."

It took Darvi only a moment to see the sadness in his eyes. In the next instant her chin tipped up. "I'll just go to her," she said, standing up as though leaving on the spot.

Brace was already shaking his head. "I don't have time to take you, and you—"

"You don't have to," Darvi cut him off. "I can get there; you know I can."

"Don't even think about it," Brace said in a voice he'd have used with his men. "I won't even discuss it."

"Uncle Marty, when are you going to realize I'm not 16 anymore?" She threw her arms up and flopped back down on the wooden seat. "For that matter," she muttered, "when are you going to face the fact that I'm not 20 anymore?"

But Brace was still shaking his head no.

"You know I can make it!" she tried again.

"I'm not willing to let you try."

"Why can't you take me? I'll just make it a quick visit. We can't be talking about more than two days on the trail, if that."

"I don't have time. I wish I did, Darvi, but my boss is coming into town, and I can't be gone when he arrives."

"When is he coming?"

"Sometime next week."

"And that's all the more specific he could be? Men!"

Brace leaned back in his chair, a big smile on his face.

"What is that grin about?"

"Oh, nothing much. Only about a niece who said she was coming back every summer and hasn't been here in four years." Brace nodded sagely. "Yes, indeed, women are much better about saying when they'll arrive and then coming on time."

Darvi stood, working hard to hide her smile.

"I believe I'll be going on my way now, since all you can do is insult me."

"Are you going to be around at lunch?" Brace asked, knowing she was not really angry.

"That all depends."

"On what?"

"On whether I've found someone to take me to Merry's or not."

The smile she gave him could have melted butter in the snow, but he knew the steel in that little backbone of hers—just like her mother's. He didn't let himself laugh, however, until she exited and shut the door in her wake.

🌿🌿🌿

Dakota hit Austin hot, dirty, and sore. There was no doubt in his mind that his first stop would be Brace's office, but from there he was headed for a bath. The dark cowboy rode easily up the familiar street only an hour past noon, stopped in front of the office, and didn't so much as wince when he climbed painfully from the saddle.

Brace's back was to him when he entered the sparse room, but that didn't change Dakota's routine. He pushed his hat back on his head, turned the chair around as he always did, and straddled it. This done, he waited for Brace to turn and acknowledge him.

Brace knew someone had come in behind him, but he'd lost a file that morning and was determined to find it. He wasn't usually so rude to folks who entered and decided he had best say something.

"I'll be with you in a moment," he called over his shoulder.

"Don't hurry on my account."

The sound of that voice caused the older man to stop. He turned slowly from the file cabinet and speared Dakota with his angry gaze. The seated Ranger looked back with a calm that was genuine.

"*What* are you doing here?"

"Coming back to work."

"I told you I didn't want to see you for six months."

"I don't need six months."

"I say you do."

The old Dakota would have stood and gone back to work without a word of apology. The new Dakota debated his next move. He wasn't certain of too many things right now, but lying low for another four months was not something he needed. He tried a new tack.

"So what you're telling me is that you have so many Rangers that you can let men sit around for months at a time."

Brace came to the desk and sat across from Dakota, his eyes thoughtful as they watched him.

"If you still feel good in another month, I'll put you back on."

"And what am I supposed to do for another month?"

"As a matter of fact, I have a personal favor to ask you. It won't take a month, but it should put you closer to home where you can go and lie low until the end of September."

Dakota was not the least bit interested in lying low, but he figured once he'd done the personal favor, he could talk Brace around.

"What's the favor?" he asked, knowing it didn't matter; he would do whatever Brace needed.

"Can you escort my niece to Stillwater?"

"Darvi?" Dakota guessed, knowing she used to visit every summer. He'd even met her one year.

"Yes. A friend of hers moved, and she wants to see her."

"Certainly. When does she want to leave?"

"Probably next week, but I'll ask her."

Dakota nodded.

"And until then," Brace said unyieldingly, "you can just enjoy the sights of Austin. If I see you working, I'll shoot you myself."

Dakota knew he had no choice, but he didn't like it. Fighting the urge to say more, he stood.

"I'm headed to get a bath."

"All right. Why don't you come to dinner some night? You name the day."

Dakota nodded. "I'll get back to you."

Brace watched him leave, looking for signs of injury. He wouldn't have admitted it for the world, but it looked to him as though Dakota was right: He was ready to come back to work.

❧ ❧ ❧

Darvi's attempt to find an escort to Stillwater was proving fruitless. For a time she had traversed the streets of Austin, hoping to find an advertisement or anything that might indicate a guide service, but she knew such possibilities were remote.

From her place in Austin's reading room, Darvi looked out the window and told herself this was not going to work. *But I don't know what else to do,* she then answered herself. *I can't exactly walk the streets looking for a man to hire—Uncle Marty would have a fit. But I'm feeling just about that desperate.*

Just about ready to give up and open a book that had caught her eye when she came in, she spotted him. Darvi was willing to bet her grandmother's inheritance that he was a Ranger. She'd certainly spent enough time around her uncle to spot the type. Not even remembering to replace the book to the shelf, Darvi came to her feet as gracefully as speed would allow and made a beeline for the door.

❧ ❧ ❧

Dakota knew he was being followed, but he wasn't overly concerned. After all, the streets were fairly crowded and the bathhouse was on a main street. Still, there was no doubt that he heard footsteps that matched his own. And unless he missed his guess, it was the light tread of a woman. He let it go a few seconds longer before stopping and slowly turning around. Sure enough, about ten yards behind him, a woman stopped as well.

"Did you need something?" he asked politely, removing his hat.

"No," she answered softly, but everything in her voice and manner said the opposite.

"Are you all right?"

This time she only nodded and looked away, clearly embarrassed.

Dakota studied her for a moment, replaced his hat, and turned back on his way. He nearly shook his head when she continued behind him.

Thinking she was simply going his way, and not wanting to make her feel awkward, he left it alone. Not until he was ready to walk up the steps of the bathhouse did he let himself look again. What he saw stopped him. The woman—quite pretty he could see from this distance—was even closer and staring right at him.

"Are you certain you're all right?"

"You are a Texas Ranger, aren't you?" the woman suddenly blurted.

"Yes, ma'am. Is there something I can do?"

Dakota watched her composure slip a little more before she visibly gathered her courage and went on.

"Do your duties happen to take you into the hills very often?"

"The hills, ma'am?" Dakota asked, completely at sea.

"Yes. I have a need to go to Stillwater, and I'm looking for someone to escort me."

Dakota had all he could do not to react, asking himself if this could actually be Darvi. Gone was the child he'd met years ago, and Dakota was left wondering how long it had been.

"You see," she tried again, this time catching herself and now standing like a woman in command, "it's rather important that I go to Stillwater. I'm terribly sorry to accost you on the street in this way, but I thought if you were to be traveling in those parts, I could accompany you and give my family ease about my travel."

Dakota was on the verge of telling her exactly who he was and that he had already been asked to see her there when gunshots were fired down the street.

"Will you excuse me a moment?" he said to the woman without hesitation as he turned and ran that way.

Gun pulled and ready, Dakota hurried toward the sound, which took him between two buildings and onto a side street. He heard shouting as he moved and sure enough, as soon as he spotted the commotion, which appeared to be a woman with a shotgun, he also spotted two officers. Even though the woman still had the gun, the men seemed to have the situation under control. Glad not to be pressed into duty just then, Dakota holstered his weapon and walked back toward the bathhouse.

Long before Dakota reached his destination, he could see that the street was empty. He debated getting back to Brace right then so that he could get word to his niece, but a spark of mischief lit inside him. He would certainly have to let Brace know that he *would* be coming for dinner. The sooner the better.

Two

DAKOTA THOUGHT HE MIGHT BE MORE comfortable at the board-inghouse, but if he wasn't going to be working for another month, he would have to be a little careful with his money for a time. That determined, he rolled out his bedding and prepared to sleep under the stars for the fifth night in a row. He could have made it to Austin in less time, but he'd taken it slow. As he now shifted around for a position that would not aggravate his wounds, he knew why.

I may not be as ready for this as I thought, he told the Lord. *I was pretty upset that Brace didn't want me back right now, but I think You must have had a hand in that.*

For a moment Dakota lay very still and wondered at this miracle that had happened in his heart. He knew God could have closed the book on him so easily; his wounds still ached in reminder, but here he was, alive and able to do things differently.

How many people get a second chance? I don't know why You think me worth it, but I'm grateful, God—more grateful than I can say.

Hot days on the trail were catching up to him. Dakota fell asleep still praying for his parents' salvation and then for Desmond and Geneva, asking God to help him remember all the things they had shared with him.

❧ ❧ ❧

"I have a surprise for you," Brace told Darvi on Saturday as they sat down to lunch.

"What is it?" Darvi asked, trying to show interest when all she could do was think about her friend. She could write, she realized, but it wouldn't be the same.

"I can't tell you. It's a surprise."

Darvi didn't like surprises, and she suspected her uncle knew this.

"Just give me a hint."

"All right. Let's just say that someone is coming for dinner tonight."

Suddenly things made sense. Milly, the woman who kept house for her uncle a few days a week and started his meals, had put a large roast in to bake that morning. With Darvi in the house, she had been leaving a little earlier in the day, giving the young woman leave to change anything she wanted on the menu. But today she had told Darvi exactly how she wanted the meat finished and what she'd wanted to go with it.

"Someone as in a family? Or someone as in one person?"

"I think I've told you enough."

"A man or a woman?"

Brace went on eating.

"What if I have plans for the night?" Darvi now tried. "What would you say to that?"

"I'd say I'm surprised. I thought you were here to visit me."

Her sharp tongue getting her into trouble in the usual way, Darvi didn't reply.

"I think that might be why I'm confused about your being in such a hurry to rush off to see Merry. You only just got here."

"I'm sorry, Uncle Marty," Darvi whispered in true repentance, her heart seeing how insensitive she had been.

"Oh, Darv," he laughed, "I'm just teasing you. You know I would wish for you to go. I'd take you myself if it were possible."

Darvi smiled at the warmth in his tone, but her head was having a little talk with her heart.

You're going to have to drop it, Darvi. He's right about this. You came to see him. Now accept that and enjoy your visit here.

Not one to feel sorry for herself, Darvi forced herself to accept the situation. She would write to Merry in the morning and be done with this plan.

🌹🌹🌹

"You look like a pincushion," the doctor said mildly as he examined Dakota's torso. "Oh, yes, I see what you mean. This one is rather red and nasty."

Dakota took a breath as the man probed around his side but didn't cry out as he was tempted. He'd woken that morning feeling warm and uncomfortable and knew it was more than the weather. He'd tried to ignore it for most of the day, but the pain had grown worse. With just two hours before he had to be at Brace's for dinner, he stopped in to see the doctor.

"I've got some powder I want you to put on this, and sleep on your other side for a while."

Dakota nodded, not bothering to mention that he'd been shot in the upper arm on the other side. It wasn't any wonder that sleeping without a mattress was fitful these nights.

"If you don't see vast improvement by Monday, get back in here."

"All right. What do I owe you?"

The doctor named a price so low that Dakota looked at him.

"My nephew's a Ranger," the man said with a sigh. "You're a breed apart—there's no denying that."

Dakota smiled a little and thanked the man. Once outside, he could tell evening was on its way; the temperature had dropped a little. A cool evening and a home-cooked meal—Dakota could hardly wait.

🌹🌹🌹

"Are you about ready to come out?" Brace had found Darvi in the kitchen and asked her for the second time.

"Almost," she said, knowing she wasn't going to have any other excuses.

"I thought you'd be more excited," he teased.

Darvi looked him in the eye, her hands going to her waist.

"I'm expected to be excited about someone I've never met?"

"I didn't say you'd never met him, but it's been a long time, and I would especially want you to be excited when I've asked him to take you to Stillwater."

Darvi stared at his mischievous eyes. "Do you mean it?" she asked, afraid to hope.

"Indeed, I do. Now come on. He's in the living room."

Darvi was suddenly all aflutter. Hair she didn't care about before was checked with careful attention, and she wiped perfectly clean hands two more times. Brace watched and waited patiently for her to join him.

"Now?" he teased again.

"Yes."

Brace let her precede him but was talking as they approached.

"Here she is, Dak. You can ask her yourself what day she wants to leave."

Darvi, whose heart had been pounding with excitement, felt the pit of her stomach plummet as they entered the small living room and the cowboy from the street the day before rose to meet her. Darvi's face flamed with mortification even as he came toward her, a kind smile on his face.

"It's nice to see you again, Darvi. You've done some growing up."

"Yes," she barely managed and then realized she did not want to explain this strange reaction to her uncle.

"You've changed a bit too," she said honestly, trying to act naturally. "I wouldn't have known you."

Dakota smiled then, a full-blown work, but Darvi was still a little too tense to join him.

"So, what day do you want to go?" he asked after reading the hesitancy in her eyes.

"What day is good for you?"

Dakota's hands came out. "My schedule is very open."

"May I think about it then, and let you know?"

"That's fine."

"Let's eat then," Brace declared, feeling he'd successfully pulled off his surprise, not to mention the fact that he was famished.

Dakota was hungry as well. He remembered his manners, but Geneva's cooking seemed much longer ago than a week. Darvi, he noticed, was not very hungry. Dakota wished he could ask her if he was causing the discomfort, but it looked as though they were going to have several days of travel where he might do that.

Partway through the meal, Brace began to tell Dakota about some cases and episodes from the last several months. Some Dakota knew of; others were new to him.

"I've got a photograph I need to show you. I think it's up in my room. I'll run up and get it, and you can tell me if you've seen this man before."

When Brace left, the dining room suddenly became very quiet. Dakota was almost through eating, and Darvi had given up pretending to eat. Dakota studied her from his seat, thinking that she had been something of a hoyden when he'd met her originally and that she had certainly grown into a refined young woman. She was poised and graceful; the only things out of place were the short curls that refused to be caught back in the elegant chignon she wore.

And that mouth! Dakota had never seen the like. Her upper lip protruded past a small shapely lower lip, giving her one of the most unusual looks he'd ever seen. In the strictest sense, she wasn't a beauty, but the soft curls around her face and those large brown eyes above her small, turned-up nose were all very eye-catching. And because she was looking everywhere but at her guest, Dakota went ahead and watched her. The moment she brought her eyes to his, however, he spoke.

"So tell me, Darvi, does your uncle know you were asking perfect strangers to escort you around the state?"

"I could tell you were a Ranger," she defended herself.

"Not all Rangers are trustworthy, and you know it."

Darvi was silent at this, her eyes moving back to her plate.

"So I take it Brace knows?"

Darvi was suddenly interested in the things on the table, straightening them just so and smoothing the already-perfect cloth.

"I didn't exactly mention it to him," she admitted. She glanced over to find those dark eyes leveled on her and asked herself if he'd always had such a powerful presence. "Are you going to tell him?"

"It's not my place, but I think you know how dangerous that could have been."

Darvi was only just able to nod before Brace came back to the table and the conversation turned to the man in the photo.

Darvi began clearing the table for dessert, thinking Dakota was right: It had been dangerous. But there was more to it, something neither man would understand. She *had* to see Merry.

☙ ☙ ☙

Desmond had not had an extra Bible to give him. Dakota had read from Geneva's when he had studied with Desmond, but when he left Wellsville there was no Bible in his gear. He'd had time the day before to look for one, but because he had woken with pain and some fever, it had completely slipped his mind.

Now Dakota sat in church wishing he had a Bible he could refer to. It wasn't that he doubted what the man was saying, but he thought if he could read it for himself, he would remember it better. Off and on each day he went over the things Desmond had told him, still somewhat amazed over how much made sense to him.

"Let me read verse 13 to you," the pastor was saying, referring to the fifth chapter of Galatians. " 'For, brethren, you have been called into liberty; only use not liberty for an occasion to the flesh, but by love serve one another.'

"It sounds to me," the man went on, "as though the Galatian church had become sloppy and willful. Remember how earlier in the chapter Paul had given them the good news that salvation was by grace alone, through Christ alone? Well, it almost looks as if they were taking this freedom, 'liberty' as the verse calls it, and treating it like an old shoe. It seems as though they no longer treated this freedom with the respect and hard work it deserves.

"Do you see how he commands them to love each other? I think selfishness has reared its ugly head. Paul is calling these believers to love each other because they were doing anything but. Verse 15 uses words like 'bite,' 'devour,' and 'consume.' Not exactly what we picture in a church family where love leads the way."

Dakota had leaned forward in his seat. He knew from his brothers that coming to Christ did not make everything perfect, but seeing that one of the churches from the Bible—one that had to be very new—had experienced these types of problems took a little getting used to.

"So what does Paul tell them to do instead?" the pastor asked. "Look to verse 14. Love your neighbor as yourself. Have you ever known someone who hated himself? We don't usually meet people like that. I can tell you that I don't do things to hurt my own body. If I so much as stub my toe, I sit down and rub it until it feels better.

"So, I have to ask myself, 'Jake, do you love your neighbors like you do yourself? Do you care for them in the careful way you look after yourself? Or are you devouring and biting?'"

This was heavy stuff for a man whose salvation was so new and who had no one with whom he could discuss what he was hearing. Dakota had seen many ugly things in his life, but he wasn't sure he could picture people in Desmond's or his brother's church acting this way. He didn't think the Bible would cover such a thing for no reason, but he was going to have to do some thinking before he made up his mind.

Getting yourself a Bible would certainly help, Rawlings.

"Let's stand for our final two hymns."

Dakota had not seen that coming. Where had the time gone? The Ranger hadn't known any of the songs at the beginning of the service or the ones they closed with, but he did his best. He didn't even take notice of his surroundings until people began to move from their seats. He was still taking in the simple wooden pews and small pulpit when from the periphery he caught someone approaching. Dakota turned to see the doctor from the day before.

"How are the wounds?" that man held his hand out and asked.

"Better, I think," Dakota answered with a return shake. "I used the powder last night and again this morning."

The older man nodded. "That's just what every doctor wants to hear—that people are taking their medicine."

Dakota smiled a little but didn't say anything else.

"Do you have someplace to eat lunch today?"

"As in the form of an invitation? No."

"Well, consider yourself invited. I'm Marcus Scott, by the way."

"Dakota Rawlings, and thank you."

"Let me give you directions to the house."

Dakota listened to the simple explanation, but before the doctor could finish, he was joined by Mrs. Scott and their two grown sons. Dakota ended up meeting them and simply following the Scotts' wagon home.

"Are you just passing through Austin, Mr. Rawlings?" Mrs. Scott asked after her husband prayed and the dishes were passed.

"In a way, ma'am, I am. I just came into town to tell my boss I'm ready to go back to work."

"And where will you go from here?"

"Just on a short jaunt into the hills, not actually working at all."

"I was going to ask," the doctor cut in, "does your boss know you're not back to strength?"

"No, but he didn't want me going back to work anyway."

"Where do you live?" one of the sons now asked, and the meal progressed in companionable conversation, doctor and Ranger taking measure of each other. Finally, near the end of the meal, Dakota found the courage to ask some questions.

"Have you gone to the church very long?"

"Years and years. Have you ever visited before?"

"No, I haven't," Dakota answered and then plunged in with what was on his mind. "Do you happen to know whether the pastor is open to questions? I have a few."

"Indeed, he is," Marcus answered as he stirred the coffee his wife had just brought to him. She returned to the kitchen to finish cutting pieces of cake. "Is there anything I can help you with?"

Dakota frowned down at his plate for a moment before admitting, "Were those verses this morning saying that the church was having problems?"

The doctor nodded. "Earlier in the chapter, Paul warns the people about the seriousness of adding anything to the gospel. Do you know what I mean by 'gospel'?"

"Salvation?"

"Yes. Their big issue was circumcision."

Dakota's brows rose on this, but he stayed quiet.

"Some people were still insisting that the men be circumcised, though Paul made it very clear that salvation comes by faith alone through Christ alone. Pastor mentioned the freedom this gave them, but they started to treat that freedom carelessly and were falling into sin toward each other."

"But the church was new! How could there be that many problems so quickly?"

Marcus smiled. "I don't know too many people who don't have problems or past experiences that affect the way they think and act. These people were no different. They had been used to blood sacrifices and circumcision. Now Christ had come along and taken all that away. And that was wonderful for these folks, but old habits—especially ones that make us feel comfortable—can die hard."

"So what type of sins are we talking about? I mean, how were they treating each other?"

"The verses that are coming up have a pretty serious list. Paul calls them the works of the flesh, and they include adultery, fornication, hatred, and much more. Maybe this was what they were saved out of, and with the way they were acting, he feared they would go back to this life. At the end of that chapter, he goes on to tell them how important it is to walk in the Spirit and gives another list, this one full of righteous acts for them to practice."

"But these people *had* heard the gospel and been saved?"

"I believe so, yes, and I don't wish to make excuses for them, but keep in mind that salvation does not take all those old temptations and actions away. We still tend to think of ourselves first and want our way much too often."

Dakota couldn't argue with that. Until recently, his own life and wants were his main concern. He cared about his family and his job, but he could now see how self-centered he'd been. At the same time, he had to admit that he was changing. The doctor was willing to talk for hours, and Dakota's questions were not about his own life, but that of Jesus Christ.

🌺🌺🌺

Thinking about how good it had been to talk to Dr. Scott, Dakota left their home and headed straight to Brace's small abode. Not until Mrs. Scott had asked if they would see him next week did Dakota realize he had no idea what his plans were. It was time to see Darvi. Because he wasn't staying at the boardinghouse, he realized Darvi had no way to tell him when she wanted to leave for Stillwater. For all he knew, they'd be pulling out of town first thing in the morning.

Dakota arrived at the house about three o'clock, knocked softly on the door, and waited. Dressed in an elegant day dress the color of dark plums, made more elegant by its unadorned lines, Darvi answered.

"Oh, Dakota!" she said in soft surprise. "I wondered when I would see you again."

Dakota stepped inside as she held the door and then understood why she whispered: Brace was sound asleep in the rocking chair.

Hat in hand, Dakota smiled a little before turning back to Darvi.

"What day did you want to leave?"

"Will Tuesday work for you?"

"That's fine. I'll check the stage schedule and get back—"

"I don't want to go by stage," Darvi cut in.

Dakota blinked.

"I thought we'd be going on horseback. I want to go on horseback," she clarified.

Dakota couldn't help the way his eyes moved over her elegant dress. "The stage will be much more comfortable."

"And also more unreliable."

Dakota nodded slowly, thinking that it was her choice but also asking himself what he'd gotten into with this favor.

"I'll check into renting a mount for you."

"Uncle Marty has two horses now. He said I can take one of his."

So Brace knows about this.

Outwardly Dakota nodded calmly, but his mind was already doing mental calisthenics as he went over the route to Blake and then on to Stillwater. The terrain wasn't bad, but it wasn't always the safest. On his own he wouldn't have given it a thought. Taking Darvi put it in a whole new light.

"What if we took the stage to Blake and then rented horses for Stillwater?"

Without so much as a moment's hesitation, Darvi shook her head no. She didn't look stubborn, just certain. Dakota decided to let it drop.

"Okay. How early do you want to leave?"

"I was thinking five."

Again Dakota was surprised but only nodded. Maybe it was for the best. He was coming to see that Darvi Wingate was one classy, sophisticated woman. More than likely they would have to take it slowly. Leaving early would help get them there in a more reasonable time frame.

"I'll see you Tuesday," Dakota supplied.

"Thank you, Dakota," she said, her face no longer businesslike but wreathed in soft, delighted lines.

Dakota couldn't help but respond. He smiled back, replaced his hat, and turned toward the door. He didn't know what the next week would bring, but he was fairly certain it wouldn't be dull.

Three

LIKE A CHILD AT CHRISTMAS, DAKOTA SAT DOWN under the large shade tree, leaned against it for comfort, and opened the package he had just bought from the general store. It had taken some searching, but he finally had it.

Moving as though touching the pages might damage them, Dakota opened a book that boasted the gold-tone title *Holy Bible* on the cover. He didn't read at first but just paged through, recognizing books that he'd discussed with Desmond and realizing he knew just where he wanted to read. He searched for a full five minutes for the book of Galatians before turning to the index in the front. After finally finding it, he settled in to study. So much was unclear to him, but he kept at it until the fifth chapter, where things fell a little more into place.

It was good to recognize things that both the pastor and Dr. Scott had referred to. Dakota read the chapter twice and sat mulling over several problematic issues. Of all the things that suddenly became clear to him, one was the thought he'd had while sitting in church the day before: The Bible didn't talk about things for no reason.

"If Paul talks about this, it must have been a problem." Dakota heard his own voice and stopped. "How did they know the writing was from Paul?"

With that Dakota was off again. He spent the next several hours reading and rereading, trying to get a grasp of the text and suddenly realizing it must have been a letter. Shaking his head at times in complete confusion, Dakota came away with one certainty: There was a way that God wanted men to act, and it was laid out in this book. It didn't all make sense, but Dakota vowed in his heart to learn that way and do his best to follow it.

※ ※ ※

"Do you want any more coffee?" Darvi asked Brace that night.

"No, thank you."

"All right. I'll go ahead and wash the pot."

Taking her uncle's coffee mug, Darvi made swift work of the kitchen detail. When she came back into the living room, she took a comfortable chair and put her feet up.

"I enjoyed coming, Uncle Marty. Thank you."

He waved at her as if she'd imagined his care of her.

"You'll have a good time with Merry," he said, ignoring her thanks. "But you've got an early morning coming up, so you'd best head up to bed."

"All right."

Darvi stood and went to his chair. She was going to lean down to kiss his cheek but suddenly stopped.

"I'm leaving after such a short time, Uncle Marty. I feel a little bad about that."

There was no ducking the issue this time. Her uncle looked her in the eye and spoke seriously.

"You're doing better, and that's all I care about, Darvi girl. And if things get rough again when you go home after your visit to Merry's, you just come right back here."

With a whispered word of thanks, Darvi did bend and kiss him. No other words were shared as Darvi left the room, mounted the stairs, and readied for bed. Tired as Darvi was, she lay awake until her uncle came up those same stairs, the sound of his steps a comfort to her. Praying for him as she felt herself relax, she drifted off to sleep some time after she heard his boots drop to the floor.

※ ※ ※

Dakota was glad that Darvi wanted to leave early and take it slow. He was still rather tender in spots and had even bled some in the night, and although he no longer wanted to sit around Austin, it was nice to know he was going to have an easy day.

All this he had decided before he saw Darvi. She and Brace were in the front yard when he arrived, and Dakota thought he'd never seen anyone so loaded for bear. Gone was the frilly dress and elegant hairstyle. In the morning light he could see that she was dressed for the trail. Darvi wore a brown dress he could only term "serviceable"

and had her hair and neck covered by an all-consuming hat and handkerchief. It was such a contrast to the day before that Dakota had all
he could do not to stare.

"Here's some money," Brace said the moment Dakota dismounted.

"I'm doing all right," Dakota replied, not taking the bills that were
being held out to him.

Brace stuffed them in Dakota's vest pocket.

"Be that as it may," he said rather softly, "you never know what's
going to happen with Darvi, and I didn't mean for you to do this
without some compensation."

Dakota opened his mouth to start to protest, but Brace cut him off.
"I mean it!"

Dakota watched him turn back to his niece. The two hugged.

"Have you got everything?" Brace asked.

"Yes. I'm sure I do."

"All right. Have a good time. Tell Merry I said hello; Calder too."

"I'll do it."

"And when you get home, tell your mother she hasn't written in
weeks."

Darvi's brow lowered. "You said you just got a letter."

"I know, but your mother always expects me to complain about
something, and I don't want to let her down."

Darvi gave him another hug and turned to the horse called Finley.
With a boost she didn't need, Brace had her in the saddle in the blink
of an eye. Dakota waited to shake Brace's hand and thank him before
gaining his own saddle, and a moment later he and Darvi were on
their way. Dakota glanced back just before they were out of sight to
find Brace reaching for his handkerchief, causing something to trigger
in his own heart. It was a good reminder that Darvi was precious
cargo.

"Hey, Darvi," Dakota called to her as they turned their horses toward the west side of town. "How soon would you like to get there?"

"Soon," she admitted. "I guess I'm not much for dawdling."

"Well, be sure and let me know if we're going too fast."

Darvi glanced at him. "Why don't I set the pace? Will that work?"

"Go to it," Dakota said with easy confidence. He knew Eli was up
to anything, and he had strong doubts that Darvi could wear him out.
With this thought in mind, Dakota simply heeled his mount to keep
pace with Darvi the moment they hit the edge of town.

❧ ❧ ❧

Calling it pride never occurred to Dakota. It was a perfect description, but the word never crossed his mind, nor did it occur to him to tell Darvi they had to slow down.

More than 12 hours after he and Darvi left Austin, they arrived in Blake, a town not far from Stillwater. Dakota was in so much pain that he didn't think he could even speak. All five of his bullet wounds were burning, and he knew the one on his waist had to be bleeding.

"I think the hotel would be good, don't you?" Darvi spoke like a woman in charge, and at the moment she was.

"Fine," Dakota managed, glad that the horses' hooves drowned out the strain in his voice.

At a later time, Dakota would think back on the way God moved to rescue him on this evening, but right now he just knew relief at how solicitous the hotel proprietress was, how swift she was to volunteer her son to take their horses to the livery, and how Darvi told Dakota she was going to eat in her room and turn in early. He fell into bed the moment he shut the door and dropped into unconsciousness for the next ten hours.

$$\text{彡-彡-彡}$$

Not feeling what anyone would term "brand new," Dakota was nevertheless at the breakfast table in a timely manner and not looking as pale as he felt. Darvi joined him just ten minutes after he sat down, and Dakota found himself feeling somewhat thankful that she had not seen him nearly swallowing his food whole. He was calmly sipping coffee when she arrived.

"I'll just have a quick bite," she explained and smiled at the waitress when she glanced their way.

"Don't hurry on my account," Dakota said, meaning it with all his heart. He'd used the powder again and tried to patch the wounds, but the job was middling at best.

"I think we're only a half-day's ride now."

Dakota nodded before asking, "How do you know this friend, by the way?"

"She used to live in Austin. We played together every summer I visited." Darvi paused. "I certainly hope she's home."

"She's not expecting you?"

"No. We never kept in touch through the mail, and I didn't even know she'd moved until I arrived in Austin."

They fell silent for a moment, and then Darvi looked at her companion.

"Did you hear any screams out your window last night?"

Dakota could have told her he didn't even remember lying down but only said no.

"I did," Darvi said. "It sounded like a woman was receiving some unwanted attention. I nearly went out to check."

This statement stopped Dakota's coffee cup on the way to his mouth.

"Tell me, Darvi," Dakota said, putting the cup down, his voice mildly curious. "What would you have done?"

"If I'd gone out?"

"Yes, and if the unwanted attentions had been turned on you?"

"With or without my gun?" she asked in all sincerity.

Dakota couldn't stop the smile that turned up one corner of his mouth, but he still managed, "With your gun."

"I'd have shot him in the foot."

Again Dakota wanted to smile but refrained.

"And without your gun?"

"I'd have tried to reason with him, and if that hadn't worked, I'd have screamed myself hoarse and tried to fight."

"It's good to have a plan," Dakota said softly, all the time trying to process whether this woman was safe on her own or not.

You never know what's going to happen with Darvi.

Brace's words from the morning before came floating back to him. Dakota would have enjoyed some time to think on them, but Darvi was pushing her plate away. Within 15 minutes, they were back on the trail.

🌣 🌣 🌣

Stillwater was a surprise. A clean, friendly-looking town that sat in the foothills, it was a good deal cooler than Austin. Since Darvi had not known of her friend's move, Dakota assumed she also did not know where this friend lived, but he kept his mouth shut and let her lead the way. She took them straight to the general store.

"I'll just be a minute," she said before dismounting and going inside.

Watching her confident stride, Dakota realized that Darvi must have wanted to make this journey on her own. He knew Brace well enough to know that man would not have even discussed it, but Darvi was clearly no stranger to being in charge. Nor did she appear timid in new surroundings.

In the middle of these thoughts, Darvi reappeared. She climbed back into the saddle and turned to him, her eyes alight with excitement.

"We're almost there."

Dakota smiled at her glowing face and said, "Lead on."

The directions Darvi received took them toward the edge of town. She hadn't been in as much of a hurry today, but now she stepped up the pace. Dakota had been on the edge of discomfort all during the day's ride but thought his body might now be nearing the end of its tolerance. His side was starting to burn, and he could only be thankful they were almost there.

"That's the house," Darvi suddenly said, their horses taking a road along the creek.

Dakota feared that she would heel her horse into a run and knew he couldn't take that. Besides, he wanted to give her some privacy.

"Darvi," he said just in time.

She turned to him in some impatience.

"I think I'll sit here by the creek while you go on up to the house."

For the first time Darvi took in his face. It was warm out, but she hadn't really noticed. She didn't think such a thing would bother him, but he looked a little strained.

"Are you certain, Dakota? You're welcome to join me."

"I would think a private reunion preferable, and beyond that, I want to stay here."

She couldn't argue much with that, so with one more glance at the man who was already turning his horse off the road, Darvi went on her way.

Heart pounding, breath coming in small gasps, Darvi rode swiftly toward the house. It was a lovely setting, not far from the creek and not very close to other homes.

"White paint, white shutters, and a large covered porch," Darvi whispered to herself, "just like the man said."

Darvi tied her horse's reins to a corner of the porch railing and went toward the steps. Things seemed so quiet—she was almost afraid to hope. Taking a breath to quell her excitement—a move that didn't work—Darvi knocked on the door. A man answered.

"Hello," he said kindly.

"Hello. I'm looking for Merry Scott. Does she live here?"

"Yes, she does. Come right in."

Darvi stepped inside when he held the door and squinted to adjust her eyes. The moment she could see, she realized her friend was standing not ten feet from her.

"Hello, Darvi," Merry welcomed with a huge smile.

"Merry," Darvi breathed, only now believing she had made it and moving forward to hug her friend.

The two women, one a soft strawberry blonde and the other a brilliant carrot top, hugged for a long time. Calder Scott, Merry's husband, stood off to one side, a wide grin on his face. The women were still hugging when Darvi heard someone call "Mama." She stepped away from her friend, her eyes huge.

"Merry?" she questioned softly.

Meredith Scott smiled the smile that first drew Darvi to her.

"Come on, Darvi. Come meet my husband and daughters."

Darvi was still mouthing the word "daughters" when Calder stepped forward.

"This is Calder," Merry began.

"Hello, Darvi," the tall man said as he held out his hand. "I've heard so much about you."

"It's so nice to meet you," Darvi replied sincerely. "I nearly panicked when I learned you'd moved away, but I found a way here."

"And these," Merry continued, "are our twins, Vivian and Pilar."

Darvi looked to where Merry pointed, through the doorway to the kitchen table, where two adorable, dark-haired moppets stared back.

"Oh, my" was all she could manage.

"Come, girls," Merry bade them. "Come and meet Miss Wingate."

"Please let them call me Darvi," that woman whispered as the girls scrambled from the chairs and ran to their mother.

"Here we go," Merry said in her quiet way. "Show your faces," she ordered the two who suddenly became shy and absorbed with their mother's skirt.

"Obey, girls," their father put in from the side, and the twins turned immediately.

"This is Vivian, and this is Pilar. Girls, this is my friend, Darvi. You may call her Aunt Darvi."

"Hello, Vivian. Hello, Pilar. It's so nice to meet you."

The girls giggled over this, and Darvi turned back to her friend.

"How old are they?"

"They were three last month."

Darvi shook her head. "So much time has passed."

"About four years," Merry confirmed. "They were born the first year we were married."

Darvi could hardly believe she was here. This friend was so special to her. Darvi didn't know if she'd ever told her that, but she would this time. This time she knew she could.

"Did you come alone, Darvi?" Calder suddenly asked.

"No," she turned to him, "but my escort seemed to think I would want a private reunion."

"Who is it, Darvi?" Merry asked.

"A friend of my uncle's. He wanted to wait by the creek."

Husband and wife exchanged a look before Calder turned away and said, "I'll just head out and invite him in to lunch."

Merry waited only until her husband was gone before sending the girls back to the table and ushering Darvi into the kitchen.

"Have a seat there, Darvi, and I'll get you a bowl of soup."

"Should I have gone out with Calder?"

"I don't think so," Merry said easily. "He'll just go out and introduce himself, I'm sure."

Merry said all of this while laying two extra place settings, making sure the bread was in reach, and then serving her friend a bowl of soup. It took a moment for her to see that Darvi was staring at her, a look of near desperation on her face.

"What is it, Darvi?" Merry asked gently, taking a chair close to her.

"I did it!" Darvi could wait no longer. "I asked Jesus Christ to save me from my sins. I wanted to pick the perfect time to tell you, but I just have to tell you now. I'm a believer, Merry, just like you."

Having prayed for this for years, Merry was surprised at her own reaction: one of tears. She tried to speak, but the words stuck in her throat. Silent tears trickled down her face, and when her little daughters saw them, their own tears began. This made the women laugh.

"Tell me everything!" Merry commanded when she finally had air again.

The words and sounds coming from the kitchen in the next minutes included an amazing blend of laughter and breathless sobs, none of which could be heard by Calder, who had finally spotted Dakota and was moving toward him. Calder was nearly to the rock the Ranger was sitting on before he realized that man had his shirt off and was trying to stop his side from bleeding.

"Hello," Calder called as Dakota glanced at him.

"Hello."

Finally at the boulder, Calder stopped and looked down on him. "It looks as though Darvi was something of a tyrant."

One corner of Dakota's mouth quirked. "She rode harder than I figured."

"Do you want me to have a look?"

Dakota took his eyes from the wound. "You a doctor?"

"Yes."

Dakota shrugged a little. "I saw a doctor in Austin. He gave me some powder."

"It wasn't Marcus Scott by any chance, was it?"

"As a matter of fact, it was."

"He's my uncle."

Dakota took a moment to compute this.

"I thought you were a Ranger."

Calder smiled. "That's my brother."

Dakota laughed a little.

"I'll get my bag," Calder said and started away.

Dakota was too weary to argue with him. He didn't think he needed any more mending, but he certainly felt worn.

Back at the house, Merry heard the door the moment it opened and went to meet their other guest. She was surprised to find her husband alone.

"He's hurt," Calder said by way of explanation.

Merry accepted this without question or comment. Darvi, on the other hand, followed Calder to the door on his way back out.

"Dakota's hurt?"

"Yes. I would guess a gunshot wound to his side."

Darvi's mouth opened. "He never said a word."

Calder's smile was full of amusement. "Somehow that doesn't surprise me."

Tempted as Darvi was to go with him, she thought she might be in the way. The blonde made herself stay put, but as soon as she saw him, Darvi would have a few questions for Dakota Rawlings.

※ ※ ※

Dakota woke slowly, his body telling him he was rested and comfortable and that everything was all right. He remembered getting to the front porch and even going through the kitchen, but almost as soon as he'd lain on the bed he had been directed to, everything had begun to fade.

Now his eyes were opening, and for the first time since he left Desmond and Geneva's, he felt truly rested. Long days and nights, hard trails, and little comfort were a way of life to him, but having bullet wounds put it all in a whole new light.

"I found it a little surprising . . ." Dakota heard Darvi say and realized she was in the kitchen, right outside his door. For the first time he noticed the door wasn't shut.

"I never thought about people in the Bible quarreling or not loving each other, but Pastor Osman's sermon spoke to that very thing. I've been reading in Galatians ever since."

"Are you understanding it?" Merry asked.

"Some of it. May I ask you some questions?"

"Of course, Darvi. Why don't we get our Bibles and sit in the living room. The girls will be waking soon, and I can hear them better if I'm near the stairs."

Dakota heard their chairs move and lay in silence. It had been like listening to his own conversation with Marcus Scott. Darvi must have been in church on Sunday. Dakota glanced around to see if his saddlebags were in sight but didn't spot them. He had a sudden need to read his Bible.

With slow but comfortable movements he eased from the bed. A glance out the window told him where the privy was situated, and he thought if he moved quietly, he might be able to get out without disturbing Darvi and her friend. It occurred to him as he pulled on boots and found the back door that he hadn't even met the woman.

♣ ♣ ♣

"I think I hear the girls," Merry said about 45 minutes later.

"Thank you for explaining some of this to me," Darvi said. "It makes sense to me now. I've sinned so many times since I believed. I'm not sure why I thought the people in the Bible would be different."

Merry smiled at her friend, still feeling rather amazed that she was even having this conversation. She had planned to go into town for some extra shopping after the twins awoke, but suddenly nothing else mattered. Darvi was here, and not just any Darvi, but a new sister in Christ.

"Mama?" A little voice floated down the stairway.

"Coming, Vivvy."

"How did you know that was Vivian?"

Merry shrugged. "I just know."

Darvi sat still in the living room after her friend walked up the stairs. She was still thinking about all the things Merry had explained and how much she had to learn when she heard a noise in the kitchen. With little forethought she stood to her feet and went that way.

Dakota, who had been reading at the table, had just put his Bible in the bedroom and returned to the kitchen when Darvi stepped into the room.

"I can't believe you did that!" Darvi attacked him without warning.

Dakota stared at her angry face, feeling rather dispassionate about her ire but thinking she looked rested and at home in these surroundings. Her yellow dress looked nice too.

"Did you hear me, Dakota?" she tried again.

"Yes, but I don't know what you're upset about."

Darvi's hands came to her waist. "You let me ride us as though there was no tomorrow and never once said you were hurt."

Dakota nodded with understanding. It took him a moment to figure out what she was referring to, but this made sense.

"I'm fine, Darvi."

Darvi looked irritated again, like a child who knew she was being patronized.

"That's why you were bleeding!" she snapped. "I know I always bleed when I'm fine."

Dakota tried not to smile at the sarcasm but couldn't help himself.

"Don't you laugh at me, Dakota Rawlings! I'm really upset about this." Her voice suddenly grew quiet; she wished she could learn to bite her tongue. "I was all het up to come here, and I didn't think about anyone but myself. I'm sorry."

Dakota couldn't help but respond to such repentance.

"I could have said something, Darvi, but I didn't. Thank you for your concern."

Darvi smiled a little at his forgiving tone. She regretted the way she'd talked to him but wasn't certain how to explain. At times she asked the Lord why He ever put up with her mouth.

All this was still rolling through Darvi's mind when she saw that she'd lost Dakota's attention. He was still standing in the same place, but his eyes were focused down and behind her; a smile was just starting across his lips.

Darvi knew what had his attention. Vivian and Pilar had come downstairs with their mother.

Four

"I'M MERRY SCOTT." THE DOCTOR'S WIFE was the first to speak and came forward to shake Dakota's hand. The girls stayed close beside her, but the shyness they had shown with Darvi was not to be found. Indeed, they seemed quite taken with this large, dark stranger.

"I'm Dakota Rawlings," Dakota said as he shook Merry's hand, catching the girls' interest but not looking directly at them. "I appreciate your hospitality. I'm sure I feel better for having come inside to lie down."

"Well, Darvi tells me you'll be taking her to Aurora to catch the train home, and you need to know that however long you're here, we expect you to use that room."

"Thank you," Dakota said, before his amused eyes swung to the strawberry blonde.

"Is that the plan? I'm taking you to Aurora?"

Darvi's mouth opened. "Didn't Uncle Marty tell you?"

"No. Maybe he thought you did."

"Oh, Dakota!" Darvi was horrified. "I had no idea. I mean, I just assumed you two had talked."

"It doesn't matter. Like I said, I have some free time right now."

"To rest up," Darvi said wryly, thinking she could cry. She had been so determined to get to Stillwater that nothing else had mattered. She now wondered whether her uncle knew of the situation.

"That was your uncle's plan," Dakota answered the unasked question, "but I don't think I'm going to be needing much rest."

"But you're not working right now?"

"No. My time is my own."

Sounding rather crushed, she said, "And I'm sure this is just how you had planned to spend it."

It was at that moment that the couple realized they were alone. When Merry and the girls slipped away, neither of them knew. Darvi moved toward the door that led to the backyard, obviously upset. Dakota followed.

"You need to listen to me, Darvi," Dakota said as soon as he followed her to the back porch. "You're upset for no reason."

"No reason?" Darvi began in outrage, but Dakota put his hand up, his face stern. Darvi subsided, something rather new for her, and waited for him to take a seat on the porch railing as she was in the only chair.

"I was hurt midsummer. Brace didn't want me back for six months. I came anyway. Since my escorting you puts me nearer my family's ranch, he said I should go there whenever we're done and check back with him in a month. The truth is, I don't feel a hundred percent, but neither am I dying. I'll probably be pacing at the ranch for three weeks before I'm supposed to report back in Austin. You may take as long as you like to get on that train in Aurora. My time is open. And unless you want me to wrestle a bear, I'm up for just about anything."

"But you were hurt some by how hard I wanted to ride," Darvi couldn't help but say.

"At any time I could have asked you to stop, Darvi, but I didn't. I have no one to blame but myself."

Darvi saw that he was right but still wanted to take responsibility. She looked away from Dakota's eyes and tried to work it out in her mind. When she looked back, he was still watching her. For some odd reason, her heart was wrung with compassion.

"How were you hurt, Dakota?"

"A gunfight. It wasn't that they outnumbered me; it was my miscalculation of where they were."

"You were shot?"

"Five times."

Darvi's hands came to her mouth.

"I'm fine," Dakota said gently. "I will tell you if I can't do something."

Darvi mentally promised to pinch herself if she cried, and it seemed to do the trick. Nodding swiftly and dropping both her hands and her eyes, she asked herself how God could stand all this weeping she did. Ever since she'd understood her own personal need for a Savior, she'd been bawling over the silliest things.

Not that Dakota's being shot is silly. I just wish I could control myself a little more.

"Are you all right?" Dakota asked. He hadn't taken his eyes from her since they'd sat down. Nevertheless, she did not look at him when she answered.

"I'm fine, Dakota, thank you. I'll just trust you to tell me if something's not right."

"All right," Dakota said as he stood. "And I'll wait for you to tell me when you're ready to go. Like I said, any time is fine."

He slipped back inside on Darvi's nod and found Merry and the girls in the kitchen. In the time he'd been gone, their fascination had melted away. They showed their faces long enough for an introduction but were terribly shy about looking at him. Dakota took pity on them and went into his bedroom and shut the door.

🌺 🌺 🌺

"How do you feel?" Calder asked Dakota the moment he arrived home that evening and found him sitting alone in the living room.

"Better. Thank you."

Dakota had been sitting and looking out the large window to the woods behind the house. It was a very tranquil scene, and as the minutes ticked by, he felt himself growing more relaxed.

Calder sat down with him.

"Any more bleeding?"

"No. Thanks for helping me earlier. I think I needed rest more than anything else."

Calder smiled.

"What does that look mean?" Dakota asked, his voice a bit dry.

"Only that you sound like my brother."

"Was that a compliment or not?"

"Or not," the doctor replied, putting it plainly. "Most days, Chet has more guts than good sense."

Dakota let himself smile over this, a smile that grew quite wide when two little girls suddenly joined them.

"Papa!" they squealed in delight as the two scrambled for his lap.

They were hugged, kissed, tickled, and snuggled in turn before settling in to stare at Dakota in adorable splendor.

"Did you meet Mr. Rawlings?" their father asked.

Both dark heads bobbed up and down. Flyaway hair fell softly around their faces, and round cheeks glowed pink below sparkling eyes. They smiled easily, and their noses were so soft-looking and rounded that Dakota wanted to tweak them.

"How do I tell who's Pilar and who's Vivian?" Dakota asked as he studied their cookie-cutter images.

The two girls stared right back, and Dakota had to shrug.

Calder stepped in.

"Show him, Vivvy."

Vivian obediently pointed to her eye. Again Dakota studied her but still had to look to Calder questioningly.

"Vivvy has a tiny scar next to her eye," the older Scott explained. "Do you see it?"

"Oh, yes. How did that happen?"

"She had just learned to walk and waited until she was next to a rock to take her first serious tumble."

Dakota smiled at both girls and then looked to Vivian.

"Did it hurt?" he asked, but Vivian only smiled at him.

Mercy, you two are cute! was all Dakota could think as he watched them. He didn't know how long he and Darvi would be in Stillwater, but he thought he could get very attached to these two girls. Though younger, they reminded him of Libby's sister, Laura.

"Dinner's ready," Merry announced from the edge of the room.

The men thanked her and stood.

Calder gave Merry a kiss, and one of the girls went into her arms.

"It smells good," Calder commented.

"Beef stew, biscuits, watermelon, and iced tea."

"Oh, my," Dakota said softly.

Merry turned to him, her eyes sparkling a little. "Don't you care for beef stew, Mr. Rawlings?"

"On the contrary, Mrs. Scott, quite suddenly I'm starving."

Having figured he would appreciate a home-cooked meal, Merry was very pleased. She was even more pleased when she saw that the girls were not going to stare at him all evening and then hide their faces when he looked their way. She was exhausted these days—she suspected she was pregnant—and in her mother's pride, she wanted Dakota and especially Darvi to see the twins at their best.

"All right, girls," Calder spoke after they had sat down. "Whose turn is it to pray tonight?"

"Vivvy's," Pilar was swift to say. "I was before."

Calder smiled at her wording and turned to Vivian.

"All right, Viv. Here we go. Dear Lord . . ."

"Dear Lor."

"Thank You for the food."

"For food."

"And all Mama's work."

"Mama."

"For friends."

This was met with silence.

"For friends," Calder repeated, his voice prompting.

Still it was quiet.

Calder finally had no choice but to open his eyes and look at his daughter. He found her staring around the table.

"Vivian, can you thank God for friends?"

"No."

"Why not?"

"Where's Beth?"

Understanding dawned. "Not *your* friends. Mama's and *my* friends. We have friends too."

The adults at the table had kept their eyes closed, but each had something over his or her mouth. Dakota's hand covered his upper lip, Darvi used her napkin, and Merry's apron helped her stem the laughter that lingered just under the surface.

"I'll go ahead and finish; you can close your eyes again," Calder stated.

Waiting until Vivian obeyed, the host went ahead with the prayer he had in mind, just barely holding his own laughter. No adults exchanged glances after Calder's amen, which was for the best. It would have been some time before anyone would have been able to eat.

❧ ❧ ❧

"I didn't have a chance to tell you until now, but I'm so excited, Calder. She's been searching for so long. I knew Darvi's search had to end in Christ, but she didn't. I'm overwhelmed with God's grace and goodness."

"It's wonderful news," Calder said softly to his wife once they had retired for the evening. "Do you know how long she plans to stay?"

"No, but however long it is, it won't be long enough."

There was something quiet in his wife tonight, and for a moment Calder studied on what it might be. She was pleased about Darvi certainly, but not like he thought she would be.

"How was your day?" Merry asked, pulling her thoughts back to her husband.

Calder started to answer but stopped.

Merry looked at him. "Did something happen, Calder?"

"No," he went on smoothly, not wanting her to know he was distracted by her manner. He went ahead and told her about his office visits and one of the curtains nearly catching fire at the general store. They weren't many minutes outside of town, but enough that she would miss the daily happenings of town life.

"So it didn't actually light?"

"No, but the smoke was a nuisance, and it drew a crowd. Is there something you're not telling me?"

His detour in the subject was so abrupt Merry laughed.

"Where did that come from?"

"I was hoping to surprise a confession out of you."

"A confession over what?" Merry asked with just enough uncertainty that Calder's suspicions were confirmed.

"Out with it, Merry. I know something is on your mind."

"As a matter of fact, there is, but I don't want to tell you now because you're going to think I'm upset."

"Are you upset?"

"No."

"But something is wrong?"

"No, it is not."

Calder's brow lowered in thought.

"For a doctor, Calder, you can be a little slow."

It didn't take long from there.

"Are you certain?"

"Not absolutely, but fairly so."

"Why didn't you want to tell me?"

"Because I knew you'd ask for my symptoms, and I would tell you I'm tired, and you would say I'm the mother of twins, like you always do."

Calder laughed. "I'm sorry I'm so predictable, but you must admit that being tired would mean that nearly every woman in town was in a family way."

Merry smiled. "You're right, of course, but I think I can tell the difference."

Calder stood up from the foot of the bed and joined her on the side. He slipped his arms around her and held her close.

"I love it when you're expecting."

"Why is that?"

"Lots of reasons that I won't try to explain, but I do know I'm going to love this pregnancy more than the first."

"Why?"

"Because I've met the girls. I know how special this baby's going to be."

"So you believe me?"

Calder kissed her.

"Certainly. You know the signs in your own body better than I do."

"Thank you, Calder."

He didn't like being thanked for what he considered to be the job of a normal loving husband; that is, trusting his wife and caring for her.

"Did you really think I wouldn't believe you?"

Merry looked up at him. "I don't know. I just feel a little uncertain. I look into the girls' faces and I can't imagine loving another baby as I do them."

"Don't forget what your mother has been heard to say: Love multiplies; it doesn't divide."

Merry sighed a little, feeling more tired than ever. "I might have to experience that to believe it."

Calder didn't comment. He knew she would love this next baby. He knew her well enough to be at complete peace on the subject. But just then he had another thought that wasn't quite so restful. What if this birth was also twins? Calder was opening his mouth to ask Merry if she'd thought of that when he looked at her face. She was nearly asleep against him. He realized he was not going to fall asleep as swiftly, but not for anything would he mention the idea to Merry, at least not tonight.

🌹🌹🌹

"Where is him?" Dakota heard one of the little girls ask before he actually spotted them.

"Where is *he?*" Calder corrected. "I think he's out back. Why do you ask?"

"I wanna see him."

Calder decided not to comment. He wouldn't mind seeing Dakota Rawlings either, but he didn't know quite how to go about it. As he and the girls walked from the back porch into the yard, Calder tried to determine why he was so drawn to the man. He knew there was something more to it than simply wanting to share Christ if he had the opportunity.

Maybe he reminds me of Chet was his last thought before Vivian spotted him.

"I see him! Hey!"

Dakota had been watching for them to come into view and now smiled as one of the twins came forward.

"How are you?" Dakota asked her.

"I'm Vivvy."

Dakota smiled. He didn't care that she'd gotten the question wrong. It was too much fun having her talk to him.

"If you were looking for peace and quiet, Dakota, you're in the wrong place."

Dakota smiled again. The huge tree stump, along with the shade thrown from a neighboring tree, was as inviting a place as Dakota had seen in a long time. He had read his Bible early that morning and was now trying to pray. He wasn't finding it as easy as he thought it would be, and that made him wonder if he might have missed something.

"Is this where the girls play?" he asked, glad for the distraction.

"Just about every day, and always 'house.' "

"Sounds like fun."

"How'd you sleep?" the doctor asked.

"Good."

"And the bleeding?"

Dakota smiled. "There's no getting around you guys, is there?"

"Not on your life. So tell me, are you still bleeding?"

"Yes, and I suppose you want to check it."

"Indeed I do, and if you don't mind an audience, I'll just look right now."

Dakota gently pulled the shirt from his waistband. Calder joined him on the stump, and the little girls moved in to watch as though it were an everyday occurrence.

"Are you sleeping on your other side?" Calder asked as he probed.

"As much as I can."

Calder looked up at him, his eyes thoughtful. "How many holes do you have?"

"Five."

Wondering how he could have missed this, Calder snorted in disgust and mumbled under his breath, "Might as well be your Uncle Chet sitting right there in front of you, girls."

"Are you hurted?"

"No," Dakota answered automatically, and to his surprise, Vivian turned to her father.

"Is he hurted?"

"Yep," Calder said mildly, a small smile on his mouth. "He just doesn't know it."

Dakota laughed a little and then winced.

"I need my bag," Calder announced and stood. "Stay put, girls."

Dakota watched him walk away before looking down at the twins. They seemed content to stare up at him, and Dakota wished he could think of something to say. He just decided to ask them if they were excited to start school someday, but he wasn't fast enough.

"I have to go," Pilar said out of the blue, her little brow furrowed as she stared up at him.

"Okay," Dakota said slowly, thinking that her father had said to stay put.

"Me too," Vivian chimed in, and Dakota watched as they walked around him and the stump but didn't go to the house. He stared after them, so he knew the exact moment they stopped and waved for him to come. Too curious not to, Dakota followed. His mouth stretched into a smile when he saw the little girls head to the privy. He had no idea why his presence was needed until they approached the building, stood still, and looked up at him. The handle was over their heads.

"Do you need me to get the door?"

Little heads bobbed in unison, and once he had the door open, they stepped inside. Wondering how he'd come to be standing there, Dakota shut the door and waited. In time he heard this:

"Look, Vivvy, a flower."

"Where?"

"Here."

"Where?"

"Here."

"Oh!"

Dakota's shoulders shook with silent laughter, but he didn't comment.

"I'm done" soon came from the privy, and not long after, the door was pushed open a bit. Dakota reached to hold it wide while the girls filed out. They came and stood side by side and looked up at him. For some reason, Dakota was speechless. He felt rescued when he saw that both of Pilar's little boots were unbuttoned.

"Here, let me get these for you."

Dakota hunkered down to do the job. Although he was not able to get all the buttons, he managed the top few. When he looked up, they were both staring at his face.

"What's your name?" Vivian asked.

"Dakota."

"Koda?"

"That's close enough," Dakota said, smiling into their eyes and thinking once again, *Mercy, you two are cute!*

The slamming of the back door brought his attention around. The threesome looked to see the doctor approaching, bag in hand.

"I guess we could do this inside," Calder commented as he followed Dakota back to the stump.

Dakota didn't answer. The yard was beautiful, full of wildflowers and tall grasses. It was a child's heaven all right, and Dakota knew why the girls played out here every day.

"Where is Darvi this morning?" Dakota thought to ask, taking his mind from the foul-smelling bottle Calder had just uncorked. Just before the painful liquid touched down, Dakota wondered if it would burn.

"She and Merry went to town. Thursdays are my mornings off. I keep the girls, and Merry gets out for half the day." This said, Calder looked into Dakota's face. He knew the stuff he was using not only smelled bad but had a tendency to sting. Dakota's face was utterly impassive, but Calder was not fooled. The big man was in pain and keeping his mouth shut in order to hide it. But Calder was in for a surprise.

"That burns," Dakota said quietly. "If I'd known you were going to treat me like this, I'd have gone to town with the ladies."

Calder was still chuckling over the comment when the girls declared they were hungry. All four went inside to find something to eat.

Five

"LOOK AT THIS FABRIC, MERRY. THE GIRLS would look wonderful in this dark pink."

Merry looked doubtful. "It would be great for trim, Darvi, but the twins need a dark background or they never look clean."

Darvi nodded but couldn't honestly say she understood. As a child she was not allowed to get dirty until she came for her annual summer visit to Austin. Her family had a yard in St. Louis, but it was all very trimmed and proper. She could pick flowers, but her fingers were not to touch the dirt. For a moment Darvi wondered how she had survived.

"What are you thinking about?" Merry asked, interrupting her thoughts.

"Just now I was asking myself how my mother and uncle could be so different and still have the same parents."

Merry suddenly looked intense and said, "You've never talked much about your mother. How is she different from Marty Bracewell?"

Darvi looked pained. "It would take less time to tell you how they're the same." She shook her head a little. "My mother must have known Uncle Marty let me run wild during those visits. I learned to ride and shoot. I came back with a tan, scratched up my arms and legs, and probably had a little dirt behind my ears, but she never said a word. She just plopped me into the tub, proclaiming that travel made one 'so dusty,' and put me back into my routine."

"And from then on you were expected to be a little lady once again," Merry guessed.

Darvi smiled wryly. "That about sums it up. I would sit in my proper little dress and shoes and long to be back climbing trees with you. Merry!" Darvi exclaimed with a sudden thought. "Will there be trees in heaven?"

"I'm not sure. I have a memory of reading something in Scripture about that, but I couldn't tell you where."

Darvi's eyes sparkled with delight. "I love all these things I've yet to learn."

Merry's eyes widened with surprise. "Most people feel just the opposite, Darv. They want to know it all right now and are frustrated that they don't."

Darvi gave a little sigh. "I was so smug, Merry—so settled in my own world and sure I knew who I was and where I was going. No matter how much I don't know right now, I do know one thing: I'll keep searching and being in wonder, but I won't ever forget that God's Son died for me, and someday I'll live forever with Him."

"I have all I can do not to hug you and burst into tears all over again."

Darvi smiled. "I don't mind. I'd probably join you, but I have a better idea. Let me take you to lunch."

"Lunch? Is it that late?"

"No, but we forgot to eat breakfast, and I'm hungry."

Merry, feeling she were walking on a cloud, tucked her arm into Darvi's and said, "I'll lead the way."

❧ ❧ ❧

"Did I mention how I met your uncle?" Dakota asked between bites of the fried egg, bacon, baked bread, and hot coffee that Calder had prepared.

"No, I don't think you did."

"I first met him when I went to his office about the wound in my side, but then I visited this church and he was there with his family. They invited me to lunch."

As Dakota was hoping, Calder took immediate interest.

"What did you think of the church?"

"I liked it. I didn't have a Bible at the time, so it was somewhat hard to follow along, but I've thought a lot about what both the pastor and your uncle said."

"So you discussed the sermon with Marc?"

Dakota answered by way of explaining what the sermon had been about and why it had been confusing. To his relief, Calder seemed to understand completely.

"I've had some of those same questions. Were you settled with Marc's answers, or do you still have questions?"

"I have questions, but not about the sermon," Dakota said, realizing as he did so that he was not very comfortable admitting this.

"About what?"

Dakota answered with his eyes on his plate. "Prayer."

Calder could see that he would need to go easy. He simply said, "If I can help, I'd be glad to."

"Thank you."

The men went on eating, Calder almost absentmindedly assisting the girls before asking Dakota a general question. The men talked easily about their jobs, neither showing outward appearances of stress.

When do I let things ride, and when do I push a little? It was a question Calder wrestled with all through the conversation. The meal ended, and Dakota even helped him clean the kitchen, but the subject of Dakota's questions on prayer did not come up again.

🌹🌹🌹

How do I really know You hear me when I pray? Dakota asked the Lord not long after the meal. *I know what Slater and Desmond have said, and at first I felt that You heard me, but right now I'm not so sure.*

Dakota stood at the window in his room, barely keeping himself from pacing. Things had not gone as he had hoped. He had wanted to ask Calder where this doubt was coming from and where the answer could be found, but Calder had the girls to handle, and Dakota also knew the women would be back at any time, since the doctor had only half the day at home.

"I can't believe You would save me like You did and then hide from me," Dakota now whispered toward the glass, his heart aching to be heard and to know he wasn't alone. "If You're listening, God, I need some answers. I need to know that this is real." Tears clogged Dakota's throat, and he didn't try to keep praying, not even in his heart. He didn't believe it was right to throw a challenge at God's feet, but he couldn't think of anything else to do or say. If only he knew where to look in the Bible for answers.

A noise coming from the kitchen beyond his closed door drew his attention. It sounded as though the women were back. The trained gentleman in him immediately sensed they might need help unloading the wagon. Glad to leave his tortured thoughts behind, Dakota went to investigate.

🌹🌹🌹

Dakota couldn't have said where Thursday went, but Friday arrived in a flurry of activity. He'd been up and dressed only a short time when he heard Darvi's and Merry's voices in the kitchen. The little girls chimed in from time to time, but the moving of chairs and other activity made it sound as if spring cleaning had arrived on September 1. Dakota stepped out to find just that. All the curtains were off the windows, and Darvi was elbow-deep in a sudsy tub, a tub of rinse water at her side.

"Good morning," Merry greeted him, setting a plate of food on the table. "How about some breakfast?"

"Thank you," Dakota replied, trying not to stare at the chaos around him.

"Sorry about the mess. I made the mistake of saying that I never got to my spring cleaning. Now Darvi's on a mission."

Dakota sat down to a high stack of griddle cakes, bacon, and hot coffee, a smile on his face.

"Trust me when I tell you that this is a feast, and washing or no washing, this beats where I usually eat."

"Where do you usually eat?" Darvi asked in genuine interest.

"On the trail. The first three things the Rangers want to know is whether you can ride, shoot, and cook."

"It's Koda!" one of the twins suddenly declared from the doorway, charging in to climb onto the chair next to his.

"All right, let me see," Dakota ordered before looking at her eye. "Ah, no scar. This must be Pilar."

That little girl smiled at him in pleasure and then settled in to watch him eat. Dakota talked to her some, but she would have occasional bouts of shyness and not answer. The scene changed entirely when Vivian showed up. The second twin looked surprised to be left out of the pleasure of watching Dakota, and with a little frown at her sister, Vivian pushed into the chair next to her in order to glue her eyes on their guest.

"What are you two doing?" their mother finally turned from the dishes she was washing to ask.

"Watching Koda."

This stopped Merry entirely. "What did you say, Pilar?"

The little girl had no idea what she was referring to, so she just looked at her. Merry tried Dakota.

"What did she call you?"

"Koda."

Merry's mouth dropped open in an unfeminine way, her head shaking in bewilderment.

"It doesn't matter," Dakota assured her. "I don't mind in the least."

"Girls," she began anyway, "I want you to call Mr. Rawlings by his name."

Their little heads bobbed just before Vivian turned to speak to him.

"Koda?"

"Yes, Vivian."

Merry's mouth was opening to scold her when Darvi's laughter rang out.

"Darvi! Do not laugh at this."

"I can't help it! They're so sincere."

Merry saw that she was right and gave up. It was not the way she wanted the girls to address adults, but she decided against fighting this particular battle.

Having finished his breakfast, Dakota suddenly stood and spoke. "Here, Darvi, let me get that."

"Oh, thank you."

Dakota took the heavy basket of wet curtains from her hands, thanked Merry for breakfast, and followed Darvi outside. He half-expected the girls to follow but soon found himself alone with Darvi at the clothesline. She plucked fabric from the basket, pegging the curtains carefully in the sun, Dakota moving with her.

"Dakota?" she said softly after a few minutes.

"Yeah?"

"Did you mean it when you said your time is your own right now?"

"Yes, I did."

Darvi looked at him before going back to work.

"Is it going to interfere with any of your plans if we stay until Monday?"

"Not in the least."

"Do you mean that?" Darvi turned to him with such hope on her face that Dakota was amazed.

"Certainly. We can stay longer if you like."

"I would like to," she said as she went back to the clothes basket, "but I think company can get old very fast. I don't want to wear out my welcome, but I do want to stay through the weekend. It's rather important to me."

"That's fine. Do you mind my asking why you want to stay?"

Darvi hesitated. This was so new to her, and she was sure if he asked her any difficult questions, she would make a complete mess of things. However, the man beside her was waiting. Seeing no help for it, she admitted, "I want to go to church with Calder and Merry."

Darvi had all she could do to keep her mouth shut when Dakota said, "I'll join you if you don't mind."

Dakota saw the surprise in her eyes, but the twins came looking for them just then and neither one had time to say another word. Less than an hour later Dakota left for town. Darvi didn't wait five minutes before telling Merry what he had said.

❧ ❧ ❧

Calder knotted his tie on Sunday morning, not quite able to grasp the last few days. He couldn't think of the last time he'd been so busy. Merry and the girls were having the time of their lives with their guests, but Calder had delivered four babies, wrapped broken bones, patched split heads, and all this among his other duties. He was starting to think the people of Stillwater were on some type of mission, one that would let them visit their doctor on a regular basis. Calder thought he would be ill as well if they kept it up, and all of this knowing that Darvi and Dakota were leaving the next day.

Dakota had even come into town and stopped at Calder's office, but he'd been with a patient and had two more waiting. The big Ranger had not looked put out, but Calder had been frustrated by it all.

There was a time when I begged You for a successful practice, Lord, and now I'm complaining. Please help me to enjoy the time I have with these folks and leave the rest to You.

"Papa?" a little voice called from outside the door.

"Come in."

Calder listened to his daughter try before he stepped over and opened the door.

"Mama says eat."

"Okay, Viv. I'll be right down."

Vivian waited for him, and when they both gained the kitchen, Calder was pleased to see that neither Darvi nor Dakota had come in yet. He didn't want to miss any more time with them. In less than five minutes everyone was gathered, and they sat down as a group. Calder prayed, and to his amazement, Dakota had a question as soon as he was finished.

"Do you ever worry that God isn't hearing you, Calder?"

"I haven't for a long time, but I used to."

"What changed for you?"

"Something my father said. He asked me if God's Word was true or not. It forced me to evaluate what I believe, and the truth is, I believe every word of the Bible. With that in mind, I looked at the different people who were devoted to prayer, including Jesus Christ. I know I can follow their lead."

"Where did you find those examples in the Bible?"

"I have some verses written in the front of my Bible that might help. Would you like me to copy them for you?"

"I would, thank you."

"Have you spent much time reading the Bible, Mr. Rawlings?" Merry asked.

"Just recently I have. I'm afraid that not all of it makes sense to me."

"I don't think anyone would claim to understand all of it," Merry added with a smile. "If he did, I'm not sure I would believe him."

Darvi was careful not to look at Merry, but she was nearly falling into her plate to listen to this exchange. Realizing she was staring at Dakota, she forced herself to eat. From there the time simply sped away. Everyone was barely finished when Merry said they were running late, and before Darvi knew it, she was sitting in church, the Scott family to the left of her and Dakota on their other side.

Some of the songs were familiar, but the sermon was something she'd never heard before or even considered. The pastor told them, with verses to support it, that God had not only saved man, but saved him with a plan. God had good works for His children to do, and His will was evident on every page of the Bible.

Darvi was still thinking about the sermon when she walked absentmindedly out the church door. She had told Merry she wanted a moment alone at the wagon. She was nearly half a block down the boardwalk when a male voice stopped her.

"Well, hello."

Pulled from her musings, Darvi turned to find two men leaning against the side of a building, both dressed in denim, clean shirts, hats, and boots. There was nothing disreputable about them; indeed, they were clean-shaven and well pressed, but Darvi thought it rude to address her without an introduction. Her chin went into the air, but they only smiled, pushed away from the wall, and started to move toward her.

"Been to church, have you?"

"You, sir," she began, but stopped before starting the set-down she was ready to give him, not certain her old tactics were a good idea.

"Sir?" The man who was fairer-haired spoke again. "Did you call me sir? Oh, I like that."

"And I'd like it if you'd move on and leave the lady alone."

Neither man looked particularly guilty or intimidated by the large, dark man who appeared behind the woman, his entire face visible above her head, but neither did they want to tangle with him. Pretty as the woman was, the dark, intense eyes of the man who shadowed her were a little more than they bargained for.

Watching them walk away, Darvi stood very still. She could tell she was shaking a little and wasn't up to facing Dakota. He didn't know this. Only a moment passed before he stepped around and faced her. Darvi made herself look up.

"Are you all right?"

"I think so," she said with more bravado than she felt.

"What did they want?"

"I don't know."

"But they wouldn't move on when you told them to."

"I didn't tell them to move on."

Dakota's brows rose on this. "Why is that?"

Darvi's face filled with frustration before she answered. "I don't know! I'm a different person now, Dakota, and I don't think I'm supposed to talk to people that way."

Dakota's eyes narrowed, his own temper rising.

"Let me get this straight. You didn't want to hurt their feelings?"

Darvi scowled at him but didn't answer. Seeing the upset and confusion in her eyes, Dakota softened. He spoke quietly, his voice compassionate.

"Unless I miss my guess, Darvi, you and I have had a recent change in our lives."

The strawberry blonde nodded.

"If yours is anything like mine, right now you don't know which way is up."

"That about explains it. It's been wonderful," she was swift to add, "but I'm so unsure about so many things."

Dakota saw that Calder was headed their way. He gave him a quick wave and turned Darvi back toward the church. As he hoped, Calder only waved back and turned himself, giving them a moment alone.

"No matter what changes have occurred, Darvi, God wants us to keep using our heads. I refuse to believe that there's some verse in Scripture that says once you accept Christ, you have to let men accost you."

"No, I don't suppose it does say that, but my tongue's been getting me into trouble for a long time."

"Nevertheless, you know what appropriate attention is and what it is not. If you wanted those men out of your face, you had every right to tell them."

"But I was angry, and I didn't want to blast them with my temper."

"That's wise of you, but you can still tell someone, quite firmly, I might add, that you don't wish to speak to him."

Darvi stopped and looked up at him.

"I'm not going to argue with you, but I'm going to have to think on that."

"That's fair enough," Dakota agreed. "What did you think of the sermon?"

Darvi sighed. "Wow."

"I know what you mean."

"I just never thought about God having a plan for us. Did you?"

"Not personally, no. My parents taught my brothers and me to believe there was a God, but it's only recently that I considered the fact that God has thoughts of me or that He would want a relationship with me. It's a little more than I can take sometimes."

Darvi was still framing a reply when Calder pulled up with the wagon. The whole family was already on board, and the girls tried to climb onto both of them the moment they were seated. Darvi ended up holding the Bibles, and Dakota took both girls on his lap.

"Koda?"

"Yes?"

But that was all Pilar wanted to say. She laid her head against him, and Dakota held her close. Vivian spent the whole ride looking up into his face but didn't care to talk either. The girls gave him such a longing for Laura Peterson, his brother's young sister-in-law, that Dakota determined to visit Slater right away. He was thinking about how he could do this when Darvi shifted beside him, and he was reminded of his present job. Working not to let his emotions take over but not quite making it, Dakota's thoughts were very determined.

I'll get Darvi off safely, and then I'll make my way home. I'll visit Cash for a while and then go see Slater and Liberty. If Brace doesn't want me back by then, I'll go back to the ranch for good!

❧ ❧ ❧

"Are you going to be all right?" Dakota asked Darvi once they had left the house. She hadn't cried when they had said goodbye, but her face was so set that Dakota knew she was in agony. The fact that she didn't answer him also told him she was just hanging on.

Not in a hurry this time, they rode easily. Dakota was very rested, and Darvi had not wanted to leave. Neither did she want to talk, at least not for some miles. Indeed, it was midmorning—they were long out of Stillwater—before she broke the silence.

"Weren't those little girls cute?" she asked quietly.

"Oh, yes," Dakota replied with a smile. "I fell in love the first moment I saw them."

"They liked you too."

"I hope so."

"Merry told me," Darvi assured him. "She said Vivian and Pilar are usually more comfortable with women. I guess their father owns their hearts, but with you they made an exception."

Dakota smiled. "They weren't very vocal, but they sure liked to look at me."

Darvi smiled as well and turned to stare at him.

"What?" Dakota wished to know.

"I'm just trying to see you through their eyes."

Dakota good-naturedly shook his head. "Well, tell me when you figure it out."

With that the two were content to ride in silence for a time. Darvi looked completely at ease, like a child who's well taken care of, and that must have been because she was well looked after. Dakota was constantly on the alert. He was mentally thinking about the roads that would take them to Aurora and also where they could lunch, as well as finding a suitable place to set up camp before dark.

Dakota had stocked up on provisions, so he wasn't worried, but when the sun was right over their heads, he decided to mention to her that they were not going to make any sort of town that night.

Upon this announcement, Darvi pulled her mount to a stop.

"We're not going back through Blake where we stayed before?"

"Not if we're headed to Aurora so you can catch the train. Blake would be out of the way."

Her hat shaded her face quite nicely, but she still put her hand up to the brim and looked around them.

"Where will we spend the night?"

"There's an oak grove about five hours from here. It's off the road, but there's a large stand of trees, and the stream there is deep and fast flowing. I think we'll be in good shape if we can make that."

"Then we'll be in Aurora tomorrow night?"

"Probably not, but if you want to ride hard, we can try."

Darvi thanked him for the information and heeled her horse back into motion; indeed, she even picked up the pace some. At the same time, her mind gave her heart a short lecture.

You had to see Merry. You couldn't live another day until you saw Merry. Would you have been quite so eager, Darvi, if you had known you were going to be sleeping on the ground? Darvi rode on without even trying to answer.

Six

"Is this the place?"

Busy scouting the area, Dakota didn't answer, but Darvi knew it had to be. He had taken them off the main road about 30 minutes back, and the trees were just as he had described. Darvi could also hear the rippling sound of water over rocks.

"Okay, Darvi," Dakota spoke as he came back toward her on foot, "Come on this way around the trees. We'll set up camp for the night and have some dinner."

Darvi did as she was directed, knowing that hotel room or not, it was going to be good to get out of the saddle. Once again she was reminded of how her determination to see Merry had clouded all else. They had certainly ridden harder *to* Stillwater, but she didn't remember feeling sore. Now as she dismounted, she barely stifled a groan.

"You weren't sore on the way to Scotts," Dakota commented from behind her.

Darvi turned to see him watching her.

"How did you know I was sore?"

A slow smile stretched across the Ranger's face.

"I just watched you get off that horse."

Darvi tried to look stern but ended up laughing a little. At least she could do that. What she couldn't do was rub the parts of her anatomy that ached with stiffness and fatigue.

"Why don't you walk down by the water? I'll take care of your horse."

Darvi looked as grateful as she felt before thanking Dakota and unfastening her satchel from Finley's saddle.

"I think I'll freshen up a bit."

"All right. Keep your eyes open and stay within earshot."

Thinking he sounded just like Uncle Marty, she went on her way, moving gingerly as sensation returned to her limbs. Pain or no pain, it wasn't long before she noticed what a lovely setting it was. The day was still plenty warm, but just the sound and sight of the water seemed to cool her, and finding a large rock right at the edge was like an answer to prayer. Darvi sat on it, slipped off her boots and stockings, and placed her feet in the water. The action seemed to cool all of her. Had it been dark, she'd have gotten all the way in, but for the moment this did the trick.

Her satchel came next. She reached for the bag and brought out a large handkerchief, one she'd borrowed from her father. After soaking it, she bathed her face and neck. In very short order she felt like herself again.

"Are you all right?" she heard Dakota call.

"Yes, thank you, I am. Do you need some help?"

"No, I'm fine, thanks."

"I have my feet in the water already."

Darvi heard the laughter in Dakota's voice when he called back, "Sounds great. I'll probably join you in a minute."

Darvi smiled in contentment, all misgivings about camping slowly dying away. She decided as she sat there that she wanted a fresh pair of stockings. Her hands were back in her bag when she heard the rattle. She stopped moving, even though she could feel the outline of her gun beneath some of her garments. Her eyes shifting frantically, she finally spotted it. A small rattlesnake was coiled on the ground about a foot away from the rock. As Darvi watched, it uncoiled a bit and started to move away from her, but Darvi still brought out her gun. She realized her mistake too late. Sensing her movement, the snake recoiled to face her, the rattles sounding off again.

"I don't think I can do this," she whispered even as she held the gun at arm's length, her finger ready to pull the trigger. Her mind raced through the things she'd heard about snakes, such as their ability to jump the length of their bodies. She wanted to gauge the distance but was afraid to take her eyes from the reptile.

"Darvi, you all right?" Dakota chose that moment to check on her. The snake still watched her, his tail now silent.

"Darvi?"

"Dakota," she managed in a small voice. Then louder. "Dakota."

"Darvi, are you—" Dakota was saying as he came into view, his brow lowering as he watched her hold something black out in front of her with both hands. He moved closer and saw that it was a stocking draped over a gun. Why it took him so long to see what had her frozen in place, he didn't know, but moving in swiftly, his gun coming clean from his holster as he walked, he fired one shot before the snake jolted with the impact and lay still.

Her eyes still huge, Darvi kept her gun trained on the dead serpent even as she watched Dakota approach.

Dakota was compassionate when he saw the fear in her face, but he still smiled and plucked at the black stocking.

"Does the gun work without this?"

Darvi slowly lowered the weapon. "I was afraid to shoot. I thought I would miss such a small target."

"That still would have scared him away."

"But then I would have wondered all night where he was." Her eyes flickered toward the snake. "Now I'll know."

Dakota then saw that she trembled a little.

"You were very brave."

"I don't feel brave. I feel like calling for my mother."

Dakota bent and put his arm around her shoulders and gave her a squeeze.

"Thanks, Dakota."

"You're welcome. I'll stomp about some and make sure he has no family." As Dakota started his search, he kept speaking. "Tell me something, Darvi, does trouble just naturally follow you around?"

"What does that mean?" she asked, working discretely to put her stockings on.

"Oh, first you follow a complete stranger down the streets of Austin, who just happens to be me, and then you have two men following you in Stillwater, and now you attract a snake. It just causes a man to wonder."

Stockings and shoes in place, Darvi turned to set him straight. "I'll have you know, Dakota Rawlings, I can take care of myself very nicely."

Dakota didn't even glance her way. "It's beginning to make sense why Brace didn't want you coming on your own."

"You're all the same," she muttered, checking around the rock before climbing down. She gathered her things, gun still in hand, and moved back in the direction from which she had come. What she saw stopped her. Darvi didn't know how Dakota had accomplished it so swiftly, but he had set up a very orderly camp. A glance to the right showed that he had tethered the horses near food and water and already had a fire coaxed along, with two bedrolls opposite each other. Darvi knew she was in good hands, but she hadn't expected this.

Dakota had told them he could cook. Darvi didn't know why she hadn't figured on the rest.

He lives his life on the trail. What did you expect?

"I think we're reptile-free for the moment," Dakota proclaimed as he joined her. "I hope you like your coffee strong. I don't know any other way to make it."

"I do like it strong, but believe me when I tell you that I'll eat and drink whatever you give me."

"Hungry, are you?"

"Well, not starved, but as usual, I've acted without thinking. It never occurred to me that we wouldn't be in a town tonight. If I was on my own, I'd be going hungry."

As though she'd just proved his point, Dakota smiled. Catching it, Darvi's chin came up.

"I would have done fine on my own," she told him firmly. "I would have come up with something to eat."

Fearing he would only get himself in trouble, Dakota didn't comment. Not fully understanding the female brain, however, he still found more than he bargained for.

"Do you doubt it?" Darvi demanded, not willing to let the matter drop.

Dakota looked at her.

"Actually, I don't. Plucky as you are, you would probably do fine, but don't ask me to condone your being out here on your own, Darvi. I won't do that."

Darvi wisely shut her mouth. She hadn't expected as much as she got, and she determined to let it drop before she pushed Dakota into saying something she didn't want to hear. *She* believed she could do fine, and that was all that really mattered to her.

※ ※ ※

The meal was very good. Merry had sent some baked goods with Dakota, and that man had a good supply of trail food. He turned dried meat into beef and gravy over rice, a biscuit on the side. They ate cookies with their last cups of coffee.

Darvi volunteered to wash dishes, and she was at the stream doing this when Dakota realized they had company. Two men approached on one horse, a small, hard-ridden beast. Their eyes watched him but were more interested in the horses nearby.

"Hello," the man on the front called.

Dakota didn't like his smile but still said, "Good evening."

"Nice horses," the second man spoke as they dismounted.

Dakota saw no reason to comment. He hoped they would move on without a confrontation, and almost at the same moment, he heard the clank of pots and knew that Darvi was returning.

"Not now, Darvi," he said under his breath, but there was no way she heard. Indeed, completely unaware of the danger, she entered the campsite talking.

"I don't know if I got this one pot clean. It was very stubborn. I hope you aren't too—"

Dakota didn't even look at her, which meant he saw every bit of interest on the visitors' faces. He decided to confront the situation head on.

"The horses aren't for sale."

The men both snickered before the first one said, "We ain't got no money anyhow."

"Well, that only leaves you one option, gentlemen," Dakota went on amiably, "and it's only fair to warn you that I'll shoot you before I let you take our horses."

They seemed to weigh this up for a time, looking at each other and then back to Dakota, who partially blocked their view of Darvi.

"She your wife?" number two asked.

"The lady is not your business," he said flatly, his hand not moving to his gun, but his whole body shifting in a no-nonsense way. "And since we're camped here for the night, I think it might be best if you head on your way."

Hesitating only for a moment, the men climbed back onto the weary animal and continued down the road. Both Darvi and Dakota watched them for some time. Darvi's imagination had them doubling back, so she kept her eyes on them for as long as she could. When she finally glanced up at Dakota, it was to find him watching her.

"I suppose you're going to say that was all my fault?" she asked calmly.

"No, I wasn't going to say that, but it would help if you didn't look so good."

Knowing she was not at her best, Darvi nearly laughed. "What do you suggest?"

Seeing the amusement in her eyes, Dakota barely kept from smiling. "Well, you could blacken a few teeth and maybe dye your hair a mud brown."

"I'll think on it," Darvi assured him before adding, "it's your size and color, by the way."

Dakota blinked.

"What's my size and color?"

"The reason the twins stare at you, and also the reason those men in Stillwater and the men today left without an argument. Depending on who they are, people either find you a great comfort or completely intimidating." This said, she turned to put the pots down and then to sit down on her bedroll, reaching for her satchel as soon as she was settled.

For a moment it was on Dakota's mind to ask which way Darvi found him, but he thought he knew the answer. She'd half-hidden behind him while he talked with the men. Somehow he didn't think she was intimidated by him in the least.

※ ※ ※

Dakota did not get into his bedroll when darkness fell and Darvi climbed into hers. There was still a small flicker of fire left, and he wanted to go back to Calder's letter, which was filled with Scriptures. He started to read the letter again, thankful that Calder had written out some of the verses.

Dear Dakota,

I want to start by thanking you for asking me about this subject. It's easy to do things by habit and not conviction. It was very good for me to be reminded why prayer is so important.

Colossians 4:12 says: "Epaphras, who is one of you, a servant of Christ, salutes you, always laboring fervently for you in prayers, that ye may stand perfect and complete in all the will of God." Epaphras is devoted to prayer.

Colossians 1:9 says: "For this cause we also, since the day we heard it, do not cease to pray for you, and to desire that ye might be filled with the knowledge of his will in all wisdom and spiritual understanding." This is Paul speaking here. Note the way he says he didn't cease; he was another person devoted to prayer. James 5 says that Elijah was such a warrior in prayer that God held the rain back for more than three years.

And then to my favorite, Jesus Himself—God's own Son—was willing to give up sleep to meet His Father to pray. Mark 1:35: "In the morning, rising up a great while before day, he went out, and departed into a solitary place, and there prayed." I don't know about you, Dakota, but I don't think Christ would give this kind of example to us if His Father wasn't listening.

As Dakota finished reading the letter, he saw that Calder had included many other verses for him to look up, as well as telling him that he would pray for understanding in the matter. He closed with God's blessing and an invitation to visit anytime.

Dakota sat for a while longer and thought about his own faith. It had been so clear to him that he was lost and that God had found him, but somewhere in the mix he'd gotten the impression that his first-time faith was all he would need.

I've got to trust You all day, every day. I see that now. Not just to save me, but that You're listening and that You care. That was never clear to me before now, but this is what Desmond was talking about when he said to match my feelings against Your Word. If they don't hold up, then I can't hold on to them.

Thank You for saving me, Lord God. I'm still amazed at this second chance, and even this second chance to understand how You work.

His heart still prayerful, Dakota went back to his Bible to look up the other verses from Calder, asking God to help him understand the truths. The flickering light made it a challenge at times, but Dakota read until he could see no more. With the last dying flames behind him, he checked on the horses, which he had moved closer to camp, and finally settled in for the night. Darvi had stopped moving around, and Dakota assumed she had fallen asleep. He knew she would be sore in the morning and that riding Finley all day was not going to help, but he saw no help for it. Dakota found himself praying for her, and somewhere along the line he dropped off to sleep. It didn't last long, though, as Darvi suddenly gasped and woke.

"Dakota?"

"Right here," came his deep voice comfortingly through the darkness.

"Did they come and take the horses?" She sounded panicked.

"No. I checked on them right before I settled in."

He heard her sigh.

"I thought my dream was real," she admitted. "I'm sorry I woke you."

"It's all right."

It was silent for a moment.

"You don't sound as though you were asleep."

"I don't sleep very soundly when I'm on the trail."

Again silence covered them, and again Darvi was the one to break it.

"Dakota?"

"Yeah?"

"I don't want to intrude, but will you tell me how it happened for you?"

"My salvation?"

"Yes. I mean, if you want to."

"It's not a very long story. You knew I'd been shot and I told you it was bad, but I don't know if I told you that while I was in that gunfight,

I thought I might die. When I realized I hadn't, I knew it was time to face what my brothers had been telling me."

"How many brothers do you have?"

"Two."

"And they both believe?"

"Yes. I thought that preachers used hell as a scare tactic to get people to church, but when I was faced with dying, I realized I wasn't ready. If hell was a real place, I was in trouble. If Slater and Cash had been telling me the truth, I knew I was lost.

"After I got hurt, I stayed with another Ranger. My brothers came to see me there, and I asked them to help me understand salvation. That's about the size of it."

"Had you been searching for a long time?"

"Running was more like it. I just didn't want to accept the fact that I sin. I'm around a lot of very desperate people, and somehow I thought I was better. I didn't like being lumped into the sinner category."

"Thank you for telling me," Darvi said softly. Dakota thought he heard tears in her voice.

"Are you all right?"

"Yes," she said, but it was on a sniff.

"How did it happen for you?"

"I won't be able to tell you without crying. It's all I've done lately."

"Well, don't let tears stop you."

"It's a long story," she replied, tears even thicker in her voice.

"I'm not going anywhere."

Dakota heard her blow her nose and cough a little. He wanted to tell her they didn't have to talk, but thinking she might fall back to sleep, he kept silent. A few minutes passed and she began.

"I don't know if you know this, Dakota, but I'm from St. Louis. And not just any part of St. Louis. I grew up in one of the nicer homes in one of the better sections of town. My family has always lived in style. In fact, I can't remember not having just about anything I wanted. We were very self-sufficient, my whole family, and because of that, I just never gave God a thought. We didn't pray at meals or go to church; we just took care of ourselves.

"But there was a woman in town, a pastor's wife, and she and my mother got to know each other through the St. Louis Ladies' Guild. I was just a little girl when I heard my mother tell Mrs. Beacher—that was her name—that she didn't believe anyone lived for eternity, not in heaven or hell. My mother believes that our life on earth is the end. You live and then you die. When Mrs. Beacher pressed her, my mother said that we live on through our descendants, and almost to prove that point, my mother has pictures of our ancestors all over the house. The hallways are lined with their paintings and photographs. So is the library and the large parlor."

Darvi fell silent for a moment.

"I grew up so smug and sure, Dakota. I didn't have a care in the world—at least not until I visited Austin in the summers and played with Merry Scott, who was then Merry Voight. She had the audacity to tell me she knew there was a heaven, and to top it off, she said she was going there."

Dakota smiled as he listened.

"I could have strangled her. I thought it was the most foolish thing, but she wasn't teasing me or acting proud. She had a deep joy about this fact, a joy I had never experienced over anything. Most of the summer I would play my heart out with her, not letting myself think too deeply, but when I went home I was miserable. Not only did I want to be back running free in a way I never could at home, but then I had time to think about what she said, and every summer I knew tremendous fear that she might be right." She sighed a little and continued quietly.

"This went on for more years than I care to think about. I eventually stopped visiting in the summer. My interests changed, and boys were noticing me. I even became engaged to be married, and then the unthinkable happened. It was just this spring. The house was abuzz with plans for a June wedding. My mother was showing the caterer through the house, and he asked about the largest portrait in the hall. Later I tried to tell myself that she was busy and distracted, but I couldn't quite convince my heart. My mother, who was going to live on through her children and grandchildren, couldn't remember Great Uncle Jenkins' name. She looked very forlorn for a moment but then passed it off with a laugh.

"Later, when I was alone, I walked through and looked at all the portraits in the house. I couldn't tell you the names of half of them. I asked myself how, if I didn't know these people and my mother was already forgetting their names, could they still be living?

"The fact that they were all very dead and always would be was like a blow to me. I walked around in a painful cloud the rest of the day, and the next morning I canceled a date with my fiancée and went to see Mrs. Beacher." Darvi sighed again, this time sounding very tired. "I understood now all the things that Merry had said to me during those hot summers in Austin, and as soon as Mrs. Beacher explained, I knew in an instant that my sin had put Christ on the cross and that I was lost without Him. I'd never known such peace, but it only lasted until I arrived home. I can't begin to tell you the mess I made of things.

"The weeks that followed were like something out of a nightmare. My parents were deeply hurt over what I was telling them. Then Mrs. Beacher, who was meeting with me each week for Bible study, asked me if my intended was a believer. I had to tell her no."

Tears were coming now, and Darvi didn't try to stop them.

"I can't tell you what it did to all of us to have me break off my engagement with Brandon. He was so hurt, and I was feeling lost and confused. My mother said it was just a stage and that I would get over it. She went right on with the wedding plans until I left for a few days to get her attention. I didn't know what else to do. And all the time Brandon was coming around, telling me he'd love me anyway, but I knew it wasn't right. I finally wrote Uncle Marty and asked if I could come. He wired me right away and said yes. I was so exhausted by the time I arrived that I ended up ill. I know my mother must have written to him, but he never said a word to me.

"In all the hoopla, I'd completely forgotten about Merry. After spending days in bed, I woke up one morning and knew I had to see her. But we had never kept in touch by mail, and I didn't know she'd moved. That's why I followed you down the street, and that's why you're stuck with me right now."

"I don't feel I'm stuck with you, Darvi, and I don't want to hear you say that again."

"All right." She sounded very contrite, and Dakota wished he could see her. He had written his parents about his conversion and received a rather surprised letter from his mother, but it was nothing like what Darvi had experienced. In fact, although admitting that she didn't understand, his mother told him that she and his father would support him in whatever he wanted to do. It had always been that way with his parents, and Dakota was just now seeing how good he'd had it. His parents' lack of faith in Christ still concerned him, but there was no anxiety as he prayed for them every day and tried to prepare his heart for the next time he saw them.

A sniff broke into Dakota's thoughts.

"Thank you for telling me, Darvi. I'll pray for you."

"Thank you. Please pray that I'll figure a way to get out of this mess I've landed myself in."

"I can't pray that, Darvi, because I don't see it that way."

"What do you mean?"

"I mean, you can't marry a man who doesn't share your faith and commitment to Christ. I'm sorry that your family has taken it so hard, but they're going to have to get used to your decision."

Darvi was so shocked she was speechless. This worried Dakota.

"Am I out of line, Darvi?"

"No, I'm just surprised that I haven't seen that before. I've got to let my mother work this out. I can't worry about her response to Christ or my decision."

"I agree with you. My parents do not share my faith in Christ, and I'm thankful they don't give me a hard time. Nevertheless, I can be tempted to worry about their eternity and choices when God says worry is a sin."

Again Darvi sighed, but not because she was overwhelmed. She knew worry was a sin, but she hadn't seen that this was what she was doing.

"Thank you, Dakota," Darvi said for the last time. "You've helped me a lot."

"You're welcome," Dakota responded, feeling very inadequate. There was so much he didn't know, and for a moment he had doubted his own words to her. He finally fell back to sleep—they both did—each one praying for greater understanding and wisdom in this new life, a life they wouldn't trade for anything, but one so foreign they might have been living in another world.

Seven

Aurora, Texas

JARED SILK'S EYES NARROWED IN ANGER as he read the newspaper column. After all this time he should have been used to it, but he knew if Annabelle Hewett had been in the room just then, he would have been tempted to strike her.

He read it yet again:

> What does Aurora's newest bank have going this time? How about loan rates that are not only too good to be true, they're impossible to believe! One can't help but wonder how owner Jared Silk can afford clothing that clearly didn't come from a catalog. We'll all be waiting with great anticipation at the town's fall festival. Will Silk's face be as red as his new cravat?
>
> A. Hewett

Had Annabelle been in the room right then, she would have seen just how red the banker's face could get. Jared was so furious he nearly barked at the person who knocked on his office door. Remembering just in time that the bank's doors were already open, he tempered his response to a terse reply and told the men to enter. Even though he'd sent for them, seeing them did nothing for his mood.

"Have you read this?" he asked one of his personal assistants.

"Yes," Seth Redding answered calmly, taking a chair as though he had all day.

"I'm sick of it! I want it stopped. Do you hear me?"

"What exactly are we supposed to do?" the other man, Eliot McDermott, asked. "She's free to write whatever she chooses, and we know from the last little job that busting up the newspaper office won't stop it."

"Shut your mouth!" Jared hissed at him as he rose to shut the door, even knowing the hall and stairway were empty.

The men, half-brothers who could have had respectable jobs, watched their boss secure the door and stalk to the window. From the second-story view, he stared down on the street, his frame tense with helpless frustration.

"What she writes is all true, Jared," Eliot added. "I don't know why you fight it."

"I don't pay you to think," Jared now said coldly, never taking his eyes from the window. The statement wasn't true, but the banker was too angry to see reason.

The brothers exchanged a look. At times like these they were tempted to ask themselves why they put up with him, but the answer was never far from their minds: the money.

"I think I'd like to talk with Annabelle Hewett," Jared said.

Seth came to his feet, and Eliot's stance became tense.

"Now, Jared," Seth began, "you can't go snatching that lady off the streets. She's too well known."

Jared finally turned to the men, his face filled with a calm they had learned to dread.

"You're right; I can't do it. But you can and you will. I don't care how you handle it. I don't even care if you hire someone else, but I want you to offer a personal invitation to Miss Hewett."

"An invitation to what?"

"Why, to my home for dinner. We'll have a nice meal and talk awhile. I'm sure I can convince her that she's quite mistaken."

The men didn't bother to hide their displeasure, but Jared was not swayed.

"Just let me know what day I'm to expect her. And boys, keep it neat. I have a reputation to uphold in this town."

Knowing they had no one to blame but themselves, the brothers filed out. They didn't linger at the bank but headed right onto the street and over to the saloon to discuss the idea. They had a plan in very little time, but later, Seth returned to the bank only to find that

Jared had come up with a plan of his own. Nevertheless, this job was going to cost the banker a little more than usual.

❧ ❧ ❧

"You don't have to stay," Darvi proclaimed to Dakota for the third time.

"So you've said." His reply was as calm as always, and Darvi gave up.

They had made excellent time getting to Aurora, and during their travels Darvi was surprised to find that Dakota's home was very near. He could be there in a matter of hours. Darvi saw no reason for him to stay the night just to put her on the train. However, he was not about to leave. Darvi was glad for the company but felt she'd been trouble enough.

"So where do you want to spend the night?"

"I've got to get my trunk from the train station, and then I'll check into the Belmont."

"Why don't I get the trunk?" Dakota started to suggest, but Darvi was already shaking her head.

"I appreciate the offer, Dakota, but I need my clothing as soon as I check in, and I'll be able to find the trunk in no time, since I know what it looks like."

"Sounds fair enough. By the way, what are we doing with Finley?"

"I'm to leave him at Garth's Livery, or some name like that. My uncle has plans to get him back. I didn't ask where it was, but I don't think it will be too hard to find."

"Have you stayed in Aurora before?"

"No, I haven't."

"How do you know about the Belmont?"

"Uncle Marty. He lectured me for a full 24 hours before I left." Darvi's voice went monotone before she went on, "What to watch for, where to go, do everything Dakota says, don't look at strange men, don't leave your room after dark, get your trunk from the station, leave the horse with Garth, and I can't remember what else."

Dakota had a good laugh over this litany but thought it sounded like Brace. He was also changing his mind about Darvi being on her own. He would never leave her to fend for herself, but she was very quick to catch on to things and as plucky as he'd first expected.

The train station was a bustling place, and it took some doing to track down the bags and trunks that were being held. Darvi had to give her name and a description of her small trunk, and then the man was gone for what seemed to be ages trying to find it. Because her name was not on the outside, he made her open the top and show her name under the lid. The fact that she had the key should have spoken volumes.

Finally satisfied, the man released the trunk to her care. Dakota hefted it onto Eli's back. It wasn't the ideal mode of transportation, but if they asked the station to deliver it, there was no telling when the heavy piece would arrive. There was a lad of 12 or 13 who stayed close to the hotel lobby and was willing to carry it to Darvi's room when she checked in. Dakota followed in their wake, his own room key in hand.

"Thank you," Darvi told the young man, slipping a coin to him.

"Thank you," he returned politely and went on his way.

"Are you on this floor?" Darvi asked Dakota.

Dakota looked at his key. "I think so, but I must be a few doors down."

"I know it's getting on in the day, Dakota, but can you give me time to clean up before we eat?"

"I was going to ask you the same thing. There's no way I'm going to enjoy my dinner until I've ordered a bath."

Darvi smiled at his understanding.

"I'll come back here in about an hour. How does that work?"

"Wonderful. I'll see you then."

Saddlebags in hand, Dakota went to find his room, not knowing that an hour was optimistic. Nevertheless, the two travelers finally sat down in the hotel dining room, both ready for a hot meal and the comfort of eating indoors.

"Dakota," Darvi asked over coffee, their order having just been taken, "how did you become a Ranger?"

Dakota smiled. "I caught the bug when I was about 13. We'd had some trouble with cattle rustling, and the Rangers came in to help. I'd never seen such tough, capable men. I was in awe of every one of them. From that time forward I dreamed of having my own sturdy mount, side arm, rope, and Bowie knife. I had access to all those things on the ranch, but they weren't mine. At the time I had no concept of the responsibility, but even when I understood the position, I still longed to work hard and uphold the law in Texas."

Dakota stopped for a moment before admitting, "It was all I ever wanted until my brother Slater came to Christ. Cash and my grandmother already believed, but I never thought Slater would. The change in him was uncanny, and then he left the Rangers to settle in one town. I was ready to string him up, but he stood up to me and told me his decision was made. The change in his life got me to thinking that I might have missed something.

"I don't know if I thought of it when you were telling your story,

Darvi, but Slater did what you need to do. Although everyone in the Rangers was telling him he didn't need to quit, he knew he couldn't stay on the trail. He stood up to me and to Brace, and I know God has blessed him for it."

It was on Darvi's mind to ask Dakota if he would stay with the Rangers now, but for some reason she held back. His salvation was as new as hers. Maybe he hadn't thought that far. Then again, she knew nothing of Slater. Maybe their situations were nothing alike.

"So are you ready to go home and face your family?"

"I think I am. I'm trying not to think of conversations in my head. I've done that in the past, and it never works. The person never says what I think he's going to, and so everything I've rehearsed is a waste of time."

Dakota was impressed. It was so easy to do just that. He'd done it many times himself.

"Well, you can go knowing that I will pray for you."

"Thank you. And I'll be praying for you. I never thought about anyone being able to have an influence on Uncle Marty. Maybe your life will touch his."

"I hope so. I care for him a lot."

Darvi found herself wanting to cry and hoped their food would come soon. Quite hungry, she suddenly realized a wave of homesickness was washing over her. The combination of hunger, her uncle, and a need to go home rained down on her with such intensity that she almost gasped.

Dakota stayed very quiet. They had talked for hours the day before, and Darvi had apologized for her tears on two occasions. Both times Dakota told her it was all right. He hoped that if he remained quiet now, she would not feel the need. It helped to have his stomach growl, and for Darvi to hear it.

"I think they've forgotten us," she said, trying not to sniff.

"I think you might be right. I'm going to have to make myself chew. Right now I think I could swallow things whole."

Neither one felt compelled to talk after that. Their food arrived about ten minutes later, and that was all they needed. By the time they finished, the days on the road were catching up. With little more than a plan to meet for breakfast, they bid each other goodnight.

❧ ❧ ❧

Darvi stood on the train station platform in a navy blue suit, her satchel open as she secured her ticket inside. Closing the top, she looked up at Dakota who stood in front of her.

"All set?" he asked.

"I think so."

"You look very nice in that suit, by the way."

Darvi looked up at him innocently and asked, "You don't think I should blacken a few front teeth?"

Dakota put his arms up in surrender.

"I'm not going to live that one down, am I?"

"Oh, I don't know about that," Darvi said playfully. "If you happen to see a certain uncle of mine and perhaps mention to him that I was a perfect angel on this trip, I might see my way clear to forget what you said."

Dakota laughed again.

"I'll do it."

Darvi smiled up at him. "Thanks for everything, Dakota. I can't tell you how good it was to see Merry and then hear of your revival as well."

"I like that," Dakota decided. "My revival. That just about sums it up."

Darvi didn't want to get teary again, so she said nothing. Not one who liked waiting for the train whistle to blow, she said goodbye right then. Dakota gave her a great hug, one that Darvi gladly returned, and then stood and watched her get on board. He searched the windows and waved when he spotted her, but as soon as she looked down at her lap, he turned away. It was going to be wonderful to get home, but he hated to see Darvi go. He walked back toward the hotel and livery, his heart a mix of emotions.

Halfway to the hotel, Dakota stopped in midstride. He didn't know why he hadn't thought of it sooner, but he could keep in contact with Darvi. The whistle had already blown, but he knew if he hurried he could get her address.

He arrived back in plenty of time, but she was not at the window. Thinking she might have moved, he quickly searched along the cars, surprised not to see her. When the train began to pull away, he comforted himself with the fact that he could get her address from Brace. Dakota turned again toward the hotel but froze before he'd walked five steps.

Moving along between two men was a woman: strawberry blonde and wearing a navy suit. Dakota wondered if he was seeing things even as his feet began to propel him in that direction. He wasn't overly concerned. After all, why would anyone take Darvi from the train?

His own teasing about trouble following her now came to mind.

With no definite plan, he picked up the pace just as they entered a crowded area of downtown Aurora.

❧ ❧ ❧

Darvi could not believe this was happening. Where the men had come from she couldn't say; she had looked up and there they were, one of them already taking the satchel from her side. Any protest she had died in her throat upon seeing the knife. The man hadn't pulled it from its sheath, but he'd made sure she saw it before their eyes met. For this reason, Darvi instantly obeyed his order to accompany them from the train.

She now walked between them, much faster than she would have on her own, the town passing rather swiftly. She nearly lost her footing at one point. Starting to gasp, she felt something hard press against her side. That these men meant business was more than clear.

Darvi was working to keep her head when they suddenly turned down an alley. They were at the side and then the back of a building almost before she could think. Almost. Deciding that she wasn't going to comply any longer, Darvi began to pull on the hand holding her upper arm, just as she opened her mouth to scream. She didn't see the fist that came down on the top of her head, so when blackness crowded in she had no idea why.

❧ ❧ ❧

Dakota had spotted them again and even knew what alley they turned down, but to his amazement, there was no one in sight. He couldn't even find three distinctive sets of footprints in the gravel. Sure that he'd misjudged, he tried the next alley down but could see that it was too far.

"I know this is where they went," he said under his breath as he continued to study the buildings. "I just don't know for sure that it was Darvi."

Dakota had a look around that brought him to a door in the back, but it was locked. Not a man given to flights of fancy, he wondered what to do next. Finding out if Darvi had actually left on that train was nearly impossible, but that would have settled his mind. He tried to assess whether or not he had actually seen anything amiss. The woman did not look upset or forced, but she certainly had Darvi's coloring.

Dakota was at a loss. He'd planned to send word to Brace that he'd gotten Darvi off safely, but right now he could not even do that. For the time being he found a bench in front of the general store and sat down to think.

🌸 🌸 🌸

"You knocked her out?" Eliot asked in outrage.

"She started to struggle," the taller of the two abductors said, defending himself, but a look from Eliot quieted him.

"When do we get paid?" the other tried, but he shut up when Seth's eyes grew as black as his brother's.

Neither man dared to comment when Eliot opened the door, his message clear. As soon as they were gone, Eliot and Seth stared down at Darvi and then at each other.

"How hard do you think he hit her?" Seth asked.

Eliot lifted one of Darvi's eyelids and shook his head. "She's out cold."

"Here, let me move her to the davenport. She's going to topple out of that chair."

Seth lifted her easily, amazed at how light she felt, his heart pumping with very real fear that they had hurt the influential Annabelle Hewett. But something else happened inside of him when he laid Darvi back against a pillow, her face so pale that he was startled. Trying not to hear his own heart pounding, Seth placed his fingers alongside her neck. He picked up a steady beat and hoped it was only a matter of time until she woke.

"She's prettier than her picture," Seth commented as he stood to full height, looking down at their guest. Eliot came over to look, his gaze somewhat dispassionate.

"Things must be better for her. Even knocked out, she looks better than the last time I saw her."

"I don't know."

"We could throw a little water in her face," Eliot joked, but Seth frowned. For some reason the idea repelled him. He knew she could be vicious with her words, but knocked out cold, Annabelle Hewett looked rather young and vulnerable.

"I'm going to get something to eat," Eliot proclaimed, heading toward the kitchen of the apartment that Jared kept in town. Its rear exit to the alley had come in handy many times over.

"I'll join you," Seth added, his eyes on Darvi until Eliot called again.

"You'd better bring that bag of hers so we can check it out. You never know what a lady like that might be packing."

🌸 🌸 🌸

Darvi woke in confusion. Before she even opened her eyes, she tried to think why the top of her head felt bruised. Her memory returned with a jolt, but she continued to keep her eyes closed. She didn't know where she was, but it might be to her advantage to let whoever had taken her think she was sleeping.

"She's coming out of it," she heard a soft male voice say. She finally gave up and opened her eyes. She did not find the men from the train. These men were tall, well dressed, and good looking. Darvi thought they might have rescued her and began to sit up.

"Where am I?" she asked.

"Don't you know, Miss Hewett?"

Darvi nearly looked behind her. "Were you talking to me?"

Both men smiled, thinking she was very good.

"We're glad you stopped to see Mr. Silk," Seth now went on smoothly. "Unfortunately you've missed him. He *would* like to see you, however. In fact he's asked us to extend a dinner invitation to his home at your earliest convenience."

"Who is Mr. Silk?"

Eliot looked cynical, but Seth began to ask himself just how hard she'd been hit.

"So when can we set a date?" Eliot pressed on.

"A date for what?" Darvi asked, beginning to wonder if she had really awakened.

"Miss Hewett . . ." Seth began patiently.

"Who is Miss Hewett?" Darvi demanded.

The men's faces grew hard, and Darvi came to her feet, albeit awkwardly.

"Where am I?" she tried again.

The men just stared at her.

Darvi walked to one of the room's windows and looked out. She knew it was still Aurora, but she couldn't quite picture where. She'd been tired the night before and eager to get on the train that morning. Was it that morning?

"Is it still Wednesday?"

"Yes."

"Do you have the time?"

"Miss Hewett," Eliot tried this time.

"Stop calling me that."

"All right, Annabelle, why do you wish to know the time?"

"That's enough!" Darvi's voice cracked with enough force to surprise even herself. She stared at them, eyes furious, her hands coming out to make her point.

"I don't know what's going on here, but you will stop calling me that name. My name is Darvi Wingate. I was on the train this morning bound for St. Louis when two men threatened me with a knife and removed me from my seat. I want some answers, and I want them now."

"I should have known she was going to make this hard," Eliot said to Seth.

"Yeah, I suppose you're right. Let's give her some time to think."

The men filed from the room then, and Darvi was completely confused. Her attention strayed around the small living area as she searched for answers, so she was startled when one of the men returned.

Seth handed Darvi her satchel.

"I thought you might want this."

Darvi took the bag.

"The gun is out," he added, holding her eyes for long moments before exiting once again.

I have to think, Darvi told herself, trying to ignore the headache. With that her eyes caught sight of the door. Bag in hand, she went to it and found it open. Hating to leave her gun and thinking she might be dreaming after all, she began to walk out onto a wooden landing that led to a tall flight of stairs. There was a door at the bottom. She was just closing the apartment door when she heard, "Did you lock that door?"

Darvi didn't even bother to catch the latch. Knowing she'd been found out, she lifted the front of her skirt and flew down the stairs as fast as she could move. She didn't make it halfway before an arm caught her around the waist. Darvi froze, waiting for him to let go, but he didn't. Not seeing any other way, she began to scream and struggle. A sound had barely escaped her when a hand was put over her mouth. The voice at her ear was quiet, almost gentle, but the words were no less serious.

"The last thing I want to do is hurt you, but I can't have you escaping or screaming." Saying this, Seth shifted her so she could see his face. The terror in her eyes nearly got to him, but he still said, "Understood?"

Darvi nodded and stayed quiet when he slowly removed his hand.

"Now, back up to the apartment you go. We have to come to some type of agreement before you leave."

"What agreement?"

"Well, it's like we said. Mr. Silk wants you to come to dinner, as you missed seeing him today."

Back in the apartment, Darvi turned to see him put her satchel on the floor while the other man locked the door.

"I don't know who Mr. Silk is, and I didn't come here on my own. I don't know how much plainer I can make it."

The men said nothing. The one nearest the door pocketed the key, and the one who had caught her on the stairs only looked at her. A moment later they exited the room again.

Eight

"Excuse me," Dakota interrupted the man at the ticket window.

"Yes, sir, what can I do for you?"

"I was just wondering if there's any chance you remember a woman buying a ticket this morning? She wore a navy suit and had reddish blonde hair."

The man nodded. "I remember her. Headed to St. Louis."

"Yes, she's the one. Do you happen to know whether she was on the train when it left?"

The man looked thoughtful. "Well, I assume she was. She didn't come back to say she missed the train. They always do that when it happens."

Dakota debated how to ask the next question delicately. "Did you by any chance happen to see her leave the station area?"

"I didn't see her go, but then I can't see as much as the men out front. You might want to check with them."

"Thank you."

Dakota stepped away from the window fighting the frustration rising within him. He'd already talked to the men who worked along the tracks. They hadn't seen anyone leaving who matched Darvi's description and told him to check with the man at the ticket window.

I don't think I can do anything else, Lord. Is it a lack of trust to wonder if she's all right? If that wasn't Darvi, then why haven't I seen another woman like her in town today? But Dakota's questions went unanswered. He honestly didn't know what to do. His money, including the funds that Brace had given him, was down to nothing. If he stayed in town, it would have to be outside tonight. He was more than willing to do this if there was a need, but if this was nothing more than a case of mistaken identity . . . On the other hand, if Darvi needed him, Dakota would never leave her.

Deciding to stay in town one more night and keep his eyes open, Dakota went in search of a cheap meal. He hadn't eaten since breakfast, and it was now way past noon. He had to assume if he didn't have answers by morning, he would have to leave well enough alone.

🌹🌹🌹

"I need to let Cassy know I won't be home tonight," Eliot said of his girlfriend.

"Maybe Nate's in town. He could tell her," Seth replied, speaking of Cassy's son.

"I'll head out and check." Eliot stood. "How is she doing?"

"The last time I looked she was reading her Bible."

The men shared a smile, and Eliot slowly shook his head. "She's good. I'll give her that."

"That she is, but I must tell you, the lady fascinates me."

"You've seen her column in the paper, big brother. Don't forget she has claws."

Eliot left to the sound of the other man's laughter. Seth went back to his paper. He had only just returned to his reading when Darvi came to the door.

"May I please leave now?"

Setting the paper aside, Seth shook his head. "We have to come to an agreement," he said, keeping his voice gentle. "You're going to have dinner with Mr. Silk, and you're even going to tell your readers about it, both before and after. You've had some pretty ugly things to say about him over the last year, and it's time to do some repair work."

Looking as devastated as she felt, Darvi turned away. Not giving her more than a few moments alone, Seth followed her. He found her sitting and looking toward the window, but since it was growing dark outside, he knew she could see little.

For a time, Seth cursed Jared Silk's very existence. None of this was going the way they had planned. Nevertheless, Seth knew he had a job to do.

"I'm sorry you won't cooperate, Miss Hewett, but if you'll just work with us, you can go home."

"Please don't call me that."

The lantern was not turned very high, but it did illumine the side of Darvi's face, catching the smooth skin on her cheek, the adorable shape of her turned-up nose, and that incredible mouth. Seth felt his heart turn over with tenderness for her and wanted to shake his head at this interest. His boss would be enraged if he knew. Annabelle Hewett was the enemy, and he would do well to remember that!

"Now listen," he spoke harshly, coming close to Darvi and towering over her as her head whipped around. "I've got better things to do than sit around here and wait for you to admit the truth. You can knock off this act and come clean. You know what I want, and I'm not going to wait forever."

Nearly growling with frustration when the light would not give him a clear view of her eyes, he turned it higher. The tears, fear, and confusion he saw were almost his undoing, but he made himself go on, albeit in a quieter tone. Reaching for an old newspaper, Seth sat next to Darvi and searched until he had found her column.

"Look at this. You say right here that Jared Silk is a con artist, but do you have any proof? You stir up a lot of trouble for one of the town's more popular businessmen. Mr. Silk just wants to know what you have against him. He believes if he could speak with you, you would see that you have him all wrong."

Darvi looked at the paper, telling herself she was not going to cry or panic. She tried to lick her lips, but her mouth was alarmingly dry.

"I didn't write this. I don't know how else to tell you. I'm not Annabelle Hewett. And if your plan is to starve me until I say that I am, then you're going to have a corpse on your hands."

Seth stopped dead in his tracks. This was not supposed to have taken all day. They hadn't given Darvi a thing to eat or drink. He was saved from falling all over himself when he heard the door open. He met his brother when he was no more than a foot inside, the smell of food enveloping him.

"*We forgot to feed her!*" Seth whispered in panic.

"I remembered that when I was out," Eliot whispered back. "I've brought some dinner from the hotel."

Seth straightened his tie and jacket and even smoothed his hair. Chin raised and determined to be all business, he returned to the living room.

"We have some dinner for you now. Come on through to the kitchen and eat."

Hoping he was not playing games with her, Darvi went ahead when he motioned for her to precede him. The room was not overly large, but she was directed to take one of the four chairs around the kitchen table. The smell of food assailed her; her mouth ran with saliva so suddenly she had to swallow several times. She'd been praying all day for strength, but if they planned to make her sit here and not eat, they might have a hysterical woman on their hands.

"Here you go." Eliot set a plate in front of her, some silverware on the side. A glass of water came next, but Darvi just sat, her hands clenched in her lap. The men had food of their own, but she was afraid to trust this situation.

Trying not to look at her, Seth started on his food. Eliot couldn't. He watched her sit there for a few seconds and then spoke up.

"You can eat."

"I don't have to do something first?"

"No."

Eliot's reply was very quiet. He had just gotten a taste of what his brother had seen. He made himself look down at his plate, but he couldn't miss the way she picked up her water, her eyes closing in relief as she drank. Drinking often, she began to work her way through the food. The rice was wonderful, but the chicken looked so good that she soon had a piece in her hand. She was just starting to feel normal when she glanced up to see that someone had filled her water glass again. Pausing only to wipe her hands, she reached for it. Not until that point did she realize the men were watching her.

For some reason, color filled her face as she slowly set down her glass. To her surprise, the men rose. They set their plates on the side counter and turned to her.

"When you're finished, come back to the living room so we can talk."

This order came from Eliot, and Darvi only nodded before they went on their way. She finished slowly, managing to eat every bite. It was during this time that her brain went back to work. She knew that the living room was out the door and to the left, but the one man had not exited that way. He'd come from the other side.

Working not to scrape her chair on the floor at all, Darvi stood up, wiping her face and hands as she went. She didn't move her plate and did everything she could to keep her feet silent. Determined not to look toward the living room, she planned to hit the doorway and head right, hopefully out the first door she came to. And it worked, right up to the moment she had her hand on the knob. It was then she noticed the large hand that had appeared just over her head. It was holding the door shut.

Darvi turned in disgust to find Seth looking down on her. Having gained back some of her old pluck, she lifted her chin into the air.

"I almost made it," she told him before slipping past and heading to the living room.

Seth was glad she couldn't see him, giving him time to wipe the smile from his face.

"Please sit down," Eliot instructed her right away, his tone firm.

Darvi complied.

"I've got a sample of the articles I want you to write. You'll put one in tomorrow's paper, and the other one will go in the day after you dine with Jared."

He tried to hand the papers to Darvi, but she wouldn't take them. Eliot let his head fall back, frustration written all over him. He didn't want to strike the woman he thought to be Annabelle; he just wanted to release her back into the alley and be done with it.

"I don't write for the newspaper," Darvi tried again. "If you want to take me down there and ask them yourself, that's fine. Maybe then you'll see I'm telling the truth."

This was getting ridiculous. Jared's scheme had seemed a little far-fetched when he'd plotted it for them, but now this attempt to execute it was just plain foolishness.

"May I leave?"

The men looked at her.

"No," Seth spoke up, trying not to be led by his heart. "I still think we can work something out."

"But it's dark out; I have to go."

"Where do you have to go?"

Darvi didn't answer. She just knew she needed to get out of there.

"Did you find Nate?" Seth asked of Eliot.

"Yes."

Seth stood.

"If you'll come with me, Miss Hewett, I'll get you settled for the night."

Darvi could not believe her ears. She could see these men did not mean her physical harm and that they truly had mistaken her for someone else, but that didn't make the whole episode any less frightening. For the dozenth time that day, Darvi was forced to push Dakota's face from her mind. He would have taken such good care of her if he were here, but he wasn't, and she had to accept that.

Following the man who picked up her satchel, Darvi left the room behind him. They went down the hallway and past the kitchen to a small bedroom. There was very little in the room. He set her satchel on the small bed.

"The window is nailed shut, but even if you do figure a way to open it, it's a two-story drop. If you need something, I'll be across the hall or in the living room."

Seth said all this while forcing himself not to look at her. He headed to the door and almost made it but looked back even as he had his hand on the knob. It was a mistake. Darvi stood looking around the room, that expression of a lost, forlorn child back on her face. Seth couldn't get out of there fast enough. He nearly ran to the living room and threw himself onto the davenport.

"Something doesn't add up, Eliot, and I don't mean maybe. If that woman is Annabelle Hewett, she's the greatest actress who ever lived."

"I was thinking the same thing. It has crossed my mind that she's playing us for the biggest fools alive, but it's getting harder to buy."

The men sat in silence until Eliot had another thought.

"Could it be a relative, even her daughter or younger sister?"

Seth shook his head. "She's never heard of Annabelle Hewett. She can't be faking that."

"I thought for a moment that she was going to tell us someone was waiting for her or that she had someplace to be, but then she stopped."

"I thought the same thing. It even looked like she wanted to make something up and couldn't think of it fast enough."

Eliot stood with a groan. "Take the first shift. I'm tired."

"All right. I didn't lock her door, so check the front again. I've got the key."

"All right. Call me before you nod off."

"Will do."

Seth was left alone with his thoughts, and they weren't happy ones. He had no idea what to do next. Not tired in the least, he determined to sit on the sofa until he had that woman figured out.

🌹🌹🌹

Darvi sat on the edge of the bed, her arms wrapped around her middle, wishing she hadn't eaten all the food. Her stomach was so upset from fear that she thought she might be ill. She had sat alone in the living room most of the day, even nodding off at times. She hadn't liked going to the kitchen; the living room seemed safer. This whole ordeal was wearing on her.

I'm so confused right now, Lord. I don't think they mean to harm me, but I want to be let out. I'm not afraid to go back to the train station and try again, but these men have me at their mercy.

Just thinking of the word mercy reminded Darvi of God's great mercy to her. She still did not have answers but was greatly calmed as she prayed. She poured her heart out to the Lord and asked Him to comfort her and provide wisdom. She didn't feel at all tired, but when

Seth checked on her some two hours later, he found her sleeping in her clothes, curled up not far from the edge of the bed.

❧ ❧ ❧

Dakota didn't leave Aurora without some misgivings, but on the whole he knew a great peace. He hadn't seen his brother, a man he dearly loved, in a long time.

He asked God to bless Darvi, trusting she was still on her way home and knowing she would face her family soon. Outside of town, Dakota picked up the pace. He would be in Kinkade tonight and home for the first time in ages.

❧ ❧ ❧

Eliot came back to the apartment, breakfast in hand. Seth had just finished shaving, and as Eliot passed Darvi's room, he saw that the door was open and she was still sleeping. Apparently Seth had covered her with a blanket. The younger man's hands shook just a little as he set the plates down, but he wasn't given much time to compose himself. Seth came into the room just a moment later. One look at Eliot's face told him something was wrong.

"What's the matter?"

"I just saw Annabelle Hewett heading into the newspaper office."

"You're sure?"

"Positive."

Seth couldn't hold his smile.

"Do not be smiling about this, Seth. What about Jared?"

"Jared or not, Eliot, this is the best news I've ever heard."

Eliot stared at his older brother. They'd been through so much together. Seth was as levelheaded a man as he'd ever met. Why now? Why her? Eliot couldn't think of worse timing. He was on the verge of telling his brother just that when a small cry came from the other room. Both men moved across the hall to investigate. They found Darvi on the floor looking very sleepy and bewildered.

"Did you fall out of bed?" Seth asked as he came forward.

Darvi, who had just awakened from a horrible nightmare about these men, tried to scoot away from him, but her legs caught in the blanket. Seeing her fear, Seth halted.

"When you're ready," he said quietly, "we have some breakfast for you."

"I'm not hungry."

Seth only nodded and cleared out of the room, shutting the door behind him.

"Let me handle this," he told Eliot as he moved to the outer door. "Don't tell her what we know. I'll go take care of things with Jared and come back here."

"What are you going to do with her?"

Seth didn't even hesitate. "Take her home."

"To the ranch?"

"Yes."

Eliot was given no time to comment. Seth slipped out the door, and the remaining brother locked it in his wake.

🥀🥀🥀

"What do you mean the plan won't work?" Jared demanded, having already closed his office door.

"Just that. We tried and it failed."

"Tried? How?"

Looking much more composed than he felt, Seth met Jared's eyes.

"We had a woman picked up who bears a striking resemblance to Annabelle Hewett. She tried to tell us she wasn't Hewett, but we didn't believe her. Then Eliot spotted Hewett in town this morning. We still have this other woman at the apartment."

Jared's look became shrewd.

"That's perfect. Now that you know exactly who Annabelle is, you can still pick her up and get her to agree to my terms."

"No."

"What do you mean, no?"

"Just what I said. The whole idea is crazy. Do you know how many people would miss Annabelle Hewett? I thought of that before, but not until we had this woman who doesn't even live in Aurora did I see that this won't work with anyone as well known as Hewett."

"But I want her stopped!"

"Be that as it may," Seth responded in a voice that had gone cold, "you'll have to find another way to do it."

Seth stood, and Jared wisely backed off. It had taken years to find men to work for him who had the sophistication that Seth Redding and Eliot McDermott displayed. He paid them well, but they were worth every dime. And over the years he'd learned some things. He knew when he could push and when he'd gone too far. The men did have their limits.

"What will you do with this woman?"

Seth shrugged as though he didn't care. "Take her to the ranch for now."

"What's her name?" Jared asked before thinking, then swiftly held up his hand to stop the question. "I don't want to know any more. Just handle it."

Seth started toward the door.

"I'll let you know when you're needed again."

"All right. We'll be in the apartment until after dark."

Jared only waved in his direction, his mind already working on the next plan. Never once did the banker's brilliant mind remind his heart that he could have used his intelligence to gather wealth honestly. This was the way he'd always done things. A different approach had never occurred to him.

❧ ❧ ❧

Darvi rubbed at her hip. She had finally climbed from the floor, but she felt stiff and sore, and her hip ached. She must have landed directly on it. She rubbed the back of her neck, glanced around the room, and noticed the steam. Moving to the pitcher and basin, she saw that someone had brought her hot wash water, soap, and towels. A wash sounded good, but to do it right, she would have to unbutton her dress and loosen her clothing. The thought alone sounded wonderful.

Darvi moved toward the room's only chair, a thin piece of furniture but her only choice. She carried it across the floor and tried to jam the back under the doorknob. She no more had it settled when someone knocked.

"Are you all right?" Eliot called from without.

"Don't you try to open that door. I've put a chair there."

"Why did you do that?"

"Because I want some privacy."

There was silence and then, "If I hear glass breaking, I'll bust the door down."

Darvi didn't answer.

"Do you hear me?"

"I hear you."

Darvi wanted to hear him walk away, but when he didn't, she still went to the basin. Hearing the splash, Eliot's suspicions about her trying to escape eased, and he went back to the kitchen to check on the two breakfasts he had set on top of the stove. He could see the food was drying out, but he thought it still looked edible.

In the room, Darvi took as much off as she dared and began to scrub with a vengeance. It occurred to her for the first time that her surroundings were impeccable, but her own fear had naturally caused her to perspire. Bathing was a definite help to her spirits.

I'm going to get out of here today, Lord, she proclaimed as she started to rinse off. *I don't know how just yet, but I'm not going to sit around here again and try to convince these men. They can take me back to the train station, or I'm going to cause such a ruckus that I'll bring the whole town down on their heads.*

Darvi hoped she could actually manage all this once she was faced with it. It was easy to be tough behind closed doors.

"You told Dakota you would do just fine on your own," she whispered to her reflection in the small mirror even as tears filled her eyes. "Oh, Dakota, I hope I didn't lie to you."

Nine

DARVI EXITED HER BEDROOM ABOUT AN HOUR after she fell out of bed. She didn't have a confirmed plan in her mind, but she was going to keep her eyes and ears open. She found one of the men in the living room, his jacket off, his feet on the table. She was grudgingly impressed when he stood and reached for his jacket. It made the whole situation all the more curious.

"What exactly do you do for a living, Mr.—"

"McDermott," he supplied. "I'm a personal assistant to Jared Silk."

Darvi nodded. She had been too stunned yesterday to act. Today she was going to learn who this Jared Silk was and why Annabelle Hewett wrote about him.

"Would you like some breakfast now?"

"No, thank you. I don't suppose it would do any good to ask you to let me leave."

"I'm afraid not."

"In that case, may I share some of your paper?"

"Indeed. Please help yourself."

"Thank you."

Darvi was scanning the pages just a moment later, but Eliot was a little slower to go back to his reading. Since she was reading attentively, he was able to study her undetected. Something had happened since the day before. She was not the least bit afraid of him right now, and he again experienced some of the fascination his brother was feeling.

Completely unaware of his scrutiny, Darvi could not believe what she was reading as she went through nearly every newspaper in the two piles that sat on the floor of the living room. Not all of Annabelle

Hewett's articles were about Jared Silk, but when his name was mentioned, the woman was nothing short of scathing. A chill went down Darvi's spine. Jared Silk must hate this woman, and these men thought they had her in captivity.

At the same time . . .

Darvi's mind worked fast. She wondered if this might not be her way out. Clearly the men believed she was a reporter. Darvi wasn't sure if there was ever a right time to lie to someone, but at the moment she was tempted. Hearing the door open and watching the man in the room get up, Darvi kept studying the newspapers and working on the plan that was budding in her mind.

❧ ❧ ❧

"Where have you been?" Eliot asked when he met Seth at the door.

"I had some things to pick up, and then I went ahead and bought lunch."

Eliot shook his head. "She never ate any of the breakfast. What did Jared say?"

"He wanted us to grab Hewett this time, and I said no."

"That sounds a little too easy."

"Not really. He pushed me, and I pushed back. He backed down and said he'd send for us when he needed us."

This Eliot could believe. Jared slid along on the edge of the law, but he never crossed Seth. Seth could find work too easily, and they both knew it.

"How has she been?" the smitten brother asked.

"She's reading through the newspapers. She's not afraid like yesterday. I swear she has something up her sleeve."

Seth looked thoughtful. "My bet is she's pretty harmless, but she did have a gun in her bag. We'll just keep on as we're doing, and hopefully I won't have to gag her before we leave here tonight."

"Seth, are you sure about this?"

"Very sure."

"This kind of thing can bring a whole lot of trouble."

Seth studied his brother's pensive face before glancing toward the doorway as if he hoped to see Darvi.

"Just go along with me, Eliot. I can't explain it, I just know what I have to do."

The men's eyes met before Seth put a hand on his brother's shoulder. A moment later he went to the living room.

"Lunch is ready."

Darvi looked up to see the other man addressing her. She set the paper aside, and much as she had done the night before, preceded him to the kitchen. Mr. McDermott was already there, the food ready and waiting. Darvi was nowhere near as starved, but she was hungry. She didn't know where they picked up the food they brought in, but the beef and vegetables on her plate were very tasty. She didn't rush. She was still asking herself if lying to the men who had her abducted was wrong when she went ahead and plunged in.

"I would like to look at those sample letters now," she said quietly, watching their faces.

The men had all they could do not to look stunned.

"You would?" Eliot questioned.

"Yes."

Eliot and Seth were careful not to look at each other as Eliot came slowly to his feet, went to the other room, and returned with the pages. Darvi took them from his hand.

Eliot, watching his brother watch Darvi, had to smile. Seth was doing everything in his power not to show it, but his heart was nearly in his eyes as he gazed at this woman, understanding exactly what she was up to.

"And if I write this for the paper," Darvi clarified, "you'll let me go?"

The men hesitated.

"Isn't that what you said?"

"There's been a slight change in plans," Seth began. "I'd have to run it past Mr. Silk."

Darvi tried not to show how far her heart sank. She had not expected this, but she was going to keep trying.

"Can you do that now? Can you check with him today?"

Seth appeared to consider this. "I think I can do that. If you're finished eating, why don't you let us talk it over and get back to you."

Darvi desperately wanted to know what he meant by a change in plans but thought she should take what she could get for the time being. Trying not to appear as uncertain as she felt, she rose from the table and left the room.

Both men remained very quiet, so they had no trouble hearing Darvi check the door in the living room. They knew it was locked. Next they heard more rattling of newspapers. Seth leaned back in his chair, a full-blown smile on his face.

"Now tell me, Eliot, had I met her under any other circumstances, would you like her more?"

"I like her now, Seth, and it's very easy to see why you're taken with her."

There was so much to add to this, but Eliot did not waste his breath. His brother was lost on this woman.

Eliot stayed where he was even after Seth went to the other room and had a few words with Darvi, obviously telling her he was headed to see Jared. Eliot even heard her thank him, her voice sweet and grateful. Not sure she should be left alone for too long, Eliot did a quick cleanup job in the kitchen and went back to reading newspapers with Darvi in the living room as soon as Seth exited the apartment.

❧ ❧ ❧

Kinkade, Texas

Cash Rawlings dusted off his jeans as he walked through the back hall of the ranch house, his ears picking up the sound of a deep male voice. His cook, Katy Sims, laughed like a girl, and suddenly Cash knew exactly who was in the kitchen.

Sitting on the counter as though he'd been there all his life, Dakota looked up when Cash entered, a huge smile covering his face.

"It's about time you got in. I've been sitting here for at least ten minutes."

The brothers met in the middle of the room, unashamedly embracing each other for long moments.

"How are you?" Cash asked, still holding the younger man by the arms.

"Good, I think. Ready for a bath and a hot meal."

"We can do both. Right, Katy?"

"As if you have to ask!" she said in her indomitable way. Cash only smiled.

"Come on," Cash invited Dakota. "Come into the den. I've got to show you something."

From the kitchen the men moved across a sprawling living room graced by a huge stone fireplace and into Cash's personal office. The oldest of the Rawlings brothers led Dakota to a framed portrait, turning to see his reaction.

"When did this arrive?"

"Just last week."

The men gazed at the beautiful picture of their parents, Charles Sr. and Virginia Rawlings. Neither parent smiled, but both had warm expressions. Dakota's eyes lingered on his mother's. Cash had been blessed with her eyes—warm and welcoming. Dakota's gaze next went to his father. It was like looking at himself in 20 more years.

"They look great," Dakota declared.

"That they do. Mother wrote that she was sending it, but I didn't know what to expect. The ornate frame and bowed glass are such a surprise. It's more elegant than ranch life, but I'll take it anyway."

"Now if Mother were here right now, she'd say it was time you had a woman's touch around here."

"She'd say the same thing to you."

"Have you been to see them lately?"

"No. I'm thinking of going just before Grandma's visit."

"How is she?"

The men fell into easy dialog about everything from their grandmother to the increasing number of cattle Cash had on the ranch. At one point Katy called that the water was hot for bathing, and Cash encouraged Dakota to go first.

"Do I smell that bad?"

Cash smiled, his eyes not bothering to disguise the love he felt.

"It's so good to have you home."

"I'm glad you feel that way. I'll probably stay for a while."

"Good. How's the new life going?"

Dakota sighed. "I have so many questions."

The men would have started on those questions right then, but Katy came from the dining area with orders.

"Cash! Are you going to let this boy bathe?"

"Go, Dak, before she has a fit."

Katy had been with the family since the men *were* boys, so the look they exchanged was a familiar one. They did as they were told. Cash followed Dakota into the large bathing chamber off the kitchen at the rear of the house so they could keep talking. Katy grumbled under her breath that they acted just like kids, but that didn't stop her from standing outside the door, listening for a moment to their nonstop talk and grinning from ear to ear.

❧ ❧ ❧

Darvi had everything she could do not to wring her hands and pace. All her brave thoughts melted as she sat and thought about the meaning of "a change in plans." Several times she had asked Mr. McDermott what could be keeping the man he called Seth, but he seemed as uninformed as she.

Another glance at the window told her darkness was crowding in. It was inconceivable to her that she had spent two whole days in this apartment, no one knowing where she was. She had not communicated a firm arrival date to her parents, and Dakota thought she was on her way home. The thought caused panic to claw at her throat. The men hadn't been threatening to her; they just wouldn't let her go. Working desperately not to crumble but to keep her voice strong, Darvi stood.

"I have to go now. It's been too long. He's not coming back, and I can't stay here anymore."

Eliot came to his feet, mentally begging Seth to return before he had to gag this woman to keep her quiet.

"I think it won't be long now."

She wasn't going to hear that again. Darvi looked toward the window, anger taking over.

"It's getting dark outside! I've probably missed my train again. Now you must let me out of here."

This said, she strode to the window and started to open it. Eliot could not stand the thought of hurting her, so he simply tried to take her by the arm.

"Don't touch me! I'm going to scream until someone comes."

"Is there a problem?" Seth's voice sounded at the edge of the room.

Darvi turned swiftly from the window, her eyes hot with betrayal.

"What kind of people are you?" she spat. "Now I want out of here, and I won't hear another excuse. Do you hear me?"

"Yes, I do hear you," Seth replied quietly, thinking a day had never been so long. It obviously had been for her as well, but certainly for another reason.

"Get your bag ready."

Darvi was surprised but went immediately to do as he bid. In less than a minute she was standing in the hallway, ready to go.

"May I take this for you?" Seth offered.

"No, thank you," Darvi said without looking at him, and Seth wondered how much ground he might have lost by staying away so long.

"Let's go," Seth said quietly and surprised Darvi again by taking her back through the living room. She remembered the stairs well, but it was getting dark and she had to take hold of the railing. A wagon was waiting in the alley, but Darvi didn't move toward it.

"Thank you," she said stiffly, thinking this entire ordeal had been a nightmare and asking God to let it be over.

"Climb in; we'll give you a ride."

"No, thank you," Darvi stated plainly. It was already quite dark, but she decided to take her chances alone. She didn't get five feet before a large arm dropped around her shoulders and steered her toward the wagon.

"What are you doing?"

"I can't let you go to the train station," Seth said, hoping she was not going to scream.

"Please, don't do this," Darvi entreated him. "Please, let me go."

"I can't," he whispered, and with that swung her up into his arms, stepped on the wheel, and sat down with her in the back of the wagon. Eliot immediately put the team into motion, and Darvi screamed. Wanting very much to put his mouth over hers, Seth had to be satisfied with his hand, only to get it bitten. At the same time Darvi's other hand clawed at his face, and it took some doing to subdue her. Unfortunately, that freed her mouth for another scream.

Eliot was cutting through alleys and behind businesses as fast as he dared, but he feared that if she sounded off again, they were going to get nabbed. He cringed at the thought of the explaining they would have to do. Some of the police force were on Jared's payroll, but no one would turn a blind eye to their abducting a woman.

Still hearing scuffling in the back, Eliot could see that they'd almost made it. Another half mile and they'd be far enough out of town that he could move the horses a little faster and not cause suspicion. From there, they would head to the ranch, some five miles out. At that point she could scream all she wanted to; no one who could do anything would hear her.

Darvi couldn't fight anymore. Seth held her very effectively, and biting his hand only lasted a few moments each time. She lay panting beside him, noticing for the first time that he wasn't trying to take advantage of her. Nevertheless, she didn't like it. She tried to speak, which caused him to ask. "Are you going to scream?"

Darvi shook her head no.

Seth let go.

"Where are we going?" Darvi pushed the words past a raw throat.

"To my home."

"Why?"

"Because we are."

Darvi tried to see him in the dark.

"Didn't Mr. Silk want to see me?"

"I didn't even ask him."

Darvi sighed. What in the world was going on?

As though he'd heard her, Seth answered. "We'll get you to the ranch, and Cassy will settle you in. Tomorrow I'll try to explain it."

"Who's Cassy?"

"Eliot's girl."

Darvi was silent for a moment.

"I'd like to sit up now."

Seth was swift to help her. He'd had her pinned to the floor of the wagon, her wrists held in one of his hands. He now put a hand to her back and helped her sit up.

"Do you want to sit on the seat with Eliot?"

"No, thank you," she said before curling into a ball, wondering if she should try to jump for it. She glanced around at the blackness and knew it would be a mistake. She'd be terribly lost out here, and they would be hunting her, not to mention the fact that the team was moving fast now. Darvi thought she might injure herself if she tried it. She placed her forehead against her upraised knees and asked God to help her think.

🌹🌹🌹

Darvi was surprised at what she could see of the house. Without permission Seth lifted her from the rear of the wagon and set her on the ground. The front door opened and the light spilled out, telling her the satchel was in Seth's hand.

"Come on in," a woman's voice called. "I've got dinner on."

Darvi entered a large, low-ceilinged room that was as well scrubbed as the apartment had been. To Darvi's amazement, a number of people were inside, almost all men. All but the woman sat eating a meal around a huge kitchen table. They turned to look her way, but a comment from the woman, something Darvi didn't quite catch, sent them back to their plates.

"I put her in with Nate and Lindy," Cassy said after Eliot kissed her.

"Do you want some dinner?" Seth asked from beside her, but Darvi didn't answer. When she felt a hand on her back propelling her forward, she obeyed.

They crossed the big room and entered a short hallway. Two doors sat across from each other.

"You're in here," Seth whispered, his voice low, "with Nate and Lindy."

"Who are Nate and Lindy?"

"Cassy's children. They're already asleep, but you won't wake them. I'll get the lamp for you."

She was doing it again, and Seth had to harden his heart. The light caught the vulnerable look in her eyes; confusion and fear were plainly evident.

"No one will hurt you here," he said, keeping his voice low, not because of the children, but because of his runaway emotions. "Keep the light burning all night if you want. Sleep as late as you like. If you need something, Cassy and Eliot's room is right across from you. My room is back out through the big room and down a bit. Just call out if you need us, but don't try to run away. We're a long way from town."

Darvi could only stare at him.

That wasn't good enough for Seth. Speaking firmly, he asked, "Did you hear me?"

Darvi nodded.

"All right. Get some sleep now."

Saying this, the tall man exited and shut the door. When he got back out to the big room, the men were finishing up and heading back to the bunkhouse. Seeing him come, Cassy put a plateful of food down in his spot and watched him sit down.

"Is she all right?"

"I think so."

Cassy looked at him for a moment. "What makes you think she'll still be here in the morning?"

"Because right now she's too afraid to run. Before she's here two days, she'll figure something out, but right now her spunk is gone."

Cassy sat down and took a long drink of her coffee. She was a beautiful woman, smart and kind and head-over-heels where Seth's brother was concerned. She ran a successful cattle ranch, and for the most part, life was good. She'd been hoping for years that Seth would find a woman to love, but not like this, not one he had to capture. What she saw as equal amounts of good and bad in the brothers still amazed her. The good she saw in Seth made her want better for him than this.

"I can't say as I like her," Cassy admitted.

"Come on, Cass." This came from Eliot. "Give it a chance."

"He's supposed to find someone who loves him in return!" Cassy shot back at Eliot, both talking as though Seth wasn't there.

"It doesn't always work that way."

"Give it time." This came from the man in question, his voice calm and confident. "If she stays long enough, she'll love us."

"I hope that's true," Cassy said, "but if she doesn't like kids, you can haul her back to the train station or wherever she came from."

"I wouldn't expect anything else, Cassy."

Much of the tension left the table at that moment. These three had lived together and been friends for a long time. It was natural that Cassy didn't want another woman coming in to upset that balance.

"I'm turning in," Seth said, finishing his food and standing up. "Thanks for dinner."

"Are you going to keep watch?" Eliot wished to know.

"I don't think so. I'll be up early, and I somehow doubt she'll be gone. If she is, I'll deal with it then. Maybe you could just check on her when you retire, Cassy. I would, but if she's still awake, it might make it even harder for her."

"I'll do it. What's her name again?"

"Darvi. Darvi Wingate." The name was said softly, a gentle smile on Seth's mouth.

"Why now? Why her?" Cassy asked of Eliot after Seth went to his room.

"I've been asking myself the same questions."

"So what are we going to do?"

Eliot shrugged a little. "Just wait and see."

Ten

DARVI'S LIDS OPENED, AND SHE STARED at the log wall in front of her face. She frowned in confusion before closing her eyes in remembrance. Tempted to pinch herself, she knew it was useless. This was no dream, and it was time she faced that.

Rolling to her back, she spotted a window above her bed, sat up, and looked out. Bright sunshine filled the sky, and she could tell it was going to be another hot day. Just as suddenly as she remembered the last few days, she recalled having roommates. Before undressing last night, she'd taken the lamp close to the room's full bed and seen two sleeping children. She now looked that way, wondering if they were still abed.

What she saw made her blink. Sitting on the edge of the bed, dressed and ready to go for the day, was a little girl. She stared right back at Darvi, her expression open and curious.

"Hello," Darvi tried.

The little girl continued to stare.

"What's your name?"

"She can't talk," a little boy said from around the door he'd just opened a bit. "But her name's Lindy."

"Thank you," Darvi told him before turning back to the little girl. "Hello, Lindy."

She gave a little wave and smiled as the boy entered the room and sat beside her.

"I'm Nate," he supplied, his face just as open and friendly as his sister's.

"Well, Nate and Lindy, I'm Darvi. It's nice to meet you."

The words were no more than out of her mouth when someone

knocked. Seth stuck his head around the door. Modest as her gown was, Darvi still reached for a bathrobe that wasn't there. She had to content herself with pulling the covers a little higher.

"Come on you two. Give Darvi some privacy."

"What did you call me?" Darvi asked as the children scrambled out.

"Darvi," he admitted, his eyes watchful.

"How long have you known?"

"Since before you fell off the bed yesterday morning."

Darvi's eyes lit with flame.

"We can talk about it," Seth reassured her.

"Oh, no," Darvi countered, her voice tight. "*We* are not going to talk about anything. I'm not saying a word. *You* have a lot of explaining to do."

Seth only nodded. "Whenever you're ready."

Darvi got up the moment he shut the door. Certain she was finally going to get on that train, she dressed yet again in her navy suit, trying to ignore some of the creases, and from years of solid habit, made her bed. After packing her bag, Darvi went out to do battle. This was all before finding the large room almost empty. The woman they referred to as Cassy stood at the stove. As soon as she spotted Darvi, she took a plate from the oven.

"I have some breakfast for you," she spoke as she moved to put it on the table.

It was on the tip of Darvi's tongue to refuse, but then she saw it was dished up and ready.

"Thank you," Darvi only replied and sat down, thanking the woman again when she was served a steaming mug of coffee. Trying to calm her now-racing heart, Darvi bowed her head and thanked God for the food. She might never see this woman again, but she wanted her impression to be a favorable one.

"Darvi, is it?" Cassy asked when her guest's head came up.

"Yes, and you're Cassy?"

That woman nodded.

"I met your children. I hope I didn't disturb them."

"Not at all. There is a spare room, but it's right across from Seth's. He felt you would feel safer in with the children. You can move if you like."

"I appreciate the offer, but I won't be needing either room another night."

Cassy only nodded, knowing it would not help Seth's cause for her to comment.

"May I ask you where Mr. McDermott is, or, um, Seth? I don't know his last name."

"Redding. Seth Redding. Eliot had to run into town, and Seth is around somewhere. I know he wants to talk with you."

The eggs and steak on Darvi's plate were delicious, and so was the thick slice of bread, but it was somewhat lost on her. She spent the entire meal searching the door and windows for any sign of Mr. Redding. He didn't appear until after she was finished. As soon as Darvi saw him come in, she went for her bag. Back in the large room, the handle in her grasp, she spoke.

"You may explain to me when you return me to town."

"I'm not returning you to town, but we can go for a walk and I'll tell you what happened."

Darvi could have stomped her foot with frustration, but as with everything else in this situation, she was helpless. She set her bag back against one wall and followed Seth outside. He walked them toward the distant woods, his stride shortened to match Darvi's. Not that she was very close to him. She walked a few steps behind and some ten feet away. Seth glanced over at her stormy face and knew he would just have to begin.

"Eliot—he's my half brother—and I work for Jared Silk; he's a banker. He's not all that honest, but he pays us well, and we're good at what we do." He glanced to see if she was listening, but she looked away when their eyes met. "Jared's sick of Annabelle Hewett's column. If the truth be told, she's often right about him, but he wants her stopped. He came up with the plan to talk to her, and our job was to convince her to have dinner with him.

"The men we sent grabbed you because you look like her, and also because she's always headed somewhere. Her job takes her all over town, so it wasn't surprising they found you at the train station. We thought we had Annabelle until Eliot saw her heading into the news office early yesterday morning. By that time, it was too late."

"What was too late?"

"I had already decided that I liked you."

Darvi stopped and gawked at the man. She could hardly believe her ears.

"It's not forever, Darvi, at least your being forced to stay here isn't forever, but I'm just so sure that if you stay for a while, you'll come to care for us."

Darvi was stunned. This tall, confident, good-looking man was staring at her with his heart in his eyes. Darvi's head was spinning. She shifted her gaze to the wide open land and the trees beyond. Even from here she could hear the low sound of the cattle and understood how they made their living.

"Mr. Redding."

"Please call me Seth."

Darvi put her hand up. "All right. Seth. Let me get this straight. You work for a man who wanted a woman abducted and threatened, but the wrong woman was taken. Now that you've met me, and even realizing I'm not Annabelle Hewett, you want me to share your life?"

"I was hoping you weren't Hewett, since working for Jared would have made that relationship impossible. Much as I hated for you to be afraid, I was very pleased to learn you weren't her."

Darvi thought about the way she'd been treated in the last 48 hours. Not once had the men given the impression that she was going to be physically harmed. They had been downright gentlemen, but it didn't make what they had done less wrong.

"I get the impression that you're a very nice man, Seth. Your family," Darvi almost stumbled over the word, knowing Eliot was living with his girlfriend and her children, "seems very nice too. So how is it that you believe you can spot a woman, desire her, and take her?"

"I know it's outrageous, but I'm sure if I let you leave, I'll never see you again."

"That's right, you won't!"

Seth put his hands out as though he'd made his point.

Darvi could not believe this. Things simply didn't happen like this these days. This was 1882. This was civilization. A man simply did not come in, pick out the female he wanted, and carry her off into the night!

"You have to take me back to town," Darvi persisted, working to keep her voice even. "You have to return me so I can catch my train home. Have you thought about what my family might be feeling when I don't show up? You can't keep me, no matter how you feel. I am a person with rights and feelings, and I want to leave."

"To my head it sounds very logical, Darvi, but my heart's just not convinced."

Darvi threw up her hands in frustration and turned back toward the house, muttering all the way. She hit the door so angry she completely forgot that she wanted to make a favorable impression on Cassy.

"Do you know," she nearly shouted when she got inside, "that he plans to keep me?"

"He said as much," Cassy admitted, turning from the stove top and wiping her hands on her checkered apron.

"And do you condone this, or are you going to help me get out of here?"

"I can't help you leave, if that's what you're asking me. I wish Seth had done this another way, but I still won't interfere."

"Then you're a part of it."

Cassy shrugged. "I guess I am."

Darvi looked as stunned as she felt.

"He's a big boy, Darvi. I don't try to tell him what to do. I'm sure you can appreciate that."

As a matter of fact, Darvi could. She knew she must not take this out on anyone but Seth. In fact, she somehow sensed that not even Eliot was involved.

"We got ten!" Nate shouted as he and Lindy came through the front door. "Ten eggs!"

"Good job. Did anyone get pecked?"

The children proudly displayed their small hands.

"Hi, Darvi," Nate said when he spotted her. Lindy waved her greeting, but Darvi offered only a limp smile in return.

"Okay, you two," Cassy chimed in. "Get your slates. We've got some arithmetic to work on."

Cassy put the eggs to one side and came to stand near Darvi, her voice low.

"Is this your traveling suit?"

"Yes."

"It doesn't look like you're going to be getting on the train today. I've got some dresses if you want to change."

"I have two more dresses with me, but I thank you."

"Let me know if you need anything," Cassy said as she moved to her children.

A way out was Darvi's only thought, but she kept this to herself.

❧ ❧ ❧

But we all, with open faces beholding as in a glass the glory of the Lord, are changed into the same image from glory to glory, even as by the Spirit of the Lord. Therefore, seeing we have this ministry, as we have received mercy, we faint not, but have renounced the hidden things of dishonesty, not walking in craftiness, nor handling the word of God deceitfully, but by manifestation of the truth commending ourselves to every man's conscience in the sight of God. But if our gospel be hidden it is hidden to them that are lost. In whom the god of this world hath blinded the minds of them who believe not, lest the light of the glorious gospel of Christ, who is the image of God, should shine upon them.

Darvi read the verses from 2 Corinthians 3 and 4 a second and third time before sitting back thoughtfully.

She would not have chosen to be in this place, but she knew from other passages that God was in control. It was hard to imagine a reason for this, but she understood now that if others couldn't see the gospel—the good news of Christ—in her, they might remain lost. Darvi read the verses again.

But does that mean I just sit here? Or do I do something to get back to town? Darvi had no answer and kept on praying. *Lord, I need You to show me a way out of this. I will never love Seth Redding because he doesn't love You, but those verses say I'm to care about the souls of these people. Part of my heart still can't believe this has happened, but I know that You have Your eye on me.*

Darvi spent a little more time in prayer and in reading her Bible before changing into an everyday dress and going back out to the big room. Cassy and the children were still working at the table. They looked up when she came in.

"Are you any good with spelling?" Cassy asked.

"Pretty good. It all depends."

Cassy raised the book when Darvi approached.

"Is there a rule I can tell the kids about adding *ed* or *ing* to a word?"

"What words do you have for examples?"

"Well, "study" for one. Stud*ied* puts an *i* in, and study*ing* leaves the *y* in place."

"Oh." Darvi was sympathetic. "That is a hard one."

While the women pored over this, the children's noses pressed close as they listened, Seth came back. He had not wanted to rush Darvi, knowing she would need time to see that, unconventional though his approach may be, he wanted only to take care of her. He thought it might be easier if he made himself scarce for a time, but it had then occurred to him that she might be giving Cassy a hard time. He knew he couldn't allow that. Seeing her working at the table with some of the people he loved most in the world did his heart a world of good.

Not waiting to be invited, Seth joined them. Lindy went right for his lap, and when Cassy had the kids go back to their spelling words, she stayed right where she was. It was not lost on Seth, however, that Darvi never spoke to him or even looked at him. This surprised him— she didn't seem to be that type of person—but considering all the circumstances, he thought she might not have seen herself as having any other recourse.

He was relieved when Cassy had something else for the kids to do and called them away. Seth spoke quietly before Darvi could get away.

"Darvi, please don't tell me you're going to spend every day not looking at me or talking to me."

Darvi finally looked him in the eye, her own gaze regretful. "I have no desire to be mean or rude to you, and I appreciate your not hurting me or threatening me, but you need to know that if I could leave here, I would. You need to understand that I'm hoping you'll come to your senses and return me to town. I'm praying for that very thing."

Seth looked thoughtful, even as he reminded himself he was going to have to be patient.

"At least I know where I stand," he finally said. "And since you're so sure of your feelings, you can't object to my trying to change them."

He wasn't listening. Darvi shook her head to clear the confusing mix of emotions.

"I'm not the woman for you, Seth, and the sooner you face that, the easier all this will be."

"Now, there you're wrong. You are the woman for me. I know you are, and given time, you'll know it too."

Darvi looked into his eyes. He was completely serious. She had been close to only one other man in love, and that had been Brandon. Seth's eyes looked the same: tender and warm, full of eagerness to please, with just enough male interest to remind Darvi that he was a man. She stood up.

"Darvi, please don't go."

She paused, making herself meet his eyes.

"I'm not running from you. I just need to get out for a little while—for your sake, I might add, not mine."

"You're sure?"

She only nodded and started away.

"Darvi?"

She turned one last time.

"You look beautiful in that yellow dress."

Darvi didn't try to hold back her sigh, but she still said, "Thank you, Seth."

❧ ❧ ❧

Even though Darvi was trusting the Lord to get her out of the mess she was in, she still set her mind to planning. She spent her first afternoon with the children, who showed her every inch of the barn. Darvi saw the chickens, the milk cow, several horses, a goat, and even two pigs. She also took note of the doors, where the saddles and tack were stored, and the access to the haymow. Her mind was working out how she could use all of this when she heard Cassy say she was taking the wagon to town first thing in the morning.

The children were already in bed, and the big room was full of ranch hands. As Darvi was eating, a plan was forming, one that she saw no harm in trying. She had told Seth she didn't want to stay there, and she meant it.

"Excuse me—" a male voice finally got through to her. Darvi looked up to see one of the hands addressing her.

"Do you still write for the paper?"

Darvi shook her head. "You've confused me with someone else. I've never written for the paper."

The man, who was very well mannered—they all were—went back to his plate. Darvi did the same, but she could feel both Seth and Eliot's eyes on her. Choosing to ignore them and wishing the children hadn't gone to bed so early, Darvi finished her meal feeling very alone. It was a relief to see Cassy starting the dishes. Darvi left the table to offer her help.

"Why don't I wash?" she suggested, knowing the dryer had to know where to put things away.

"All right. Did you have enough to eat?"

"Yes, thank you, it was delicious." Darvi glanced at the half-dozen ranch hands still eating. "Did they come in for breakfast and lunch and I miss them?"

Cassy laughed. "No. My cook has been with me for years, but he's getting on. He wanted to retire, so I made a deal with him. If he would do the breakfast and the noon meals in the bunkhouse or on the range, I'd do supper for everyone, including him. He didn't even hesitate. He knew supper was the hardest meal of the day."

Darvi nodded, knowing what she meant. The platters that held the meat and side dishes were huge, not to mention the dozens of plates, bowls, and cups, along with all the flatware. Trying not to think of how her hands were going to feel when she was done, Darvi started in. She was impressed when she heard the men thanking Cassy on their way out, and even more so when both Seth and Eliot offered to help.

"I think for tonight we have it under control," she said kindly, "but don't forget us in the future."

The brothers also thanked her and went on their way. Unknown to Darvi, Cassy did this on purpose. She wanted to talk to the newest houseguest alone.

"Are you all right?" she started by asking.

"Yes," Darvi answered, but she didn't elaborate.

Cassy tried not to rush her feelings, but she couldn't help it. Only a few minutes had passed before she said, "I hope you know how much Seth wants this to work."

"I probably don't fully understand it, but then no one seems to understand my position either."

"What makes you say that?"

Darvi turned to look at her.

"Was this originally your ranch or Eliot's?"

"It was mine."

"So you brought Eliot here and held him until he fell in love with you?"

Cassy had the good grace to drop her eyes in shame, but it didn't last for long. The longing she was seeing in Seth's eyes was killing her. The other men had all they could do not to gawk at Darvi tonight, even though some of them had steady girls, but their eyes weren't filled with love the way Seth's were. Cassy knew how little they could promise. Seth could hand Darvi the world on a platter, and probably would.

"I guess I wish you'd give him a chance. I know it's just been a few days, but if you got to know him, you might feel differently."

"I already know some things I wish I didn't know."

"Like what?"

"I have no desire to show disrespect to you or the people you love, Cassy, but I'm horrified by what Seth and Eliot do for a living, and I'm sure I don't know the half of it."

"Talk to Seth. Your affection might mean that much to him."

"That's just it, Cassy, if I bring this up to him, he's going to think that if he changes, I'll love him. That's not going to happen."

Cassy's face clouded with anger. "What are the men like where you come from, Miss Wingate, that Seth Redding is not good enough?"

Darvi knew she should have held her tongue, but they had gone this far and she was going to finish it. She turned from the wash water and faced the other woman.

"Just a few months back I realized I was a sinner and needed to have a personal relationship with God. Because of God's Son, I'm a different person. I didn't have to do this; it was my free choice. But now that it's done, I'm working to live my life in a way that's pleasing to God, and one of those ways is not marrying a man who does not share my faith. The Bible is very specific about that.

"If Seth were to know Christ someday, that would be great, but he can't do that just to win me. He's got to do that for his own soul's sake. It's a matter between him and God. If I still sound to you as if I think I'm too good, I'm sorry, but God as my witness, my only desire is to do what I know to be right."

Cassy was stunned. Of all the things she expected to hear, this was not it. She had not an argument left in her head. She was not a religious woman, but she had high respect for anyone who was. Cassy dried a pot and watched Darvi's profile. She had to say something so Darvi would not think her upset. Absolutely nothing came to mind, but the dishes were almost done and she *couldn't* let it end like this.

"Thank you for telling me, Darvi."

Darvi turned in relief. She had remembered too late that this woman hadn't even bothered to marry the man she loved. Darvi had been wishing the tongue right out of her mouth. Cassy's words were an olive branch she was not going to turn down.

"I think we're about set here, Cassy. Is there anything else I can do?"

"No, thank you, Darvi. I think you've earned the right to put your feet up for the evening."

The women didn't exchange any more words, but both left the wash area with the small comfort that the strange relationship they found themselves in was still intact.

Eleven

"ARE YOU ALL RIGHT?" ELIOT ASKED CASSY when he retired that night.

"Um hm" was her only answer as she rocked in the chair. She was ready for bed but not there yet. For dozens of reasons Eliot knew her answer was not the end of it, but he was tired and just wanted to sleep, so he found himself somewhat cross with her.

"If you don't want to talk about it, Cass, that's fine, but don't say you're all right when you're not!"

Cassy didn't answer. She stayed in the chair even after Eliot climbed into bed, her heart pained and uncertain. She hadn't felt this way in a long time, not since after her husband had died and left her with a baby and a toddler and a ranch to run on her own. Those were black days, and she didn't want to go back there again, but some of the old feelings were returning.

"Cassy," Eliot said softly now, not able to sleep with her upset. "What is it?"

"She has strong religious beliefs."

"Darvi?"

"Yes. It's more than just being taken against her will; it goes against her belief in God. That really bothers me."

"Has she told Seth?"

"She won't do that," Cassy stated and went on to explain Darvi's reasons.

For a time the couple was silent.

"It's gotten me to thinking about the days after Chad died, about God and the way I was raised." Cassy turned to look at him for the first time. "I was raised to know better than to live with a man I wasn't married to."

Eliot was out of the bed in a flash, over to her chair and turning it so he could see her face in the light. With his hands tenderly holding her face, he whispered the words in his heart.

"I'm the one who's been asking you to marry me for five years, Cassandra. I can't promise I won't die, but I'm the one who's always wanted marriage. You'll get no argument out of me."

"Oh, Eliot. I don't know what I've been waiting for, but I think it must be time."

He leaned down and kissed her very softly.

"I also need to tell you, though," he knew he had to add, "this has nothing to do with God. I'm not sure there is a God. I think the only heaven we'll ever know is right here—good or bad—this is it. The only thing I know for sure is that I love you."

Cassy nodded. Her own beliefs were not that far distant from his. Her grandfather had been a preacher, but her own father had wanted nothing to do with God. He was moral to a fault over issues like drinking, wife beating, adultery, and fornication, but God was never mentioned. In truth, Cassy didn't know exactly what she believed. She only knew right now that she was tired. She finally climbed into bed, comforted by Eliot's presence beside her but wondering what it would be like to have the peace that Darvi Wingate seemed to own.

❧ ❧ ❧

Darvi knew she would not be able to hold her breath, so she didn't even try, but by reciting her family's names very slowly, she was able to keep her breathing shallow. As she hoped, Cassy checked on the sleeping children before she left, not realizing Darvi was under the covers in her clothes and ready to make a run for the barn the moment the woman exited the room. She had done this and was now under the blanket behind the seat, barely able to hold her wits about her as she felt the team pull the wagon from the barn.

I'm going to make it! I'm really going to make it! Darvi had all she could do not to shout with delight. She'd been forced to leave her bag behind, but she would remedy that when she got to town and made a little call to the sheriff's office. She didn't have malicious thoughts toward these people, but what had happened to her could not be allowed without repercussions.

If she remembered correctly, she had spotted the law office when she and Dakota were trying to find the livery. She thought it might . . .

Darvi's thoughts were cut short, and her whole body jumped

when the report of a rifle shattered the silence. She heard Cassy mutter, "What in the world?" and then felt the wagon slow and halt as a fast horse galloped up and stopped as well. Darvi's heart sank.

"I think you have a passenger."

It was Seth's voice.

"You're kidding" came from Cassy just before the blanket was tugged on and Seth came into Darvi's view.

"I'm going to town with Cassy." Darvi stated the obvious.

"No, you're not," Seth replied firmly, his hand already out to help her. Darvi ignored it. She climbed awkwardly from the wagon, none too pleased about being caught.

"Seth," Cassy began the moment Darvi stepped down, "I don't know if this is a good idea. She doesn't want to stay."

"There hasn't been enough time, Cass. You can't expect—" Seth stopped because Darvi was headed for the horse. It had no saddle, but she didn't care. He caught her around the waist and hauled her back to the wagon with him.

"I'll see you when you get back," he told Cassy, but she was far from pleased. She watched Darvi struggle in his arms but knew there was nothing she could do.

Clicking to the team, she set the wagon in motion just as Darvi landed a strong backward kick against Seth's shin. He grunted in very real pain but didn't let go until he had the horse's reins securely in his hand. That little move got him glared at, but he couldn't find it in his heart to be angry. He had brought this on.

"Do you want a ride?" he volunteered, even as the creak and rumble of the wagon faded in their ears.

Darvi didn't answer. She was too disappointed with her foiled plan. She thought that getting as far as she had meant she would actually make it.

I'm giving up, Lord. I thought it was a great idea, but we're just too isolated out here. At times I think I'm going to lose my mind. I'm trying to trust, but right now I just want to scream and run from here as fast as I can.

Darvi was so intent on her praying that she stumbled into a hole. Seth's hand was right there to catch her. She hadn't realized he was so close.

"How's your leg?" she asked, eyes ahead as she walked swiftly back.

"It hurts."

Darvi had all she could do not to smile, but she knew that would have been wrong. Was it wrong to kick the man who was holding her? That one she couldn't answer.

Returning to the house and going straight to her room, Darvi tried not to start planning again.

☙☙☙

Kinkade, Texas

"This church family is wonderful," Dakota said sincerely as he and Cash rode home together from an all-church Saturday afternoon picnic.

"I certainly think so. I mean, we're not without our problems, but God has greatly blessed in this place."

"Is Grandma's church like this?"

"Very much so, just smaller. Her pastor is a younger man with a young family. We've had some great talks, and he's very grounded in the Word and eager for his congregation to grow. Grandma adores him, and he never stops telling her what an encouragement she is."

Dakota was silent for a moment, the clop of the horses' hooves the only sound.

"Do you ever think about our situation, Cash?" the younger man asked thoughtfully. "I mean, the way God reached down for you and Gram, and now Slater and me? Sometimes it's almost more than I can take in."

Cash couldn't speak. He too was amazed at what God had done, but as always, his heart went to his parents.

I know You want their salvation more than I do, Father. Please help Dak and me to be the examples we need to be. Help my folks to find You before it's too late.

"I was just praying for the folks," Dakota said.

"So was I."

From there, the men rode home in silence.

☙☙☙

Aurora

Darvi was tired of sitting in her room with no place to read but her bed. She had only her Bible with her, but she wasn't going to sit in this bedroom anymore. She didn't think Cassy was back—somehow she thought that woman might be leaning toward her side—but she was still going to go out to one of the chairs by the fireplace to read. To her relief, she found the room empty. Taking a comfortable chair, she welcomed the opportunity to look around.

It was an interesting layout. Only two rooms led off of the main room, and from what Cassy had said, they were both hallways to bedrooms. The big room held everything else: kitchen area, dining area, and living room furniture set up around the fireplace. There were windows on two sides. The kitchen table was long and wide with a variety of mismatched chairs. The two davenports and three rocking chairs were well worn but clean looking.

Darvi settled back with her Bible and turned a little to catch the light from the window. She had covered only two chapters when Eliot, Seth, Nate, and Lindy came in. Lindy came right to her, her eyes intent on Darvi's Bible. Darvi smiled and watched her touch the book and then pat her little chest.

"Do you have a Bible?"

She shook her head no and patted the Bible and her chest again.

"Do you want me to read to you?" Darvi wasn't long in catching on.

Her little head bobbed again, this time in excitement.

"I would be happy to read to you, Lindy, but you need to ask Mr. McDermott first."

The men couldn't help but overhear the conversation. After the events of that morning, Seth was keeping his distance, but Eliot came right over.

"Do you mind if I read the Bible to Lindy?"

The man looked completely untroubled. "Not at all." Even his voice was unconcerned. "It's just stories."

Eliot was on his way back across the room when Darvi asked Lindy a question.

"Do you have another book I might read to you, Lindy?"

The little girl frowned in confusion.

"I want to read to you, Lindy," Darvi clarified, "but I don't think these are just stories."

Eliot came back.

"Darvi, Cassy won't mind if you read the Bible to Lindy."

Aware that every eye in the room was on her, she still said, "But if I have to tell her this is just another storybook, *I* mind very much."

"Run and get a book from your room, Lindy."

When the little girl scampered away, Eliot met Darvi's eyes.

"So you think the Bible is from God?"

"Yes, I do," Darvi answered, glad that he understood what she was saying.

"I can't speak for Cassy on that, so if you don't mind reading something else . . ." Eliot let the sentence hang, as Darvi was already nodding.

"Not at all."

That was all the more time Lindy needed to come back with a

thick book of nursery rhymes, stories, and poems. Darvi saw nothing wrong with the book, but it was something of a letdown for her. She sincerely hoped to read to Lindy from the Bible one day but invited the little girl into her lap and read from the story Lindy opened to. It was a familiar one from Darvi's childhood, and she had to fight the homesickness that welled up inside of her.

She wasn't usually prone to missing home so much, but she had been primed and ready to go back, even if there was a battle, and now having been cheated out of that, her heart yearned for home more than it ever had before. For a time she read without thought, her mind on how she and her parents had parted. She knew things would never be completely settled unless they came to Christ, but she also thought it was right to have as little tension as possible between them.

Not aware of the little girl's drooping lids, Darvi read through the entire story before she noticed that Lindy's head had fallen to the side. She set the book down, but because they were both comfortable, Darvi kept rocking and holding her. It was a bit warm to be cuddling, but the amazement of how kind and sweet these children were to her, a virtual stranger, wrung Darvi's heart. While they were sitting quietly, Seth joined them.

"Do you want me to take her?" he offered.

"She's fine, thank you." Both adults whispered.

Seth worked to keep the emotions from his face, but seeing Darvi with a child was doing wild things to his heart.

"Tell me, Seth, why aren't the children in school in town?"

"Nate was," Seth explained, "but when it was Lindy's turn to go, the teacher didn't believe that she couldn't talk. He believed she *wouldn't* talk. He hit her until she bruised and even bled. When Cassy learned of it, she nearly went after him with the shotgun but realized that it was violence that had gotten Lindy hurt. Instead, she never took either child back, determined to teach them on her own for all their school years if she had to."

Darvi could have cried. It was so sad and painful to think of someone hitting this mute little girl.

"Has she ever talked?" Darvi asked the question that suddenly came to mind.

"Yes, but when she wasn't yet three, she watched a bull gore her father to death. She hasn't uttered a word since."

Darvi couldn't take any more. She didn't want to care for these people. She didn't want to get attached to this place. She wasn't supposed to be here, not really.

Making herself speak normally, she closed the conversation.

"Thank you for telling me." With that Darvi laid her head back and closed her eyes. She didn't hear whether Seth left; she didn't care if he did, but she had to be finished hearing about this family.

I'm so totally off balance right now, Lord, I don't know what I'm doing. What is my place here? How do I deal with my captors? Lindy and Nate are innocent of what Seth has done and what their mother and Eliot are a part of. Help me to never take my frustration out on them, but I do ask You to take me from this place. I don't want to be here.

Darvi thought she might cry and made herself stop thinking such thoughts. She was very warm and uncomfortable and felt sweat starting to break out where Lindy lay against her. It was with nothing but relief that she heard a wagon approach. Lindy heard it too.

Perking up as if to say, "It's Mama!" she was off Darvi's lap in a flash.

Darvi stayed where she was, fanning herself slightly with her hand. Even Seth had gone to meet the wagon, and somewhere in the commotion she heard Cassy through an open window saying something about the next day being Sunday.

Where had the days gone?

Praying for renewed strength to make it through, Darvi put her Bible back on her bed. Not seeing any other help for it, she went out to join the family.

🌹🌹🌹

"Oh, Darvi." Cassy spoke her name the moment she came from her room Sunday morning. "Do you have a moment?"

"Yes," Darvi said, noting absently that no one else was around.

"The men have gone into town and taken Nate along," Cassy volunteered, answering the unspoken question.

Determining not to start planning an escape and working hard not to think about how much she wanted to be in church, Darvi accompanied Cassy to her bedroom. Lindy was already there, sitting on the bed with a book. Cassy walked to the wardrobe, pulled a dress out, and hung it outside the door. This done, she stepped back.

"What do you think?"

"It's beautiful," Darvi said sincerely of the lavender gown with the long sleeves and high neck. It wasn't overly done with frills, but the bodice, neck, and cuffs were all trimmed in dark purple lace and strips of satin. The effect was very attractive, and it wasn't hard to imagine Cassy, with her blonde hair and blue eyes, looking very lovely.

"It's my wedding dress."

Darvi turned to look at her.

"You're getting married?"

"Yes, and it's all because of you."

Darvi didn't know what to say. She had questions but was afraid of the answers. What had she said or done to compel Cassy to get married? And what did Eliot think?

Watching her search for words, Cassy thought she might be more comfortable if Lindy left the room. Using gentle words, Cassy asked her daughter to take the book into the other room for a few minutes.

"I've shocked you," Cassy said when they were alone.

"You have, yes. I can't imagine what you mean."

Cassy became rather fascinated with her fingers and nails.

"I put it to Eliot this way: I was raised better than to be living with a man who wasn't my husband. Your convictions about God reminded me of that fact."

"And Eliot's not angry with me?"

"No. He's been asking me to marry him for five years, and I wouldn't. It's stupid on my part. I already buried one husband and somehow thought it wouldn't hurt as much to lose Eliot if we weren't married, so I didn't want to take any vows. It's ridiculous, I know. I can see that now."

Darvi was stunned. Cassy had not wanted to be married, but Eliot had. Where Darvi came from, catching a handsome husband was all young women could talk about; the men, on the other hand, until they were smitten, seemed to dread the very thought.

"Congratulations, Cassy," Darvi said suddenly, realizing she was being watched carefully. "When is the day?"

Cassy smiled. "We haven't gotten that far. I just happened to spot this dress yesterday, so I went ahead and bought it. Eliot likes it a lot, but we haven't really made further plans. But the kids are thrilled," she added swiftly, "and Seth hugged me and said it was about time."

This was not St. Louis. And never was Darvi more reminded of that. Women who took up residence with men without bothering to marry them were a shame and a disgrace in the community. Darvi didn't think she was too sheltered, but she couldn't honestly think of one woman who would admit to being intimate with a man outside of the bonds of matrimony. Texas wasn't as settled as Missouri certainly, but right and wrong were still right and wrong.

"Well, I'm happy for both of you, Cassy. I really am."

Cassy forced herself to say only a quiet thank you. She knew for a fact that Eliot was going to try to talk some sense into Seth, but knowing how stubborn the oldest brother could be, Cassy did not want to get Darvi's hopes up.

To distract herself, she offered breakfast and hot coffee to the other woman, not to mention she always cooked a slab of beef on Sunday afternoons, and time was awasting.

❧ ❧ ❧

"Do I look all right to you?" Seth suddenly asked Eliot.

Eliot frowned at him. "You look like you always do. Why, are you feeling sick?"

"No."

Seth's answer was short and he broke eye contact with Eliot, but Eliot was not done. He'd been hoping all morning for a lead-in of some type.

"Why did you ask?"

"I don't know. I was just wondering if maybe she finds me repulsive or something."

"They don't think like we do, Seth. When are you going to see that?"

The other man didn't answer. Eliot tried again.

"You can't expect to hold her body and have her heart follow."

Seth's eyes closed. The words about holding Darvi were a little too much for him right now. He had been tempted so many times just to grab her and kiss her until she knew she was loved, but her eyes held him at bay. She was not a woman to be trifled with, and he didn't want to do anything now that might mess up his chances later, not to mention the fact that he could still feel where she kicked him in the shin.

"I just need to give her some more time," Seth repeated in honest belief. "I can already see that Cass and the kids care for her. Her heart is tender and sweet. She'll come to love us. She'll come to love me. She won't be able to help herself."

Eliot knew the door was closed. He didn't agree, and he knew Cassy hated it this way, but this was not his call.

Five minutes later the men left the dining room of the hotel. Jared had scheduled a meeting.

❧ ❧ ❧

Darvi had told herself not to plan. She had scolded and carried on in her heart, but that hadn't stopped her feet from taking her toward the barn. She had helped Cassy with some things in the house for a time, even going to get eggs from the barn and vegetables from the garden with the children, but now her mind was on escape, and she was not going to be stopped. If only she could get out right after everyone went to bed for the night. She knew she couldn't hide in the bunkhouse—that could be disastrous—and if she hid in the barn, that would be the first place they would look. Then she thought of the outhouse. Would anyone ever think to look behind it? Darvi surreptitiously moved around the outside of the barn now to have a look, rounded a corner, and ran smack into Eliot.

Not bothering to hide her frustration, she crossed her arms over her chest and looked very stern.

"I thought you were in town."

"I was, but I dispensed with my business and I'm back."

She watched Eliot smile at her and knew he'd figured her out.

"Will you please talk to him?" she entreated quietly. "Will you please tell your brother he can't do this?"

"It won't do any good, Darvi. He loves you."

"He can't love me." Frustration rose in her voice. "He doesn't even know me."

Eliot shrugged. "Sometimes it works like that. I set eyes on Cass five years ago, and I've never gotten over it."

It was one of the most romantic things Darvi had ever heard, but it wasn't right—not here, not now.

"Why me?" was all she could think to say.

Again Eliot smiled. "Maybe if he had seen you on the street and not met you like he did, you would feel differently. He's not going to let you go, Darvi, so you might try to figure out if there's something about him you can love."

"Eliot, it doesn't work that way. Surely you can see that?"

"I can, yes, but then no one is trying to take Cass and the kids away from me. I know I wouldn't be so reasonable then."

Darvi could see that no amount of words would sway him. They stared at each other for a few moments before Eliot, still dressed up for town, moved and held out an arm for her to lead the way. Darvi wanted to argue that she didn't want to go back inside just yet, but mentally her mind was growing strong. She'd let them think she was going along with everything they asked, but if she ever got a chance to leave, she'd be gone before anyone could take another breath.

Twelve

Kinkade

"I THINK I'LL HEAD OUT TOMORROW AND visit Gram," Dakota said after dinner on Monday night.

"Okay," Cash agreed quietly, setting his paper aside.

Dakota was not looking at him, which gave the older brother a chance to study him. Something was wrong. He didn't know what. Indeed, he couldn't imagine what was troubling him, but Dakota was clearly tense. Cash had never been anything but direct in the past and saw no reason to change now.

"Out with it, Dak," he ordered.

That man looked up and frowned.

"Out with what?"

"That's just it; I don't know. But something is wrong. I can tell."

Dakota looked at him. It didn't take long to admit, at least to himself, that something was on his mind.

"You're going to think I'm crazy."

"I already do."

Having Cash tease him was all he needed. In the next few minutes he offered a rundown on his time with Darvi and ended it by explaining what happened after he put her on the train.

"So you never saw this woman's face?"

"No, and if I think about it long enough I go around in circles. It hasn't been that many days, but I just wish there was some way to get word about whether she arrived safely." Dakota stopped and stared at his brother. "Will I trust more when I've been at this longer, Cash? I want to leave it in God's hands, but if anything should happen to Darvi, it would be all my fault."

"How do you figure?"

"I was responsible to get her home."

"No, you weren't. You just told me you had to get her on the train in Aurora. If you hadn't had it in your heart to keep in touch with her and gone back for an address, you wouldn't know a thing. None of what you've described is your worry. I can see why you're concerned, but you did your job."

Dakota honestly couldn't argue with him there.

"Did you see anyone else in town who you could have mistaken her for?"

Dakota shook his head. "Not in the brief time I looked around, but it's a good-sized city. It's hard to know just how far to track."

Cash could see his point, and it was unsettling.

"Have you sent word to Brace?"

"You mean asking if he's heard from Darvi?"

"Right."

"No, I didn't want him to think anything was wrong when I had no proof. I guess I could ask without voicing any of my doubts."

"Why don't you do that? It's a normal enough question."

Dakota thanked Cash for the advice and decided to stop at the telegraph office on his way to his grandmother's the next day. He asked for a section of the newspaper and both men settled in to read.

☙ ☙ ☙

Dakota felt better having talked to Cash and went to bed with a light heart. He didn't figure on what would happen in the morning. Cash was in his room before he even finished dressing.

"I'm not a man given to foolish notions," he said without greeting his brother. "You would agree with that, wouldn't you, Dak?"

"Absolutely."

"So what I'm about to say to you might seem strange."

"Okay."

"Go back to Aurora and check again for Darvi."

Dakota stopped all movement.

"Do you mean it, Cash? You really think I should go?"

"Yes, I do. I can tell you want to, and I ache at the thought that Darvi might be in trouble. I don't want you to head off on a wild goose chase, but the truth of the matter is she could have been taken from the train. If you don't find her, we'll have to wait until you get word from Brace as to whether or not she arrived. If she does need you, you'll be there all the sooner."

Dakota was thoughtful. His brother was certainly not given to impulsive or rash behavior. It had been on Dakota's heart off and on that Darvi might need him, but he had felt so helpless. Having Cash be so practical about checking back in Aurora was all the permission he needed.

"I'll start right after breakfast."

"All right. I'll make sure Katy has provisions for you. Do you have any money?"

"Yes, I went by the bank yesterday."

Dakota had been enjoying his time with Cash very much, and he loved working the ranch, but the incident with Darvi and the train had left him doubting himself. He thought it had been God's way of testing him to see if he was truly trusting, and it might have been, but it was with a light heart that he headed back the way he had come. He asked God for wisdom and strength but also found himself talking to the woman herself.

If you need me, Darvi, I'm on my way.

❧ ❧ ❧

Aurora

"What is it?" Darvi asked Seth without taking the box he held out to her. They were alone by the trees to the west where Seth had found Darvi walking.

"Just take it," he urged.

"Not until you tell me what it is."

"It's a gift for you."

Darvi's hands went behind her back.

"You've got to stop bringing me gifts, Seth. This is not going to work."

"Just take it."

Darvi eyed him and the box.

"I'll take the box and look in it, but that doesn't mean I'm accepting this gift."

His eyes were warm with amusement, and Darvi almost wished that he would grow angry.

He wasn't constantly around, but since Sunday, if he was anywhere in the vicinity, he was courting her. He had brought her flowers, both from town and along the roadside. A book of poems arrived one day, and a comb for her hair the next. Gifts would come to the ranch even when he hadn't gone to town but Eliot had. This told Darvi that Seth was planning ahead.

Darvi had started to mark the days in her Bible as they passed. She had been on Cassy's outlying ranch for eight days, and each day she had to work at trusting God to bring this nightmare to an end.

"Take it, Darvi," he urged one last time, and Darvi did so.

She opened the box and peeked inside. What she saw made her eyes huge before she nearly threw the gift at him and tried to run. She didn't get far. His arms came around her, and for the first time he attempted to hold her close. Darvi tried to get away, but there was no possibility of overpowering him. When Darvi saw escape wasn't going to work, she planted her palms against his chest and held herself away from him as much as she could. When she looked up, he spoke.

"The ring isn't for now," he panted slightly, "but it's to show you that I'm serious about us."

Darvi started to shake her head.

"Don't say no. Give us a chance. I know we could have a wonderful life together, and the ring is to prove that to you. You say the word, and we'll be married. That's how strongly I feel about you."

Darvi could only stare at him. What in the world was she to do?

When she froze, Seth's head started to descend.

"Don't!" Darvi commanded with some force, and he stopped with several inches still separating them.

Seth studied her features very slowly, his eyes warming noticeably.

"That upside-down mouth of yours is going to drive me crazy."

Darvi's chin came up. "Let me go."

Seth did so, although very slowly, his eyes never leaving her face.

"I'll never marry you," Darvi said quietly, "and if that's what you're waiting for, then you can release me now."

Their eyes met for long seconds, and for the first time Darvi saw a flicker of something other than patience. To her surprise, it didn't frighten her.

"Keep your hands to yourself, Mr. Redding," she added in low fury, "or I won't be responsible for my actions."

Still meeting his eyes to tell him she meant business, she took several more seconds before turning and walking back to the house. She wasn't a dozen feet along when she heard him behind her, but he did not attempt to catch up to her or to engage her in conversation, all of which was fine with Darvi. She had nothing else to say to the man.

❧ ❧ ❧

"She doesn't want him," Cassy whispered in frustration. "Why can't he see that?"

Eliot didn't answer. Cassy had just taken her hair down, and he was rather preoccupied with the way it looked. He leaned over the bed to kiss the side of her neck, but she turned and glared at him.

Seeing it, Eliot shook his head in longsuffering.

"Let me get this straight. You're mad at Seth, so you're going to take it out on me."

Cassy frowned. That was exactly what she'd been about to do. Now feeling upset with herself, she turned back away from him. Eliot didn't want to talk about Seth and Darvi right now, but he made himself join her on the edge of the bed and even took her hand when they sat side by side.

"What is it you want me to do?"

"That's just it—I don't know. I know they're both unhappy, and I feel so helpless. It would be great if she could stay. She's so sweet with the kids and willingly helps out, but this isn't where she belongs, and as much as I want Seth's happiness, I can't agree with what he's doing to Darvi."

Cassy turned her head to look at him. "If someone took Lindy and wouldn't let her go, I'd be out of my mind with worry. Seth has got to see that he's doing the same thing to Darvi's family."

Eliot didn't like this comparison at all. Lindy was like his own child, and this analogy hit a little too close to home for him.

"I'll talk to him again."

Cassy did not look grateful.

"I'd better warn you, Eliot McDermott," she threatened. "If I get a chance to help Darvi get out of here, I'm going to do it."

Eliot put gentle arms around her, but the voice at her ear was very firm.

"You will do no such thing."

"Do *not* tell me what to do!"

She suddenly wanted nothing to do with him, but Eliot did not let her pull away. In fact, he slipped an arm under her knees and deposited her on his lap. Cassy's eyes were filled with betrayal as she looked at him, and Eliot almost wished she would struggle some. He smoothed the hair from her face, his hands gentle and his heart filled with love.

"I'm sorry that Darvi is caught in the middle of this and that you're hurting over it too, but I'm not going to betray my brother, and if you think about it, you don't want to either."

Cassy's eyes filled with tears.

"It's a lousy excuse, but Darvi is not in any danger here. Seth's intentions toward her are honorable. I do think he's going to see pretty soon that she's not going to change her mind, but taking her from him is not the answer. He's got to come to it on his own."

Cassy still wanted to be angry, but Eliot was right.

"Cassandra . . ." Eliot's voice came softly to her ear.

Cassy looked at him.

"What day are you going to become my wife?"

Feeling almost shy, she fiddled with the apron she still had on and refused to look at him.

"I don't know."

"You have the dress, which means we're halfway there. I'm not going to let you get away from me now."

Cassy looked up with a smile. She loved him so much.

"You name the day," she was able to say, knowing it was time.

"October 30."

"Oh!" Cassy had not been prepared for such a definite answer. "When is that?"

"Two weeks from this Saturday."

A measure of panic clawed at her throat, but she wasn't able to talk about it as Eliot was lifting her and setting her on her feet. He then bent, kissed her brow, and started toward the door.

"Where are you going?"

"To the spare room."

It took a moment for Cassy to catch on, and when she did, her eyes softened with emotion.

"I love you," she said.

Eliot smiled. "And I love you, Cassy girl. I wouldn't be heading out this door for any other reason."

Cassy let him leave, but her heart was ready to burst. She couldn't possibly explain what had just happened to Darvi but wanted once again to thank her. Had it not been for Darvi, Cassy might not have seen the misguided direction of her entire life. She was convinced that she would have gone on for years living in sin with Eliot and not thinking about the right thing to do.

She got ready for bed very slowly, missing Eliot's presence already but knowing it was for the best.

Seth is the same kind of man, Cassy thought as she settled under the covers. *His and Eliot's jobs are not always the best, but they're good men who know how to love.* Completely forgetting Darvi's beliefs, her heart was quiet for a moment before wishing: *If only Darvi had met him some other way.*

❧ ❧ ❧

"My name is Dakota Rawlings," Dakota said to Aurora's sheriff. "I'm a Texas Ranger."

The other man stuck his hand out to shake Dakota's.

"Joe Laverty. What can I do for you?"

"Actually, I just wanted to let you know I'm going to be in town for a few days, maybe longer. I've lost track of someone, and I think this person might be in your town."

"Who is it?"

"I'm not at liberty to say right now, but I wanted you to know that I plan to stay out of the way and do my job as quietly as possible."

The sheriff, who had respect for most Rangers, thought Dakota seemed genuine. He was a curious man and didn't like not knowing exactly what was going on, but since the Ranger had stated his willingness to stay out of the way, he knew he'd have to let it go.

"Well, if we can be of any help from this office, be sure to let me know."

"Thank you, sir."

"Where will you be staying?"

"I'll probably camp outside of town. I noticed you have a bathhouse and a number of eating establishments." Dakota smiled a little. "It looks as though I'll be able to stay clean and fed."

When Dakota turned on the charm, it could be very effective, and it worked now. Sheriff Laverty smiled reluctantly and only waved when Dakota moved to the door and went on his way.

He'd arrived the day before, not late in the day by any means, but late enough to put off a visit to the local constabulary. The day was fresh, the visit to the sheriff was taken care of, and now Dakota was headed out into the streets of Aurora to see what he could find. He sensed that it was a well-settled town with what appeared to be many successful businesses, and as a rule the folks seemed friendly.

Not wishing to draw any undue attention to himself, Dakota had arrived in clothing a little less suited to his work than usual and having already let his beard go a few days. It didn't take him long to look scruffy, and that was just what he wanted. Eli was at one of the liveries, and Dakota now prepared to move about on foot and have a closer look around Aurora. Not knowing exactly what he was looking for made things a bit tricky, but he was certain that if something was amiss in this town, he would spot it.

A horrible feeling of dread came over him as he thought about how easy it would be to take a woman and disappear with her, but

Dakota forced himself away from those thoughts. It would only disturb his concentration and hinder his goal. He didn't know when or where he would find answers, but look he would.

It occurred to him very suddenly that he could wire Brace and Darvi's family from Aurora and ask after her, but he hesitated. If she'd made an appearance, he could return to his life. If she hadn't . . . Deciding to give it at least a few more days, Dakota began his tour.

❧ ❧ ❧

Cassy was nearly pacing before Darvi emerged from her room the next morning. The strawberry blonde had been very quiet at dinner the night before and retired to her room the moment she was able. Cassy had not witnessed the exchange with Seth, but she knew from watching both people that something had gone on. She and Eliot were to be married in only two and a half weeks, but Cassy was not waiting to tell Darvi that. She just wanted to make sure she was all right.

Breakfast was long over, cleanup was done, the men had headed into town, the hands were out with the stock, and the children sat reading books. There were dozens of things Cassy could do, but she wanted to see Darvi first. All of Eliot's talk was not doing her any good at the moment. His telling her that they couldn't take Darvi from Seth and that deep in her heart she wouldn't really want that was sounding very hollow in her ears right now. If she didn't want to, then why did she wish she could load Darvi into the wagon and take her to the train? She and the children could give her a nice send-off.

Cassy was beginning to get quite worked up over this idea when the bedroom door opened. She turned to see Darvi enter, her mouth set.

"Where is Seth?" she wasted no time in asking.

"He and Eliot went into town."

Darvi's shoulders slumped. She had been ready to do battle with the man, and now he was gone.

Just the sight of Darvi turned all of Cassy's intentions to dust. It wasn't that she hadn't seen Darvi in the pale blue dress in the past, but today her cheeks were blooming with color and her eyes sparkled. And it wasn't just that. Darvi was one of the sweetest women the ranch owner had ever known.

Cassy had never been in such a quandary. It was so easy to see why Seth loved Darvi, and for that reason, Cassy could not interfere. She found her heart reasoning that Seth might be correct: Maybe Darvi would come to love him and wish to stay.

"I don't suppose there's anything I can do," Cassy finally voiced, knowing that she could, but wouldn't.

"Not unless you're willing to take me back to town," Darvi said, not bothering to read the other woman's expression or to wait for an answer. She headed out the door then, around the house, and toward the barn.

As yet, Cassy had never hindered her from looking around. Knowing that both brothers were gone left her free to look a little. She told herself she wasn't exactly planning, but if something just happened to jump out at her, she'd be foolish not to give it notice.

Once inside the dark reaches of the barn, she looked out at the house. The bedroom window above her bed appeared to be some four feet off the ground. She had tested the window just that morning and been surprised to find that Seth had not nailed it shut. There was nothing to step on when she climbed out, so it would be a bit of a drop, but neither was there a prickly bush to fall into.

"Darvi!" Cassy called from near the house.

Darvi waited a moment and emerged into the sunlight.

"Yes?"

"Would you like something to eat?"

"Is it near noon?"

"No, but the children are hungry, and you didn't get breakfast."

Darvi waved. "Thank you. I'll be right in."

Still feeling as though she might have one person on her side, Darvi was pleased to see that Cassy didn't hesitate but turned around and went directly back inside. Darvi followed at a snail's pace, taking note of the layout of her window at close range. She had no idea if the information would ever be useful, but somehow she felt better for being prepared.

🌿🌿🌿

Sitting down in the hotel to treat himself to a hot meal for lunch on his third day in town, Dakota ate slowly and gave himself plenty of time to think. He was not discouraged, but he was starting to wonder a bit. Were things in this town just a little too neat, or was he getting overly suspicious with his line of work and Darvi's disappearance? Was the law doing its job in Aurora?

Two days had passed, two full days of watching, waiting, and making subtle inquiries, and still he had no leads as to what might have happened to Darvi. He'd all but stalked the alley where he thought she might have been taken, but there was nothing of even the slightest interest going on.

He learned that at least five stills were set up in full operation, quietly attended but working nevertheless. He found two homes where men came and went at all hours of the night, but the saloons appeared only to have some dancing and lots of cards and drinking.

What he'd seen of the law in action had been impressive. He had watched an officer haul a man off for spending a little too much time outside the home of Mrs. Gillham, who gave piano lessons to the town's young ladies. Several drunks had made trips to the jail, and when one of the general stores had a customer who refused to pay, the law answered in great haste.

"What can I get you?" a friendly woman in a clean apron asked as she appeared at his table.

"How about the special?"

"With or without gravy?"

"With gravy, please, and coffee."

"For one?" she asked with more than a little show of interest.

Dakota smiled. "Yes, thank you."

She was smiling in return, her eyes inviting, causing the Ranger to shake his head as she walked away. He hadn't shaved in days.

Maybe she likes scruffy, half-started beards, he speculated even as his stomach growled. Glancing around to see if she was bringing his coffee, Dakota froze.

He forced himself to look down at the tablecloth before shifting his gaze again. He could hardly believe what his eyes were telling him. His coffee was delivered, but he took little notice. He didn't even pick up the mug. All he could do was ask himself why he had thought he needed to come back to Aurora.

Thirteen

I CAN'T BELIEVE THIS, LORD. I HAVEN'T BEEN ABLE to get Darvi from my mind. I told Cash all about it and made him concerned, and here . . .

Dakota stopped and tried to slow his racing thoughts before glancing over at another table in the hotel restaurant. Sitting with two male escorts was a woman of striking appearance. She was also a near twin to Darvi Wingate. Dakota had all he could do to keep his teeth in his mouth.

Was this the woman I saw that day? Had the incident at the train all been completely innocent?

Dakota made himself take a few deep breaths. He didn't want to overreact, but that was taking some effort. By sheer force of will, he kept himself from dashing to the other table and demanding from the woman her whereabouts the day he put Darvi on the train.

"Here you go." The waitress had returned, placing a steaming plate of food in front of him, the edges nearly running over with a huge cut of beef and a heap of mashed potatoes, both covered with a dark gravy, which also ran into a mound of cooked greens.

"Thank you," Dakota said quietly, too distracted to miss her disappointment at not gaining more eye contact.

The Ranger ate slowly. After the initial shock wore off, he noticed that by using a large oblong mirror right across from his table, he had an almost perfect view of the woman and two men.

Already planning to wire Cash about his mistake and then head home in the morning, Dakota ate in a leisurely fashion, his heart calming some even as he glanced in the mirror from time to time. He was nearly through with his meal when he noticed something else. A man, fine in dress and manners, sat a few tables away from the strawberry blonde, a newspaper propped in front of him. Even though the man never lowered the paper from reading level, neither did he look at it. With remarkable consistency, he kept his eyes on the woman's table. No one sat at the tables in between, and the woman's table was against a wall. There could be no other person holding his interest. And if that hadn't been enough to convince the Ranger, he eventually watched the woman and two gentlemen exit, just 15 seconds before the lone man got up to follow.

Dakota left a coin on the table to cover both meal and tip and did a little following of his own. He still planned to wire Cash and tell him he had it all wrong, but he didn't think he'd say he was headed home, at least not yet.

❧ ❧ ❧

"Why didn't you go to town today?" Darvi asked in frustration.

"I wasn't needed," Seth told her calmly, completely ignoring everything she'd said that morning.

Arms crossed tightly, Darvi tapped her foot impatiently and nearly shooed him as she would the dog. The children were helping their mother bake a cake, and to get out of the house and away from Seth's watchful eyes, Darvi had volunteered to get the eggs. It hadn't made any difference. Seth tagged along right behind her, even though she had let him have a good piece of her mind that morning over her captivity.

"I don't need help getting eggs, Seth," Darvi said as she turned her back and walked away from him.

"You never know," he replied, bringing up the rear with this assurance. "Some of those hens can be pretty feisty."

Darvi didn't answer, but Seth didn't care—he much preferred her to be like this. When she got all quiet and sad, he had to make himself continue with his plan. When she was fiery and told him what for, he knew he'd never let her go.

He was still shaking his head about how he'd found her. Never in his life had he imagined such a woman existed. Never had he known such a mix of fire and uncertainty. He knew he would love her for the rest of his life.

"And why don't you just tell me," Darvi suddenly spun and demanded, "just what is it you do for this Jared Silk?"

Seth shrugged. "Whatever he needs."

"Like what?"

"Oh, a little of this and a little of that."

Her arms crossed again. "I hope you know that was ridiculously vague."

"Was it?"

Darvi's eyes narrowed. "It's rude to answer a question with a question."

Seth stopped just short of saying, "Is it?"

"Go ahead and ask me about my work," Seth encouraged her. "I'll try to answer."

This took Darvi by surprise. She didn't want to get close to this man. Her chin rising, she laid it on the line.

"No matter how you answer me, it's not going to stop my wanting to leave."

"I understand that. Go ahead and ask."

"Is he a banker?"

"Yes."

"Why would a banker want you to take a woman from the train unless he's hiding something? What gives either one of you the right to do such a thing?"

Knowing she wouldn't like the answer, Seth hesitated. Jared's view—as well as his own—was that a man did what he had to do. Seth knew he didn't look the part of a criminal, and rarely did he use the word to describe himself, but deep in his heart Seth Redding knew what he was. He also knew that wherever Darvi Wingate was from, she did not socialize with people who considered themselves above the law. Not having Jared here to defend himself, Seth let him take the heat.

"Jared feels that sometimes we do what we have to do. It's not too much more complicated than that."

"Not complicated?" Darvi said in disbelief, her mouth open. "You step in and turn people's worlds upside down, and I'm supposed to see that as simple?"

Seth had nothing to say. He hadn't expected her to respond like that and knew anything he might tell her just now was only going to push her further away. He was glad when she turned again for the barn. He hadn't liked the little shake of her head, the one that said she was offended by his actions, but at least he didn't have to explain himself anymore.

Quite suddenly he found himself wishing he had let her gather eggs on her own.

❧ ❧ ❧

It didn't take long to see that the redheaded woman was well known and liked in Aurora. Dakota kept his distance behind both the woman, who now walked alone, and the man who followed her from the hotel, but he still thought he caught a name now and again.

Ann Bell. Dakota was certain he had heard right. He had stopped in front of the bank—looking for all the world as though he was window shopping—and was quite sure this was what people were calling her. Neither she nor the man stopped near the bank, but Dakota had caught up a little too swiftly. He took his time fixing his boot, hoping no one was onto him, and in less than a minute was on the move again.

His work paid off. The woman went into the newspaper office, and the man took up a position to watch everything that went on behind the large front window of the building. Dakota could see that even a rear exit would be detected. Dakota decided to go for his horse. The woman was distinct enough that he'd be able to describe her to the sheriff and get some answers, but the man was another story. If the man sat all afternoon and watched the news office, Dakota would regret retrieving Eli, but if he made a big move, Dakota wanted his horse.

Knowing that the man could be long gone before he returned, Dakota nevertheless fetched Eli, tied him in the alley, and went back to stalking the stalker. As Dakota watched him, he felt a grudging admiration. The man was cool, very cool. When a lady passed, be she 15 or 50, he raised his hat and gave a polite bow. He didn't appear to be observing anyone, but he keenly noted any activity involving the door of the news office.

Dakota was beginning to think that the life of a detective was a curse. His restless limbs were begging to move when the man consulted his pocket watch and walked down the street. Dakota left Eli where he was and moved just enough to watch the man enter the Aurora Bank. Dakota wondered how long he could take the inactivity. He knew very well that the man could leave out the back somewhere and he would never be the wiser. Heavily exhaling with relief, Dakota noticed the man had reappeared and was headed into the very livery where Dakota had boarded his horse. Dakota moved again, this time to mount up and be ready. Again, his patience paid off.

Coming from the livery on a fine animal—a city horse, as Rangers thought of them—the man rode south down the main street of town. He was not a short man, and his horse was of a size that made it easy to track. Dakota was careful to look disinterested as the man hit the edge of town and kept right on moving. He never picked up the pace but rode easily, his attitude that of a man without a care in the world.

Down the road some five miles, Dakota watched the rider calmly turn down a well-worn side road. Dakota kept his eyes forward and allowed Eli to plod along, but only until a group of trees hid him from view, whereupon he doubled back through the woods, working to gauge just where the man might be headed.

Long before he was close enough to see anything, Dakota heard cattle. Only a few hours of daylight were left, so he moved swiftly along, dodging branches and low limbs in an attempt to see where the man might have gone. It took some doing. While still trying to stay out of sight, he made occasional visits to the edge of the tree line and checked the view. At last he saw something just at the edge of a barn. A few more feet and maybe . . .

Dakota stood and stared. In a remarkably picturesque setting sat a large, low farmhouse and a huge barn. The buildings were in fine condition, and as he watched, it looked as though a child was running in the yard, a little girl with flowing blonde hair.

Tying Eli up the hillside a bit, Dakota dug his field glasses from his saddlebags and climbed a tree. With enough light to still see things clearly, he methodically went over every building and scrap of ground. No one was visible until a man emerged from what appeared to be a bunkhouse to throw out a pail of water. An outhouse stood beyond that structure, as did one for the main house.

Dakota was in the process of planning how to get into the barn when he saw her. The hair was the first thing to catch his eye, and then the field glasses did the rest. Never taking his eyes from her, Dakota watched Darvi stand at the corner of the porch, her gaze locked on the road that led to the ranch. A moment or two passed before she looped an arm around the porch support and leaned there.

Dakota was still watching when the little blonde girl appeared, held something out for Darvi to see, and then took her hand to lead her back inside. Dakota scanned the windows of the house but saw no sign of life. Shaking just a little, the big man climbed from the tree and moved to Eli. Once next to the horse, his arm went across the saddle and he buried his face. A sob broke in his chest as he prayed.

You knew she was here; You knew. Please help me. Please let me rescue this woman before she comes to any more harm. I want to ride down there and take her and defy anyone to stop me, but something isn't right here. I've got to go slow and use my head.

Dakota took some moments to compose himself before climbing back up into the tree. He watched until darkness filled the sky but caught no further sight of anyone he could be certain was Darvi. The decision to camp in the woods was no decision at all. Scouting the area for safety and privacy, Dakota settled down early. He didn't dare light a fire and was glad he'd eaten a large lunch, but in fact, his stomach was not really on his mind.

Not interested in lying down right away, he sat for a long time in the dark and thought about what might have gone on at the ranch. It seemed a good sign that at least one child appeared to live in the house. That didn't mean the adults in the situation could be trusted, but the child appeared happy and carefree as she played. And at least from a distance, Darvi looked all right. Dakota was thankful for that much, but he knew even without getting closer that she didn't want to be there. And for that reason alone he was intent on getting her out just as soon as he could manage it.

It was well and truly late by the time Dakota sought his rest, but it was a peaceful sleep. He hadn't been able to read his Bible, but he prayed off and on for hours. He also fell asleep with a plan. He would put it into action in the morning.

ふふふ

Darvi groaned a little as she bent over to pick up the spoon she'd just dropped. Nate had finished his breakfast but not cleared his place. Darvi stooped, and sticky as the utensil was, she managed only to lose it again.

"You sound stiff," Cassy commented.

"I am."

"Is it your mattress?"

"It might be," Darvi guessed, not having thought of it.

"Nate slept on that one for a time and said it was a bit lumpy."

Darvi decided not to comment. She didn't think it would do any good to complain about the mattress, but more than that, she had just noticed that Seth was in the room. She was not giving him the cool treatment or anything too dramatic, but if he was in the room, which was too often for her comfort, Darvi was careful with what she said and did.

"I'll check it for you, Darvi," Cassy now offered, thinking that her silence meant she was a bit unhappy about it.

"Thank you. Do you want me to do anything special with this water?" Darvi asked from her place by the sink.

"Why don't you just dump it? I'll send Nate for fresh."

Seth had learned not to take things from Darvi—he knew she did not want him to coddle her—but that didn't stop him from following her outdoors. He stayed well back when she poured the water on the flowers at the side of the house but was right close when she turned.

"You can always try my mattress," he said gently, his gaze tender and inviting. "It's not lumpy at all."

Darvi barely hesitated before drawing her foot back and kicking him in the shin. Her foot hurt with the impact, but having him double over with pain was well worth it. Darvi didn't speak until his red face came up again.

"Where I come from," she gritted, "a gentleman does not make such suggestions to a lady! If you ever say such a thing to me again, I'll not only repeat the kick, I'll slap your face until your ears ring." This said, she turned on her heel and stomped into the house.

"Good girl," Dakota Rawlings found himself saying aloud from the tree he had staked as his own. As he watched, the man—not the one from town—straightened up and put a hand to the back of his neck, his face thoughtful. When he did move, limping slightly, he didn't go into the house but toward the barn.

Dakota planned to hit town while it was still early and then realized it was Sunday. He would still try the telegraph office and the sheriff but thought later might be best. Witnessing Darvi in action gave him great hope that, at least in some ways, she was not completely at the mercy of others.

Gathering his gear and making his way back to town, all out of sight of the ranch house, Dakota washed up and then went looking for the sheriff. He was pleasantly surprised to find him alone in his office.

"Well, Mr. Rawlings, how is your search coming?"

"I found the person I was looking for. May I ask you a few questions?"

"On one condition."

"What's that?"

"You tell me who it is."

"It's just a friend," Dakota stated, still not willing to give Darvi's name. "I put her on the train in your station, thinking she was headed for St. Louis, and then I realized someone had other ideas. I've spotted her now, and I'm making plans to get her."

The lawman came to his feet. "You mean to tell me that a woman was taken against her will from the train?"

"Yes, I do."

"But how do you know? How can you be sure she isn't visiting friends?"

"She would have told me. Her plan was to head home and see her family. If she had even known anyone in Aurora, I would have been aware of it."

All idle curiosity about this woman melted away. "Ask your questions," the sheriff directed. He knew people thought he was soft when it came to crime in this town, but that wasn't true. He even suspected that some of his own men were dirty, but he had never turned a blind eye to it. He just couldn't move without proof.

"There's a ranch about five miles south of town. Who owns it?"

"Cassy Robinson."

"A woman?"

"Yes. She has two children, and her boyfriend lives with her, as does his brother, not to mention about six ranch hands who keep the place going. She has a good-sized spread." The man stopped and speared him with his eyes. "Why?"

"Because that's where she is. I don't want to shoot anyone to rescue my friend, but if I have to, I will. How many children did you say?"

"Two. The girl never comes into town, but I see the boy now and again."

The sheriff had much more he could add, starting with Seth and Eliot's connection with Jared Silk, but he kept this to himself. He had no way of proving if they were involved in an abduction, a pretty serious charge, and decided to refrain from comment, at least for the moment.

"I think I'll head out there tomorrow and see if Miss Robinson needs any more hands."

"It's Mrs. Have you done any ranch work? I have an undercover man I could send."

Dakota thanked him but explained that he would do fine. He asked the names of the men who lived there but kept the conversation short. He wasn't willing to discuss this overly much, and if he kept looking for answers, the man might expect him to return the favor.

"I will tell you one more thing," Dakota said as he moved toward the door. "I want whoever is behind this to answer for it, but not until I have my friend at a safe distance. If I get a chance, I'll take her and run, but you can bet I'll be back in town at some point."

For a moment the sheriff was put off but then realized this was the very thing he wanted in his own men: determination to see justice done and a concern for the innocent.

Unfortunately, before he could comment one way or the other, Dakota had gone on his way

❧ ❧ ❧

"He's dead?" Cassy asked in disbelief. "You can't mean that."

"He is, Mrs. Robinson. We all slept in 'cause he didn't wake us, so when Timmy woke first and didn't find any coffee to clear our heads, he checked. I checked too. Q is gone."

Cassy was in shock. Q had been cooking for this ranch since her husband had been a little boy. A more loyal, hardworking cook she couldn't imagine. She knew he had been tired and worn out lately but thought that her offering to take the big meal on Sunday and evening meals during the week would be enough.

"Mama," Nate said from beside her, and she turned to find both children with very large eyes.

"Wake Eliot," she said softly. The children were swift to obey.

The next few hours were spent confirming the news, comforting the children, going for the preacher and setting up a time for the funeral the next day, and going about the day's activities and chores in quiet shock. The men were very subdued, many still feeling the effects from Saturday-night drinking, but the family was also quiet. The children tried to attach to Eliot and Seth, as all Cassy wanted to do was lie on her bed.

Darvi felt at a complete loss and wandered around as lost and confused as everyone else. She could offer no words of comfort. She hadn't known the man; in fact, she'd only seen him a half-dozen times. The children were very upset, and she wondered if it was over their mother's distress or if they had known and cared for the old man as well.

"Are you all right?"

Darvi turned to see Eliot. She nodded.

"How are Cassy and the children?"

"All resting on the bed. Lindy is almost asleep, and Nate is drifting."

"Did the children know him well?"

Eliot smiled. "If they knew he was cooking hotcakes and their mother was only serving oatmeal, they would eat as little as they could get away with and make a visit to the bunkhouse. That, and he always had something sweet for them."

Darvi only nodded, again at a loss for words.

"Well, I guess he's in a better place."

Darvi had all she could do to keep her mouth shut. Why did people always say that? Why did people who gave God absolutely no place in their life on earth assume that someone dead was now at peace and rest? Darvi wanted to comment or at least ask what he meant, but she didn't think this was the time to attack the man's views.

She was doubly glad she'd kept her mouth shut when she looked up to see that Cassy had come from the bedroom. Eliot went to her. They spoke quietly for a moment and then Eliot went to the bedroom and shut the door. Cassy approached.

"You don't believe that, do you, Darvi?"

"Believe what?" Darvi asked, a bit afraid of the answer.

"I heard what Eliot said. I saw your face. You don't believe that Q is in a better place."

Darvi's head cocked a bit in genuine confusion.

"Tell me something, Cassy, why do my beliefs mean so much to you?"

The blonde woman shrugged. "I don't know," she admitted, "but they do. I'm so cut off out here. The days just tend to run together. Not until Eliot reminded me that the preacher wouldn't be available until after church did I even remember it was Sunday. I mean, I knew it was Sunday because of the extra cooking, but not because it was the Lord's day. We didn't actually attend church, but I was still raised differently. Your being here has reminded me of that."

Darvi nodded but didn't reply. Cassy was not put off so easily.

"You didn't answer me."

The women's eyes met.

"Do you think," Cassy repeated the question, "that Q is in a better place?"

Darvi put a hand on the other woman's arm.

"There are a lot of things I don't understand in God's Word, Cassy, but this one I know. God says the way to Him is through His Son, Jesus Christ. When we humble ourselves and accept His free gift of salvation, then we are assured of a better place when we die. If, um, if this man—"

"Q."

"Q?"

"Yes. That's all we ever called him.

Darvi's nod was decisive. "If Q accepted God's gift to him, then yes, I think he's in a better place."

Cassy saw what she had done. Rather than start a debate about what she believed, Darvi had very neatly put the responsibility on Q.

And where else should it be? Cassy asked herself, knowing that the same reasoning applied to her own heart.

Cassy suddenly looked to Darvi and found anxious eyes studying her.

"You've given me something to think about, Darvi."

"I don't want to overburden you when you're hurting, Cassy. I honestly don't."

"It's all right."

Darvi wasn't sure that Cassy's words matched her eyes, but when the ranch owner gave her a small smile and moved to go outside, she knew that, for the time being, that was the end of it.

Fourteen

"THE LORD GIVETH AND THE LORD TAKETH AWAY. Blessed be the name of the Lord."

The preacher's final words fell hard on Darvi's ears, causing her to wonder what they actually meant, or rather, what the preacher had meant. She'd heard those same words many times, but as with Eliot's overused cliché about Q being in a better place, she wondered if the man speaking actually believed that God was to be praised, even in the midst of death and loss.

"Are you all right?" Seth asked her quietly as the few mourners broke up and started to move away.

"What does my face look like that everyone keeps asking me that?"

Seth hesitated before saying. "In truth, I'm not sure. If I knew you better I might have an answer, but you almost look as though you disapprove, and since I can't think why you wouldn't approve of giving a man a proper burial, I assume I've read you wrong."

Darvi was shocked. *Am I really so transparent?* She didn't want everyone to know that she didn't approve of the things being said. Her frustration had nothing to do with burying this man but with all the ridiculous concepts about God. Cassy had seen it in her face and so had Seth.

"You're right, you have read me wrong," she tried to say gently. "I'm not looking with disapproval because this man was buried. I'm very sorry for your loss, but there are some things I find confusing."

Seth was on the verge of asking what they were but stopped himself. He was certain this woman was for him, but he was also certain if they talked right now, they'd disagree. His brother had hinted at

Darvi having some strong religious beliefs. That was fine with Seth— she could believe anything she wanted—but he didn't want her knowing that he might not agree. Once they were married they could talk on all the issues, but not now, not when he was still trying to get close and gain her trust.

"We have a visitor," Darvi heard Eliot comment from behind her, but she didn't look up. She walked straight into the house and hoped that Seth wouldn't follow her. To keep from having to face him when she realized he had indeed trailed her in, Darvi picked up a cloth and began to wash the crumbs from the table. She would have dropped it in an instant if she could have seen the pleasure on the man's face behind her, so certain was he that her actions meant she was beginning to see this as home.

❧ ❧ ❧

"I'll handle it for you," Eliot offered as they watched a rider come up the road. His offer was born of compassion, as the running of the ranch was all Cassy's.

"It's all right," Cassy declined, squeezing his hand a little.

"Are you sure?"

"Yeah. Maybe you could just check on Lindy for me. She didn't eat much breakfast."

"Will do."

Cassy moved away from the porch and waited for the rider to near. He swung from the saddle, dropped the reins, and covered the distance between them on foot, removing his hat as he approached.

"Good morning, ma'am," he said even as he took in her mourning garb. "I think I've come at a bad time."

"It's all right. Did you need directions?"

"No, ma'am. I'm looking for Cassy Robinson because I'm hoping to find work. The name's Rawlings, Dakota Rawlings, and someone in town said Mrs. Robinson might need an extra hand."

"I'm Mrs. Robinson, but I don't need more hands right now."

Dakota nodded respectfully but did not have to feign his disappointment.

"We'll be eating in about an hour," Cassy offered hospitably, "if you care to join us."

"I appreciate that, ma'am. Thank you."

Cassy began to turn away but stopped abruptly and faced Dakota again.

"Can you cook?"

"Yes, I can. I do better as a ranch hand, but I can cook."

"All I need right now is a cook."

Again Dakota gave that humble, polite nod. "If you're willing to try me, I'll do my best."

Cassy was won over in a heartbeat.

"Where're you from, cowboy?"

"Originally, St. Louis, but lately I tend to roam around."

Cassy smiled at him. "Come on in. I just need to check on something, and then I'll show you the bunkhouse and introduce you to the men."

Dakota did as he was told, glancing back to see that Eli was watching him and ready to follow right up to the house.

"Stay put," he ordered the horse as he would a dog. Then he walked into the ranch house, heart pounding and praying at the same time.

"Thank you," he said when Cassy held the door for him.

"I'll be right with you, Mr. Rawlings."

"Please call me Dakota."

Darvi, still bent over the kitchen table, became very slow in her movements. She heard the door behind her, Dakota's voice, Cassy's voice, Cassy's footsteps, and then quiet. But even knowing that no one else was in the room, she knew better than to turn around. Working at keeping all expression from her face, she returned the washcloth to the counter and found the solace of her room.

Hands shaking as they came to her face, Darvi sank onto the bed, her heart pounding beneath her dress.

He's here! He's actually here. I didn't know how You were going to do this. I couldn't imagine how I would ever be rescued.

Darvi was so overcome that she couldn't move. She sat on the edge of the bed and worked to muffle her sobs. Not until she saw Cassy come from her own room, saying a word to Eliot before she shut the door, did she think to stand up and shut her own bedroom door, thankful that the other woman hadn't even glanced her way.

The door finally shut, she stood still and tried to assess her emotions. It came to her that she could not just go to him. Even though the men who slept in the bunkhouse had eaten at the dinner table every night, Darvi had had literally nothing to do with them. She had exchanged a few words with Cassy, Seth, or Eliot, but rarely did she even look at the men. It wasn't anything personal, just her constant attempt to keep some distance from the situation.

Darvi heard voices and turned toward the window. Moving the sheer curtain just a bit, she watched as Cassy, now changed into a cotton workdress, walked Dakota to the bunkhouse. Darvi watched until they were out of sight before sitting back and praying, her mind coming to grips with one main fact.

His being here doesn't take care of everything, Lord. Help him to be wise and not get hurt. I know he's here for me. I know You sent him, but this won't be easy. You've brought us this far, Lord. Please help us all the way out of here.

❧ ❧ ❧

"Gentlemen," Cassy spoke quietly after she knocked on the bunkhouse door, heard someone's call to enter, and then stepped inside with the new cook, "this is Dakota Rawlings. He's going to be cooking for us."

Dakota watched five men either come to their feet or turn to look at him.

"This is Timmy," Cassy began. "Next is Scooter, then Roy, Adam, and Gordie."

"Howdy," Dakota said quietly and watched the men nod or utter a quiet greeting. No one looked particularly glad to see him, but neither did he feel threatened.

"Plan to join us for lunch today," Cassy said, turning back to the ranch's new cook. "Then you can get started tonight."

"All right."

"Your bunk is around here," Cassy directed him, taking him through an open doorway to the kitchen area. It appeared to be a well-stocked kitchen, and across from the stove was a bed and a small dresser. Dakota thought the space must be too hot for sleeping when it was midsummer and a meal had been cooked, but he didn't plan to be there next summer, so that was the least of his worries.

"I have an account at Dawson's General Store. When you need supplies, make a list and let me check it, but Dawson's is where you'll head for nearly everything. Breakfast is at 6:30, lunch at noon, and dinner at sundown or when the men come in. At times you'll need to cook on the range. For those times there's a cook wagon in the barn. Any questions?"

Dozens was Dakota's first thought, but he said only, "I'm sure I'll have some, but for the moment I'll just settle my horse in the corral and have a look around. Oh! I guess I'd better ask how you want me to work the meals. Do I decide what we have?"

"In the future, yes, but Q had meals set up for a month in advance. He kept a list—oh, yes, here it is—nailed to the pantry door. If you follow it, you'll probably have all the supplies you need. However, keep in mind that this list was for noon dinners. You'll probably run short since you'll be cooking evening meals too."

Dakota moved with her and saw the schedule.

"Thank you."

"No problem," Cassy said quietly, having been affected just by seeing the dead man's handwriting. She moved slowly back to the doorway. "You and the boys all come in for lunch—maybe 30 minutes."

"Thank you."

Dakota wasn't far behind his new boss when she exited, walking slowly back to the front of the house to get Eli. The horse was within five feet of where Dakota had left him and came to him like a big dog as soon as he spotted him.

Not until he had Eli settled and was headed back to the bunkhouse with his saddlebags did Dakota think about how hard this was going to be. He didn't want to stay here, and he didn't want to work here. He wanted to walk into that house, take Darvi, and ride as fast and far as they could go.

Still praying for patience and wisdom about how to act and when, Dakota hung around in the kitchen of the bunkhouse until it was time for lunch.

🌹🌹🌹

When she first realized Dakota had come for her, Darvi had been sorry that she'd never developed any kind of relationship with the ranch hands, but now that fact was standing her in good favor. It would have been nothing short of disastrous if she had even allowed herself to gaze in Dakota's direction, but since she never looked at the ranch hands, she didn't have to do any pretending.

The men usually ate rather quietly in the evening, but today, during the noon meal, they were doubly so; everyone was. It had to have been Q's death, and Darvi didn't blame them. At the same time, Cassy hiring Dakota as cook probably meant that the men wouldn't be in for supper. Darvi wondered when she would ever have an excuse to speak to the man when she realized Seth was addressing her.

"Were you speaking to me?" she asked to give herself time to school her features.

"Yes." Seth looked amused. "Do you want pie?"

"Yes, please." Darvi took dessert for the first time, wanting to be close to Dakota for as long as possible.

Seth's gaze became rather hopeful. He took this as another good sign. Darvi usually ate and started on the dishes or disappeared into her room as soon as she was through. He passed her a large slice of pie and then tried to engage her in conversation, but she wasn't going for it.

"Are you upset with me about something?" he finally asked.

"You know I am," Darvi said plainly. "I've never made a secret of it."

"I mean other than the obvious."

"The obvious is all that matters to me right now," she said quietly, not wanting to draw attention. A glance into Seth's face told her that he wanted to say more but was hesitating. She shouldn't have been surprised that he wanted to speak with her almost as soon as the meal was over, but surprised she was.

"I'm helping with the dishes," she explained.

"You help with them every day. I want to talk with you."

"Go on, Darvi," Cassy urged her. Cleanup wasn't that bad, and right now she didn't want Seth to be sad. She didn't want anyone to be as sad as she was. If Q's death could somehow open a door for Seth and Darvi, she would be thrilled.

"Lindy can help me," she added. "You go on."

Darvi did so reluctantly. She laid her towel down and preceded Seth out of doors.

"Walk this way," he directed and started toward the woods. The last time she walked to the woods with him, he tried to kiss her, but Darvi was not going to be caught out this time. She kept her distance as well as a watchful eye.

"I've noticed that you've stopped asking me to let you go," Seth began, making Darvi's mouth open in surprise and then shut before he could notice. "I know you didn't want to come here originally, but I guess I'm hoping that your silence means you're getting somewhat adjusted."

He stopped talking, and Darvi realized his head was turned to look at her. He was doing it again, watching her with such tender anxiety that Darvi was amazed. She shook her head a little and tried to think.

"Seth," she began but got no further.

I'm going to have to tell him. I'm going to have to share my belief and not worry if he tries to emulate it for the wrong reason.

"I can't give you any hope, Seth." Darvi put it on the line. "I don't even know if I'm supposed to be married, but—"

"That's ridiculous," Seth cut in with quiet conviction. "Do you have any idea how envied I am?"

Darvi blinked, not having expected this.

"Do you really not know how much you're meant to be cherished, Darvi? It's so clear to me, I just assumed you would understand."

"It's not that simple, Seth. I want to marry a man who shares my beliefs."

"How do you know I don't?"

"Because you've abducted me, Seth!" she said with some heat. "It doesn't take a genius to figure it out."

"But if I had met you some other way, it wouldn't have been like this."

"But you still felt you had the right, and you don't."

Seth looked slightly discouraged and spoke softly, almost to himself.

"Why can't we ever talk about things?"

"I'll tell you why," Darvi spoke up, not caring if he'd really asked her or not. "You can't steal a person and then expect to find her reasonable. It's reasonable to me that you return me to town this instant, and your idea of reason is that I fall for you because you're handsome and polite."

"You think I'm handsome?" he asked with such great hope that Darvi threw her arms into the air.

"I'm done!" she announced, turning and striding toward the barn.

"Darvi, come back."

"No! Leave me alone, and I mean it."

"Darvi!" he tried again, but she kept walking.

Darvi was so angry she thought she could spit. All the excitement over Dakota being there to rescue her had drained away. She thought she would go crazy if she had to spend another moment on this ranch.

Willing to be anywhere but in the house, Darvi stalked into the barn and stopped suddenly to let her eyes adjust in the dimness. She heard movement at the rear, but before she could investigate, she glanced over and spotted Lindy.

"Hello, Lindy," Darvi said softly, always wishing to be kind to the little girl. "What are you doing?"

Lindy looked up at her and then toward the rear.

"Is someone working back there?"

The little girl nodded.

"You want me to go with you so you can see?"

Lindy nodded at once and slid off the barrel she'd climbed onto.

As Darvi half-expected, Dakota was doing something with the cook wagon. Still angry at Seth, Darvi didn't find it too hard to keep her other emotions at bay. Earlier she'd have burst into tears and sobbed out her whole story, but not now.

"Hello," she said as they neared. "We came to watch you work."

"You did?" The Ranger came out with a smile, wiping his hands on a handkerchief. "Who's this?" he smiled down at Lindy, his attention entirely on her.

"This is Lindy."

"Hello, Lindy."

"She doesn't say too much with her mouth, but her eyes and hands do a lot of talking."

"I'm Dakota." Dakota put a hand out and smiled hugely at her when she shook it. "It's nice to meet you, Lindy. Are you Mrs. Robinson's daughter?"

Lindy nodded, her cheeks dimpling in delight before tugging on Darvi's hand. After observing a few hand movements, Darvi turned to translate.

"I think she wants to know what you're doing."

"I'm just looking at the cook wagon today in case I need to make a meal for the men when they're out on the range. Have you ever eaten out on the range, Lindy?"

The little girl shook her head no.

"It's pretty fun. Especially if you get to sleep out under the stars."

Lindy smiled and moved to climb up onto the wagon. Dakota helped her, and Darvi stayed to the side. She listened as he talked and explained things, but suddenly Darvi's breath quickened. What if they didn't make it? What if he couldn't figure a way to get her out? Darvi wondered if she might need to be the one to put together a plan; after all, she'd been there longer.

Her mind raced with what might be the best method: full confrontation or slipping away quietly after dark? Now, or when everyone had been lulled into thinking Dakota was a real cook? Darvi was so intent on her ideas, she didn't even hear Nate calling his sister but suddenly saw Lindy run past.

"The thing to remember—" Dakota's voice came softly to Darvi, and she looked up to find him bent over the back of the wagon, not even looking at her, "is that there will be no heroics. Some night when I tell you, you'll climb out your window, I'll be there, and we'll leave for Kinkade. No shooting. No one chasing us. We'll just leave."

This said, Dakota tucked things away, moved toward the rear door, and exited the barn. Darvi stood with her mouth open, wondering if she might have imagined the entire episode.

"Darvi?" Eliot called from outside.

"I'm in here," she answered, hoping she sounded normal.

Eliot came to the double doors and stopped.

Watching him, Darvi waited for him to speak. She almost began to question him, but he was finally ready to talk.

"When are you going to stop running from Seth?"

Darvi found her mouth open again in shock. She shut it swiftly in irritation.

"Don't you start with me, Eliot McDermott! Don't you do it!" Darvi spat out her words with instant vehemence. "You know as well as I do that it was wrong for him to take me. And I've made it very clear to everyone that I wish to leave. So don't you dare stand there and tell me to be nice in order to put his or anyone else's mind at rest."

"Have you heard him out?" Eliot asked.

"Regarding what?"

"How he feels about you."

"Eliot." Darvi tried to temper her voice. "He's just infatuated, that's all. The man barely knows me."

"If you knew him better, Darvi, you'd see how wrong you are. He's in deep."

Darvi only shook her head, knowing it was pointless to keep up this line of conversation. She wanted to sigh in frustration but thought she might be doing a little too much of that lately.

Eliot, on the other hand, did a little sighing of his own and then admitted, "The truth is, Darvi, I'm getting married a week from Saturday, and I want it to be a happy day."

Darvi blinked. "I didn't know that. Cassy said you didn't have a date."

"Well, we do now."

His tone and face spoke volumes. Darvi's hands came to her waist and she went to him, her eyes hard and determined.

"There's a simple answer to your problem, Eliot, and we both know it. You can return me to town so we can all get on with our lives."

He was shaking his head, and Darvi's brows lifted.

"You have some nerve," she said quietly, "coming and asking me favors when you're just as much to blame for this as Seth is."

As Darvi stepped around him and moved toward the house, she wondered what would happen if she just started walking down the road. Then she remembered Dakota's words.

I must be patient.

Rounding the house, Darvi found Seth on the porch, his facing lighting up at the sight of her. Darvi knew that more prayers for patience would be forthcoming.

❧ ❧ ❧

Having left the interior of the barn, Dakota was still leaning against the side, fixing a boot that was just fine but hearing enough from inside to put a few more pieces into this puzzle. Right now he hoped for one of two things: a chance to either get Darvi out or run low on supplies and have an excuse to head into town and hopefully see the sheriff. He found he had a few more questions for that man.

Fifteen

"Come and get it," Dakota told the men that evening, thinking he would have to start some bread; they wouldn't miss it tonight since he'd made biscuits, but they would surely expect it in the morning.

The men were slow to join him, but in time they gathered around the table at the far end of the kitchen area, no more talkative than they had been at the noon meal; that is, until they tasted the food.

"This is good," Gordie said, shoveling in more spoonfuls of the beef, potatoes, and thick gravy.

"So are the biscuits," Roy added.

Dakota reminded himself to thank Katy when he got home. She was the main reason he knew his way around the kitchen.

"You boys worked here long?" Dakota now felt free to open some conversation.

The answers varied, one man as many as ten years, the others somewhat less. The youngest of the group, Dakota remembered his name to be Scooter, said that Q had been on the ranch the longest, way back before Mrs. Robinson had married her husband.

"So this is his ranch, but he lets her handle it?" Dakota asked, thinking about the man he'd first seen in town.

"Robinson's dead. You're thinking of Eliot McDermott."

Dakota nodded as though that explained everything. It didn't, but he still refrained from asking any more questions.

He was sitting quietly over his own plate of stew when Roy announced to the group that he was going to ask his girl to marry him come Saturday night. Dakota knew that a longstanding joke was in play because his comment brought gales of laughter, something he could see they all needed.

"Will we be invited to the wedding?" Adam asked. "I'll polish my boots if you let me dance with the bride."

Dakota had to put up with a few comments about the other things Adam wanted to do with the bride, but overall he could see that the men respected each other. He also caught a note of respect for Mrs. Robinson and the others living in the house.

Thinking of the house shifted Dakota's thoughts back to Darvi. Though he didn't know it, he was experiencing some of the same emotions she had struggled with, especially that of not wanting to get too close to these people.

What's the balance here, Lord? I want to be a witness for You, but I've had to come here under pretense to get Darvi. What is my main role?

The answer was not obvious to Dakota. The men thanked him and left him to the cleanup. Dakota was glad to be on his own.

❧❧❧

"Is there anything else you need from town, Mrs. Robinson?"

"No, Dakota. I didn't think you'd need to be going this soon, but I'm low on flour too," Cassy said, standing next to the wagon. "No, Lindy, you can't go." The mother directed this to her daughter, who was tapping her and looking up with pleading eyes. Cassy looked back to Dakota. "Why don't you grab a little candy or something?"

He smiled. "I'll do it."

Dakota put the team into motion, finding he wasn't enjoying this at all. From what he could figure out, Darvi's predicament all revolved around the wants of one man. He didn't know his name yet, but clearly the man wanted Darvi.

At moments like this Dakota had to remind himself that the other people at the ranch might have been able to help her escape. He needed to think this way to keep things in their proper perspective. Most things could not be blamed on just one person. The man, a brother to Eliot McDermott if their looks could be trusted, must have instigated the abduction, but Cassy Robinson was a capable woman. If she had wanted to help Darvi, she would have.

Dakota pushed these thoughts aside. He was determined to speak with the sheriff but knew that at least one of the men and the boy had gone into town earlier. It could get a bit tricky. He was thinking about how to handle it when he realized he was on the edge of town and had better look for Dawson's. Then something wonderful happened.

About a block from his destination he spotted Joe Laverty, who had spotted him as well. They had managed just enough eye contact to give Dakota hope, and sure enough, when he was almost through with his list, the law man appeared at his side.

"Is there somewhere we can talk?" Dakota said without introduction.

The sheriff was right glad to see this Ranger after so many days. Without a word he moved toward the back room. Dakota waited a moment and followed.

"I thought you might have moved on by now."

"No, but that's my plan for the end of the week."

"And you need me," the sheriff said with some satisfaction.

"In a way I do. Can you answer some questions for me?"

"Maybe," he said thoughtfully, not wanting the younger man to sense his need to be needed.

"Is there a woman in town who works for the newspaper named Ann Bell?"

"Her name's Annabelle. Annabelle Hewett. She writes for the paper every week."

"What contact does she have with the men from the Robinson ranch—Eliot McDermott and the other man?"

"The other man is Seth Redding, and they're half-brothers. They work for Jared Silk, a banker whose dealings are called into question by Annabelle on a regular basis."

"But the brothers themselves," Dakota went back to them. "You've never brought them in for anything?

"No, they always have airtight alibis."

"What kind of things do you suspect of them?"

The sheriff's smile was bitter.

"That's the problem. They don't often get their hands dirty, and neither does Silk. The brothers have connections who give them what they want and still let them come out smelling like a rose. I've never heard of them having someone murdered, but I'm not too sure they're above much else."

Dakota nodded, but the sheriff wasn't about to provide information without gaining some in return.

"Now it's your turn. What does this have to do with the woman you're after?"

Dakota knew it was time. "Her name is Darvi Wingate, and she's a near mirror image of Annabelle Hewett."

The sheriff let out a low whistle. "Abduction is not the brothers' style, but it sounds as though they tried it and grabbed the wrong woman."

"And decided to keep her," Dakota finished. "Do you think this banker is behind that?"

"I don't know, but I'm going to find out."

"I would appreciate your sitting on that until I get Miss Wingate out of there."

"I can do that."

A creak in the floor caused the men to cut the conversation short. Dakota left the room first, and the sheriff hung around just long enough to let him get on his way.

Neither man noticed the way Nate Robinson kept behind the shelves, his eyes peeking just above the large sacks of meal as he watched the men's mouths move and listened to their words. He eventually left the storeroom as well, but by the time he got out front, both men were gone.

❧·❧·❧

Darvi opened her window very slowly, listening for creaks and groans. Not hearing any this night or the previous nights, she pushed it all the way up and settled back into bed. The first two nights she'd done this, she'd heard other noises in the house and even someone outside, but not now. Whoever was checking on her must have figured that she was just sleeping with her window open, which was partly true.

She had started opening her window the day after Dakota had arrived, all the while hoping not to draw suspicion. After Dakota's words that day, she acted the scene out in her mind. It all worked beautifully until she thought of opening the window with a loud creak and bringing the entire house down on her head.

Darvi stiffened suddenly when out the window she heard a door open and close. Was tonight the night and had she missed it? Another door, farther away, opened, and Darvi knew someone was using the outhouse.

She made herself breathe normally and tried to pray. At moments like this she wondered if she was going to make it. Helplessness and frustration had begun to be the norm in her world as Seth would not listen to reason. Now all of that was replaced by tension and fear. She didn't think anyone was noticing—Seth and Eliot both went off to work as usual, and Cassy and the kids had nothing but the wedding on their minds—but inside Darvi felt like a tightly stretched thread.

Doors moved again, and Darvi knew all would be quiet now. One of the children shifted in bed, and Darvi was once again set to wondering how she'd come to be in this place. It was all so unreal at times, and altogether too real at others. Sleep finally came, but not before Darvi muffled unexpected tears. Dakota had come to rescue her; she was still so amazed over that fact that she could hardly believe it would happen.

❧ ❧ ❧

When the plan hit his mind, Dakota wanted to laugh. It was so simple, and yet it took some days to perfect. He had discovered that every man in the bunkhouse went to town on Saturday night. Dakota would simply join them. He knew they all drank, visited friends, or played cards and came back with great hopes that their horses could find the way. It couldn't have been more perfect if he had planned it with them.

Dakota had meant what he said. There would be no guns fired nor anyone chasing them, not even Seth Redding. That the man was besotted with Darvi was more than obvious, and Dakota had no doubt he would take action to keep her, but the Ranger wasn't going to give him that chance.

Letting Darvi know had been tricky. He hadn't been certain just how he would do it, but burning the biscuits and needing to have all doors and windows open gave him an excuse to be outside by the barn and available when Lindy came to see about the smell. Even Mrs. Robinson had checked on him. The single word *tonight* had been easier to pass than he'd figured, and the brief moment of eye contact with Darvi told him he'd been understood.

Now as he made his way to town, having told the men he would bathe last and to go on without him, it felt like child's play to cut off the road and double back through the woods to the place near the ranch where he'd spent that first night.

Even though it was dark, Dakota still climbed the tree, field glasses in hand, actually quite pleased with so little moon. He couldn't see much, but sound carried well, and it would be easy to count the men as they returned. The hours would be long, possibly until two or three in the morning, but in the end Darvi would be safe. Right now that was all that mattered.

❧ ❧ ❧

Darvi could feel sweat breaking out all over her body. It didn't help to be under the covers with her clothing on, but she was sure it was more than that. The first sounds she heard outside caused her to gasp in fear, and she knew she was going to have to keep still or ruin the whole thing. Had the men come in so noisily on the other Saturday nights? Darvi had never noticed, but right now each sound of hooves, each low voice or laugh, made her feel as though she were being struck.

And the children were more restless too, which eventually told Darvi that a closed window had been keeping the noise out. She didn't want them to waken, but neither would she shut that window. Darvi had to force herself not to think of them. Against her will she had come to care for them. She had to leave here—there was no other option—but she didn't think she would ever forget Cassy and the . . .

"Darvi."

It was said so quietly that she almost missed it, and for a moment she hesitated before reminding herself that no one else would be calling her name. Reaching for the satchel that was packed and ready next to the bed, she sat up and started to put it through the window. Her heart nearly came out of her chest when she felt Dakota take it.

On legs that would not stop shaking, Darvi stood on the bed and leaned out, wondering how she would stay quiet and climb out at the same time. She need not have worried. Dakota's strong arms were there and almost before she could guess his intentions, he lifted her and stood her against the side of the house.

Taking her cue from him, she stood very still beside him. She thought that all might be quiet, but her breathing was so labored she couldn't be sure. However, Dakota must have been. He suddenly took her by the hand and began to walk with her across the field. They were more than halfway to the woods when Darvi realized her other hand was empty.

"My bag," she said on a soft gasp.

"I have it."

And on they went, right into the trees, Dakota leading the way, ducking and moving branches from her path. Then suddenly, when they had climbed several dozen feet, he stopped. Darvi couldn't stop shaking and jumped nervously when he whistled. Again she had to stifle a gasp when something moved and started toward them. The next thing she knew, Dakota's horse had drawn abreast of them, and Dakota was lifting her. Climbing into the saddle behind her, he maneuvered Eli through the woods.

Darvi had no sense of time. She tried to listen for the sounds of pursuit but could hear only the horse and the sound of her own breathing and pounding heart. She said nothing. A thousand thoughts rushed through her mind at once, but not one would stop and make itself heard. For a time she thought she might sleep, but the pounding inside was giving her a headache, so she sat very still, Dakota's chest at her back, and tried not to give in to the temptation to cry hysterically or leap off the horse and run.

She knew some relief when they came from the woods and began moving down the road. She wished she knew where they were and hoped Dakota did, but as with the other questions, she kept this one to herself.

At last the sky began to lighten. Darvi was not glad to see it. The darkness made her feel safe; it made them untraceable. She had not been afraid of the people she'd been forced to live with for these weeks, but having them pursue her and take her back was nothing short of terrifying.

All these tempestuous thoughts took their toll. Darvi was near to bursting by the time Dakota pulled off the road and into a wooded area. He climbed down and brought Darvi down after him. It was light enough for him to see that she was deathly pale, her eyes huge. He had wanted to give her time, knowing her stay had to have been traumatic, but he needed to check on her before they went another step.

"Are you all right?"

"I think so," she said softly, eyes looking up at him in amazement. "You came for me." Her voice held wonder. "I can't believe you came for me."

A nearby falling branch caused her to start and move toward him.

"Is that him?" she asked in panic.

"No." Dakota's voice was soft and reassuring as he watched her keenly. "No one is following us, and even if someone was, I wouldn't let him have you."

Darvi couldn't hold back. She wanted to be so brave, but she couldn't do it much longer.

"Please don't let him, Dakota," she said on a soft sob. "I'll do anything you ask, but please don't let Seth or anyone take me back."

Dakota's heart couldn't stand it. He moved and wrapped his arms around her, not at all surprised when the dam burst forth. Dakota didn't remember ever hearing anyone cry like Darvi did. She choked several times, but not even that stopped her. Not until she seemed too weary to make a sound did the tears stop, and by then she was like a limp rag. Dakota felt her legs buckle and bent to lift her in his arms. Darvi worked to catch her breath, looking up at him through swollen eyes.

"Do you want something to drink?" he asked, not letting his mind dwell on all she'd been through; it wasn't time for that yet.

"Not right now."

Dakota took her back to the horse. It occurred to him after they'd started back down the road that she might have wanted a few minutes of privacy, but he didn't check with her. She would tell him if there was a need. And no doubt they would stop at some point, but home was just a few hours away. Darvi didn't know where they were heading, but Dakota found it comforting beyond words. No matter what had happened, no matter how awful things had been, he would take her home to the ranch and take care of her. He couldn't think of a safer place in all of Texas.

🌼 🌼 🌼

Kinkade

"Cash, I think you'd better come," Katy called out, interrupting the rancher's newspaper reading at the kitchen table. They had not been home from church that long, and Katy was still preparing Sunday dinner. She had been in the kitchen with him but suddenly left. Cash now followed her through the house and into the front yard.

Dakota rode toward them, a woman in the saddle in front of him. He came to a stop before Katy, and Cash could see that the woman was asleep. Both Dakota and Darvi looked very spent.

"Darvi," Dakota said softly, but she remained limp in his arms.

Cash stepped forward, and Dakota handed her down to him. The moment his feet were on the ground, however, he took her back. Katy led the way through the house and to an upstairs bedroom. Dakota had just stepped across the threshold of the guestroom when Darvi woke up. She started violently and reached for the front of his shirt. There was no disguising her panic.

"Where are we?"

"In my home in Kinkade."

He started to bend down a bit.

"I'm going put you on your feet, and Katy will see to you. All right?"

Darvi nodded, working hard to clear the webs from her mind. She felt Dakota let go of her and put her arms out to steady herself. His hands were instantly back.

"Are you there?" he asked, a small smile in his voice. Darvi looked up into his familiar face and felt peace stealing over her.

"Yes, I'm here. Did my bag make it?"

"Right here," Cash said from the door, his eyes not missing a thing.

"Darvi," Dakota began, "this is my brother Cash, and behind you is Katy."

"Land sakes! I don't know why they can't just introduce me as the housekeeper. That's what I am, and proud of it, but you would think they're afraid to say the word. Land sakes!"

Katy smiled at the woman and got just what she wanted: a smile in return.

"Now you boys get," she ordered. "Miss Darvi and I have things to do, and we don't need you. Cash, you check that meat if I don't get down soon. I will not have that dinner ruined."

"I will," he said with an amused smile.

"You do that. Keep an eye on the top."

Dakota caught Darvi's eye one more time before they exited and was pleased to see her looking a little more normal. However, he didn't get far down the wide hallway. After exiting and shutting the door, he leaned against the wall. Cash stood with him.

"Do you want to talk about it?"

"I would," Dakota admitted, "but I don't know anything, at least not much. It seems a man in Aurora got it into his head to keep her. I think it started with a case of mistaken identity and then rolled into a full-blown abduction. She didn't seem to be abused by them."

"Them?" Cash frowned, working to follow.

Dakota slowly shook his head. "It's one of the strangest things I've ever encountered." His voice died off, and he stood there.

"Come on," Cash ordered. "Let's get you cleaned up and fed."

Dakota went willingly, but his mind was still in the room with Darvi. He knew she was in good hands, but he felt rather helpless right now. If they could talk he might be able to reassure her about any remaining fears, but if he knew Katy, she was probably tucking her into bed at this moment.

Thank You, he suddenly remembered to pray. *You got us out of there, Lord. I know this. Thank You that Darvi's all right. Help her to heal and be at peace in the days to come.*

"By the way," Cash began once they had reached the downstairs, allowing Dakota to go ahead of him to the washbasin in the corner of the kitchen, "you got a telegram from Brace."

"Did you read it?"

"Yes. He was just checking on you."

"Any mention of Darvi?"

"No. I assumed her family hasn't missed her yet."

Dakota shook his head. "I'd almost forgotten about her family."

"How long did it take to find her?"

Dakota's shirt was off, and he lathered his face and neck while he spoke.

"Not long, and I'll tell you something, Cash, the only explanation for how things went is that God led the way. I was sitting in a hotel when I saw this woman who looked like Darvi. Then I noticed a man watching her, so I followed him. I ended up asking for a job at a ranch where the cook died the day before, and I was hired. That led to waiting until late last night while the men were coming home from town. I took Darvi out a bedroom window and we walked away."

Cash was silent with thanks over what Dakota had just revealed. He'd prayed the whole time his brother was gone, thinking for part of the time that he might have sent him on a wild goose chase. He was so relieved that Dakota had been there for Darvi that for a moment he couldn't speak.

"She refused to be babied. I'm trying to mother her, and she won't have it!"

Katy's words preceded the woman herself, who was closely followed by Darvi.

"Did you check this meat?" she demanded.

"Six times," Cash told her with wide eyes.

Katy turned away toward the oven so as not to be caught smiling. Slipping into a clean shirt that Cash had handed him, Dakota headed to see Darvi, who was still in the doorway.

"How are you?"

"I'm okay. I keep thinking about my Uncle Marty and family. I need to send word."

"Brace has been in touch." Dakota told her, "and it doesn't sound like anyone has missed you. Did your family know when you were headed back?"

Darvi looked surprised. "As a matter of fact, I didn't say, but I would like to wire them."

"We'll go to town tomorrow and take care of it."

Darvi nodded. She still looked a bit under the weather, but he could see that she was coming along.

"Hungry?" Cash stepped forward and asked.

"Very. Is there anything I can do to help?"

Something akin to a growl escaped Katy's throat, and Cash only shook his head.

"I think that means no. Why don't you come on through here and get comfortable in the living room? We'll eat in no time."

Cash led the way, and Dakota brought up the rear. They took Darvi to the large living room, warm with earthy colors and deep, comfortable furniture. Darvi sank down in the first chair and thought she could lay her head back and go to sleep.

"Go ahead," Dakota directed.

"Go ahead and what?"

"Sleep. I can see you want to."

Darvi smiled at being so transparent. "I am tired, but it can wait. It feels too good to be awake and know that I'm not trapped anymore."

"When you're up to it, I really would like to hear what went on."

"Well, I'll tell you, Dakota, as soon as I've had a little something to eat. I'll tell you everything."

As though on cue, Katy called them to the table. No one needed to be asked twice. And Darvi was good at her word. Before her plate was even half-empty, she began to talk.

Sixteen

Starting with "They thought I was a woman named Annabelle Hewett," and ending with hearing Dakota's voice in the ranch house, Darvi chronicled her adventure. She grew emotional at times, but as they shared a wonderful Sunday dinner, Darvi explained the details she could recall.

Listening to her, Dakota knew his own range of emotions. At some times he thought he could string up Seth Redding, and at other times he felt Cassy and Eliot were to blame as well. That they hadn't harmed her physically was a remarkable relief, but it didn't get them off the hook. He would see to that personally.

"It's your turn, Dakota," Darvi finally said. "How did you find me? How did you know?"

Dakota smiled. "I have Cash to thank for that."

Darvi looked to the tall redhead and waited for someone to explain. When Dakota did, she was as amazed at his story as he was at her own.

"So this woman, this reporter, does look like me?"

"Remarkably so. I had all I could do not to ask her where she'd been the day you boarded the train, thinking I'd made a complete mistake."

Darvi shook her head a little. "That day feels like such a long time ago."

"It was," Cash said gently. "Not in actual chronological days, but in events, and those are far more emotionally draining than just time moving along the clock or calendar."

"I can't honestly say that I've ever thought of it before, but I think you must be right. I don't know when I've been so tired."

Not having meant to hint, Darvi was surprised when both men pushed back their chairs.

"Head out, Darvi," Dakota spoke to her surprised face. "Go get some rest."

"I didn't mean for you . . ." But they didn't give her a chance to finish.

"I'll look forward to talking with you later, Miss Wingate," Cash said, his voice and expression very warm and kind.

Darvi looked into his eyes and smiled.

"Thank you for a wonderful meal and for allowing me to stay with so little notice."

"Well, don't hurry off. I think you'll find Kinkade and the Rawlings Cattle Company very much to your liking."

Cash went on his way then, and Dakota came to get her chair.

"I'll walk you up," he offered, and Darvi allowed herself to be cared for. As her legs took the stairs, however, they began to feel weighted. By the time she reached her room, she was nearly wobbling.

"Will you get some rest too?" she couldn't help but ask before going into the room.

"We take it pretty easy around here on Sundays, so I'm planning on it."

Acute disappointment sprang into Darvi's eyes.

"I missed church again," she said with a small shake of her head. "It feels like it's been forever."

"It's over now," Dakota told her very gently.

"You're right," Darvi agreed, a part of her heart still trying to process this.

"Come on down to the living room when you're ready. We'll ride out and see a little of the ranch."

"All right. Thank you, Dakota, for everything."

"My pleasure."

Dakota turned for the stairs, hearing Darvi's door close behind him. He sought out his favorite chair in the living room and reached for Cash's Bible. He was asleep before he could read five verses.

🌹🌹🌹

"And this," Dakota pronounced dramatically as they rounded the trees, "is the pond."

"Oh, my," Darvi breathed. "It's beautiful."

"We think so."

The two sat astride their horses and took in the scene. The pond was almost a perfect circle, a good 300 feet across, bordered on two sides by pecan trees.

"Do you want to walk awhile?" Dakota asked, all the time trying to gauge how she was doing.

"That sounds nice. Where shall we leave the horses?"

"Right here. We'll tie Toby, but Eli will stay put."

Darvi looked at him. "You whistled for Eli in the woods, didn't you, just like a dog?"

Dakota smiled. "That about describes him. He's always been like a big puppy. If you look behind us right now, you'll find him watching me, as though he doesn't want me out of his sight."

Darvi did as he suggested and laughed out loud at how accurately he had called it. Dakota loved hearing the sound of her laugh and joined her when her face began to turn red.

"And you say he's always been like that?"

"Yep."

Darvi bit her lip to keep from laughing again. She didn't know if it was that funny or if she was still tired. She was trying to figure it out when she spotted a half-circle of wooden benches that sat around a fire pit and gave a perfect view of the pond. Going to a seat and getting comfortable, Darvi let her mind drift back. It didn't take much coaxing. The people she'd left, most especially Cassy and the children, were never far from her thoughts.

"It was strange," Darvi began as though they'd already been speaking of it.

Dakota had taken a seat across from her, but she hadn't looked at him. He watched and listened in silence.

"Cassy and the children were so sweet, and even the men were kind, but Seth would not see reason. I woke up every morning shaking my head that this had happened. I just didn't think such a thing could go on in this day and age, and certainly not to me."

Darvi finally looked at him, and Dakota asked the question he dreaded, fearing that the answer would make him want to shoot the man in question.

"Did he hurt you?"

"No. I didn't feel threatened in any way."

Darvi suddenly frowned.

"He wanted to kiss me. I wouldn't let him!"

"You did the right thing."

"One time I kicked him."

"That was good. Your kisses are yours to give, not someone else's to take."

Darvi melted a little. It was such a nice thing to say, but as she was finding, memories continued to flood back.

"He said I had an upside-down mouth."

Dakota looked at her.

"It's a very kissable mouth."

Emotions chased across Darvi's features in rapid succession: first surprise, then pleasure that softened her features as she looked at the man across from her. But before long that softness was replaced by a look of uncertainty and then another frown.

"Dakota Rawlings," she said in soft rebuke "a gentleman does not tell a lady that her mouth is kissable."

Dakota wished he'd kept the thought to himself.

"You're right. I'm sorry I said that."

An uncomfortable silence fell over them, neither looking at the other. The water proved to be a helpful neutral point, and both took advantage of it.

Several minutes passed. A breeze stirred the trees, and as always, the low sound of cattle could be heard from the distance. Not certain how she felt about what had just happened, Darvi did not like sitting there with a strain between them. She was the first to chance a peek and was glad the Ranger's gaze was on the water. She transferred her own gaze back before saying, in as normal a voice as she could manage, "I've been meaning to ask you, Dakota, how are your bullet wounds? Has all of this mess with me kept you from going back to work?"

"No, it hasn't. My wounds are fine. I feel I could go back at any time, but Brace said he didn't want me for another month after I dropped you off."

"How long has it been?"

"Let me see. I think I had dinner with you and Brace in Austin just four weeks ago yesterday, and after that we were in Stillwater with Calder and Merry and then in Aurora, so that makes it about two and a half weeks ago."

"We were in Austin just a month ago?"

"As far as I can figure."

Darvi stared at him, looking upset.

"Is that right?"

"Yes. You can check the calendar when we get back to the house."

"That means I haven't been home for more than a month."

Dakota, who was on the road most of the year, understood completely. At times he missed home so much he ached. Darvi's face told him she ached right now.

A bell rang in the distance.

"That's for us," Dakota told her as he stood. "Katy must have supper nearly ready."

By the time they reached the horses, Eli was rather anxious, starting Darvi's laughter all over again.

Dakota listened in silence, hoping to find other ways to hear her laughter in the following days. In his opinion, she'd been frightened and sad for much too long.

ॐ-ॐ-ॐ

"Are you just a little bit amazed by it all?" Cash asked kindly. Dinner was over, and they were having coffee in the living room. "I mean, I thought about it most of the day, and it's almost too outrageous to be true."

"I was just telling Dakota that very thing. Even in the midst of it, I could hardly believe it."

"I don't find it so hard to believe," Dakota stated calmly.

The two other occupants of the room stared at him.

"You don't know her, Cash, but things have a way of following Darvi around."

"Things?" Cash questioned, even as he caught the gleam in his brother's eye.

Dakota shook his head in pity. "Yes, things. They just mange to follow Darvi around. I'm not sure why, but there's no doubt about it."

"Do not believe a word he says, Cash," Darvi finally cut in, having gotten over her shock to see she was being teased. "Dakota is very imaginative; that's all there is to it. Those other incidents were just circumstances beyond my control."

"Following a stranger down the streets of Austin?"

"I knew you were a Ranger," Darvi defended, trying not to laugh.

"Then there were the men in Stillwater who just *had* to talk with you and wouldn't let you pass?"

"I think," Darvi responded, growing as outlandish, "that they were wanting to ask directions to the sheriff's office, and we didn't give them a chance."

"The snake?"

Darvi shook her head, her expression one of pity over his shortsightedness.

"The snake simply misunderstood the time schedule and that it was my turn at the creek. It's all very easily explained."

Dakota gave a huge sigh of mock exasperation and looked back to his brother.

"You see, Cash. Things happen to Darvi, so I'm not at all surprised she was mistaken for another woman. She just can't seem to help herself."

"And if that wasn't bad enough," Darvi added, almost taking Dakota's side against herself, "even after those people realized their mistake, they decided to keep me."

"That's the part!" Cash came forward in his seat and exclaimed. "I can't get over that—I can't imagine what they must have been thinking."

"It was more Seth than anyone else. If it had not been for him, the others would have let me go."

"Are you angry about that?" Cash asked.

Darvi had to think on it.

"Not exactly angry, but amazed—like you are. Seth's and Eliot's jobs are not aboveboard, and the fact that they believe they can do things outside the law leaves them open to any whim. They have their own standard, which they feel gives them the right to take someone."

"Did this Seth really think you would eventually wish to stay?" Dakota now asked.

"That's exactly what he thought," she replied, shaking her head, and suddenly wanting to laugh a little more. "Did I tell you that I tried to sneak out in the wagon?"

Both men smiled but said no.

Darvi nodded. "I did, but Seth caught me, and Cassy went to town without me."

"Tell us about Cassy, Darvi," Cash urged her. "Did she not have trouble with what the men were doing?"

"Actually, she did. In fact, my telling her about my faith somehow prompted her into marrying Eliot. They just set a date after being together for five years."

Both men gawked at her.

"You had a chance to witness to this woman?" Cash asked to be sure.

"Yes. We were talking, and she was saying how sorry she was that I'd come to be there under those circumstances, but that Seth was a fine man. I told her I didn't want him, and thinking that I meant he wasn't good enough for me, she became angry. I had no choice but to lay it on the line. She took it very well. It actually got her to thinking. The next time she went to town she bought a dress to be married in and showed it me. Then later I heard they'd set a date."

"When is it?"

"Let me see. The days were so full and anxious at the same time that they tended to blend together, but I think it's this Saturday."

Dakota looked thoughtful, and Cash was the first to catch on. "She's going to have to go back, isn't she?"

"Eventually, yes, but I think it can wait until after she goes home."

"Why do I have to go back?" Darvi asked with a sinking heart.

"Because anything that happened to you is hearsay without your testimony." Dakota looked at her. "You do want these people to answer for this, don't you?"

Nate's and Lindy's faces sprang into her mind, but she still nodded her head yes.

"I can't say that I'm thrilled to return, however."

Dakota caught her eyes and told her plainly, "I'm not going to let anything happen to you."

"You'll be there?"

His brows rose as though he'd been insulted, and for a moment they only looked at each other.

"But first," Cash cut in, "you'll get in touch with your family and tell them you're spending the rest of the week here resting up before starting for home." Cash paused and smiled at her. "At least that's what I hope you'll do."

Darvi smiled back. "I would like to rest a little before traveling again. Are you sure I won't be imposing?"

"Very sure."

"Does the train run from Kinkade?"

"Twice daily. You'll connect at Dallas and then be on your way."

"I'll telegraph tomorrow."

"I'll take you in," Dakota offered.

At that point the evening came to a very quiet close. Darvi found herself watching Dakota yawn and needing to do the same. Cash rescued both of them and said he was turning in.

Darvi lay down in bed just a short time later, hardly able to remember that she'd taken a nap. She thought she might lie there for long minutes, still in wonder over how God had used Dakota to rescue her, but the strange sounds and surroundings took little time to fade.

❧ ❧ ❧

"So when did you tell them you'd be home?" Dakota asked when Darvi was finished in the telegraph office. He saw her inside but took a seat to give her privacy.

"I'm going to take Cash's offer and stay until Friday or Saturday."

"Why not Sunday or Monday?"

Darvi looked up at him. "I don't want to wear out my welcome."

Again she received that look; Dakota's brows went up as though he was insulted for his brother.

"I told them to look for me sometime next week," she admitted.

Dakota smiled complacently and offered to show her around town, pointing out the bank and the new hotel. Kinkade had a fairly good-sized school, and Dakota told her all about it.

"I love Texas," Darvi mentioned at one point.

"Why is that?"

"The diversity. Some areas are huge and flat; others are hilly and dense." She looked up at him. "Uncle Marty even took me to Houston one summer and down to the Gulf of Mexico. It was so exciting."

"I've never been," Dakota admitted.

"Oh, you've got to go, Dakota. It's beautiful."

"I think I'll do that sometime," he said with quiet conviction.

Watching him, Darvi noticed for the first time how handsome he was. His eyes were very dark and oftentimes serious, but when he was smiling or amused, they were beautiful. She took in the square line of his jaw to the thick black hair atop his head. His features were strong, something she found very appealing. Suddenly feeling shy with him, Darvi dropped her eyes, hoping he had not caught her gawking.

"I just spotted someone I need to speak with, Darvi. Come on over with me, and I'll introduce you."

Feeling rescued, Darvi looked up to see they were in front of the general store.

"Would you mind very much, Dakota, if I stopped in here first? I'll come find you afterward."

She watched him hesitate but didn't know why.

"All right. I'll come back for you, okay?"

"Okay."

Dakota waited until she went inside before crossing the street. Darvi didn't look back but headed inside with good intentions. Unfortunately, they didn't last very long. She wasn't in the mood to shop, just in the mood to think about this new awareness of Dakota. She wandered the aisles of the store for a time but couldn't keep it up. With a smile to the proprietor, she exited.

There was no sign of Dakota. Darvi was getting ready to sit on one of the empty benches out front when she spotted a small dog as he went limping into the alley. She changed her mind and trailed after the stray.

"Hey, there," she said softly when she found the dog had gone just halfway down the alley and stopped against the mercantile wall. The dog's tail thumped at the sight of her, but he still held his right foreleg close to his body.

Darvi approached without fear and stroked his small head. He didn't look to be more than a pup. Nevertheless, she knew she would need help. Darvi made a swift trip back out to the boardwalk and immediately spied a pair of teenage boys. She stopped them with a word.

"Excuse me."

The boys stopped and came to immediate attention; this lady was pretty, and she had spoken to them first.

"There's a dog in the alley that seems to be hurt. Could you tell me where I could take him?"

"We'll help you," the taller of the two boys said.

Darvi didn't know why they did this but still showed them the dog. It was no trouble for the first one down the alley to lift him, and Darvi was glad to see that he was gentle.

They took the dog to Dr. Wilcox, whose sign Darvi remembered seeing earlier. His speciality was people, the boys told her, but he had compassion for dogs. That was enough for Darvi.

She was a little surprised that the boys did not drop off the dog and leave, but she didn't mind the company as long as the little dog was helped. Darvi was still sorting through some of her thoughts when the doctor joined them in the waiting room.

"What can I do for you?" Dr. Wilcox asked.

"I found this dog in the alley," Darvi explained. "His leg seems to be hurt."

The wise doctor took in the scene at a glance before kneeling down to examine his canine patient.

"I think this is Rickmans' dog. Why don't you boys run down the street and let them know he's here?"

The youths agreed readily enough, but neither one moved. Darvi had been too busy watching the dog to notice.

"So what's your name?" one of the boys now asked.

The strawberry blonde answered without looking up.

"Darvi Wingate."

"Darvi. That's a nice name. You new in town?"

Darvi finally caught on. She looked up to find keen interest in both sets of young eyes. Hers had been for the dog; theirs were for her.

"I think I should tell you, gentlemen, that I'm old enough to be your, well, your older sister."

They both smiled at her.

"Where do you live?" was the next question, telling Darvi they were not put off.

Darvi's chin came up, but she turned away from them, opening her purse as she moved.

"I'd like to leave payment with you if I could," she said to the doctor and held out a coin.

"Thank you," he said graciously, "but I'm sure Mr. Rickman will be happy to take care of it."

Putting her money away, she asked, "Will the little dog be all right?"

"He'll be fine. We'll have him wrapped up and back to his owner in no time."

"Thank you," she said to the doctor and then to her helpers.

As she moved to the door, she heard the physician say, "Stay here, boys." With that she moved outside and almost into Dakota's chest.

"Oh, Dakota, I'm sorry I couldn't tell you. I found a dog in the alley and he was hurt. We just brought him down here."

"Is the dog all right?"

"He's going to be fine. The doctor is taking care of him."

"Are *you* all right?" he asked, thinking she looked a little flushed.

Darvi nodded quietly, and Dakota was willing to let the matter drop, but he'd caught the word we and noticed the two young men who stood at the doctor's office window watching them.

"Ready to head back to the ranch?"

"Yes, please."

Dakota saw her to the wagon, but before he could assist her, she stopped and looked up at him.

"There were two young men who helped me. I think they were more interested in me than the dog."

Dakota nodded, his eyes telling her he cared.

"I think you might be right," she said in a soft little voice. "Trouble seems to follow me around."

"It's not your fault, Darvi. If I know you, you didn't do anything improper. Their interest is not your doing."

"Why were they interested?" she asked in genuine confusion. "I'm clearly no longer a teen, and they don't even know me."

"You're very pretty and very sweet, and that's a combination most men can't resist."

Darvi smiled a little at the compliment and allowed herself to be helped into the wagon even as her heart asked, *What about you, Dakota Rawlings? Can you resist?*

Seventeen

THE NEXT FEW DAYS BROUGHT AN EASY routine with them. Cash and Dakota worked for a good portion of the day while Darvi worked around the house with Katy, read, prayed, baked, took naps, or sat thinking about the changes in her life.

Come late afternoon and evening, the men would return, clean up, join Darvi and Katy for a wonderful meal, and then spend the evening visiting or playing games. Darvi couldn't remember when she'd had such a restful, peace-filled time. Both she and Dakota accompanied Cash to a Bible study he attended on Tuesday nights, and the three spent the next two days talking about the passage they'd studied in Genesis.

In fact, they were still doing this on Thursday night when someone knocked at the door. Cash rose to answer it. On his doorstep he found a remarkable sight: a refined woman, not young but elegantly dressed, whose eyes betrayed worry. She also bore a startling resemblance to Darvi.

"Good evening," Cash began, telling himself not to gawk.

"Good evening. I'm so sorry to call on you without notice, but could you please tell me if Miss Darvi Wingate is here?"

"Yes, she is here."

The woman's eyes closed momentarily in relief.

"May I see her?"

"Certainly. May I tell her who's calling?"

The woman hesitated, the fingers of one hand coming up to her mouth in uncertainty.

"Please excuse my horrid breach of manners, but I would really like to introduce myself."

Cash smiled and stood aside.

"She's right in here."

"Thank you."

Cash followed the woman back to the living room and watched as Darvi looked up at her.

"Aunt Renee?" the younger woman exclaimed, coming to her feet.

"Hello, Darvi," the older woman said, her voice thick with emotion.

The nearly identical strawberry blondes met in the middle of the room in a huge embrace.

"How did you know I was here?" Darvi asked in astonishment. "And what are you doing here? Mother had a fit when she couldn't find an address for you, so she could tell you about the wedding."

Darvi's aunt held her at arm's length.

"You're getting married?"

"Not anymore."

Renee's brows rose.

"It's a long story."

The two women stared at each other.

"My mother used to tell me that I looked like my father's sister," Darvi said, "but it's been so many years since she's mentioned it, and I just lost track."

The older woman smiled. "It's all right, Darvi. As long as you're safe from Seth Redding."

"You know about that?"

"Darvi," her aunt returned, becoming very serious, "I'm Annabelle Hewett."

Darvi's hand came to her mouth. "Oh, no. You're not serious."

"I'm very serious."

"So that's why . . ." Darvi began, but she had already started to laugh. Renee joined her.

The men stood and stared as both women collapsed with laughter onto the davenport. They didn't know if they should stay or go; both were too fascinated to move. Darvi finally noticed them standing side by side across the room.

"Oh, I'm so sorry," she began and stood. Renee followed suit. "Dakota, Cash, this is my aunt, Renee Comstock, or should I say Annabelle Hewett?"

"As long as you don't call me Aunt Renee in Aurora, I don't care."

Renee was now poised and gracious as she faced them.

"I'm so sorry to have come in this rude way, gentlemen. Please forgive me."

In the next few seconds, official introductions were made all around, and then the four sat down to talk.

"How did you know Darvi was here?" Dakota had to ask.

"Sheriff Laverty. I guess both Eliot and Seth came tearing into town on Sunday morning, acting and looking as though they'd lost a trunk of gold. Because you had told the sheriff your plan, he wasn't too surprised. I came in wanting the story for the paper, and he told me." The woman looked at her niece. "I nearly fainted when he said the name Darvi Wingate."

"And I wouldn't have thought that Annabelle Hewett was related to me in a million years. What are you doing in Aurora?"

"You knew that Sam died, didn't you?"

"Yes. Mother told me. I'm sorry."

"Well, he left me in a very comfortable position, so comfortable that I could have sat back and had ladies in for tea, and little else, for the rest of my years. I didn't want that. I wanted to make a difference. I found a way to do that very thing through the paper. It's been the most fascinating experience of my life."

"But you're not married again?"

"Not yet. I became engaged about two months ago to a man who lives in Kerrville, but we haven't set a date."

"I'm glad," Darvi told her sincerely. "I know it hasn't been easy."

Renee smiled. "Now that was your mother talking."

Darvi blinked. "Why? What did I say?"

"You said it's been hard for me. That's the type of thing she would say to explain away the embarrassing behavior of the black sheep of the family. If I'm off acting wildly for no reason, they must not talk about me, but if I'm getting things out of my system because of grief over losing my first husband, then there's no family shame."

Darvi sat back and crossed her arms. "I had no idea anyone else had Mother so well figured."

The men took their cue at that point. Unnoticed by the women, they rose and quietly left the room, going out the front door and onto the porch. The sun was setting fast, but there was still enough light to see each other.

Dakota took the large rocking chair, and Cash sat on the double swing.

"I wonder how the sheriff knew to send her down here," Cash pondered aloud.

"He knew my name was Rawlings, and the Rawlings Cattle Company of Kinkade, Texas, is pretty well known."

"Maybe. I'll have to ask Darvi's aunt."

Dakota's chair creaked as it moved, the swing giving off its own low groan.

"It wasn't that long ago I was teasing you about finding a woman, Dak," Cash said thoughtfully. "Mother would be awfully glad to see you two together."

"What two?" Dakota asked in genuine confusion.

"You and Katy," Cash replied sarcastically. "Who do you think?"

Dakota gawked at his older brother and then shook his head.

"I don't know anyone who does ranching better than you do, Cash, old buddy, but you need to stick with cattle."

"I don't think so."

"Cash," Dakota began again, this time his voice very serious, "Darvi is one of the sweetest women on the face of the earth, but she's like a sister I want to protect. I assure you, there's nothing more."

"Dakota, old buddy," Cash said, taking on the same tone as Dakota, "You can deny this all you want, but I've seen you two. Darvi Wingate may be a lot of things to you over the years, but a sister isn't going to be one of them."

Dakota had no reply. Cash had been utterly serious. His mind reeled with the implications, and he shook his head a little. He'd told Darvi her mouth was kissable and meant it with all his heart. He'd also said she was very sweet and pretty and meant that too, but not in a romantic way—at least he didn't think it was. In truth, having Darvi smile and be lighthearted was something he'd very much come to enjoy. Being with her was just plain fun.

"You riled at me, Dak?"

"No, just thinking."

"I'm right, aren't I?"

"I don't know, Cash. I honestly can't tell you right now."

"Do you mean you really haven't seen it?"

"Seen what?"

Cash was silent for a moment.

"You two have something special going. I know you just rescued her, and I can't say that that's not what I'm seeing, but she looks at you with hope and confidence. And I know you're used to taking care of people and wading into the fray to see justice done, but there's something different where Darvi is concerned. Mother saw to it that she raised three gentlemen, Dak, but what I'm seeing is above and beyond the call of duty."

Again the men fell silent, each alone with his thoughts. Cash prayed for this brother he loved so much, somewhat afraid he'd said too much. Dakota prayed for understanding and wisdom over these new thoughts and feelings.

He was rather drawn to Darvi, but did that mean he was falling in love, or did it just mean that he'd spent some time with her? He was not made of stone. He had held her in his arms a few times and even dried her tears, his heart deeply affected by her emotions. Were his own emotions more involved than he suspected? And what did she feel? Was Cash really seeing interest on her part? Dakota wondered how he could possibly know, wishing he could see her right now but knowing it would have to wait. She was still talking to her aunt.

❧ ❧ ❧

"So you were engaged," Renee prompted after they'd talked for some time about all that Darvi had been through.

"Yes. His name is Brandon Young."

"What happened?"

"I've gone through a lot of changes in the last few months, and I knew that Brandon was not the man for me."

"What kind of changes?"

"Spiritual ones."

A cynical gleam entered Renee's eyes. "So, you found religion. Your parents must be having a fit."

"I did not find *religion*," Darvi corrected in a firm voice. "This is different. This has been life-changing for me."

Renee took the reproach very well. The cynical gleam disappeared, and she only nodded.

"How did you know my parents would be upset?" Darvi questioned, suddenly hearing what she had said.

"Well, maybe not both your parents, but I knew your mother would be."

"Why?"

"Because your mother's world is perfect. By your needing God, you're saying she did something wrong."

"Oh, Renee," Darvi said softly, "that perfectly describes the situation. You would have thought I had committed murder. She wouldn't even let me discuss it with her."

"Your mother is a wonderful person, Darvi, and I'm so glad my brother married her, but her standard is higher than God's."

It was a very irreverent thing to say, but Darvi had to bite her lip to keep from laughing.

"Family is everything," Renee continued. "A good face must be put on at all costs. You must marry well. You can grieve someone's passing, but in a quiet way. And whatever you do, remember the ancestors!"

Darvi thought she could become very depressed at the moment. She found herself praying very hard for her mother, thinking that if she could please her mother, she would have an opportunity to share her new faith. She prayed for Renee as well, and in the midst of that, the men returned.

"I'm sorry we chased you out of your own living room, Cash," Darvi said.

"Not at all," he replied dismissing her words.

"Well, I'm glad you came back. I was just about to ask my aunt about her connection to Jared Silk."

Renee gave an unladylike snort.

"That man," she spoke as both Dakota and Cash found seats. "He calls himself a banker. I think before this is over, his entire operation will be disclosed. At least I hope it will be."

"How did you get onto him?"

"I used to bank with Jared, and I would see the most interesting people coming and going while I would be in his building, men who were not known for abiding by the law. I did a little snooping and found out that he wasn't always honest in his dealings. I pulled my money from his bank, and it's been war ever since."

Renee glanced over just then and found her niece smiling rather hugely at her.

"What are you grinning at?"

"You. And thinking about my father's reaction to your new life."

Renee shuddered. "We might have to have a talk, my dear little niece. There are some things the family does *not* need to know." Renee shifted her gaze to the men. "Do you two have a younger sister?"

They both shook their heads no.

Renee did a little head shaking of her own. "It's not fun. It doesn't matter that I've been grown and gone for years—I'm still Stanley Wingate's baby sister."

The people in the room laughed at her aggrieved expression, but each one also caught a bit of longing in her eyes. She might fuss and fume about her sister-in-law's views on family, but family was important to her too.

"I hope you'll stay with us," Cash suddenly said. "I hope Darvi invited you."

"She didn't, but I would appreciate the offer. When I arrived I didn't even look around to see what the hotels were like."

"How did you find us in the first place?" Dakota asked.

"I got as much information as I could from Sheriff Laverty. Then my boss at the paper knew of the Rawlings Cattle Company, and I came down with great hopes."

"And here I was," Darvi said with a smile.

Renee became a bit emotional but hid it very well. She hadn't known she had such a beautiful niece. Darvi was in the same boat. She had only seen an old photo of her aunt as a younger woman and heard of their likeness over the years.

But Renee didn't have to leave until the next afternoon, so the two renewed old family ties. In fact, Darvi was so caught up in her aunt's visit that the time rushed away. Her aunt had been gone only an hour when Darvi remembered that she had decided to leave on Saturday, which happened to be the very next day.

※ ※ ※

"Are you all set, Darvi?"

"Yes. Thank you, Cash, for everything. And please thank Katy for me too. I tried, but she only shooed me away with the towel."

The two stood on the train station platform while Dakota went to the ticket booth. Cash laughed at Darvi's description, knowing it had to be very true.

"If she let you say goodbye, she might become emotional, and we can't have that."

Darvi smiled in understanding.

Dakota joined them in short order, and Cash gave Darvi a hug. She turned to Dakota, who smiled and hugged her as well.

"Thank you for everything."

"You're welcome. Here's your ticket. Have you got everything?"

Darvi nodded, her throat suddenly very tight.

"I hate goodbyes, so I'll just go."

Not even waiting for them to reply, Darvi turned and went on her way, swiftly taking the conductor's hand and boarding with her satchel. So she wouldn't think about the men behind her, Darvi made herself think about where her trunk might be after all these weeks.

Having watched her out of sight, Cash turned to his brother.

"Why didn't you tell her you were going?"

Dakota gave him a quick glance.

"The truth?"

"I wouldn't expect anything else."

"I wanted to hug her."

Cash had all he could do not to shout with laughter.

"Go on, Dak," he said with a chuckle and a slap on Dakota's back. "Chase her down until she catches you."

The men embraced, and Dakota, bag in hand, one that Darvi hadn't even noticed, went to board the train. It wasn't hard to find the person he was determined to sit with; she was on the opposite side from the platform, face to the window. Dakota stowed his bag up top, his eyes on Darvi as he worked. Not until he sat down did she turn, her eyes so full of vulnerability that he immediately apologized.

"I'm sorry I didn't tell you I was coming. I didn't mean to startle or deceive you."

"Why are you, Dakota?" she asked, honestly needing to know.

His eyes shifted away, but he still answered.

"It bothered me quite a bit to have you taken off the train like you were in Aurora. When I think of how long ago you started home, and you're still not there, it upsets me even more. As much as it's within my power to do so, I'll see to it this time that you arrive safely in St. Louis."

Darvi put a hand on his arm for a moment before once again turning back to the window. Dakota let her have the silence. He was more confused than ever about almost everything—his feelings and his job as a Ranger, just to name two. But right now he didn't need to dwell on those. He had a goal, and it was not complicated: Get Darvi home. Once he had done that, he would wait and see what the future might bring.

❧·❧·❧

The telegraph for Darvi actually arrived a few hours ahead of her. Completely sealed in an envelope, it was from Annabelle Hewett, telling Darvi when she would be needed back in Aurora as a witness in Jared Silk's trial. It was all very businesslike and proper, allowing Renee to keep her cover yet still remain in contact with her niece.

Darvi, however, did not know this as the hired hack pulled up in front of her house and she listened to Dakota tell the man to wait. She stood on the sidewalk while he fetched her bag from the rear and proceeded to walk her up to the front door of the large, blue two-story house that loomed above them. Darvi went to that door and opened it without hesitation.

"Mother," she called as Dakota brought up the rear, closing the door behind him.

"Darvi!" a deep male voice came in reply, just moments before a tall, well-dressed young gentleman rushed to the front door and took Darvi in his arms.

"You're home! You're home!" the man kept repeating as he

appeared to be squeezing the life out of her. He let her go for a moment but then snatched her right back into his arms.

Darvi caught Dakota's eye and tried to communicate her helplessness, wishing at the same time she could read his expression, which was very bland.

"Brandon," Darvi got out at last.

That man stepped back and looked at her.

"Where are my parents?"

"Your mother had to run uptown for a minute. And your father is at work."

She nodded and put a hand up so he could not hug her again.

"Brandon, I'd like you to meet Dakota Rawlings. He's the man who brought me home."

Brandon turned with a huge smile.

"Thank you so much, Mr. Rawlings." His hand came out for a shake. "I can't begin to tell you how I've missed her."

"My pleasure," Dakota assured him as they shook hands. He then turned to the strawberry blonde, who was watching his every move.

"Well, Darvi, I'd best be on my way. You take care of yourself."

Darvi's mind screamed that it wasn't supposed to be this way. Brandon wasn't supposed to be there. She and Dakota had just spent two and a half more days together, and Darvi was more taken than ever. He couldn't leave now, not before meeting her parents.

"Thank you" was all she could manage, her voice coming out in little more than a whisper.

"It was nice to meet you," Dakota told Brandon before giving a last goodbye that encompassed them both.

Darvi watched in shock and amazement as he went to the door, exited, and shut it behind him.

Out on the sidewalk, Dakota returned to the waiting hack, spoke to the driver, and climbed on board. Not even after he'd taken a seat and the driver put the horse into motion did he look back at Darvi's house. His gaze swung here and there as they moved, but for the most part, his eyes were down the road.

The driver navigated a few turns, and some three blocks later, Dakota finally spoke.

"The big white one," he said quietly.

"Yes, sir."

Just moments later the driver halted again. Dakota alighted this time, paid the man, reached for his own bag, and went up yet another sidewalk. Much like Darvi, he too opened the front door without hesitation, stepped inside, and closed it softy.

Across the wide foyer stood an elegantly dressed woman, hair perfectly coifed, face turned to the housekeeper as they studied a list together.

"And you found two broken chairs?" the lady of the house inquired.

"Yes, but Croft is fixing them right now. It shouldn't be a problem."

"What about the glasses? Any more broken?"

"Not a one. That new girl from down the street is a marvel. She has the nicest touch of any girl you've ever hired."

"Good, good," the lady said absently, her eyes once again on the paper. When she glanced back at her housekeeper, however, she found her eyes on some distant spot, a smile on her lips.

Virginia Rawlings turned to the front door for the first time, her own smile bursting forth.

"Dakota," she said softly.

"Hello, Mother." That man's smile mirrored her own.

"You're home," she spoke again, this time moving forward.

The two met in a warm embrace, Dakota's heart echoing her words.

Yes, Mother, I'm home.

Eighteen

"How are you?" Virginia finally asked. At first she hadn't talked. She just wanted to hug him, not caring the reason he was suddenly in St. Louis and not Texas.

"I'm doing fine. How are you?"

"Worried about you."

"Why?"

She looked him in the eye.

"The last I'd heard you had five bullet holes in you."

Dakota grinned. "And you thought that might slow me down?"

Virginia only shook her head.

"Mother," he said, changing subjects quickly to what was on his mind. "Have you had your fall fling yet?"

"If you mean my Autumn Garden Party," she told him patiently, "no, I haven't. It's in 18 days."

"Can you invite the Wingates?"

His mother's brow furrowed. "Three blocks over, the large blue house?"

"That's the one."

"Why?"

"I want to see a little more of their daughter."

After dropping that tidbit of information, Dakota started for the stairs.

"Oh, and Mother," he now tossed over his shoulder, "can you send for the tailor? I need a new suit."

A moment later the bell rang at the front door.

"Dakota James Rawlings," his mother said in a no-nonsense way, "you come back here this instant!"

Dakota turned with a smile. "I've got to clean up if I'm going to be fitted for a suit."

"That can wait. Tell me about this girl."

"Get the door, Mother," he teased her, turning to go on his way.

Virginia had all she could do not to laugh. He was a rascal, just like his father, but she adored him.

The matter at the door only took a moment, and the second she was free Dakota's mother made a beeline for the stairs. Long before she reached his bedroom, she heard Dakota and his father talking. Not bothering to even knock at the door he had only partially closed, she barged right into her son's room. Dakota was already shirtless, bent over the washstand, Charles Rawlings Sr. talking to his back.

"So how's the ranch?"

"Doing great," Dakota spoke as he scrubbed. "I worked with Cash the days I was there. Everything looks fine. I think he's got a sale coming up soon."

"I've been following the prices. He should do well at market right now," Charles commented.

"How can you be talking about the ranch at a time like this?" Virginia demanded, arms akimbo.

"At a time like what?" Charles questioned in confusion.

Virginia pointed to Dakota. "The boy is in love."

"He didn't tell me he was in love," Charles stated. He then mumbled, "No one tells me anything."

"Of course he didn't tell you he was in love, you're only interested in the price of beef. Did you even ask about your mother?"

Charles looked sheepish, and both Virginia and Dakota had to fight smiles as they looked at him.

"How is your grandmother?" he ventured at last.

"I didn't get a chance to go see her, but as far as I know she's doing fine."

"And Cash?" This came from Virginia.

"Great. I've been at the ranch quite a bit these last few weeks. He's doing well."

"Slater and Liberty?"

"I haven't seen them, but I think everything is fine."

"Good. Now, about this girl," Virginia started. "What's her name?"

Dakota grinned but still said quietly, "Darvi."

Virginia's eyes widened with memory. "Darvi Wingate? Isn't she engaged to Brandon Young?"

"Was engaged," Dakota corrected.

"Did you have something to do with the breakup?" Charles asked.

"No. It all happened before we met."

Virginia was frowning again. "Before you met? She's Marty Bracewell's niece, isn't she? You've known each other for years."

"Met again," Dakota explained and waited for the barrage that wasn't long in coming. His mother wanted to know everything. Dakota did not volunteer every detail but gave his parents a fairly clear picture of the situation. His mother was stunned into silence, and he was rather relieved. It had been an emotional time.

"Is she all right now?" Charles asked kindly.

"Yes. She's doing very well."

"Good. I forgot to ask how long you can stay," Charles continued, reading his son's face very easily.

"I should head back to Aurora tomorrow, but I'll return for the party. The timing hasn't been right to talk to Darvi about some of what I'm feeling, and I may never have a chance, but I wish to do my own talking."

Both parents nodded in agreement, understanding completely.

"I'll get an invitation out today. I'll also send for the tailor, or if you'd rather, you could go to him and speed the process a bit."

Dakota nodded. "I'll do that. Thank you, Mother."

Virginia went to hug him again. "It's good to have you here, scars and all, even if it's just for a day."

Dakota looked over his mother's head to see his father looking pleased. It was at that moment he realized he'd missed a vital opportunity. This was the first time he had seen his parents since coming to Christ. By coming in and mentioning Darvi he had lost his chance, at least for the moment, of bringing up the changes in his life.

His parents left him alone, and Dakota prepared to go uptown. As he did so, he prayed for yet another opportunity to share his faith. If not now, then in a few weeks when he returned to St. Louis.

❧ ❧ ❧

Darvi would eventually kick herself for not making the connection, but they had never socialized with the Rawlingses before, and she simply gave their last name no thought.

Accompanying her parents to the party, she wore a dress of dark apricot. Made for her, it was lightweight and full-skirted. It fit perfectly, displaying her lovely shape and slim arms and neck. She didn't go for too many ruffles or much lace, but her gown was elegant.

A group of six arrived just ahead of Darvi and her parents, Stanley and Clarisse Wingate, forcing them to wait in line for just a few seconds. Nevertheless, the moment Darvi caught sight of Mr. Rawlings, her mind began to work. She didn't have time to develop any ideas—they were inside more quickly than she expected—but as soon as she spotted the man who had occupied many of her thoughts for the last two and a half weeks, it all made perfect sense.

Dakota was slightly taller than his father, who was an older version of the Ranger, and Darvi's eyes drank in the sight of him in a formal suit. His shirt was a snowy white, a black tie at his throat, and to Darvi he looked taller and larger than ever.

Her parents went through the receiving line first, and almost before she was ready, she was standing in front of him. Dakota held her eyes as he bent over her and kissed the back of her hand.

"May I see you on very short notice?"

"Yes." Darvi's soft tone matched his own.

"This evening? After the party?"

All she could do was nod. She thought it might be time to move away, but Dakota still held her hand. Her mind scrambled for something to say.

"I've heard from Annabelle Hewett," she got out.

"She told me she'd been in touch."

Darvi's eyes widened. "You've seen her?"

"I just got back."

Darvi nodded, even as her heart sank. "And that's why you want to see me."

Dakota studied her face.

"Are you seeing Brandon again?

Looking surprised, Darvi said no.

Dakota couldn't stop his smile. More people were coming in the door, so Dakota turned to his mother.

"I'm going to walk Darvi to the punch bowl. I'll be back shortly."

Virginia sent a beaming smile at the small strawberry blonde, who smiled in return. Dakota offered his arm and led her away.

If Darvi expected more of his time, however, she was to be disappointed. Dakota walked her directly to the punch table, got her a glass, and bent slightly to catch her ear.

"What time may I call for you later? I thought we might go for a walk."

"What time are you available after the party?"

"I think about six."

"Will seven o'clock work then?" Darvi asked, wishing it could be now.

"I'll be there."

Darvi forced herself not to watch him walk away. Most people knew she was no longer engaged, but she hated it when people talked about her.

There was someone talking about her right now, but had she known about these two and how kind their words were, she would have relaxed.

"Is Darvi all right?" Virginia asked as soon as Dakota was back at her side.

"Why do you ask?"

"She was clearly surprised, Dakota, and she looked rather pale."

"I noticed that too. I'll be seeing her later and hopefully I can clear everything up."

More guests arrived, and they went back to work. They spent another 20 minutes receiving people and then joined their guests in the huge garden at the rear of the house. It was a large group, but Dakota had little trouble finding Darvi with his gaze. He forced himself not to stare at her, much as he wanted to, but to mill around and talk with his parents' guests, some of whom he hadn't seen for years. And he enjoyed himself. He was even able to have a brief conversation with Darvi's father, who watched him rather closely but did not seem to object to him as a person. Dakota's heart, however, could not see seven o'clock coming fast enough.

❧ ❧ ❧

"Did you have a good time at the party?" Dakota asked when they were barely out Darvi's front door.

"Yes, I did. Your parents are very nice." She glanced sideways at him while they walked. "We've never been invited to anything at your parents' home before."

"Haven't you?"

"No. Did you have anything to do with today's invitation?"

"Yes, I did."

Darvi stopped and turned to him. "Why, Dakota? Why did you never tell me you're from St. Louis?"

"Because I'm not," he began, but seeing how stunned she was over that statement, he didn't go on. He glanced down the sidewalk just then and saw they were almost at the park.

"Would you mind if we sat down?"

"No, that's fine."

A few minutes later they took opposite ends of a bench in the middle of the park so they could turn and see each other. Darvi said not a word but waited and hoped that this man wasn't about to hurt her. She worked to keep her emotions from showing, hoping he would explain everything.

"The first thing I need to tell you is that I've never intentionally kept something from you. I knew you were from St. Louis, but where I was born just never came up."

She looked confused, so Dakota tried again.

"I left St. Louis when I was five, Darvi. My home is Kinkade, Texas. I'll always think of it that way. My father worked the ranch until just six years ago, when he and my mother moved back here. I'm 26 years old, and for most of those years my parents lived in Kinkade. My grandmother is still in Texas. She loved it so much she didn't want to move back, even though her only son did.

"On top of that, St. Louis is a sprawling city. If you had looked at my face when we pulled into your neighborhood and then up to your house, you would have seen that I was stunned to see how close you lived to my parents."

"Why didn't you say anything then?" Darvi asked. It was not an accusation, just an honest appeal for understanding.

"I was all ready to meet your parents, Darvi, but they weren't there. Brandon was. I could see that you didn't want him hugging you, but for all I knew he'd had a life-changing experience of his own, and the two of you would be engaged again by the time we next saw each other. I wasn't even convinced that he might not be with you at the party today."

For a moment they stared at each other, and then Darvi looked at her lap. She fiddled with the folds in her skirt before speaking.

"He didn't understand. He offered to take me to church every day if I wanted, but he just couldn't see how our not sharing the same beliefs could make that much difference. It took two days to convince him, and now I think he hates me." Darvi paused, her voice growing thick. "It also didn't help to have my parents just as confused. My mother is barely speaking to me."

"What did they have to say about the abduction?"

Darvi shook her head a little. "In order to protect Renee's privacy, I didn't go into much detail. I'm not sure that's fair to them since I don't think they understood the full gist of what happened, but I didn't know what else to do." Darvi paused before adding, "Not that I'm sure it would matter. All my mother seems concerned about right now is my breakup with Brandon."

Dakota's face clouded with compassion, and Darvi tried not to cry. Instead, she shifted her attention to Dakota.

"How did your parents take the news of your conversion?" she asked Dakota.

"We haven't discussed it. I wrote them as soon as I was able to sit up, and Mother mentioned it in her letter back to me, but when I got home, I didn't bring it up. I was gone less than 24 hours later and just arrived back yesterday."

"And you've been in Aurora?"

"Part of the time, yes. Jared Silk has been charged for money laundering, fraud, and embezzlement, but so far Seth and Eliot are still at the ranch. Something tells me they are behind Silk's arrest."

"But they're not in jail?"

Dakota shook his head no, even as he read the worry in her eyes.

"When does your aunt suggest you come back?"

"Suggest?" Darvi exclaimed. "She says I'm to *be* there by the twenty-eighth."

"A week from today."

"Yes."

"There's no point in my going all the way there and back. I'll just stay and go with you."

"You don't have to do that."

They stared at each other.

"I have a lot of things going on inside of me right now, Darvi," Dakota confessed. "But it's only fair to warn you that I'm not a St. Louis type of person. I love Texas."

"I love Texas too, but it's only fair to warn you that I've never been so confused about anyone as I am about you."

Dakota laughed a little.

"It's good to hear that someone else is in the same boat."

Darvi smiled, and again they found themselves regarding each other.

"Aunt Renee's telegraph was at the house when I arrived," Darvi said quietly. "I read it and remembered your telling me you were going to be in Aurora with me. I didn't see how that was possible, since you'd just left."

"If I had it to do over again," Dakota said, "I'd have asked to see you a moment before I left, so you would have known of my plans to return to Aurora."

"Would you have told me about your parents too?"

"That one's a little harder, Darv," he said comically. "I can never remember when Mother has that fall garden thing of hers, and for all I knew, she and my father were on a trip somewhere. They don't exactly check in with me."

Darvi had to laugh, and not just at Dakota's expression. She was beginning to see that he was from a different world. He teased her about trouble following her around, and she knew she was somewhat sheltered, but never once had he treated her like a child the way her parents and Brandon were wont to do. She was just a year younger than Dakota, but he'd been out of the nest and on his own for ages. She, on the other hand, was still treated like a little princess, one who had suddenly discovered her wings and was not living up to the life her parents had planned for her in the palace.

"I should get you home," Dakota said. "It's getting dark."

Darvi sighed. "I feel terrible that I'm in no hurry to go home."

"I feel bad about that too, but I'd feel worse if your reputation suffered because of my keeping you in the park too long." Dakota had a sudden thought. "Would you like to stop by your house and ask your parents if you could spend the evening with my family?"

Darvi perked up but then thought better of it. "Won't your parents be rather tired?"

"Yes, but we always play cards when we're home on Saturday nights, even when everyone is weary. You could be our fourth."

"I would like that," Darvi said. Dakota stood and offered his arm, his heart swelling over the chance to spend more time with her. He still didn't know if that meant love, but he was enjoying every moment of it.

And his parents enjoyed it too. Darvi's parents were willing to let her go, and Dakota's parents were delighted to see her. They brought her in and made her feel very welcome, even going so far as to tell her how sorry they were for all she'd been through. Dakota's heart squeezed with thankfulness for their kindness and hospitality. It was a fabulous evening, and Dakota had all he could do not to take Darvi's hand when he eventually walked her home.

To Dakota's surprise, his parents were still up when he got back. They called him into the living room when they heard the door.

"I thought you'd be asleep by now, Mother."

"I should be, but the game perked me up a bit."

Dakota sat down, kicked his shoes off, and put his feet on the ottoman.

"She's a sweet girl," Charles opened. His shoes were off, his feet up as well. "A lot of fun."

"Yes, she is," Dakota agreed, his eyes a little distant.

His mother then proceeded to astound him.

"Have you fallen for her because of her beliefs, Dak?"

Dakota had all he could do to answer in a normal voice.

"That has played a part, Mother, I'm sure of it, but that's not the only reason." He stopped and looked at her. "Have you heard something?"

"Only that she broke it off with Brandon, not the other way around, and that the reason had something to do with religion."

Dakota nodded but didn't know what to say. Was this the opportunity he had been looking for?

"Your grandmother wrote to us, Dak," Charles put in. "She made no secret of her excitement over what she calls *your salvation*. This is the third, no fourth, time we've heard this. First Cash, then my mother, then Slater, and now you. I don't know what you think you all have that the rest of us don't."

Dakota was no longer left wondering. There was no getting around the fact that his parents were ready to talk. But was he prepared to tell them? With a quick reminder that he was only responsible for what he knew, he tried to start.

"No one's ever wanted you to feel left out, Father. I hope you understand that. And I know in the past you've said you've been to church all your life." Dakota paused. He was already starting to ramble. He took a breath and began again. "There's so much I don't know or understand, but this much is clear to me: I was lost in my sin. It took awhile, but I finally saw that I *do* sin, and that my sin separated me from God."

Dakota looked into their faces, encouraged that they were listening so closely.

"You've seen my scars, and I know Cash wrote you. I nearly died. When that happened, I knew I wasn't ready to die. If I had been forced to face God in person at that moment, I would have had no excuse. Cash and Slate had both told me that my sin separates me from God, and that the only way to cover the separation is through His Son, Jesus. I accepted Jesus as my own Savior, and I no longer fear death or judgment." Dakota's eyes met those of his father's. "It's not about going to church all your life or being a good person. It's more personal than that."

When they said nothing, he went on.

"And to answer your question, Mother, the same thing happened to Darvi. Brandon wanted no part of it, so she broke it off. Darvi and I didn't fall for each other because of that, but knowing that we believe the same lets us explore this relationship. If she didn't share my belief, I wouldn't have a choice but to ignore my feelings, no matter how much it might hurt."

"But you do think you're in love with her?"

"I don't honestly know, but I'm willing to find out."

Again, they silently regarded him.

Dakota suddenly hated this. He had never known such peace as he had now, but not having his parents being in one accord with him was very painful. They had raised him to be independent and think for himself, so he knew they would never be harsh with him over this or any decision, but he wasn't sure they had the slightest inkling of what had happened to him.

"Well, Dak," his mother finally said, although her tone was sober. "We're glad to see you home and safe. Any little difference in our beliefs is nothing in light of your being safe. That's all we care about."

Dakota held his tongue. The "little difference" his mother spoke of was nothing short of a life-and-death matter, but Dakota knew there was no sense arguing. Reminding himself to stay respectful, Dakota kept praying and asking God to work in their hearts and open doors of opportunity.

Nineteen

"WHAT IF HE'S RIGHT?" CHARLES ASKED Virginia after they had retired.

Dakota's mother turned from the bottle of lotion she had been reaching for and stared at her husband.

"About what?"

"About facing God. Can I honestly say I'm ready?"

"Of course you're ready, Charles. You're a good person. What more can God want?"

He stared at his wife. Had she not heard what Dakota had said? Had *he* misunderstood?

"Charles?" Virginia ventured, her voice so tentative that the senior Rawlings wondered what his face looked like.

"I'm going to go ask Dakota something. I'll be right back."

Virginia was stunned. What had he been thinking? Her brow furrowed with deliberation. She didn't like the children coming home and upsetting things. If Dakota left chaos in his wake, it would put such a damper on his visit. Confrontation was the last thing she wanted.

Down the hallway Charles' thoughts were far different. His heart almost in dread over some of the things his son had said, he knocked on Dakota's door, working to remember what Cash and Slater had shared as well. Dakota answered before anything came to mind.

"Are you going to church tomorrow?" Charles asked without preamble.

Dakota nodded. "I was going to go early in the morning and get a note to Darvi to see if I could attend church with her."

"What about your mother's and my church?"

"In truth, Dad, I don't know anything about it, but because you don't agree with my beliefs, I'm assuming there won't be anything there for me."

"And what do you hope Darvi's church will have?"

"Some type of message and challenge from God's Word. Something I can learn from and put into practice in my life."

"And that's all part of not being afraid to die?"

"My peace about death does not come from a sermon I might hear, but from knowing that I have a relationship with Christ. However, salvation is only the beginning. There's a whole life to be lived, and I won't know how to live it without study in the Word."

The older Rawlings studied his boy's face, their eyes meeting and holding.

"I'll go with you! Your mother too!"

Dakota blinked. "All right," he said slowly. "But I'm not sure what Darvi will say. I mean, I haven't checked with her."

"What if," Charles began, his pride rubbing him a bit, "it turns out she goes to our church, and the preacher explains it just like you did?"

"Then I'll wonder how you could have been missing it all these years," Dakota replied before he thought.

Charles wasn't happy with this disrespectful statement, and his eyes communicated that with ease.

"I'm sorry, sir. I shouldn't have said that."

"No, you shouldn't have, but it's what you believe, isn't it?"

Dakota dropped his eyes before admitting, "Yes, sir."

Charles didn't like the shame he felt over the way he'd gained the upper hand. It was true that he had taught his boys to respect him, but he had come knocking on Dakota's door, not the other way around.

"It's all right," he said quietly. "Sleep well, Dakota."

"Thank you. Goodnight."

Charles made his way back down the hall, unaware of the way Dakota stood and watched him retreat into the darkness. He gained his own room, where Virginia still had a light on, and floored her with his announcement.

"We're going to church with Darvi and Dakota in the morning."

"What church?"

"I don't know yet, but we're going."

Her mouth opened a little. "You don't mean that."

"I do mean it."

"Charles, what will our neighbors who go to our church say?"

"I don't care."

Virginia knew very well how true that statement was. Charles Rawlings Sr. never did anything because someone thought he should. She watched him settle into bed, not at all comfortable with his plan. The lantern was still on, so Charles caught her gaze on him when he turned on his side. Virginia dropped her eyes and reached for the lamp, but his hand stopped her.

"Ginny," he said quietly, "he's got me to thinking."

"About what?"

"I'm not a kid anymore."

"You're not old, either."

"Neither was Ben down at the bank, and he dropped without warning."

"So that's what this is all about," she said in a mothering tone. "You've just realized you're not going to live forever."

"Exactly."

Virginia had not expected him to agree. She had even used a tone with him that usually angered him.

"All right, Charles." She gave in more out of confusion than anything else. "I'll go with you."

Charles had not thought anything else. Virginia went nearly everywhere with him. But her answer gave him pause. Would he go if she refused? It took some time before Charles fell asleep, but even then he wasn't sure he would go without her.

$$\text{\textmd{❧·❧·❧}}$$

"I'm sorry to call at your back door at such an early hour," Dakota said to the woman at the Wingates' kitchen door. "I didn't want to disturb anyone, but could you please get this note to Miss Wingate as soon as possible?"

"I will, sir. Is there anything else?"

"No, thank you."

That was how the morning had started. Dakota had awakened early and gone swiftly to Darvi's, hoping she would get the note as he directed, and she did. Just an hour later a return note arrived from her, telling Dakota what church she attended and that if he liked, she would come for him at ten o'clock. One more message from Dakota established that his parents would be along and also offered to include her in their carriage.

Now, Dakota, Charles, and Virginia rode in silence to the Wingate home. Virginia was tense, her mind filled with uncertainty over this outing. Charles seemed so certain, and Dakota was calm, his expression relaxed, but she felt completely out of her element.

It helped to have Darvi join their group. That young woman began a conversation with her the moment she took a seat, and Virginia actually relaxed a little before they arrived at the church.

"I want you to meet a friend of mine," Darvi continued to talk as they walked up the steps, the younger woman having taken the older woman's arm. "Her name is Mrs. Beacher, and she's such a dear. In fact, she lives just a few blocks from you."

"Martha Beacher?"

"Yes!"

"We've known each other for years. She goes to your church?"

Darvi smiled. "This is her church. She was the one who introduced me."

Virginia relaxed a little more. Martha Beacher was a wonderful woman, always kind and ready to lend a hand. Up to that moment Virginia had not known what to expect, but suddenly she wasn't worried, at least not about meeting the people. However, the sermon, or whatever the service entailed, still had her somewhat concerned.

❧ ❧ ❧

"Can you tell what your parents thought?" Darvi asked Dakota as they walked in the garden behind the house.

"Not exactly." His voice was deep and soft. "I think my father understood, but I'm not sure what Mother was thinking."

"How is it that they wanted to come?"

"My father decided. I'm not sure he gave Mother much choice."

"Does she do everything he says?"

Dakota smiled. "What do you think?"

Darvi smiled back. "I think the Rawlings men are used to getting what they want."

Dakota looked very innocent. "I can't imagine what you're talking about."

"Of course you can't." Darvi's voice was indulgent. "You always *ask* me and give me lots of choices. You never *tell* me to do anything."

Dakota worked at not smiling. "Regarding what?"

" 'By the way, Darvi, we're not going to make the next town. Would you like to camp here for the night?' " she began to tease him. " 'Darvi, you've been through a lot. Would you like to lie down and rest awhile?' " Her brows rose in a way that told him she was very pleased with herself just then. "You're used to giving orders, Dakota Rawlings, and I suspect your father is the same way."

"You little pill," Dakota growled playfully and began to reach for her. Darvi darted away from him and around a bush.

"Did I hit a little close to home, Mr. Rawlings?"

Dakota told himself not to laugh as he came around the bush toward her. Darvi evaded him nicely and slipped across the paved path around an arbor. She peeked through and watched him approach. She was about to dart off again, but he stopped. Bending just a little to watch his face, Darvi waited.

"I just thought of something," he admitted, his eyes on hers. "I can't really do anything if I catch you."

Darvi's smile grew rather wide, her expression downright smug.

"On second thought . . ." Dakota reconsidered and started forward again.

Virginia chose that moment to call from the kitchen door, telling them she was serving coffee and cake in the living room.

"We're coming," Darvi took advantage and answered, her eyes gleaming with amusement as she sauntered triumphantly up the path.

"You're an impudent piece of baggage, Miss Wingate," Dakota growled close to her ear as he drew up beside her. Darvi smiled for a moment but suddenly stopped and turned worried eyes up to his. Her brow lowering in concern, she studied him a moment.

"You knew I was teasing just now, didn't you, Dakota? I mean, you do know how much I appreciate everything you've done, all your care and such?"

Dakota's finger swept through the soft tendrils of hair that refused to stay off of her forehead, pleased when her brow softened a little.

"Yes," he said softly. "I do know that you're thankful. You've told me in dozens of ways."

Darvi's head tipped to the side in a way Dakota found irresistible. "What kinds of ways?"

In a flash Dakota was back on the roadside, having rescued Darvi from Cassy's ranch. He had stopped to check on her and soon found her sobbing in his arms. Never had he felt so needed.

"Let's just say," Dakota began, working to dispel the image, "in your own special way you've made it very clear."

Darvi studied him. "Will I ever get a straight answer to that question?"

Dakota could feel himself falling, his heart squeezing and filling all at the same time as he looked into eyes that held such trust and honesty.

"I hope so" was all he was willing to say just then, and Darvi understood. She smiled a little and nodded.

They walked on to the house, Dakota doing all he could not to place an arm around her slim waist. He hadn't been glad to see Brandon at the house a few weeks back, but he couldn't say he blamed the man for trying.

❧ ❧ ❧

"Have you been at church this whole time?" Clarisse Wingate spoke rather primly the moment Darvi walked in the door. It was almost two o'clock.

"No, the Rawlings asked me to lunch, and I accepted. I didn't think you'd mind."

"And does my minding mean anything to you these days?"

"Of course it does, Mother. I thought you enjoyed the Rawlingses and approved of them."

Her mother sniffed, not wanting to admit that her daughter was right. Another tact was needed.

"You've certainly transferred your affections swiftly enough."

"Swiftly?"

"Yes, swiftly! You just broke off with Brandon a few weeks ago."

Still managing to keep her voice kind, Darvi said, "I broke up with Brandon early this summer, but no one would listen to me."

Her mother shook her head. "I don't know you anymore."

Darvi felt cut to the quick but stayed quiet. Why her mother would want the "old Darvi" back was unimaginable. The old Darvi pouted if she didn't get her way. The old Darvi was never happy, constantly wanting more things, parties, or excitement. The new Darvi was very glad to be rid of her.

"Did I see Mr. and Mrs. Rawlings in the carriage earlier?" her mother asked next, working hard to sound as though she didn't care.

"Yes."

"Does Mrs. Rawlings go to that church?"

"She did this morning."

Her mother's face was so stiff it looked as though it might crack.

"May I tell you something, Mother?"

Clarisse Wingate nodded but looked no less unyielding.

"Our ancestors are so important to you, but I can't remember half of them. I'm your only child. If I don't remember, who will?"

"You could make more of an effort."

"I suppose I could, but even you have forgotten some of them, and when that happened, I finally understood that we do not carry on through our ancestors."

Her mother's face went from stony to livid.

"How can you say such a thing? Why, you were named after your dearly departed Uncle Darwin and Uncle Virgil!"

Clarisse stomped away at that point, leaving the foyer area and retreating to her small sitting room on the south side of the house. It was her sanctuary, her leave-me-alone spot, but Darvi did not take the usual hint. She followed right behind.

"Please, Mother. Please discuss it with me."

"I will not! I've never heard such nonsense. You're going against everything we've ever taught you."

But her mother did turn to her, and even though her eyes did nothing but accuse, Darvi tried again.

"I have so much I want to share with you and Father, so much in my heart. But it seems to me that you only want to look good on the outside, not take time to see inside to the real person."

"You will not speak to me in such a way!"

The words were all but shouted, and Darvi retreated in defeat. Her face a mask of pain, she uttered her final words. "Uncle Marty told me I could live with him anytime I needed. I leave Wednesday for Aurora. I think I'll just go on to Austin from there."

Darvi waited for her mother to ask her not to go, to order her or demand that she come right home, but nothing was forthcoming. Feeling as though her insides were breaking into little pieces, Darvi took her pain over this rejection to her room, where fighting tears of horrible pain and confusion, she began to sort through her things and pack.

🌺 🌺 🌺

"I want you to do me a favor," Virginia said to Dakota the moment he came home from returning Darvi. Setting her book aside, she turned a little to face him squarely.

"All right," Dakota said as he sat down, watching his father put his paper aside and figuring that he was in the dark as well.

"When do you leave?"

"Tuesday or Wednesday."

Virginia nodded. "I want you to write me a letter."

Dakota forced a dozen questions to stay inside.

"You can write it now and leave it here for me, or you can write it after you leave and mail it."

Dakota only looked at her; Charles did the same.

"In the letter, I would like you to explain to me what that man was talking about this morning. What does he mean when he says we have to be born again?"

"May I ask you a question?" Dakota put in before she could go on.

Virginia gave a brief nod.

"Why can't we talk about this face-to-face?"

Virginia looked away and kept her eyes averted while she answered.

"I haven't told anyone how much it bothers me that all of you boys have something with your grandmother that I don't have. And now your father is interested, and I'm going to be left all alone."

"I would never leave you all alone," Charles said quietly.

"Not physically—I know that—but this is bigger than our living together, Charles. You must see that."

"Yes, I do," he admitted out loud because she was still not looking at either one of them.

"But why a letter, Mother?" Dakota persisted.

"Because I need time to think. I feel rattled when you start to talk of this, and I want to panic and run." She finally turned to him, and Dakota was shocked to see tears in her eyes. She managed to speak, but her voice was filled with self-deprecation. "Wouldn't the women in town be amazed to find the invincible Virginia Rawlings all shook up over her son's religious convictions?"

"I'm not sure I agree with you there, Mother. If you were to get any of them alone to talk about their own mortality, I think you might see something different. Maybe all the parties and committees are a way of covering their own fears."

"But you and that pastor honestly think I deserve to go to hell, don't you?"

"*I* deserved to go to hell," Dakota countered. "Why God saved me from that I'll never know, but that's what He did, and I know He's waiting to do the same for anyone who will call on Him."

Virginia's heart lightened within her. She had felt so helplessly condemned, but Dakota's tone had been understanding and humble. And she did want to comprehend, but it was frightening to her as well. At the same time, he had made it sound as though there was hope.

"So you'll write the letter?"

"Absolutely. I'll leave it in my room."

Virginia wanted to cry in earnest then. He was so much like his father: used to taking charge but sensitive with those he loved. She didn't know why she'd expected the worst, but she had.

Stifling a yawn, Virginia suddenly felt very weary. Not getting her son's wrath or scorn was so relieving that all she wanted to do was sleep.

Having been married to her for 30 years, Charles detected the signs. She had yet to look at him, which told him she was either embarrassed or still felt betrayed, but even in profile he watched her lids grow heavy over the pages of the book she had reopened. Before long she was trying to read with her head laid back, finally giving up and placing the book in her lap. Moments later her eyes were closed.

Father and son were on their own, but neither spoke. Dakota had questions but sensed they should wait. His father hadn't looked his way before going back to the newspaper, but Dakota had watched the way he'd studied his wife. It came to him without warning, and he was not sure his parents were aware of the fact, but Dakota saw for the first time that God had certainly blessed their marriage.

Dakota didn't join his parents in reading or napping just then. He was too busy wondering how he'd never seen this before. Not moving an inch from the living room, Dakota talked the whole thing out with God and determined to ask Cash the next time he saw him whether God blessed those who wanted nothing to do with Him. Dakota thought He must, but that wasn't good enough. The Texas Ranger wanted verses to prove it.

❦ ❦ ❦

"How are you today?" Dakota asked quietly as he and Darvi walked from her front door on Monday evening.

"I'm fine," she said quietly.

"Was your mother a little cool just now," he asked before getting to the carriage, "or did I imagine things?"

"Frozen better describes her," Darvi said so quietly that Dakota let it drop. He had asked her to join him for dinner and knew that this conversation would wait for the restaurant.

They rode in silence; Dakota at the reins, Darvi beside him. Thinking as they moved along that Dakota was one of the most restful persons she'd ever known, Darvi felt not the slightest anxiety whenever she was with him. If he looked at her a certain way, her heart would pound and her pulse race, and his nearness affected her no small amount, but never did she know danger or fear. It was an amazing thing.

Sitting beside her, having already pulled the carriage over to the curb in front of the Grayson Hotel, Dakota studied Darvi's profile and waited. He smiled just studying that captivating mouth and little-girl-turned-up nose. She was in a far-off place right now, but the half-smitten Ranger saw no reason to disturb her. Not even the horse's shifting brought her attention around, and Dakota waited several minutes in silence. When he saw her noticing where they were, he just waited for her eyes to swing to his. Darvi smiled as soon as they met.

"We're here," she grinned a little.

"Yes."

"How long?"

"I didn't keep track."

"But we didn't just get here, did we?"

"No."

For a few seconds they just watched each other. Dakota's heart felt a little fuller every time he was with her. Darvi's was doing the same.

Dakota climbed down at last, moved to her side, and assisted Darvi to the walk. Offering his arm to her, he said, "May I escort you to dinner, Miss Wingate?"

"Yes, please," she said.

Dakota led her inside. It was going to be a wonderful evening.

Twenty

"I WAITED FOR HER TO TELL ME I COULDN'T go to Uncle Marty's, but she was silent. She's been silent ever since."

"Oh, Darvi, I'm sorry it's gone like that. Is it the same with your father?"

"No," Darvi said with relief. "I think he's a bit upset with Mother. In fact, he talks to me more than he has in years. He's nonstop at the dinner table and in the evenings. He even asked me to breakfast this morning. We had a wonderful time."

Darvi bit her lip suddenly, and Dakota let the subject drop. They had enjoyed a sumptuous meal of veal cutlets, baked potatoes covered with dill and cheese, baby peas, and dark rye biscuits. Now they had hot coffee in thin porcelain cups with French pastries headed their way. The gas lighting was soft, and the table was set in a horseshoe booth. There were couples on either side, but all voices were quiet, the waiters moving silently over the brightly colored rugs, making the setting more elegant.

"Will it work for you to leave here tomorrow afternoon instead of Wednesday morning?" Dakota inquired.

"I think so. Is there some problem?"

"No, but we have to go back through Kinkade, as I need my horse, and it might be nice to have a little extra time on the other end."

"Would it be easier if we split up at Young Springs?" Darvi made herself ask. "I could go on to Aurora on my own and meet you there."

"I'm not letting you out of my sight," Dakota said bluntly.

"But then you'll have the trouble of getting whatever horse I ride back to your brother's."

"I'm sorry I didn't tell you, but I planned for us to ride the train.

I'll just pay the price to put Eli in with the stock. You won't have a horse to worry about."

Much as Darvi wanted to bask in the warm glow of knowing that he had planned all this to take care of her, she couldn't get Eli from her mind. She bit her lip to keep from smiling, but it didn't work.

"What's that for?"

"Eli."

Dakota rolled his eyes.

"What will he have done all this time without you?"

"Probably driven Cash crazy. My brother has better things to do than entertain my horse, but Eli will be keeping a close eye out for me, and as compassionate as Cash is, he will have probably ridden him a time or two."

Darvi suddenly smiled. "Admit it, Dakota."

"Admit what?"

"You miss him too?"

Dakota grinned but didn't have to answer; the pastries had arrived. They talked for another hour, eating slowly and enjoying endless cups of rich coffee. It was like a dream come true for both of them as they covered various subjects and beliefs, some held very dear and others still under inspection. They talked about their moments of salvation again, both reflecting on the way God had been working behind the scenes and how obvious that was now. Dakota told Darvi nearly every word of the letter he had written to his mother and appreciated her encouragement. After hearing about Dakota's letter, Darvi thought she might write to her own mother and wondered if that might not be easier for her to take.

"Dakota," Darvi asked as they finally rose from the table to go, "would you mind giving me the Scriptures you wrote to your mother, the exact ones?"

"Not at all. Do you want them tonight, or can I bring them tomorrow?"

"Tomorrow is fine. I think I need to put some distance between us, so I won't write until I get to Texas."

Her words had the strangest effect on his heart. He didn't say anything, but knowing she was returning to Texas with him and that she was so matter-of-fact about it filled him with hope and happiness. Though she was deeply affected by this fallout with her mother, he still wanted her with him. He wanted her close, not just to protect and keep an eye on her, but to be with her, to hear her voice, listen to her laugh, watch her smile, and talk with him about a thousand different subjects. He was afraid to let his heart move too fast, but at times it was so hard.

Such a moment came upon him when he dropped her off. He wanted to spend more time with her. He wanted to hold and kiss her but knew that such actions at this time would be a mistake. Instead he held her hand for a moment and lightly kissed the back of it, much like he had done at his parents' house that first afternoon. He looked up to see Darvi's smile.

"Is something funny?"

"No, it's just a little hard to remember the Ranger when I see you dressed like this and using manners one would expect to find only in the city."

"Well, we are in the city," he teased a little. "I thought it appropriate."

"Is that the only reason you did it?"

Dakota's white teeth gleamed as he smiled, but no answer came to her question.

"I'll see you tomorrow. I'll be here around one o'clock, and we'll take the 1:45 train."

"All right. Thank you for a wonderful evening."

"Thank *you*" was all Dakota said, and he moved on his way.

Darvi's father was in the living room, but she was glad he was busy with a newspaper. She wanted to be alone and to cherish the memories of the evening.

❧ ❧ ❧

They were silent for the first time in hours. The conversation that had started at dinner in St. Louis the night before only continued as the train moved south and west. Dakota had been good at his word: He had brought the list of Scriptures he'd put in his mother's letter for Darvi. Darvi's mouth was dry, and she was tired of talking, but her brain was still moving faster than the train. Dakota had put his head back and fallen asleep, but Darvi took her Bible from the satchel at her feet and turned to the first verse.

The list started with Romans 3:23: *All have sinned, and come short of the glory of God.* Next was Romans 6:23: *The wages of sin is death; but the gift of God is eternal life through Jesus Christ our Lord.* Dakota had also written some notes. One was about the jailer in Acts who had asked Paul and Silas how he could be saved. Darvi found their answer in Acts 16:31: *They said, Believe on the Lord Jesus Christ, and thou shalt be saved, and thy house.*

The book of Ephesians came next with 2:8,9: *By grace are ye saved through faith; and that not of yourselves: it is the gift of God, not of works, lest any man should boast.* Romans 10:9,10 went on to add: *If thou shalt confess with thy mouth the Lord Jesus, and shalt believe in thine heart that God hath raised him from the dead, thou shalt be saved. For with the heart man believeth unto righteousness; and with the mouth confession is made unto salvation.*

Second Corinthians 6:2 left no doubt as to the urgency of the decision: *I have heard thee in a time accepted, and in the day of salvation have I helped thee: behold, now is the accepted time; behold, now is the day of salvation.* The last verse Darvi looked up was from John 20:31: *These are written, that ye might believe that Jesus is the Christ, the Son of God; and that believing ye might have life through his name.*

Thank You, Lord, Darvi's heart now prayed. *Thank You for saving me and showing me all of this. Help me to write to my own family. I want them to have this hope. I want them to know and believe.*

Darvi felt tired now. She hadn't slept all that well in the night and had woken early, hoping her mother would offer an olive branch before she left. No such offer was made. Darvi had said goodbye to her father and mother, but only her father had replied. Her father had started to scold his wife even before Darvi was out of earshot, but that hadn't made her feel any better.

Quite suddenly Darvi wasn't certain if the letter was a good idea. She had already said enough. What she needed right now was for her mother to speak to her. Anything she said short of that time would surely fall on deaf ears.

Thinking she would have to discuss it with Dakota, and hoping that he hadn't written all of those references out for no reason, Darvi drifted off to sleep.

❧ ❧ ❧

Never had Texas looked so good. Dakota had sent word from Dallas that they were on their way, but not until he saw Cash on the platform was he certain the telegram had arrived.

The brothers embraced just before Cash hugged Darvi.

"Welcome back," he told her with a huge smile.

Darvi would have replied, but Dakota stepped over and hugged her too.

"What was that for?" Darvi asked, even as she wished he would do it again.

Dakota looked innocent. "I was adding my own welcome to Texas."

"But you came with me," Darvi pointed out, eyes just short of laughter.

Still managing to look innocent, Dakota asked, "So does that mean it doesn't count?"

"Come on you two," Cash cut in, his voice dry. "Dakota needs to visit a certain horse."

"How is he?"

"Completely depressed. He must think you're dead."

As they moved to the wagon that would take them to the ranch house, Dakota could only laugh at the description; he knew it had to be all too true.

ॐ ॐ ॐ

"How was your trip?" Cash wanted to know as soon as Darvi had returned from freshening up in her room.

"It was fast. Very few delays. We stayed over in Oklahoma City one night but otherwise just slept and ate on the train."

"Where did you stay in Oklahoma City?"

"The big hotel. I can't recall the name."

"The Oaks?"

"That was it," Darvi said with a smile. "You've been there?"

"Several times. Oh!" Cash remembered. "A package came for you."

"From whom?" Darvi asked as Cash moved to his office and came out again.

"I don't know."

Darvi took the package from Cash's outstretched hands, her movements somewhat cautious. Cash offered his pocketknife, and a moment later the strawberry blonde had it open. A letter came first and then, surprisingly enough, a black-haired wig.

Darvi read the note, her eyes growing huge just before Dakota came in the front door.

"You're not coming in here," he said sternly to Eli, who had clopped right onto the porch. "Now get back before I put you in the barn."

With this he shut the door, but a glance out the window told Dakota that the horse had stationed himself in the yard, where he could see inside. The Ranger only shook his head and joined the others, surprised to see Darvi looking rather sober.

"What's going on?" Dakota asked.

"She wants me to wear this wig."

"Who wants you to wear a wig?"

"Aunt Renee. She wrote, reminding me that Jared Silk is locked up but Seth and Eliot are still free men. She doesn't want Seth to recognize me and get it into his head to snatch me again."

Dakota shook his head a little. "That's not going to happen."

Doubts assailed Darvi in a horrible rush. It was so easy in this place, at this ranch, to forget how helpless she'd been, but for a moment the memories came flooding back. A shudder ran over her as she pictured Seth's calm, implacable face. He had been completely serious about keeping her until she fell for him.

Seeing her uncertainty, Dakota sat next to her, his head turned to watch her. Cash had quietly left them alone. Darvi did not look at Dakota, so Dakota sat a moment, giving her time to think.

"I tell myself you won't let anything happen, but in truth, Dakota, you can't be with me every moment."

"That's true."

Darvi finally looked at him.

"But you're still sure he's not going to get me, aren't you?"

"Yes, very sure."

She looked so troubled and confused that he took her hand.

"Listen to me, Darvi. I'm not trying to play God here, but I'm very good at what I do. I assume your plan is to stay with your aunt, and I'm hoping that will work out, but if we need to take rooms in the same hotel in order for me to be close by, that's what we'll do. Seth Redding is not going to take you against your will again."

Tears filled her eyes before she whispered, "I didn't like it, Dakota."

"I know," he said softly before reaching up with his free hand to touch her cheek. "We'll be thinking very clearly; we'll take all the necessary precautions; and in truth, I just don't think he's that stupid. As soon as he spots me, he'll put the situation together."

Darvi looked surprised. "He will, won't he?" she said in soft amazement.

"I certainly think so. He's not a fool, or he wouldn't be working for Silk. In fact, they probably know now. After all, we both disappeared at the same time."

Darvi shook her head. "Why didn't any of this occur to me before?"

"I don't know, but there's no point in worrying. We're going to do everything we can to keep a lid on this. I'm not expecting any trouble." Dakota reached for the wig, his mouth just beginning to smile. "Your aunt is quite a character." He fingered the hair for a moment and then looked at her again. "You might look good with black hair, but I prefer what you have."

Darvi smiled but didn't reply. She wanted to say something about the way he looked too—his size, his handsome face, his gentle manner—but she thought someone might be headed their way.

Dakota watched her, wanting to speak as well but holding off for the same reason. Dakota didn't know when the time would be right, but it wasn't now.

"I've got dinner on," Katy called from the edge of the room.

"Thanks, Katy," Dakota responded and stood with Darvi. "Are you all right?" he asked as soon as Katy turned away.

"Yes, thank you. I can't say that I'm looking forward to it, but I think I'll be fine."

Dakota took her arm to escort her to dinner, thinking she was the most courageous woman he knew.

He would have laughed if he could have heard Darvi's prayer at the moment: She was asking God to give her strength and to help her be brave.

❧ ❧ ❧

"It's almost completely dark now," Darvi commented, her head tipped back a little. Dakota followed her gaze.

"I love a Texas sky," he said quietly. Having eaten dinner, he and Darvi had taken a walk. The sky was clear this night—huge and full of stars.

They were silent for a moment, both still looking up and trying to take it all in.

"There's a man who runs the general store in Shotgun where my brother lives," Dakota began. "He's huge. He has to duck for every doorway, and if he's coming through, no one can walk beside him. Not too long ago I read in Isaiah 66 where it says that heaven is God's throne and the earth His footstool, and I thought about what a big God He is. I love a Texas sky. I think it's the biggest in the world, but even at that, God has to duck His head to enter my world, because He's so huge." Dakota looked down at Darvi, who was staring up at him in the shadowy light. "But that is what He did for me, Darvi. He ducked His head and entered, so I could be saved."

"Oh, Dakota," was all she could say.

He reached out his hand and she took it, finding comfort in his touch. Darvi was not at all looking forward to returning to Aurora, not even to see her aunt, but Dakota's hand and words reminded her that she was not alone. Dakota wasn't all that thrilled himself, but he wanted closure to the situation so Darvi would not have to look over her shoulder in fear.

And the sky only helped. If God could create a universe this big and perfect, He could surely handle the relatively small court case that awaited them in Aurora.

***

"You still awake?" Dakota asked Cash after bedtime that night, barely taking time to knock.

In truth Cash had just dropped off, but he was able to wake swiftly.

"What's up?" he asked as he threw the covers back and swung his legs out to sit on the edge of the bed. Dakota sat down as well.

"I haven't had a chance to tell you what happened with the folks."

"Why, what happened?"

In great detail Dakota explained the way Charles had shown interest in the things Dakota shared, his visit to Dakota's room that night, and the way they had attended church together. Dakota recounted almost word for word the letter he had written to his mother while Cash sat in stunned silence.

"They went to church with you?" the older Rawlings clarified in wonder.

"Yes. Mother was not happy about it, but you can tell she's thinking. Father, for all his interest, is not asking too many questions. I'm not sure if Mother's lack of enthusiasm has tempered his response, or if the whole thing was a flash in the pan."

Again, there was silence in the darkness. Cash had been praying for his parents for years, but the door had never opened as it had for Dakota. Of course, the change in Dakota was more drastic, so it wasn't hard to see that this might have had an effect. Still, the whole thing took some getting used to.

"Tell me something, Cash," Dakota went on.

"Okay."

"Is the folks' marriage blessed by God?"

"Certainly."

"How do you know that?"

"Matthew 5 says God allows the sun to rise on the evil and on the good. He sends rain on the just and the unjust. What made you think of that?"

"Seeing Father and Mother . . . they love each other more than they ever have, but they haven't had the Lord to lead them. I can't imagine making a marriage work without God."

"But God does bless those who want nothing to do with Him, Dak; that's the kind of God He is."

Dakota nodded.

"I take it you've been thinking about marriage lately."

Dakota looked at him.

"I don't know what I'm thinking exactly, but I do know I've never met anyone before Darvi who actually made me think about giving up the Rangers."

"And you're certain you have to give up that job if you marry?"

Dakota's nod was decisive. "It's no life for a family man. I'd never be home."

"What would you do?"

Dakota smiled.

"I rather like this ranch."

Cash could only laugh.

"I won't tell you I could use you or you'd be welcome, little brother. I expect you to already know."

The two looked at each other.

"I'm going to bed," Dakota announced as he stood.

"All right. I'll see you in the morning."

Cash waited until the door closed and slipped back into bed. He didn't let his mind drift too far, but it wouldn't hurt his feelings to have Dakota around more often. Thinking that Darvi would be a nice addition to the picture too, he fell back to sleep.

Twenty-One

DAKOTA AND DARVI HAD TALKED FOR THE first part of the journey to Aurora, but now both were silent with their thoughts. Darvi was fine when she was distracted by conversation, but alone with her thoughts, she felt something akin to panic creeping up on her.

Part of her mind simply could not accept the fact that she was headed back to Aurora. And not just to the town, but to the very train station where those two men had taken her.

A glance at Dakota's profile told Darvi he was as confident as any man could be in his ability to protect her, but going back to Aurora was causing her no end of anxiety. And the wig in her bag didn't help!

She shook her head at her aunt's scheme. What could the woman be thinking? Darvi hated pretense. She honestly didn't know how her aunt stood such a life. A spark of anger flashed inside her, and it was all directed toward her aunt. Darvi knew it was wrong and worked for the remainder of the journey to calm down.

I'll just explain when I get there that I didn't want to wear the wig, Darvi finally calmed and told herself. *Aunt Renee will understand. I don't have a thing to worry about.*

❧ ❧ ❧

"Where's your wig?" were the first words out of Renee's mouth.

Darvi's mouth opened a little with hurt and surprise and for a moment she lost her train of thought. When she recovered, she was glad to hear that her voice was normal.

"Are you going to ask us in, Aunt Renee?"

"Oh, yes." The older woman was momentarily flustered by being caught off guard, and the result was a breach of manners. "Come in. I'm sorry. You took me by surprise."

Renee invited them into her living room. Moving silently, Dakota and Darvi entered and, when directed, sat on the comfortable red sofa. Most of the furniture was red or pink, but it wasn't gaudy as Darvi might have expected had she only heard about it. The room was warm with family photos and bits of lace and ruffles here and there.

"Why aren't you wearing the wig?" Renee asked as soon as she had taken a seat across from Darvi. She had known her own anxieties concerning the pending court case, and having Darvi show up looking like her wasn't helping.

"It's in my bag," Darvi told her quietly.

"You didn't feel you needed it?"

"No. I think Dakota is all the protection I need."

"What about my privacy—did you think of that?"

Darvi hadn't, but didn't say that. Why had she thought her aunt would understand? They had gotten on well at the ranch in Kinkade, but in truth, they didn't know each other at all. Working not to lead with her emotions, Darvi spoke.

"There's something I need to tell you, Renee. If, when I'm done, you want me to wear the wig, then I will, but I hope you'll hear me out."

"I will, Darvi," Renee said sincerely, seeing that she had come across rather strongly.

"Thank you," Darvi replied. "I think that even if I wear the wig, people will be able to see that we're related. I don't think it can be helped. I know you value your privacy, but at what price?"

"What do you mean?"

"I mean, if you believe in what you're doing here, it shouldn't matter. It shouldn't make any difference if people know that Annabelle Hewett is an assumed name. Everyone comes from somewhere. Surely people know you have family."

Renee blinked at her. Never had she looked at it that way. She then looked slowly at Dakota to gauge his reaction, but his face was unreadable. Watching her, Darvi thought Renee looked so surprised that it made her feel guilty.

"I'm sorry, Aunt Renee," She said quietly, sorry that she had even tried to explain. "I hate subterfuge, and having to wear that wig scares me more than taking my chances on the street. I couldn't even tell my parents the whole story because they would have wanted to know who this woman was that looked just like me. If you're hurt, I'm truly sorry, but I did mean what I said: Why must you hide who you really are?"

Renee looked upset, her fingers coming to her lips.

"I never thought about your not being able to tell your family, Darvi. Honestly, I didn't. Please tell them. If I had a daughter who had been through what you've experienced, I would want every detail. Tell them whatever you need to."

Darvi nodded, and in the moment Renee thought she looked very young and vulnerable. She also looked a bit pale. She wanted to speak more on the issue, but Dakota had a question of his own.

"There's something else bothering you, Darvi." Dakota's deep voice rumbled out, his head turned to study her. "What is it?"

Darvi closed her eyes for a moment and then looked at him.

"This whole thing—the trial, having to see Seth and Eliot again . . . all of it." Darvi glanced at her aunt. "I know you can't wait to see Jared Silk pay for his crimes, but in truth, I don't even know the man."

"You should still want to see justice done," Renee stated plainly.

"I do, but in the process I'm sure others are going to be hurt. I don't feel good about that at all."

"What others?"

"Cassy Robinson for one."

"Cassy's no child, Darvi." This time her aunt's words were blunt. "She knows exactly what type of man Eliot McDermott is."

"Be that as it may," Darvi went on quietly, "she loves him and so do the children. You may want justice served so badly that nothing else bothers you, but I can't make the same claim."

Renee sat back in her seat. She wanted to tell her niece to grow up and stop walking around with her heart on her sleeve, but maybe Darvi had a point. For the first time in a long time, Renee wondered if she might have become a bit hard.

"So, what is it you want to do, Darvi?" Dakota surprised both women by asking. "For that matter, what is it you want your aunt to do?"

Seeing that he was right, Darvi sighed very quietly.

"I guess I want her to do just what she's doing. Jared needs to answer the charges against him, and she's right, Cassy's made her choices with her eyes wide open." Darvi's gaze dropped to her lap. "Nevertheless, it still hurts my heart to be involved in all of this."

As Dakota had gotten in the habit of doing, he reached for her hand and held it tenderly.

"I'm glad to hear that, since this whole thing should hurt your heart," he assured her softly. "Justice is a must, but there are ways to go about it. There's nothing I hate more than coming across a Ranger who's lost his compassion, one who's mean and thoughtless. He gives the rest of us a bad name."

A distinct whinny outside the house suddenly set Dakota's gaze to the window.

"I'm sorry, ladies," he said with genuine regret. "I have to see to my horse. Would you please excuse me for a moment?"

"Certainly," Renee offered graciously, and a moment later she was alone with her niece.

"I appreciate all you've said, Darvi, and I plan to think on it."

"Thank you."

"I also don't want you to wear the wig. I think your point is very valid."

Darvi nodded with relief, as they both heard Dakota's voice outside. Darvi glanced that way, and when she looked back, her aunt was smiling.

"I certainly hope you're not going to let that one get away."

Darvi surprised her when she only smiled. Renee waited a moment for her to reply, but it didn't happen.

"No comment?" the older woman prompted, and Darvi laughed.

"Aunt Renee, I think you might be one of the most private people I know, but you expect me to bare my heart to you."

Renee grinned. "It's the reporter in me. I can't stand not knowing something."

Darvi smiled back, and Renee's eyes widened when she realized her niece wasn't going to answer. The older woman actually moved to the edge of her seat, reminding Darvi of a six-year-old.

"So tell me, how do you feel about him?"

Darvi laughed and watched her with amusement.

"Darvi Leigh Wingate!" She was very stern now. "This is your aunt speaking, and I expect an answer."

Darvi hadn't even opened her mouth when they both heard the front door. Dakota was returning. The younger of the two women had all she could do not to laugh at her aunt's aggrieved expression.

❧ ❧ ❧

"So you've never attended this church?" Darvi asked Dakota the next morning as they walked toward the end of town.

"No. I've never attended any church in Aurora." He glanced down at her and then back up the street. "I found myself looking for a certain strawberry blonde when I was last here. I'm afraid I thought of little else."

Darvi studied the firm, clean-shaven line of his jaw from a shorter vantage point and knew she'd been complimented. She shifted her gaze away again before speaking.

"My aunt seemed pleased that you asked her to join us."

"True. But if you'll notice, she's not here."

"No, she's not. She would say that my mother can't deal with the fact that I need a relationship with God, but I'm not sure she can either."

"It's easiest to be blind to our own sins."

Darvi silently agreed as the church came into view. The boardwalk would end in another 30 feet, and the church was still a block from there. They were nearing the end of the board slats when a horseman rode up. Dakota turned swiftly and brought them to a halt, but Darvi, whose hand was tucked in his arm, felt him relax.

"Sheriff," the Ranger greeted the rider.

"How are you, Rawlings?"

"Fine, and yourself?"

"I'm fine, thank you." With that the man tipped his hat toward Darvi. "You must be Miss Wingate."

"Yes," Dakota spoke up. "Darvi, this is Sheriff Laverty."

"It's a pleasure to meet you," Darvi greeted him.

"Your aunt tells me you're headed to church."

"Were you at the house this morning?" Dakota asked, his mind working so fast that he did not let Darvi answer.

"No, she came by my office as soon as Seth Redding showed up at her door looking for Miss Wingate."

Darvi's eyes grew large at this announcement.

"I'm not worried that he's going to try anything stupid," the law man went on smoothly, "but I'd just as soon not have you out and about today, Miss Wingate. In fact, if you wouldn't mind, the lawyer representing some of the bank customers was tied up yesterday when you came into town and would like to speak with you today. He's at my office."

"How did Seth know I was in town?" Darvi asked.

The sheriff's smile was lopsided. "Seth and Eliot seem to have eyes everywhere. Your coming in on the train would be no secret."

"And he was actually bold enough to go to my aunt's door?"

"Yes. She said he was very polite about it all, but that he seemed determined to speak with you."

From that point onward, Darvi's Sunday plans fell into a heap around her. Her expectation of spending some time in church and possibly fellowshipping for a time with the congregation was swiftly put aside. Knowing it was best to do as the sheriff asked, Darvi went with Dakota to a back room at the sheriff's office to meet with a Mr. Danby. He was a polite man, but all business. Some of his terms confused Darvi, but she asked enough questions to understand what her role would be the next day.

"All of this will be quite unnecessary," he said more than two hours later, his papers already in his case, "if Mr. Silk will simply admit to guilt—something we don't expect. But one can always hope."

Darvi could think of nothing to say to this, but something niggled at the back of her mind, even as the man stood, thanked her, nodded to Dakota, and went on his way. Dakota, good at his word, was with Darvi the whole time. He had been silent during the proceedings and was still quiet, giving Darvi time to think. A few minutes later she knew what was bothering her.

"This is all about Jared Silk, isn't it?"

"What do you mean?"

"No charge is being brought against Seth and Eliot for abducting me."

"Not at this time. Your testimony is about their involvement with Silk."

Darvi looked thoughtful and said with quiet conviction, "I'm going to have my say in that courtroom, Dakota. Even if none of the lawyers asks me about it, I'm going to tell them what happened to me."

Dakota smiled. "Go to it."

That smile was all Darvi needed until she had one more thought.

"Dakota," she asked, "why aren't Seth and Eliot in jail? Why is Seth allowed to roam the streets and look for me?"

"Because the law is imperfect, Darvi. I also suspect that his lawyer might have had something to do with it, along with the fact that you weren't here to file any charges."

Darvi knew she would have to be satisfied with this. She wasn't really content with it, but right now nothing could change her helplessness in the situation.

"I guess we'd better head back to my aunt's," Darvi was saying as the door suddenly opened.

"Oh! You *are* here," Renee spoke with relief as she entered. "I wasn't certain what could be taking so long, and I had myself convinced that Seth Redding had found you."

"He might find her," Dakota put in calmly, "but he won't take her."

Renee looked up at the Ranger's face and suddenly knew why Darvi was so trusting of him. Darvi's aunt liked Dakota—she liked him a lot—but there was no missing the steel in his eyes right now. Renee almost shook her head. She would not choose to tangle with this man if she was on the wrong side of the law. She thought anyone who did was a fool.

"Well, let's go home," she said quietly, simply wanting to see Darvi safe behind closed doors.

"That's fine," Dakota confirmed, "but if you don't mind, I'll answer the front door for the rest of the day."

All Renee could do was nod, but in her heart she was more determined than ever to see Darvi marry this man.

🌹🌹🌹

Sunday turned out to be a very quiet day, which made the noise and crowded courtroom all the harder to take the next morning. It seemed that every person in town had turned out for this event, and Darvi knew that, as his witnesses, if the lawyer had not saved seats for them in the front row, they would have been outside with dozens of others who were denied entrance.

The courtroom was set up with a center section of seating flanked by two angled sections. Renee, Dakota, and Darvi had seats in the far right side. Once situated, Darvi settled her skirts around her, Dakota on her right and her aunt on her left, before glancing around. She had barely shifted her eyes when she spotted Seth in the far left section. The way the seats angled, they had nearly perfect views of each other.

He was looking straight at her, his eyes reflecting caring and interest. Darvi didn't look at him for long but shifted her own gaze back to the front. Dakota, on the other hand, kept watching.

The moment Darvi turned away, Seth leaned and spoke to a man—assumably his lawyer—who shook his head no. He then wrote a note and gave it to his lawyer. He read it, handed it right back, and once again shook his head no. At that point Dakota turned away, but not before seeing that Seth's eyes came right back to Darvi, who was still watching for the judge to enter. That the man was desperate to see the woman across from him was only too clear.

Dakota gave one more glance Seth's way, and that was when he spotted Cassy and the children in the front row of the middle section. All three looked pale and sober, and Dakota was glad for Darvi's tender heart. His own felt a little broken as well. He had chosen to deceive Cassy in order to rescue Darvi. Given a choice, he would do it all over again, but it wasn't something he enjoyed.

The judge finally arrived. He was a large man with stern eyes, and the audience was very quiet as he took his place and cast those penetrating eyes over the room. No time was wasted, however, and in less than five minutes, things were underway. Mr. Danby, whose strict business manner seemed to have melted into something a bit more dramatic, called many witnesses forward to testify, but the defense offered no cross examination until Annabelle Hewett was called to the stand.

Darvi watched her aunt move to the witness stand in graceful confidence. The defense was out to prove that the reporter's testimony, which was quite damaging, was nothing more than the rantings of an overemotional female. Their tactic fell very flat. Renee kept her cool, calmly answering all questions and putting holes in several theories. From her vantage point, Darvi thought Jared Silk looked angry enough to kill.

The day moved on slowly, and Darvi, to her surprise, wasn't actually called to the stand until the next morning. She thought she caught the softening of the judge's eyes at one point, but in her nervousness she couldn't be certain. She took the stand and tried not to feel the awful pounding of her heart.

"State your full name, please."

This came from Mr. Danby, and Darvi did as she was told.

"Darvi Leigh Wingate."

"Address, Miss Wingate?"

"49 Brighton Road, St Louis, Missouri."

"Thank you, Miss Wingate. Correct me if I'm wrong, but were you not taken against your will from a train in the Aurora train station on the sixth day of September?"

"Yes, sir, I was."

"And am I right in thinking that two men took you from the train?"

"Yes, sir."

"And am I also right in believing that those two men are in the courtroom today?"

Darvi's heart froze and then pounded on, making her feel breathless. She was certain she had told him this. Had he not heard her, or had he misunderstood?

Mr. Danby, who thought she would answer immediately, seemed to freeze as well. He looked at Darvi's stunned face and tried again.

"Would you like to me repeat the question?"

"Yes, please."

"Can you point out the two men who took you from the train?"

Darvi's heart sank. "No, I cannot."

Mr. Danby blinked.

"Maybe you need a little more time," he said, his face going slightly red, his eyes showing some strain. "Look around the court-room again. Take all the time you need."

Darvi had all she could do not to look at Dakota and nowhere else, but she made herself take stock of the entire room. She had not been with those men for very long, but she was very sure they were not in the room. She looked back to Mr. Danby.

"Did you see them?"

Darvi began to shake her head no and then verbally answered.

"You're sure?" Mr. Danby tried again, but Jared Silk's lawyer had had enough and came to his feet.

"The woman has more than answered the question, your honor. What more could the man need?"

The judge waved him back down.

"Do you have another line of questioning, Mr. Danby?" the judge asked, his tone almost bored.

That man came just short of tugging on his collar.

"No, your honor," he admitted at last.

"Your witness, Mr. Robbins," the judge said to Jared's attorney.

"Thank you, your honor."

Darvi watched him come forward, a kind smile on his face, but it didn't fool her. She knew that all men had a right to a fair trial, but this man was out for blood.

"Now then Miss Wingate, there seems to be a bit of a misunder-standing here. You don't even know Jared Silk, do you?"

"No, sir, I don't."

"Have you even been into his bank or laid eyes on him before to-day?"

"No, sir."

"So anything you might have heard about Jared Silk is what you've read in the newspaper or been told by someone else. Isn't that right?"

"Yes."

The man's smile was just short of benevolent as he said, "That will be all."

"You're dismissed, Miss Wingate," the judge told her.

Darvi looked down just then and into Dakota's eyes. While he held her gaze, he raised his chin.

"Your honor," Darvi said a bit loudly, causing the judge to turn in surprise.

"Yes, Miss Wingate?"

"I would beg your indulgence, sir. I do have something to say, if I could just say it without having to answer questions."

"This witness has been dismissed!" Mr. Robbins nearly shouted, his calm face deserting him in a flash. Even Jared came to his feet.

"Sit down, both of you," the judge said in a frigid voice. "I want to hear what the lady has to say."

Darvi's eyes were huge in her pale face as she turned to face the judge, who was leaning toward her in full attention. Darvi made herself swallow and start.

"It's true, your honor, that I've never met Jared Silk, and that the men who took me from the train are not here today, but the two men who held me captive against my will are here today and have told me they work for Jared Silk." Darvi glanced their way and kept on. "Their names are Seth Redding and Eliot McDermott. I never saw the two men from the train again, but Mr. Redding and Mr. McDermott kept me in an apartment and made it very clear that I couldn't leave until I agreed to meet with Jared Silk."

"Why would they do that if you don't know the man?"

"They thought I was Annabelle Hewett, and even when they learned I was not, Mr. Redding decided to keep me. I was held at the apartment for two days and then taken against my will to Cassy Robinson's ranch. I had no idea where I was and no way to leave there."

"But you did get away?"

"Yes, a friend found me and got himself hired onto the ranch as a cook. We left one night after dark."

The eyes that the judge turned on the defense lawyer and Jared were colder than ever.

"Thank you, Miss Wingate. If there's nothing else, you may step down."

Darvi did so on shaking legs. She made her way back to her seat to the sound of the courtroom buzzing around her. Mr. Robbins was on his feet again, protesting the judge's interference and unorthodox behavior at the top of his voice. From their seats with the rest of the audience, the accused brothers and their lawyer had their heads close together, the lawyer doing all the talking. All three seemed to be completely unaware of the courtroom's state of pandemonium. The judge finally pounded his gavel to gain order and make an announcement.

"This court will adjourn until nine o'clock tomorrow morning, whereupon I will hear final testimony and make my decision. I will be available today until five o'clock for questions or further information."

With that he stood and exited the room. People talked even louder, babies cried, and in the midst of it, Dakota had Darvi's arm in a steel grip. Getting her outside as swiftly as he could manage, he moved her along through town, cutting off on a side street in hopes that it would be a shortcut to Renee's house.

In better time than he'd figured, the house came into view. Both still moving silently, Dakota took Darvi up the front steps, through the front door, and into the house, not even waiting a full heartbeat before he pulled her into his arms.

Twenty-Two

"YOU WERE WONDERFUL UP THERE," Dakota said softly, his arms still holding Darvi close.

Darvi let her head rest against the solid wall of his chest, thinking about how much she needed this man.

"I almost broke down," she said at last. "Could you tell?"

"No."

"It was when I caught sight of Nate and Lindy. I was so angry at Cassy for putting them in this position that I almost cried."

"You hid it very well, and you said everything that needed to be said. The judge was furious with Robbins." Dakota's chest vibrated a little with silent laughter. "You could see he believed every word you said, and Jared Silk looked as if he were going to explode."

Darvi put a few inches between them so she could look up into his face.

"I'm so glad you were there."

"I told you I would be," he said, thinking he wouldn't have missed it for the world. Seth Redding was still a free man, and for a moment, Dakota's thoughts clouded with all Darvi had been through and how much he wanted to protect her. He looked into her face and studied her eyes with tenderness before bending and kissing her very gently. Still holding her gaze with his own, he kissed her again.

"I was right," he whispered.

"About what?" Darvi breathed.

Steps outside drew them apart, and just after that, Renee came inside.

"How are you?" Renee asked Darvi as she came to hug her.

"I'm all right."

"You did so well. I was so proud of you."

"What do you think that judge will say tomorrow?"

"I think he'll end up throwing the key away where they're concerned. At least I hope he will." Renee hung her hat on the mirrored hat stand hear the door. "I've even heard that some of Aurora's crooked police will eventually be dragged into this." Smoothing her still-perfect coiffure, she finished, "Come to the kitchen. I'll make us some lunch."

Renee sailed ahead, clearly pleased with the way the morning had gone. Dakota brought up the rear, and as he held the door for Darvi, he bent and whispered close to her ear.

"Your mouth is very kissable."

By the time Darvi arrived next to the kitchen table, her face was the color of ripe watermelon. Renee turned to say something, took in that pink glow, and changed her mind. She went back to her lunch preparations with a huge smile on her face.

❧ ❧ ❧

"Are you going to try to see her?" Eliot asked Seth as he studied that man's back.

Seth stood at one of the windows in the apartment living room, his eyes on the street.

"I want to," he said at last.

"But you won't," Eliot guessed.

Seth turned. "No, I won't. I know this is our last day of freedom, but I can't take the chance that that Ranger will shoot first and ask questions later."

"He didn't do that when he was at the ranch."

"No, but jail time or not, I can't take that chance."

Seth turned back to the window. Eliot watched him in frustration. He hated this. It was never supposed to be this way. Jared was not supposed to mess up and get caught, bringing them down at the same time. And Darvi. She was supposed to love his brother and make him smile again.

A moment later Eliot told Seth goodbye and went on his way. They had just met with the judge. He had told them both to stay in town that night, but Eliot couldn't. If this was his last night of freedom, he wanted to be with the woman he loved.

❧ ❧ ❧

"I've made a decision," Darvi told Dakota that night. Renee had some business to attend to at the news office, so Darvi and Dakota were doing the dishes.

"About the trial?"

"No. Believe it or not, I've been thinking about my mother, and your mother is the reason."

"How's that?"

Darvi paused with her hands in the soapy water.

"You have such a wonderful relationship with your mother—she could even ask you about what you believe. I've so put off my mother by not marrying Brandon that she can barely stand the sight of me. I'm all ready to give her verses and share my faith with her, but she's barely speaking to me."

Dakota listened to the wonder in her voice and kept silent.

"I've been putting the cart in front of the horse. My next letter isn't going to say anything about Christ. I'm just going to try to get her to speak with me. What do you think?"

"I think you're right. Your mother is only going to see God as the problem unless you repair the relationship."

"I think so too. Our relationship has always been based on our pleasing each other. The moment one of us didn't do what the other wanted, we were in a fight. That's got to be fixed before anything else happens!"

With that Darvi went back to washing. Dakota watched her, not able to stop smiling.

You're like that to Your children, Lord—always giving us new insight and expanding our worlds with more knowledge, not just about You, but about how to live this life. I still marvel at how I survived without You, how I made a single decision on my own. But You must have been leading in those situations too.

And help my parents as they read my letter. Help them to see their need for You. Give Darvi just the words for her mother. Help her mother to read with an open heart and accept Darvi back.

"What are you thinking about?"

"I was praying."

"Oh, I'm sorry to interrupt."

"It's all right. Somehow I think God understands."

Darvi kept washing, but she looked very content. Dakota didn't think there was another place on earth he'd rather be than in Texas with Darvi.

❧ ❧ ❧

For the third day in a row the courtroom was packed. From their front-row seats, Renee, Darvi, and Dakota noticed that things became very quiet when the judge entered, and in just a matter of minutes, the charges were read and the courtroom heard that Jared Silk was going to jail for a very long time.

On the adjournment, Darvi and Dakota stood, Darvi wishing that her abductors were going with Mr. Silk. She was still thinking this when a police officer approached with Seth Redding, his hands cuffed behind his back. Seth stopped and looked down at her, his eyes as warm and caring as always.

"Hello, Darvi."

"Hello, Seth."

He studied her a moment, and Darvi thought he would move on, but he spoke again.

"Eliot and I turned state's evidence against Jared. Our time inside will be very short."

He paused now, as though giving her time to think about it.

"Please tell me I can contact you when I get out, Darvi. I swear, I'll never hold you captive again."

"I can't do that," Darvi whispered, her heart in terrible pain over this whole ordeal. She shook her head and tried to find words. She ended up saying, "For so many reasons, Seth, it just won't work."

The temptation was very strong to say cruel things and make her feel as bad as he was feeling, but Seth couldn't do it.

"You're quite a lady, Darvi Wingate," he now said, a small smile in his eyes. "Don't ever forget that."

The officer led him away then, Eliot and another officer some ten feet behind. Seeing Eliot brought Darvi's eyes to where she'd last seen Cassy. That woman's devastated face was staring after the departing brothers. Lindy's face was buried in her mother's skirts, and Nate's little visage was nothing short of tragic. Darvi glanced up at Dakota, who nodded as he guided her in Cassy's direction.

"I'm sorry I had to deceive you, Cassy," Dakota said to the ranch owner the moment she looked at them.

"Don't be, Dakota." Her voice was resigned. "You only did what you had to do."

An uncomfortable silence fell over them as Darvi cast about desperately for something to say. She then noticed Cassy's dress. It was her wedding dress.

"Did you get married?"

Cassy actually managed a smile. "Yes, we did."

"Was it nice?"

The other woman nodded, her eyes softening in remembrance, before becoming direct as she looked into Darvi's face.

"I've been doing a lot of thinking, Darvi. I need to hear more. I've been trying to read my Bible, but I'm not understanding. I need to hear more about the way you believe. Will you write to me?"

"I'd be happy to meet with you, Cassy," Darvi volunteered. "I'll tell you anything you want to know."

But the blonde was already shaking her head. "No. I need to be able to read it and think it over."

Cassy's gaze dropped, her face looking tired and ashamed. She moved as though she would turn away and leave, but Nate was pulling on her arm.

"Oh, yes," she stopped to say, looking back to Darvi. "I almost forgot. Nate wants you to know that at the end he knew everything. He saw and heard Dakota talking with the sheriff, and he even heard you leaving out the window the night you left."

Darvi looked down at him.

"And you didn't say anything, Nate?"

"Not for a while," the boy told her. "Not until after you left, and then only to Mama."

"Why, Nate? Why didn't you wake the house?"

He shrugged a little. "You weren't happy. I know Seth wanted to keep you, but you were sad. And I didn't think you should have to cry in your bed anymore."

Tears flooding her eyes, Darvi took him in her arms. The little boy held on for dear life. When he let go, Darvi looked down and smoothed his hair. Lindy came next, hugging Darvi with all the sweetness she'd always shown her.

When at last they stood apart, Darvi knew that Cassy would have to make the move. Darvi's heart was ready to burst when Cassy stepped forward to hug her. She and the children then left without another word.

"I think maybe we should head to your aunt's," Dakota said quietly, and Darvi only nodded.

Halfway there, she had a thought and said, "Too often I can't see why God does things or lets them happen, but right now I'm willing to admit that I had to go through all of this to open a door between Cassy and me."

"I think you might be right."

"I'm going to use those verses you gave me for Cassy instead of my mother. Do you think that's all right?"

"I think that's perfect."

It was good to cover the rest of the way in silence. Upon arriving, both were surprised to find that Renee had reached home first.

"Aunt Renee," Darvi said the moment she saw her, "thank you for everything. It's been wonderful seeing you and getting to know you, but I'm going to leave for Austin tomorrow. I hope you won't think me rude, but I want to go see Uncle Marty."

Renee hugged her niece.

"That's fine, dear. I was hoping you could meet my James, but maybe another time."

"You could always invite me to the wedding."

Renee smiled.

"I'll do that, Darvi Wingate, just see if I don't."

The three spent the remainder of the day in relaxed pursuits. Renee took Darvi and Dakota out to dinner and spent the evening regaling them with stories of her reporting escapades. Dakota had plenty of his own tales, and they laughed until way too late.

Nevertheless, Darvi stood by her word. Dakota still acting as protector and guide, they left the next morning for Austin.

Epilogue

Austin
One Month Later

Dear Darvi,
THE CHILDREN LOVED THE LETTERS YOU WROTE *just for them. You
would not believe their excitement. They are working on letters back to you,
but I wanted to reply first.*

*I can't thank you enough for your words to me. We miss Eliot terribly,
Seth too, but your letter gave me some hope and peace for my own heart. I
must admit that for a time I felt I'd sinned too badly to ever be forgiven by
God, but the verses you gave me would indicate otherwise.*

*I think we are going to take your advice and start going into town for
church on Sunday mornings. When I was shopping last week, I met a woman
at Dawson's who was very kind. I don't recall ever seeing her before but
found out that she's a pastor's wife. I know the church she goes to, and I
thought if she was typical of the congregation, we might be welcome. I'm
scared of such a move, but I'm more afraid of doing nothing.*

*Well, I've run out of words. Thank you again for the list of verses. The
Bible does make it very clear; I just need to figure out what my heart should
do. Take care, Darvi, and I'm sorry for all the pain we caused you. I wouldn't
mind hearing from you again.*

Sincerely,
Cassandra McDermott

Darvi lay her head back, her heart so blessed that she could barely
think. She'd received four letters and hadn't known where to start. A
little afraid of what her mother's letter might say, and certain that

Merry's letter would be good news, she had put them aside in favor of Cassy's. The one from Dakota's mother intrigued her; nevertheless, she saved it until last, glad that after she read her mother's letter, she could tell her uncle it was good news as well.

❧ ❧ ❧

Dakota was doing some letter-reading of his own. Having finally gone back to work on a job that put him under new command with a group of Rangers toward the south, he was just getting into Austin for his first leave. Upon his arrival he did two things: got a bath and checked to see if the post office had mail for him. A letter from his mother, which Cash had forwarded, awaited him. It was short. She thanked him, told him she would think about all he said, and went on to talk about some plans she and his father were making for the winter, possibly even a trip to Texas.

Dakota put the letter away with great hope. He didn't think he would belabor the point in his letters back to her, but she hadn't slammed the door in his face. His heart content, he heeled Eli toward Marty Bracewell's house. It had seemed like years since he'd ridden on official business, but in truth, once he was on the trail, it had felt like forever since he'd seen Darvi.

He used the kitchen door because he knew it would be open, and surprisingly enough found his boss sitting at the table reading his own mail.

"Well, Dakota, when did you get in?"

"Only just."

Brace smiled. "Your hair get that wet on the trail?"

Dakota smiled back. "It can get mighty hot out there."

Brace only laughed.

"Where is she?" Dakota felt he had waited long enough.

"In the living room. Her mother has asked her to come home for a time, so she's going next week, but right now she's reading a letter from your mother."

"*My* mother?"

"Yes," Brace responded, looking very pleased as he answered. "It was a pretty thick envelope. I suspect she's telling Darvi every rotten thing you did as a child. That would take more than a few pages."

Dakota had heard enough.

"Darvi," he called firmly as he moved that way, not missing the sound of someone scrambling and papers crackling. He went through the dining room, and sure enough, the living room was empty.

"Darvi." His voice was coaxing now, even as his eyes searched for some sign of her. He hadn't heard her on the stairs, and it took some doing to spot a bit of her skirt sticking out from the door that opened into the dining room. The door was open against the wall, and he could now see that she had scooted behind it.

He moved it slowly and tried not to laugh at her attempt at an innocent face.

"Dakota! When did you get in?"

He came close and put his hands on the wall on either side of her head.

"Just now."

"How nice," she said a little too brightly, all the while keeping her hands behind her back.

His eyes dropped down for a moment before coming back to hers.

"A little bird told me you got a letter."

"A letter?" Darvi appeared to think on this. "Now, let me see. Have I received any letters lately?" With that Darvi couldn't hold on. She laughed and brought out several pages.

"Is this really from my mother?"

"Yep," she teased him. "Every word. I'm learning an awful lot."

For a moment they just stared at each other. Darvi felt her cheeks grow warm and tried to divert his gaze with a question.

"Do you know when you head out again?"

"No."

"How about where you'll be going?"

"I don't know."

Darvi playfully shook her head.

"You don't know much, do you?"

"I know that I love you."

For Darvi, time stood still. She had never pushed this man to say those words, knowing she'd wanted it to be in his time and not her own, but she had been feeling love for him for a very long time.

"When did you decide this?"

"When I was near the river. It reminded me of the night we stayed on the trail and you met the rattlesnake."

"And that made you love me?"

He nodded. "It caused me to remember how many times I could have lost you. I don't want to lose you, Darvi. Not now—not ever."

Her heart filling her eyes, Darvi said, "I love you, Dakota Rawlings."

Moving very slowly and gently, Dakota leaned forward and kissed her. Darvi sighed when he pulled away. Dakota wanted to kiss her again but told himself that would have to wait.

"Brace tells me you're headed home next week."

"Yes, I prayed you'd get here before I left."

"I made it." He then added. "I'm glad your mother wants to see you."

"I am too, but I don't really want to leave Texas."

"But this time you'll leave knowing that I love you."

Darvi smiled. "And you won't forget my love, will you?"

"Not a chance."

This time Dakota didn't kiss her but took her gently into his arms. It was the sealing of a promise that both of them would keep.

LORI WICK

City Girl

HARVEST HOUSE PUBLISHERS

EUGENE, OREGON

Cover by Dugan Design Group, Bloomington, Minnesota

Cover photos © Walter Bibikow

CITY GIRL
Yellow Rose Trilogy
Copyright © 2001 by Lori Wick
Published by Harvest House Publishers
Eugene, Oregon 97402

ISBN-13: 978-0-7394-9555-1

Printed in the United States of America.

Acknowledgments

❦ ❦ ❦

Bob Hawkins Jr. It's a delight to work with you and be a recipient of your warm, wonderful humor. My Bob and I love laughing with you. We treasure both you and Beth more than we can say.

Kathi MacKenzie-Foster, Nina Stianson, O.J. Acton, Walt Seward, Mike Bailey, Vince Attardi, John Hurley, Phil Fleming, Marion Smith, and Bob Boyne. I always enjoy any time we can spend visiting at CBA. Your hard work does not go unnoticed.

Vivian Danz. So many people fill my life with joy, and you are one of them. Thank you for your precious friendship, joyful spirit, and also your words of wisdom.

Jayne Wiese. Your quiet, gentle spirit is beyond precious to me. I learn something from you every time we visit. Thank you for keeping on and for helping me do the same.

Todd Barsness. We are often blessed by your words, hard work, and laughter. The coaching is just an added bonus. Thank you for hours of compassion and creativity, and for putting God first.

My Bob. Well, we made it! The Texas trilogy is complete. Thanks for cheering me on along the way. I tried recently to imagine doing a book without you and decided it can't be done. Fun as it is to write a romance about another couple, you're still the only romance I want. It's funny, but even when I'm furious with you, I'm still head-over-heels in love. Thank you for 20 years of patience, love, laughter, and especially your guidance.

Prologue

REAGAN SULLIVAN PEDALED HER BICYCLE down the busy neighborhood street, calling greetings to everyone who spoke to her and trying successfully not to run over anyone's dog or child. She was tired after her day in the factory but jubilant over the news she'd received at the beginning of the week.

"You'd better watch yourself," a familiar voice called as she passed old man Cannon's house.

"I will, Mr. Cannon. How's your wife?"

"Pretty as the day I married her."

It was their standard exchange, and with a wave and a smile, Reagan moved on. She was almost home and sighed when she saw the sign for Mrs. Banner's Boardinghouse for Girls come into view. She hoped Mrs. Banner had a good meal for the night, one that included chocolate cake.

Pulling along the curb and swinging her leg over the bar to hop down, Reagan had the bike stopped and parked in the blink of an eye. She laid it against the stone steps that led up to the boardinghouse, and with the usual jog in her step, started to ascend.

A hand grabbed her arm suddenly as a voice called her name, but she wasn't too surprised.

"Just hold on now, Reagan," Tommy said, the usual smile in his voice. "You can just talk to me before the lady of the house catches you and says dinner is hot."

Reagan turned with a smile and looked up at Tommy Amhurst. He lived two doors down the block, and they had been friends for years.

"But dinner might be hot," Reagan returned in her normally straightforward way, "and I'm hungry."

"Never mind your stomach," he chided. "Tell me it isn't true. Tell me right now."

Reagan's smile grew by inches.

"But it is true," she replied, not feigning ignorance or able to conceal her excitement. "I'm leaving New York after the first of the year."

"For where?"

"Texas!"

"Texas? What in the world will you do there?"

Reagan nearly danced in her excitement.

"You happen to be looking at the newest nanny in town."

Tommy couldn't stop his mouth from dropping open.

"Nanny? Did you say nanny? As in a person who takes care of children?"

"That's right."

"But Reagan, you don't know anything about children."

The dark-haired, dark-eyed, petite woman only smiled.

"I'll just have to learn then, won't I?"

Tommy's finger came up to wag in her face. It almost touched her nose.

"You have had some mad schemes in your day, but this tops them all. What has come over you?"

"Nothing," she told him sincerely. "I just saw a way to get out and experience life a little, and I'm going to take it. I answered an ad, and the man even sent half my fare. I may never get an opportunity like this again." She suddenly smiled. "Not to mention, he's a widower. Maybe I'll find love."

Knowing Reagan as he did, Tommy's head fell back with his laughter.

"Reagan, are you out there?" a motherly voice called from the window. "Dinner's hot."

"Thank you, Mrs. Banner," Reagan called in return. She turned back to Tommy. "I've got to go in."

The man on the step below her only shook his head.

"You're really going to go?"

"Yes, I am, Tommy. I've run out of room for adventures in New York. I need the wide open spaces. On top of that, I'm not getting any younger."

Tommy knew he would miss her terribly, but in a way he envied her. He didn't know anyone half as gutsy or hardworking.

"I've got to go in," Reagan repeated as she started to turn away. "You'll tell me the exact date?"

"As soon as I know for sure." Reagan turned with one more saucy smile. "And besides, if I don't tell you a date, you won't be able to put together a big send-off party in my honor."

Reagan slipped inside just as her stomach started to growl, still managing a smile at the sound of Tommy's laughter.

🌹 🌹 🌹

One Month Later

"You'll send my bike? I'm too rattled to bring it right now."

"I said I would," Tommy assured her again.

"But you didn't promise."

"I promise."

"You have the address?"

"In my pocket."

"All right. Do it right away."

"I will. Have you got everything?"

"Yes. I'm fine."

The two stared at each other before both smiled.

"I envy you a little," Tommy admitted and then added, "but not enough to join you."

Reagan laughed and hugged him.

"You've been a good friend, Tommy. Write me if you get married or something big happens."

"You do the same," he said, knowing she never would. She hated letters and anything else that made her feel sentimental.

The two hugged once more, this time to the accompaniment of the train whistle. Reagan boarded, and Tommy turned away. He didn't want to watch her go. He almost stayed on the busy platform, thinking she might want to wave to him one more time but then remembered that it was Reagan. She would want no such thing.

And he was right. That westbound, determined woman had already found her seat and sat with eyes straight ahead, only occasionally glancing out the window. She was off to new sights and adventures. And tempted though she was, she reminded herself that there was no room in her heart for looking back.

One

St. Louis, Missouri
January 1883

SLATER RAWLINGS CAME QUIETLY INTO the room where he hoped his wife, Liberty, would still be sleeping, but as soon as he neared the bed, he could see that her eyes were open. She lay flat on her back, staring at the ceiling.

"How are you?" he asked quietly.

"The nausea was supposed to go away after three months."

Slater sat on the edge of the mattress, bent over, and kissed her cheek. He knew she wouldn't actually be sick—it might be better if she could be—but at this particular time in her life, mornings were not very fun.

"How about some juice? My mother always has some."

"Fruit juice?"

"Yes."

"That sounds good."

"Coming right up."

Liberty lay still and listened to the sound of her husband's footsteps. They were muffled on the thick carpets that lined all the hallways of Slater's parents' home. Charles Sr. and Virginia Rawlings had a wonderful two-story home in a fine neighborhood of town. Liberty had only visited one other time since marrying Slater nine months before. The first time she hadn't been expecting. She had hoped this visit would be as enjoyable as the last, especially since they had come for such a special occasion, but right now she was having her doubts.

Working at not being discouraged, she thought of the family that was gathered. The oldest brother, Charles Rawlings Jr., better known as Cash, had come from Kinkade, Texas. The middle brother, Dakota, was present; he had just resigned from his position as a Texas Ranger to take a sheriff's job in the small town of Jessup, Texas. And their grandmother, Gretchen Rawlings, from Hilldale, Texas, had also made the trip. Liberty reminisced over the time they had all gathered in Shotgun, Texas, for her wedding to the youngest brother, Slater.

"Here you go," Slater said, coming into the room with a large glass of juice in his hand. "How does orange juice sound?"

"Wonderful," Liberty said sincerely, scooting up against the headboard to drink. The first sip was just what she needed, and already feeling better, she drank more than half the contents.

"Thank you," she finally said, setting the glass aside and looking into her husband's eyes.

"I'm still asking myself if we should have come," Slater admitted.

Liberty opened her mouth, but Slater cut her off.

"And before you say anything about what Duffy had to say, you can let me have a second thought or two."

Liberty shut her mouth but still smiled a little.

Duffy was her stepfather. He was also her doctor. When word had come that there was to be a wedding after the first of the year, Liberty's heart had sunk, thinking it would be too close to her due date to travel, but then a second letter had come, saying the wedding would be in January. Liberty assumed they would go. Slater had other ideas. Liberty smiled as she remembered the conversation.

"Oh, Duffy and Slate, I was hoping I'd find you together," Liberty said as she entered Duffy's office with a letter in her hand.

"What's up?" her husband asked.

She waved a letter. "It's about the wedding; he's getting married in January. Isn't that good news?"

"We knew he was getting married, Lib, so why is this good news?" Slater asked.

"Now I can go with you," Liberty stated what she thought was the obvious.

"Let's get one thing straight," Slater said firmly. *"I'm not going to the wedding without you, and since you can't travel, I'm staying home."*

"But with the wedding in January, we don't need to stay home."

"It's still too close."

Liberty looked at her stepfather. "Will you please tell him?"

"It's fine, Slater," Duffy said, his bedside-manner voice becoming rather matter-of-fact. *"With her due date, it shouldn't be a problem."*

Slater's eyes grew suspicious. "Did she put you up to this?"

Liberty laughed out loud over this, Duffy joining her.

"Slater, Slater," Liberty said, her voice loving. "I'm fine, and the baby's going to be fine."

"You feel sick every morning," he argued.

"That's normal."

"It is, Slater," Duffy put in. "The stage ride to Keyes would be the most stressful part, and that's only 17 miles. Taking the train makes it a very easy journey."

"You did remember that we're talking about St. Louis, didn't you, Duffy? It's a long way."

The older man only smiled. Slater's eyes swung to his wife to find her smiling too. At that moment his face told them he was giving in.

"What's that smile for?" Slater now asked, breaking into Liberty's thoughts.

"I'm just remembering how panicked you were about my coming here."

"I have good reason. It's a long way in your condition."

Liberty could only grin.

"You are impertinent," Slater told her, but it was no use. As poorly as she had felt a few minutes earlier, she was glad she'd come, her smile attesting to that fact. Slater could frown all he wanted, but Liberty was delighted to be here for Dakota Rawlings' wedding.

🌹 🌹 🌹

"You have that tense look again," Dakota said to Darvi Wingate, the woman who was scheduled to be his bride in less than a week. He had just arrived at her house, and they were sitting alone in the parlor.

Darvi was from St. Louis, and if the guest list was any indication, a boatload of family had come to wish her well. That, along with the wedding paraphernalia that could be seen everywhere, indicated it was going to be quite the occasion.

"I am tense," Darvi admitted. "The caterer informed us this morning that he didn't know we wanted candelabra."

"Do we want candelabra?"

"My mother does," came Darvi's standard reply.

Dakota couldn't stop his smile as he teased her.

"I'm not going to let you forget that it was my idea to elope."

"And have my mother hunting us down for the rest of our lives?" Darvi reminded him with a theatrical shudder. "I know you'll forgive me. I'm not too sure about her."

Dakota suddenly leaned forward and kissed her.

"What was that for?"

"Do I need a reason?"

"This time, yes."

He studied her. "You're fun, and I'm in love with you."

Darvi gazed at him, her own heart in her eyes.

"That was a nice reason. I'm glad I asked."

"Oh, Dakota," Mrs. Wingate said from the doorway of the room; the couple had not even heard her approach. "I'm so glad you're here. Did you take care of the carriages?"

"Yes, ma'am." Having come to his feet, Dakota answered politely, not bothering to remind her that she had already checked with him on this subject. "They're all set."

"Good. There's no problem with your suit or those of your brothers, is there?"

"No, ma'am. Everything is in order."

Clarisse Wingate stared blankly at Darvi and Dakota for a moment before giving a small gasp and hurrying on her way.

"Is your mother going to make it?" Dakota asked compassionately when she had left.

"I hope so. When you consider that she wasn't even speaking to me in the fall of last year, we've come a long way. Having me marry in style has always been important to her. I took the chance away from her once; she's not going to be denied again."

"Well, if I have anything to say about it," Dakota said, sitting back with a smile, his eyes still on his fiancée, "she'll see you married."

"Is that right?" Darvi's smile held a teasing glint. "And what makes you so eager, Mr. Rawlings?"

Dakota tried to look nonchalant. He studied the ceiling with interest. "I'm just thinking that our trip to the gulf sounds nice. I've never been to the gulf."

Darvi laughed. She wasn't fooled in the least. He was looking forward to being alone and on their honeymoon as much as she was.

Dakota was reaching for her hand when Darvi had a sudden thought.

"Oh, Dakota, I just remembered something. Uncle Marty sent us a gift."

"That was nice. What is it?"

"I didn't open it. I wanted to wait for you."

Dakota watched her move from the room, loving how graceful and feminine she was. The uncle she spoke of had been Dakota's superior in the Rangers. He hadn't been happy when Dakota had wanted to leave but in the end had admitted that he understood.

"Let me get that," Dakota said as Darvi came back into the room, a large box in her arms.

Dakota waited for her to take a seat on the sofa and then set the box down so it would be positioned between them. Darvi had opened a few gifts already, presents from people Dakota did not know, so it was special for her to watch him open this box and remove the gift. It was a beautiful wall-mount coffee grinder.

"Oh, my," Darvi said as she took in the size and heavy cast-iron make. "This is wonderful. I think Uncle Marty knows how much you like your coffee."

"I think you might be right." Dakota suddenly stopped and stared at Darvi. "Are we thanking all these people at the wedding for this stuff or what?"

Darvi laughed until she was red in the face.

"Leave it to a man," she finally gasped, "not to know what's going on. If a gift arrives early, it's usually because the giver can't attend the wedding. I've been sending out thank-you cards as things come in."

Dakota looked rather sheepish but still laughed a little.

"Thanks for taking care of all this, Darv."

"You're welcome."

The couple's eyes met and held for long moments. Dakota was glad the box separated them. Darvi wished she could move it. Both were thinking: *Just a few more days.*

🌹 🌹 🌹

Cash Rawlings sidestepped a running child and the woman darting after him and made his way into the downtown shop. Each and every time he was in St. Louis to see his parents, he took a gift to his housekeeper, Katy. Knowing her personality, it had always been something practical. This time he was going to surprise her.

"May I help you, sir?" asked a friendly woman who met him in the middle of the store.

"Yes, please. I'm looking for something for someone who is a little older. I'm not even sure she'll welcome the idea," Cash added with a smile, "but I'm going to give it a try."

The perfume shop owner's smile was genuine, her eyes twinkling as she said, "I believe I have just the thing." She turned and led him to one of the three perfume counters, slipped behind it to face him, and from under that glass countertop withdrew a tray full of tiny bottles.

"Try this," she said, uncorking a small vial and waving the lid in his direction.

"That's nice," Cash said, but it had a scent he would term romantic. He almost shuddered as he pictured Katy's reaction.

"Too romantic?" the woman shocked him by saying.

Cash looked down at her and blinked. "As a matter of fact, I was thinking that very thing."

"I was hoping you were, in case you realize you have a second lady at home who would enjoy some perfume."

She was openly flirting, and Cash's smile was kind, but he stuck to the business at hand.

"I'll just shop for my housekeeper this time," he said, not unkindly. "Have you something else in mind?"

"I do," she stated, all at once becoming very professional. She put the first tray back under the counter and had Cash follow her to the next counter.

"This is what I should have shown you in the first place. I believe you will like it."

The woman was right. Cash inhaled the gentle scent and thought that not even Katy would be able to hide her pleasure.

"This is perfect," he stated quietly. "I need it gift-wrapped and able to travel."

"Right away," the woman agreed with a smile, wondering why some woman had not snatched up this charming, redheaded cowboy. His manners were faultless, and if the cut of his clothing was any indication, he was not living on the streets. But the thing she was most drawn to was his eyes. A deep shade of brown, they were so warm that even a stranger was made to feel as though he cared.

The package wrapped and secured for travel, the proprietress walked Cash to the door as if it were an everyday occurrence. It wasn't, but she couldn't deny herself the sight of watching him put his hat back in place and then seeing his long legs take him down the street. She knew her business would never survive out of the city, but for a moment she wondered just how far west she would need to go in order to find a town where the men were all like that.

❦ ❦ ❦

"How are you, Libby?" Virginia asked as soon as she returned from meeting with the dressmaker. Virginia's dress was done, but she had caught some of the excitement that surrounded this wedding and had gone in person to make sure it was being delivered that very day as promised.

Having removed her hat and gloves, she now came over to hug

the younger woman and kiss her cheek. "I'm sorry I wasn't here when you came down."

"That's fine. I'm feeling much better, thank you. I had a good breakfast, and I just came back from a walk."

"Did Slater go with you?"

"No, a message came for Dak, so he went to Darvi's to deliver it."

Virginia took a seat but didn't bother to get comfortable.

"At moments like this, I wonder if any of us are going to survive this."

Liberty smiled with compassion. "When we went to dinner the other night, Darvi told us her mother wanted her to have a wedding she would never forget."

Virginia's eyes rolled. "She's sure to have that, and if it will keep peace in the family, then it's worth it."

Liberty didn't comment but was well aware of the story. Liberty also knew that at times Dakota found *his* mother rather stubborn on issues she felt were important. Virginia Rawlings was not as worried about St. Louis' opinion as Darvi's mother seemed to be, but when it came to spiritual truths, she was almost stiff with fear and pride. Mr. Rawlings had been more open, and the discussions with his sons had given them great hope, but Virginia still seemed to be digging her heels in on the subject. So much so, in fact, that Dakota had told Cash and Slater, *If it wasn't for Mother's hesitance, I think Father would have come to Christ by now. He won't have anyone to blame if he waits too long, but I do think Mother is holding him back.*

"Is there anything I can do to help?" Liberty asked, even as she prayed for Slater's parents.

"I can't think of anything just now. Be sure you get your dress to Winnie so she can press it for you."

"She came for it yesterday."

"Oh, that's right. I saw it in the back hallway. It's beautiful, by the way."

"Thank you."

Virginia sighed. "I've got so many lists in my head, I can't keep track."

One of the staff came to the door just then with a question for the lady of the house. Virginia stood as she answered, moving toward the doorway, but then remembered her daughter-in-law.

"Oh, Libby, how rude of me to leave like this, but the truth is, I'm going to be so busy today. Are you going to feel terribly neglected, dear?"

"Not at all, Mrs. Rawlings. Slater and his grandmother have plans this afternoon to show me where she used to live. Darvi and I will see you at dinner tonight," Liberty reminded her. "Your sons are going out on their own."

"I'd forgotten about that," she said with a laugh. "Look out, St. Louis!"

❦ ❦ ❦

"Do you remember the time you tried to hide from Father in a stall full of hay?" Dakota asked Slater that evening.

The three Rawlings brothers were in a small St. Louis dining establishment. Their table was quiet, as was the rest of the place, and the smells coming from the kitchen told them their father's recommendation had been a good one.

"How could I forget?" said the youngest brother, shaking his head at the memory. "I still have the scars from that pitchfork I never saw coming."

"I came into the house and thought you were dead," Cash added. "All because Dak stood in the hallway and howled all the way through the doctor's examination of you."

Dakota shook his head and smiled. "I hated the pain of one of Father's spankings, and I thought a pitchfork in the seat must have been a hundred times worse."

"At least I didn't get both," Slater added.

"He wouldn't have done that," Cash added with confidence. "I heard him and Mother in the kitchen later. He was too shaken up about the blood all over your pants."

Cash suddenly looked at Slater. "What had you done?"

"Ridden Father's horse after I'd been told not to. I thought Father had gone to town, but when I came past the pond, I saw him headed into the barn. He came out a second later shouting my name, and I knew I'd been caught. He wasn't even looking for me in that stall, he said later, but he decided to fork some hay into one of the stalls before he turned the ranch upside down to find me."

"Father's probably hoping you have a son that gives you twice the trouble."

"Me?" Slater looked to Dakota in amazement. "I was easy compared to you, especially after you'd decided to join the Rangers. Why, you arrested the dog every day over something. You practiced holding your toy gun on Mother and Katy so much, the two of them still don't flinch at the sight of a weapon."

Both Slater and Cash had a good laugh at Dakota's expense, and he couldn't help smiling as well. The threesome fell quiet for a moment, and after several seconds, Cash realized his brothers were exchanging a glance. Cash was about to ask what was going on when Dakota gave some instructions to Slater.

"All right, Slate, you go first."

Slater nodded and looked to his oldest brother.

"You have to get married, Cash."

"Is that right?" Cash asked calmly. He didn't know whether he should be laughing or his mouth should be hanging open at this unannounced change in topics.

"Yes. Marriage is wonderful, and now that Dak is taking the plunge, it's your turn."

"To any lady in particular?" Cash asked congenially.

Slater turned back to Dakota.

"Go ahead, Dak, you've been in his church. Who could he marry?"

With this, Cash started to laugh.

"Be serious now, Cash," Slater scolded him. "You have to let Dak think."

"You two are crazy. Do you know that?"

"Never mind now," Slater directed, starting to smile too. "Let Dakota think."

"There was that one woman," the black-haired brother said thoughtfully. "She was sort of tall with blonde hair, I think. Is she available?"

Cash shook his head in amazement.

"Maybe Libby and I need to go home by way of Kinkade, so we can find someone for you," Slater said so matter-of-factly that Cash began to laugh again.

"Let me ask you one thing, Cash." Dakota's serious face was almost comical. "Have you been looking?"

"Not specifically, no."

"She's not suddenly going to drop into your lap," the middle brother chided.

"She did for both of you," Cash stated mildly.

This silenced the younger Rawlingses. They looked at Cash and then at each other in surprise. The waiter came to their table before anyone else could comment further, and all three men realized they hadn't even glanced at the menus. The waiter stood by while they looked over the choices. It didn't take long, and after they'd given their orders and the man had gone on his way, Cash spoke in a voice tinged with laughter.

"Shall we start this evening over again, gentlemen, or does someone want to tell me what that was all about?"

"We honestly want you to get married, Cash," Slater admitted, his smile lopsided. "It's nothing more than that."

Cash gave a moment's thought to this and then asked, "Is there something in my life that makes you think I'm not trying?"

Both men shook their heads no.

"Then I don't know what else I can do. I certainly talk to the Lord about it, but in truth, there is no one at my home church, and I don't want a mail-order bride. You both found love, and I have to be honest and tell you I'm looking for the same thing."

Forgetting where he was for a moment, Dakota sat back in his chair, the front legs lifting from the floor. His dark gaze was intent on his brother.

"Darvi did drop into my lap, didn't she? I hadn't really thought about it like that."

"Yes," Cash agreed, "and Slater dropped into Libby's. It doesn't always happen that way, but since there aren't any single women my age at church right now . . ." Cash shrugged as he let the sentence hang.

"Well, I still think you should," Dakota said, his brow drawn down in a stubborn way.

"If you find someone for me, I'll listen to you."

"Darvi's cousin is a believer, and she's pretty too," Slater said.

"Who's that?" Dakota was all ears.

"I can't recall her name. She's the one we met the other night."

"If you're talking about Wendy, Mother told me she's 17." Cash put his oar in, wondering if he should stop them or just listen.

Thankfully, their food came in record time, and from there the conversation turned to business, Dakota's new job and the town it was in, where he and Darvi would live, Slater and Liberty's life in Shotgun, and finally the ranch.

Either by design or by oversight, the topic of a bride for Cash was put on the back burner, and Cash was rather thankful that it was. His brothers wanted answers. He had none. In his mind there was nothing to talk about.

Two

"THANK YOU FOR DINNER," Charles said, following Virginia to the kitchen and kissing her cheek after she set a large bowl down on the counter.

"You're welcome," she replied, smiling as she looked up at him. "Do you think the girls liked it?"

"Very much," he returned, his voice warming perceptibly. "I would say our boys have done very well."

"And a grandchild, Charles!" She grabbed his arm. "I'm so excited. I don't suppose we could talk Slater into moving back to St. Louis."

Charles laughed. "He loves Texas, Ginny, not to mention that you told me you were in as much a mood to travel as I was. We already put off our trip to Europe for the wedding. I was hoping we could leave after Dakota and Darvi are off on their wedding trip."

Virginia looked at him in horror. "I can't leave now."

"Why not?"

"The baby!"

"The baby's not due until June."

Virginia opened her mouth but quickly closed it again. She had just seen a side of herself that she did not like. For years women in her association had been making fools of themselves over grandchildren; something she had vowed never to do. She and Charles had only recently learned that Liberty was going to have a baby, and here she was trying to fit her life around this grandchild instead of the man she'd been married to for more than 30 years.

"You're right," she said quietly. "The baby's not due until summer, and I did want to see Europe in early spring."

Charles put his arms around her and held her close. He didn't say all that was in his heart, but he was very proud of her. Unbeknownst to either of them, they were thinking of the same sets of friends who were grandparents. On Charles' part, he was picturing men whose wives would not stray from their grandchildren. The men were forced to sit and listen to tales of travel from other husbands whose wives accompanied them or who simply chose to travel without them.

Suddenly weary, Virginia thought she could rest in her husband's arms all night. But her daughters-in-law were waiting for coffee and dessert in the next room. After a warm kiss for the man she loved, she moved to get the good china teacups.

🌺 🌺 🌺

"How are you feeling?" Darvi asked Liberty.

"Most of the time, I'm fine. Mornings are still rough."

"Was the trip a bit long for you?"

"At times, but I worked to hide it."

Darvi smiled. "Why was that?"

"Slater wasn't really sure that he wanted me to do this, so I was trying not to worry him."

"Tell me something, Liberty," Darvi suddenly sat forward and asked. "Were you surprised when you first met the brothers, how little they look alike?"

Liberty had a good laugh over this.

"It lasts until you get to know them and watch them interact. They become so similar then that you forget about their looks."

"I haven't had much time with all three," Darvi noted, wondering if there would be such a time. She had enjoyed some great visits with Cash in Texas but had only just met Slater and Liberty.

"Are you all set for the wedding?" Liberty asked.

"I think I am. I've told myself I can't go crazy over every detail, and that seems to help. I don't know if my mother is sleeping at all, but most of the time I'm peaceful."

"Are there days you wish you'd just up and married?"

"Every day," Darvi said dryly, as both women heard their hosts returning. And the timing couldn't have been better. Charles and Virginia had no more arrived with the tray full of coffee and cake than Cash, Dakota, and Slater showed up.

"How was dinner?" Charles asked first.

"Excellent," he was told, his sons thanking him for the recommendation.

"How are you?" Dakota asked, having sat close to Darvi and taken her hand.

"Fine. We had a wonderful meal."

The two smiled into each other's eyes for a moment.

Slater had slipped into the seat next to his wife, his eyes studying her as they often did, first her face and then her waistline. Following his eyes and train of thought, Liberty smiled, and he caught her. He was giving her a stern look for laughing at his concern when his mother offered him coffee.

"Yes, please."

"So did you boys do anything else?" Virginia asked when she had served everyone and taken her seat.

Slater gave the details of the evening, which did consist only of eating a leisurely meal and coming home. He ended by teasing his mother. "We looked over the desserts at the restaurant, but we knew we'd get a better offer here."

This said, he took a bite of cake, his eyes sparkling over his mother's laugh.

"Is that so?" She tried to sound outraged, but she was still chuckling.

"It worked, Mother," Dakota reminded her, and everyone laughed at her look of surprise.

"This sounds fun," said a voice from the edge of the room, and everyone turned to see Gretchen Rawlings in the doorway.

"Come in, Mama," Charles invited, standing to give her his seat. "Have some cake."

"I couldn't eat another bite," she told him, having just returned from dinner with friends and taking the chair he offered.

"What restaurant did you visit?" This came from Cash, and in the time that followed, the eight of them fell into good conversation. The topics ranged from old family stories to the latest political subject. Some resorted to filibuster tactics to keep the floor, and with plenty of cake and coffee, it seemed they would go all night.

Darvi didn't want it to end, but she knew that her coming in would disturb her parents and thought that an early getaway from the Rawlingses might be better. All were sorry to see her go, but everyone was gracious as she and Dakota walked to the door and made their way outside.

"Have I mentioned that I'm sick of walking you home?" Dakota offered, his hand holding Darvi's as they covered the distance between his parents' house and hers.

Darvi tried not to be hurt by his words but found herself glad that it was dark out.

"No," she said quietly, working to keep her voice normal. "I don't think you've said that."

They had arrived on Darvi's front porch, a dark place at this time of the night. Dakota waited only until they had stopped moving to bring her gently against his chest and whisper in her ear, "I want to keep you with me. I'm sick of leaving you at your door and having to walk away."

Darvi relaxed in his arms, so enjoying his tender hold.

"It's not long now," she said as she felt him kiss her brow.

"Forty-eight hours."

Darvi tipped her head back and tried to see him in the dark.

"Mrs. Dakota Rawlings. I like the sound of that."

Dakota bent and kissed her, not a long kiss—that had to wait—but one filled with the tenderness he felt for her.

"I'd better let you go in."

"All right. I'll see you tomorrow evening at the family dinner, and then on Saturday . . ."

Dakota laughed. "I'll be there."

With one more hug, he stepped off the porch and walked into the night. Behind him, he heard Darvi's door open and close. Just a few more days and she could be with him, but in the meantime, his family was gathered as they hadn't been for a long time. He was eager to get home and share in that celebration too.

❧ ❧ ❧

"Cash," his mother said to him much later that night. The family had laughed and talked until some were drooping in their seats. When people started to head off to bed, Cash grabbed the serving tray for his mother and walked it into the kitchen. He hadn't planned to linger, but she caught him before he could leave.

"Yes?"

"It's time you got married," she said without warning.

If Cash hadn't contained himself, he would have laughed.

"Why is that?" he managed, a small smile coming to his mouth.

"Well," she tried, her brow furrowed a little as if she expected him to already know. "I was just watching your brothers with Libby and Darvi tonight, and I thought, 'I want that for Cash too.'"

"I appreciate that, Mother, but sometimes it's easier said than done."

Virginia looked thoughtful. "I suppose it is." Her eyes shifted around the room, gazing lovingly at the contents before looking back to her son. "Between this house and the ranch house, I prefer the ranch house. Did you know that, Cash?"

"No."

Virginia smiled. "You father built that ranch house for us. This house was already built. I love the kitchen at the ranch house and all the rooms. I love the way it's laid out. We've had some great times in this house, and I wouldn't want to move back to Texas, but I do miss that house." She looked Cash in the eye. "But even with all of that, I have no problem with another woman living there. I want you to marry someone who will enjoy the ranch with you. I want your children to grow up there, as you boys did."

Cash so appreciated his mother's words, but he couldn't exactly promise to give her what she wished. He wondered what she would say if he told her what her other sons had said to him that very evening. He ended up smiling at her and saying nothing at all.

"Well, dear," she said quietly, in what Cash knew to be her *mother's voice*, "when the time comes, remember that your mother will be delighted."

"Thank you, Mother," he said sincerely, knowing no end of relief that she didn't expect to hear a plan to make this happen. And her eyes, just before she hugged him, told him how deeply he was loved. He took himself off to bed, his heart wondering if God was trying to tell him something or if Dakota's wedding had just put everyone into a matrimonial mood.

❧ ❧ ❧

"You look a little pale," Cash said to Dakota just an hour before the big event.

"Do I?" Dakota asked, looking vague and not quite focusing on his brother's face.

"Sit down, Dak." Slater took his arm and led him to a chair.

"All right," Dakota agreed, but he sat for only a matter of seconds. "Is it hot in here to you?"

Thinking that letting him pace might be the best thing, Slater and Cash stood back while Dakota moved to open the window.

At the same time, all three men heard laughter from the next room.

"It sounds like the ladies are having a party," Slater said casually, but Dakota did not appear to have heard.

"How are you?" Virginia asked as she sailed through the door, Charles at her heels.

"We're fine," Slater replied, his eyes sparkling. "Aren't we, Dak?"

But Dakota wasn't listening. He had finally sat down and was staring blankly out the window.

His father found this highly amusing and started to laugh. His whole family was nearly hysterical before the groom noticed.

"What did I miss?"

No one could answer him. It had been a busy time for everyone, which left a certain level of fatigue on each person's part, making the incident seem funnier than it might have been. Nevertheless Dakota began to smile. His father's face was getting red, and he laughed a little in return.

"I think they're ready for you," one of the wedding coordinators said to Charles and Virginia as she stuck her head in the door.

"Thank you. We'll be right there," Virginia responded agreeably, moving swiftly to hug Dakota and say something quietly in his ear. Charles didn't hug him, but he smiled as he moved out the door, an older version of the groom himself. Dakota had been watching him and smiled in return.

The room was still quiet after the older Rawlingses went on their way, but the tension was gone. Cash, Dakota, and Slater sat quietly and talked—something they never seemed to tire of doing—until it was their turn to join the wedding party.

❧ ❧ ❧

Dakota's quiet and distracted state before the ceremony had not been the result of second thoughts. Not for a moment did he doubt whether or not he and Darvi should be married. But his heart had been prayerful, asking God to bless this union and help him to be the husband he needed to be. For this reason and many more, he was now able to stand in great joy and excitement and watch Darvi come up the aisle toward him.

Darvi's dress was a stylish creation of satin and lace, the very latest in fashion with a bustle that was just coming back into style. But the groom, had he been willing to admit it, didn't take much notice. His eyes intent on hers, he offered his arm when she neared, barely aware of the way Mr. Wingate let her go and took a seat with his wife.

Hundreds of people from St. Louis and family from far and wide had turned out to see these nuptials, but the bride and groom were hardly aware of them. Darvi heard someone sniff and thought her mother might be tearful, but she herself didn't want to cry at all. She worked to keep her eyes on Pastor Daniel Cooper, a man she had come to love and deeply respect since her conversion, but her gaze strayed repeatedly to Dakota, who was just as distracted by her presence.

They both grew solemn when it was time to repeat their vows, promises they were taking very seriously, and in rather short order, they were pronounced husband and wife. Mr. and Mrs. Dakota Rawlings turned to face the church and found smiles at every glance.

The couple led the way out of the sanctuary to the large hall where a banquet had been prepared. Taking their seats at the head table, they were joined by the family, and the merrymaking began.

"She looks beautiful," Liberty said to Slater, her head bent forward slightly to see down the table.

"Um hmm," he agreed, looking at his wife's face. "Like another bride I remember."

Liberty smiled as they leaned to kiss each other.

Down the table, Darvi was saying to Dakota, "It went so fast. Beforehand it felt like forever, and now here it's all behind us."

Dakota smiled at her enthusiasm just as his stomach growled.

"Didn't you eat breakfast?" she asked him.

"I can't remember."

Darvi looked very pleased with herself. "Well, you have a wife now. She'll see that you don't go hungry."

And down the table some more, Cash was sitting with Darvi's youngest bridesmaid, a sweet girl of 11 who wanted to know all about ranching.

"How do the cattle get to market?"

"We round them up and load them onto the train."

Not wishing to be impolite, she tried not to show her dismay.

"Doesn't it smell rather bad?"

Cash smiled. "In summer it does."

"What do the people do, just ride with a hankie over their noses?"

"Well, the cattle are not with the people. They have special train cars."

Cash watched as she bit her lip and giggled.

"I thought they were right in with the people."

"That *would* smell rather bad," he said and made her laugh again.

🌹 🌹 🌹

Hours later, after good food and lots of hugs and good wishes, the bride and groom climbed into a covered carriage and settled against the plush seat.

"You know," Dakota said for his wife's ears alone, his arm holding her close, "I couldn't help but notice that this dress has a lot of buttons down the back."

Darvi turned to look at him.

"It does, doesn't it? Do you think that will be a problem?"

"Not for me." He sounded very satisfied. "I'm a very patient man."

Darvi started to laugh, but Dakota caught it with a kiss before they both settled back to finish the ride to the hotel.

❦ ❦ ❦

"I've been reading the Bible," Charles told Cash at breakfast the next morning.

"What have you been reading?"

"Genesis," the older man answered and then seemed to be searching for words. "I'm a businessman, Cash. I try never to lead with my heart."

Cash waited, sure his father was going somewhere with this.

"I guess I'm just trying to say that I never saw God as logical before, but I'm very impressed with how He laid out the world and commanded Adam to care for it. And even after Adam and Eve had to leave the garden, God had plans for them. He never set them adrift, as it were."

"No, He sure didn't. Genesis is a great place to start, Father. That was wise of you to start at the beginning."

"There are some things that confuse me, though. I mean, why would Noah, after being so disciplined to do this huge job God gave him, get drunk?"

Cash smiled a little. "And why do I, knowing I was bought with a price, Christ's precious blood, commit sins and want my own way?"

"Why do you?" Charles persisted, truly needing an answer.

"Because I'm still a sinner. Scripture says the spirit is willing, but the flesh is weak. I've been saved from eternal death, but as long as I'm on this earth, the battle with my flesh will continue. I can choose not to sin at any time—God's Spirit inside of me gives me the strength to do that—but I don't always choose it. I sometimes want to sin and don't care that I've put myself out of fellowship with God."

"What does that mean, 'put yourself out of fellowship'?"

"My faith in Christ's life, death, and resurrection made me clean before God, but sin separates us from God, so when I sin, I lose communion with Him. I'm still His child—it's impossible to lose that—but until I confess my sin and repent of it, there's a barrier between God and me. He's a huge, forgiving God, so I have no excuse. I just need to agree with Him about my sin, and all lines of communication become open again."

Charles nodded, his face intent. He was opening his mouth to speak again but suddenly stopped. Cash saw his father's eyes dart across the room before the older man shifted his gaze to his coffee cup and took a drink.

Cash turned to see his mother had come in and let the door swing shut behind her. Cash watched her as she came to the table.

"You're talking about God, aren't you?"

Charles looked a bit sheepish, but Virginia sat down, her face open.

"It's all right, Charles," she shocked him by saying. "I've been doing some thinking of my own."

"On what exactly?"

Virginia turned and looked at Cash. "I've been patting myself on the back about this wedding." She smiled a little wryly. "I'm not sure why—Clarisse Wingate did all the work—but for some reason it's given me great pride that two of my boys have found wives. But in the midst of those thoughts, you came to mind. It's not that you're not married, Cash; it's what you believe. I was just short of taking bows over Dakota and Darvi's marriage, and then I thought you wouldn't feel that way. You would thank God for putting them together."

Cash only looked at her, still too surprised to speak.

"You would, wouldn't you, Cash?"

"Yes, Mother," he said gently. "I would."

Virginia sighed a little, her gaze going upward. "I just don't know if He wants me. I know Charles is interested, and I want to be, but I feel as though God is hiding."

"The God I believe in, the God of the Bible, doesn't play hide-and-seek with anyone. He's not capricious. Deuteronomy 4:29 tells us God can be found if we search for Him with all our heart and soul."

"Where does it say that?" Charles asked, standing as he spoke and moving to the small desk in the kitchen where he'd been keeping the Bible. When he came back, Cash opened the book and showed him the verse. Virginia pressed in to see as well.

For the next few minutes Cash took them to passages that spoke of God and His expectations of the people He created. Both Virginia and Charles were very attentive. Cash didn't press his parents, and after just a short time, he sat back and was quiet.

Virginia was the first to speak. "Charles, would you mind terribly if we didn't leave for Europe this month?"

"No, I wouldn't, but why wait?"

"I just want to hear more of what Pastor Cooper has to say. I want to go this morning and next week too. If we're leaving soon, I might be distracted."

Charles took her hand, and for a long time they looked at each other.

"I'm a stubborn old man," he said, having forgotten Cash's presence.

"You're in good company then," Virginia said, her eyes still on his. "You're married to a stubborn old woman."

Charles raised Virginia's hand and kissed it, but they weren't distracted with each other for very long. This subject was too urgent in their minds. Only seconds passed before they had more questions for their oldest son.

🌷 🌷 🌷

"What are you doing?" Liberty asked her husband when she found him poised outside the closed kitchen door. She was ready for the service long before she needed to be, and because she'd already had some juice, she was hungry.

"Cash is talking to the folks about spiritual issues," Slater responded, his voice low. "I don't want to interrupt."

Liberty nodded. She couldn't really hear what was being said, but she was quiet with her husband. They stood for a moment longer until Slater glanced at his wife's face. As usual she looked a little pale in the morning. He knew it would help if she could eat.

"How about," he started, "I take you out to breakfast?"

"All right. Do I need a sweater?"

"I'll keep you warm."

Liberty smiled in delight as he took her hand and led her to the front door. An impulsive outing was always fun in her mind, and she loved having time with her spouse, but even as they left, both husband and wife remembered to pray for the people in the kitchen.

Three

"YOUR FATHER GAVE ME THE LONGEST hug he's given me in years," Gretchen Rawlings told Cash, Slater, and Liberty after the train pulled out of the St. Louis station. "I don't know when I've seen him so tender."

The older woman's eyes misted over, and her three grandchildren let silence fall, but they understood just what she meant. The questions and discussions they'd had in the last few days and the interest they saw in Charles and Virginia had given them all renewed hope that someday they might set their faith, their future, in Christ.

It was five days after the wedding and time for all of them to head home. Before catching their own train back to spend a week on the gulf, Darvi and Dakota had spent a few days on their own and then come back to the Rawlingses' house to open gifts. Now these other four would ride together as far as Dallas before Slater and Liberty would connect to one train and Cash and his grandmother to another.

Everyone was on the quiet side. It had been a tiring time—fun, but draining both physically and emotionally. The family was weary. And Liberty was not just tired—she was hungry. She had not felt up to eating before they left, so it wasn't surprising that she was ready for food not too many miles down the tracks. The young couple asked the others to join them in the dining car, but both Cash and Grandma Rawlings declined.

"I'm rather glad we're on our own for a moment, Cash," Gretchen turned from the window to say.

"Why is that?"

"I've been meaning to tell you that you need to get married."

Cash looked at her, hardly able to believe his ears.

"You're the fourth person to tell me that in a week," he admitted quietly and found his grandmother's eyes widening in surprise.

His face was so serious that she put a hand on his arm.

"I'm sorry, Cash. Truly I am. That was very insensitive of me."

And that was all. No "buts," no explanation of good intentions or having only his happiness and well-being in mind—just an apology.

Cash smiled at her and she smiled in return, and although they shared no other words, Cash's heart was very thoughtful.

It was never my intention to be the last one, but it's not as if I'd planned it. I couldn't be happier for my brothers, but seeing them get married doesn't change anything in my life. Cash let his heart be quiet for a moment, and then he spoke to the Lord. *You don't have this for me yet. I don't need to even ask about it. I can see it with my own eyes. I feel I'm ready to be married, but You know me best.*

Cash could see that this was all he could say to God. He could thank God and trust Him for the future, but he couldn't expect God to act on something just because he felt the time was right in his human mind.

Cash's own sense of weariness suddenly intensified. He was so glad for the time he'd had with the family, but right now he was tired. A glance at his grandmother, whose stamina always amazed him, told him she was settling in for sleep too. Cash had no problem joining her. Even knowing he would have to move when Slater and Liberty came back, he stretched his long legs toward the seat across from him and let his body slouch down into comfort so he could sleep.

ॐ ॐ ॐ

Kinkade, Texas

There weren't too many trains into Kinkade each day, but Reagan had taken an early one. She had a name, William Harmond, and an address, and in her mind that was enough. She wasn't as fresh as she would like to have been for a first meeting with her new employer but felt sure he would understand.

The platform cleared swiftly, and Reagan was glad to have a moment to look around. She liked what she could see of Kinkade. It looked to be on the quiet side and nowhere near as large as her neighborhood in New York; she could tell that it was a town just her size.

"Excuse me," Reagan said when a man in uniform passed by. "May I ask you a question?"

"Certainly, miss. What can I do for you?"

"I'm looking for a Mr. William Harmond. Could you possibly tell me where he lives?"

"Yes, ma'am, it just so happens he lives next to my aunt. You go to the middle of town, and then a block to the north, turn left, and he's the third house on the right."

Reagan beamed at him. She never dreamed she would hear such clear directions.

"Thank you, sir."

The man watched her walk away, a small smile on his face as he shook his head a little. She had smiled at him as though he'd given her a sack of gold.

Reagan did not look back. She moved toward downtown, a woman with a mission, her eyes swiftly scanning the storefronts. She watched the door of the general store just being opened, reminded again of the early hour. It was a brisk day, but not at all cold like New York. Reagan had everything she could do not to smile and greet everyone she saw.

A bit of preoccupation over one advertisement in the barber shop window almost made her miss her turn, but with just a few maneuvers, she was on her way again. It didn't take long to find that the instructions had been perfect. Doing exactly as she'd been told, she stood in front of a large, well-kept home and saw the name Harmond on the porch. Thinking there was no time like the present, Reagan started up the walk.

A brisk knock on the wide wood door produced a woman. She didn't look like a servant, and Reagan could only hope he hadn't hired someone else.

"May I help you?" the woman asked.

"Yes, please. I'm Reagan Sullivan. I'm looking for Mr. William Harmond."

The woman nodded, and Reagan thought she looked at her oddly.

"I'll get him for you" was all she said before leaving Reagan on the front porch.

"Well, at least she didn't shut the door completely," the nanny muttered, wondering what to think of what had just happened. She wasn't given much time. Within seconds the door opened wide and a man stood there.

"Miss Sullivan?"

"Yes. Are you Mr. Harmond?"

"I am. Won't you please come in?"

"Thank you."

Her heart surging with excitement, seeing now that it was all going to work out fine, Reagan stepped across the threshold.

"You didn't get my letter," Mr. Harmond began before Reagan could even set down her bag.

"Yes, I did," she said plainly. "I wouldn't be here otherwise."

William Harmond hesitated, his mind scrambling for words.

In that instant, Reagan knew something was wrong, and it wasn't hard to figure that the woman at the door had something to do with it. Nevertheless she was going to wait for this man to admit it.

"How is it you got my letter if you're just now arriving? I mailed it two weeks ago."

Reagan smiled. "I left early and took a little time to see the country."

Mr. Harmond nodded. He had hoped to avoid this, but now he had no choice.

"I must tell you, Miss Sullivan, that since I contacted you the first time, I've taken a wife."

"Have you now?" she asked calmly.

"Yes."

"And that would have been mentioned in this letter that I missed?"

"Yes. I'm sorry you've had to come all this way."

Reagan eyed him for a moment and then let her gaze take in the foyer. It would have been a nice place to work.

"Well, I guess that's the end of it," she said, not with a stinging tone but one that spoke of regret.

"I'm sorry."

Reagan smiled at him and started toward the door. Mr. Harmond was there ahead of her, his gaze anxious as he watched her. For this reason he saw the exact moment she stopped. He froze when she turned to him, not at all sure what she might do or say.

"Who did you marry?"

Nearly flabbergasted at the question, the man still managed, "Beth Barton."

"Where did she work?"

"She was a cook at the hotel."

Mr. Harmond was awarded one of the smiles that drew people to Reagan.

"I'll have to head there then, won't I? They'll be needing a cook."

William Harmond couldn't stop his shoulders from shaking. He'd never encountered anyone with such charm and pluck.

"Good day," Reagan said as she moved out the door, across the porch, and down the steps. She was halfway down the walk when he called her name. Reagan turned to see him approaching.

"This is for you," he said, his hand outstretched to offer money to her. "I only sent half your train fare because I didn't know if you'd really come, but this should be enough to get you home if the hotel has already hired someone."

Reagan took the money without hesitation.

"I thank you, Mr. Harmond. As I don't even know where I'm sleeping tonight, I thank you indeed."

They parted company then, Reagan back to the main street of town and Mr. Harmond back to his wife. Mr. Harmond was not sorry he'd married; indeed, he was quite content, and Reagan, although sorry the job didn't pan out, felt it was early enough in the day to still land on her feet.

2. 2. 2.

Russell Bennett, a mountain of a man, wiped the sweat from his brow, put down his hammer and tongs, and stepped away from the forge in his blacksmith's shop. He needed a drink and a rest from the fire. Business was brisk, and this was his day to work in the shop. He wouldn't make calls to the ranches until Monday. Not only taking a drink but pouring some on his neck as well, Russell had only just set the water jug aside when he spotted her.

Standing in the middle of the double doorway, right where the horses came and went, was a small, dark-haired woman. She stood erect, a single bag grasped by both hands and held in front of her.

"Can I help you?"

"I don't know, but I was wondering what I need to rent one of your stalls for a time."

"You need a horse."

Reagan nodded.

"Would you say a horse is a pretty expensive item, something a person would want watched with care?"

Trying not to smile, Russell said, "I would agree with that, yes."

"Well, that being the case, would it be possible to leave my bag in a stall for a time? I've got business here in Kinkade, and the bag's heavy enough to add inches to my arms."

Russell did smile then. He also pointed toward a stall.

"No one will disturb your bag if you leave it right there."

"Right here?" Reagan asked, setting the bag down so that it couldn't be seen from the door.

"That's the place."

Regan brought up the small purse that hung from her wrist to look for a coin.

"You don't need to pay me."

Reagan eyed him.

"Are you going to rent that stall and let some animal step on my things?"

Russell laughed at this, a booming sound that made Reagan smile.

"No," he told her, still chuckling. "I close down at five. Just be back before then so you can get your things."

"I thank you, sir."

"What's your business?" he asked her as she began to walk away.

Reagan answered with only a glance over her shoulder. "I'm job hunting."

That said, she continued on her way.

Russell stood still for a moment, a smile on his face. His own dear Holly would have to meet this one. Unless he missed his guess, she was too independent by half and just might need a friend in Kinkade.

☙ ☙ ☙

"I need to see the manager," Reagan said for the second time.

"What about?" the little man at the rear of the dining area asked again. She hadn't been willing to give her name, and he thought this might work.

"I'll tell the manager when I see him."

It went a long way toward strengthening Reagan's resolve to hear pots crashing behind the closed door to the right of her and a woman's voice above it all. It didn't take any great skill to hear that she was unhappy.

"Do you have an appointment?"

"Do I need an appointment?"

The little man gave up, saying with long-suffering, "Wait here."

Going through the very door Reagan knew led to the kitchen, the man disappeared. As Reagan watched, her eyes caught a glimpse of a kitchen she felt sure had seen better days. For a moment she doubted her idea, and at that moment a woman appeared.

"Meddlesome busybody," she muttered. "As if I can't use a few minutes out of that steaming kitchen." The flushed woman didn't see Reagan until she was almost on top of her, but she didn't look sorry, only hot and cross.

"Are you the manager?" Reagan asked.

"I am. What can I do for you?"

"I hear you need a cook. I'd like to apply for the job."

Much as the woman looked as though she needed relief, she still asked, "Do you have any experience?"

"Not much, but I'm a fast learner."

The woman's eyes rolled heavenward. "As if I have any time to teach you."

Reagan eyed her, taking in the stains on her apron and the beads of sweat over her upper lip.

"Maybe you're right. It doesn't look like much fun."

Reagan was turning away when the manager said, "It pays well if you're experienced."

Reagan turned back in surprise. Had she not heard her say she wasn't?

"What does it pay if you're not experienced?"

The manager smiled. "I like your honesty."

"I won't promise something I can't give you."

The two eyed each other.

"So how much experience have you had?"

"I can cook anything. I've just never done it for a large group."

"Well, that's a start."

"You didn't answer me about the pay."

The woman quoted a wage that was so low Reagan was outraged.

"*A week?*"

"That's right."

"I'm used to twice that."

"Where are you from?"

"New York."

"This is not New York."

"I know that, but I don't even have a place to stay. It could cost a fortune to live in this town!"

"It's not that bad, especially since you can eat here anytime you cook. That would leave most of your pay for rent."

"And clothing. Kitchen work is murder on fabric."

The manager smiled; this one was as dumb as a fox.

"I'm Sally March, by the way." The woman offered her hand.

"Reagan Sullivan."

"Megan?"

"No, Reagan with an *R*."

"That's different."

"*I'm* different."

"I can see that. I'm willing to give you a try, but it's only fair to warn you that my cousin from Cincinnati is supposed to be coming to take this job. If he ever shows up, I might not need you."

"Well, at least for the moment I'll have work, but I'd better warn you, I plan to eat plenty."

Sally's eyes twinkled. She didn't know what the food would taste like, but the new cook was sure to lighten the load and the atmosphere. There wasn't much to her, but over the years Sally had found that the plucky applicants worked the hardest. Indeed Sally was getting ready to put her to work when Reagan moved as if she was leaving.

"I thank you for trying me, Mrs. March. I'll see you tomorrow."

"It's Miss, and you can call me Sally. I was thinking you'd be start-ing right now."

Reagan faced her squarely.

"I just got off the train. I don't have a place to live, and I haven't eaten yet today. If I find a place to stay, I'll come back as soon as I can, but for right now, I've got to make plans for tonight."

"Fair enough. Plan to eat when you get back here, even if you don't have a chance to work. The least I can do is feed you."

Reagan smiled and left without another word. She wasn't at all sure where to start, but start she would.

"A place to stay on only my new salary," she said quietly to no one but herself. "This could take awhile."

❧ ❧ ❧

"Whose bag is this?" Holly Bennett asked of Russell when she brought him his lunch.

"Some little gal's. I didn't get her name."

"Did she take a horse?"

"No. She said she was job hunting and the bag was heavy."

Russell smiled at his wife's wide eyes.

"She knew what she wanted, Holly. You would have liked her."

Holly looked at him teasingly. "I don't know what you're talking about, Mr. Bennett. You speak as though I've been strong-willed in the recent past."

She chose to turn her back on him and jumped a little when he landed a swat on her seat.

"Russell Bennett! Someone could have seen that."

But the blacksmith had just put half his sandwich in his mouth and managed to look innocent as he chewed.

Holly only shook her head. He was always so much fun.

"Where's Alisa?" Russell asked.

"Mrs. Ellis stopped in and offered to stay with her, but I should probably get home."

"Thanks for lunch."

"You're welcome. I'll see you tonight."

A quick kiss later, Holly went on her way. Russell watched as she turned back at the door and waved at him the way she always did. He waved in return, but as soon as she was gone, his eyes landed on the bag that had been left. He wanted to laugh all over again. He also wondered how the mystery woman was doing.

🌹 🌹 🌹

"This door has no lock on it."

"You want how much a week?"

"I have to share a bed?"

Those were Reagan's three responses to the three places she checked. Kinkade not lacking for rooms to rent, but it was also clear why some of them were empty. Nevertheless she was undaunted. At the moment, Reagan was following directions she'd been given at the general store and found herself wishing she'd started there. The lady had been kind, almost motherly, and not asked a dozen questions that Reagan did not have time to answer.

"This must be it," she said, still talking to herself.

Knock on the door of the big house, not the little one.

"I don't even see a small house," Reagan mumbled as she remembered the woman's words and climbed resolutely onto the porch. She was about three blocks from Mr. Harmond's place and thought that if this didn't pan out, she might have to ask him for help, at least for the night.

"Of course Sally might have an idea. That would probably be . . ."

"Hello."

Reagan had not heard the door open, so she was startled to hear someone speak to her.

"Hello. My name is Reagan Sullivan, and the woman at the general store said you might have a room to rent."

"Oh, I do, yes. Did you say your name was Megan?"

"No, it's Reagan with an *R.*"

"It's nice to meet you, Reagan. My name is Holly. Would you like to see the house?"

"It's a house?"

Holly Bennett smiled. "A small one."

"How much is the rent?"

She named a price that made Reagan's heart sink.

"Would you still like to see it?"

"Well," she said honestly, her truthful nature rising to the surface, "it's a little steep for my pay right now."

To her surprise the woman smiled.

"Why don't you see it anyhow?"

Not sure if this was wise or not, she agreed.

Holly Bennett led the way around her own house and down a short lane. About 20 yards behind the main house was a small structure. A shed might have been the best description, but it was in good shape and had windows and a front door that made it look like a small house.

Following the woman, Reagan walked over the threshold behind her host, and in the space of one heartbeat fell in love. All in one room, this tiny house had every amenity. In one corner was a brass bed, and next to it was a low table. Opposite the door was an overstuffed chair with an ottoman, and behind the chair was an oak dresser. A tiny stove sat next to a table for two and there were even shelves for a pantry. Holly opened a closet that had been built in behind the front door, and Reagan could only stare.

Reagan had never imagined such a place. Visions of living alone, something she had never done—quiet mornings and no one snoring in the night—floated through her mind.

"How much did you say it was again?"

Seeing her face, Holly made herself quote the price she and Russell had decided on. It was hard to do because she wanted this woman to move in, but she remained true to her agreement.

Reagan licked her lips. She would probably be in rags because she wouldn't be able to afford new clothes, but she couldn't let this get away.

"Is there a lock on the door?" she remembered to ask at the last minute.

"Of course," Holly answered in surprise.

Reagan felt a smile building up inside of her. She wouldn't even have a blanket for the bed that night, but the thought of being chilly didn't stop her. Before she headed back to the livery for her bag, she gave Holly Bennett the money for one month's rent.

Four

RUSSELL REALIZED SHE COULD HAVE taken her bag and left, but she didn't do that. He had been busy shoeing a horse when she returned, and when he looked up she was standing there, the bag at her feet.

"Thank you for watching my bag."

"You're welcome," the big man said as he used his handkerchief on his face. "How did the job search go?"

"I found one, and a place to live as well."

"Well, now, you've been busy."

Reagan couldn't hide her pleasure and didn't try.

"So where do you work?"

"At the hotel, in the kitchen."

Fearing that her skills would be inadequate, she hesitated to call herself a cook and then find herself out of work in a week.

"So you cook?"

Reagan smiled. "I hope so."

The big man laughed again.

"And where did you find a place to live?"

Reagan's guard went up in a hurry. She had learned many survival skills living in New York City, and one clear law was not volunteering information to strangers. Her hand came out as if he hadn't spoken. Russell shook it automatically.

"Thank you again for watching my bag."

"You're welcome."

With that she moved on her way.

The blacksmith was not exactly sure what had happened, but a customer came in the door looking for his horse, and he ran out of time to speculate.

🌿 🌿 🌿

"Well, you certainly can eat a lot, can't you?" Sally said about an hour later, having watched Reagan methodically polish off a large plate of food.

"It's good food."

"We certainly want the customer to feel that way," she said pointedly, but Reagan only smiled.

"Actually," Sally started again, "I need to tell you that I want you to come in the mornings and bake. If the truth be told, I don't mind the cooking. It's the baking I hate."

"All right. I can do that. What time?"

"You'd best be here by four, since the first breakfast customers come between five and half past. You'll bake all the bread, rolls, pies, and cakes for each day."

"All right, and when do I get my first raise?"

"Raise? You haven't even started."

"I know that, but you said my pay was because of inexperience. I just figured when I had some experience, it would be worth it to you."

Sally's look was shrewd, but Reagan met it unflinchingly.

"I'll let you know" was all she would say.

"Oh, don't worry about it," Reagan replied lightly, "I don't mind asking again."

Sally was taken off guard and found herself laughing. She'd have kept on laughing if she hadn't heard an impatient sniff. She turned to see her front-desk man standing nearby, his face disapproving when he saw that Reagan was eating. It told him she'd been hired.

"What is it, Pierce?"

"I was wondering if you'd had a chance to look at those ledgers yet."

"Yes, they're done and on my desk."

"Thank you."

After he walked away, Sally shook her head.

"He drives me crazy."

"Why do you keep him on?"

Her brows rose as if Reagan should know.

"His manners at the front desk are excellent. The customers love him."

She sounded so aggrieved that Reagan smiled.

"Well, if you're finished eating, you can clear out."

"You don't want help tonight?"

"Tonight's all done—that's what you're eating. I'm always done cooking by three, and the waitresses, who will be here any minute, do the coffee and small stuff."

Reagan stood. "So I'll see you in the morning."

"Four o'clock."

Reagan stared at her for a moment.

"Thank you, Sally, for everything."

"You'll earn it, Reagan," the older woman said confidently, albeit kindly.

Reagan retrieved her bag from near the door and stepped outside. It was time to head home.

🌿 🌿 🌿

"Here you go," Holly said to her daughter that evening as she handed her a piece of bread.

"Thank you, Mama."

"How about you, Russ?"

"Yes, please. Elly, would you please pass me the butter?"

The ten-year-old handed it to him and then realized she needed it back for her own bread. They spent a little time working together and then laughed when seven-year-old Jonah realized he needed bread with butter too and the passing began all over again. Nine-month-old Alisa sat in the high chair, smiling at anyone who would look her way and cheerfully eating whatever was offered.

"Someone is in the little house, Papa," Jonah announced to his father.

"Mama told me," Russell said. "Did you meet her?"

"No, she's not home now, so we can't meet her."

"I think I might have met her earlier today," Russell told his children. "A woman asked me to watch her traveling case, and I think it might be the same one."

Having said this, Russell found his wife's eyes on him.

"What's the matter?"

"Is that the only bag she has—the one you watched for her?"

"I don't know."

Holly worried her lower lip for a time.

"Russell, she probably doesn't have sheets or blankets or anything. I left a lantern, but would she find it and the matches if she didn't return until dark?"

Husband and wife finished eating as soon as they could, and leaving Elly in charge of her siblings, took their own lantern to the rear of the lot toward the little house. Even from a distance they could see a light burning. Holly knocked on the door but still called out so as not to frighten their new tenant.

"Reagan, it's Holly."

The door opened.

"We're sorry to disturb you, but we thought you might need some things."

Reagan didn't answer. She was too busy staring at the large man behind Holly. When he smiled, she recalled her manners.

"Come in," Reagan invited and stepped back. Even so, Reagan took a moment to recover, especially since the room shrank visibly with the blacksmith inside.

"We wanted to make sure you had everything you need, Reagan," Holly said again, having already taken in the things laid on the dresser, but also seeing absolutely nothing on the bed. The room was warm from the fire Reagan had lit in the stove, but Holly was not comforted.

"I'm doing fine," Reagan assured her landlady. "But if I could impose upon you for one thing, I would be very grateful."

"Just name it."

"A pillow. I don't think I'll sleep well without it."

"But you do think you'll sleep well without blankets and sheets?" This came from Russell before he realized they'd never been introduced. "I'm Russell, Holly's husband."

"I'm Reagan," that lady told him. "Did you put this little house together?"

"Yes, ma'am."

Reagan took in the way his head almost touched the ceiling.

"How did you manage that?"

"It wasn't easy," he replied, smiling in a way that belied the words.

Reagan and Holly laughed a little just before both of them heard a small voice.

"Papa?"

It was Elly. Russell opened the door for them, and Reagan smiled as Elly entered with Alisa in her arms and Jonah coming just behind.

"It looks like the whole family is going to welcome you, Reagan. I hope you don't mind."

"Not at all."

"This is Elly, and next to her is Jonah, and the baby is Alisa. Children, this is Miss Sullivan."

Holly plucked Alisa from Elly's arms as the two older children came over to shake Reagan's hand.

"You're the first one to live here," Jonah informed her. "I wanted to live here, but my room is in the house."

"Well, you'll just have to come and visit me. Will you do that?"

Jonah was only too happy to nod in agreement, and he might have had more to say, but Russell was ready to bring the party to an end.

"All right, children, let's give Miss Sullivan a little privacy now. We'll head back to the house and leave the ladies alone."

"Thank you," Reagan said when they all turned to tell her good-night. In just a moment she was alone with Holly.

"Reagan, do you have pots or pans or even anything to eat?"

"I don't, Holly, but I'll be doing most of my eating at the hotel, so that's not really much of a concern. I guess it would be nice to have a blanket, but I've got plenty of clothes and the stove is going to keep me nice and warm."

Holly didn't comment on that particular remark but did say, "I'll head back to the house and gather some things for you. We have plenty to spare, so there's no need for you to be going without."

"Are you certain, Holly? I mean, you have three children."

The other woman was already shaking her head.

"It's not a problem."

Reagan stood in a mix of emotions when her landlady left, so pleased to have a place to live and a job, but also feeling the effects of a long day. She was tempted to sit down but knew it would be too hard to get back up. It was with relief that she heard Holly returning.

"Okay," Holly said when she was back inside, a basket overflowing with a pillow, a quilt, one blanket, a set of sheets, and several sizes of towels. "I took you at your word about the food, but you can't sleep on a bare bed."

Reagan smiled at her adamancy.

"Oh!" Holly suddenly remembered, her hand going to the pocket of her apron. "Russell sent this out to you."

Reagan looked at the money in Holly's hand but didn't take it.

"What is it?"

"Russ has lowered the rent, and this is the difference."

"Why is he doing that?"

"I told him it was a bit steep for you, and he doesn't want you to struggle."

Reagan didn't speak, but she was thinking, *Could these people be real?*

"Take it, Reagan." Holly pushed the money toward her. "He won't want it back."

Reagan took the offered money, not sure what she thought.

"Can I help you with anything, Reagan? We could have this bed done in no time."

Reagan looked into her kind face and thought she really had landed on her feet in this town. Almost all the people in Kinkade had been kind, and her landlady was especially so.

"Thank you, Holly, but it's no trouble. You've been very kind, and before it's over I'll probably need something else, but for right now, I'm doing fine."

"I'm glad, Reagan. Just come right to the back door if you find you do need something, even if it's in the middle of the night."

Holly took her leave, and Reagan found herself alone once again. Not until that moment did she remember the money in her hand. She looked down at it, her brow furrowed in thought. Had the blacksmith asked where she'd found a place to live only out of curiosity and kindness, or was there something more?

"His wife is beautiful," Reagan said quietly, "but more than one man has wandered in spite of that."

She hoped she had read the situation all wrong, but why would he return about a quarter of her money in exchange for nothing?

Reagan had a sudden need to check the already locked door. She went to each window and found them secured as well. Not liking the thought in her mind, Reagan nevertheless faced the fact that Russell Bennett might not be as respectable as she first thought.

※ ※ ※

"Is she settled, Holly?" Russell asked once the children were in bed. He'd taken his bath and gone to the bedroom to find Holly changing into a nightie and starting on her hair.

"I think so. She looked tired to me, but she didn't want help with the bed." A huge yawn escaped her. "If she's like me tonight, she'll sleep hard."

"What did she say about the returned rent?"

"Not much, but I'm not sure she liked it."

Russell was quiet over this. He had debated what to do about the rent, and in the end was glad he'd given some back, but there was a chance he could have given the wrong impression, or even that they would find themselves taken advantage of. He wasn't all that keen about being a landlord in the first place, and he and Holly had both decided that if it didn't work out, they would not rent "the shack," as they called it, to strangers again.

"Of all the people I tried to imagine would be our first tenant, Holly, I don't think Reagan fit the bill."

"What type of person did you expect?"

Russell's smile was lopsided. "Some homeless man with a drinking problem, maybe. I don't know."

Holly only watched him climb into bed.

"Did you get to know anything about her?" he asked as he lay down on his back.

"Not before I let her rent the place. I mean, she mentioned that she couldn't afford it, and just now she told me she's working at the hotel, but you had already mentioned that." Holly chewed on her lip, a sure sign she was worrying. "Did I mess things up, Russell?"

"No," he said quietly. "But when I'm feeling tired, like I am tonight, having someone else in my life to take care of makes me weary."

Holly was now ready for bed and joined her husband.

"Well, you might have emotions involved simply because she's the type of person who causes that, but something tells me that Reagan is used to taking care of herself."

"You're probably right."

Both husband and wife had run out of steam. Neither one moved to kiss the other goodnight. Russell simply reached for Holly's hand to squeeze it, and Holly mumbled a goodnight. Russell was thinking that he loved her and should say so, but sleep was rushing in fast.

🌹 🌹 🌹

"Have you got those biscuits in?" Sally asked a little before five the next morning.

"In and almost done," Reagan informed her, her arm still mixing the batter for two cakes.

"How much longer?"

"Only about five minutes. The bread is rising nicely."

Sally stood back in approval, thinking Reagan was going to work out fine. Sally had all but taken the morning off, since the baking had to be done first, and for the first time in a month, she wasn't tense before she started to cook.

Even if Cousin Leslie shows up, I might just keep Reagan too.

"We have customers," Pierce put his head in the door to announce.

"Well, where is Missy?" Sally demanded.

"I haven't seen her."

Sally's face went red very quickly as she whipped her apron off and went out to the dining area to do someone else's job. Her peaceful thoughts about Reagan's hard work evaporated.

Reagan noticed the exchange but kept her thoughts to herself. She wondered at people these days who didn't have enough pride in their work to show up on time and do a good job but then remembered that it was none of her business. The event lingered on her mind, however, so when she finished her work in the kitchen, she removed her own apron and went out front to see if she could help. Sally was still taking orders, so Reagan started around with the coffeepot and a tray of mugs.

"Well, now," one cowboy spoke amid a table full of cowboys, straightening when she got to his table. "You must be new."

"I might be." Reagan was noncommittal. "Do you want coffee?"

"I do, ma'am, yes, but only after you tell me if you're on today's menu."

"Do you want the coffee on your head or in your cup?" was Reagan's only reply as she counted heads, set mugs on the table, and began to pour. The men at the table had a good laugh over her words, but to a man they tried to catch her eye.

"You have flour on your cheek," the man alone at the next table told her.

Again Reagan was nonchalant.

"Do I?"

"Yes."

"Would you like coffee?"

"Here, let me get the flour off for you."

Reagan was two arms' lengths away from the table before the man saw her move. He sat with his handkerchief in hand, just staring at her.

"All I'm offering is the coffee," she clarified. "Do you want some?"

Not able to get anything more than an impassive stare from her, the man gave in. He nodded and watched as she poured but wasn't able to miss that she left his table without a backward glance.

"They seem to like you," Sally commented when Reagan came back to the kitchen to help dish up eggs and bacon.

"I'm the new girl, that's all."

Sally took in that head of dark wavy hair, the dark sparkling eyes, and the small but shapely figure, and wasn't convinced. And she was right. Two weeks passed, and the men still watched for Reagan. She had a way of lighting up the dining room with her candor, her quick smile, and her no-nonsense service. Sally had been smart enough to offer her a little more money, so each morning when she was finished with the baking, she moved to the dining room to wait tables. She was already used to being proposed to and took it in stride, but she didn't tolerate unwelcome caresses. More than one mess had to be cleaned up because Reagan had been forced to discourage a suitor by dumping his food on top of him.

The Wednesday of her third week began just this way. Reagan had not slept well and was not in the mood for games. A man whom she had not met before wouldn't take no for an answer, and Reagan had thrown his water in his face. The man was outraged, but Reagan had had enough. Exiting to the kitchen, she spoke as she gathered her things.

"I'm leaving for the day, Sally. I'm tired of being treated like something on the auction block." She turned and gave her employer a hard look. "From the outside this place looks classy, but some of your breakfast customers act like animals."

Not sure she still had a job, Reagan moved to the door. She headed down the alley, not really keeping track of where she was headed. She wasn't upset so much as she was tired. The man really hadn't been that obnoxious, but she hadn't been in the mood to deal with him.

A good walk; that's all I need. Without my bicycle I just don't get out enough.

"Good morning, Reagan," a voice suddenly called to her, and she realized she'd walked all the way down to Russell's livery.

"Hello, Russell," Reagan said easily enough, approaching where he stood in the alley behind his shop. She still didn't know the man very well, but at the moment he was a kind face, and Reagan felt very alone.

"Did you work today?"

"I did, yes, but I left early."

"Are you not feeling well?" he asked with genuine concern. "Holly has everything you can think of if you're under the weather. Just stop and see her."

"No, I'm all right."

The big man studied her.

"Your face says you aren't."

Reagan smiled and laughed a little.

"Sometimes men are so rude!" she suddenly blurted, and Russell had all he could do not to laugh.

"I can't disagree with you there."

They were silent for a moment.

"What happened?" Russell finally asked.

Reagan shook her head in wonder. "One of the hotel patrons could not keep his hands to himself. I threw his water in his face."

Russell's booming laugh brought a smile to Reagan's face.

"Good job. You keep them in their place."

Reagan was fascinated. This was the last thing she'd expected from him.

"Do you really think it was all right that I did that?"

"Of course I do. A woman alone can't let her guard down for an instant."

Reagan couldn't have felt better if he'd offered her the moon. Smiling a little, she thanked him and turned to go on her way.

"Oh, Reagan," he said, stopping her. She looked back. "How are things in the little house? Everything working well?"

"It's wonderful," she told him honestly.

"Well, if you need something, you know where to come."

With a wave Russell went back inside, and Reagan moved toward home. She was inside the safe walls of her little house a short time later, feeling as tired as if she'd worked her regular day.

Sitting down in her chair and putting her feet up, she found herself thinking of New York and growing sad over what she'd left behind. It hadn't been much, but it had been familiar. Tommy hadn't even sent her bicycle yet, and for one ridiculous moment Reagan thought she might cry.

"This won't do," she said quietly. "I must be more tired than I first thought."

But not even hearing the sound of her own voice could convince Reagan. She dozed off for a nap before she could put her finger on what was truly wrong.

Five

"I'M SUPPOSED TO BE WATCHING CHILDREN," Reagan muttered in low fury just two weeks later, her arm scrubbing furiously at a pot. "Kind, gentle little children who adore me. I'm supposed to be sitting under shade trees and reading storybooks. I should be eating little cakes and fanning myself if I'm warm." Reagan shook her head in irritation, blew the air from her brow, and picked up the bucket of water that needed dumping.

It wasn't enough that waiting on tables had been added to her original job as baker. Now, added to those jobs was pot scrubbing. It didn't matter that she was being paid more. She didn't like it! Nearly stomping to the back door, Reagan took barely a step outside before she tossed the bucket of water into the alley. She would have turned right around and gone back in, but a deep gasp stopped her. Peeking around the doorjamb that hindered her view, Reagan caught sight of a tall cowboy. He was dripping wet from his mid-chest to his knees. Reagan's hand came to her mouth.

"I'm sorry!" she exclaimed. "I didn't see you."

"It's all right," he said, still looking surprised but not angry.

"What were you doing back here anyway?"

The apologetic, concerned face of the woman with the bucket was transfigured into a frown. The wet man looked a little taken aback but still answered, "Just taking a shortcut, ma'am."

Reagan did little more than nod, not aware that she was still frowning in ill humor. Not until the cowboy went on his way without another word did she think she could have at least apologized again. She had not only soaked him with dirty wash water but intruded into his business as well.

I've got to get out more, she decided as she went back into work. *I'm wilting here in Texas, and it's only been a month. If Tommy would just send my . . .*

"Reagan, what are you doing just standing there?"

Sally had not asked in outrage, but Reagan was not in a pleasant mood. She caught herself before she snapped at the woman.

"Just emptying the bucket. And yes," Reagan added before Sally could ask her usual question, "everything is either baking or cooling."

Sally smiled and teased her.

"What put a burr under your saddle?"

"I don't know," Reagan admitted as she put the bucket down. "I don't like scrubbing pots—that much I know—but other than that I'm not sure."

"If you don't like scrubbing pots, why did you agree to do it?"

"The money."

"Well, is it worth it?"

Reagan looked at her, thinking for the first time that she *had* been a fair employer, not overly harsh, but at times single-minded in purpose because she had a business to run and reliable people were not always available to help her. Reagan smiled for the first time all day.

"Actually, it is, but I just needed to complain for a time."

Sally shook her head in mock exasperation and went to peek into the ovens. Reagan got fresh water and went back to scrubbing pots.

❧ ❧ ❧

Holly was hanging out the wash when Reagan arrived home. They hadn't seen too much of each other outside of Reagan's paying the rent and returning the borrowed things as she'd purchased blankets, sheets, and towels of her own.

"How are you, Reagan?" Holly asked. Reagan smiled at the sight of Alisa asleep in a basket at the end of the clothesline.

"I'm doing fine. How are you?"

"Very well, thank you. Jonah found a handkerchief in the bushes," Holly said as she plucked a small white cloth from her pocket. "Is it yours?"

"It is," Reagan said after she studied it. "Thank you. It must have blown away when I pegged out my own wash."

"Are you free to come to dinner tonight?" Holly offered on the spur of the moment. "I've got a chicken stewing, and you're welcome to join us."

"Why, thank you, I am free tonight."

Holly smiled at her.

"Is there something I can bring?"

"Just yourself."

They didn't talk much longer, but after learning the time to arrive, Reagan went to her little house, her mood very light.

"That's it," she concluded as she prepared to bathe. "I don't have any friends here. That's why I'm so down. Tommy hasn't sent my bicycle, and I have no friends. Who wouldn't be down?"

Having concluded this, Reagan stopped worrying about her mood. She had a plan now, and that was all she ever needed.

🌹 🌹 🌹

"I don't like school as much as Elly does," Jonah informed Reagan that evening. Holly would not accept her help with dinner, so she sat in the living room with Alisa in her lap and Jonah visiting at her side.

"Why is that?" Reagan asked the seven-year-old boy.

"Elly can read lots better than me."

"But you'll learn, won't you?"

"That's what mama says."

Reagan smiled down into his dejected little face and thought she might be seeing herself. Most things came easily to her. When they did not, she wasn't very patient.

"What *do* you like about school?"

His face lit up in an instant.

"I like taking lunch in the tin with Elly, and I like to hear the teacher read, and I like it when Timmy Bolthouse plays with me."

"Who is Timmy Bolthouse?"

"He's my friend from school. He can spit water out his teeth!"

"I can do that."

Jonah's eyes and little open mouth spoke of his awe.

"Can you teach me?"

Reagan saw her mistake.

"Well . . ." She tried to find words.

"Can you teach me?" he asked again, thinking she might not have understood.

"Jonah," Holly suddenly called from the kitchen, "please come help Elly with the table."

The little boy was clearly in agony. Reagan barely kept her mouth shut as she watched Jonah look between her and the door that would lead to the kitchen.

"Go on now, son." Russell suddenly appeared to give his boy the urging he needed.

"I'm sorry," Reagan began as soon as the child was gone. She had shifted Alisa in her lap, but that baby had yet to do anything but sit complacently and play with her toes.

"For what?" Russell asked when he took a seat across from their guest.

Reagan gave him a quick rundown and watched him laugh in delight.

"I'm glad you're laughing," she said when her host quieted.

"So what did you tell him?"

"I didn't."

"Well, I think you should," Russell surprised her by saying. He grinned boyishly. "Then he could teach me."

Reagan laughed so suddenly that the baby jumped.

"I'm sorry, Alisa," she said quietly, and for the first time Alisa caught sight of the silver necklace that hung down the front of Reagan's dress. The baby's hand was reaching for it when her father called her name.

"Alisa, don't touch that," he said, and she looked at him and looked back at the enticing locket.

"Alisa," he called her name again.

She looked at him.

"No," he said quite firmly when they had made eye contact.

For a moment she looked as though she would pout or cry, but another look from her father put an end to that.

Reagan didn't know if she was impressed or concerned at how stern he had been. She had to admit to herself, however, that it was nice not to have her necklace grabbed and possibly broken.

A glance at the baby gave her further pause. She was smiling across at her father as though he'd hung the moon. In fact, just a moment later her pudgy arms went out to him. When he took her, Alisa giggled and snuggled up against his chest as though she'd been waiting to do so all day.

"I think we're ready in here," Holly called from the kitchen before Reagan could comment. And just a few minutes later, Reagan found herself at the kitchen table set for five, with Alisa's high chair close by her mother's seat. The rolls were directly in front of her, and she was about to take one so she could pass the basket when Russell's voice stopped her.

"I think it's my turn to pray tonight," he said.

Reagan was glad she'd not made a move. She bowed her head along with everyone else and waited for one of the memorized prayers she'd heard off and on over the years.

"Father in heaven," Russell began, "thank You for this wonderful day and the way You blessed us each hour. Thank You for all Holly's hard work and this great food we can eat. Thank You that Reagan could join us. What a blessing to have her live in the little house and be such a good neighbor. Bless us as we eat and spend the evening together, and may we ever be mindful of Your presence and blessing in our lives. In Christ's name I pray. Amen."

Reagan managed to raise her head, but the rolls and other food were forgotten. No one had ever prayed for her before. She hadn't even known that a person could talk to God like that. If she hadn't known better, she'd have wondered if Russell might not be a man of the cloth.

"Would you like some potatoes, Miss Sullivan?" Elly was asking, and Reagan was jerked back to the present.

"Thank you," she said, her head bent low to cover her red face. What had she done in those seconds of distracted concentration, and had this family noticed?

"I think I'll hold this chicken platter for you, Reagan," Russell was saying. "It's rather hot."

"Thank you," she said again, and for more than one reason: It seemed they hadn't noticed anything odd in her behavior.

"How is work at the hotel, Reagan?" Holly asked when everyone had been served.

"Most days, it's fine."

"Is that what you did in New York?"

"No. I worked at a factory. It was monotonous, but at least we had one day off a week."

"That must have been nice," Russell put in. "I'm not sure all factories do that."

"No, they don't. Many of the girls in the boardinghouse worked seven days a week."

"Where is your family?"

"They're all gone. I've been on my own for some time."

"What do you do at the hotel?" Elly asked, and Reagan began to fill her in.

"And then today," she concluded, her eyes rolling at the memory, "I needed to change my wash water when I was scrubbing pots, and I threw a bucket of water on a man in the alley."

"Oh, no!" Elly gasped, her eyes large.

Reagan shook her head in self-deprecation.

"Was he angry?" This came from Jonah.

"No," Russell answered, and all eyes turned to him.

"Did you see it happen?" Reagan asked.

"No, but the man was a friend of mine, and he was on his way to see me."

"Who was it, Russ?" Holly wished to know.

The big man's eyes sparkled. "Cash."

Holly and the children all laughed over this, and Russell turned to Reagan to explain.

"Cash is a good friend. We've known each other for years."

"And he wasn't angry?" Reagan asked with a small amount of anxiety.

"Not at all. He was laughing by the time he got to me."

Reagan sat back with a sigh. "I'm glad to hear it, but he would have been more than justified."

"He doesn't anger easily."

"I've never seen him angry," added Holly.

These comments were of great interest to Reagan. She didn't have much of an impression of the man from the alley, having only seen him for a few moments, but these people she rented from were somehow different; she figured their friends must be too. Reagan couldn't put her finger on an exact incident, but something here was not what she was used to. For an instant she remembered the way Russell prayed.

"We have cake for dessert," Holly announced. "Anyone interested?"

Even Alisa seemed to light up over these words, and Holly gave out generous slices of cake just a few minutes later. As coffee cups were refilled, the conversation started up all over again.

"I had a big one come in today," Russell began. "One of the biggest horses in town."

"Was he nice or mean?" Jonah, who loved his father's work, wished to know.

"What was his name?" Elly stuck in.

"His name was Sam, and as for temperament, he was somewhere in the middle. I've had some big ones you could swing by the tail and they wouldn't blink, but this one liked me in his sight and was happy as long as I kept talking."

"Have you ever been seriously injured?" Reagan found herself asking, fascinated.

"Yes. I have a cavity on the outside of my leg from a severe kick more than ten years ago."

"And you still wanted to be a blacksmith after that?"

"Yes, ma'am," the big man replied contentedly. "I can count on one hand the number of days I've wanted to quit."

There was something in the way he said this that made Reagan smile. She couldn't think of anything more wonderful than having a job she loved. The question was, would *she* ever feel that way?

Hours later Reagan climbed into bed, tired but not exhausted, that question and the whole evening still on her mind. It had done her heart a world of good to have some fun. Typically her friends from New York were single men or women, but getting to know a family here was a wonderful new experience.

The thought of family suddenly made her lie very still.

Maybe I haven't gotten too close to a family in the past because I didn't want to know what I've missed.

Almost afraid to let her thoughts go on but not able to stop them, Reagan thought about how she'd grown up, and how cruel life could be. If she had learned anything, it was this: To love someone was to give them the power to hurt you. Not by plan or design did Reagan live this out, but by instinct.

Her thoughts unsettled, Reagan rolled into a ball to get comfortable, reminding herself that morning came whether she was ready or not, and she would be a bear if she didn't get her sleep.

🌿 🌿 🌿

"What was *that?*" old Hank Demby exclaimed. He stood at the checkout counter at the general store, his eyes on the large glass window that overlooked the street.

"That was Reagan on her bicycle," Lavinia Unger, the proprietress said. "Have you not see her before?"

The older gentleman didn't answer. He'd gone to the door to try to catch sight of it again. Lavinia joined him and, sure enough, they were swiftly rewarded with a view of Reagan as she left the bank, hopped on her bike in the most amazing way, and began to ride toward them.

"Good afternoon, Mrs. Unger," she called when she was abreast of them.

"Hello, Reagan."

Pedaling along as if she hadn't a care in the world, Reagan gave a wave and kept going.

"How long has that been here?" Hank asked, his mouth still slightly agape.

"I think only about a week. It came in on the train. Reagan had told the boys at the station to watch for it, and when they sent word that it had arrived, she was down there in a flash—didn't even remove her apron."

"Disgraceful!" a woman sniffed as she came up the boardwalk toward the door. "Completely improper! These easterners coming west with their strange and unprincipled ways."

"Now, now," Lavinia tried to soothe her. "Reagan's a good girl. She works hard."

"Where's she work?" Hank found himself curious about the rider as well.

While this exchange took place, Reagan, who was uncaring of any attention she might draw, finished her errands. She was down to her last stop, and that was the livery. She found Russell shoeing a horse, lifting the animal's leg as though it weighed like a coin.

"Hello," Reagan greeted him when he heard her and glanced up.

"Well, now," he said as he finished with the last nail, dropped the hoof, and straightened to look at her. "Been riding that bike?"

Reagan smiled.

"How can you tell?"

Russell didn't answer, but he always knew. Her eyes would be especially bright, and if the day was brisk, her cheeks would redden, but the real giveaway was what it did to her hair. Always a bit unruly, Reagan's coiffure had been blown around until black curls and wisps finally fell on her forehead and down her neck.

"I've just come to tell you that Holly wasn't home when I got there, so I left the rent on the table."

"She goes to Bible study on Wednesdays, and then sometimes the women visit," Russell said almost absently. "You did the right thing. She'll find it."

"All right."

It had been on Reagan's mind to ask why Holly was studying the Bible, but she decided against it.

"So, are you out on business or just getting some exercise?" Russell asked.

"I'm doing errands until I meet the children at school."

"Oh, that's right. Elly said you were coming to walk them home."

"She's getting quite good on my bicycle."

Russell grinned. "Only one scraped knee."

"It helps that she's tall."

"Has Jonah ridden yet?"

"Not on his own. The pedals are too far away."

"Well, be sure and tell me if they don't thank you for all this fun."

Reagan only laughed at what had been a serious comment from him and started on her way. Somewhere along the line she had decided that Russell and Holly took obedience a little too seriously. They had good kids. Reagan could see that. It seemed to her that they need not worry so much about all the little details.

Hopping on her bicycle yet again, Reagan rode toward the schoolhouse. She was running a little late, and the school was uphill, but she arrived just as the children were dismissed for the day. Several of them stopped to see her two-wheeled conveyance and were suitably impressed, but in short order she was walking along with the Bennett children.

"How was your day?" she asked them.

They both tried to answer at once, but then Jonah let his sister talk. Reagan listened with genuine interest until they were over halfway home, then agreed to take Elly's books so she could ride the rest of the way. Once Reagan and Jonah were alone, the little boy told her about his day.

"I had to spell words up front."

"How did you do?"

"I got them all right. Jimmy got one wrong, but teacher let him do it over."

"That was nice of her. What word was it?"

"What."

"What word was it?"

"What," he said again, turning his head to look at her, and Reagan began to laugh. Hearing her laugh, Jonah caught on and laughed too.

"We could have gone on with that for a long time," Reagan commented as both her little house and Jonah's came into view. Out front, Elly was still atop the bike, going in big circles. Reagan heard Jonah sigh.

"I wish I had long legs."

"You will before you know it."

"That's what my mother says too."

Reagan smiled at his sweet little face. She had never yearned for a family, but this little boy touched something inside of her that she had never felt before.

"Watch me, Miss Sullivan," Elly called just as Holly came to the porch with Alisa.

The adults clapped and cheered while Elly leapt off and stopped the bicycle. Reagan then gave Jonah a ride, basically pushing him while he steered. Elly cheered her brother on from the porch, and Reagan was again struck by the closeness of these two children.

A moment later Holly told the children she had a snack for them on the kitchen table. She invited Reagan, who declined. Much as she enjoyed being with this family, at times she was oddly uncomfortable.

Not willing to think on it, Reagan took herself home. She had no specific plan, but she needed to do something to elude the feelings that seemed to pester her.

Six

A Sunday morning off! Reagan could hardly believe her luck. Not that she would ever want anyone to be harmed, but having a small fire in the hotel kitchen on Saturday night had meant the dining room would be closed all day Sunday. It hadn't allowed her to sleep in because she didn't know about it until she arrived for work, but that didn't diminish her joy. She hadn't had a morning off since arriving in Kinkade, so she wouldn't have wanted to lie in bed anyway. There was too much to see and do!

For the first time since her bicycle had arrived, Reagan left it at home. She had ridden to work but now returned home, spent time mending a torn seam, puttered around her small house, and eventually put on her better dress and set off on foot. It occurred to her somewhere along the line that she had not had breakfast, but she dismissed the thought for the moment. If she got desperate, she could throw herself on Sally's mercy to let her use the kitchen long enough to prepare a meal.

Thoughts of all she might do with a full day ahead raced through her mind. Because her business rarely took her to the east end of town, she decided to head that way. She was enjoying a few new sights when she heard singing.

Reagan stopped and listened to what sounded like a choir in full voice. It was in front of her somewhere, and after a few seconds, she moved toward the sound. A small white church came into view. Reagan didn't know why the idea of a church hadn't immediately occurred to her, but now that she saw where the sound was coming from, she smiled at her own surprise, shook her head, and started to turn away. At almost the same moment, she remembered that she had nowhere else in particular to go.

Walking slowly and enjoying the voices, Reagan went ahead to the church and stopped a few feet from the closed door. The closer she neared, the more beautiful it sounded. Church was not a place she'd visited much, hardly at all if the truth be told, but she felt mesmerized by the music she was hearing. Even when the singing stopped and didn't start up for a few seconds, Reagan remained still. The singing resumed, and the congregation must have been on their fifth number when Reagan's feet moved again, this time all the way to the door. Working not to be noticed, she opened the portal and slipped inside. To her surprise, no one turned. They were all standing, facing front, hymn books in hand, singing their hearts out.

Reagan couldn't say exactly what compelled her, but she slipped into the last pew and sat down just as they finished. There was no one directly in front of her for two pews as she moved as far to the wall as she could get, and the people in the next two pews were closer to the aisle.

Reagan gazed at the man up front and listened to the sound of his deep voice. He was reading from the book in front of him, and although the words were not familiar to Reagan, she knew it must be the Bible. With almost no idea how she'd come to be there, Reagan found herself quite rapt.

" 'The angel said unto him, Fear not, Zacharias; for thy prayer is heard; and thy wife Elisabeth shall bear thee a son, and thou shalt call his name John. And thou shalt have joy and gladness; and many shall rejoice at his birth. For he shall be great in the sight of the Lord, and shall drink neither wine nor strong drink; and he shall be filled with the Holy Ghost, even from his mother's womb. And many of the children of Israel shall he turn to the Lord, their God. And he shall go before him in the spirit and power of Elijah, to turn the hearts of the fathers to the children, and the disobedient to the wisdom of the just, to make ready a people prepared for the Lord. And Zacharias said unto the angel, Whereby shall I know this? For I am an old man, and my wife well stricken in years. And the angel answering said unto him, I am Gabriel, who stands in the presence of God; and am sent to speak unto thee, and to show thee these glad tidings.'

"This news from Gabriel was huge," the pastor intoned, looking up from the pulpit and smiling kindly at the people in the pews. "A special child is about to be born to Zacharias and Elisabeth because Zacharias and Elisabeth are special. Verse six describes them as blameless. They had clearly shown God that they were up to the task of raising this child.

"John is going to be a man with a very special job. The angel compares him to Elijah, one of the most powerful prophets of the Old Testament. We've taken a few weeks to come to these verses because I didn't want to rush. I wanted you to be prepared for the special words here."

Reagan watched as the man paused, his eyes scanning the pews.

"Look at verse 17. It says John is going to go before Him. Do you understand who the verse is talking about here? Who that *Him* is?"

Reagan could see some heads nodding, but she didn't have a clue.

"It's Jesus Christ," the pastor continued. "John is coming to prepare hearts for Christ when He starts His earthly ministry. God's Son, who has come to bring salvation to mankind, is going to be announced by John."

For a time, the man's words were lost on Reagan. She had never heard of this, but she found it riveting. It was almost as if her questions were being answered, but she hadn't asked any questions.

"The events that follow in the book of Luke have paved the way for what we believe today, and we will get to many of those in the weeks and months to come, but don't rush past verse 17. Let me read it to you again. 'And he,' that's John, 'shall go before Him,' Jesus Christ, 'in the spirit and power of Elijah, to turn the hearts of the fathers to the children, and the disobedient to the wisdom of the just, to make ready a people prepared for the Lord.'

"What is the first thing Jesus is going to address? The fathers! Of all the things that could be at the top of the list during this time, we find that God wants fathers to father their children. I don't know about the rest of you men in the room, but this gives me a wake-up call. Are my children hearing from me the way of salvation? Do my children know that my main priority is to teach them of their Creator, their Savior, their God?"

The pastor shook his head in wonder, smiling a little as he leaned forward on the pulpit. "I'm excited about this verse. God never demands something of me that is impossible for me to do. He came to turn my heart to Him, and to help me, as a father, put my children in the right direction as well. With God's help I can do this."

Again Reagan was swept out of the room as her own father's face sprang to mind. The pastor concluded with a final prayer and an announcement, but Reagan did not hear much of it.

"Father in heaven, thank You for bringing each one here today. We praise You for Your Word and Your love for us. May we go from this place better prepared to serve You and return next week if You do not come for us before that time. In Christ's name I pray. Amen.

"Don't forget now, come out the side door today and see all the remodeling in our home. We'll meet in the side yard for prayer in a few minutes, and then we'll eat. It looks as though we have enough for an army, so don't hesitate to join us."

The pastor, his family, and almost the entire congregation moved forward to a side door to exit, but Reagan was still in New York as a child. She was aware of things around her but felt apart and separate, her heart a little bruised. It took a few moments for the room to quiet down, and when it did, Reagan finally realized someone was standing in the aisle staring at her. Her head whipped over, and her eyes met those of the cowboy from the alley.

"Do you have your bucket with you today, or am I safe?"

Reagan relaxed in the light of his humor and laughed. When she did, Cash came forward.

"I'm Cash Rawlings," he said, putting his hand out.

Reagan shook it.

"I'm Reagan Sullivan, and I've wanted to tell you again how sorry I am about the water."

Cash shrugged. "Accidents happen."

Reagan shook her head. "You might be more understanding than you should be."

"I don't think so."

"Actually," Reagan admitted, "Russell Bennett told me you weren't angry."

"Do you know Russ?"

"Yes."

"They're here," Cash told her. "Come on. I know they'll want to see you."

"They go to this church?" Reagan asked as she moved out into the aisle between the two pews and toward the door where the others had gone.

"Yes, they do. Did they know you were coming?"

"No, it was a last-minute decision," Reagan said, her voice having dropped some. She also had come to a halt.

Cash watched her stare at the pulpit as though Pastor Ellis were still standing there. She then looked to him.

"I think there might be something to this salvation thing."

"I certainly think so."

Reagan's eyes widened. "Then you've done it? You know about salvation?"

"Yes, I do."

"Salvation from God, from His Son?"

"That's right."

Reagan could only stare at him. Her mind moving faster than she could keep up, Reagan was unaware of the way she gawked at the man, making him feel that he shouldn't question her.

"Cash!" a voice called from without before Russell Bennett came through the door. "Reagan?" he said in obvious surprise.

Reagan seemed to snap out of her trance.

"Are you a Christian?" she blurted, nearly accusing Russell.

"Yes."

"But you didn't get your Bible out and try to convert me as soon as we met."

"No." Russell was as calm as ever. "I wouldn't have done that for a number of reasons."

"Like what?"

"Well, for one you're a woman, and I wouldn't want to give the wrong impression. Also, you didn't show any interest, so why would I shove it down your throat?"

"That didn't stop certain people in my old neighborhood," Reagan grumbled.

"Listen, Reagan," Russell said, having come to a swift decision as the entire church was waiting, "we need to talk about this, but right now Cash has to come and pray for our meal."

"Oh, right," Reagan began as she started to back away.

"Come and eat with us," Russell invited as his huge hand took Reagan's wrist. "Holly is right out here."

Cash smiled at the stunned look on her face as she was hauled out the door. Russell landed her next to Holly and then walked with Cash to the front.

"That was subtle," Cash teased him.

Russell smiled. "I had her this far. I didn't want to let her get away."

"Oh, here's Cash now," Pastor Ellis said as the men neared.

"Let's pray," Cash said when he stepped up front next to the pastor and his family. After a few moments of silence, he began. "Father in heaven, thank You for the work that was done here. Thank You for the willing hands and hearts that made all of this possible. We are so blessed, Father, to have Pastor and Noelle with us, and their children, and by giving to them we have an even greater blessing. We pray, Lord, that they would enjoy this wonderful home for years to come.

"Thank You for this food, Father. Thank You for all who worked to make it. May we remember Your goodness to us as we enjoy it. In Your name I pray. Amen."

In the back, Holly opened her eyes and looked over at Reagan. Their renter was a bit shorter than she was, so it was easy to watch her expression. Holly had not really had time to find out how Reagan had come to be there, and she desperately wanted her to stay but knew that forcing her would never work.

"Reagan," she finally called her name.

Reagan looked at her.

"I hope you'll want to stay, but please don't feel you must."

"I didn't bring anything to share."

"If you mean the food, I brought two dishes, a pie and a beef and bean casserole. We always have plenty at these gatherings."

"So you've done this before?"

"Eaten together, you mean?"

"Yes—I mean, you don't just come and sit in the pews and then go home?"

"Sometimes we head right out, especially if the children have had trouble sitting still and we need to get home and talk about it, but the majority of the time we visit, and often we eat with another family or have a family to our house."

Reagan was on the verge of saying she'd never seen anyone there and then remembered she was always working. As though she'd said this out loud, Holly asked her about it.

"Did you get the morning off?"

"Yes. There was a fire in the hotel kitchen last night, and Sally shut the dining room for the day."

"Was anyone harmed?"

"No, nothing like that."

"I'm glad. Will it be open tomorrow?"

"I think Sally was planning that. I'll check with her later."

"Hi, Miss Sullivan," Jonah, who had suddenly run up, greeted her. "Are you going to eat with us?"

"I think I am, yes," Reagan said, and it was the last thing she said for a while. What followed was a celebration unlike anything she'd ever known. With everyone laughing and talking, the group lining up to eat couldn't have been more friendly or generous. Men allowed their wives to go first and then stayed to help with the children, much the way Reagan had seen Russell and Holly interact. It was interesting to watch one family in action; it was nothing short of amazing to watch a hundred people acting the same way.

Reagan caught male eyes on her from time to time, but none of the men had inappropriate looks on their faces, and none of them stood with a woman at his side.

"Have you seen the house?" Russell asked Reagan as the event was starting to wind down.

"No. Why did the pastor want everyone to do that?"

"Because we've been doing some remodeling for the past nine months, and it's finally done. The house is not that old, but the original owner had skimped in some areas, so there was rain damage in a number of places. Once we started working, we found even more places that needed repair, and so we did the whole job. You should go in. It won't be as good as seeing it before, but you'll still enjoy it."

Once Reagan left the table with Holly and Alisa, Cash joined Russell.

"I've set up an elders' meeting for the twenty-fifth. Is that going to work for you?" Cash asked.

"That should be fine. I'll tell Holly, and she can remind me."

"Okay. I've got to let Jarvis know before I leave."

"Are we going to be discussing the widow and orphans' fund at this meeting?"

"Yes. I've got that on my list. Have you had more feedback?"

"Yes, some good comments. I've made some notes, and I'll bring them with me."

"All right."

Jonah, who had played with his friends but was now tired, had made his way into Cash's lap, and for a time the tall cowboy let everything else slide.

"How are you, Jonah?" he asked, his arms holding the boy close.

"I rode a bike."

"A bike?" Cash frowned as though he'd not heard right.

"It's Miss Sullivan's."

"Oh."

Cash was so stopped by this that Russell began to laugh. Cash looked up at him.

"She has a bicycle?"

"Yes. Elly can ride it alone, but Jonah needs a push."

"Well, now." Cash looked down into the little face again. "That sounds very fun. Have you done it very often?"

"Every week."

"Wow. And you don't fall?"

"No. Elly has, but Miss Sullivan hangs onto me."

"She sounds very nice."

"She's here today! She ate with us."

"I saw her."

Jonah suddenly laughed. "She threw water on you."

"Did she?" Cash asked angelically while his fingers found Jonah's ticklish sides. The little boy squirmed with laughter as Cash took his revenge.

"I didn't have any cake!" Jonah announced. Cash had stopped tickling him, and he had remembered his stomach.

"Well, go have some."

The little boy was off in a flash, and the men went back to talking. Cash had horses that needed shoeing and some work on a few broken wagons.

"I can come out Tuesday," Russell told him. "Will that work?"

"Yeah. Come at noon. I'll tell Katy to plan on you."

"How are you for hands these days?"

"I have plenty of men. Brad is the best foreman I've ever had. As you well know, I didn't even have to help with roundup this year. He can charm the hat off the most cantankerous cowboy and still get two more hours of work out of him at the end of a long day."

Russell was chuckling at this description when Holly and Alisa joined them. Reagan was not with them.

"Did you lose Reagan?" Russell asked as soon as Holly sat down.

"In a way, yes. I think she was a little overwhelmed by all of this. It seemed to come on her rather suddenly. I could tell she wanted to think and take it all in. When we finished in the house, she said she was headed home. I don't think she ate much, but I didn't want to say anything."

"It's hard, isn't it?" Cash interjected. "We don't want to come across as crazed, but we believe we have the best news in the world to share."

The Bennetts were in full agreement with that sentiment.

Jonah chose that moment to return with his cake. His baby sister saw it and all but crawled from her mother's arms to get at the plate. Cash volunteered to go for the dessert and rescue all of them. They stayed to visit until Alisa's cake was gone and she was drooping in her father's arms.

If someone had reported the event in the local paper that week, it would have said, "A good time was had by all."

❧ ❧ ❧

"What do you mean you need Sundays off?" Sally asked in surprise. "What for?"

"Not the whole morning, just long enough to go to church."

Sally looked clearly skeptical. "And who takes the cakes from the oven when you're gone?"

"That's what I've been trying to tell you. I'll come early enough to have the baking done. When I come back, I'll clean up and help with tables."

"Reagan, you don't strike me as the type who needs religion. What's gotten into you?"

"I don't know," the younger woman said honestly, her dinner plate forgotten in front of her. She had been too nervous to eat much at the church gathering and had found herself hungry that evening. She'd gone to Sally's without a backward glance and found her in the kitchen fixing her own meal. The way she'd welcomed Reagan had done the younger woman's heart a world of good.

"I just found myself at that church this morning. I'm not even sure how. And once I got inside, I was just so drawn to what the pastor was saying."

"Pastor Ellis?"

"Yes. Do you know him?"

"No, but his wife is a real person—I know that."

"Noelle. I met her too. Even their children are nice. Just like Russell and Holly's family."

"They go to that church too, don't they?"

Reagan nodded.

"And you want to find out why they live the way they do."

Reagan stared at her.

"You've wanted to as well, haven't you, Sally?"

The hotel owner shrugged. "Maybe."

"Why haven't you looked into this?" Reagan demanded. "You've lived here for years!"

"Reagan," she said with a shake of her head. "I don't have time for church. This place takes every minute of every day. Can't you see that?"

Reagan's eyes narrowed. "Of course I can see that, Sally, but you're not going to be here forever! You can say something to shut me up for the moment, but when you're on your own, are you happy with who you are, fine hotel or not?"

Sally's eyes narrowed right back, but she didn't say anything right away.

"You can take off on Sundays to go to church unless it doesn't work."

"Why wouldn't it?"

Sally shook her head in amazement. "You have more guts than anyone I know, Reagan. I hand you a favor, and you're ready to argue."

Reagan didn't reply. In her haste to have her own way, she often forgot that Sally was her boss.

"Thank you for giving me time to go to church."

"If you get all religious, are you going to start carrying your Bible and drive us all crazy?"

In a heartbeat, Reagan thought of the difference between the two Christians she'd known in New York and Russell Bennett. It was not hard to answer Sally.

"I won't say anything unless you ask me."

"Fair enough. Had enough to eat?"

"No," she said, tucking back into her plate. "Let me finish, and I'll clean up for you."

Sally, who'd had a long, arduous day, was not going to argue with that idea.

❧ ❧ ❧

"Was she here this morning?" Russell asked Cash before their meeting started at the church just two weeks later.

"Yes. Just like last week. I think she must slip in just before we start and back out again on the last song. Have you had a chance to ask her about it?"

"Not really. Holly and I are both afraid of pressuring her. We're both praying that she'll know where to come if she has questions."

Both men would have been delighted to know that Reagan was on her way to Holly's door right then. She was not aware that Russell was not at home, but she had some questions and could only hope that someone in the big house had the answers.

Seven

"Holly, are you busy?"

"Not at all, Reagan. Come right in."

Reagan entered the familiar home, but unlike the first time, she didn't enjoy her surroundings. She was too distracted for that.

"Have a seat," Holly invited. She had a word with one of her children in the kitchen and then joined her guest.

"What can I do for you?"

"I have a few questions."

"All right."

"I went to church this morning—last week too."

Holly nodded. She hadn't been certain of this, but she was glad nevertheless.

"If I believe as your church does, do I have to get married?"

Holly had all she could do not to look surprised. This was the last thing she expected.

"May I ask you a question?" Holly said after a moment's recovery.

"Yes."

"What do you mean, 'believe as my church does'?"

"Become a Christian—be saved—like Pastor Ellis talked about."

"Like the Bible explains?" Holly questioned again, hoping they were talking about the same thing.

"Yes. Believing on the Lord Jesus Christ and living for Him."

Holly nodded, now feeling satisfied that she and Reagan were on the same track.

"No one in our church is going to force you to get married, no matter what you believe."

Reagan looked so relieved that Holly smiled.

"Why did you ask, Reagan? Can you tell me?"

"It's not something I want, Holly. Marriage, that is. I don't want a husband. I don't want a man to rule over me and control my life."

"What about a man to love and cherish you?"

Reagan smiled a little. "I don't think I'm the love and cherish type."

Holly could not have disagreed more, but she didn't argue with her.

"Is that all that's on your mind, Reagan? Are you understanding what you're hearing in church?"

"Yes," she said with excitement, leaning forward a little. "I've never heard any of this, and I think it's wonderful. What Christ did was wonderful. I don't think I could have done it."

"I know I couldn't have," Holly agreed. "Only God could do that for us."

"How do we really know that Jesus is God?"

"The Bible."

"But what if the Bible's not right?"

"That's a good question, Reagan—one that many people have asked. I think the first thing we have to establish is whether or not we take the Bible as God's Word or something less than that. The answer to that question determines our response to the answers for all the other questions we ask."

Holly had believed this for so long that she'd started to take it for granted, but Reagan looked amazed.

"That's it, isn't it? It's all about how I view the Bible!"

To Holly's surprise, Reagan got up and began to head to the door. The hostess watched as she had her hand on the knob and then caught herself.

"Oh, Holly, I'm sorry. I just have so much to think about. I didn't mean to be so rude."

"It's all right. Can I help with anything else?"

Reagan looked at her. "Do you have an extra Bible I could read?"

"Yes, I do. Let me just get it."

It sounded as though someone dropped a plate in the kitchen just then, but Holly didn't go there. She disappeared into another room and returned to give Reagan a dusty Bible.

"This was my father's. You read it for as long as you like."

"Thank you, Holly. I'll take good care of it."

"I'm not worried about that. May I tell you something, Reagan?"

"Sure."

"I'm praying for you."

Reagan didn't know what to say. She wasn't overly surprised, but she still didn't know how to answer.

"I've been meaning to ask you, Reagan," Holly continued, "do you have Sundays off?"

"Not the whole day, but Sally has given me enough time to go to church."

"That was kind of her."

"It was, wasn't it?"

Reagan left then. She had not known exactly how to thank Holly or say goodbye, but it seemed to Reagan that she understood.

❧ ❧ ❧

"What is it that makes her tick?" Russell asked that night.

"I don't know. She hasn't really said anything about herself, and she certainly shows no sign of hating men, but she's not going to trust one to be in charge of her."

"I can honestly say that I've never known anyone like her."

"I wish you could have seen her face when I made that statement."

"About the Bible?"

"Yes. She was flabbergasted. And then after she left I realized there was so much more I could have said."

"Maybe it was best that you didn't."

"Maybe."

A very sleepy Alisa sighed softly from her quilt on the floor just then, and Holly remembered that she wanted her in bed early. Russell volunteered to do the honors, and Holly sat down in the living room to read a book to Jonah and Elly.

"Did Miss Sullivan come today to talk about God?" Elly asked before the book was opened.

"In a way she did. She's been coming to church and had a few questions."

"Does she love God like we do?"

"I'm not sure what she believes, Jonah. I think she's searching for answers to things in her heart."

"Do I have questions in my heart?"

"I think you must."

"What are they?"

Holly smiled. "Well, the first would be if you have questions in your heart."

The little boy smiled then, and Holly bent to kiss his adorable face.

"We didn't pray for her at dinner tonight," Elly said, her little brow furrowed in thought.

"Didn't we?" Holly honestly couldn't remember.

"I don't think so."

"Well, we can pray right now. All right? Jonah, would you like to pray?"

The little boy nodded and began.

Returning to the living room while Jonah prayed, Russell listened quietly.

"And please God, help Reagan to be saved. Help her to want Jesus in her heart. Help her not to be afraid anymore. Amen."

Russell looked at his son.

"Do you think Reagan is afraid of something, Jonah?"

"Well, maybe she's not, but she might be afraid that God wouldn't want her."

Russell smiled at him very tenderly. The little boy had summed up so neatly what many people believed. His own sister felt that she had to clean herself up before she could approach God. Nothing Russell and Holly had ever said could sway her. His sister was still trying to work on her life so she would be "saveable" in God's eyes.

In truth Russell and Holly didn't know if this was Reagan's problem or not, but when the quiet time was over and their two older children were in bed, they prayed for Reagan about that very thing.

🌱 🌱 🌱

Reagan had all she could do not to growl with frustration. She had thought the Bible would be so easy to read and understand, but the different passages she turned to were about as clear as mud. She read that evening until she had to turn in and even tried again before work the next morning, but it was no use.

She wasn't in the best of moods to be heading to work, but she was liking her job more and more, having found the best method to do things and settling into her routine with Sally very nicely. And of course the dining room always made for a change. One could never anticipate exactly what would happen.

For all Reagan's sarcasm and sometimes-sharp tongue, she knew she was genuinely liked by the men who ate breakfast at the hotel each morning. Some were rather persistent about her joining them for a cup of coffee. She always said no but never grew angry or irate as long as they kept their hands to themselves. Indeed, she took it all in so calmly that they found her all the more intriguing.

Reagan had learned early on never to tell a man that she had no plans to ever be married. Men could be counted on to respond in one of two ways. Some said they were fine with that plan since they were only looking for a little fun and not a ball and chain—something Reagan found highly insulting. She thought the term "ball and chain" fit a man much better. Others attempted to talk Reagan into agreeing with them on the spot that every woman needed a husband. The term "ball and chain" was the last thing on their minds. Reagan had learned that both conversations were futile.

Nevertheless, some days she was flattered. A few men were so charming and persistent that Reagan had to stop herself from smiling for fear of encouraging them. One such man was Tyrone Arnold. He went by the name of Ty, and there was no getting around his good looks and fine manners. He looked at Reagan as though she were the last woman on earth, and never once had he intimated that he was just out for a few laughs. At the same time, he never once proposed or asked to take her out for the evening. He always made Reagan feel as though she'd made his day simply by waiting on his table.

Today was about to be different.

Reagan worked on pies until it was time to go out front. As always, the door opening from the back brought the delicious smell of food along with Reagan's presence, and the men loved it.

"We thought you'd never come," one young cowboy complained. He would take Reagan out every night if she would only agree.

"I can see you've suffered greatly," she said dryly, filling his cup without giving him any encouragement.

"When do I get a ride on that bicycle?" he asked, but Reagan didn't answer. She was getting coffee, talking to a little girl who was out for breakfast with her father, and taking an order from Ty, who had just sat down.

"Whatever Sally has hot and ready," he said congenially.

"Hungry this morning?" Reagan knew she could ask this man and not get a lewd comment.

"Starving."

"I'll get her right at it."

"Hey, Reagan," someone else called in full voice as she moved back to the kitchen. "You still haven't answered the question I asked you yesterday."

Reagan glanced over her shoulder to answer but kept moving.

"I can't remember what you asked, but whatever it is, the answer's no."

Reagan exited on a wave of laughter.

"They sure like you," Sally said as she entered the kitchen.

"That's because they don't know me."

With no time for chitchat, the women sped headlong into the

morning. Reagan waited tables, finished the baking, and was scrubbing pots when the back door to the kitchen opened. Ty was standing there.

"Hello, Ty," Reagan greeted him. "Are you looking for Sally? She's in her office."

"Actually, I came to see you."

Reagan's guard went up, but she tried to brush it off.

"Did I leave a strip of bacon off your plate?"

"No," he said with a smile. "You never make mistakes with my breakfast."

There was a warm tone in his voice that Reagan didn't like, but she only looked at him.

Ty was swift to see that she wasn't smiling at him in return and knew it was time to get to the point. He did so, keeping his voice even and businesslike.

"I didn't want to ask you in front of the others, Reagan, because I wanted you to take me seriously, but I was wondering if you'd have dinner with me some evening this week?" Reagan was already shaking her head when he added, "I want to talk to you about a job."

Reagan was suddenly all ears.

"A job?"

"Yes."

"What kind of job?"

"I want to tell you about it over dinner."

Reagan shook her head. "You've got the wrong girl, Ty. Any job that has to be discussed over dinner . . ." She let the sentence hang.

"It's not like that, I assure you, Reagan. I have tremendous respect for you and a job that would be perfect for you if you're interested. It's not a job I'm offering to anyone else, so you let me know if and when you want to hear about it."

To Reagan's amazement, he turned for the door and exited. He was only a dozen feet down the alley when Reagan, whose curiosity had gotten the best of her, made it outside and stopped him with one question.

"Can I meet you somewhere for dinner?"

Ty turned.

"What do you mean?"

"I don't want to be picked up at my house. I'll come to dinner and hear about the job if I can meet you."

"That's fine," Ty agreed, coming toward her a ways and gaining tremendous ground by agreeing to this term.

"How about this Saturday night?"

"How about Tuesday next week?"

Ty grinned, knowing he was doing the right thing.

"Tuesday, it is. Where do you want to meet?"

"Right here in front of the hotel."

Ty tipped his hat. "Tuesday, seven o'clock. I'll be here."

Reagan watched him walk away without a single romantic thought in her head, but she didn't think his handsome face would be hard to look at if she actually went to work for him.

🌹 🌹 🌹

"Okay, Reagan," Russell said the next evening as he did odd jobs in the little rental house. "Try that."

Reagan opened the cupboard door and found it working fine.

"It's perfect, Russell. Thank you."

"With all your independence," he teased her, "I'm surprised you didn't fix it yourself."

Reagan grinned.

"I left my tools in New York."

Russell smiled in return.

"Okay. What was next?"

"This window. The lock is a little loose. I've been thinking about buying a gun, but I haven't done it yet."

On his way toward the window, Russell stopped and turned to look at her.

"Are you saying that if you had a gun, you wouldn't need window locks?"

Reagan looked thoughtful.

"No, but I wouldn't be as concerned about them."

"Have you ever handled a gun?"

Reagan met the eyes that were trained on her and answered slowly.

"No, but I didn't think it could be too hard."

Russell's finger came up. "You do not make one move toward a gun without talking to me first. Do you hear me, Reagan?"

"Yes, Father."

"You can *Yes, Father* me all you please, but you do as I say."

Reagan's head tipped as she looked at him.

"What do you fear would happen?"

Russell looked shocked enough to cause Reagan to laugh.

"This is not funny, Reagan," he responded, trying to be stern. "You could shoot yourself or someone else."

"I think that would be the point."

Russell leveled her with a look.

"I'm not fixing another thing in this house until you agree to consult with me about any and all weapons."

Hands to his hips, the hammer held easily under one huge thumb, Russell waited.

"All right," Reagan said with a tolerant shake of her head. "I'll be sure to tell you, but you don't need to be such a tyrant about it. I don't know how Holly stands it."

"Holly isn't wandering around with a naive view of guns," he muttered as he went to work on the window. "Sometimes you scare me."

"I can take care of myself."

"That's what scares me."

Any stinging retort Reagan might have had was interrupted by Jonah's arrival. He'd been helping his father by finding a needed tool.

"Have you got it?"

"I think so. Is this it?"

"That's the one," Russell congratulated the little guy as he took the tool from his open palm.

"How are you, Reagan?"

"Miss Sullivan," his father corrected, his back to them as he worked on the latch.

Reagan only winked at Jonah and brought out a jar of candy she had bought at the general store.

"Would you like a peppermint drop?"

"Yes, please."

"How was school today?"

"It was fun," he answered around the ball of candy swelling his cheek. "I like school, but sometimes I miss Alisa."

"She probably misses you too."

Jonah gave her his shy smile, and, as always, Reagan's heart melted a little.

"Jonah," Russell called to him then, "climb up here and hold this for me, will you?"

The little boy was swift to help, his eyes catching Reagan's one more time and with one glance telling her how proud he was to be asked to help his dad.

The Bennett "men" finished up at Reagan's a short time later, and as nice as it was to have everything repaired, Reagan hated to see Jonah go. Quite suddenly she wanted to be with that little boy whenever she could.

🌸 🌸 🌸

"You're coming on Saturday, aren't you, Reagan?" Jonah asked as Reagan walked him home from school, forgetting again to call her Miss Sullivan.

"What's on Saturday?"

"The party at Cash's ranch!" Jonah looked up at her with huge eyes, as if her not knowing was some type of crime. Elly had ridden ahead on the bike, and Jonah and Reagan walked slowly along behind her.

"I don't think I'm invited, Jonah," she said, feeling a need to be honest.

"Everyone is! Pastor Ellis said so."

"Is it a church party?"

Jonah nodded with great enthusiasm. "We have lots of fun. We get to swim in the pond, play games, and even ride horses all by ourselves! And then we eat dinner under the big shade trees by the house."

"That does sound fun. Are you sure everyone is invited?"

She was treated to another nod. Huge eyes punctuated his words. "Pastor said. He was about to tell everyone they could stand, and then he reminded us."

"So this has been planned for a while?"

"We always go. Every year. Mama says it's tramition or something like that."

"Tradition?"

"Yeah. Tradition."

The house was in sight now, as were Elly and the bike. The little girl was jumping off, however, and running to hug her mother, who stood on the front porch.

"I think Miss Sullivan spoils you," Holly said as she wrapped her arms around her oldest child.

"She's so nice, Mama. Jonah and me like her so much."

"Jonah and I. And your father and I like her too."

"Mama," Holly heard Jonah calling as he ran, "Reagan can come to the party, can't she? I asked her and told her about the pond."

"Reagan," Holly asked as soon as she was within earshot, "did you not hear the announcements these past weeks?"

"I guess not. The whole church is invited?"

"Yes. It's a wonderful time. We go every year. It starts at about two o'clock, and we often stay until dark."

"This Saturday?"

Holly nodded, trying to gauge by Reagan's face whether she would attend. Holly would have been doing well to figure it out as Reagan was not certain herself. She had a meal with the Bennetts almost every week and saw the children daily, but other than a brief exchange about how the Bible reading was going, neither Holly nor Russell could gain an idea of what Reagan thought of the church family.

They shared little more conversation just then. Reagan gave Jonah a quick ride on the bike and then went home.

Once in her house, Reagan sat at her little table trying to figure out the yearning inside of her. She desperately wanted to attend the party and be with these people as she had the first morning when she hadn't needed to rush off for work. At the same time the idea terrified her, and she had no idea why.

Before walking back to the hotel, she sat for just a few minutes more, all the while telling herself she just wouldn't go. No one was forcing her, and she didn't have to!

"But I'm sure not going to show up without a cake or something," she muttered as she hit the back door of the kitchen, knowing she would have to borrow a pan from Sally or go empty-handed. She was also sure that if anyone could have read her befuddled thoughts just then, they'd have committed her to an asylum.

Eight

IT HADN'T BEEN EASY, BUT SHE HAD done it. Still vacillating right up to the end, Reagan ended up having to ride her bike to the Rawlings Cattle Company—not a long journey, but made a good deal more challenging by the need to carry a frosted layer cake in one hand.

Reagan rode under the arch of the gateway at the head of the driveway, not letting herself do more than glance at the sign, and in no time at all the house and many wagons came into view. To Reagan's surprise, Cash Rawlings himself came down the driveway to meet her.

"Well, hello," he said, managing to take the cake and catch and steady the bike all in one smooth movement. "Welcome to the ranch," he continued, as if people always arrived in just that manner.

"Thank you," she said as she jumped down, still breathing hard. "I'm a little late."

"Not at all. The games are just getting started. Thank you for bringing the cake, by the way."

"Oh, you're welcome. I wasn't sure what to bring."

"The cake is fine," he said, not willing to tell her that this was not a potluck.

"Something sure smells good."

"That's the beef we've got turning over the fire. It does smell good, doesn't it?"

"Spoken like a man who eats beef every day."

Cash laughed. "It kind of goes with the job."

"Where should I put my bike?" Reagan suddenly wanted to have her hands free.

"Why don't you put it there by the Bennetts' wagon? Then you can hop a ride home."

Cash waited for Reagan to come back from propping it against the wheel. He kept the cake and escorted her up the drive.

"How did you know which wagon belonged to the Bennetts?" she asked.

Cash smiled. "I don't know."

"How about the others?"

Having never given a moment's thought to this, Cash was nevertheless able to stop, look down the line, and name the owners of every wagon or buggy.

"Is it that you're a rancher or that I'm a city girl?"

"I don't know." Cash was again at a loss. "Can you pick a woman out by just the color of her dress?"

"Of course. What does that prove?"

"Maybe nothing, but maybe it's about interests and not just about living out of the city. I can't say that I would know a woman if I caught sight only of her dress."

Reagan looked up at her tall, redheaded host. She saw a kindness and a humility in him that she hadn't encountered very often. She was still thinking on it when the house, with many empty tables in front of it, came fully into view.

"Where is all the food?"

"Still in the kitchen."

"How did you make it fit?"

"Well, most of it's still in pots or in the oven. And don't forget, the beef is on the spit out back."

Reagan was not long in putting two and two together.

"This wasn't a potluck, was it?"

"No."

"Were you going to tell me?"

"Certainly not! You might have taken your cake back."

Reagan found herself laughing. She hadn't expected to. She was ready to be embarrassed about bringing food to a gathering when it was not needed, but suddenly that didn't matter.

"Hello," a woman called from up near the house. "Did you make that cake? She didn't have to make a cake, Cash," the woman said to him as though it was all his fault. "Land sakes alive! Give it to me now and go join the games. This one's going to make my cakes look terrible. Look at all that frosting."

Reagan stood with her mouth open as the scrappy little woman had her say, took the cake, muttering the entire time, and disappeared inside the huge ranch house. She finally looked up to see her host smiling at her and remembered to shut her mouth.

"That was Katy," Cash supplied. "She takes care of me."

"Do you need someone to take care of you?"

"Constantly," he said dryly. "Come on, Reagan. Let's join the party out back."

❧ ❧ ❧

"Is it me?" Reagan asked of Holly a few hours later, "or is everyone here extremely nice?"

Holly smiled. The two women were walking alone near the pond. People were milling everywhere, but no one else was a part of their conversation.

"That's a hard one to answer, Reagan," Holly said, opting for complete honesty.

"Why is that?"

"Because I don't want to lead you to believe that we're perfect. We all have feet of clay."

"Feet of clay?"

Holly was swiftly reminded of how Christians can fall into using clichés that aren't helpful to others.

"That saying comes from the book of Daniel in the Old Testament. The passage is talking about a statue that's made of fine gold and silver, but its feet are made partly of clay and partly of iron, so it's vulnerable in that area.

"I just now used the phrase since I'm afraid that your brief time with us has given you the wrong impression. Yes, people are nice—very nice—but that's only because of the work God has done in our hearts. We still sin, and sometimes we're not kind to each other, but most of the people here have made a personal commitment to God through His Son, and because of that, we're changed."

Reagan nodded but didn't comment. The women continued to circle the pond, sometimes walking among the pecan trees that bordered two sides. Holly kept glancing at Reagan's face, and when she could read her expression, she had to ask the question in her heart.

"Have I said too much, Reagan?"

"No, but it takes a little getting used to."

"What does?"

"People who call themselves Christians but are humble about it."

"Reagan," Holly said firmly, "I think it's time you tell me what kind of Christian you've known in the past."

"I thought the usual kind," Reagan admitted, "but you're smashing all those notions."

"How am I doing that?"

"By admitting that you still sin. The Christians I've known made me feel as though I was the only sinner in the world. They never once talked about not being perfect."

"And you knew better."

Reagan stopped and stared at her. Holly stopped with her.

"They would carry their Bibles everywhere but not stop to give a coin to someone starving in the street! They went to church and talked with each other, but they only came near the rest of us when they were ready to preach a street sermon. I told myself that if that's what becoming perfect means, they could have it!"

"And well you should," Holly shocked her by saying.

"You agree with me?"

"Of course I do. Clearly these people hadn't spent much time looking at the life of Jesus Christ. He went wherever He was needed. He was thronged by the sick and helpless. His own comfort was never foremost in His mind. He always looked for a way to teach. At times He preached, but often He healed the sick with just a word or two about who He was. He saw to the physical needs as well as confronting the spiritually sick time and again, but anyone who did call on Him, anyone who wanted to know the way of salvation, was never turned away. It's the same today. We can call on Jesus Christ, and He will save."

"When did you call on Him, Holly? When did you believe all of this?"

"When I was a child. My parents believed in Christ, and one night when I was frightened by the dark, my father talked with me about God's being everywhere, whether it was dark or light. Then he said God wasn't in one place that he knew of, and I naturally wanted to know what he meant. My father was talking about my own heart. So that night he explained to me the way Christ died for me, and I believed."

"The next race is starting!" The loud call came to everyone within earshot of the pond. "Line up behind the house, and we'll group off by ages."

Holly glanced up and then back to Reagan.

"Do you want to keep talking about this, Reagan, or join the race?"

"Let's go watch the race," Reagan said without hesitation, but then asked, "Is that okay?"

"It sure is, as long as you know where you can come with your questions."

"I know, Holly." Reagan put a hand on her arm. "Thank you."

The women moved with the group toward the rear of the house, and for the moment, the subject was dropped.

❧ ❧ ❧

"She rents from you?" Jerome Hill, one of the single men from church, clarified as he sat at a table with Russell and Cash.

Russell nodded. "Since the middle of January."

"And how did she end up at our church? Has she said?"

"It wasn't by her design, I know that. She was walking through town on a Sunday morning and heard us singing."

"And what does she think?"

Russell smiled. "Last I knew she was still trying to figure us out."

"So you don't think she's a believer?"

"No, I don't. She's searching—Holly and I can see that—but I can't tell where she'll end up."

Jerome nodded, his face not giving anything away, but Russell understood the questions. Theirs was a church unlike others in that they had a surplus of single, interested-in-marriage men. There was not one single young woman in the church, for the simple reason that nearly all who entered found themselves courted and married. This didn't happen all that often, but when it did, it gave the waiting men more hope that God might have a bride for them, one who shared their beliefs.

"I wish I could tell you she was a believer, Jerome; not just for her sake, but for yours as well."

"Well, I can still pray for her, can't I? Even if nothing ever comes of it for me, I can still ask God to save her."

"Indeed, Jerome. Someday she might even thank you for that."

Jerome didn't stay at the table too much longer, but the moment he left, Russell confronted Cash.

"Why haven't you asked me about Reagan?"

"I was the first one to meet her that Sunday, Russ. I know the situation."

"True, but you've never mentioned her need for salvation."

"But you know I'm aware. I pray for her every time God brings her to mind."

"And how often is that?" Russell asked, watching him closely.

Cash smiled. This was the crux of the matter, and they both knew it.

"There are two problems here, Russ, and you know the first one."

"Yes, I do," he admitted quietly, knowing this conversation was one between good friends. Russell Bennett would never wish for his friend to marry an unbeliever, no matter how endearing. He now stated it plainly.

"You can't go falling for a woman who isn't a believer."

"Exactly."

"But I don't know the second reason."

"That has to do with Reagan herself," Cash explained. "Even if she did come to Christ, I can see that she doesn't want a man of her own. She doesn't mind being friendly to all of us, women and children included, but she isn't looking for a husband."

Considering that neither Russell nor Holly had told Cash this, Russell thought him rather astute.

"You're right. She fears having a man control her."

"I thought as much. I would say she's wise about living life on her own, and because of that, I think she's a little short on trust."

"She's used to taking care of herself; I can tell you that."

Cash suddenly laughed. "She rode up the drive on that bicycle, the cake held in one hand . . . I was very impressed."

"Did she think it was potluck?"

Cash nodded.

Cries from Alisa stopped the conversation. They both looked up to see Holly coming with the baby in her arms, a red-stained handkerchief held against the child's head.

"She pulled herself up next to a tree," Holly explained, "and then proceeded to fall against it and cut her head on the bark."

"Go on into the house, Holly," Cash instructed as Russell rose to hold the door. "Katy's in the kitchen."

Cash smiled at the big, tragic eyes that looked at him from Alisa's tiny face just before she buried it against her mother again.

"How is she?" Reagan asked, coming up as they went into the house, a baby's blanket in her hands.

"I think she'll live."

"You're sure to be right. She's the third, and they're usually pretty tough."

"Do you speak from experience?"

"Not personally, no, but several large families lived on my street in New York. I was close to one of them, and we ended up with the saying, 'There's no one tougher than the youngest Caminiti.'"

"And who was the youngest Caminiti?" Cash asked, working to get his mouth around the different-sounding name.

"Tony," Reagan said with a smile. "An adorable, round-faced two-year-old who had a smile for everyone."

"You miss them, don't you?"

"The people, yes, but not New York." Reagan glanced around. "The sky here is so big, even at night. There's more dust than I thought existed anywhere on the earth, but I can live with that."

Cash looked down into her earnest face, the creamy complexion, the dark, curly hair and intense dark eyes, and found himself praying for Jerome. There was no doubt about the right thing to do, but if the men in the church weren't careful, they were going to succumb to this woman's charms.

🥀 🥀 🥀

"Thank you for everything," Reagan told Katy at the end of the evening. Her bike was already loaded in the rear of the Bennetts' wagon, but Reagan didn't want to leave without thanking the woman who had done so much work.

"Well, don't be a stranger," the ranch housekeeper said. "You come back anytime. That cake was a good one. Have you got your plate?" she asked for the third time.

"Yes, ma'am. Thanks again."

Katy waved her off, dismissing the words—something, Reagan noticed, she did with everyone. A few minutes later Reagan found herself in the back of the wagon with the Bennett children, darkness coming fast. They made the ride home in near silence, the children almost asleep at the end of the drive, and the adults alone in their thoughts.

Reagan enjoyed picturing the ranch in her mind. She thought it was a wonderful place, so wide open and grand. The trees that sat in front of the large two-story ranch house had provided abundant shade. Reagan had walked through the barn, which had dozens of horse stalls, and stood at the corral fence. This city girl wasn't any judge of horseflesh, but Cash's horses seemed very fine indeed. And the pond. Reagan smiled at the memory. Pecan trees, wooden benches, and a nice expanse of water all lingered in her mind as she watched the children swim, sat with the adults to visit, or walked with Holly around the perimeter.

Some of her conversation with that lady came back to mind, but her brain was too weary to take it in.

Had she but known that Russell and Holly were in the same position, she would have laughed. Both of them wondered if she'd had a good time and what she'd thought of the day and the people, but neither one had the energy to ask.

Home came into view when all were more than ready to arrive, and with only the briefest words of good night, they unloaded the wagon and went their separate ways.

❦ ❦ ❦

"You're meeting who for dinner tonight?"

"Ty. He says he has a job for me. And you know I'm always trying to better myself."

Sally's brows rose. "What's the job?"

"He wants to discuss it with me then."

Sally looked more than a little skeptical, and Reagan was not going to let that pass.

"Should I not trust him?"

"I didn't say that."

"But you're thinking it."

"No, I'm not. Ty is utterly respectable, but he doesn't have the type of job that would need a woman's help."

"What does he do?" Reagan asked, knowing full well she should have asked the man himself.

"He builds houses."

Reagan blinked.

"Like with a hammer and nails?"

Sally laughed. "Yes, just like that."

Reagan chewed her lip a moment. The breakfast crowd was long gone, and she was working on cleanup. A moment later, the same dry pot in her hand, she told herself to go through with the evening's plans.

"Well, I'm going to meet him and at least hear him out."

"Why isn't he picking you up? In my day, a lady didn't meet a man on the streets."

"You make it sound clandestine. I just feel safer not having men know where I live. 'In your day,'" she went on to mutter. "You sound 102."

"I feel 102, believe me."

That night, as Reagan stood and waited for Ty to arrive, she remembered the conversation from the morning. She wasn't really worried, but she was early for the meeting in hopes that her escort would come soon and she could ask him about his business and the job he had in mind.

"Well, Reagan," said a male voice to her right side.

Reagan turned to see Cash coming up the street.

"Hello," she greeted him.

The tall cowboy came up the boardwalk and stopped as Reagan turned to speak to him.

"You look as though you're meeting someone."

"I am."

"What's her name?"

"It's not a woman."

Cash frowned. "A gentleman asked you out for the evening but didn't offer to escort you from home?"

His tone put Reagan off a bit, but she still admitted, "I asked to meet him."

"Why would you do that?"

Reagan's gaze shifted away and back again before she answered. "I didn't want him to know where I lived."

Cash's face told her she'd shocked him.

"Let me get this straight," Cash said, a little too calmly. "You're going to spend the evening with this man, but you don't trust him enough to tell him where you live?"

Reagan's gaze shifted again. She started a little when Cash suddenly moved and sat on one of the benches in front of the hotel.

"What are you doing?" Reagan asked as she turned to watch. He was only ten feet away.

"I'm sitting here to make sure you're going to be all right."

"You might be used to people taking care of you," Reagan informed him, her mood growing dark, "but I do just fine on my own."

"That's why you're sitting safely at home waiting for this man to escort you safely to dinner."

Reagan frowned at him.

"Who is it, by the way?"

"Tyrone Arnold."

Cash didn't comment, and Reagan got angry.

"You don't have to do this," she hissed at him.

Cash only stared back at her, crossed his booted ankles, and settled in, looking for all the world as though he was staying the night.

"You have a huge nerve, Cash Rawlings," Reagan told him, clearly not happy with his actions.

"And you have more guts than good sense."

Reagan's gaze narrowed. Russell Bennett had said something very similar to her, and she didn't like it. Who did these men think they were?

"I want you to leave."

Cash shrugged. "I'm just sitting on a public bench in front of the hotel."

"We both know that's not true."

"We also both know that you're more worried about this meeting than you're letting on."

Reagan's chin rose in the air, but she didn't deny it.

"If you're not," Cash pressed her, "move down the walk a ways. I'm sure Ty will still find you."

Reagan turned her back on him. She didn't know when she'd been so angry. She did not, however, move down the walk. She told herself she didn't have to. If anyone should move, it should be Cash! But even in her anger she wasn't quite convinced. It was on her mind to simply turn and walk home. She didn't have to meet Ty. No one was forcing her, and she certainly didn't have to answer to Cash Rawlings.

Reagan decided to make her move. She would give Cash a few more words to put him in his place and then walk home. In her mood, she'd be there in a matter of seconds.

But in truth, more time had passed than she figured. Before she could do anything, she looked up to see that Ty was nearly upon her.

Nine

"HELLO, REAGAN," TY SAID, A HUGE SMILE on his face. "You look nice."

"Thank you," Reagan said, relaxing a little. Why hadn't she just told Cash that she didn't fear Ty and let it go at that? Indeed, looking into his handsome, smiling face, she couldn't think why she hadn't told him to come for her at the house.

"Are you ready to go?" Ty asked; he hadn't even noticed Cash's presence on the bench against the building.

"I am, yes, but I do have one question. What kind of work do you want me to do?"

Ty licked his lips. "Can't we talk about it over dinner?"

"Well, in truth," Reagan improvised, trying to keep her voice normal, though she was suddenly nervous, "you shouldn't have to spend money on a meal for me if I wouldn't be suited for the job. Why waste your time and efforts?"

"It's no waste of time, Reagan." His voice grew perceptibly warmer. "I want to buy you dinner."

Reagan caught the tone and stiffened her resolve even as she sensed the whole evening was about to fall into a heap around her ankles.

"Please tell me."

Clearly he didn't want to, but there was no missing the set line of her jaw.

"Reagan, if only . . ." he began, but Reagan shook her head. "All right," he conceded, his voice sounding weary and cautious. "I want you to become my wife and take care of my children."

Reagan couldn't keep her mouth shut.

"You have children?"

"They're my sister's kids. She died a year ago, and I can't do it on my own anymore. That's the job I'm talking about—being my wife and mother to Sammy and Kara."

Reagan felt sick to her stomach thinking about all his smiles, warm looks, and kind manner. He wasn't being friendly. He wanted to marry her!

"I'm sorry, Ty. I have no interest in being married, not to you or anyone else. It's nothing personal, and I can certainly understand why you didn't want to discuss this while I was on the job, but I'm not the woman you need."

Tyrone Arnold was a desperate man. He needed a wife very badly. But he was also proud. With little more than a brief nod of his head, he turned and went on his way. He had thought the children would sway her. He'd worked for hours on the meal they would eat, not willing to tell her until the last moment that they wouldn't be going to a restaurant, so sure that meeting his niece and nephew would help her to see his position.

As he walked on, he determined that she'd never know how hurt he was. As tears of frustration and helplessness filled his eyes, he determined to walk away and never look back.

Still standing just where he'd left her, Reagan stood like a statue, her heart a lump of iron in her chest. It wasn't supposed to happen this way. He wasn't supposed to look so hurt and vulnerable. She didn't want to marry. Had he offered her a nanny's job, she would have heard him out, but not wife—not now, not ever.

"Are you all right?" Cash asked from her side. Reagan had all but forgotten him.

"I'm always all right," she answered without thought.

Cash made a small sound in his throat and took her arm. "Come on."

"I want to go home."

"You will, eventually."

"Where are we going?" she asked.

"We're going to see Holly and Russell."

"How do you know they're home?"

"Because I was already headed there."

Reagan didn't respond, but neither did she argue. At the moment there wasn't any fight in her at all.

🌿 🌿 🌿

"Reagan, why did you agree to go out with this man?" Holly asked, trying to gain a clear picture with the little bit that Cash had shared. The four adults were sitting in the Bennetts' living room.

"He offered me a job."

"Ty Arnold?" Russell questioned. "He builds houses."

Reagan glanced at Cash.

"I found that out only this morning. The job he had for me was to be his wife and take care of his children."

"I didn't know he had children."

"He said they're his sister's kids. He said she died a year ago and he couldn't do it on his own anymore."

The Bennetts were quietly shocked. They had been expecting Cash, but not with Reagan in tow. And not just any Reagan, but a subdued Reagan who had frowned at Cash at least once and looked over at him often. That she found him highhanded was obvious, but they both understood why he'd brought her with him. Had he not been coming for the evening, he probably would have dropped Reagan off and left.

"Why were you looking for another job, Reagan?" Holly asked.

"I'm trying to better myself, Holly. I don't want to bake cakes and wash pots for the rest of my life—not unless I'm running my own place."

Holly nodded in understanding.

"I mean," Reagan went on, warming a little to her subject and hoping that Cash was listening, "the secret to this life is knowing what you want and going after it. No one is going to take better care of me than I am, so I've got to do it to the best of my ability."

No one in the room commented on this, and Reagan knew exactly what they were thinking. She stood, her movements agitated.

"Yes, you can all stay very quiet, you who have this knowledge about God, but not all of us share in that."

"But you can, Reagan," Russell said. "It's yours for the asking."

Reagan knew that now was the perfect time to admit to them that the Bible had been as clear as mud to her, but pride kept her mouth shut.

"May I ask you something, Reagan?" Holly put in when Reagan remained silent.

The other woman nodded and sat back down. She had other friends in this town, but it wasn't her choice to be at odds with anyone, and these people had been more than kind to her; not to mention they were her landlords.

"I don't know what you have come to understand and what you

aren't getting," Holly began, "but I'll start by asking if you realize that *you* have to make a step here? God is waiting for you to humble yourself and believe. Does that make sense to you, Reagan?"

"I think so."

"Why aren't you sure?"

Reagan looked at her lap. "The Bible hasn't been very clear to me."

"That's no surprise," Holly said, and Reagan was amazed at how often Holly took her off guard.

"What do you mean?"

"I mean, the Bible is a love letter to believers. I can understand if it's not clear to you. Prior to someone coming to Christ, he doesn't have God's Spirit to help him. I'm not saying that a person can't understand, but when he doesn't, I'm reminded to whom the Bible is written. It's for Christians."

"So how do I stand a chance?"

"You stand a chance because God says that anyone who asks may receive, and God never lies. You've told me that you understand what's being taught on Sunday mornings, but what I think you're missing is that you have to own that belief yourself. You can't just spend time around Christians and hope that what they have will rub off on you.

"You can admire us and be fascinated all you want, but until you reach out in faith to God, you won't have the eternal life we possess. We aren't going to love you less, Reagan, if you don't believe, but I would be no friend to you if I didn't tell you plainly what you need to do."

"Like God being everywhere, but not in my heart."

"Exactly. God doesn't force Himself on us. He'll only be in your heart if you'll open it to Him."

Reagan was quiet for a moment, and the others let her be.

"May I think about it?"

Sitting across from Reagan, Russell and Holly both smiled. Naturally Reagan looked surprised.

"We're smiling," Holly explained, "because I used to feel that a person must believe on the spot. Russell was the one to point out to me what a huge step believing is. God takes it very seriously, and so should you. You should not jump into this blindly. God requires no less than full commitment from His children."

Reagan closed her eyes. She wasn't sure she wanted to hear this. Fear about what God would require of her filled her, and she wanted to escape.

"Would you care for anything to eat, Reagan?" Russell suddenly asked. "You didn't get dinner, did you?"

"I'm not very hungry, but thank you."

With that she stood, knowing she could do so without offense. "I thank you for your hospitality, but I think I want to go home."

"That's fine," Russell said, his deep voice calm.

"Reagan," Cash spoke. The small woman turned to him. "I'm very sorry if you're upset with the way I handled things. I just didn't want to see you hurt."

"It's all right, Cash. I was upset, but I do understand, and I thank you for caring."

Reagan moved to the door, thanking her hosts again, but Russell caught up with her on the front porch.

"Reagan, if you do decide to read the Bible again, work on the third chapter of John."

"The third chapter of John? Is that the same as St. John?"

"Yes. The New Testament starts with Matthew, then Mark, Luke, and John. John 3. It's all there."

Reagan sighed a little.

"Don't be discouraged, Reagan. Holly is a good friend to lay it on the line to you. Trust us when we tell you, God never hides from those who seek Him."

Reagan looked into his smiling face and smiled in return as her heart reminded her that this man had been different from others she'd known. His life did not contradict his words. She could say the same for his wife and his friends.

Not willing to tell him that at present, she went on her way, thinking she might actually do as he suggested.

🌹 🌹 🌹

Katy Sims headed into the general store a day earlier than usual. Saturday was her usual day to stock the pantry and get supplies, but the big party always depleted her stores, and she thought Friday afternoon was as good as Saturday morning when she was low on sugar.

"Hey, Katy," Lavinia called when she entered.

"How are you for raisins right now, Lavinia?"

"Just in."

And with that they were off. Katy was one of the proprietress's favorites. She was picky to a fault and would brook no nonsense, but that she patronized her store spoke volumes to the other establishments in town.

More than an hour later, Katy finished and was ready to leave.

She left instructions about the way she wanted things loaded into the wagon, telling Lavinia she had business down the street and she would return.

"You keep an eye on things, Luke," she said as she did most weeks, addressing the new ranch hand who had been chosen to drive her. "I won't be long, so you wait for me right here."

"Yes, ma'am," Luke responded with the utmost respect, having taken his cue from a certain ranch owner, who, although he teased his housekeeper, still treated her like a cherished family member.

As usual Katy was in a hurry. The day was warm but not hot, and she was due for an outing, but having come into town in the afternoon put a damper on any kind of window shopping. She needed some molasses candy, the kind Cash liked, and only Reynolds carried it.

Katy was almost to the other store when Reagan sailed by on her bicycle. The older woman stopped in surprise. Reagan caught the movement out of the corner of her eye, and when she glanced back, she saw it was Katy. Reagan quickly turned and rode up parallel to the boardwalk.

"It's you!"

Reagan smiled, glad to see Katy. She had liked the outspoken older woman. Not sure why, she was nevertheless very drawn to her.

"How are you, Katy?"

"You're going to kill yourself!"

Reagan laughed. "No, it's fun. You should try it."

Katy's eyes grew huge, but in truth she was fascinated.

"No," she said, having regained her good sense. "I'd fall and break my neck."

"No, you wouldn't. I'd help you." Reagan glanced around. "No one's watching."

"Oh, go on with you! I can't do that in town."

Reagan smiled again.

"I'll have to come out to the ranch."

Katy only waved her off, but Reagan thought she had seen a sign of genuine interest. Not even bothering to return Reagan's goodbye, Katy went into the store, found the candy for Cash, and went on her way. It didn't take long before she was back at the wagon, and after Luke helped her aboard, they started home.

In less than a minute, town and all she had seen were forgotten. Dinner had to be made and supplies put away. Anyone listening to Katy's thoughts would have said that she took her job too seriously. Katy would have scoffed at such a notion. There was nothing serious about it. It was her job, and it had to get done!

"You can help me unload, Luke," Katy announced when they returned to the ranch house, the hand having taken the wagon around back so they were closer to the kitchen. His reply was a simple "Yes, ma'am." He'd been told by the ranch's foreman, Brad Johns, to expect anything and to stay until he was dismissed.

The ranch house at the Rawlings Cattle Company was as modern as any home in the area, and the kitchen was no exception. It was a cook's dream for meals and baking. Spacious, with work area and floor space and a pantry you could walk into, the kitchen area allowed Katy to put out a meal for 30 without even breaking a sweat.

"How about these sacks of sugar?" Luke asked, both shoulders laden.

"Bottom shelf on the right. You'll see the space."

"Do you need some help?" a male voice asked from the doorway. Katy turned to see Max, the ranch hands' cook.

"I think there's still some in the wagon," Katy told him. "Wipe your feet."

"Yes, ma'am," he drawled, having known just what she was going to say.

Katy had washed her hands and was getting ready to mix biscuit dough when Max returned.

"Why'd you go today?"

"I'm out of things," she said, as if it was the most logical reason in the world.

"I'm goin' tomorrow."

"Good. If I remember I've forgotten something, I'll put it on your list."

"My own list is plenty full."

"Well, one more item won't hurt. What are you making the men tonight?"

"Fish stew. Luke's brother caught a slew of bluegills and landed them all in my kitchen."

"I thought they hated fish stew."

"No, they don't!" His voice grew indignant. "It's that lamb stew I tried! I had a revolt on that one," he muttered, but there was a twinkle in his eye. Katy smiled a little herself.

Max Reed and Katy Sims had been friends for more than ten years. Max wasn't as old as Cash's housekeeper, but age had never been a factor. Their jobs—the very nature of being at the ranch nearly every day and not out on the range—simply drew them together.

"Is that wagon done?" Katy asked Luke when he came back with yet another load.

"Just about."

"Well, when you finish, you just get yourself over to that jar and get some cookies. Do you hear me?"

"Yes, ma'am," Luke replied, just barely holding his smile.

"And you get out from under foot, Max Reed. I've got Cash's dinner to put on."

"I'm goin'. I'm goin'. I got my own work to do."

Katy snorted as though he didn't know the meaning of the word and kept on with her dinner preparations. Cash came on the scene about an hour later when supper was just about ready.

"How were things in town?" he asked while having a quick wash at the basin. She'd told him that morning she was going a day early.

"Did you know that Reagan Sullivan rides a bicycle?" she demanded, turning toward him.

Cash laughed. "I take it you saw her?"

Katy shook her head in amazement. "She's going to break her neck!"

"I don't think so," Cash said confidently. "If anyone can take care of herself, it's Reagan."

Katy looked at Cash, her eyes narrowing.

"You sound interested."

"In what?"

"Reagan."

"You mean as a woman?" He looked confused.

"No, I mean as a horse. Of course, as a woman!"

Cash was already shaking his head.

"Now don't you say no to me, Charles Rawlings! She couldn't be sweeter, and something tells me she's a hard worker."

"I'm sure she's all of that, but she doesn't share my faith, Katy," Cash told her soberly.

The woman's eyes widened.

"But she came to the church party, and I've seen her at church too."

"Well," Cash kept his voice gentle and worked not to show his surprise, "we both know that attending church does not mean you believe."

This shut Katy's mouth. Cash had not intended to put her in her place, but she simply had no argument, and they both knew it. And the reason was a simple one: Katy had been attending church off and on with Cash for a couple of years, but never once had she been willing to talk about what she was hearing.

One Sunday morning Cash had asked her outright if she had ever gotten serious about her relationship to God. Katy had not pretended ignorance. She told him plainly that she didn't think she was a sinner and didn't believe God would condemn anyone He had created. And that wasn't the end of it! She had made it very clear to Cash on that day that she didn't wish to discuss it anymore.

But they had been sharing the same house for a long time, and he knew from other comments she made that a lot of her beliefs stemmed from her relationship to his parents. When he had first come to Christ, she had naturally wanted to know how his beliefs were different from his parents'. His explanation had not been well received. She thought the sun, moon, and stars rose and set on the senior Charles Rawlings and his wife and would hear no word to the contrary. Cash could still recall the scene.

How could you say such a thing, Cash Rawlings! Why, your mother took me in when I didn't have a thing. We've worked side by side in this house since the first year it was built, and now with them in St. Louis and not even here to defend themselves, you say they're not Christians!

"Dinner's ready," the housekeeper announced, her voice sounding completely normal.

"It smells good. What is it?"

"Veal medallions in peppercorn sauce. And if you'll check the little bowl in the living room, I've got your favorite molasses candy in there."

"What would I do without you, Kate?" Cash asked as he sat down to eat.

"Just curl up and die, I 'spect."

Katy didn't stick around to eat with him as she often did, and tonight Cash was thankful. He had little choice but to leave the subject of faith alone, but not having her in the kitchen allowed him to spend a little extra time in prayer. As he did often throughout the day, he asked God to soften Katy's heart so that she could see her need of Him.

Cash finally tucked into his meal but had only taken a few bites when his foreman knocked on the back door.

"Come in," he called.

Brad entered, taking his hat off before seeing that Katy was not in the room. Cash smiled when he replaced it and sat across from him.

"I'm headed out now."

"All right. Who're you taking with you?"

"Dusty and Zeke."

"Zeke?"

"I'll tell you, Cash, if you can get past that baby face, there's a lot of man there. He never complains, and because he was raised in the hills, he's a good man to track those coyotes."

Cash nodded. "I'll leave it up to you."

"One of the girls has a cold by the way," Brad added, talking about one of his two daughters. "I told Brenda to come up here to the big house if it gets worse."

"Good. I'll have Katy check on her tomorrow."

"All right, boss," the cowboy stood, his hat still in place. "I'll see you next week."

Cash waved him on and went back to his meal. Of all the changes he'd made since taking over the ranch from his father, the best was putting in a house for his foreman. Prior to that, his father had been through several foremen. They had been young and lacked experience. Men with better qualifications usually had wives and children. With no place for another family to live at the ranch, it was very difficult to offer the job to such a man.

"Where did she get that bicycle anyhow?" Katy demanded, suddenly coming on the scene. Cash nearly choked on his food for laughing.

"Are you still thinking on that?"

"Have you seen her?" the woman asked, as though that explained it all. This said, she went on her way, leaving Cash to wonder just what kind of impact Reagan Sullivan was going to have on them all.

Ten

REAGAN HAD MEANT WHAT SHE SAID. She had no doubt in her mind that anyone could ride a bicycle, and now she was headed to the ranch to let Katy try. This trip to the ranch, however, was a bit different. There was no cake in her hand, and she was not late and in a big hurry. Letting herself look all around, Reagan rode as though she didn't have a care in the world. And if she worked hard enough, she could even convince herself that she didn't.

It had been more than a week since she'd been scheduled to meet Ty and ended up in the Bennetts' living room. She hadn't touched her Bible or gone to church since she left them. She wasn't angry, but she just didn't think she could agree with their way of thinking. The whole idea of letting God rule over her ran her blood cold. What if He demanded more than she could ever give? What if she had to give up what she found most dear—her freedom?

Reagan's thoughts were interrupted when she realized the gateway to the ranch had come into view. She could hardly wait to see the surprise on Katy's face. Indeed, she was still laughing at the older woman's proclamation that she would break her neck.

She picked up the pace a little, excitement running in her veins, and before she knew it, she was hopping off the bike, bounding up the steps, and scooting across the wide porch to knock on the big wooden door. Feeling antsy, she wiggled around a bit when no one came. Making a harder ball with her fist, she came close to pounding this time, and sure enough, she heard someone speaking as she approached.

"You'd think it was locked," Katy muttered as she pulled the door open and found a smiling Reagan on the porch.

"I'm here with the bike!" she announced, her dark eyes sparkling.

Katy stared at her.

"You said you wanted to ride."

"Land sakes! Have you lost your mind?"

"Not at all. You can do it, Katy. A woman in my neighborhood in New York learned to ride, and she was much older than you."

"How old?" Katy shot at her.

"Very old," Reagan assured her.

"Oh, for pity's sake!" Katy exclaimed, but she also came onto the porch and walked to the top of the steps where she could look down to where the bike leaned against the railing.

"You do it," Katy suddenly turned and demanded.

Not saying a word but smiling hugely, Reagan descended the steps, put the bicycle into position, gave it a little push, hopped on with the ease of breathing, and rode in a little circle as though she'd been doing it all her life.

"Where did you get that?"

"I sent for it," she called from the leather seat. "It was in a catalog."

"How did you learn to ride?"

"I just did it. I held onto the side of a building when I first got going. It took only a few hours. It'll be easier for you, since I'll be here to help and steady you."

Katy licked her lips. Cash was always teasing her about being old and set in her ways, but what if he came off the range tonight and found her riding a bike? Reagan could stay for dinner, and Katy could greet Cash from the seat of that metal contraption.

Having convinced herself, Katy moved down the steps. Reagan all but shouted with enthusiasm and jumped off the bike to let her have a try.

"Okay," she urged the older woman, who was smaller in frame and height than she was. "Gather your skirt to one side with your left hand, and take this side of the steering bar with your right. Okay? Good. Now, let the bike roll a bit and then make a quick jump, releasing your left hand very fast, and grabbing the bar, just as you land on the seat."

"You must be out of your mind," Katy said with complete conviction.

"Here." Reagan took the bike from her. "Watch me. I don't have to hold my skirt over anymore, but I'll do it so you'll understand."

Katy stood back and watched as Reagan made it look very easy. She even hopped off and started again to show her.

"What if I tip over?"

"I'll run alongside and catch you."

Katy just about said no but then remembered how hard it was to surprise Cash.

"You'll stay right with me?"

"Yes. I won't let go unless you tell me."

Her mouth pursed with determination, Katy tried it and was surprised into a breathless gasp that it actually worked. Reagan kept her hand on the bar and seat, running alongside and encouraging her all the way. Katy made it several feet before she got wobbly and had to jump off.

"It just about jars your teeth out!"

Reagan smiled. "I know! Isn't it fun?"

Katy couldn't help but laugh as she said, "All right! Let's go again."

This time they got down to real business. The housekeeper even commanded Reagan to let go. She did very well for a good ten yards before taking a spill. Recovering very nicely, she even fussed over the dirt on her dress.

"Are you hurt?" Reagan asked as she rushed up.

"No. I want to ride some more."

Reagan laughed. It had been the same for her. Once she'd gotten the hang of it, she hadn't wanted to do anything else. In the next half hour the two had more fun than either could remember in a long time. Reagan even showed Katy a few tricks she had taught herself. Not warm by nature, Katy was thinking that she didn't ever want this girl to go home.

"I'll have a try at one of those tricks," Katy said.

"Maybe you'd better give it some more time, Katy," Reagan cautioned.

"I didn't mean it," she said as if Reagan should know. "I just want another ride."

Reagan stood back and watched her hop on. She headed down the driveway and then turned to come back. The turn was what ended the fun. She started to fall, and just as Reagan had taught her, put her foot out. This time, however, she was moving too fast. Her leg could not support her and down she went at an awkward angle. Reagan thought it looked painful and swiftly rushed to her side.

"Are you all right?"

Katy didn't answer.

Reagan moved so she could look right down into her face. The housekeeper's complexion had gone very pale.

"It hurts," she said.

"Where, Katy?"

"My leg. I can't move it."

Reagan could have died on the spot. That Katy might get hurt had honestly never occurred to her.

"I'll go for the doctor," she said, her voice rising in panic.

"No, send Max."

"Where is Max?"

"In the bunkhouse. You know the one?"

But Reagan didn't answer, she was already running, her skirts hitched up to give her freedom. She was fairly certain which building was the bunkhouse, but when she pounded and yelled, a woman answered.

"Where's Max?" Reagan demanded.

"In the bunkhouse. What is it?"

"Which one's the bunkhouse?"

"There," the woman pointed. "What's happened?" she called again, this time to Reagan's retreating back.

"Katy's hurt! We need the doctor," she yelled as she moved to the other building, not waiting to see if the woman heard her or not.

♞ ♞ ♞

Today they were branding calves. Normally Cash would not have been directly involved, but with Brad gone, he felt he needed to be on the job. That morning he had met with a man who hailed from the east and wished to go into ranching. Cash didn't think he would actually do it—he'd been too horrified by the smell of cattle—but Cash had been more than willing to answer his questions and offer help in any way he could.

The event caused Cash to think about the type of man his father was. Charles Rawlings Sr. had been born and raised in the city, but when an opportunity came to turn his hand to Texas ranching, he had jumped at it and been successful in the bargain. The ranch he handed down to his son was very prosperous.

Working without having to give the branding any thought, Cash let his mind wander to his family. He'd been with all of them just that January, but it seemed so long ago. He'd received a letter from Darvi the week before saying she and Dakota were doing well and settled in a small house in town. Cash was glad that the town was small. He liked thinking about his brothers ensconced in small, close communities like Kinkade.

"He's loose!" one of the men yelled when his rope slipped. Cash jumped to his feet—lariat in hand—to rope a runaway whose mother bellowed to him from outside the makeshift pen.

It was while Cash was finishing rounding up this stray that he looked up and saw Brenda riding toward him at a furious pace, her hair and clothing blowing out behind her. Cash's heart plummeted with fear, knowing she wouldn't be out here for anything short of an emergency.

"It's Katy," she called as she reined the horse to a hard stop. "She fell hard."

"Todd," Cash ordered, his voice belying the feelings inside, "go for Doc Bruce."

"Max went," Brenda told him, still breathless.

"Who's with Katy?" Cash asked, even as he moved toward his mount.

"Some woman. I didn't have time to get her name."

With this cryptic news, Cash's horse left Brenda's in the dust as he rode for all he was worth back to the main house. He went in the back way, and when he couldn't find her inside, he rushed for the front yard.

A mixture of surprise and concern filled him when he saw the bike, Reagan, and his housekeeper, who was still lying in the dirt.

"Katy!" he said, running fast and dropping to her side.

"I've done it this time, Cash," was all she said, her eyes clouded with pain.

Afraid to move her or even touch her, he naturally turned to Reagan for answers.

"She fell off the bike," Reagan told him, her face showing her own measure of misery. "She was doing so well . . ."

"It's all right, Reagan," he said, hoping it was true. "The doctor is on his way. He'll get her all fixed up."

Part of which proved to be true. The doctor was on his way, and when he arrived, they moved Katy, a terrible ordeal for the older woman, to a bed in the small downstairs bedroom. But fixing her up was not going to be so easy.

"Her hip is broken," Dr. Bruce told Cash, Brenda, and Max after they'd waited outside the closed bedroom door for about 20 minutes. Reagan had gone in to help. "She'll be laid up for a good long time."

"How much pain is she in?"

"Right now it's intense. She needs to lie still and not worry."

The doctor continued to speak with Brenda and Max, but Cash needed to see Katy. He slipped past the threesome and entered quietly.

The curtains were pulled back, allowing plenty of light to filter in. Cash found Reagan sitting next to the bed gently bathing Katy's face and hands. The fact that his housekeeper allowed this spoke volumes to him concerning her condition.

Cash took the other side of the bed. There was no chair, so with a hand to the oak headboard, he leaned down to speak into her face, asking himself as he did if she'd looked that old at breakfast that morning.

"How is it?"

"I've never broken anything, Cash."

He nodded. All three of the Rawlings boys had broken and cracked various bones, and although Katy had been as compassionate as they'd ever known her in her ministrations of them, she had not experienced this pain before.

"The doctor says you have to lie still and not worry."

"How am I supposed to do that? Who's going to take care of you?"

It was her standard line, and Cash smiled at her, glad to hear she had at least one small tease left.

"Maybe it's time I grow up."

Katy sighed. "I should have insisted that you take me to my house," she said, referring to the small bungalow that sat next to the foreman's house.

"Then I wouldn't be able to take care of you like I can now," Cash reasoned.

"You've got a ranch to run."

"Brad will be back in two days. When he's here, I'm not even needed."

Had Katy not been in so much pain, she would have given her customary snort. Instead she closed her eyes, thinking she might cry for the first time since Virginia Rawlings moved back to St. Louis.

Seeing her eyes closed, Cash motioned to Reagan. The two left the room together. The doctor slipped back in to check on his patient, and Cash was glad for a few minutes alone with his guest.

"You're not to blame yourself for this," he said to Reagan's set features.

"She didn't ask me to bring the bike. I just thought it would be fun."

"So you forced her?"

"No, but—"

"There are no 'buts.' It was an accident. She'll be fine."

"She's not a young woman, Cash. Why didn't I see that?"

"She'll be fine. It will take awhile, but she'll be back to her old self again."

Reagan only half heard him. She was already making plans to fix things, and her mind had shifted away from the man who faced her.

"All right, Cash," the doctor interrupted him, "come in here, and I'll tell you what she needs."

Without being asked, Reagan joined them. She listened in silence, but with every word the doctor spoke to the rancher, her resolve strengthened.

Cash did not comment as Dr. Bruce mapped out his expectations, but he could see that it was going to be a lot of work in the weeks and months ahead. The doctor had a powder for the pain, but not enough with him. The men eventually exited the room so Cash could send a man to town to get the medicine.

Reagan went back to the edge of the bed. Katy's eyes were still closed, but her mouth was open and her breathing told Reagan she was lying in very great pain. Without a word, the small, dark-haired woman exited—not just the room, but the ranch house itself, heading for her bike. She was back on the road just a minute later and headed for town. She had a lot of work to do before nightfall.

※ ※ ※

"You're not riding back there in the dark!" Sally said for the second time. "And I mean it."

"But don't you see, if I go now it won't be dark."

"That's not true, Reagan. The day has gotten away from you. It'll be dark in an hour, and you said you haven't even gone home."

Reagan sighed.

"I know what this is about," Sally guessed. "You haven't told Cash Rawlings that you're going to do this, and if he hears a wagon, he'll send you packing before you can even climb out."

Reagan looked away from her and admitted, "I'm going to do this, Sally, with or without your help."

"That's just it, Reagan. I am willing to help you."

She turned back.

"So you understand?"

"Completely. Now, I think you should head home and get your stuff. Talk to Holly or Russell if you can so they won't worry, and then come back here. I can take you almost all the way there, and you can ride yourself the rest of the way."

"I don't know what I'd do without you, Sally."

"Well, I know what I'm going to do without you," she retorted. "I'm going to get up before dawn tomorrow and start baking."

Reagan gave her a hug. She couldn't help herself.

"Get out of here," she ordered, and Reagan hurried on her way.

Just 30 minutes later she was back, not having been able to speak with her landlords. Sally promised to tell them about the change. As soon as Reagan was ready, they settled into Sally's buggy and that woman, good friend that she was, took Reagan as far as the gate.

Reagan put her carpet bag handle over the bar on her bike and rode as steadily as she could manage. It was almost fully dark, but she could see what she needed. Heart pounding in her chest, she knocked hard on the door and waited.

"Reagan," Cash said with surprise. He answered the door, a lantern in his hand. "I wondered where you'd gone."

"I had to go home to get my things."

This said, she scooted past him and walked to the living room, looking for all the world as though she was there to stay. A moment later, Cash learned that she was.

"I'm here to take care of Katy and to do her jobs until she mends."

Cash stared at her, finally taking in the bag.

"You don't have to do that," he tried.

"But I'm going to. I've quit my job; I have money to live on for a time, and I'm here to do whatever needs to be done."

"You will not quit your job," he started to declare, but to his surprise, Reagan turned her back on him and started toward Katy's room. Cash was hard on her heels.

"Reagan," he began again, but she marched resolutely away.

"Reagan?" This time the name came from Katy as Reagan crossed the threshold of her room. "I was looking for you."

"Well, you don't have to look anymore. I'm here to take care of everything."

"You're not," Katy said, hoping above hope that it was true.

"Yes, I am. I'm going to take care of you and this house until you're up again and as bossy as ever."

Cash had entered the room right behind Reagan, so it would have been impossible for him to miss the sob that broke in the old woman's throat.

"I didn't know what I was going to do," she cried softly. "I've got to take care of Cash and this house. It's my job."

"It's all right," Reagan said gently, coming to take her hand. "I'm here now, and I'll see to it."

Cash had never seen this woman cry. He didn't know she was capable of such an act. He stood still while Reagan bent over her, talking in soothing tones and bathing her face again. Even in the lantern light he could see some of the worry lines easing around Katy's brow and temples.

He had no idea how it could possibly work to have Reagan living and working in his home, but sending her away from Katy right now was just not something he was willing to do.

Eleven

REAGAN SULLIVAN IS SLEEPING DOWNSTAIRS with Katy, Cash told God that night, speaking as though this would be news to Him. *I'm not sure I can do this. I'm not sure I can have her here. There's so much I don't know about her, and she doesn't know anything about us either. I understand that she's here because of what happened, and I can see why she'd blame herself, but in the space of a few hours, she quit her job and moved here!*

For a moment Cash only lay on his back and stared at the ceiling. The events of the day had put him in a near state of shock. It broke his heart to see Katy as he never had: broken and flat on her back. And then to have Reagan show up at the door! It was all too fantastic to be real.

Help me, Father. I need to take care of my Katy. Maybe this is what will draw her to You, but before I can help her spiritually, I have to figure out a way to help her physically. Brenda is willing to help, but she has the girls to care for, and if her changing shape is any indication, she has another one on the way. I'm willing to do anything Katy needs, Lord, but I'm not a woman and . . .

Cash's mind came to a complete stop. He had been staring up with his eyes open, but they now closed as he remembered Reagan.

I think You must have sent her, Lord. I would never have asked her to come, but Katy was so glad to see her. I have never seen Katy cry.

Cash's own throat closed at the memory. It had been awful to see her vulnerable and tearful, but the more he thought about Reagan's presence, the way she comforted Katy, and the fact that that woman even accepted it, the more a peace stole over his heart. He would not have planned to end the day the way he did, but he now chose to be thankful.

In a moment of time things change so quickly, Lord, but You're never surprised. Whatever You have for tomorrow, help me to be ready and thankful for Your care.

Suddenly realizing he wasn't the least bit tired, Cash relit the lantern and opened his Bible. He read for almost an hour, and when he did fall asleep, it was with the sweet knowledge that God was still very much in control.

🌹 🌹 🌹

"I wasn't sure how you liked your eggs" were the first words that greeted Cash the next morning; he had barely taken two steps into the kitchen. "I scrambled them. Will that be all right?"

"Yes," Cash said, not used to having his opinion asked. Katy knew his likes and dislikes very well. Neither was he accustomed to having such a young, attractive woman flushed and working over the stove in his kitchen, but clearly she had found her feet. As efficiently as if she did it every day, she laid the table service where he always sat, set his plate in front of him, and filled his coffee cup while he watched.

"I found a small pitcher of cream and assume you take it in your coffee."

"Yes, I do. Thank you," Cash said, getting over his surprise enough to sit down.

Reagan put both sugar and cream in close reach, her movements relaxed but very capable.

"Now she might eat something for me," Reagan muttered good-naturedly, turning away to replace the coffeepot and lift a waiting tray that held a second breakfast.

"Katy's awake?"

"Yes, but she wouldn't eat a thing until you'd been served."

Cash's mouth tightened. "Well, this is the last day for that. Here, give me that tray."

Upon seeing his expression and hearing his tone, Reagan knew better than to argue. She stayed where she was, and realizing she needed to eat as well, fixed herself a small plate.

Cash, on the other hand, did not give his own stomach or cooling food a second thought. Tray held firmly in his large, work-roughened hands, he headed in to straighten a few things out with a certain stubborn old woman.

"Cash," Katy said in soft surprise. "Did you finish your breakfast already?"

"No, I have not," he said, his voice sounding more angry than she had ever heard him. Cash set the tray on her bedside table, pulled the chair close, sat down, and looked at her. "We will have one thing straight right now, Kathleen Sims. I am not the one in need of tender care."

"Well!" Katy said with a small spark of her old indignation. "What did she fix you that you're so put out?"

"I mean it, Katy," he said in a no-nonsense way. "You can lie in this bed and tell Reagan how you want things done until you're blue in the face, but you'll not tell her to feed me and take care of my needs first."

"What will you do?" Katy challenged. The pain was riding her hard, but she could not let this pup have his way.

Cash sat back and crossed his arms.

"That's easy. I'll forbid her to see to a single one of my needs. No food cooked, no clothes washed, nothing."

"I'll just tell her otherwise."

Cash stood, moved the tray so she could reach everything and then put his hand on the headboard to lean over her once again.

"This is still my home," he said with deadly calm. "It was a surprise to see Reagan at the door last night, but after a few hours of thinking it through, I see her as a blessing. But her main purpose here is to take care of *you*. If she doesn't understand that, I'll get someone who does." Cash straightened, his voice returning to normal. "Start your breakfast, Katy, and I'll ask Reagan to check on you as soon as I've explained the situation to her."

Cash left the sickroom without a word. He found Reagan in almost the same position as he'd left her. As he sat back down at his now-empty place, movement caught his eye. He looked to see Reagan using the corner of her apron, and taking his meal from the oven. She set the hot plate before him.

"Please sit down, Reagan. I need to tell you a few things."

Reagan obeyed, her face sober, but rebellion growing in her heart. She was not leaving here, no matter what he said!

"You're not here to take care of me," Cash stated. "I can understand Katy's distraction with that since she's done nothing but see to my needs and the needs of others for many years, but if she's ever going to get out of that bed and walk again, she needs to take care of herself."

Reagan's heart turned with pain at the thought that Katy might not make a full recovery.

"If it makes her feel better to have you changing beds and doing other household chores, that's fine. But you're never, and I repeat, never, no matter what Katy says, to set her needs aside for mine. You won't hear this from her, but it's what I expect."

"What do I do if she tells me otherwise, like this morning?"

Cash looked her in the eye and admitted, "After getting over my surprise, I'm glad you're here, Reagan, but I know how I want this done. Katy sometimes forgets who's in charge. If you can't do as I expect, I'll find someone who can."

Reagan had no argument for that. Indeed Katy's very commanding presence had caused Reagan to forget whose home she was in. All remaining fight drained out of her. It was more than reasonable that Cash get his way in this matter, especially in light of the fact that he only wanted his housekeeper to be well.

"Do you have any questions?"

"No. I should tell you, though, that she was awake in the night and has some pretty aggressive plans."

"Like what?"

"She says she hasn't done the windows in a while, the rugs need beating—things like that. She also said your bedroom and office need turning out, and she was going to get to it next week."

Cash shook his head a little. "I think you should run everything through me for a while. You can take notes or whatever you need to keep track of what she wants done, but before you start any large projects, see me."

"All right."

"I need to tell you, Reagan," Cash added, "I'm very thankful that you've come to help her."

"It's all my fault, Cash. No matter what you say, I'll believe that." She shrugged and added, "There was nothing else I could do."

The rancher knew there was no point in arguing with her.

"Nevertheless, I thank you for your willingness to come and help." He paused suddenly, as he fully realized what a huge job they would both have. "Reagan," he went on, "the doctor said that Katy must keep still if her hip is going to heal properly so she can walk again. I don't want you to lie to her, but between the two of us, we need to keep her as calm and happy as we can manage. I'm not sure she'll make it easy, and I'm not going to let her run you ragged, but—"

Cash cut off when Reagan put her hand up.

"I know what you want, and I'm willing to do that."

Cash stared at her. He genuinely liked her, he realized, and at the moment he was more grateful to her than he could say. That it had been her bicycle that caused the accident was of little importance to him. She was willing to help, and he was very glad to have her.

"I did tell Katy that you would check on her after I talked to you."

Reagan pushed out of the kitchen chair.

"I'll go right now."

Cash ate his again-cool breakfast, his mind covering the things he had to do. Reagan could not keep sleeping on the floor of Katy's room, and his family needed to know what had happened. He ate without giving much thought to the taste, his mind on the full day ahead.

🌺 🌺 🌺

"What is that noise?" Katy demanded not long after Reagan started giving her a bath. She'd eaten a small breakfast and had been fairly subdued. Reagan had been the one to suggest washing up when she noticed the hair around Katy's temples and forehead was matted with sweat.

"I don't know."

"Well, go check!"

"As soon as we're done and you're settled."

"Oh, for pity's sake!" the old woman exclaimed in very real frustration. "I tell you, Cash does not know what he's talking about! I'm fine. Go see what that is!"

Reagan stood to full height, a glint in her eye and, surprisingly, a smile on her face.

"As me Irish father would say," she said, dropping into a remarkable Irish brogue, " 'Dinna fash yourself, woman.' "

"What?" Katy was so taken aback, she forgot about the noises.

" 'Dinna fash yourself.' In other words, don't fret yourself, don't worry."

"Easy for you to say," the older woman sniffed, turning her head with as much dignity as she could muster.

Reagan ignored her and went back to the bath. She made swift work of it, and by the time someone knocked on the door, Katy was bathed and in a fresh gown.

"Come in," Reagan called.

Cash's head came around the corner.

"I need to show you something, Reagan. Do you have a minute?"

"Coming right up."

"What were those noises?" Katy demanded.

"I'll tell you as soon as I get finished talking with Reagan," Cash said, waiting for Reagan to come to the door so he could take her out into the hall.

"If you're stirring up a bunch of dust, Cash Rawlings . . ." they both heard Katy begin, but neither one turned back to hear the rest.

"There's a small storeroom around here next to the pantry," Cash said, as they headed down the hall. "It was never meant for a bedroom, but if the closet door in Katy's room is open, you can hear everything in that room."

Reagan suddenly smiled at him.

"You sound as though you speak from experience."

Cash smiled at being caught out and laughed when he volunteered, "My mother's great uncle visited one time. With the way he snored, you could hear it all over the house, but my brothers and I did hide in this room one night just to get the full effect."

Reagan had a good laugh over this as they finished the journey to the room. She passed odds and ends of furniture and even some sacks of food that had been stacked against one wall of the narrow hallway. When she got to the room, she could see that someone had been busy.

The room was very small, but already there was a bed with a small table near the head. Suddenly, from behind Cash and Reagan, one of the ranch hands showed up with a small dresser.

"Right in the corner there, Luke," Cash directed. "Now, Reagan, we've got rugs to spare and just about anything you want to make this liveable. I don't want you sleeping on the floor for the next six weeks. It's simply not practical, and I don't think you'll be able to move around comfortably if I put another bed in Katy's room."

"But I can't be too far away and still hear her if she calls in the night," Reagan finished for him.

"Exactly. Now right here, on the other side of the wall, is the closet. We're going to try a few experiments and see . . ." Cash stopped talking, his voice trailing off for a moment.

Reagan watched him, as did Luke, both waiting for further instructions.

"Do you sleep soundly?" he finally asked.

Reagan shrugged. "I don't know. I've never given it much thought."

"Did you wake easily when Katy called you in the night?"

"I think so."

"But you were sleeping on the floor," Cash said as he did some thinking out loud, "and that couldn't have been very restful."

"Reagan?" Katy's voice suddenly came through the wall.

"Is that closet door open?" Cash asked as he turned to Reagan.

"I don't think so."

Cash worried the edge of his lip for a moment.

"I'd better see what Katy wants."

"Right!" Cash was brought back to reality. "Before you go, though, do you think you could be comfortable in here, Reagan?"

Reagan couldn't stop her smile, her eyes sparkling and white teeth flashing at him.

"You haven't seen my house, have you, Cash?"

With that she turned and went on her way. Not until then did Cash notice that Luke had not taken his eyes from Reagan. Remembering that night with Ty in front of the hotel, the ranch owner had all he could do not to pat Luke on the back and warn him that the lady would not be interested.

🌣 🌣 🌣

"I spilled my water!" Katy all but snapped at Reagan when she crossed the threshold. "Cash should just come in here and put me out of my misery. I can't even get myself a drink!"

Reagan did not comment. The thought of Katy dying horrified her, and for a moment she could not speak. She came close to the bed, lifting a towel from the basin on her way past. She mopped the water without overdo fuss, but inside she was shaken.

I've caused all of this. Katy's misery and all the inconvenience are my fault.

"Okay," Cash stated with enthusiasm, coming through the open door unannounced. "Here's the plan, Kate. Reagan and I are going to clear the stuff from this closet and then shut the door. You're going to hear a lot of cutting and pounding because I'm going to put a doorway through on the other side."

"Whatever for?" Katy asked, mouth open.

"Reagan's going to sleep in the little storeroom by the pantry, and the new door will give her access in here. I don't want another bed in this room, but she needs to be able to hear you."

The older woman looked so upset that Cash went to her. Reagan felt they needed time alone, but for some reason she couldn't move.

"Katy." The big cowboy said her name quietly, taking the chair and leaning close. "I want you better, and to do that you can't get out of this bed. Reagan has to be close to help you, but she can't sleep on the floor."

"But it's little more than a closet. Never has a guest in this house been treated that way."

"I know, and if things were different, it wouldn't have to be this way now, but Reagan understands."

"Maybe we should move to my house. I wanted Reagan here to take care of you, but maybe we should get out of your hair."

Cash picked up her hand.

"This is where you're staying until you can walk out on your own. When you're on your own two feet—bossy as the day is long—you can go home. Until then we're going to live together and probably drive each other crazy at times, but that won't change the facts. The three of us are going to do everything we have to do to get you out of that bed."

Listening to him from where she felt frozen in place, Reagan saw for the first time how much Cash loved this old woman. This kind of love was foreign to her. She didn't know what to do with it; indeed, it frightened her, but at the same time she was strangely touched by what she was witnessing.

"Okay." Cash stood, clearly ready to get to work. "We'll make it as fast as possible, but it will be noisy."

"Who's helping you?" Katy demanded.

"Luke."

"Well, that's at least something."

Cash went on his way, and Katy decided to take her mind off what she thought of as an intolerable situation.

"Have you met Luke?"

"I don't think so," Reagan said. She wasn't ready to talk, but keeping Katy's spirits in mind, she answered.

"I think he's about your age."

"Now, what would you be knowing about my age?" The brogue was back, and Reagan was smiling.

Katy snorted. "You can't be more than 20."

Reagan had a good laugh over this, and without even knowing it, Katy was drawn away from her pain as curiosity got the best of her.

"You don't mean to say you're older!"

"Indeed, I do," Reagan said as she straightened the room and even dusted the dresser.

"Twenty-one?"

Again Reagan laughed.

"No!" Katy exclaimed. "I refuse to believe it."

"I'll have you know," Reagan informed her, brogue still in place as she came to the end of the bed, "that I will be 24 later this year."

Katy's mouth opened and with good reason. Reagan did have a youthful appearance about her. And with her gutsy, sometimes zany, approach to life, Katy naturally thought her younger.

"What year were you born?" Katy prodded, certain Reagan could not be telling the truth.

"Eighteen fifty-nine. How about yourself?"

The number on the tip of her tongue, Katy opened her mouth but caught herself just in time.

Reagan smiled, and Katy shook her head a little in mock despair. But all of this fun came to an end just moments later when pounding and lots of movement started on the other side of the wall. Reagan went over and swiftly began to empty the closet so she could shut the door, but there had been no missing the pained look on the bedridden woman's face.

※ ※ ※

Reagan had never been so glad to sit down. Prior to speaking with Cash, she had been determined to clean the entire house *and* see to Katy's needs, but right now she saw that in no uncertain terms Cash had rescued her.

Katy was finally asleep. There was now a new passageway between Katy's room and her small bedroom. Katy had eaten and told Reagan she wanted to sleep, and Reagan had figured out that if she left the doors open, she could sit on the porch in a rocking chair and still hear if Katy called.

Her feet throbbing, even though she'd put them up on a small wooden bench, Reagan let her head fall against the high-backed rocking chair, her eyelids lowered just enough to find the horizon going to dusk. In that position, she was ready to think about the day.

Katy had received a surprising number of visitors, almost all food-bearing: the Bennetts; Max; Brenda and her daughters; two other cowhands; Pastor Ellis and Noelle; Lavinia from the general store; and Dr. Bruce again. Reagan had been introduced to the ones she did not know, but she did not visit with any of them or even stay close by. Katy still had things she needed from her little house, and finding them had taken some searching. Reagan also had her own room to clean and put together, wanting it done before nightfall. All had been accomplished, but by the time Reagan had started dinner, she'd been nearly cross-eyed with exhaustion, and the day wasn't done. Cash had turned out to be a marvelous help in the kitchen, but he'd gone to be with Katy while Reagan worked on the dishes. Never had Reagan been so glad to hear anyone say she wanted to sleep than when Katy made this announcement not long after the dishes were completed.

Reagan now shifted a little in her chair, thinking she should just head to bed, but before she could do that, her thoughts went back to the way Cash had dealt with the patient all day. Panic almost gripped the new caregiver. Cash's tenderness was still too much for Reagan to take in.

For the first time in a very long time, Reagan found herself asking her own heart why she could not let people love her. As a child she'd been starved for love and affection, but when she'd grown into womanhood and men were actually willing to marry her, her young heart had felt frozen in her chest.

And then today, having to watch the love between a pair who were like mother and son had been just as painful. *When*, Reagan asked herself, *had all love become a threat? When did I go from needing it so badly to being terrified by it? And where, if anywhere, does God fit into the whole picture?*

Not having answers to these questions was so confusing and painful to Reagan that she didn't even want to think about them, but one question would not go away, and that one was directed at God.

Do You really love people in a way they can survive?

The question repeated itself over and over again in Reagan's mind until she thought her head might burst. When she knew she couldn't think on it anymore, she rose wearily to her feet and made her way inside. A swift check on Katy told her that for the moment she was still off duty.

Trying not to long for the little house behind the Bennetts', Reagan took herself off to bed.

Twelve

Dear Slate, THE LETTER STARTED, the third one of the evening. *Katy has fallen and broken her hip. The doctor predicted that she will be laid up for about six weeks, but if she remains still during the healing process, she should be able to walk again with very little trouble.*

I won't try to go into details on how it happened, but there is a young woman from town who has moved in to help her. At first I didn't want her, but Katy was so glad to see her that I didn't feel I could send her away. I will keep you informed of Katy's progress, but if any business should bring you into the area, I know she would appreciate the visit.

Greet Duffy and the family and give my love to Libby. You're to take good care of her right now. God bless you all.

Love, Cash

Cash had deliberately kept all the letters short, but it had still been a lot of writing for one day. He would ride into town first thing in the morning and get them posted. Thoughts of town caused him to remember that, between him and Reagan, they would have to keep tabs on the pantry and other house supplies and needs. Max might be a help in that area, and he had offered to do all he could.

Cash sat up straight and thought about what a long day it had been. From his office he'd heard Reagan go onto the porch and now rose to check on her.

The porch was empty.

Lantern in hand, he made a swift check on Katy, found her sleeping, and knew it was time to close up for the night. He had no more gotten to her doorway, however, when she called Reagan's name.

"No, it's Cash," he whispered, going over to shut the closet door so Reagan would not be disturbed. "Do you need something?" he asked, approaching the bed.

"No. What time is it?"

Cash told her as he sat down.

"Why aren't you in bed?" she wished to know, but her voice was calm.

"I was just headed up."

"Good. You need your rest."

"I just finished letters to the family, letting them know you'd been hurt."

"You didn't have to do that."

"How do you figure?"

Katy had no reply. She knew very well that if she said anything, he would only remind her of what she would have done if the situation had been reversed.

"Cash?" she asked quietly.

"Yeah."

"Do you pray for me?"

"Yes, I do. What made you ask that?"

"Do you think God let this happen because I've sinned?"

"Not specifically, I don't, but at some point we all have to face the fact that we sin. If the fall you took helps you to do that, then I would say that was good."

"So you don't think I'm being punished?"

"No, but you know how I feel about God getting your attention, Katy. I think you've needed Him for a long time."

"What if it's too late?"

"I don't believe that, and God's Word doesn't support that idea either."

Again Katy had no reply. Cash wasn't sure what he should add or say, so he opted just to pray this time so that she could hear.

"Father in heaven," he began quietly, "thank You for Katy. She means so much to me. I ask You to help her heal well so she can be on her feet again, but even more than her body, Lord, I know her heart needs to be healed of sin, like mine did before I found You. Bless Katy this night and in the days to come. Thank You that Reagan could be here to help. Help us all to sleep so we can work hard tomorrow. In Your name I pray. Amen."

Cash stood, bent over the bedridden woman, and kissed her brow.

"Good night, Kate."

"Good night, Cash."

Cash opened the closet door again and then made his way from the room and up the stairway, thinking that his own bed was never going to feel so good. And he was right. Much as he was thankful for an opportunity to pray with Katy, knowing she was thinking about God, he could not stay awake to give it much contemplation.

❧ ❧ ❧

"Did I see Reagan at the church party?" Brenda asked of her husband the morning after he arrived home. He had surprised her by coming in very late on Thursday night when she hadn't expected him until Friday.

"I don't know," Brad said. "Did you?"

"I thought I did. Did you happen to notice her?"

Brad smiled, his eyes flirting with hers.

"You're the only woman I notice."

Brenda shook her head. "When I start believing that, Bradley Johns, it'll be a cold day in August."

Brad only laughed.

"Why did you want to know?"

"Because I'll go over and give Reagan a break with Katy if she wants to attend church."

"It's only been a few days, Bren," he said out of genuine concern for his wife's current condition. "I mean, it's a nice thought, but you're tired yourself these days."

"Nevertheless . . ." she said pointedly, hands going to her waist. Brad raised his own hands in surrender.

"You do whatever you think is best. I'll be talking to Cash about what he wants done on the ranch, but if you want to help out on Sunday, I'll watch the girls."

Smiling with pleasure, Brenda slipped her arms around his neck and kissed him. Brad found himself rather glad he'd agreed.

❧ ❧ ❧

"How does Doc say she's doing?" Brad asked of Cash later that same morning.

"He says she'll be all right if she keeps still."

Brad's brows rose.

"I know," Cash said, having read the foreman's mind. "We're doing all we can."

"What can I do?"

"Take care of the ranch."

Brad nodded, not surprised, and more than willing and capable. The foreman was about to ask some detailed questions when Reagan came through the kitchen door, set the tray down very hard on the table, and turned to both men, eyes blazing.

"There is *nothing* wrong with this food."

"Did Katy say there was?"

Reagan's voice grew tight with sarcasm.

"This isn't the way she bakes her bread. She likes a firmer loaf."

With a hand to his employer's arm, Brad went on his way. Cash waved him off and then went to the tray.

"Is this the same bread that I had for breakfast?"

"Yes, it is."

"I thought it tasted fine, very good even."

"But my patient doesn't."

Cash nodded, looking down into her flushed face. She was awfully easy on the eyes, especially when the color was high in her cheeks.

"I'll tell you what, Reagan," he said quickly to get his mind back on the business at hand. "When she gets hungry enough, she'll eat. Just give her a little time."

Reagan sighed. "The last thing you need me to do is get upset at her." She glanced up at him. "If I'm not careful, you'll have two unreasonable females on your hands."

Cash's smile seemed to say *I'm not too worried about it.*

"You don't upset easily, do you, Cash?" Reagan couldn't help but ask.

"Not as a rule."

"How have the two of you worked together all these years?"

Cash smiled again but didn't answer.

"Well, I'll try again." Reagan picked up the tray and went back to work. Cash told her he'd be in the office and left her on her own.

Reagan heard him go and thought that if she wasn't careful she could become very depressed. She was a people person. She liked to take care of things, and under all her bravado was pleased when folks were happy. Katy's dislike of the bread she made every day was a little hard to take.

But she still has to eat, and you've got to feed her.

This little pep talk over, Reagan started on another meal.

🌹 🌹 🌹

"Cash," Brenda called when she spotted him outside. Both of her girls were healthy again and back in school. Brenda had appreciated her husband's concern for her, but she was feeling fine and very much wanted to help Katy, who had helped them out so many times in the past.

"How are you, Brenda?" Cash asked as the two covered the distance and met between the two houses.

"I'm doing well. How's Katy this morning?"

"I think she's already tired of that bed. She wasn't too happy with what was on her breakfast tray, so Reagan was going to try again."

"I'm glad I caught you then, because I wanted to tell you that if you and Reagan want to go to church on Sunday morning, I'll stay with Katy."

"That would be great, Brenda. Thank you," Cash said with genuine relief. He had been thinking on that very problem as he wondered whether he should offer a wagon to Reagan so she could attend or simply go without her. This solution allowed him to go no matter what she wanted. "I'll let her know of the offer, and one of us will get back to you."

"All right. Or if Reagan just needs some time off, please come and tell me, Cash. Brad is rather fussy about me right now, but I'm sure I could give Reagan a half day's break with no problem, especially if the girls are home from school. They can always cheer Katy up."

"Thank you, Brenda. How are the girls, by the way?"

"Doing well. Robin's cold was nothing serious. I think she might have been a little worked up about her father's trip."

Cash smiled in compassion, albeit a bit distractedly, and Brenda said goodbye, sensing his need to get back to work.

"Thanks again, Brenda."

"You're welcome."

Cash moved to go on his way but ended up just walking back to the house. He couldn't remember the last time he'd had so much on his mind. He'd been headed somewhere when Brenda stopped him, and right now he couldn't recall what his destination had been. It didn't help to walk in the front door and hear Katy yelling. Cash figured that Reagan was tied up somewhere, so he rushed to her aid.

To his surprise and dismay, Reagan was standing at the foot of the bed, taking Katy's ill humor with a placid face.

"What in the world, Katy?" Cash began.

"She won't do it!" Katy nearly shouted. She was puce in color, her eyes bulging with rage. She looked as if her heart could fail at any moment. "I'm telling her she has to start in the office, and she won't go!"

"Please calm down," Cash began, trying not to think about how many weeks they had to go.

"But she won't listen. Did you hire her to take care of things or not?"

Cash knew right then that all those years of ignoring Katy's moods had been a mistake. He had let Katy have run of the house—much as his mother had—and now it was coming around to haunt him. He had never wanted to be too hard on her when she bossed him and everyone else. Indeed, it was something of a joke around the ranch, even with the woman herself, but now he could see that he'd not done any of them favors by letting it continue.

If he hadn't been afraid she might try to get out of that bed and hurt herself worse in the process, Cash might have called Reagan from the room and left Katy to stew in her own juices. Right now he didn't want to take the chance.

"Please explain to me exactly what you want Reagan to do."

"Your office!"

Cash paused and nearly shook his head. Katy had been on the verge of hysterics over his office not getting cleaned? Knowing that he had to get more sleep this night, Cash worked to question her calmly.

"What about my office?"

"It's got to be cleaned! She has to go over every shelf and book."

Cash turned to Reagan, whose eyes gave nothing away but whose face was pale.

"And is there a reason you don't want to do that?"

"You said that Katy's needs came first, and she still hasn't eaten a thing today." Reagan gestured rather helplessly with her hands. "That and the fact you've been trying to work in there."

With sudden clarity of thought, Cash turned stern eyes to Katy and knew that he was long overdue in explaining some things to his housekeeper.

"What gives you the right to put us all through this?"

Katy blinked in surprise. Cash's voice was utterly normal, but his words were astounding.

"Reagan comes out with her bicycle to give you a good time, you get hurt, and now you somehow think you have the right to make all of us fit into your agenda. I couldn't be more sorry that you got hurt, Katy. I wish it had been me. But it hasn't even been 48 hours, and you're doing everything in your power to make us all miserable."

Katy was still silent with shock.

"If you don't want anything to eat, that's fine, but Reagan isn't here to listen to you rant and rave. From now on, whatever you tell her to do, she'll do, even if you lie there and starve, but not once will you raise your voice to her or be disrespectful in any way. Do I make myself clear?"

The housekeeper was too shocked to answer, and Cash's mouth tightened in anger.

"I said, do I make myself clear?"

Katy could only nod.

Cash turned to Reagan now, not caring that it was right in front of Katy.

"You're here, Reagan, because you feel guilty. You're here because you think this is all your fault, and I understand and appreciate that, but no one should have to put up with what Katy is handing out. I'll understand if you want to move back to town. I'll even take you. Just say the word, and I'll find someone else."

"No, it's all right," Reagan responded, swiftly shaking her head. It had been a terrible scene to witness, and she just wanted to get away and be alone with her thoughts, but she made herself stay and listen. After all, this was her fault. "I'll be all right. As soon as you're done in your office, I'll start in there."

"Fine. I'm headed to the barn, so you go right ahead."

Cash left without another word.

Reagan was left alone with the bedridden woman.

"I'll just be across the way in the office, Katy. Call if you need me."

Still feeling very awkward about the entire scene, Reagan had not actually looked Katy in the eye as she said this, so she didn't notice whether the other woman nodded or acknowledged her in the least. Either way she was glad to escape. She was so tense she thought she might burst.

Dusting cloths and broom in hand, Reagan entered Cash's office a few minutes later and, at a first glance, could not find a speck of dust. Nevertheless, she got to work, thinking that when she was done, the room would never have been so clean.

☙ ☙ ☙

Cash finally remembered what he'd needed to do in the barn, but when he got there, he didn't start to work. Familiar sights and smells surrounding him, Cash stood and prayed.

Do I go back and apologize for speaking to her as I never have before or for letting her have her way for so long? Or do I let it go and hope I haven't ruined the relationship for all time? I don't know what to do, Father. I said what needed to be said. Katy needed to hear it, but she's not used to that from me. I'm not going to let her lie there and pout, and I can't let her slowly tear Reagan apart.

Cash tried to think. He couldn't be certain, but it seemed to him that Reagan was looking very tired. And why wouldn't she? Her hours at the hotel had been from morning into the early afternoon. Here she was on duty almost 24 hours a day.

After a few more minutes in prayer, Cash opted not to say anything else to Katy about the incident. When he finished in the barn, he would return to the house and carry on business as usual. He wasn't certain what to expect from Katy, and he was willing to allow her to deal with this in her own way, but only as long as the rest of them could still stand to live with her.

❧ ❧ ❧

Reagan's back hurt a little—there had been a lot of books to move—but the office looked great. She had polished, dusted, and swept, even going so far as to wash the inside panes on the windows. Now on her way out the door, Reagan took a moment to study a portrait on the wall.

A man and woman looked back at her. The woman had Cash Rawlings' eyes, and Reagan didn't have a hard time figuring out who they were. Neither one smiled, but Reagan thought that to have had a son as caring as Cash, they must be very kind.

"Reagan," Cash said as he came through the door, "I'm glad I caught you . . ." He started again but stopped talking without warning.

Reagan watched him walk around the room, not touching anything but smiling with pleasure at the job she'd done. He turned to face her when he was finally behind his desk.

"The office looks great. Thank you."

"You're welcome," she said with a smile, glad she could please someone.

"Those are my parents, by the way."

Reagan's eyes went back to the frame.

"I figured as much. You have your mother's eyes."

"So I've been told," Cash said as he moved to join her by the picture.

"What are their names?"

"Charles Sr. and Virginia Rawlings."

"Who's Junior?"

"I am."

Reagan frowned up at him.

" 'Cash' was all the better my brothers could manage, and the name just stuck."

"How many siblings do you have?"

"Two brothers, both younger. In fact, if you look at my father, you'll just about see an older version of Dakota."

"Dakota? That's an unusual name."

"It is, but it fits him."

Reagan looked back at the portrait, and Cash studied her. Again he found himself feeling rather drawn to her.

"Reagan's not all that common either."

"No," she said with a smile, "but I think it fits me too."

"It does," Cash had to agree. "What's your middle name, by the way?"

"Reagan."

Cash laughed. "Okay, what's your first name?"

"Eileen."

"Eileen Reagan Sullivan?"

"That's it. A fine Irish girl must have a fine Irish name," she told him, brogue in place.

Cash was delighted and wished she'd do it again.

"Who were you quoting? Your father?"

"That's the one. Mother got away with Reagan as a middle name only because it was her maiden name."

"How did you get away with not going by Eileen?"

"I didn't—not around my father at least."

"Why didn't you like Eileen? It's a beautiful name."

"It is, but I wanted the connection to my mother."

Cash saw the sadness in her face and was certain he knew why.

"Did she die, Reagan?"

"No, she left my father and me not long after my ninth birthday." Reagan looked up at him, her look almost daring him to pity her. "My father finished drinking himself to death three years later."

"I'm sorry."

"I'm not," she stated flatly. "After that, there was no one to stop me from being Reagan."

Cash thought it was the kind of comment she would exit on, but she stayed right where she was, her face still set.

"Before I forget," Cash said, changing the subject as tactfully as he could manage and walking back to the desk to pick up an envelope, "I have your pay ready. You can expect it every Friday."

"Pay?" Reagan asked as she moved to the desk and took the packet from his outstretched hand. She looked inside, not believing him until she saw the bills. She set the envelope back down.

"You're not paying me."

"Says who?"

"Says me."

Cash laughed. "Let's get something straight right now, Reagan Sullivan. I didn't hire you in the same way I did my other employees, but you've got yourself a job."

She began to shake her head, and Cash's brows rose.

"Don't even think about saying no to this, Reagan." He handed the money packet to her again. "You won't win."

Now Reagan's brows elevated.

"We'll just see about that, Mr. Rawlings."

Cash smiled at her tone.

"I'm not trying to play power games with you, Miss Sullivan. It's just that I'm a businessman with a ranch to run, and you are one of my employees. It's no more complicated than that. You're doing your job, and I'm paying you for it."

"But you wouldn't even need me if I hadn't—" Reagan began, but Cash wasn't listening. She could see that by his face.

"Take the money, Reagan," Cash stated for the last time, not really caring if he sounded high-handed. "I won't hear of anything else."

Cash went to his desk chair then, and Reagan knew the conversation was over. She did leave with the money as she exited the office, but even as she cleaned up so she could check on Katy, she was thinking of ways to get around her new boss's having to pay her.

Thirteen

"I COMPLETELY FORGOT TO TELL YOU something yesterday, Reagan." Cash started Saturday morning with these words.

"What's that?"

"Brenda says she'll stay with Katy while we go to church."

There was no mistaking the relief on her face.

"Did she really?"

"Yes. I usually leave around 9:20 if that will work for you."

"That would be fine," she said, but then hesitated. "Should I ask Katy?"

Cash shook his head no. "Has she spoken to you yet?"

"No. She had a good meal last night and again this morning— better than she has eaten—but other than thanking me, she hasn't said two words."

Cash's unconscious sigh told of the pain he was feeling. Katy hadn't spoken to him either.

"Just leave her be," he finally said. "You can't read her mind, so unless she asks for something, let her alone."

"I'll work on the house some more and check on her often."

"Good."

And they both discovered that it *was* good. Cash ate his breakfast, and Reagan went to work on Katy's regular chores. That it was Saturday and she should have gone to town for supplies was lost on her. She dusted, swept, and started the meat for dinner, all the while checking on Katy at regular intervals.

Cash went about his day as well. As usual on a Saturday night, the boys would be done a little early so they could head into town with their pay, and his own schedule was one he liked to keep monitored so that he was fresh for Sunday morning.

He worked in his office for a time and then went to check the livestock in the barn. It didn't take long, and as he made his way back to the house, the Bennetts' wagon came up the drive. He stopped, a big smile on his face, as it drew abreast of him.

"Well, hello," he greeted Holly and all three of the kids, even as he lifted Elly so he could swing her down from the wagon bed. Jonah scrambled behind his sister.

"Hello, Cash. I hope you don't mind the intrusion, but I have two little people who need to see Reagan."

"I don't mind at all, and she's going to be very pleased. Here, let me get Alisa."

The baby smiled at him as soon as she was in his arms, and Cash kissed her soft, pudgy cheek.

"How is Katy doing?" Holly asked after Cash had given her a hand down.

"She's having a pretty hard time with it all, I would say. How are things in town?"

"There she is!" Elly suddenly cried before Holly could answer, and both adults turned to see Reagan come out the front door. From across the yard they could hear Reagan laugh as Elly and Jonah ran to hug her. The three sat down on the front porch steps together, heads close as they snuggled and talked.

Cash looked back at his guest just as Alisa reached for her mother.

"And you, Cash Rawlings," Holly said as she settled Alisa on her hip, her voice low to give them privacy. "How are you doing?"

Cash smiled, knowing she could read him well after all these years.

"I think I'm still surprised that it happened at all. I keep expecting to see Kate in the kitchen and bustling through the house, but it's Reagan."

"How is Reagan doing? Is it dreadfully uncomfortable?"

"Actually, it's not. She's very competent, and she works quietly and effectively. Compared to Katy's bossing me around, the place is silent."

"So you're not sorry she came?"

"I was at first. I didn't think I could manage it, but she did so well with Katy that I didn't feel I had a choice." Cash laughed a little. "Katy's not even speaking to us right now, but Reagan just keeps on."

Holly's face told him she sympathized.

"We're praying for you, Cash."

"I can tell. I'm getting very little sleep, and it's probably the only way I'm holding up. But tell me, why did you visit when we'll see you tomorrow?"

"We weren't sure if Reagan would come."

"She's planning on it," Cash was glad to tell her. "Brenda Johns is going to fill in for her. You should have seen Reagan's face when I gave her the option."

"Relieved?"

"Definitely. I'm not certain if she's coming because she wants to be in church or get away from Katy, but either way, she's coming."

"I'm glad."

Up on the porch, Reagan was glad too. She had missed the children so much, and she thought if she had to go another hour with Katy's silent treatment she just might scream. She had just about decided to take a spin on her bike when she looked out the window and saw the children.

"How is school?" she asked them.

"It's good. We still like it."

"But we miss you, Reagan," Jonah told her. "And not just for rides on the bicycle."

Reagan laughed and hugged him a little closer. She thought about taking them in to see Katy, but if that woman was still pouting, the children would be hurt by her actions and wouldn't understand the reason.

"You know what?" Reagan said as she stood, taking the kids' hands in hers. "I need to see that baby."

Holly and Reagan hugged when the groups joined, and as everyone had come to expect, Alisa had a smile for whoever was holding her.

"I've missed you, Alisa," Reagan told her softly, and not for the first time Holly was struck by the fact that this woman did not want a husband and family. It didn't make sense to her.

The baby only smiled at Reagan and reached for her face.

"Is Katy up to company?" Holly asked.

Cash's and Reagan's eyes met. Reagan shrugged, and Cash nodded in decision.

"Why don't I just go in and check with her?"

Cash didn't wait for anyone to acknowledge his idea but headed to see his housekeeper, a few things on his mind. Without preamble he stepped into her room and began. "Holly Bennett and the children are here to see you. Do you want visitors?"

Katy's eyes swung to Cash and then away. The cowboy stood

where he was for a full minute, but the prone woman did not look back at him.

"I'm not going to put up with this much longer, Kate."

"What are you going to do about it?" she shot right back, her eyes turning to him and showing her frustration.

Cash shook his head. "Is that what this is about, Katy? Not speaking to the people who are bending over backward to help you is your way of having a say?" He shook his head again in very real regret. "You ought to be ashamed."

Not giving her any time to reply, he turned for the door.

"Cash!" she called to him.

That man stopped and looked back, his brows raised in question.

"Please tell them to come in."

"I'll get them right now," he said, all rebuke gone.

Standing in her little room down the back hall where she'd dashed to get a small music box to show the children, Reagan stood very still, having heard a good bit of the exchange. Fresh waves of something foreign and frightening came over her, and she was again filled with wonder over this man's care of his injured housekeeper.

"Hello, Katy," Reagan heard Holly saying. She realized she'd been missing for some minutes. She made her way around through the kitchen, going slowly to give herself time to settle down.

🌹 🌹 🌹

"And then what did you do?" Katy was saying just as Reagan entered the room.

"We ran a race around the schoolhouse, and Elly almost won!" Jonah filled her in.

"How did you do?"

"I was first after all the big kids."

A fond light entered Katy's eyes, and unbeknownst to her, both Cash and Reagan knew comfort at the sight of it.

"Reagan," Katy suddenly said, "there's a tin of salty peanuts in that cupboard over the large counter. Go and get some of those for the children, will you?"

"Coming right up."

What followed was a wonderful half hour. Katy spoke with some of her usual brusqueness, but all the remarks were kind with very few orders given, and more than one sentence was directed to Cash or Reagan. By the time Holly and the children headed back to town, things seemed to have righted themselves.

"I've got a roast in the oven, Katy," Reagan popped in to say after having seen the guests off and claiming four more hugs. "I'll check on it and then be back."

"That little Jonah is a corker and a half."

"Yes, he is. He can't wait to have legs long enough to ride—" Reagan cut off, but it was too late. Katy knew just what she was going to say.

"Now that's enough of that, Reagan Sullivan. We'll have no bad feelings on this. What's done is done!"

Reagan only nodded and slipped from the room, but she was distracted as she checked the meat and put some vegetables into a pot. She was getting ready to make gravy when Cash came on the scene.

"How was she after they left?"

"Back to herself, only nicer."

"Good."

Reagan turned fully to him.

"How did you convince her to see them?"

"I reminded her of all that's being done for her, and it seems to have softened her."

Reagan nodded. "When does the doctor come again?"

"I'm not sure. Do you think he's needed?"

"By Katy, yes. She needs to have hope that her hip is coming along and this whole thing will come to an end."

"Maybe I'll pop in tomorrow after church and let him know that she could use a visit."

Cash went back to work then, this time in his office, and Reagan went back to the meal. As she had come to expect, fatigue hit her at this time every day, but she kept on. At least her patient was speaking to her. Reagan found that made all the difference in the world.

🌺 🌺 🌺

Katy listened for the wagon wheels to pull away on Sunday morning but could hear nothing. Brenda had brought the girls with her, and they were both eager to visit. Utter sadness filled Katy over the loss of her mobility. Many were the times these girls had come to the back door and she had had cookies for them. Now she lay in bed, more helpless than a baby. Never had she been so frustrated. Her good sense had told her to take a quick ride on that bike and be done, but she had wanted to show off for Cash.

For a moment Katy's eyes closed on his memory. Prior to her accident, he had never spoken harshly to her, but he was right, she needed to be shamed. Giving Reagan a hard time when she had quit her job to come and help and then repaying her with orders and anger was simply not to be tolerated. Katy didn't know what had come over her.

"All right, girls," Brenda said, entering with a fresh pitcher of water. "You've talked enough. Go see how your father is doing and if he's still in bed, tell him it's late."

"'Bye, girls," Katy called to them as they hurried away.

"I forgot how much they talk. I hope they didn't wear you out."

Katy only smiled, but it did the trick. Brenda assumed she was tired and left her on her own, but in truth, the older woman just needed time to think. For a woman who only darkened the door of the church out of guilt, she was certainly having a strange reaction to not being able to attend this morning. It wasn't guilt that filled her right now but longing. She could hear Brenda moving around not far outside the door, sounding as though she might be headed back her way, but still Katy wanted to pray.

I've spent so much time trying not to think about You that I don't know how to do this. Cash says You're there for everyone, even sinners, and I can see now that I am. She paused, her breathing coming hard as she tried to find the words to say what was in her heart, feeling more fear than she had been prepared for. *I think I might need to know more about this before I can do anything, but if You'll help me to get out of this bed, I'll try to learn about You and not run away anymore.*

Almost on that exact note, Brenda reentered the room. Had Cash been home, Katy would have asked for him, but he had only just left. She made herself lie still, even as Brenda moved quietly around the room, hoping she could fall asleep and not have to think about it when there was no one there to help her.

🌹 🌹 🌹

"Is God always in control?" Pastor Ellis asked on Sunday morning. "I mean, constantly, 100 percent of the time? Or is He a God who decided one day to wind up the universe, stand back, arms crossed over His chest, and watch to see what happened?"

Reagan's mouth opened a little. That was exactly the way her father had believed. When she was a child, he had said time and again that God might have created things, but He was not a part of the everyday dealings of humans.

He just wound up the universe and let it run. And who could blame Him? That's what I would do if I were God. I wouldn't want to be bothered with humans any longer than I had to.

"Do you think God really cares about the people He's created?" Pastor Ellis now queried. "The answer to that question might tell you about your view of God. Is He a sovereign ruler who enjoys seeing His creatures suffer, or is He a sovereign ruler who's there to love and aid His people in hard times? Maybe He's a God who isn't completely in control. Maybe He loves His creation, but He can't actually help it."

Reagan watched Pastor Ellis smile.

"I'd like to read to you from the book of Jeremiah. Don't turn there. Just let yourself listen for a moment. This is Jeremiah 32:17-19, and then verse 27. Just listen now to some of my favorite verses in all of Scripture.

"'Ah, Lord God! Behold, thou hast made the heaven and the earth by thy great power and stretched out arm, and there is nothing too hard for thee. Thou showest lovingkindness unto thousands, and recompensest the iniquity of the fathers into the bosom of their children after them; the Great, the Mighty God, the Lord of hosts, is his name, great in counsel, and mighty in work. For thine eyes are open upon all the ways of the sons of men, to give every one according to his ways, and according to the fruit of his doings.'

"Now to verse 27: 'Behold, I am the Lord, the God of all flesh. Is there anything too hard for me?'

"If you'll open your Bibles to the last chapter of the book of Job, I'd like to read to you again, but this time I want you to follow along. Job had been through so much, but the Word says he trusted God through it all. If you still doubt God's ability to be in control, follow along as I read from the first few verses of Job 42."

Not until that moment did Reagan realize she'd left the Bible Holly had loaned her in the little house. She searched around, hoping someone had left a Bible nearby, but saw that Cash already had his open and was holding it between them.

Reagan smiled at him; she had not even remembered he was there but now leaned a little to read along, even as the pastor began.

"'Then Job answered the Lord, and said, I know that thou canst do everything, and that no thought can be withheld from thee.' Now skip down to verse 12. 'So the Lord blessed the latter end of Job more than his beginning, for he had fourteen thousand sheep, and six thousand camels, and a thousand yoke of oxen, and a thousand she-asses. He had also seven sons and three daughters.' Now to verse 15: 'And in all the land were no women found so fair as the daughters of Job, and their father gave them inheritance among their brethren. After this lived Job an hundred and forty years, and saw his sons, and his sons' sons, even four generations. So Job died, being old and full of days.'"

Again the pastor smiled at the congregation. "You might be tempted to say that was the least God could do. After all, He allowed Satan to touch Job's life. But don't miss the point I'm trying to make: God is powerful, loving, and able. He did not sit back once He created us, happy to just watch us struggling to survive. Even today He's active and very much a part of any life that will allow Him room.

"But maybe you don't know what I'm talking about. Maybe you've never experienced what a personal God we have. Don't wait another day to find out. Don't be uncertain about tomorrow ever again. Don't be frightened of death for one more moment.

"I want you to bow your heads right now—no one looking around so all have privacy. This is not something I do very often, but all week I've felt a great burden to share this with you. Some of you don't know me very well, so you might not come to me or anyone else in this church, but you might be desperate to settle this issue between yourself and God. If you are, then I would urge you to pray this prayer with me. Just say the words in your heart after I say them. If you mean them, God will save you. You'll be a new believer in Jesus Christ.

"Just pray like this," Pastor Ellis continued, and then proceeded very slowly. "Father in heaven, I know I am a sinner. I know I am lost without You, but You sent Your Son to die for my sins, and I want to believe on You right now. I know You are willing and able to save me, and at this time I wish for Your salvation, so I can live my life for You.

"Dear friend," the pastor started, but needed to add, "let's keep our eyes closed for just a moment more. Dear friend, if you prayed that prayer with me, you are a new creature in Christ, a new believer. You don't need to tell me about it, but I would urge you to tell someone, and if you do tell me, I have a list of verses from God's Word that will help you understand what you've done and help you grow.

"We're just going to have a moment of silent prayer right now. I won't keep you too much longer, but let us just be quiet a moment to give all of our hearts some time to think."

Another minute passed, this time in silence, and finally Pastor Ellis closed the prayer with a few words. He then invited the congregation to stand and join him in a closing song.

"Is it really that simple?" Reagan turned to Cash and whispered. Her eyes were huge. She had not even made a pretense of reaching for the hymnbook or attempting to stand. All she could think about was the prayer she had just prayed. She had not planned to, but suddenly she'd wanted to so much that she ached. To her amazement, the ache was gone.

"Yes, Reagan, it is," Cash confirmed, keeping his seat as well, glad they were in one of the last pews.

"But there's so much I don't know," she told him, feeling slightly overwhelmed.

"That comes in time. When a person truly believes, he's new in

Christ. The desire to learn fills him because God's Spirit now indwells him and can teach him all about the Word."

"You mean the Bible."

"Yes. A desire to know more about the Lord and live for Him is one of the ways we know that true salvation happened. It doesn't mean we never sin again, but our attitude is changed about sin, and we don't want to live in it anymore."

Reagan bit her lip just before she admitted, "I prayed the prayer."

Cash's smile was as warm as a spring day. "Did you, Reagan?"

She nodded rather helplessly.

"I hadn't planned to—not really—but suddenly my heart wanted to so badly. He said I would never have to fear again, and he said I could get this settled between God and me right now, and I wanted that."

"That sounds like great news, Reagan," Cash said sincerely. The congregation was milling around, but neither one noticed. "Our God is a saving God, and the benefits of knowing Him are without measure."

"That's the way Holly has talked."

"And she's right. Tell me something, Reagan; what happened to your fear of someone else being in control?"

"What do you mean?"

Cash looked her in the eye. "Listen to me, Reagan. I do not want to put a damper on your prayer in any way, but there is something we all have to understand. We need to understand who we are accepting when we are saved. God is huge, and He is a righteously jealous God. He does not want to share us. This needs to be a whole-heart experience for you, or me, or anyone who desires that relationship. Does that make sense?"

Reagan nodded.

"Your life will be taking a new direction. You won't be living for self, but for God. It's a wonderful life—there is none better—but I want to be sure you understand. I wouldn't want you to be confused about that."

Reagan stared at him for a moment and then began without warning: "There was a girl I knew in New York. She worked with me at the factory, and I was there on her first day. I remember her hands were bleeding by the time we broke for lunch. She'd obviously never worked a day in her life. Some of the girls asked her about it, but she didn't say very much."

Cash was hanging on every word, his face intent.

"Over time Veronica and I talked. I found out that she was from one of the wealthiest families in the city. She didn't want all the girls to know since they would never have understood. They would never have grasped why she would walk away from all that money to work like a dog in the factory, but she summed it up for me in a few words. She said she couldn't take the responsibility anymore."

Knowing that Reagan understood him so clearly caused Cash's heart to thunder in his chest.

"That's it, isn't it, Cash? My father, God, is the wealthiest man in the city, and I've got to act as though I belong to Him."

"Yes, Reagan, but our God doesn't leave us alone to do that. Just as Pastor said, He doesn't wind us up and let us go. He helps us every step of the way. He makes the changes in us. His love makes it worth living for Him—as you put it, 'acting like we belong to Him.'"

Reagan's heart and mind were so full she didn't know what to do or think. She sat quietly, trying to pray, but all she could do was express her gratitude.

"Do you thank God for saving you, Cash?" Reagan suddenly asked.

"Not as often as I should," he admitted. "I think that might be something I should thank Him for all day."

"He really does save, doesn't He?"

"Yes, He does," Cash agreed, that warm smile back in place. "When I first came to Christ, I had times when I didn't think it was real, but there was no denying the changes going on inside of me. God has a way of affirming us when we most need it."

"You weren't saved as a child?"

"No. I've only been saved for about five years."

"So you know what I'm feeling?"

Cash could only laugh at her look of wonder.

"Am I interrupting?" a voice cut in, and both turned to see Holly Bennett had come to stand just behind the pew where they sat.

Reagan rose to her feet, her face alight with wonder as she faced her friend.

"Oh, Holly," the younger woman whispered. "I'm so glad you came over. I have something wonderful to tell you."

Fourteen

"I DON'T HAVE TO GET MARRIED NOW, do I, Holly?" Reagan asked suddenly. She had talked with Russell and then Pastor Ellis, and now Holly was walking her to the wagon.

"What has you so worried on that issue, Reagan?"

The young woman sighed. "I don't know exactly, but the whole idea repels me. I can see how Russell loves you, but it's just not something I want."

"What if a man loved *you*?"

Reagan shook her head no.

"What if you loved a man?"

Reagan looked surprised.

"I've never been in love," she admitted, "but I've seen it happen and don't think it's for me."

Holly knew she should not debate this with her. As far as she knew, there was no command in Scripture that all women and men must find spouses. And Holly couldn't help but think that a person's preference was valid. At the same time, there was a correct way to view marriage, an institution God Himself created.

"You're worrying about this, Reagan, and there's no need. If God has marriage for you, He'll prepare your heart. Don't get in the habit of telling Him what He can and cannot do, and also don't fall into the sin pattern of worrying over what He *might* do."

This said, Holly smiled at her, and Reagan relaxed. She hugged the older woman and thanked her.

"I certainly have a lot to learn."

"You're not alone in that."

"Thank you, Holly. Thank you for everything."

"You're welcome. And don't give the little house another thought. I keep a close eye on it, and it's waiting for you whenever Katy's back on her feet."

The women hugged again before the men showed up and they parted. Once in the wagon, Russell told the children what had transpired, and they were very pleased. Elly, however, had a question.

"Will one of the men marry Reagan now?"

This wasn't an unusual question for a child in this situation who had watched it happen in the church family several times before.

"Reagan doesn't wish to be married," Holly told her gently. "So we'd probably better not watch for that."

But as soon as they arrived home and Russell had a moment alone with Holly, he returned to the subject.

"Maybe she won't feel that way after today."

"Yes, she will," Holly informed him. "She brought it up to me the moment we were alone."

"Did she really?" Russell asked, clearly surprised.

"Yes. I told her not to panic. But if the men in the congregation are smart, they'll keep their distance, because the lady is not in the market for a mate."

When Russell and Holly took so long, Jonah came looking for them, so they dropped the subject again. But for some reason, it lingered in the minds of both adults.

❧ ❧ ❧

By the time Reagan had talked with Holly, Russell, Pastor Ellis, and Holly again, and then she and Cash had asked the doctor to visit, they did not return to the ranch until quite late. Brenda met them at the door, something that caused momentary alarm, but all fear melted in the light of her smile.

"How did it go?" Cash asked.

"Just fine. She was a little tired, I think, but we got along just great."

"Thank you, Brenda," Reagan told her sincerely.

"Anytime, Reagan. Just let me know."

"Next Sunday?" Reagan said, a lilt in her voice.

"I'll plan on it."

Cash saw Brenda on her way and then went to check on Katy. Reagan was already in the room.

"Cash," Katy said as soon as she saw him, her voice urgent. "I need to speak with you."

"All right."

As he brought the chair close, Reagan bowed out with a few words.

"I'll be in the kitchen working on Sunday dinner."

"Thank you, Reagan," acknowledged Cash before he turned back to Katy, who surprised him by reaching for his hand.

"I did something," she said, her eyes anxious as they searched his.

"Okay."

"I made a deal with God."

Cash was surprised and didn't bother to hide it. "What kind of deal?"

"I told Him if He'll let me get out of this bed, I won't run from Him anymore."

Tenderness filled the rancher's heart. With his free hand, he reached over and carefully smoothed the iron-colored hair from Katy's brow.

"And tell me what you'll do with God if you never get out of this bed?"

Her hand tightened on his. "Do you think He would do that to me?"

"Not *to* you, Katy, but maybe *for* you."

Her brow deeply furrowed with confusion, she asked, "How could that be?"

"I can't say that I know God's mind on this matter, Kate, but maybe you've been running so long that this was His way to slow you down and get your attention. Maybe by staying in this bed, you can grow to be more help than you ever dreamed of."

All she could do was ask again, "How can that be?"

"Ask me what I want, Katy." Cash bent closer to her face to command in tender urgency. "Ask me whether I want clean clothes and a hot meal or to have you with me in eternity?"

For only the second time in his life—the incidents within a week of each other—Cash watched Katy cry. He didn't know when he'd felt so helpless, but he moved gently and put his arms around her. This act was not a first, but it had been years since he'd felt welcome to help her.

"I don't know what to do!" she finally wailed. "I thought this was God punishing me, but if I'm going to be punished, why did He send His Son to die?"

Cash smiled amid Katy's pain.

"You've been listening in church after all, Katy."

She sniffed and tried to calm herself, but it was a struggle.

"I'm going to get Reagan," Cash told her.

"Why?"

"Because something happened to her this morning, and she needs to tell you about it. Will you let me get her?"

Katy nodded, and Cash pressed his handkerchief into her hands before he left. Seconds later he was in the kitchen.

"Reagan, would you mind coming in and telling Katy about your decision this morning?"

"No, not at all," Reagan said right away but then hesitated. "She looked so glad to see you when you came in. I could tell something was bothering her."

"Yes, it is, and I think it would help to hear about this morning."

Reagan put aside the food she was working on, wiped her hands clean, and preceded Cash as he politely waited to follow.

"Take the chair, Reagan," Cash directed as soon as they were in the housekeeper's room.

"What happened this morning, Reagan?" Katy asked the moment she sat down.

Reagan could see that she'd been weeping and hoped she could explain this thing that was almost too huge to take in.

"I prayed to receive salvation from God. The pastor prayed, and I prayed with him."

"Why, Reagan?" Katy asked almost desperately. "Why now? Why today?"

Reagan shook her head a little. "I hadn't really planned on hearing what I did this morning, Katy, but Pastor Ellis said something my father used to claim. It was about God not being involved in people's lives. But Pastor showed us how involved He really was and is, and I knew a spark of hope for the first time. I've been asking myself if it could be true. I've been wondering if God could really want a relationship with me, and today it was so clear that He did."

Reagan sighed and went on quietly. "I'm a hard worker, Katy. I can do anything you ask of me, but sometimes when the lantern is dark and I can't get right to sleep, I ask myself who I really am. You have Cash. You have a place. You belong to someone. I've been on my own since I was a child. Most of the time it didn't matter. It couldn't matter, or I wouldn't have been able to keep on. I would ask myself why I needed God at all, and it took awhile, but eventually I figured out that it's not really whether or not I need God. The biggest worry was whether or not He would reject me. After I admitted that was the problem, and then someone showed me He *does* want me—" Reagan gave a little shrug. "There was nothing else I could do."

Katy's eyes filled with sadness.

"Look at me, Reagan. I'm old and worn out. Why would God want me?"

Reagan smiled at her. "I want you," she admitted. "I wanted your friendship so badly that I rode my bicycle out here so you could ride it." Again Reagan gave that little shrug. "Unlike God, I'm just a person with all kinds of faults. His reasons for wanting you wouldn't be selfish. Mine probably were."

It was Katy's undoing. No one had ever told her she was wanted as a friend. She cried, her hip hurting with how tensely she held her body, but her heart hurting more. It was some time before she could calm down enough to ask for help, but in the next half an hour, Cash questioned Katy and answered her questions in return before praying with her as she made the same choice Reagan had made earlier.

For a time the three sat in silence. Cash didn't know when he'd been so drained, but there was no denying the peace that filled his heart. He remembered the wonder he felt when his grandmother had come to Christ, and then Slater and Dakota. He knew his family was going to be stunned and delighted when they learned of Katy's salvation. It also gave him great hope for his parents.

And Reagan! Cash was still in a state of shock over that. Her heart had been so open, and she had been completely unguarded for the first time since he'd met her.

"Did Brenda give you lunch, Katy?" Reagan asked with wonderful practicality.

"No, I wasn't hungry."

"I'll bring something in."

"You go ahead and eat, Reagan," Katy said quietly. "I'm not that hungry, so go ahead."

"Okay."

"Do you want me to set up a table in here for the three of us?" Cash offered, not having thought of it before.

Katy smiled at him, an unusual sight. "I'm tired, Cash. Maybe later."

"All right."

The redhead bent low and kissed her cheek. Reagan did the same thing. The two exited on a quiet note, each feeling his own level of weariness. Reagan put Sunday dinner on the table and they ate together, but there was not a lot of conversation.

After the meal, Reagan checked on Katy and found her sleeping. She then felt free to spend some time on her own. Cash did the same, both understanding that the last few hours had given them a lot to take in.

※ ※ ※

Katy was settled in for the night, and Reagan was headed to her room. Earlier, Cash had come to the younger woman with a Bible and told her she could use it for as long as she liked. Reagan didn't bother to tell him that Holly had done the same thing for her, but now that the house was completely quiet for the day and Katy's closet door was shut against the lantern light, Reagan sat in her room, the lantern turned high, and started on the verses Pastor Ellis had given her.

The first was in Romans 10, and when Reagan read it she saw that that was just what she'd done: confessed Christ and believed on Him. But the next verses were of a different sort.

Romans 8:38,39 said, *For I am persuaded, that neither death, nor life, nor angels, nor principalities, nor powers, nor things present, nor things to come, nor height, nor depth, nor any other creature, shall be able to separate us from the love of God, which is in Christ Jesus our Lord.*

Reagan read this in quiet amazement. She didn't know when she'd read such a comprehensive list. And if the list missed anything, it was covered in the last part about "any other creature." Reagan was so pleased and surprised about this that she sat on the edge of her bed and smiled. Truly it had never occurred to her that God might rescind His love, but if the thought ever tormented her, she now knew where to turn.

Reagan found the next verses on the list just as amazing. She read John 10:27-30. *My sheep hear my voice, and I know them, and they follow me. And I give unto them eternal life, and they shall never perish, and neither shall any man pluck them out of my hand. My Father, which gave them me, is greater than all; and no man is able to pluck them out of my Father's hand. I and my Father are one.*

Reagan had not been positive who it was that was speaking until the last verse. *This has to be Jesus Christ,* she thought, *or He would not be claiming to be one with God.*

Without warning Reagan knew she shouldn't read anymore. She had been growing tired, a good tired that meant she would sleep well, but now questions were coming to mind that were going to keep her awake.

Setting the Bible aside, she readied for bed, her heart amazingly full of what she was learning, but her brain trying to maintain control so she would sleep. Eventually her mind won over. Reagan fell asleep in the darkness, her heart never once wondering who she was.

🌿 🌿 🌿

"Well, now, Katy, have you been lying still like a good girl?" the doctor asked Monday morning a few hours after breakfast.

"I've been out dancing," she told him, a small twinkle in her eye.

"How's the pain?"

It was on the tip of Katy's tongue to brush it off and say she'd had worse, but that wasn't true.

"More intense in the morning."

"That's the usual complaint. Another three weeks and we'll have you up in a wheelchair."

"Not walking?" she asked, wondering how she'd missed this.

"No. You'll have to stay off your feet for another three weeks after that. You don't want to risk falling again. And even when you start to walk, it's going to have to be slow."

Katy was stunned. She had thought that Reagan could go home as soon as she could get out of the bed, but the housekeeper knew she would never be able to help herself in and out of a wheelchair.

"We don't have a wheelchair," she reminded the doc, wondering why Cash remained quiet through this whole exchange.

"I've got one you can use," he said calmly. "And by the way, you're coming along fine. This is all very normal."

Katy felt herself relax. The news of the wheelchair wasn't a surprise she enjoyed, but there was no doubt that she found comfort in the doctor's other words.

❧ ❧ ❧

Reagan was doing laundry. She'd meant to attack the kitchen that morning but realized the laundry was piling up. The washing and dusting would still be waiting for her, but at least their clothes would be clean.

I didn't think a task as mundane as the laundry could be done with such peace, Reagan thought to herself, even as she washed. The same strength was needed for the hard wringing-out after rinsing and the lugging of wet, heavy clothes, but knowing God loved her somehow made the burden lighter. Nothing had changed around her, Reagan understood, but things were certainly different on the inside.

Even while pegging out the wash in the swiftly warming air on the clothesline at the back of the house, Reagan's thoughts lingered on what she knew about God. Sheets went up amid thoughts of God's Son. As towels and tablecloths were hung, she wondered about heaven. Jeans, shirts, dresses, blouses, skirts, and underclothing were pegged out in tidy order, but the work was done rather unconsciously. In fact Reagan didn't even hear her employer approaching.

"Move along," the rancher ordered mildly.

"Move where?" Reagan stopped and asked, having misunderstood.

"I wasn't talking to you."

Reagan frowned at him.

Cash nodded his head, and Reagan looked behind her. Four ranch hands were walking away, two of whom still turned to look behind them.

"You don't want them outside?" Reagan innocently guessed.

"They can be outside all they want, but I didn't think you needed an audience."

Reagan's brows rose, and she asked before thinking, "Why were they watching me?"

Cash laughed. "They have great hopes," he explained.

Having been confused by men's reaction to her for a long time, Reagan asked with candid curiosity, "Of what exactly?"

"Of catching your eye."

Reagan nodded and Cash went on.

"You might smile or speak to them. If you do that, you open the door so one of them could ask you out on Saturday night."

Reagan shook her head a little, and Cash misunderstood.

"Come now, Reagan. Were there no men who wanted to court you in New York?"

Reagan looked to where the men had been, her eyes thoughtful. "Do you really think one of your ranch hands wants to court me?"

"He might. His intentions might not be honorable, but this can be lonely country. Some cowboys don't figure they could ever support a wife and don't even try, but some work a ranch like this, dreaming of a time when they could own their own. When a man does that, he wants a woman by his side."

Reagan almost asked if Cash wanted that very thing but decided she might not like the answer. She wasn't blind. She could see that men stared at her, but she also figured that they knew, just by looking at her, that she was not the love-and-cherish type.

"Doc just left," Cash said, appearing not to notice Reagan's hesitation.

"What did he have to say?"

"That she's doing well, and all is as it should be. Right after the fall she didn't hear him when he talked about her time in the wheelchair, so that was a surprise to her."

"Where will you get a wheelchair?" Reagan suddenly thought to ask.

"The doc has one, but what I want to know from you is, did you hear that she'll not be completely back on her feet for about six weeks?"

"No, but it doesn't matter."

"You're sure? I didn't know what arrangements you made with Sally or Russ and Holly."

"I'm still paying my rent, and Sally wants me back no matter when I can come."

"She's a good employer, isn't she?"

"Yes, she is," Reagan said. Then her eyes grew huge. "I've got to tell her. I've got to tell her about Christ!"

Cash blinked at her sudden vehemence.

"Just this morning I read a verse in Matthew about letting people see your light. I've got to tell her!"

"Do you think she wants to hear?" Cash asked with maddening calm.

"Does that matter?" Reagan's face and question were so comical that Cash laughed all over again.

He knew they would have to discuss her evangelism tactics, but Reagan was already calming. Her mind had gone back to the Christians in New York and the first time she realized Russell Bennett was a Christian.

"I could turn her away from me, couldn't I?" she asked quietly. "If I don't tell Sally the right way, she won't want anything to do with me."

"It's entirely possible, and I don't think you want to take that risk."

Reagan's head tipped to one side.

"How did you tell people?"

"I told a few without invitation, but my family started asking why I'd changed. Then the door was open. The same thing has happened with some of the other ranchers in the area."

Reagan was asking herself if that might happen between her and Sally when she spotted something that made her gasp.

"What is that?" she asked in horror, moving a little closer to Cash and trying to get behind him.

"Go on now." Cash raised his voice and waved his hand.

The armadillo that had wandered into the yard stopped his clumsy progress and stared over at them, so Cash waved him on again. Reagan's eyes nearly swallowed her face as she looked at the strange armor-plated creature as he waddled back the way he'd come.

"What is it?" she gasped out loud.

"An armadillo. Have you not seen one yet?"

"You mean, they live around here?"

"Sure."

Her hands to her waist, she turned fully to face Cash Rawlings, her eyes filled with astonishment. In a brogue as thick as though she'd just arrived from Ireland, Reagan demanded, "What kind of employer are you not to let a girl know about such creatures? My heart could have been scared into stopping on the spot."

Cash could only smile, wishing she would do it again.

"Were you born in Ireland?"

"We were discussing armordillos!"

"Armadillos," he corrected softly, his eyes alight with amusement.

"That is entirely beside the point! I want to know that one of those creatures is not going to visit me in my room some night."

"No, they don't like the house. It's too active."

"They?" The brogue was back. "How many might there be?"

To which Cash could only laugh. "I've got to get back to work, Reagan," he responded, turning with a wave. "I'll talk to you later."

Reagan was not at all sure she wanted to end this conversation, but she was given little choice. She also knew her employer was right. Katy hadn't been checked on since the doctor left, and some of the laundry was still in the basket. The day was moving on, and if she wasn't careful, it would move without her.

Fifteen

"I'VE GOT TO GO TO TOWN tomorrow," Reagan told Katy later that day. "We're low on supplies. Do you go to Mrs. Unger's?"

"Always. And for everything except the molasses candy that Cash likes."

"Is that what's in the bowl in the living room?"

"That's it."

"I've got paper here." Reagan sat down and began to read what she had on her list.

"We're low on brown sugar? Have you checked the tall cupboard by the door?"

"No. I'll do that," Reagan said, head bent, making notes.

"Are you sure you're saved, Reagan?" Katy suddenly asked quietly.

The younger woman looked up at her. Their eyes held for a moment, and then Reagan nodded affirmatively.

"Are you having doubts, Katy?"

"A few. I just don't feel saved. I want to get out of this bed. I want to do so many things, and I can't! Would I be feeling this restless if I was really saved?"

Reagan had no idea what to tell her. "Why don't you ask Cash? You know he'll help you."

Katy sighed with relief.

"Maybe I will. I know from church that Satan is a powerful enemy. He lies all the time. Maybe he's lying to me, and I'm lying to myself, and God knows that I'm just fine with Him."

"Except . . ." Reagan began but halted.

"Except what?"

"Isn't worry a sin?"

Katy's eyes got big.

"I think it is."

"Talk to Cash, Katy. Don't lie there without answers."

The older woman nodded, and Reagan smiled at her. As Reagan bent back over her list, Katy found herself thanking God for the younger woman and almost instantly realized she'd never done such a thing before.

"Okay," Reagan said. "How about beans? We're very low. Is there another bag I'm not seeing?"

The conversation went back to the matter at hand, namely, Reagan's trip to town. They covered the entire list before Katy told her that Lavinia would expect the order to be charged and that if Cash needed his candy from Reynold's, the money jar was in the big cupboard.

Reagan finally left the sickroom, a dozen thoughts filling her head, the first one being that she would have to tell Katy how much she was needed. She ran the house with ease, seeing to every need. Did anyone ever tell her how vital she was to the ranch? It seemed like something Cash would do often, but whether or not he did, Reagan decided that at some time she needed to add her own voice of admiration.

🌾 🌾 🌾

"I appreciate this, Brenda," Reagan told the other woman the next morning.

"It's my pleasure, Reagan. Do you need anything special done?"

"No. She's had her bath, which made her a little cold, so now she's under an extra blanket and reading a book."

"All right. I'll check on her and see if she wants anything from her house."

"Good. I've been over a few times, but I'm always in a rush."

This established, Reagan took her list and small coin purse with money from the jar and walked outside to the barn. The day felt as if it was going to be hot. Little by little, as the weeks passed, it had been warming up, and Reagan knew that very soon she would have to look into some lighter-weight clothing. Today however, she had supplies to purchase. She wasn't comfortable spending someone else's money, but if this was what it took to get Katy back on her feet, she would do it.

Reagan worked all of this out in her mind before she got to the barn. Never very comfortable around horses, she forced herself not to think about what must be done. If she could have figured a way to get supplies back to the ranch on her bicycle, she would have done it.

The barn was scarier than she thought it would be, and not until she was inside did she remember that the horses were kept in the paddock outside. The thought of having to catch one gave her no comfort, but as she walked down the length of the barn, a horse's head came out over the door of its stall. At first Reagan was startled but realized suddenly that she'd been rescued.

"Hey, fella," she began coaxingly, not missing the gray muzzle and sunken eyes. "You look about my speed."

The horse stretched his neck out in a friendly fashion, but Reagan was still uneasy. She glanced around and spotted a buggy, one that looked light and manageable. She went into that stall and, taking the shaves, manhandled the buggy out into the lane between the two long rows of stalls.

"Okay," she panted, still speaking to the horse, which looked half asleep, "we'll just get you out of there, and you can take me to town."

Reagan flipped the latch, and as soon as the horse heard it, his ears perked up and he moved to come out. A moment later, the door swung fully open and the horse came straight at Reagan, his nose smelling her clothing for sugar or a handful of oats.

"Oh, no!" Reagan cried as she backed up. "Stay back now; stay back."

But the old horse just nuzzled the front of her dress and then stood still. When Reagan saw that she was not going to be trampled, she relaxed a little and began to give orders.

"All right now. You just back yourself up to the buggy."

The horse's ears twitched, but already his eyes had half-closed again.

"Come on, now. I've got things to do. Just get hitched to this buggy, and we'll go."

Reagan reached out and pushed a little on the horse's side, but the animal didn't appear to notice.

Reagan cast about for some other plan, and that was when she spotted him. Watching her intently, Cash Rawlings stood about 20 feet away, shoulder propped against a column.

"Oh, Cash," Reagan began, "I didn't see you."

"Reagan, what are you doing?"

"I'm trying to get this horse hitched to the buggy. I have to go to town."

Cash could only laugh.

"And what were you doing just standing there, Cash Rawlings?" Reagan wanted to know. "I could have been trampled."

"Not by Misty. I think she's older than I am."

"Oh, it's a girl?" She looked with new interest at the animal's face. "How can you tell?"

Cash's laughter echoed off the barn's interior, even as Reagan turned red and refused to look at him.

Pushing away from the column, the rancher finally took pity on her and came forward.

"Didn't Katy tell you I always assign one of the men to take her to town?"

"No. We never got to that." Reagan glanced at him. "How did you know I was out here?"

"I saw Brenda in the kitchen, and Katy told me where you were headed. I was actually getting ready to saddle my horse and head after you, sure you'd taken off on your bike."

"I would have if I could have figured out a way to do it!" she told him indignantly, a slight brogue entering in.

"I'll take you," Cash told her, moving to put Misty back inside with soothing words and a handful of oats.

"But you're busy, Cash, and the whole point of my being here is to help."

"I need some things in town too, Reagan. If I didn't have time, I would send someone else."

Reagan looked suspicious but let it go. He was a big boy. If he didn't want to go to town, he didn't have to.

"By the way," Cash began again, "were you really hoping Misty would just back her way into the harness?"

Reagan's chin went into the air. "As old as she is, I thought she must know how."

"But Misty's never been a cart horse. She's a cattle pony."

"Oh, there are different types?"

Her eyes were so big with interest that Cash couldn't find it in his heart to laugh again, but he wanted to. The things he'd taken for granted nearly all his life were so wondrous to her. In fact, it wasn't all that unusual to spot armadillos in the barn, but he didn't think he would mention it.

"So, are you ready to go?"

"Yes, I have my list and some money for your candy."

"Are we out of candy? I haven't been eating it much."

"Katy didn't want to run out."

"She spoils me."

I'm glad someone does was the first thought that sprang to Reagan's mind.

Because she had no idea where it had come from, it disturbed her all the way to town.

❧ ❧ ❧

"Okay, Reagan," Lavinia said, having checked over the list again and been even more picky than Katy. "I think that's the lot. Anything more?"

"I don't think so."

"Here—" The proprietress grabbed a tin of lady's powder—it was scented with flowers—and pressed it into Reagan's hands. "Take this to Katy; no charge. Tell her to come back soon."

"I'll do that, Mrs. Unger. Thank you."

"Sally misses you," Lavinia said, acting as though she had all day even though there were other patrons in the store.

"I miss her too. If Cash doesn't get back before I'm done, I may go down to see her."

"I can always tell him where you went."

"I'll do that, then. Thank you again."

Lavinia waved Reagan away, but in truth she was just barely holding her tongue. Had she seen something in Cash Rawlings' eyes when he'd dropped Reagan off?

"He's tall and she's not, and I always think that makes for a cute couple."

"I don't need a couple," Mrs. Guthrie said in Lavinia's ear. The woman's hearing was not what it used to be, and she also had a habit of starting conversations in her head. "Don't try to sell me more than I need, Lavinia Unger."

Lavinia only shook her head, moved to assist her customer, and held her peace yet again.

❧ ❧ ❧

"You look tired," Sally told Reagan, hugging her again. "How much time do you have?"

"Not much, but I wanted to see how you were doing."

"I'm tired too, but then we both knew I would be. How is Katy, by the way?"

"She's coming along. It's hard to be in that bed all day, but she's coping."

"I thought she'd be verbally tearing the house down."

"She started out that way, but there's been a change in her."

"Good. Do they give you any time off?"

Reagan smiled. "I have as many days off as you gave me."

Sally had a good laugh over this, and both women saw Cash come in the front.

"I just wanted to tell you I'd be at the livery," he told her as he started to turn away.

Reagan stopped him.

"Cash. I don't want to leave Brenda alone too long."

Cash waved in understanding and went on his way.

Reagan would have enjoyed going to see Holly, but she still had to get the candy her boss liked.

"I'd better go."

"Are you and Cash starting to get along?" Sally asked suddenly.

Reagan frowned at her. "We've always gotten along."

Sally only nodded, her face impassive. She thought the relationship was changing, but maybe she was wrong. Then again, she figured she might be right and Reagan didn't see it.

"Take care," Sally said, not bothering to answer the question that was still in Reagan's face.

"All right. You do the same."

Reagan went on her way but wondered what might have come over Sally. She dismissed it before she reached Reynold's, however, where she made her purchase and was the first one back to the wagon. Cash was just behind her, and in good time they were on their way.

"Was I hard to get along with before?" Reagan asked Cash out of the blue; they hadn't even cleared downtown.

"Before?"

"Before I came to Christ."

"Not really hard to get along with, Reagan, but a little closed off to certain topics."

"So you didn't find me rude?"

"No."

Reagan sat staring straight ahead, and after a moment Cash glanced at her profile.

"Did I say something that made you think that?" he asked after a time.

"No, but Sally said something about our getting along, and I thought we always had."

"Ahh."

Now it was Reagan's turn to look at Cash.

"What did 'ahh' mean?"

At first Cash didn't answer, but Reagan continued to look at him.

"I'm afraid, Reagan, that people are going to talk. They're going to see us together and make wrong assumptions."

Reagan took no time to catch on. She thought Sally would have known better, but clearly she'd misjudged her. And because Reagan wasn't a woman who went in for coyness and flirtations, she came right out with her feelings on the matter.

"You don't make wrong assumptions about us, do you, Cash?"

"No, ma'am, I don't," he told her, his voice as it always was.

Reagan sighed with relief, not caring if she was heard or not. The last thing she needed was her boss mooning over her. If he started that—Katy or not—Reagan would be on her way.

Reagan's mind was still on the matter—that is, men in general and their relationship to women—when she and Cash pulled down the long driveway, and for that reason she knew without having to be told why their wagon was met by three cowhands.

"Hello, boys," Cash greeted them as he pulled up.

All three men had removed their hats, but the tallest of the three stepped forward to speak.

"When we realized that you hadn't assigned anyone to go to town with Miss Sullivan, we thought you might want help with the unloading."

"Well, boys, that's right kind of you. Miss Sullivan can tell you where things go."

The pointed look Reagan gave Cash was rewarded only with a smile.

"I'll just go in and check on Katy and tell Brenda she can go."

"Thank you," Reagan told him, her eyes saying otherwise.

As soon as Cash left, two of the hands came forward to help her down, but Reagan told them she could manage. When she caught sight of one trying to get a glimpse of her ankles, she became all businesslike. In a matter of minutes the job was done, and the men were thanked and sent on their way.

"Did you give them cookies?" Katy asked when Reagan told her of the episode.

"They weren't looking for cookies," Reagan stated in no uncertain terms, and Katy chuckled.

"You can laugh all you want, Katy, but I could have done without them."

Cash, who had just entered the room, exchanged a look with Katy, both sets of eyes holding laughter.

"So how was Lavinia?"

"She misses you and sent you some powder."

"Now wasn't that nice! What scent?"

"Wildflower, I think."

"Mmmm . . ." Katy showed her appreciation after Reagan had handed her the tin and she had opened it enough to get a whiff. "Who else did you see in town?"

"Before Reagan fills you in," Cash inserted, "I saw Pastor at the livery, and he wanted to know if the three of us are planning to have a Bible study together. I told him we hadn't gotten that far."

"I want to," Reagan said without hesitation. While reading her Bible that morning, she'd had several questions.

"I do too," Katy added.

"All right. We'll start this week. How's Thursday night—in here after dinner?"

"What will we study?" Katy wished to know.

"I'm not sure just yet. Do you have an interest?"

Katy looked thoughtful. "I missed some of the work Pastor Ellis did on God's promises. Can we go over that?"

"Sure. Is that going to work for you, Reagan?"

"Anything," she told him. "I feel completely lost in the Bible."

"Okay. Thursday night it is."

Cash went on his way, and Reagan turned to Katy.

"Did you talk to him about your doubts?"

"No, because I remembered what he would say."

"What would he say?"

"That all feelings have to follow the truth of Scripture. If I don't feel saved, but I know in my heart that I took care of things between God the Father and me, then I'm saved forever."

"You know so much, Katy," Reagan said in amazement. "How do you know so much?"

Katy did not look pleased. "I sat in that church just trying to be good enough to get God's notice without admitting that His way was the only way He would accept. I did my level best not to listen, but a few things got in!"

Reagan bit her lip in an effort not to laugh, but it didn't work. A giggle slipped out and then another.

Just realizing what she'd said, Katy began to laugh as well. Before many moments passed, the two of them were having a loud session of laughter and giggles.

Across the way, Cash sat in his office and listened. He was in the midst of trying to catch up on his correspondence, but for a time he couldn't lift the pen. This miracle that had happened in his own household was just too big to take in.

❧ ❧ ❧

One week and six days after Katy was hurt, Dakota and Slater Rawlings rode up the drive to the ranch. They hadn't planned on arriving together but had met up on the road and come in at the same time. It had been a good time to catch up as Dakota had taken a new job, but both men were preoccupied with the news about Katy. She was not a young woman anymore, as they knew all too well.

Dakota and Slater quickened their pace when the ranch house came into view, but a scene in front of the house—Cash and a young woman arguing—caused them to finish the ride very slowly. When they got close enough, they saw that a contraption stood between the warring couple—one they'd both seen in St. Louis but never in Texas.

"Why have you brought me out here?" Reagan asked loudly enough for the visiting Rawlingses to hear. "And why do you have my bike out?"

"I want you to go for a ride."

"To town?"

"No. Just for pleasure."

"Why?"

"You need a break."

Reagan's hands came up.

"I have work to do, Cash."

"It can wait. Get on the bike."

"What if Katy needs me?"

"I'll keep an eye on her. Get on the bike."

"This is ridiculous."

"No, it's not. What's ridiculous is that you haven't had a moment to yourself since Katy fell, and I know you love to ride. Now get on the bike."

"Stop saying that."

"As soon as you get on the bike, I will."

With eyes that told him she thought him demented, Reagan took the bicycle handles and, with the ease of breathing, hopped on and began to ride. Planning to keep it short, she started around the house, fully intending to stay in the barnyard.

"Make it a long one," Cash called after her, "or I'll send you out again."

Not until that was settled and Reagan was riding out of sight did Cash look up to see his brothers. They were both smiling hugely, and

Cash shook his head, not looking forward to explaining the situation to the two men with the Cheshire cat smiles.

"Well, now," Dakota began. "Who was that?"

"You can get that gleam out of your eye, Dak. It's not what you think."

"What do we think?" Slater asked, smile still in place as he dismounted, went forward, and hugged his oldest brother.

Dakota was next, and the middle brother's mouth was opening to say more when he spotted Reagan again on the bike. His gaze drew the others, and for a moment all three watched as she made a wide circle by the barn and headed once again toward the back of the house, looking for all the world as though she was having the time of her life. Dakota finally spoke when she disappeared.

"Is that the woman from town? The one in the letter?"

"Yes. Her name is Reagan Sullivan."

"A woman who owns her own bicycle, Cash," Dakota said, eyes hopeful. "Just the kind of girl you need. Any chance she's a believer?"

Cash had all he could do not to shake his head. Since their marriages, his brothers had one thing on their minds: to see him married as well.

"Well?" Slater put in now. "Is she?"

"As of about nine days ago, yes."

"She's not taken, is she?"

"You two take the cake, you know that? I strongly suspect you're here for Katy, but all you want to know is whether or not I've found someone to marry."

The younger brothers' faces became very sober, and Cash saw in an instant that he should not have teased them.

"Come on in," he said. "Katy will be surprised speechless."

"How is she, Cash?" Slater said seriously. "I mean, really?"

Cash smiled, absolutely delighted to be able to say, "I'll let her tell you herself."

Sixteen

"That was just what I needed!" Reagan announced as she spotted Cash in Katy's room, rushing in before seeing that they had guests. "At first I thought you needed your head checked, but then I just—" Reagan came to an abrupt and awkward halt. Two men were in the room, both cowboys, and Reagan had interrupted.

"I'm sorry," she said as she began backing toward the door. "I'm sorry," she said even more softly before anyone could speak.

"Come in, Reagan." Katy's voice stopped her; she had never heard her so excited. "These are my other two boys!"

Reagan looked to Cash.

"My brothers," he supplied. "Dakota and Slater, I'd like to introduce you to Reagan Sullivan."

"Hello," Reagan greeted them, still embarrassed. The men were perfect gentlemen, however, and came forward to shake her hand, neither one seeming the least bit put out.

"It's a pleasure," Dakota said, his smile genuine.

"Cash and Katy have been telling us about all you do. We can't thank you enough."

This had come from Slater, and Reagan blinked in surprise. She had known that Cash was a gentleman, but three in the same family was almost too hard to believe. And they were all so different in appearance!

"You're not from Texas, are you?" Dakota now asked, his voice a deep drawl.

Reagan smiled. "How could you tell?"

"No one else here rides a bicycle."

Reagan couldn't help but laugh at that; she knew it was probably true. But as much as the men genuinely seemed to enjoy her company, Reagan wanted to leave them on their own. If the light in Katy's eyes was any indication, she was near to bursting with pleasure over having them there.

"I've got some things to do in the kitchen," she said, backing toward the door. "I'll see you at dinner."

"Thank you, Reagan," Cash said, even as he hoped she wasn't leaving for another reason. He had caught a glimpse of vulnerability in her face, something he was not accustomed to seeing in Reagan. It left him uncertain about how to respond.

Reagan was feeling very much the way Cash had guessed. She knew that she was still needed, but interfering with this family reunion was the last thing she wanted. Katy needed to see "her boys" on her own. And too, she just hadn't spent much time with families. She thought that Russell and Holly's family was unusually close, but now she was seeing it again in Cash and his brothers.

To get her mind off the feelings she didn't understand and didn't know how to handle, Reagan threw herself into a wonderful meal, one that would celebrate the return of the brothers. Glad she'd baked a cake earlier that day, she frosted it and then worked hard on the potatoes and vegetables to go with the meat.

"We're going to eat in Katy's room tonight," Cash announced about 15 minutes after Reagan got down to work, Slater right behind him.

"That's a wonderful idea. Katy will love that."

While Reagan remained over the stove and oven, the men took a small table and four chairs to Katy's room. Reagan did not understand the complete plan, however, until after they came and took all the bowls of food as well. Reagan was getting ready to serve herself from the pot when she heard a voice.

"I'll get her," Slater called over his shoulder as he came back to the kitchen. "Come on, Reagan. We're waiting for you."

Reagan shook her head.

"I'll be fine in the kitchen, Dakota. I see Katy all the time."

"I'm Slater, and Katy wants you to come."

Reagan looked suspicious. "Did she say that?"

He nodded like a schoolboy, and Reagan had to laugh. Nevertheless he was very persuasive, and before long Reagan found herself in Katy's room. A prayer was said and dishes were passed. The men bantered constantly, teasing Katy almost nonstop and still managing to compliment Reagan on the food.

"I made cake," she said at one point, and the men were appreciative to the point of making Reagan think they had never had it.

"We have molasses candy too, don't we, Reagan?" Katy put in.

"Yes, ma'am. I just filled the jar."

"I may never go home," Dakota said outrageously.

"I'll go home," Slater added, "but I might have to take that candy dish with me."

Cash snorted in disbelief. "If I know you, Slate, there won't be any candy left in the jar when you leave tomorrow night."

Slater looked innocent at this remark, and even Katy laughed.

"Do you have to leave so soon?" Reagan asked. These three had a way of making everyone feel right at home.

"Yes. My wife is having a baby soon, and I don't want to miss anything."

"You shouldn't have come," Katy worried from the bed.

"It's all right, Kate. You're too important to me not to be here, and Duffy says that Libby probably has another week at least, maybe two."

"Libby is Slater's wife, and Duffy is her stepfather and doctor," Cash supplied for Reagan.

"Do you hope for a boy or a girl?" Reagan asked the blond brother.

Slater smiled. "My wife has three younger siblings, a brother and two sisters. They are the sweetest kids in the world, which makes it impossible for me to choose among them. For some reason I feel the same way about the baby. I know if it's a little Laura or Jeanette, I'll love her, and if the baby's a little Zach, that would be just as great."

"You should have brought them with you," Dakota said. "I could go for a conversation with Laura or Zach at just about any time."

"Then you're going to love the latest, Dak," Slater filled them in. "Just before Libby and I moved into our own place, Laura would come into our room in the mornings and look around. At first she wouldn't tell Libby why, but then Libby got her to admit that she was looking for a nest."

"A nest?" Cash asked. "What was that about?"

"We think it was about Duffy teasing Liberty and her mother one night, saying that he always knew when Katie was going to give birth because she'd start nesting up a storm."

All the occupants of the room had a good laugh over this. Slater went on to tell of some other conversations with Laura and Zach and how fast Jeanette was growing, and Reagan could only sit in quiet amazement. It was with nothing short of relief to be able to serve the cake, have a small piece herself, and then escape to the cleanup needed in the kitchen.

She was almost halfway done when Cash joined her. He picked up the dish towel—something he did for her often—and began to dry the heavy pots she'd used. Tonight, however, instead of talking to her about general topics or answering her questions on Scripture, he came right to what was on his mind.

"What happened in there, Reagan?"

"What do you mean?" she asked, head still bent and hoping it wasn't what she feared.

"You looked about ready to cry when Slater was talking about his wife's siblings."

"I never cry," she told him, as though that were the end of the subject.

"Why is that, do you think?"

"It doesn't do any good."

"I don't know about that."

Reagan looked at him but then went right back to washing.

"So answer my other question. Why was it upsetting to you when Slater was talking?"

More than anything in the world, Reagan wanted to lie and say she wasn't upset at all, but she couldn't do it. She knew it was wrong, and this was Cash. She would never lie to him.

"I don't want to talk about it," she opted, her voice tight.

"All right," Cash said easily, his voice as calm as ever.

"Are you always so nice?" Reagan demanded, turning to him, her face red with emotion. "Aren't you ever grouchy or mean?"

Cash looked at her for a moment and then spoke, his voice filled with wonder.

"What possible reason would I have for being mean to you, Reagan? You're my sister in Christ. You're a part of my household. You take care of Katy and me as though you've been doing it all your life. You give of your time and energy all day long. What possible reason could I have to reward all your kindness and hard work with meanness?"

Feeling very shamed, Reagan went back to the dishes. She thought Cash would walk away and leave her to finish on her own, but even though she'd acted like a shrew, he stayed. They were almost done when Reagan began to quietly admit what was on her mind.

"I've never had a family like yours, Cash. I've always wanted one, but just the thought of it scares me to no end."

"Why does it, Reagan?"

"Because families take something from you."

"What do you mean?"

Reagan turned to face him.

"Your brothers and Katy are here now, but they're not going to live forever. What will you do when they're gone?"

"I'll be very sad. I'll grieve for a long time, but I still won't hold back on my feelings for them today. I'll still pour my heart into them so that today can be all God intended and so when they do ride away from here—even if it turns out to be the last time I see them on this earth—I'll have no regrets.

"You're right, Reagan, families do cost something, but they're worth every cent."

Reagan was so shaken that she almost dropped her washcloth. Her complexion went very pale, and she looked helplessly at Cash.

"Reagan." Cash's voice was the kindest she'd ever heard. "I'm sorry to upset you. I promise it was the last thing I wanted to do. You didn't want to talk about it. I should have let it go."

"You did let it go," she reminded him. "I brought it back up." She turned to the dishpan and admitted softly, "I don't know why I'm the way I am."

"It's not hard to guess, the way your mother left and your father turned to drink."

Reagan nodded. "But there's no excuse for worry or fear, is there, Cash? You told us how huge our God is and how powerful and able to look after our every need He is. You told Katy and me that last Thursday night, and Pastor Ellis said something about it on Sunday too."

"That's true, Reagan, and it's great you remembered, but don't be harder on yourself than God is. When you fall into the sin of worry or fear, confess it to God as you would any other sin, and ask Him to change you."

They heard laughter coming from Katy's room, and Reagan listened to it in silence. Cash was right. Those men with her had no guarantee that Katy would be alive the next time they visited, but they'd traveled—one leaving an expectant wife—to see her because she was loved, because she was family. Even if she died an hour after they left, they would not be the least bit sorry they had come. In fact, Reagan thought with a sudden certainty, it would probably be quite the opposite.

Without warning the young woman relaxed. She had not been thinking logically. Her fear had clouded her judgment. If she knew that she had a last chance to see Sally or Holly, she would not stay away. She would go to her side and be with her no matter how hard it was to say goodbye at a later time.

For a moment Reagan was transported back to the day she realized her mother was not returning. For a long time she had blamed herself. She convinced herself that her mother would have stayed if she'd only been a better little girl. Then her life became consumed with her father's drinking, and some of her mother's memory faded into the background. She had started to wonder if she'd caused her father to drink, but by then a wall had grown around her heart, and she didn't care if she had or not.

Today she was able to see that she had not been responsible. Just by thinking about her own life, she knew that she couldn't blame someone else for the choices she made, no matter how tempting that might be.

With a heartfelt sigh, Reagan turned to thank Cash for the help his words had been but found herself alone.

And isn't that just like him, Reagan thought with pleasure. *He's so thoughtful and caring. It's too bad he doesn't have children*, she said to the Lord. *Their upbringing would be far removed from my own.*

🌹 🌹 🌹

"We have to talk."

Cash had been dead asleep. He was emotionally drained these days, and most nights when his head hit the pillow, he was gone.

"Dakota?"

"Yeah. Slater too."

Cash heard the strike of a match just as light came into his eyes. Both his brothers were standing fully dressed at the side of his bed. For a moment he wondered what time it was and then realized they must have stayed up talking after he'd gone to bed.

"Is something wrong?"

"No, but with Slater leaving tomorrow night, who knows when we'll get to talk again?"

Cash was finally awake enough to look into their eyes. He caught steely determination.

"Talk or browbeat me into agreeing with you?"

"He knows us too well," Dakota said without repentance and proceeded to sit on the edge of the bed. Slater took the floor.

"I know she's a new Christian and that these things take time," Dakota began. "But Slate and I want to know if you've noticed Reagan."

"She lives in my house," Cash stated calmly.

"That doesn't mean you've noticed her," Slater said. "Dak told me that if you hadn't pointed out to him that he was falling for Darvi, he might never have given it a thought."

"And you think I've fallen for Reagan?"

"No. We think she's fallen for you."

Cash had no trouble shaking his head.

"Now there you're wrong. If ever there was a woman who did not want a family, it's Reagan Sullivan."

This stopped both men. Their brother's voice told them he was completely serious.

"Listen," Cash went on, "I appreciate your caring—you know I do—and as I've told you, I want to fall in love and get married. But it doesn't seem to consume my thoughts like it does yours. I'm happy and at peace with who I am right now. If God has someone for me, you'll be the first to know, but for now, I can't push this, especially not with Reagan. Her heart can't take it."

"We're sorry we woke you," Dakota said sincerely. "Thanks for telling us, Cash. We'll keep praying."

"Thank you. I'll see you in the morning," he murmured, sounding as tired as he felt.

"All right. Good night."

Slater said his goodnight as well, but the moment the two men were out in the hallway, Dakota signaled his brother into his room. They shut the door so they could finish the conversation.

"He's in love with her," Slater stated.

"I think so too, but he doesn't know it, and right now it looks like that's for the best."

"Do you think he does know but has held his feelings in check? I mean, she did *just* come to Christ, and Cash would not even entertain the notion of marrying an unbeliever."

"He might have, but I don't think so. I think his heart is as tender as it's always been, and Reagan is just another one of the many recipients."

The younger Rawlings brothers were tired as well and didn't have much more to say. With few other words, each man sought his own bed, but before they could rest, each was convicted of his thoughts and actions.

A major miracle had happened with both Katy and Reagan coming to Christ, and all they could do was play matchmaker. In the morning, both men planned to seek Cash out and apologize.

❧ ❧ ❧

"You want to ride?" Reagan asked in surprise, staring up at Slater.

"Sure. I've seen them in St. Louis but never been close to one. Or don't you think I'll fit?"

"Oh, no, you'll fit. I'm just surprised."

"Why?"

Reagan looked uncertain and then knew she had to come out with it.

"I'm the reason Katy broke her hip. I brought the bike out and talked her into riding."

"That's not what Katy said," Slater told her with a smile.

Reagan blinked.

"What did Katy say?"

"She said that she knew she should have stopped and didn't. She was getting tired but wanted to show off for Cash, so when she put her leg out, it couldn't support her."

Reagan's mouth opened and Slater grinned. Her hands came to her waist, and the accent slipped into place.

"So you've been chattin' behind Reagan's back, have you now? Well, I'll tell you a thing or two, Mr. Rawlings," Reagan began, stopping when she saw that Dakota had come on the scene and was staring at her.

"Do it again," he ordered, but Reagan only laughed.

"I thought you were here to visit Katy," she accused them, her voice returning to normal.

"She's asleep. I think we wore her out last night and then again this morning."

"I still want to ride this thing," Slater put in, and Reagan acquiesced and gave him a quick demonstration.

"She just hops right on! Did you see that?"

"Yes, I did. I think I'll have a try."

"Wait your turn, Dakota."

Before long Cash joined the threesome, and in little time they had Reagan in near hysterics with their antics on the bike. To the amazement of all, Cash was the most proficient.

"Have you been practicing in the barn when I wasn't looking?" Reagan challenged him.

"Every night," he teased. "I sneak down after dark and ride among the horses."

"Wouldn't Darvi love to see this," Slater called as Dakota took a turn.

"I was thinking of some of the Rangers I used to work with. I'm glad they're not around now."

"Rangers?" Reagan questioned Cash.

"Dakota and Slater were both with the Texas Rangers."

Reagan's mouth dropped open as she did nothing to disguise her amazement.

"Real Texas Rangers?"

Cash smiled.

"Who's a real Texas Ranger?" Dakota asked as he rode up and stopped.

Reagan could only stare at both of the younger Rawlingses.

"What's so amazing, Reagan?" Cash asked her.

"I don't know. I just never thought I'd meet any. I've been hearing about the Texas Rangers since I was a little girl."

Once again Cash was given a glimpse of life through Reagan's eyes. The very things he thought nothing of were special and amazing to her.

"Is it too personal to ask why you're not with the Rangers anymore?"

"Not at all." Dakota filled her in, explaining the way Rangers had to be on the move and how hard it was to meet that expectation and also be with his family.

Reagan was still looking stunned over who they had been when she realized she hadn't checked on Katy for a time.

"I'd better get inside."

"Thanks for the lesson," they called to her, but Reagan only waved them away. Once inside she found Katy still asleep and thought it might be a good time to dust and sweep upstairs. She tried to make quick work of it but found it was quite warm and was reminded that she still hadn't gotten a chance to shop for cooler clothing. Having arrived in this hot country in January, she had not made summer clothing a priority, but suddenly Reagan felt awful.

Not caring whether or not she was needed, Reagan moved down to Katy's bedroom and sat quietly in the chair. The window was open, and for a time she let what little breeze there was blow in on her as she prayed for Katy's hip to heal.

"Are you all right, Reagan?"

Reagan turned from the window to find Katy looking at her.

"I'm just a little warm."

"Have you nothing cooler to wear?" the older woman asked, taking in the long sleeves and dark material of Reagan's dress.

"No. I haven't had a chance to shop."

"Well, go today."

"No. I'll just take some time the next time we need supplies."

"Oh, stuff and nonsense! It's only April, Reagan. You're going to need cooler clothing. Go now while I have the boys to look after me."

"It's not the same," Reagan informed her, knowing Katy would understand her meaning.

"I don't have any needs like that right now. I'm fine. Now go. No, wait. Get Cash in here. I'll ask him to take you. Do you have money?"

"Yes, thank you, I do have money, and I'll just ride my bike."

"How will you get your dress home?"

"Mrs. Unger will wrap it, I'm sure." Reagan smiled before adding, "Dinna fash yourself, woman."

Before it was over, Cash ended up hearing about Reagan's plans and did offer to take her into town, but she would have none of it. Before lunch, so the sun was not quite as fierce, Reagan—with instructions to take all day if she needed—took herself off in the direction of town, her mind already going over what she should buy. She also had a letter in her pocket from Katy. It was to be delivered to Lavinia. Reagan assumed it was a thank-you note for the powder.

And she was partially correct.

Had Reagan but known it, Katy was plotting against her. All her life Katy Sims had had tender thoughts for the ones she loved, but never before had she felt she could express them or do anything about them. It had been her lot, or so she felt, to cook and clean as a way to say the words she could not utter.

Now she knew better. And the letter to Lavinia was only the start.

Seventeen

"I'M HAVING A SALE FOR SPECIAL customers," Lavinia whispered to Reagan not many minutes after she was handed the letter. "Buy two dresses, get one free."

Reagan's eyes rounded.

"When is the sale?"

"Today only."

Katy had not asked the mercantile proprietress to lie to Reagan; nevertheless, in handling it her own way, she was going to accomplish Katy's goal.

That Lavinia had received a note from Katy thanking her for the powder and telling her to talk Reagan into buying an extra dress and putting it on her bill was enough to surprise her into sitting down, but she fought the urge. Staying on her feet and helping Reagan, Lavinia was able to see that in just under an hour's time, the younger woman left the store with three new dresses, all very lightweight and comfortable, and some new underthings and stockings too.

Never in her life had Reagan been able to afford more than two dresses. Her shoes were not going to last another year, but for the moment, Reagan felt as though she was set for life. She was so excited about her purchases that she wanted to tell someone. At the same time, she wanted to ignore Katy's orders to take her time. Telling herself she would just take a few minutes, she rode her bicycle toward Holly's house.

As Reagan knew she would be, Holly was very surprised but also pleased to see her.

"You came in on your own? Cash didn't have one of the men bring you?"

"No, I rode my bike."

"I'm surprised Cash didn't do the job himself."

"He wanted to, but his brothers are visiting, one of them just until tonight, and I didn't want any of them to have to come to town with me."

"Will you be able to get things back on your bike?"

"Yes. It's just a small bundle of clothing."

"For you?"

Reagan nodded.

"Show me!"

For a time the women enjoyed looking at the purchases, but before long Reagan put her hand on Holly's arm and spoke intently about what had been lingering in her heart on her ride into town.

"I understand now, Holly, why you wanted this for me. I was reading my Bible on Monday morning and realized that your prayers were answered with a yes. You knew how much God's Son would do in my life, and you wanted that for me."

"Oh, Reagan," Holly said quietly, "you have no idea what you do for my heart."

"I don't know how," Reagan said with a laugh. "There's so little I know."

"But you want to know, and that's such a blessing, Reagan."

Reagan frowned a little.

"Think of how delighted you were when the children loved your bike and Elly wanted to ride it. You were thrilled to have them share in something you love."

Reagan nodded with new understanding.

"It's coming up on noon. Do you have time to walk with Alisa and me to give Russell his lunch?"

Reagan hesitated, but she wanted to see the large blacksmith who was missing from her life on the ranch.

"All right, but I'd better take my bike and go right from the livery."

Holly pushed the bike so Reagan could hold Alisa. They walked swiftly to the livery, talking all the way, and when Russell saw Reagan he gave her a hug.

"We miss you. How is it going at the ranch?"

"It's going well. Cash's brothers are visiting. Slater leaves tonight, and I'm not sure when Dakota leaves. Katy was so glad to see them."

"I'm sure she was. How is she coming?"

"She's doing very well. I think she'll be in that wheelchair right on time, and once she gets out of that bed, there will be no stopping her."

Russell and Holly were both very glad to hear it, and with Alisa going from one adult to the next and even spending some time falling in the dirt on her own, the three of them had a quick session of catching up.

The time flew swiftly, however, and all too soon Reagan said she had to go. Getting hugs from both Holly and Russell and a grimy one from Alisa, she hopped on her bike and started out of town.

It didn't take long to see that the sun was going to be very hot for her ride back, but it was good to know that she could wash the dress she was wearing and put it away for a time. Come next winter, she would be glad to have its extra weight.

Without really planning to, Reagan stopped riding. There was some shade ahead, and she walked the bike and stood for a moment in it. The thought of winter caused something like sadness to come upon her. She didn't know why, but the future—even knowing that God loved her and would take care of her—was somehow daunting. She couldn't put her finger on the exact reason, but she feared that the sameness of her life, the day in and day out working at the hotel and dealing with the customers, would eventually grow old and tiresome.

Reagan was still thinking on it when a rider came into view. She stood still and watched as Dakota Rawlings came abreast of her.

"Hello," she greeted him with a smile.

"Hello, yourself."

"Where are you off to?"

"To find you."

Reagan looked concerned. "Is something wrong with Katy?"

"No, but she wanted me to look for you."

"You didn't have to do that."

"She was growing anxious," Dakota explained. "She was doing her best not to show it, but she just kept asking after you."

"I knew I should have stayed and seen to her needs."

"I don't think that's it. She felt that she pushed you into going and said that you looked overheated even before you left. She also said she told you to take your time but didn't believe you actually would. I think your being gone this long convinced her that you must have collapsed on the side of the road."

"I'd better get right back."

"I'll go along with you. In fact, we can just walk. She started to relax as soon as I volunteered to go."

"Oh, all right."

Dakota swung down from the saddle, took Reagan's parcel and hung the string on his saddle horn, and then took the handlebars of her bike. That he did nothing to restrain his horse or prompt him to follow was not lost on her.

"Will he just come?"

"The puppy? Yes."

Reagan laughed at the term, but in a moment saw what he meant. Dakota's horse did not want him far from view.

"So how did your shopping go?"

Reagan looked pleased when she said, "Very well. It's fun to get new things, isn't it?"

"Yes, it is. Too bad my wife wasn't here to go with you. She loves to shop."

"How long have you been married?"

"Since January."

"Well, congratulations."

"Thank you."

At any other time Dakota might have been tempted to tease her a little about a marriage of her own, but Cash's words were still strong in his mind. For some reason, this woman's heart was vulnerable where marriage or men were concerned. Maybe she'd been married before and deserted. Dakota didn't know, but after he'd apologized to Cash that morning, he realized his first concern needed to be for Reagan's spiritual growth, not whether or not she wanted to marry his brother.

"Do you miss New York?" he asked.

"Just some of the people. I like Texas."

"What brought you here?"

"I applied for a job as a nanny, but then it was taken when I got here."

"I think Cash told us you work at the hotel."

"I did until Katy got hurt."

"What will you do when she gets back on her feet?"

"Go back to the hotel."

Dakota glanced her way and wondered if he caught a note of sadness.

"How do you like having Russ and Holly as landlords?"

"They're wonderful. I love the children too."

"I haven't seen much of the baby, but that Jonah is a keeper."

"Yes, he is. He can't wait for the day when his legs are long enough to ride the bike like his sister does."

"Isn't that just like a little boy?"

"What's that?"

"To wish his childhood away."

"You sound as though you speak from experience."

"I do."

"What was your wish?"

"To be a Texas Ranger."

"But then you gave it up."

Dakota smiled. "You haven't met Darvi. If you met her, you'd understand."

A wave of such longing swept over Reagan that she almost gasped. The thought of having someone speak like that of her, his voice sounding so caring and intimate, was almost more than she could take in. It was nothing short of relief to see the gate to the ranch come into view.

"My feet are starting to hurt," Reagan said honestly. "I hope you don't mind if I ride the rest of the way, Dakota."

"Not at all. Just leave your package with me."

"Thank you. And thank you for walking me."

"My pleasure."

Reagan was off just a heartbeat later, her mind gearing up to get back to work. Dakota didn't waste any time, but he did follow more slowly. He didn't want to tarry too long since Slater was leaving later in the day, but suddenly he had much on his mind.

❧ ❧ ❧

"You'll take care of yourself and get out of this bed as soon as possible, right?" Slater asked quietly as he leaned close to the woman who had helped raise him, knowing he needed to leave very soon.

"I will if you'll take care of Libby and that baby."

"I'll do it."

"Send word as soon as he's born."

Slater smiled. "What if it's a she?"

"I never had one of those to chase," she said, her voice almost wistful. "I'm not sure I'd know what to do."

"Well, we'll bring him or her as soon as we can so you can find out."

Slater gave her a warm hug, his heart squeezing with love.

He made his way from the room, his thoughts in a quandary. His wife needed him, and he very much wanted to be with her, but Katy's joy at seeing him had been impossible to miss.

His horse was saddled and waiting for him out front, but the only people he could see standing in the yard were his brothers. A swift check in the kitchen told him Reagan was elsewhere, so he tried upstairs. When he still didn't find her, he checked the kitchen again and found her coming from the pantry.

"Thank you for everything," he began.

"Oh, you're welcome. Did you get the food I wrapped for you?"

"Yes, ma'am. I appreciate it very much."

Reagan smiled. "Have a good trip."

"Thank you, Reagan, and I do mean thank you for everything."

Not wanting to be made over, Reagan only nodded and gave a little wave when he turned and went on his way.

Outside his brothers waited, and Slater found it hard to leave them as well. He made his goodbye a brief one, but the older brothers stood in the yard for a time.

"I sure hope that baby doesn't come before he gets back."

"It doesn't sound like that will happen."

"But he looked a little anxious."

"I thought he did too."

The two looked at each other.

"When are you pulling out?" Cash asked.

"I'll go Friday. Darvi isn't looking for me too soon."

"I'm glad you're staying. It'll do Katy's heart good."

"From what I can see, you and Reagan are about all she needs."

Cash shook his head. "When I think of how panicked I was when she showed up at the door . . ." Another shake accompanied this. "I could not have done this without her."

"Any word from the folks?"

"No. I'm not certain they're home. I know Mother would have been in touch if she'd gotten my letter."

"Yes. She would have."

The conversation dwindled to a comfortable silence as they both watched Slater and his horse ride out of sight. Neither man needing any further words, they both turned for the house.

🌹 🌹 🌹

Reagan was working hard in the kitchen when Cash came down the next morning. She had scrambled eggs, a large pot of coffee brewing, and also hot biscuits and sausage staying warm in the oven.

"It smells good in here," Cash commented.

"Are you hungry?" Reagan asked with a smile, turning as Cash approached.

She didn't see his hesitation as she spun his way. Since she was a good deal shorter, all she noticed was the blood on his chin.

"Are you cut?" she said moving closer, her face showing concern. "Your chin is bleeding."

"Oh, is it still bleeding?" His hand came up. "I nicked myself while shaving."

His voice conveying it was nothing, Cash walked toward the mirror that hung over the washbasin to inspect his chin.

Reagan stayed where she was, but it was happening again. Her heart had an odd feeling around it, as though someone were squeezing it hard. It hurt her to breathe deeply, and she had the funny feeling she might need to cry. Since she never cried, this was very foreign to her, but she thought if she didn't stop thinking about him being hurt, she would weep on the spot.

"Do you want anything?" Reagan asked in a voice she didn't recognize. She cleared her throat in an effort to hide the squeak.

Cash turned to her.

"No, it's fine. Thank you. I already washed it off."

When Reagan didn't answer, Cash watched her for a moment, his brow showing that he was somewhat puzzled. Reagan quickly schooled her features and went back to work on the meal. Cash spoke again, but she did not turn.

"If my lazybones brother ever gets out of bed, tell him I'm headed out for a quick check on the stock."

Reagan only nodded, and Cash felt he needed to add, "I'll grab a plate when I get back in."

"I'll leave it for you in the oven."

"Thank you."

Reagan didn't see that her hands were shaking until after she heard the door close on his exit.

What is the matter with me? I'm going to drop something or burn myself if I keep this up! He said he was fine. Men cut themselves shaving every day.

But Reagan was not convinced. She was still feeling upset about the whole episode even as she put a full plate of food in the oven for her employer and took a tray to Katy. She did so hoping the older woman was in a chatty mood. She would welcome anything that would get her mind off the way her heart was acting.

❧ ❧ ❧

She had to buy new dresses, Cash thought as he heeled his mount a little harder. *As if she didn't look good enough the way she was, she's now decked out in flowers and gingham. And that yellow dress next to her hair. I could barely take my eyes off her face.*

Cash refused to let his mind go any further. He rode his horse across the flats of his land, praying and trying hard to clear his thinking. He had known that Reagan was headed to buy clothing, but he didn't think she would find anything quite so attractive.

"Katy shops in that same store, and she never looks like that," Cash muttered, his mind missing the obvious.

The rancher had come out to check on some fence line and the stock and now forced his mind to those tasks. As he was riding out, he had passed his foreman, who said he would join him soon. In the distance Cash could see him on the way.

Brad's horse covered the distance in an easy gait, and Cash waited in the saddle for him to arrive. The two addressed ideas to repair some fences, and Brad filled him in as to his plans for the next few weeks.

Cash rode back to the ranch house, confident that his foreman had things under control. As to his own control, that was yet to be seen. Reagan had made her view of marriage very clear. He knew she wasn't against men in general, but she certainly wouldn't welcome the warm thoughts he'd had about her earlier. If he continued to feel the way he did, his intentions would be more than honorable, but no more welcome.

Giving his horse a break even as his stomach rumbled with hunger, Cash made his way slowly back to the house, asking God to help his confused heart.

❧ ❧ ❧

"Good morning," Dakota greeted Katy as he came into her room and found both women inside.

"Have you eaten?" Katy asked, some of her mothering ways coming to the surface.

Dakota looked to Reagan.

"Have you ever known such a woman for wanting to feed a man? Does she constantly try to put food into you all day?"

Reagan laughed but also added, "There is food in the kitchen. Did you find it?"

"I found a plate in the oven."

Reagan's mouth opened a little, but she wasn't sure what to say. That had been Cash's food. Neither Dakota nor Katy seemed to notice her thoughtful face, and just as soon as she had an opportunity, she made her way from Katy's room to the kitchen, but it was too late. Cash was scooping the remains of the pan onto a plate.

"I'm sorry," Reagan began.

"For what?"

"Dakota ate your food. I just found out."

Cash smiled. "If Dak ate it, then why are you apologizing?"

"Because I should have put two plates in the oven. Are those eggs even warm?"

"They're fine."

"So you've tried them?" Reagan pressed him.

"Not yet."

"So how do you know?"

"I know I'm hungry enough to eat anything."

Reagan closed her mouth while he took his plate to the table, but she wasted no time in bringing him a cup of coffee. She was going to set it next to his plate and start on the dishes when he invited her to sit down.

Reagan did so, always a little wary when this happened, but Cash looked completely at ease.

"How are you?" he asked, his eyes on hers.

"Fine."

"Are you sure? You don't get a lot of time off, and I don't want you wearing down."

Reagan made herself think about it. She was often too fast in answering questions about herself as it was a subject she never wished to discuss.

"I'm fine."

"Not too tired?"

"At times I am," she admitted, working to be honest. "But not right now."

"Okay. For a time a couple of women from town were coming out to help Katy with some of the housework, but for one reason or another, they both had to quit. I'm thinking about getting someone else in, just to lighten the load, and if I do that soon, it will relieve you a little."

"How will Katy be with that?"

"I think she'll be fine," Cash said, even as his heart was asking how Reagan would deal with it. "Doc should be out today," he added. "I know Kate is hoping for a good report."

"She says the pain lessens all the time. I think she'll be out of that bed next week."

"That would be right on schedule. I'm going to do a little rearranging of furniture so she'll be able to get around in that chair."

"All right. There was a woman in New York who lived in a wheelchair. She wouldn't allow anyone to help her. She moved the wheels and propelled herself anywhere she wanted to go."

"Sounds independent."

"She was."

"That must be common to New Yorkers," Cash said with a small smile, his eyes watchful.

Reagan looked at him.

"Was that a compliment or an insult?"

"Depends."

"On what?"

Cash didn't answer. He only smiled and stood, getting ready to take his plate to the counter.

"You're pretty confident, you know that?" Reagan said to his retreating back.

"How's that?"

"You think you can tease me and still get a hot meal tonight."

Cash smiled, much as he had at the table, his eyes warm as he looked at Reagan for a moment and then went on his way.

The housekeeper didn't move for a time. She had work to do certainly, but for the moment she wanted to figure out her enigmatic employer. Her eyes half-closed in thought, she sat and looked at the place where he'd been sitting.

It didn't help, and after just a few minutes, she pushed to her feet. Time was wasting, and she still didn't know what to think of the man.

Eighteen

"Okay, Katy," Cash directed after dinner that night. "You read the verses in John 14, and Reagan, you put your finger in 1 Corinthians 10:13 so you can read that in a minute."

Katy took a moment to find the passage and began. " 'In my Father's house are many mansions; if it were not so, I would have told you. I go to prepare a place for you. And if I go and prepare a place for you, I will come again, and receive you unto myself, that where I am, there ye may be also.' "

"Did you see all the promises in there?" Cash asked the women. Dakota's own head was bent as he studied the verses with them.

"But the word 'promise' isn't in there," Reagan said quietly.

"That's true, but God can't lie, so anything He tells us in His Word can be taken as a promise."

"That's the part!" Katy exclaimed. "When Pastor Ellis said that in church, I didn't understand it. And both times he and Mrs. Ellis have visited, I haven't known how to word the question."

"But it's clear to you now?"

"Yes."

That settled, Cash had Reagan read her verse.

" 'There hath no temptation taken you but such as is common to man; but God is faithful, who will not suffer you to be tempted above that ye are able, but will with the temptation also make a way to escape, that ye may be able to bear it.' "

"Do you understand what that means?" Cash asked and watched Dakota nod.

Reagan and Katy were still studying their Bibles, so he waited.

"I think it means that I have no excuse to sin," Reagan said.

"That's true, Reagan, but there's more to it than that. God always provides a way out. We never have to be slaves to sin again, because He always gives us some way to escape every time we're tempted."

From there, Cash took them into Psalms. For the next hour they studied verse after verse on the promises of God. Only when Katy began to flag did Cash bring things to a close.

"Thank you, Cash," Katy told him as the men kissed her and left the room. Reagan stayed to ready her for the night.

"Did you learn as much as I did?" Katy wanted to know.

Reagan smiled as she filled the water glass and put everything within reach.

"I might have learned more. You keep forgetting, I haven't heard any of this."

Katy patted the chair, and Reagan sat close to her. The older woman took her hand and held it.

"Tell me about Wednesday."

"Wednesday?"

"Yes. Isn't that the day you went shopping?"

"Yes, but I don't think there's anything to tell."

"How did you end up with three dresses?"

Reagan smiled. "Lavinia was having a one-day sale." Reagan paused and looked deflated. "I should have shopped for you too."

Katy grinned in delight and confessed to Reagan what was in the note she'd sent. The younger woman looked shocked but also very pleased.

"Go on now," Katy finally shooed her away. "You've had a long day. Go sit and put your feet up."

Reagan kissed her goodnight and then walked out to find the men talking in the living room. She had rarely let herself sit on one of those beautiful sofas—she never felt she had time—but did so now, hoping she was not intruding.

"I'm glad you joined us," Cash said. "Put your feet up."

He smiled at her when she settled in and then turned to his brother.

"What will Darvi be doing tonight?"

"She'll probably have dinner with some of the friends we've made. The church family there is small, but it's very close. The townsfolk are kind too."

"What do you do for a living now?" Reagan felt free to ask.

"I'm filling in for a sheriff who's been hurt, so I'm still in law enforcement."

"And what will you do when the sheriff comes back?"

"I just heard that that's not going to happen for a while, but when he does return, I have two options: I could get another job in law enforcement, or Darvi and I could come back to the ranch, build our own place, and work with Cash."

Reagan turned immediately to her employer.

"Will you be expanding if that happens?"

Cash blinked. "As a matter of fact, I will, but how did you know that?"

"Well, you have things completely under control right now. If you're going to add another full-time man, I assume you'll be letting your foreman go or expanding your herd."

"And what would you be knowing about herd expansion?" Dakota asked, his mouth open a little.

"Well, sometimes I look at the books Cash has on the office shelves, the ones that talk about ranching," she answered, clearly embarrassed, and then looked to Cash. "I hope that's all right."

"Of course it's all right. Do you have any questions?"

"Actually I do." She leaned forward a little, her eyes alight with interest. "Do you brand just in the spring or more than once a year? And why do you brand when you have fences? I thought branding was going out of style with fences becoming so popular."

Cash had all he could do not to gawk at her as he answered.

"Brands are still important when we go to market. Also, fences don't always hold, and with more ranchers moving into the area, I want to be certain I can claim my own herd. We're also not immune to rustling."

"I wondered about that. How often do you come across head that have lost some of their brand?"

"Off and on."

"Do you redo it?"

"Yes, ma'am."

"You sound rather interested in ranching, Reagan," Dakota put in.

"Oh, I am," she told him honestly. "I think it would be wonderful to own my own ranch. Even a small place would be exciting."

"And how would you work things?"

"Like Cash does. He does a great job. Although I would probably put the barn and paddock further from the house to cut down on the dust."

The men smiled.

"Our mother felt the same way, but by the time she realized it, it was too late."

A few moments later, Reagan stifled a yawn and asked to be

excused. Out of courtesy, the men stood when she rose and left, but sat back down to talk some more.

"How long has she lived here?" Dakota asked.

"Since January."

"And she's from New York?"

"Yes."

Dakota stared at his brother. "She reminds me of Father. He was so city bred, but he sure took to Texas."

"I hadn't thought of it, but you're right. Other than the heat before she got lighter clothing, she hasn't batted an eyelash over much of anything."

Cash had no more said this when he remembered the armadillo. He laughed as he explained to Dakota.

Dakota had all he could do not to mention how well suited she seemed for his brother, but he restrained himself and remembered once again to pray only for God's will and not his own concerning his oldest sibling and the two women living in his house.

🥀 🥀 🥀

On their way to church, Cash was thinking about the good time he'd had with his brothers, and how nice it would have been if Dakota could have stayed to see the church family. He did this in an effort to ignore how Reagan looked in another one of her new dresses, this one a medium blue that made her skin look like fresh cream.

He was praying for both his brothers, their wives, and the new baby—whether he or she had arrived or not—when he realized that Reagan was staying very close even after they'd arrived at church and walked into the building. Brenda had filled in with Katy as she had before, and Cash and Reagan had come at a good time to visit. Reagan, however, seemed unwilling to move from his side.

"Everything all right, Reagan?"

"Um hmm."

Cash looked down at her profile; she was worrying her lip a bit, her eyes watchful.

"Why do I have a hard time believing that?"

"I don't know," she said with a complete nonchalance that Cash wasn't buying.

"All right," he said, his voice dropping as he stepped in front of her. "What's going on?"

"Can't I stand with you?"

"You know you can."

"It's just until Holly comes."

"What happens then?"

"I'll have someone to stand with."

"Why must you stand with someone?"

With that, Reagan's mouth shut. She looked up at him and then away, but said nothing more.

"You may stand with me all morning if you want to."

"Thank you."

There was no missing her relief, and Cash was glad he didn't press her, but he wasn't done. Almost as soon as they left the church, he asked her again.

"Has someone at the church seemed threatening to you?"

Reagan's eyes grew.

"No."

"Has someone made improper advances?"

"No."

"Has someone done anything that I need to know about?"

"I don't think so."

"You didn't sound as sure that time."

Reagan fiddled with the fabric in her lap and fingered the Bible she'd brought.

Cash waited in silence for her to speak.

"It's hard to explain."

"What is?"

"Why I stayed close to you."

"I'd really like you to try, Reagan."

Not for the first time she noticed that his voice was always kind. Even when he was giving orders, he managed to use a tone that never frightened her.

"I think some of the men have heard about my decision for Christ. And so I think some of them want to catch my eye, like you said about the ranch hands."

"And that doesn't happen if you stay with someone?"

"Well, it might happen if I'm talking to Holly, but I know it won't happen if I'm with you." Reagan suddenly heard what she'd just said, and her head turned swiftly to look at him. "I'm sorry."

"For what?"

"I think I just admitted that I used you this morning," Reagan said with some exasperation, thinking he should know.

"No, you didn't. If I ever feel used, I'll tell you."

"So you don't mind?"

"That you stand with me? Of course not. I can't honestly think of a single man at church who would mean you harm, but if you don't wish to encourage any of them, that's fine."

Without warning, Reagan's head filled with one question: *What if I wish to encourage you?* She was horrified by this thought and put a hand to her face just thinking about it.

"Are you all right?" Cash asked as he watched her go quite pale.

"Yes. Well, sort of."

Cash continued to study her.

"I will be," she said at last, feeling her face flush. She never remembered blushing in New York, but it happened here quite often. What was the matter with her?

"I think I need more sleep," she said out loud, not really intending to voice that thought.

"Well, you'll be glad to know that I spoke with Meg Patton today, and she would be happy to come and relieve you one day a week. When I spoke to Katy about the idea this morning, I could tell she wanted only you but also that she understood."

"I was going to talk to you about that, Cash. I think I'll be fine to keep on as I'm doing. It's only a few more weeks, and I know just how Katy wants things done."

Cash didn't reply.

She looked a little more worn each day, and Cash was growing concerned about her health.

"I worked every day for Sally," Reagan reminded him.

"Not all day, you didn't. And unless I've missed something, you were never called in at night."

Reagan chewed her lip some more, the ranch gate coming into view.

"Let me tell you what I have in mind," Cash began gently. "I thought if Meg came on Saturdays and gave you the entire day off, and Brenda still took over for you on Sunday mornings, you would get a nice long rest each week."

"I've been meaning to talk to you about that, Cash."

"About what?"

"About Brenda's filling in for me. I feel badly that she and Brad can't go to church."

"Brenda and Brad have no interest in church, Reagan. He's been my foreman for several years now, and we've had many conversations on spiritual matters. He feels his life is fine. He believes in God and even says he prays to Him, but Brad doesn't believe he needs more than that."

Reagan nodded. She thought that might be the case but hoped she was wrong. She enjoyed Sunday mornings off, but not at someone else's expense.

"Would I go back to my house on Saturdays?" Reagan asked.

"I hope not, but you could if you wanted to."

It was on Reagan's mind to ask why he wanted her to stay when she wasn't working, but for some reason she thought the answer might be unsettling.

"Well," Reagan said at last, feeling as though she needed to be rescued. All spunk was gone from her these days. Maybe she was more tired than she realized. "You tell me what you want me to do, and I'll do it."

"All right," Cash agreed without hesitation as he pulled up to drop her in front of the house. "You'll work Monday through Friday, as you have been, but come Saturday, Meg will arrive and give you the entire day off. You'll stay here on those days, but you won't work. Someone can take you to town; you can go for a ride on your bicycle; you can sleep late; lie around and read, visit with Katy, or any number of things; but you can't clean, wash clothes, or even cook for yourself. On Sundays Brenda will come, and you'll go back on duty after church until the next Saturday. And we'll do things that way until Katy is completely back on her feet."

Had Cash not been a strong man, he'd have kissed Reagan on the spot. Her mouth was hanging open in a way he found adorable.

"Is that clear?" he finally asked when she only stared at him.

"I think so. You may have to go over it again."

"Anytime," he said easily and climbed down to help her out of the wagon.

She looked at him, still feeling slightly amazed, but he only smiled.

Reagan made her way into the house, telling herself not to try and take it all in at that moment.

☙ ☙ ☙

"How are you doing?" Russell asked Cash at the elders' meeting that Sunday afternoon.

Cash looked at him, knowing if he could tell anyone what was going on, he could tell Russell.

"I'm all right, I think."

"How is it going having Reagan living under your roof?"

Cash stared at him. He should have known this friend would be perceptive.

"It has its moments."

"I'm sure it does."

Cash stood still, his mind on the woman who was wreaking havoc in his heart.

"Have you fallen for her?"

"I'm not sure, but something is happening."

"In both of you or just you?"

"That's a good question. Sometimes I see a softening in Reagan when she's with me, or maybe 'interest' would be a better word, but I can't be sure."

"Are you even sure of your own feelings?"

"Not to describe them. I do feel very protective of her, but at the same time I'm afraid of her."

"Why would you be afraid of her?"

"Not of her, I guess, but for her. Because she doesn't want a relationship. I've asked myself if she feels that way because of where she's been and how she's been treated, and maybe I would be different for her, but if that doesn't happen—if she doesn't see it that way—I would be in love alone."

It was not the clearest sentence, but Russell got the full meaning.

"I'm praying for you, Cash. Holly and I both are."

"Thank you. If Holly has any insight into Reagan that she thinks would help, I'd be glad to hear it."

The meeting was going to be starting soon, so the men joined the others. The first thing the elders did was take prayer requests and pray together. Cash asked the other men to remember his unusual situation and felt a peace over having them pray for him without having to go into specific details that might have embarrassed Reagan. And then Cash was the first to pray. He started by thanking God for allowing him to work with the caring elders of the church.

🌹 🌹 🌹

The rocking chair moved swiftly under Reagan's body as she tried not to think about all she could be doing in the house. Before Cash had left for his meeting, he told her he just wanted her to see to Katy's needs on Sundays and to keep the cooking light. And that was all.

"But I was going to get a jump on the washing," she'd argued.

Cash had shaken his head.

"That might be why you're getting so tired. You need to take a day off. I don't work on Sundays any more than I have to, and that's how I stay strong the rest of the week."

Reagan could hardly argue with that, but at the moment she

wasn't tired. Katy had dozed off, and normally Reagan would have been flying around to get a head start on the week.

"And why did Cash wait until this week to tell me?" Reagan muttered, wishing he was there so she could have it out with him.

But her feelings didn't last long. The longer she rocked, the more slowly she moved. She thought she should check on Katy before she got too comfortable but couldn't manage it. She nodded off while thinking about the work she would have waiting in the morning.

❧ ❧ ❧

Reagan opened her eyes to find she wasn't alone. Cash was in the other rocking chair, his feet up on the stool.

"I'm sure glad you got a jump on that wash today," he teased her.

Reagan blinked owlishly at him.

"How long have I been asleep?"

"I don't know."

Reagan leapt to her feet. "Katy!"

"I just checked on her. She just woke up too."

Reagan sank back into the chair with relief.

"I must have really conked out," she said, her hands wiping her face as she worked to remove the last vestiges of sleep.

Cash only stared at her.

"How was your meeting?"

"It was fine."

"What do you do?"

"Well, the elders are responsible for the church family. We need to make certain that folks are taken care of, both spiritually and physically, but we can't do that unless we're taking care of ourselves, so we meet once a month for prayer and Bible study, and then we discuss the needs of the rest of the church family."

"And that's right in Scripture?"

"Yes. The Bible asks the question, If a man can't order his own life, how can he lead the church? I can give you the passage if you want."

"Thank you."

A short silence fell, but Reagan was still thinking.

"Will I ever know what you know?"

"Certainly," he was able to answer honestly. "You study very hard, Reagan, and there's nothing slow about you."

Reagan was pleased to hear this, and she wanted to thank him, but at the moment the thoughts in her head made her embarrassed to even look at him.

"I'd better check on Katy."

"Reagan." Cash stopped her when she was right in front of him.

She reluctantly looked at him.

"This is how I want you to spend every Sunday, taking it as easy as possible."

"But now you're giving me Saturdays off, Cash. Before it's over, I'll be working on Wednesday from noon to three and that will be my whole week!"

Cash could only laugh.

"I wasn't making a joke," Reagan told him, her hands coming to her waist.

"But you're still funny."

This got him frowned at, so he added, "Why don't you ride your bike or go back to sleep for a while?"

"I have to check on Katy."

"I told you I just did. She's reading and making a list for town next time you go."

This put Reagan completely out of her element. She cast around for something to say and ended up storming off the porch. She stopped at the bottom of the steps and glared back at her employer.

"I'm going for a walk, Cash Rawlings, but not a pleasure walk. I'll be thinking about all the work I have to do this week and planning how to get it done in less time!"

This said, she stomped off. Much as he wanted to, Cash didn't follow or comment. He had all he could do not to laugh again.

Nineteen

REAGAN'S FIRST SATURDAY OFF WAS a fiasco. Meg came and worked hard, but Reagan could not keep still. Katy had been in her wheelchair for two days, and Reagan felt she had to be on hand at all times. Cash watched his plan fall apart and put a new one into action for the very next week. When Reagan got up he told her to change into an older dress and meet him in the yard.

Reagan did as she was told and arrived expecting him to ask her to wash windows, but instead, she found two horses waiting, both saddled and ready.

"We're going for a ride?" she asked, her skepticism showing in every way.

"Yep. I'll show you some of the land."

Reagan did not look pleased.

"I've never ridden a horse before. I don't like horses."

"Why not?"

"Because."

"Because why?"

Reagan's face told him he should already know this, but she still explained.

"What if it decides to bite me or buck me off?"

"I didn't choose a horse that would do that to you. This animal is very gentle."

"You want me to break my neck, don't you?" she asked, but it was apparent to Cash that she wasn't really speaking to him. She was circling the animal and mumbling to herself.

"What if I don't want to?" she demanded as she came to stand in front of Cash.

"How are you going to run your own ranch someday if you can't ride?" the cowboy countered, and Reagan bit her lip.

"It might happen," she said quietly.

"Yes, it might."

"I mean, it would take a miracle, but God can do that, can't He?"

"Yes, He can."

Cash watched her reconsider. While she was doing that, he reached for the hat that he'd hooked on her saddle horn and plopped it on her head.

"You'll need this."

"Oh, my," Reagan said as she took off the cowboy hat and examined it. "It's a woman's, isn't it? Where did you find it?"

"It's my mother's. She leaves it here."

"And she won't mind?"

"Not at all."

Cash watched her set the hat in place and adjust the rim. She then smiled up at him, and he had to ask himself what he'd been thinking to believe this was the answer to getting Reagan to relax on her day off. If the day continued as it started, he would be so weary from fighting his emotions, he wouldn't be able to stand.

"You're sure I won't get hurt?" she asked, her little face looking up at him trustingly.

"I can't say for sure, Reagan, but as much as it's within my power, I won't let you be harmed."

"You promise?"

"I can't do that. I'm not God."

Reagan's eyes grew a bit.

"Are we not supposed to promise?"

"It's not a good idea. Our word needs to be trustworthy, but I can't promise because circumstances might enter in that are out of my control."

Reagan thought on this for a time.

"God promises. He promises all the time. But then He can do anything He needs to make the promise happen."

Cash was glad he'd stayed quiet so she could come to this on her own.

"All right," Reagan said after another moment of quiet. "I'll ride the horse."

Without ceremony Cash boosted her into the saddle and watched her immediately panic. She gripped the horn with white-knuckled fingers and said in a voice that was very high and soft, "It's too far up. I'm going to fall."

"I'm right here, Reagan," Cash comforted, but it took a moment to get through to her. She stared at him in horror until she realized his hands were still holding her waist.

"You're still holding me."

He smiled the smile that had become so familiar, and Reagan relaxed a bit. When Cash felt and saw it, he gave her some directions on what to do and stepped back. She looked ready to panic again but didn't say anything.

Cash climbed into the saddle of his own horse and maneuvered him close to hers. As he expected, Reagan's horse didn't even shift.

"Are you set?"

"I can't remember what to do first."

"Give her a little bump with your heels. That's it."

"We're moving!"

"You're doing fine."

Inside of an hour, Reagan was as relaxed as if she'd been riding for years. She joined Cash when he stepped up the pace a bit and in little time found the rhythm of the horse's gait. Her hat flew off to be caught by the tie at her neck, and her laughter could be heard from afar.

"I had no idea! The horse really does just what you tell it."

"She's a good mount. Her name's Bessy, by the way."

Reagan reached down and patted the side of the horse's neck. They rode on for some time before Cash wanted to show Reagan some sights from the top of the hills. They left the horses staked below and walked up a slope.

On the way up, however, Reagan lost her footing. With a small cry she began to fall. Cash steadied himself to catch her, but he was too late in responding. Almost before he knew it, he was tumbling backward. The slope wasn't extremely steep, and he'd have probably rolled down and laughed about it if not for the tree that got in his way. The back of his head slammed against the trunk and set his ears to ringing.

"Oh, Cash!" Reagan cried. Having righted herself, she began running as fast as she could to get to his side. He had already sat up by the time she got there, but he was shaking his head to clear it.

"Are you all right?"

"I think so, but that hurt."

Reagan knelt next to him, her hands clenched in fear. She wanted to touch his head and see if he had a bump, but she was afraid of hurting him more.

"Why don't you lie back," she suggested. "Maybe you'll feel better."

Cash was feeling poorly enough to take her suggestion. He scooted forward a little, not caring about his clothing, and lay back. There was a slight rise at the base of the tree that was comfortable for his neck, and he settled in and shut his eyes.

"How is it?"

"It still hurts, but it did help to lie down. Thank you."

"It's all my fault. I fell right into you."

"It's not your fault, Reagan. I couldn't get my footing."

Reagan didn't really feel any better, but it helped to have him sound normal to her. His eyes were closed, but he was still talking. Thinking it would help to change the subject, Reagan asked some questions about where they were. Cash told her what he'd been taking her to see and said that if he rested for a time, they could still go.

"Is there anything you want me to do?" Reagan asked when Cash fell quiet.

Cash opened his eyes for a moment, put his head up, and looked back down the hill.

"Do you remember how far back it is to the horses?"

"Yes. It's not far at all."

"Would you mind getting the water I have on my saddle?"

"I'll go right now."

Reagan hurried, so it didn't take long, and after Cash drank, he closed his eyes again. By then Reagan had run out of words. She felt awful. She wouldn't have wanted it to happen to anyone, but especially not to Cash. Cash, who was always so strong and ready to take care of others.

Reagan looked into his face—it was rather pale—and felt her heart squeeze. She watched the even rise and fall of his chest and thought he must have gone to sleep. She didn't know if that was safe, but clearly his head hurt, and she didn't wish to disturb him.

Moving carefully, she picked up his hand and held it in her lap. It was a hand much larger and rougher than her own, and with gentle movements she touched his fingers and even laid her own palm against his. She prayed while doing this, asking God to heal him and not let him be permanently harmed. She was still holding his hand and praying when she looked over to find his eyes on her.

Reagan let go of his hand as though she'd been burned, color leaping into her face.

"You're in love with me, Reagan," Cash said softly, and for a moment she froze.

It didn't last long. In less than a minute her face crumpled, and try as she might, the tears would not be stemmed.

"I didn't mean for it to happen. I really didn't," she cried quietly, a few tears actually falling down her cheeks. "I just couldn't seem to help myself."

The quiet tears deserted her then, and she cried the real ones, the ones that hadn't been shed in more years than she could remember. She was near to choking when she realized that Cash was sitting up and trying to speak to her.

"It's all right, Reagan," he said. "Listen to me."

"But it's not all right," she told him, sniffling and shaking all over. "I have no right to love you."

"How do you figure?"

"I just don't. I don't have any right to think that I could have Cash Rawlings for my own."

"What right do I have to think I could have Reagan Sullivan?"

Reagan shook her head. "It's not the same."

Cash smiled that warm, wonderful smile. "If the men at church are any indication, it's very much the same."

Reagan looked into his eyes.

Cash looked right back. With slow movements, he reached forward and brushed the tears from her cheeks. "You've been very hurt by someone," he said quietly.

All Reagan could do was nod.

"I'm not that man, Reagan."

"No, you're not," she agreed without hesitation. "You're nothing like my father."

"Was he the one?"

"Yes. I see him differently now that I understand what a sinner I am, but the way fathers treat their children—good or bad—lasts a long time."

"Can you tell me about it, or is it too painful?"

Reagan gave a mirthless laugh. "Even in that you're different. My father would have demanded an answer, not given me a choice."

Cash waited, knowing he needn't say any more.

"All I can tell you," Reagan started, "is what I know. I don't know the details. I just know how it affected me. Not long after my ninth birthday, my parents had a terrible fight. There was yelling and screaming, and I was locked out of the apartment. When my father came storming out, I ran in to find my mother on the floor.

"To this day I don't know if he struck her or forced himself on her or what, but she was crying and her hair was a mess, and she sat up and said she couldn't take it anymore."

Reagan looked up and found Cash listening carefully.

"She was gone when I woke up the next morning, and I never saw her again. For a time I tried to be a very good little girl, certain that would bring her back, but no one even noticed. On top of that my father was addicted to the bottle, and that only grew worse after Mama left. He was angry all the time, and I became afraid of him when he came close to backhanding me. That only happened once, and he stopped short, but I remember it. I didn't answer him quickly enough about where I'd been, and he almost hit me.

"Day after day I would watch him drink until he couldn't move in the chair any longer, and I'd leave him alone until he roused again. I don't know how we ate or even stayed in the apartment, but one day he didn't rouse, and I went for the neighbors. He was dead, and I was alone. I wasn't going to let it get me down, so before I was even a teen, I found work. I worked hard and did my best to find adventure around every corner so I could forget the things that hurt me. That's why I took the nanny's job that didn't work out. That's why I was willing to come to Texas."

Reagan looked him in the eye.

"But there's one adventure that terrifies me. I never wanted to be married. I never wanted a man to have control over me or to love me and then leave me or hurt me."

Cash put his hand out, just holding it open and waiting. After a moment, Reagan placed her hand in his palm, but Cash did not enclose her hand. Still moving carefully, he put his thumb on the back of her hand, not too tightly, and not attempting to pull her toward him in any way.

"I must know your views on marriage better than anyone, Reagan. I've had to be very careful."

"What do you mean?"

With his thumb stroking gently over the back of her hand, Cash said, "You're not a woman a man can rush. Not that I tend to be reckless, but I knew I had to be extra careful with your heart."

"Oh, Cash," was all she could think to say. Her thoughts felt scrambled. He was so wonderful—her heart knew that—but her mind was still afraid. Even the way he held her hand was undemanding. She didn't think she had ever met anyone like him.

"You need to know, Reagan, how much I want to take you in my arms right now and kiss you." Cash shocked her with his words; the hold on her hand had given no indication. "But you may not want to be my wife. You may never accept my love, and as much as I want to kiss you, I'm not going to do that if you're not going to marry me."

"I've never been kissed."

"When I was 16, I had a girlfriend and we used to kiss. When I got a little older, I saw what a mistake that was, but I've not had anyone in my life since I came to Christ."

Reagan's face told Cash she was thinking again. Thankfully, she wasn't long in saying what it was.

"Kissing leads to other things."

Even though his head still hurt, Cash had to laugh. She was always such a surprise.

"Well, doesn't it?"

"Yes, it certainly can—it never has for me—but even talking about it can lead to temptation, so I think the two of us had better get back on the trail."

Cash came awkwardly to his feet, and Reagan touched his arm.

"How is your head?"

"It hurts, but my heart knows I'm not in love alone, and that's enough to make me ignore the pain."

Reagan smiled. She was not a woman who dreamed about a man falling for her and telling her how he felt, but if she were, this would not be what she imagined.

You've been fighting this for years, Reagan girl—it's the least you deserve.

The two made their way down the hill to the horses and then very slowly back to the ranch. Reagan kept a close eye on Cash, but he didn't look as if he was going to pass out as she feared. She offered to go for someone to help with the horses, knowing she was useless in the barn, and Cash accepted. One of the hands, looking very pleased to be following Reagan, came in a hurry and offered to help Cash to the house as well.

Cash said he could handle it but was glad to get to the living room.

"If this isn't the worst," he commented quietly as he dropped onto the sofa.

"What's that?" Reagan asked. She had remained close by, hoping for a bit more conversation.

"Finding out you love me and having a headache all at the same time."

Reagan smiled. She had never heard him sound so disgruntled.

"Should I go for the doctor?" Reagan asked, making herself be practical.

"I don't think so."

This was no more than said when they both heard the bunkhouse cook coming through the kitchen. Max had come to see Katy on occasion, but Reagan had never had much interaction with him.

"Cash," he called again. "Where are you?"

"In the living room."

Max's voice brought Meg from Katy's room, so she was standing nearby when he arrived.

"You hit your head?" the older man demanded.

"Just a bump."

"Let me see it," he grumbled, as though Cash were a pesky child. "You've got a good egg there. What were you doing?"

"I lost my footing and fell against a tree."

Max shook his head.

"You'll have to keep an eye on him tonight," he said to Reagan. "Don't let him sleep too long."

Cash tried to object, but Reagan was taking it all in. As though the ranch owner weren't even in the room, plans were made around him. Reagan was told to wake him twice during the night, three times if he went to bed early, and Max would check him again in the morning. Max then proceeded to Katy's room, where she had just gotten back into bed, to fill her in as well.

"I'm fine," Cash said for the umpteenth time and then gave up trying to convince anyone. Meg was busy putting lunch on as both Reagan and Cash had missed it, and Max headed out to tell Brad about the head injury.

Cash was sitting in the living room feeling as though the house were falling apart around him when he realized all was quiet and that he was not alone. He looked over to see Reagan sitting on a chair watching him.

"Do you feel like you've lost control of your own home?"

"That was perceptive of you."

"Not really."

Cash's brows rose in question.

"You're always the one in charge, always the one to take care of everyone else. Having anything happen to you makes the rest of us fall apart."

"You seem pretty calm right now."

"I'm not as calm as I look. I'm afraid you're not all right, but you won't admit it or don't realize it."

"May I be honest with you?"

Reagan nodded.

"My head hurts a little, but my real problem is my frustration in not being able to talk to you more."

"What would you say?"

"I would ask you if I can talk to Pastor or Russell about us. I know how I feel, and I know how you feel, but there are things to be worked out because of your fear."

Reagan nodded in understanding.

"Once in a while," she admitted, "I would have a vision of living here for always and being yours too, and sometimes it would feel scary to me and sometimes not."

"What does it feel like right now?"

Reagan had to shake her head and confess that she wasn't sure.

"I just wish," she whispered, her heart ripping a little around the edge, "that you could have someone who's not me. I think you deserve better."

Cash didn't say a word, but Reagan got the distinct impression that he was not happy with this idea. She suspected that he might even have addressed the issue, but Meg came through the living room just then to tell them she had lunch hot and ready on the table.

Cash and Reagan thanked her and moved to the kitchen, both knowing that the end of this conversation was going to have to wait.

Twenty

"ARE YOU SURE YOU WANT TO TRY this?" Cash asked Katy again.

"I'm sure. Are you sure?"

Cash smiled when her tone begged him not to say no.

Reagan had awakened him in the night, but even so he'd slept well. Now, after having assured the woman repeatedly that his head was fine, Cash had rigged up a ramp in order to push Katy's wheelchair into the back of the wagon. The plan was not without risks.

"What do you suppose the doc would say?" Katy asked conversationally as Cash tied her chair to the sideboards to steady it.

"You do know how to panic a man, don't you, Kate."

Katy gave a crack of laughter just as Reagan came from the house with all of their Bibles.

"Are we set?" she asked, her eyes alight with excitement. This scheme had been all her own, and even though Cash had originally been horrified by the idea, he was once again won over by Katy's pleasure.

"I think so. Are you still riding back here?"

"Yes. I have a quilt to sit on, and I'll just keep the chair steady."

Cash shook his head when she looked mischievous and then stepped forward to help her when she moved to climb aboard. She smiled down at him, and his eyes held hers for a moment.

"It's about time you two found each other," Katy stated, shocking them a little. She looked at the couple staring at her and snorted.

"My hip is broken," she reminded them. "Not my eyes."

"Katy," Cash began patiently, feeling very protective of Reagan, "it's not that simple. We're going to give this—"

"I know," she cut him off. "Reagan has to get over her fear of being married, but she will. And I'm not going to spread the news until the two of you do."

"How did you know, Katy?" Reagan asked from her place on the floor of the wagon bed.

The older woman's face was kind. "I live with the two of you, Reagan. Cash didn't even know it, but as soon as you came to Christ, his feelings toward you started to change. And you didn't want this, but no woman has ever been able to resist Cash Rawlings. He's never encouraged them, mind you, but when that man walks the streets of Kinkade, female heads turn from all directions."

It was an interesting start to the morning. They had to get going because the ride was going to be slower, but both Cash and Reagan were somewhat shocked by all of Katy's observations.

"I've been praying for you both," she added when the wagon was finally set into motion.

"And what exactly have you been praying?" Cash asked over his shoulder from his place behind the reins.

"That you would grow in the Lord, so that if He did bring you together you'd be ready. I prayed in God's will, but I must admit I've wanted to see it happen."

"Why did you never say anything?" Reagan asked.

"That wouldn't have been wise. If I had been mistaken, it would have just made you uncomfortable around each other."

"But why did you say something now?" Cash asked.

"Because something more went on yesterday than you bumping your head. I don't need to know what, but Reagan doesn't have to try not to look at you anymore, and you touched her arm twice last night, Cash. That's not something I've ever seen you do to any woman before."

Cash turned around and met Reagan's wide gaze before both started to laugh. Katy joined them, not knowing when she had felt so good. Her hip was mending, and she was headed to church—and not out of fear—but because God now lived inside of her. This thought, however, reminded her of something she needed to take care of with Cash.

"Cash," Katy called to him just as her chair shifted a little and her hip experienced some pain.

"Am I going too fast?"

"No. I've got something to apologize to you about."

"All right. Did you want to talk to me later?"

"No. Reagan can hear this. Remember how angry I was about your view of your parents' salvation?"

"I remember."

"Well, I can see what you were talking about now. I know your mother would have come if she'd received the letter you sent. She's that type of person. But I do see what you meant before. Being a good person is not what God has to say."

It had been said in Katy's way, but Cash understood her.

"Thank you, Kate. I appreciate that very much."

The three went on to church and had a wonderful morning. Less than a handful of folks missed the chance to greet Katy and wish her well, and she thought that if she died that day, she would do so the happiest person on earth.

"How many folks get a second chance at my age?" she asked Noelle Ellis.

"Not many take it like you have, Katy. Even at the eleventh hour God saves, but it seems that not many folks see their need in time."

Katy was so excited she could hardly speak. She was still sitting there smiling when Cash came to claim her.

"Are you about ready to head out?"

"Yes, I am. Is Reagan ready?"

"I believe so."

Several men were on hand to help Cash load Katy and her chair back into the wagon. It wasn't without discomfort to her, but if the truth be told, that lady barely even noticed.

🌹 🌹 🌹

"Katy!" Cash called to her after he made a trip into town on Thursday morning.

"In the kitchen," she called back.

Cash just about ran to find her and saw Reagan in attendance as well.

"My parents are on their way!" he told them. "Davis at the telegraph office caught me just as I was leaving town. They had been out of the state, and while away my father had taken ill, but now they're on their way."

"We'll have to shop," Katy said decisively. "Do we have time?"

"I'm not sure," he spoke as he tried to scan the contents of the message again. "With this date, they could be coming in today."

Amid Katy's and his own excitement, it took a moment for Cash to notice that Reagan was missing. He called for her and began to check around the house, but not until he walked through the living room did he spot her out front, bicycle in hand, getting ready to hop on and ride. Without having to be told, he knew she was not headed out for exercise.

He was out the door in a flash, running faster than he had in years. He caught up with her just as she was giving the bike a push to jump on. He was thankful she heard his approach and stopped.

"Oh, Cash," she said quietly, her features strained and tense, "I have to go home for a little while. I should have told you, but you're here now, so now you know."

"Can I take you?" he offered, his chest still heaving some.

"No, no," she said, her eyes filling with panic. "I'll be back sometime."

"Reagan, honey," Cash said gently, "what's wrong?"

"I just need to go home. It's been a long time."

"Does this have anything to do with my parents' coming?"

"I have to go," she told him, not even looking at him. "I'll be back."

"Reagan," he tried again, but she just shook her head and started on her way.

Cash wasted no time. He moved swiftly back to the house, spoke with Katy, ran over to see Brenda, and then went out to the barn. He saddled his horse and was riding at a full gallop just ten minutes later.

He had waited a long time for that little black-haired woman to walk into his life. He wasn't going to let her escape him that easily.

❧ ❧ ❧

Reagan's heart was near to bursting by the time she reached the street on which she lived. For the first time since she could remember, she hoped Holly would not spot her and come to the porch to visit. She needed to talk to only one person at the moment, and she had run away from him. Outside of Cash Rawlings, she wanted to be alone.

For the last half block she had been off the bike, just pushing it along. Now she was almost to the yard and already wanting to cry. She thought if she could just get inside, she could let go. It would feel good to cry. It might give her a headache the way it had when she cried with Cash, but in the end she had been glad she allowed herself the release.

"Cash!" Reagan said his name when she spotted him, stopping short to see him leaning against her front door. After a moment she continued pushing her bike up to him.

"How can you possibly be here ahead of me?"

"I have a fast horse, and I know a shortcut."

Reagan looked into his eyes and then away.

"I shouldn't have run. I know that now, but I just panicked."

"Why did you?"

Reagan made herself admit the truth. "When your brothers came, I hadn't yet faced my feelings for you. Now it's different. What if I don't like your parents? What if they don't like me?"

Reagan gestured helplessly with one hand, wishing for some way to make herself clear.

"I've never had what you have, Cash," she tried. "Most people would be dying for it, but I'm afraid of it. You have brothers who love and care for you. They came from miles away to see Katy. Now your parents are on their way. I don't even have to see them to know that they won't be anything like my parents, but that doesn't mean we'll like each other."

"And what happens if they don't like you?"

Reagan's smile was sad. "It will no longer be an issue of me getting over my fears. The issue will be that you would never marry a woman your family didn't approve of."

"Here," Cash said. "Give me your bike."

He took it and leaned it up against the side of the house. He then directed Reagan to the bench in the yard. Once they'd sat down, he prayed and tried to gather his thoughts.

"It's funny, but I think many husbands and wives come from very diverse backgrounds. Have you ever noticed that?"

Reagan said she hadn't.

"I sometimes wonder if that isn't by design. I mean, you've been hurt by your family, but mine is very loving and supportive. I can see how you might find that threatening, but it could also serve to give you strength."

Cash turned his head to study her, and he could see that she was thinking.

"Do you remember last Saturday when I said I wished you could find someone better?"

"Yes."

"You didn't like that, did you?"

"No, I didn't because it's not true."

"But this is what I'm talking about. A woman should be glad to meet your family. I mean, a little bit of nerves is normal, but not panic and thoughts of escape."

"But I don't want just *any* woman. I want you. Even if you panic and run away. I want to give you as much time as you need to see that you have nothing to fear, but I don't want anyone else, Reagan."

The little Irish woman next to him said nothing, and Cash was suddenly glad that this had happened. There were some things she didn't know about him. It was time she did.

"Have you caught on yet that my parents are not believers?"

"Yes."

"It's interesting to me that all of their sons and even my father's mother have come to Christ, but they haven't. Now ask me Reagan—ask me why it's interesting."

"Okay. Why is it?"

"Because Charles Rawlings Sr. set out to raise three of the most independent children you could imagine. He hoped one of us boys would want the ranch, and I did, but he's always insisted that we step out and follow our dreams. He loves to travel and have adventures, and he's dragged my mother halfway around the world, but not in all of his ventures has he found Jesus Christ.

"He and my mother are starting to ask some questions, but it's taken a lot of years for that to happen."

"But God saved all three of you boys after you were grown and gone?"

"Yes, and that brings me back to us. You're right, I do value my parents' opinion. But you need to understand their expectations. Slater met Libby and fell in love before any of us met her. We all went to the wedding, but he was a man in love long before my parents knew.

"Dakota and Darvi had known each other for years but hadn't seen each other. He was escorting her back to St. Louis just last fall, and on the way they came here. I was the one to point out to Dakota that he was in love. He told me later that our mother came right out and asked him if he fell in love with Darvi because she shared his faith. They were married in January.

"You see, Reagan, my parents know exactly the type of woman my brothers and I are going to fall for. They know the women will share our belief in Christ because that's the life we've chosen for ourselves. They also know that the wives we choose will be people who are strong and independent because that's what they instilled in us from the time we were small.

"Hair color, where you grew up, how tall you are, what type of books you like—those are all just details. Everyone who meets you falls in love with you. My parents won't be any different. My love for you will cause them to love you, and when they see that you share my faith, they'll just see that as normal, even though they haven't embraced it themselves."

The couple's eyes met.

"All this to say, Reagan, that it's still about your fear of marriage. My parents are wonderful. You'll love them, and they'll love you in return. What is yet to be determined is whether or not you want to be my wife."

Reagan looked into his face and found what she always did: a wonderful man. His eyes were filled with caring, and she knew he was not a man to play games with a woman.

"I can't promise that the fear won't come back, Cash."

"So what does that mean? Do you want to wait until all fears are gone or what?"

She chewed her lip. "Can I think on it?"

"No," he teased. "I need to know right now."

Reagan smiled.

"Come on." Cash stood. "Let's get back to the ranch. I asked Brenda to fill in, but I don't want to be gone too long."

"I shouldn't have run like that. Will Katy be upset?"

"Furious."

They did stop to greet Holly but didn't find anyone home. They continued on to the edge of town where Reagan was going to ride her bike ahead of Cash's horse. The sound of the train heading out of town reminded Reagan of the Rawlingses' visit. She stopped and turned to Cash.

"Is that the last train today I hear?"

"No, I think there's one more."

"But your parents could have come in already."

"True."

"They could be at the ranch."

"Yes."

Reagan's mouth opened. "What are they going to say when they find you gone?"

"Nothing."

She began to shake her head.

"Reagan," he began patiently, "they really do want my brothers and me to live our own lives. They don't expect me to drop everything because they're coming."

Reagan was intrigued for the first time. Until now she'd been too wrapped up in herself to give them much thought, but now she realized she would be gaining a glimpse into Cash's life in a way that had not been possible before.

Wordlessly climbing back onto her bike, Reagan continued on her way to the ranch. Cash followed her with a smile, just glad she was still going in the right direction. It was hard to wait at times like this, but Cash asked God for patience.

It's my dream to have the ranch be her home, her permanent home, Lord,

where she would feel safe and loved, but You know what You want here. Help
me to trust, and help Reagan to see that I want only to treasure her.

❧ ❧ ❧

"Reagan," Cash said with a huge smile, just moments after they
arrived back, "these are my parents, Charles and Virginia Rawlings."

"Oh, Reagan!" Virginia shocked her by coming forward to hug
her. "I can't think what Katy and Cash would have done without you.
Katy's told us all about it. You dear, sweet thing."

Charles smiled into the wide, dark eyes that met his and was
there to shake Reagan's hand as soon as Virginia released her.

"It's great to meet you, Reagan. Did I see you come up on a bicycle?"

"Yes."

"You're not from Texas, so where are you from?"

Reagan laughed a little. "New York."

"I love New York. Were you right in the city?"

"For most of my life, yes."

"Great place. What brought you to Texas?"

Reagan smiled. He was like an older version of Dakota.

"Adventure."

"That's my kind of answer. Have you found some?"

"Yes. Sometimes more than I bargained for."

"Tell them what you think of armadillos," Katy directed, and both
senior Rawlings enjoyed her face of horror and general description of
what she called a "creature."

"You look a little thin," Cash said of his father when there was a
break.

The older man shook his head and admitted, "I haven't had the
flu like that in a long time. And it certainly wasn't fun not being at
home."

The two fell into easy conversation, and before long Virginia was
up wheeling Katy into the kitchen and signaling for Reagan to join
them.

As elegantly as Mrs. Rawlings was dressed, Reagan was surprised
to see her dig right into the kitchen work. She took over dinner preparations as though she had done so all her life, and Reagan was reminded that this had been her home.

Reagan listened to her talk to Katy, and even though they included her, it was clear that they were old and dear friends. Reagan
found herself praying that Katy would have an opportunity to share
the change in her life, but for the most part she just listened and
laughed at some of Mrs. Rawlings' stories.

Everyone was on the tired side, so they had an early dinner. Again Reagan laughed at the easy banter and camaraderie. And it was just as Cash said it would be: They seemed to accept her wholeheartedly and without question.

Mrs. Rawlings insisted on cleaning up, coaxing her husband to help her, and as much as Katy was glad to see them, she was perfectly content to have Reagan settle her for an early night. She was enjoying the freedom of the chair, but her body still ached, and she grew fatigued in fairly short order.

Cash bid Katy good night and then waited for Reagan to appear. Without asking, he whisked her onto the front porch and spoke as soon as he had her alone.

"How are you? Do you wish you'd stayed in town?"

"No. I'm fine. They're both so kind, just like you said they would be. Why did I run away and act so foolishly?"

Cash bent and kissed her cheek.

"I don't want you to be too rough on yourself. It's a lot to take in, and I've told you I don't have a timetable that you have to meet."

"Maybe you should."

He shook his head, took a seat, and asked her to join him.

Reagan sighed, feeling as tired as everyone else. They talked for a short time, but Cash didn't try to dissuade her when she said she was ready to head to bed. He knew that emotional issues were the most wearying kind. He was tired as well.

"Thank you, Cash," she surprised him by saying just before she slipped inside.

"For what?"

"For coming after me."

"My pleasure," he said, able to mean it with all his heart.

🌹 🌹 🌹

"You're in love with that girl," Virginia said to her son much later that night. They were the last ones awake in the house. Always the rancher, Charles had gone to the barn to check the stock, and the two were visiting in the upstairs hall.

"You think so, do you?"

Virginia laughed a little. "I may be tired, Cash, but I can still see straight."

The rancher laughed with her. "We're not moving very fast," he said.

"Is that your choice or hers?"

"It's ours."

Virginia smiled with pride. She loved knowing that she had raised three gentlemen. It meant the world to her.

"How long are you staying?" Cash finally remembered to ask.

"Probably just a few days before we head out to see your grandmother and brothers, but I think we'll be back on the way home."

"I'm glad. It's good to have you here, Mother. I know it means so much to Katy."

"She's changed," Virginia said, her voice thoughtful.

All Cash did was nod before Virginia said she was going to bed. Mother and son went to their rooms shortly after that, and until Cash fell asleep, he asked himself whether he should have told his mother why Katy was different or let the lady do it herself.

Twenty-One

"Now, DIDN'T YOU TELL ME THEY HAD seemed open earlier this year?" Pastor Ellis asked Cash the next Sunday afternoon. The Ellis family had invited Cash, Reagan, Katy, and the Bennetts to lunch.

"Yes. When my brother was married in January, my parents were both very open, and I told them to write if I could be of help. I know they were planning to keep going to the church I visited while I was there, but they haven't brought the subject up, and I don't know how to go about it. They didn't even say what they thought of the service here last week."

"I didn't have a chance either," Katy put in. "I found out after they left that Mrs. Rawlings noticed a change in me, but I didn't have any opportunities to tell her the reason."

"It might still come," Pastor encouraged her. "Did you say they were still coming back this way?"

Cash nodded, and they all listened as Katy gave the schedule Virginia had shared with her.

"Maybe one of your brothers will have a chance to ask how they're doing, or even your grandmother." Russell added this hopeful note just before Noelle said she had cake for dessert.

"How are you?" Holly asked of Reagan as they finished with dessert a short time later. The two were sitting side by side, and there had been a lull in the conversation. The other people went back to talking, but the two women had a moment alone.

"I'm doing fine. How are you?"

"Doing great. Do I miss my guess, or are you and Cash getting rather close?"

Reagan smiled. "Cash has talked to Pastor, and I think he even spoke to Russell, but they must have taken him seriously when he said we were keeping it quiet right now."

Holly had all she could do not to squeal with excitement. Instead she asked with a false calm, "And what did Cash speak to Pastor and Russ about?"

"Just that we're starting to talk about a relationship."

The word was enough to jolt Holly back to earth.

"Reagan, are you all right with this? I mean, really?"

Reagan's face was wreathed with softness as she thought about this question.

"He's so patient, Holly. I didn't know anyone like him existed."

Holly Bennett knew she was going to burst into tears at any moment, and she had to get out of the room.

"I'm going to check on the children," she announced, raising her voice some to be heard by Russell.

He nodded and thanked her.

Reagan only let her get to her feet before saying she was going to join her. She followed Holly onto the front porch where the older woman stood with her hand over her mouth.

"Holly?"

"I'm sorry, Reagan." She was just barely holding tears. "I've just wanted this for you for so long. I've wanted you to know how loved you are, and if Cash can do that, I just—" She couldn't go on, but Reagan didn't really need her to.

"Thank you, Holly," she said when she hugged her.

"Hi, Reagan," Jonah called as he ran by, and that gave Holly the push she needed to dry her tears. She looked down at Reagan for a moment and then smiled and hugged her again.

"I just want you to know," Holly ended up saying, "that whatever you do, I'll love you like a sister forever."

Reagan had never had anyone say such a thing to her. For a moment she was speechless.

"Thank you, Holly. It's a wonderful thing to know."

Wanting to rejoin the group, Holly made a swift check on the children, but as soon as she was finished, she and Reagan went back inside.

❧ ❧ ❧

"What are you up to?" Cash asked Reagan after he'd taken her to the general store for supplies.

"Nothing," she said innocently, but Cash saw what she was trying to hide.

A thumb went up to push the brim of his hat back as he asked, "Wrinkle cream, Reagan?"

She frowned at him. "I'm not exactly a teen any longer, Cash."

The cowboy had all he could do not to shout with laughter.

"Let me see this stuff," he said as he took it from the hand she held behind her back.

Reagan looked innocently around as he read, but there was no escaping when he leaned close to her face.

"Now, show me these wrinkles you're trying to get rid of."

"You don't see any?" She looked up at him in that trusting way he was coming to know.

"No."

"What about those little lines next to my eyes?"

"Where?"

Reagan squinted, and this time Cash had to laugh.

"Shh . . ." she got after him, fighting laughter of her own.

"You don't need this," he said, plunking it decisively on the shelf.

"This dry heat is hard on the skin."

"I agree with you, but some regular lotion will do." Cash grabbed a jar from the shelf and handed it to her. It was a brand that he'd seen Katy use in the kitchen.

"This stuff?"

"I think Katy uses it."

Reagan read the description on the bottle before looking up to ask Cash if Katy needed any. The question was never voiced. Cash's eyes were on something further down the shelf, and as Reagan followed his gaze, she smiled. Never before had she noticed the full line of feminine apparel that covered half of those shelves. Clearly Cash had never noticed either. Reagan just stood and watched him.

"Reagan?" he asked before making eye contact with her.

"Yes?"

Cash turned to see that she'd been staring at him. His smile was full blown in an instant, and Reagan wanted to laugh.

"Do all women wear those pretty things?" he asked when they were finally back in the wagon and headed to the ranch.

"Well, maybe not as lacy and pretty as some of those, but something like them."

Cash nodded, still looking thoughtfully out over the horses' heads.

"Honestly, Cash, you do have a mother. Certainly you have seen some of those things before."

"Honestly, Reagan," he copied her, "a man doesn't give much

thought to what his mother wears. The woman he's in love with is a different matter."

"I guess that makes sense, but don't you ever go down that aisle?"

"For what?"

"I don't know. Where do they keep the men's underthings?"

"In a different spot, and you can trust me when I tell you that they don't have the same effect. By the way," he asked, "do certain things come in certain colors?"

"No. That was all a mixture. There were blue bloomers, but also blue shifts and camisoles. All those things come in a variety of colors."

"What's a camisole? I've never heard of that."

Reagan cleared her throat, wondering how they had come to talk of this.

"You wear it under your blouse."

"Do you have a blue one?" Cash asked before he thought.

"Am I allowed to tell you that?"

Cash turned to look at her, his eyes straying a bit before he caught himself.

"Maybe you shouldn't," he said, fixing his gaze over the horses again.

In truth Reagan had a pink one, but she wisely kept this to herself.

"Don't decide to marry me too soon, Reagan," Cash said suddenly.

"Why is that?"

"Courting you is an education."

As she'd wanted to in the store, Reagan allowed herself a nice loud laugh.

❧ ❧ ❧

"Have I ever missed you," Sally said on the first morning Reagan went back to work at the hotel. Katy was back on her feet and going strong; Reagan had even stayed on for an extra week just to enjoy working with Katy in her element. It had been hard to leave the ranch, but everyone knew it was for the best.

Reagan smiled.

"Did your cousin ever show up?"

"No, and I've got bunions the size of eggs to prove it."

"Well, I'm here now."

"True, but I suspect it won't be for long."

"What do you mean?"

Sally looked innocent. "Rumor around town has it that you and Cash Rawlings are getting mighty friendly."

"Is that right?" Reagan asked, already tying on an apron and setting to work.

"Yes, that's right."

Reagan didn't respond.

"Well?"

"Well what?"

"Is it true?"

Reagan smiled. "I happen to think he's very special."

"And does he share that same opinion of you?"

Reagan looked at her. "He has said something along that line."

Sally grinned. "He's been a sought-after catch in this town for a long time, Reagan. A few hearts are going to break when word gets out on this."

"According to you, word is already out."

"I mean official word, the church bells ringing and all that."

Reagan only laughed and went to work in earnest. She was slightly out of practice after eight weeks off the job, but things were coming back fast. And indeed the morning flew. Long before she was ready, it was time to head to the dining room.

Reagan had to laugh. The men acted as if she'd been gone for ages, and their pleas for dinner or an evening out with her were more ardent than ever. Reagan was wondering how many more days of this she could take when she looked up to see Cash Rawlings come in the door.

He took a seat at an empty table, his eyes trained on Reagan, and when she was done with the order she was working on, she went to him.

"Well, now," she said softly, eyes on his face. "What brings you out this morning?"

"A man's got to eat," he said, his own eyes smiling right back.

"But you've got someone to cook for you," Reagan said, even being so bold as to sit down for a moment.

Cash leaned close, aware that every eye in the room was on them.

"I thought maybe these gentlemen needed a little notice that you're not up for grabs any longer."

"I never was."

"But they didn't know that."

Reagan smiled. "True. I think they believed if they just asked long enough, I would eventually succumb."

"That's what I'm hoping," he said as he reached up and brushed a finger down her cheek.

Reagan bit her lip to keep from laughing and stood, not bothering to take his order before exiting to the kitchen and returning with just the breakfast she knew he liked.

❧ ❧ ❧

About ten days later, Reagan and Cash walked along the pond, their hands linked. It was dreadfully hot, but dusk was beginning to fall, and they were happy just to be together. It was a Sunday, and Reagan had come after work for a late lunch that Katy had prepared and to spend the day at the ranch.

"I miss you," she said suddenly.

"The feeling is more than shared, Reagan."

"Mine's different."

"How's that?"

"It just is."

Cash's hand brought her gently to a halt. He looked down into her face, and in just a matter of seconds understood that she was there to stay. He studied her eyes, and with complete openness found her eyes staring right back.

"If I wanted to talk about the future, Reagan, would you run away?"

"Nope," she said, giving the word her best Texas drawl.

"How about children? Would you be afraid to discuss having a family?"

"Nope."

Cash's smile was tender beyond belief.

"And marriage, Reagan," he whispered. "How scary is marriage these days?"

"Not at all."

Moving ever so carefully, his hands coming up to cup her face, Cash leaned forward until their lips touched for the first time.

"Oh, my," Reagan breathed when he broke the contact.

"I was afraid of that," Cash said, his forehead laid against hers.

"What's that?"

"Of liking this no small amount."

Reagan laughed and went on tiptoe to kiss him again.

"I hope you know what this means," he warned her.

"What?"

"I'll be asking very soon, and I'll expect a yes answer."

Reagan stepped back, her hands going to her hips in that familiar way.

"You mean you're not going to ask this minute?"

Cash could only snatch her into his arms and hold on tight, his laughter coming in great waves that echoed over the pond. But they couldn't keep this event to themselves. In just a few moments, like children let outside to play, they ran for the house to see Katy.

"How did you know?" Katy asked after Cash shared their conversation. The three sat in the living room. "What changed for you, Reagan?" the older woman asked. "Why aren't you afraid any longer?"

"It's been coming for a long time, Katy," Reagan answered, her eyes on Cash. "I watched Cash deal with you and everyone in and around this ranch. Even people he didn't know very well were treated with such care and kindness, and then he said he loved me and wanted me to be his wife. If folks just passing through could be treated with kindness, what would he be like to a wife he loved? I realized I was a fool not to have seen it sooner."

Cash looked into her eyes, and for a moment the young couple forgot anyone else was in the room.

Katy sighed as if she herself had just fallen in love, and Reagan looked at her.

"Will you stand up with me, Katy?"

"Me?" her voice squeaked, giving Reagan the giggles.

"Yes. I want a big wedding. I'm planning on asking Holly and Sally too."

"You're going to have me bawling," she said.

"Do you want to know what else?" Reagan said, her eyes alight with mischief.

"What?"

"He hasn't even asked me yet."

Katy looked at her employer in shock and then came to her feet.

"Well, I'm getting out of here. You, Cash Rawlings, have work to do."

The couple had a good laugh as Katy took herself from the room. Reagan was about to say something to Cash, but he was coming to his feet as well. She watched as he slipped into his office and returned with a box in his hands.

"What's this?"

"A little gift for you."

Reagan loved gifts and swiftly opened it. Her mouth opening in surprise, she took out a small silver-colored bell.

"For my bike?"

"Yes, indeed."

"Where did you find it?"

"Lavinia had it."

Reagan gave the bell a little ring and then looked at him.

"What would I do without you, Cash?"

"Marry me and you won't have to find out."

Reagan smiled, her eyes thoughtful.

"Reagan Rawlings. It sounds kind of funny, doesn't it?"

"Not to me."

"Oh, Cash, just name the day."

"I'll take that as a yes," he said, just before pulling her close and sealing her agreement with a kiss.

❦ ❦ ❦

"It's a boy!" Virginia said as she burst in the front door of the ranch house and found the spacious living room empty. "Is anyone here?"

Katy came from the kitchen, not moving as spryly as she once did, but on her own two feet.

"What's that?"

"Libby had a boy! We were only going to stay a short time, but then she was so close, so we just waited. I held him, Katy," she said, her voice taking on a note of wonder. "I held my own little grandson, Reese Rawlings."

"A boy." Katy shook her head in surprise. She had been praying for Liberty just that morning. "How is Libby? How is Slater?"

"Everyone's doing great. Where's Cash?"

"In the barn, last I knew."

Virginia took off in the direction of the kitchen to use the back door, and only then did Katy look up to see that Charles had come in the front door behind his wife. He was standing just inside, a smile on his face.

"A boy," Katy said. "Now isn't that good news?"

"Yes, it is," Charles agreed, albeit a good deal calmer than his wife. He came forward, his eyes on the housekeeper.

"Sit down, Katy," he invited. "I want to talk to you."

Katy sat in complete comfort. They'd known each other too many years for anything else.

"You've changed, Katy."

"I have," Katy admitted without hesitation. She had been asking God for open doors with people and boldness when they came. "Do you want to hear about it?"

"Yes, I do."

"I believe the way Gretchen, Cash, Slater, and Dak do. I know I'm a sinner, but I'm saved from punishment."

Charles nodded, his face serene. He bent forward, his voice low as he admitted, "I am too, Katy."

Katy's mouth opened.

"But you've not said anything. Cash can't know. He'd have told me."

"No one knows."

"Why, Mr. Rawlings?"

"Virginia. She still doesn't know what to do with it all." He paused, his face so troubled. "Do you know all the places I've dragged her, Katy? She's been everywhere with me because I told her when we got married that I wasn't going to do things on my own. She agreed with me, and that's the way it's always been. But now I've done this without her, and I don't know how to tell her."

Katy's heart broke over this news. "When did it happen?"

"When I was ill. I honestly thought that was the end for me. I knew I was lost if it was, so I took care of things, and just like Dakota, God gave me another chance."

"He's good that way," Katy said. "I know all about second chances, Mr. Rawlings. I'll pray for you," she said suddenly. "I have been, but now I'll pray that you'll find a way to tell Mrs. Rawlings. Maybe just hearing from you will turn her heart."

"Thank you, Katy. I don't know if I've ever told you what you mean to us, and I don't think I could find the words now, but I do thank you."

Katy smiled at him, and Charles wanted to shake his head in amazement. The old Katy would have hushed him and left the room. The peace and serenity that surrounded this Katy was unmistakable. He had seen it even before they had left but had not had a chance to speak with her.

"Charles!" Virginia could be heard coming back through the house now.

"In the living room."

Mrs. Rawlings came rushing through, pulling Cash, who was laughing at her excitement, with her.

"Tell him, Cash!" she demanded, looking ready to burst all over again.

Cash smiled at his father.

"I've asked Reagan to marry me, and she's accepted."

Charles went to his son. The men embraced, and the older Rawlings found himself quite choked up. He knew he had to tell Virginia soon, so he could share his news with his son, this precious first child who loved the ranch as he did.

But the time didn't come. Anxious as she was to return home,

Virginia wanted to spend only one night at the ranch, and then head to Dakota's before going back to St. Louis.

Cash, however, did find a letter on his desk after his parents left. He read it and then laid his head down on the desktop and cried with a mixture of joy and heartbreak. That God would save his father was the most amazing thing Cash had ever known. In years past, whenever he had pictured one of his parents coming to Christ, it was his mother, and here his father had been the first to believe.

A note on the bottom of the letter said that Katy knew also but to be careful of his mother's feelings in any future dealings with her. Cash went to Katy, glad she was close by, to see if she knew about the note.

"I didn't think he'd had a chance to talk with you, so I'm glad he wrote it," she said. "They were gone so fast."

"I just wish my mother knew."

Katy looked at him, her chin thrust forward a bit.

"You're not doubting, are you, Cash?"

"What exactly?"

"I know your father hasn't told your mother yet, but you don't doubt that she'll believe, do you?"

"I do at times, Katy. I want it very badly, but God does give us a choice."

"That He does," she said with conviction, "and I have to trust Him no matter what, but I think your mother will come around. I'm praying for that very thing."

"I am too, Katy. It's good to know I'm not alone."

Katy smiled even after he left the room. Neither one of them was alone. They would never be alone again.

Epilogue

Christmas 1883

DAKOTA AND DARVI HAD BEEN IN their new house at the ranch for almost a month, but they would still have Christmas in the main house. And the whole family would be gathered. Slater, Liberty, and Reese were already at the ranch, as was Grandma Rawlings. Charles and Virginia were due that day.

Married just four months, Reagan Rawlings had decorated to her heart's content, and her husband had even bought her a dark green dress that she was saving for Christmas day. She had been somewhat nervous about hosting this special day for the whole clan, but as usual, Katy was a lifesaver, and Cash took it all in stride.

Over at Dakota and Darvi's, Darvi held her little nephew, dreaming of when it would be her turn. Liberty and Darvi grew closer each time they saw each other, and the men always had catching up to do.

In the kitchen of the main house, Gretchen Rawlings and Katy were talking and working away, both elated to have the family gathered under one roof. They each knew the favorite dishes of the family and worked on what they termed their "secret" recipes.

Coming in on the train—due to arrive in just 45 minutes—were Charles and Virginia Rawlings. They were laden with packages, even though they'd sent many ahead of time, and Virginia worked at not worrying.

"Are you going to make it?" Charles asked, his eyes searching her face.

"I don't know. I almost wish I had written first. They're all going to cry, and that's not what we need to do at Christmas."

"When someone comes to Christ, especially when it's someone you love dearly, you can cry anytime."

Virginia leaned to kiss him.

"Why did it take me so long?"

He slipped an arm around her.

"I don't care how long it took. I just love knowing I never have to leave you behind. That's all that matters to me."

Virginia relaxed completely then, her husband's embrace telling her it was going to be all right.

In the main house at the ranch, Cash was looking for his wife.

"Reagan?" Cash called to her as he mounted the stairs toward their room. She didn't answer, but he found her sitting on the side of their bed.

"Hi," he said as he sat down next to her, scooped her into his arms, and settled her in his lap.

"Hello," she said, still giving him her profile.

Her voice told him she was thinking.

"What's up?"

"I was just thinking," she admitted, finally meeting his eyes.

"About what?"

"Your Christmas gift."

"What about it?"

"I couldn't stand for you not to like it, Cash, at least not in front of anyone else." She turned to look at him. "I want to give you your gift now."

"Now?"

"Now."

Cash started to laugh.

"Reagan, I know I'll like it."

He tried to reason with her for some minutes, but she had that stubborn tilt to her chin.

"I want to give it to you now."

"No."

"Yes."

This went on for a short time before Cash realized he didn't care. Looking like a conspiratorial child, Reagan took his hand and led him quietly down the stairs. At the bottom she peeked around the corner, and when it was clear, rushed him to the room that Katy had used to recuperate.

Cash was laughing so hard that he tried to hold his breath. Reagan was taking this all the way. She darted inside, shut the door, and leaned on it, breathing theatrically.

"What are we doing?"

"Shh," she told him. "They'll hear us."

Cash wanted to shake his head but found himself dragged along to the closet. It creaked a little when it opened, and even Reagan started to laugh.

"Come on," she urged him, having picked up a lantern. "Come through here."

"It's dark."

"Just hold onto me."

"Gladly," he agreed just before finding himself in pitch blackness.

"Okay, now close your eyes."

"It's dark, Reagan," he said indulgently.

"I know, but I'm going to light the lantern. Are they closed?"

"Yes."

He heard the strike of the match, and from behind his lids could tell that Reagan's little room had been illumined.

"Okay," she said, watching him carefully.

Cash opened his eyes and then blinked.

"You bought me a bike?"

"Yes. Do you like it?"

"You bought me my own bike?"

"Yes. It's taller than mine. It should fit you very well."

He walked toward it like a child on his tenth birthday.

Reagan watched him, her hands clasped in front of her.

"You bought me a bike," he said with such pleasure that Reagan beamed.

"Look at me. I'm a city boy!"

Watching as he tried to straddle it in the tiny room, she suddenly realized what she'd done.

"Oh, no," she suddenly said.

"What's wrong?"

"You like it."

"That's bad?"

"No, but now I don't have anything to surprise you with for Christmas."

Cash set the bike aside and came to her. His arms were gentle around her as he gathered her to his chest.

"My entire family is coming for Christmas in the home I share with my new wife, and you think I need more gifts."

Reagan threw her arms around his neck, her lips seeking his own. She suddenly felt exactly the same. He was all the Christmas gift she would ever need again.

About the Author

LORI WICK is a multifaceted author of Christian fiction. As comfortable writing period stories as she is penning contemporary works, Lori's books (6 million in print) vary widely in location and time period. Lori's faithful fans consistently put her series and standalone works on the bestseller lists. Lori and her husband, Bob, live with their swiftly growing family in the Midwest.